Many t

From fea

CW00393311

NIGHTMARES:

Three Great Suspense Novels by Ira Levin

NIGHTMARES

Three Great Suspense Novels by Ira Levin

An Omnibus Edition containing
ROSEMARY'S BABY, THE STEPFORD WIVES
and
A KISS BEFORE DYING

London
Michael Joseph

First published in Great Britain in this
omnibus edition by Michael Joseph Limited
44 Bedford Square London WC1
1981

ISBN 0 7181 2034 5

Printed and bound in Great Britain by Billings, Guildford and Worcester.

Contents

Completed in August, 1966, in Wilton,
Connecticut, and dedicated to Gabrielle

Rosemary's Baby

PART ONE
1

Rosemary and Guy Woodhouse had signed a lease on a five-room apartment in a geometric white house on First Avenue when they received word, from a woman named Mrs Cortez, that a four-room apartment in the Bramford had become available. The Bramford, old, black, and elephantine, is a warren of high-ceilinged apartments prized for their fireplaces and Victorian detail. Rosemary and Guy had been on its waiting list since their marriage but had finally given up.

Guy relayed the news to Rosemary, stopping the phone against his chest. Rosemary groaned 'Oh *no*!' and looked as if she would weep.

'It's too late,' Guy said to the phone. 'We signed a lease yesterday.' Rosemary caught his arm. 'Couldn't we get out of it?' she asked him. 'Tell them something?'

'Hold on a minute, will you, Mrs Cortez?' Guy stopped the phone again. 'Tell them what?' he asked.

Rosemary floundered and raised her hands helplessly. 'I don't know, the truth. That we have a chance to get into the Bramford.'

'Honey,' Guy said, 'they're not going to care about that.'

'You'll think of *something*, Guy. Let's just look, all right? Tell her we'll look. Please. Before she hangs up.'

'We signed a *lease*, Ro; we're stuck.'

'Please! She'll hang up!' Whimpering with mock anguish, Rosemary pried the phone from Guy's chest and tried to push it up to his mouth.

Guy laughed and let the phone be pushed. 'Mrs Cortez? It turns out there's a chance we'll be able to get out of it, because we haven't signed the actual lease yet. They were out of the forms so we only signed a letter of agreement. Can we take a look at the apartment?'

Mrs Cortez gave instructions: they were to go to the Bramford between eleven and eleven-thirty, find Mr Micklas or Jerome, and tell whichever they found that they were the party she had sent to look at 7E. Then they were to call her. She gave Guy her number. 'You see how you can think of things?' Rosemary said, putting Peds and yellow shoes on her feet. 'You're a *marvellous* liar.'

Guy, at the mirror, said, 'Christ, a pimple.'

'Don't squeeze it.'

'It's only four rooms, you know. No nursery.'

'I'd rather have four rooms in the Bramford,' Rosemary said, 'than a whole floor in that – that white cellblock.'

'Yesterday you loved it.'

'I liked it. I never loved it. I'll bet not even the architect loves it. We'll make a dining area in the living-room and have a beautiful nursery, when and if.'

'Soon,' Guy said. He ran an electric razor back and forth across his upper lip, looking into his eyes, which were brown and large. Rosemary stepped into a yellow dress and squirmed the zipper up the back of it.

They were in one room, that had been Guy's bachelor apartment. It had posters of Paris and Verona, a large day bed and a pullman kitchen.

It was Tuesday, the third of August.

Mr Micklas was small and dapper but had fingers missing from both hands, which made shaking hands an embarrassment, though not apparently for him. 'Oh, an actor,' he said, ringing for the elevator with a middle finger. 'We're very popular with actors.' He named four who were living at the Bramford, all of them well known. 'Have I seen you in anything?'

'Let's see,' Guy said. 'I did *Hamlet* a while back, didn't I, Liz? And then we made *The Sandpiper . . .*'

'He's joking,' Rosemary said. 'He was in *Luther* and *Nobody Loves An Albatross* and a lot of television plays and television commercials.'

'That's where the money is, isn't it?' Mr Micklas said; 'the commercials.'

'Yes,' Rosemary said, and Guy said, 'And the artistic thrill, too.'

Rosemary gave him a pleading look; he gave back one of stunned innocence and then made a leering vampire face at the top of Mr Micklas's head.

The elevator – oak-panelled, with a shining brass hand-rail all around – was run by a uniformed Negro boy with a locked-in-place smile. 'Seven,' Mr Micklas told him; to Rosemary and Guy he said, 'This apartment has four rooms, two baths, and five closets. Originally the house consisted of very large apartments – the smallest was a nine – but now they've almost all been broken up into fours, fives, and sixes. Seven E is a four that was originally the back part of a ten. It has the original kitchen and master bath, which are enormous, as you'll soon see. It has the original master bedroom for its living-room, another bedroom for its bedroom, and two servant's rooms thrown together for its dining-room or second bedroom. Do you have children?'

'We plan to,' Rosemary said.

'It's an ideal child's room, with a full bathroom and a large closet. The whole set-up is made to order for a young couple like yourselves.'

The elevator stopped and the Negro boy, smiling, chivied it down, up, and down again for a closer alignment with the floor rail outside; and still smiling, pulled in the brass inner gate and the outer rolling door. Mr Micklas stood aside and Rosemary and Guy stepped out – into a dimly lighted hallway walled and carpeted in dark green. A workman at a sculptured green door marked 7B looked at them and turned back to fitting a peepscope into its cut-out hole.

Mr Micklas led the way to the right and then to the left, through short branches of dark green hallway. Rosemary and Guy, following, saw rubbed-away places in the wallpaper and a seam where it had lifted and was curling inward; saw a dead light bulb in a cut-glass sconce and a patched place of light green tape on the dark green carpet. Guy looked at Rosemary: *Patched carpet?* She looked away and smiled brightly: *I love it; everything's lovely!*

'The previous tenant, Mrs Gardenia,' Mr Micklas said, not looking back at them, 'passed away only a few days ago and nothing has been moved out of the apartment yet. Her son asked me to tell whoever looks at it that the rugs, the air conditioners, and some of the furniture can be had practically for the asking.' He turned into another branch of hallway papered in newer-looking green and gold stripes.

'Did she die in the apartment?' Rosemary asked. 'Not that it—'

'Oh, no, in a hospital,' Mr Micklas said. 'She'd been in a coma for weeks. She was very old and passed away without ever waking. I'll be grateful to go that way myself when the time comes. She was chipper right to the end; cooked her own meals, shopped the department stores . . . She was one of the first women lawyers in New York State.'

They came now to a stairwell that ended the hallway. Adjacent to it, on the left, was the door of apartment 7E, a door without sculptured garlands, narrower than the doors they had passed. Mr Micklas pressed the pearl bell button – *L. Gardenia* was mounted above it in white letters on black plastic – and turned a key in the lock. Despite lost fingers he worked the knob and threw the door smartly. 'After you, please,' he said, leaning forward on his toes and holding the door open with the length of an outstretched arm.

The apartment's four rooms were divided two and two on either side of a narrow central hallway that extended in a straight line from the front door. The first room on the right was the kitchen, and at the sight of it Rosemary couldn't keep from giggling, for it was as large if not larger than the whole apartment in which they were then living. It had a six-burner gas stove with two ovens, a mammoth refrigerator, a monumental sink; it had dozens of cabinets, a window on Seventh Avenue, a high *high* ceiling, and it even had – imagining away Mrs Gardenia's chrome table and chairs and roped bales of *Fortune* and *Musical America* – the perfect place for something like the blue-and-ivory breakfast nook she had clipped from last month's *House Beautiful*.

Opposite the kitchen was the dining-room or second bedroom, which Mrs Gardenia had apparently used as a combination study and greenhouse. Hundreds of small plants, dying and dead, stood on jerry-built shelves under spirals of unlighted fluorescent tubing; in their midst a roll-top desk spilled over with books and papers. A handsome desk it was, broad and gleaming with age. Rosemary left Guy and Mr Micklas talking by the door and went to it, stepping over a shelf of withered brown fronds. Desks like this were displayed in antique-store windows; Rosemary wondered, touching it, if it was one of the things that could be had practically for the asking. Graceful blue penmanship on mauve paper said *than merely the intriguing pastime I believed it to be. I can no longer associate myself*—and she caught herself snooping and looked up at Mr Micklas turning from Guy. 'Is this desk one of the things Mrs Gardenia's son wants to sell?' she asked.

'I don't know,' Mr Micklas said. 'I could find out for you, though.'

'It's a beauty,' Guy said.

12

Rosemary said 'Isn't it?' and smiling, looked about at walls and windows. The room would accommodate almost perfectly the nursery she had imagined. It was a bit dark – the windows faced on a narrow courtyard – but the white-and-yellow wallpaper would brighten it tremendously. The bathroom was small but a bonus, and the closet, filled with potted seedlings that seemed to be doing quite well, was a good one.

They turned to the door, and Guy asked, 'What are all these?'

'Herbs, mostly,' Rosemary said. 'There's mint and basil . . . I don't know what these are.'

Farther along the hallway there was a guest closet on the left, and then, on the right, a wide archway opening on to the living-room. Large bay windows stood opposite, two of them, with diamond panes and three-sided window seats. There was a small fireplace in the right-hand wall, with a scrolled white marble mantel, and there were high oak bookshelves on the left.

'Oh, Guy,' Rosemary said, finding his hand and squeezing it. Guy said 'Mm' non-committally but squeezed back; Mr Micklas was beside him.

'The fireplace works, of course,' Mr Micklas said.

The bedroom, behind them, was adequate – about twelve by eighteen, with its windows facing on the same narrow courtyard as those of the dining-room-second-bedroom-nursery. The bathroom, beyond the living-room, was big, and full of bulbous white brass-knobbed fixtures.

'It's a marvellous apartment!' Rosemary said, back in the living-room. She spun about with opened arms, as if to take and embrace it. 'I love it!'

'What she's trying to do,' Guy said, 'is get you to lower the rent.'

Mr Micklas smiled. 'We would raise it if we were allowed,' he said. 'Beyond the fifteen-per-cent increase, I mean. Apartments with this kind of charm and individuality are as rare as hen's teeth today. The new—' He stopped short, looking at a mahogany secretary at the head of the central hallway. 'That's odd,' he said. 'There's a closet behind that secretary. I'm sure there is. There are five: two in the bedroom, one in the second bedroom, and two in the hallway, there and there.' He went closer to the secretary.

Guy stood high on tiptoes and said, 'You're right. I can see the corners of the door.'

'She moved it,' Rosemary said. 'The secretary; it used to be there.' She pointed to a peaked silhouette left ghostlike on the wall near the bedroom door, and the deep prints of four ball feet in the burgundy carpet. Faint scuff-trails curved and crossed from the four prints to the secretary's feet where they stood now against the narrow adjacent wall.

'Give me a hand, will you?' Mr Micklas said to Guy.

Between them they worked the secretary bit by bit back towards its original place. 'I see why she went into a coma,' Guy said, pushing.

'She couldn't have moved this by herself,' Mr Micklas said; 'she was eighty-nine.'

Rosemary looked doubtfully at the closet door they had uncovered. 'Should we open it?' she asked. 'Maybe her son should.'

The secretary lodged neatly in its four footprints. Mr Micklas massaged his fingers-missing hands. 'I'm authorized to show the apartment,' he said, and went to the door and opened it. The closet was nearly empty; a vacuum cleaner stood at one side of it and three or four wood boards at the other. The overhead shelf was stacked with blue and green bath towels.

'Whoever she locked in got out,' Guy said.

Mr Micklas said, 'She probably didn't need five closets.'

'But why would she cover up her vacuum cleaner and her towels?' Rosemary asked.

Mr Micklas shrugged. 'I don't suppose we'll ever know. She may have been getting senile after all.' He smiled. 'Is there anything else I can show you or tell you?'

'Yes,' Rosemary said. 'What about the laundry facilities? Are there washing machines downstairs?'

They thanked Mr Micklas, who saw them out on to the sidewalk, and then they walked slowly uptown along Seventh Avenue.

'It's cheaper than the other,' Rosemary said, trying to sound as if practical considerations stood foremost in her mind.

'It's one room less, honey,' Guy said.

Rosemary walked in silence for a moment, and then said, 'It's better located.'

'God, yes,' Guy said. 'I could walk to all the theatres.'

Heartened, Rosemary leaped from practicality. 'Oh, Guy, let's take it! Please! Please! It's *such* a wonderful apartment! She didn't do *anything* with it, old Mrs Gardenia! That living-room could be – it could be *beautiful*, and *warm*, and – oh, please, Guy, let's take it, all right?'

'Well sure,' Guy said, smiling. 'If we can get out of the other thing.'

Rosemary grabbed his elbow happily. 'We will!' she said. 'You'll think of something, I know you will!'

Guy telephoned Mrs Cortez from a glass-walled booth while Rosemary, outside, tried to lip-read. Mrs Cortez said she would give them until three o'clock; if she hadn't heard from them by then she would call the next party on the waiting list.

They went to the Russian Tea Room and ordered Bloody Marys and chicken salad sandwiches on black bread.

'You could tell them I'm sick and have to go into the hospital,' Rosemary said.

But that was neither convincing nor compelling. Instead Guy spun a story about a call to join a company of *Come Blow Your Horn* leaving for a four-month USO tour of Vietnam and the Far East. The actor playing Alan had broken his hip and unless he, Guy, who knew the part from stock, stepped in and replaced him, the tour would have to be postponed for at least two weeks. Which would be a damn shame, the way those kids over there were slugging away against the Commies. His wife would have to stay with her folks in Omaha . . .

He ran it twice and went to find the phone.

Rosemary sipped her drink, keeping her left hand all-fingers-crossed under the table. She thought about the First Avenue apartment she didn't want and made a conscientious mental list of its good points; the shiny new kitchen, the dishwasher, the view of the East River, the central air conditioning . . .

The waitress brought the sandwiches.

A pregnant woman went by in a navy blue dress. Rosemary watched her. She must have been in her sixth or seventh month, talking back happily over her shoulder to an older woman with packages, probably her mother.

Someone waved from the opposite wall – the red-haired girl who had come into CBS a few weeks before Rosemary left. Rosemary waved back. The girl mouthed something and, when Rosemary didn't understand, mouthed it again. A man facing the girl turned to look at Rosemary, a starved-looking waxen-faced man.

And there came Guy, tall and handsome, biting back his grin, with *yes* glowing all over him.

'Yes?' Rosemary asked as he took his seat opposite her.

'Yes,' he said. 'The lease is void; the deposit will be returned; I'm to keep an eye open for Lieutenant Hartman of the Signal Corps. Mrs Cortez awaits us at two.'

'You called her?'

'I called her.'

The red-haired girl was suddenly with them, flushed and bright-eyed. 'I said "Marriage certainly agrees with you, you look marvellous",' she said.

Rosemary, ransacking for the girl's name, laughed and said, 'Thank you! We're celebrating. We just got an apartment in the Bramford!'

'The Bram?' the girl said. 'I'm *mad* about it! If you ever want to sub-let, I'm first, and don't you forget it! All those weird gargoyles and creatures climbing up and down between the windows!'

2

Hutch, surprisingly, tried to talk them out of it, on the grounds that the Bramford was a 'danger zone.'

When Rosemary had first come to New York in June of 1962 she had joined another Omaha girl and two girls from Atlanta in an apartment on lower Lexington Avenue. Hutch lived next door, and though he declined to be the full-time father-substitute the girls would have made of him – he had raised two daughters of his own and that was quite enough, thank you – he was none the less on hand in emergencies, such as The Night Someone Was on The Fire Escape and The Time Jeanne Almost Choked to Death. His name was Edward Hutchins, he was English, he was fifty-four. Under three different pen-names he wrote three different series of boys' adventure books.

To Rosemary he gave another sort of emergency assistance. She was the youngest of six children, the other five of whom had married early and made homes close to their parents; behind her in Omaha she had left an angry, suspicious father, a silent mother, and four resenting brothers and sisters. (Only the next-to-the-oldest, Brian, who had a drink problem, had said, 'Go on, Rosie, do what you want to do,' and had slipped her a plastic handbag with eighty-five dollars in it.) In New York Rosemary felt guilty and selfish, and Hutch bucked her up with strong tea and talks about parents and children and one's duty to oneself. She asked him questions that had been unspeakable in Catholic High; he sent her to a night course in philosophy at NYU. 'I'll make a duchess out of this cockney flower girl yet,' he said, and Rosemary had had wit enough to say 'Garn!'

Now, every month or so, Rosemary and Guy had dinner with Hutch, either in their apartment or, when it was his turn, in a restaurant. Guy found Hutch a bit boring but always treated him cordially; his wife had been a cousin of Terence Rattigan, the playwright, and Rattigan and Hutch corresponded. Connections often proved crucial in the theatre, Guy knew, even connections at second-hand.

On the Thursday after they saw the apartment, Rosemary and Guy had dinner with Hutch at Klube's, a small German restaurant on Twenty-third Street. They had given his name to Mrs Cortez on Tuesday afternoon as one of three references she had asked for, and he had already received and answered her letter of inquiry.

'I was tempted to say that you were drug addicts or litter-bugs,' he said, 'or something equally repellent to managers of apartment houses.'

They asked why.

'I don't know whether or not you know it,' he said, buttering a roll, 'but the Bramford had rather an unpleasant reputation early in the century.' He looked up, saw that they didn't know, and went on. (He had a broad shiny face, blue eyes that darted enthusiastically, and a few strands of wetted-down black hair combed crossways over his scalp.) 'Along with the Isadora Duncans and Theodore Dreisers,' he said, 'the Bramford has housed a considerable number of less attractive personages. It's where the Trench sisters performed their little dietary experiments, and where Keith Kennedy held his parties. Adrian Marcato lived there too; and so did Pearl Ames.'

'Who were the Trench sisters?' Guy asked, and Rosemary asked, 'Who was Adrian Marcato?'

'The Trench sisters,' Hutch said, 'were two proper Victorian ladies who were occasional cannibals. They cooked and ate several young children, including a niece.'

'Lovely,' Guy said.

Hutch turned to Rosemary. 'Adrian Marcato practised witchcraft,' he said. 'He made quite a splash in the eighteen-nineties by announcing that he had succeeded in conjuring up the living Satan. He showed off a handful of hair and some claw-parings, and apparently people believed him; enough of them, at least, to form a mob that attacked and nearly killed him in the Bramford lobby.'

'You're joking,' Rosemary said.

'I'm quite serious. A few years later the Keith Kennedy business began, and by the twenties the house was half empty.'

Guy said, 'I knew about Keith Kennedy and about Pearl Ames, but I didn't know Adrian Marcato lived there.'

'And those sisters,' Rosemary said with a shudder.

'It was only World War Two and the housing shortage,' Hutch said, 'that filled the place up again, and now it's acquired a bit of Grand-Old-Apartment-House prestige; but in the twenties it was called Black Bramford and sensible people stayed away. The melon is for the lady, isn't it, Rosemary?'

The waiter placed their appetizers. Rosemary looked questioningly at Guy; he pursed his brow and gave a quick headshake: *It's nothing, don't let him scare you.*

The waiter left. 'Over the years,' Hutch said, 'the Bramford has had far more than its share of ugly and unsavoury happenings. Nor have all of them been in the distant past. In 1959 a dead infant was found wrapped in newspaper in the basement.'

Rosemary said, 'But – awful things probably happen in *every* apartment house now and then.'

'Now and then,' Hutch said. 'The point is, though, that at the Bramford awful things happen a good deal more frequently than "now and then". There are less spectacular irregularities too. There've been more suicides there, for instance, than in houses of comparable size and age.'

'What's the answer, Hutch?' Guy said, playing serious-and-concerned. 'There must be some kind of explanation.'

Hutch looked at him for a moment. 'I don't know,' he said. 'Perhaps it's simply that the notoriety of a pair of Trench sisters attracts an Adrian Marcato, and his notoriety attracts a Keith Kennedy, and eventually a house becomes a – a kind of rallying place for people who are more prone than others to certain types of behaviour. Or perhaps there are things we don't know yet – about magnetic fields or electrons or whatever – ways in which a place can quite literally be malign. I do know this, though: the Bramford is by no means unique. There was a house in London, on Praed Street, in which five separate brutal murders took place within sixty years.

18

None of the five was in any way connected with any of the others; the murderers weren't related nor were the victims, nor were all the murders committed for the same moonstone or Maltese falcon. Yet five separate brutal murders took place within sixty years. In a small house with a shop on the street and an apartment overhead. It was demolished in 1954 – for no especially pressing purpose, since as far as I know the plot was left empty.'

Rosemary worked her spoon in melon. 'Maybe there are good houses too,' she said; 'houses where people keep falling in love and getting married and having babies.'

'And becoming stars,' Guy said.

'Probably there are,' Hutch said. 'Only one never hears of them. It's the stinkers that get the publicity.' He smiled at Rosemary and Guy. 'I wish you two would look for a good house instead of the Bramford,' he said.

Rosemary's spoon of melon stopped halfway to her mouth. 'Are you honestly trying to talk us out of it?' she asked.

'My dear girl,' Hutch said, 'I had a perfectly good date with a charming woman this evening and broke it solely to see you and say my say. I am honestly trying to talk you out of it.'

'Well, Jesus, Hutch—' Guy began.

'I am not saying,' Hutch said, 'that you will walk into the Bramford and be hit on the head with a piano or eaten by spinsters or turned to stone. I am simply saying that the record is there and ought to be considered along with the reasonable rent and the working fire-place: the house has a high incidence of unpleasant happenings. Why deliberately enter a danger zone? Go to the Dakota or the Osborne if you're dead set on nineteenth-century splendour.'

'The Dakota is co-op,' Rosemary said, 'and the Osborne's going to be torn down.'

'Aren't you exaggerating a little bit, Hutch?' Guy said. 'Have there been any other "unpleasant happenings" in the past few years? Besides that baby in the basement?'

'An elevator man was killed last winter,' Hutch said. 'In a not-at-the-dinner-table kind of accident. I was at the library this afternoon with the *Times Index* and three hours of microfilm; would you care to hear more?'

Rosemary looked at Guy. He put down his fork and wiped his mouth. 'It's silly,' he said. 'All right, a lot of unpleasant things have happened there. That doesn't mean that more of them are going to happen. I don't see why the Bramford is any more of a "danger zone'' than any other house in the city. You can flip a coin and get five heads in a row; that doesn't mean that the next five flips are going to be heads too, and it doesn't mean that the coin is any different from any other coin. It's coincidence, that's all.'

'If there were *really* something wrong,' Rosemary said, 'wouldn't it have been demolished? Like the house in London?'

'The house in London,' Hutch said, 'was owned by the family of the last chap murdered there. The Bramford is owned by the church next door.'

'There you are,' Guy said, lighting a cigarette; 'we've got divine protection.'

'It hasn't been working,' Hutch said.

The waiter lifted away their plates.

Rosemary said, 'I didn't know it was owned by a church,' and Guy said, 'The whole city is, honey.'

'Have you tried the Wyoming?' Hutch asked. 'It's in the same block, I think.'

'Hutch,' Rosemary said, 'we've tried everywhere. There's nothing, absolutely nothing, except the *new* houses, with neat square rooms that are all exactly alike and television cameras in the elevators.'

'Is that so terrible?' Hutch asked, smiling.

'Yes,' Rosemary said, and Guy said, 'We were set to go into one, but we backed out to take this.'

Hutch looked at them for a moment, then sat back and struck the table with wide-apart palms. 'Enough,' he said. 'I shall mind my own business, as I ought to have done from the outset. Make fires in your working fireplace! I'll give you a bolt for the door and keep my mouth shut from this day forward. I'm an idiot; forgive me.'

Rosemary smiled. 'The door already has a bolt,' she said. 'And one of those chain things and a peephole.'

'Well, mind you use all three,' Hutch said. 'And don't go wandering through the halls introducing yourself to all and sundry. You're not in Iowa.'

'Omaha.'

The waiter brought their main courses.

On the following Monday afternoon Rosemary and Guy signed a two-year lease on apartment 7E at the Bramford. They gave Mrs Cortez a check for five hundred and eighty-three dollars – a month's rent in advance and a month's rent as security – and were told that if they wished they could make occupancy of the apartment earlier than September first, as it would be cleared by the end of the week and the painters could come in on Wednesday the eighteenth.

Later on Monday they received a telephone call from Martin Gardenia, the son of the apartment's previous tenant. They agreed to meet him at the apartment on Tuesday evening at eight, and, doing so, found him to be a tall man past sixty with a cheerful open manner. He pointed out the things he wanted to sell and named his prices, all of which were attractively low. Rosemary and Guy conferred and examined, and bought two air conditioners, a rose-wood vanity with a petit-point bench, the living-room's Persian rug, and the andirons, firescreen, and tools. Mrs Gardenia's rolltop desk, disappointingly, was not for sale. While Guy wrote a cheque and helped tag the items to be left behind, Rosemary measured the living-room and the bedroom with a six-foot folding rule she had bought that morning.

The previous March Guy had played a role on *Another World*, a daytime television series. The character was back now for three days, so for the rest of the week Guy was busy. Rosemary winnowed a folder of decorating schemes she had collected since high school, found two that seemed appropriate to the apartment, and with those to guide her went looking at furnishings with Joan Jellico, one of the girls from Atlanta she had roomed with on coming to New York. Joan had the card of a decorator, which gave them entrance to wholesale houses and showrooms of every sort. Rosemary looked and made shorthand notes and drew sketches to bring to Guy, and hurried home spilling over with fabric and wallpaper samples in time to catch him on *Another World* and then run out again and shop for dinner. She skipped her sculpture class and cancelled, happily, a dental appointment.

On the Friday evening the apartment was theirs; an emptiness of high ceilings and unfamiliar dark into which they came with a lamp and a shopping bag, striking echoes from the farthest rooms. They turned on their air conditioners and admired their rug and their fireplace and Rosemary's vanity; admired too their bathtub, doorknobs, hinges, moulding, floors, stove, refrigerator, bay windows, and view. They picnicked on the rug, on tuna sandwiches and beer, and made floor plans of all four rooms, Guy measuring and Rosemary drawing. On the rug again, they unplugged the lamp and stripped and made love in the nightglow of shadeless windows. 'Shh!' Guy hissed afterwards, wide-eyed with fear. 'I hear – the

21

Trench sisters chewing!' Rosemary hit him on the head, hard.

They bought a sofa and a king-size bed, a table for the kitchen, and two bentwood chairs. They called Con Ed and the phone company and stores and workmen and the Padded Wagon.

The painters came on Wednesday the eighteenth; patched, spackled, primed, painted, and were gone on Friday the twentieth, leaving colours very much like Rosemary's samples. A solitary paperhanger came in and grumbled and papered the bedroom.

They called stores and workmen and Guy's mother in Montreal. They bought an airmoire and a dining table and hi-fi components and new dishes and silverware. They were flush. In 1964 Guy had done a series of Anacin commercials that, shown time and time again, had earned him eighteen thousand dollars and was still producing a sizable income.

They hung window shades and papered shelves, watched carpet go down in the bedroom and white vinyl in the hallway. They got a plug-in-phone with three jacks; paid bills and left a forwarding notice at the post office.

On Friday, August 27th, they moved. Joan and Dick Jellico sent a large potted plant and Guy's agent a small one. Hutch sent a telegram: *The Bramford will change from a bad house to a good house when one of its doors is marked R. and G. Woodhouse.*

3

And then Rosemary was busy and happy. She bought and hung curtains, found a Victorian glass lamp for the living-room, hung pots and pans on the kitchen wall. One day she realized that the four boards in the hall closet were shelves, fitting across to sit on wood cleats on the side walls. She covered them with gingham contact paper and, when Guy came home, showed him a neatly filled linen closet. She found a supermarket on Sixth Avenue and a Chinese laundry on Fifty-fifth Street for the sheets and Guy's shirts.

Guy was busy too, away every day like other women's husbands. With Labour Day past, his vocal coach was back in town; Guy worked with him each morning and auditioned for plays and commercials most afternoons. At breakfast he was touchy reading the theatrical page – everyone else was out of town with *Skyscraper* or *Drat! The Cat!* or *The Impossible Years* or *Hot September*; only he was in New York with residuals-from-Anacin – but Rosemary knew that very soon he'd get something good, and quietly she set his coffee before him and quietly took for herself the newspaper's other section.

The nursery was, for the time being, a den, with off-white walls and the furniture from the old apartment. The white-and-yellow wallpaper would come later, clean and fresh. Rosemary had a sample of it lying ready in *Picasso's Picassos*, along with a Saks ad showing the crib and bureau.

She wrote to her brother Brian to share her happiness. No one else in the family would have welcomed it; they were all hostile now – parents, brothers, sisters – not forgiving her for (*a*) marrying a Protestant, (*b*) marrying in only a civil ceremony, and (*c*) having a mother-in-law who had had two divorces and was married now to a Jew up in Canada.

She made Guy chicken Marengo and *vitello tonnato*, baked a mocha layer cake and a jarful of butter cookies.

They heard Minnie Castevet before they met her; heard her through their bedroom wall, shouting in a hoarse mid-western bray. 'Roman, come to bed! It's twenty past eleven!' And five minutes later: 'Roman? Bring me in some root beer when you come!'

'I didn't know they were still making Ma and Pa Kettle movies,' Guy said, and Rosemary laughed uncertainly. She was nine years younger than Guy, and some of his references lacked clear meaning for her.

They met the Goulds in 7F, a pleasant elderly couple, and the German-accented Bruhns and their son Walter in 7C. They smiled and nodded in the hall to the Kelloggs, 7G, Mr Stein, 7H, and the Messrs Dubin and DeVore, 7B. (Rosemary learned everyone's name immediately, from doorbells and from face-up mail on doormats, which she had no qualms about reading.) The Kapps in 7D, unseen and with no mail, were apparently still away for the summer; and the Castevets in 7A, heard ('Roman! Where's Terry?') but unseen, were either recluses or comers-and-goers-at-odd-hours. Their door was opposite the elevator, their doormat supremely readable. They got air mail letters from a surprising variety of places: Hawick, Scotland; Langeac, France; Vitória, Brazil; Cessnock, Australia.

They subscribed to both *Life* and *Look*.

No sign at all did Rosemary and Guy see of the Trench sisters, Adrian Marcato, Keith Kennedy, Pearl Ames, or their latter-day equivalents. Dublin and DeVore were homosexuals; everyone else seemed entirely commonplace.

Almost every night the midwestern bray could be heard, from the apartment which, Rosemary and Guy came to realize, had originally been the bigger front part of their own. 'But it's *impossible* to be a hundred per cent sure!' the woman argued, and, 'If you want *my* opinion, we shouldn't tell her at *all*; that's *my* opinion!'

One Saturday night the Castevets had a party, with a dozen or so people talking and singing. Guy fell asleep easily but Rosemary lay awake until after two, hearing flat unmusical singing and a flute or clarinet that piped along beside it.

The only time Rosemary remembered Hutch's misgivings and was made uneasy by them was when she went down to the basement every fourth day or so to do the laundry. The service elevator was in itself unsettling – small, unmanned, and given to sudden creaks and tremors – and the basement was an eerie place of once-whitewashed brick passageways where footfalls whispered distantly and unseen doors thudded closed, where cast-off refrigerators faced the wall under glary bulbs in wire cages.

It was here, Rosemary would remember, that a dead baby wrapped in newspaper had not so long ago been found. Whose baby had it been, and how had it died? Who had found it? Had the person who left it been caught and punished? She thought of going to the library and reading the story in old newspapers as Hutch had done; but that would have made it more real, more dreadful than it already was. To know the spot where the baby had lain, to have perhaps to walk past it on the way to the laundry room and again on the way back to the elevator, would have been unbearable. Partial ignorance, she decided, was partial bliss. *Damn Hutch and his good intentions!*

The laundry room would have done nicely in a prison: steamy brick walls, more bulbs in cages, and scores of deep double sinks in iron-mesh cubicles. There were coin-operated washers and dryers and, in most of the padlocked cubicles, privately owned machines. Rosemary came down on weekends or after five; earlier on weekdays a bevy of Negro laundresses ironed and gossiped and had abruptly fallen silent at her one unknowing intrusion. She had smiled all around and tried to be invisible, but they hadn't spoken another word and she had felt self-conscious, clumsy, and Negro-oppressing.

One afternoon, when she and Guy had been in the Bramford a little over two weeks, Rosemary was sitting in the laundry room at 5.15 reading *The New Yorker* and waiting to add softener to the rinse water when a girl her own age came in – a dark-haired cameo-faced girl who, Rosemary realized with a start, was Anna Maria Alberghetti. She was wearing white sandals, black shorts, and an apricot silk blouse, and was carrying a yellow plastic laundry basket. Nodding at Rosemary and then not looking at her, she went to one of the washers, opened it, and began feeding dirty clothes into it.

Anna Maria Alberghetti, as far as Rosemary knew, did not live at the Bramford, but she could well have been visiting someone and helping out with the chores. A closer look, though, told Rosemary that she was mistaken; this girl's nose was too long and sharp and there were other less definable differences of expression and carriage. The resemblance, however, was a remarkable one – and suddenly Rosemary found the girl looking at her with an embarrassed questioning smile, the washer beside her closed and filling.

'I'm sorry,' Rosemary said. 'I thought you were Anna Maria Alberghetti, so I've been staring at you. I'm sorry.'

The girl blushed and smiled and looked at the floor a few feet to her side. 'That happens a lot,' she said. 'You don't have to apologize. People have been thinking I'm Anna Maria since I was, oh, just a kid, when she first started out in *Here Comes The Groom*.' She looked at Rosemary, still blushing but no longer smiling. 'I don't see a resemblance at all,' she said. 'I'm of Italian parentage like she is, but no *physical* resemblance.'

'There's a very strong one,' Rosemary said.

'I guess there is,' the girl said; 'everyone's always telling me. I don't see it though. I wish I did, believe me.'

'Do you know her?' Rosemary asked.

'No.'

'The way you said "Anna Maria" I thought—'

'Oh no, I just call her that. I guess from talking about her so much with everyone.' She wiped her hand on her shorts and stepped forward, holding it out and smiling. 'I'm Terry Gionoffrio,' she said, 'and *I* can't spell it so don't *you* try.'

Rosemary smiled and shook hands. 'I'm Rosemary Woodhouse,' she said. 'We're new tenants here. Have you been here long?'

'I'm not a tenant at all,' the girl said. 'I'm just staying with Mr and Mrs Castevet, up on the seventh floor. I'm their guest, sort of, since June. Oh, you know them?'

'No,' Rosemary said, smiling, 'but our apartment is right behind theirs and used to be the back part of it.'

'Oh for goodness' sake,' the girl said, 'you're the party that took the old lady's apartment! Mrs – the old lady who died!'

'Gardenia.'

'That's right. She was a good *friend* of the Castevets. She used to grow herbs and things and bring them in for Mrs Castevet to cook with.'

Rosemary nodded. 'When we first looked at the apartment,' she said, 'one room was full of plants.'

'And now that she's dead,' Terry said, 'Mrs Castevet's got a miniature greenhouse in the kitchen and grows things herself.'

'Excuse me, I have to put softener in,' Rosemary said. She got up and got the bottle from the laundry bag on the washer.

'Do you know who *you* look like?' Terry asked her; and Rosemary, unscrewing the cap, said, 'No, who?'

'Piper Laurie.'

Rosemary laughed. 'Oh, no,' she said. 'It's funny your saying that, because my husband used to date Piper Laurie before she got married.'

'No kidding? In Hollywood?'

'No, here.' Rosemary poured a capful of the softener. Terry opened the washer door and Rosemary thanked her and tossed the softener in.

'Is he an actor, your husband?' Terry asked.

Rosemary nodded complacently, capping the bottle.

'No kidding! What's his name?'

'Guy Woodhouse,' Rosemary said. 'He was in *Luther* and *Nobody Loves An Albatross*, and he does a lot of work in television.'

'Gee, I watch TV all day long,' Terry said. 'I'll bet I've seen him!' Glass crashed somewhere in the basement; a bottle smashing or a windowpane. 'Yow,' Terry said.

Rosemary hunched her shoulders and looked uneasily towards the laundry room's doorway. 'I hate this basement,' she said.

'Me too,' Terry said. 'I'm glad you're here. If I was alone now I'd be scared stiff.'

'A delivery boy probably dropped a bottle,' Rosemary said.

Terry said, 'Listen, we could come down together regular. Your door is by the service elevator, isn't it? I could ring your bell and we could come down together. We could call each other first on the house phone.'

'That would be great,' Rosemary said. 'I hate coming down here alone.'

Terry laughed happily, seemed to seek words, and then, still laughing, said, 'I've got a good luck charm that'll maybe do for both of us!' She pulled away the collar of her blouse, drew out a silver neckchain, and showed Rosemary on the end of it a silver filigree ball a little less than an inch in diameter.

'Oh, that's *beautiful*,' Rosemary said.

'Isn't it?' Terry said. 'Mrs Castevet gave it to me the day before yesterday. It's three hundred years old. She grew the stuff inside it in that little greenhouse. It's good luck, or anyway it's supposed to be.'

Rosemary looked more closely at the charm Terry held out between thumb and fingertip. It was filled with a greenish-brown spongy substance that pressed out against the silver openwork. A bitter smell made Rosemary draw back.

Terry laughed again. 'I'm not mad about the smell either,' she said. 'I hope it works!'

'It's a beautiful charm,' Rosemary said. 'I've never seen anything like it.'

'It's European,' Terry said. She leaned a hip against a washer and admired the ball, turning it one way and another. 'The Castevets are the most wonderful people in the world, bar none,' she said. 'They picked me up off the sidewalk – and I mean that literally; I conked out on Eighth Avenue – and they brought me here and adopted me like a mother and father. Or like a grandmother and grandfather, I guess.'

'You were sick?' Rosemary asked.

'That's putting it mildly,' Terry said. 'I was starving and on dope and doing a lot of other things that I'm so ashamed of I could throw up just thinking about them. And Mr and Mrs Castevet completely rehabilitated me. They got me off the H, the dope, and got food into me and clean clothes on me, and now nothing is too good for me as far as they're concerned. They give me all kinds of health food and vitamins, they even have a doctor come give me regular checkups! It's because they're childless. I'm like the daughter they never had, you know?'

Rosemary nodded.

'I thought at first that maybe they had some kind of ulterior motive,' Terry said. 'Maybe some kind of sex thing they would want me to do, or he would want, or she. But they've really been like real grandparents. Nothing like that. They're going to put me through secretarial school in a little while and later on I'm going to pay them back. I only had three years of high school but there's a way of making it up.' She dropped the filigree ball back into her blouse.

Rosemary said, 'It's nice to know there are people like that, when you hear so much about apathy and people who are afraid of getting involved.'

'There aren't many like Mr and Mrs Castevet,' Terry said. 'I would be dead now if it wasn't for them. That's an absolute fact. Dead or in jail.'

'You don't have any family that could have helped you?'

A brother in the Navy. The less said about *him* the better.'

Rosemary transferred her finished wash to a dryer and waited with Terry for hers to be done. They spoke of Guy's occasional role on *Another World* ('Sure I remember! You're married to *him*?'), the Bramford's past (of which Terry knew nothing), and the coming visit to New York of Pope Paul. Terry was, like Rosemary, Catholic but no longer observing; she was anxious, though, to get a ticket to the papal mass to be celebrated at Yankee Stadium. When her wash was done and drying the two girls walked together to the service elevator and rode to the seventh floor. Rosemary invited Terry in to see the apartment, but Terry asked if she could take a rain check; the Castevets ate at six and she didn't like to be late. She said she would call Rosemary on the house phone later in the evening so they could go down together to pick up their dry laundry.

Guy was home, eating a bag of Fritos and watching a Grace Kelly movie. 'Them sure must be clean clothes,' he said.

Rosemary told him about Terry and the Castevets, and that Terry had remembered him from *Another World*. He made light of it, but it pleased him. He was depressed by the likelihood that an actor named Donald Baumgart was going to beat him out for a part in a new comedy for which both had read a second time that afternoon. 'Jesus Christ,' he said, 'what kind of a name is *Donald Baumgart*?' His own name, before he changed it, had been Sherman Peden.

Rosemary and Terry picked up their laundry at eight o'clock, and Terry came in with Rosemary to meet Guy and see the apartment. She blushed and was flustered by Guy, which spurred him to flowery

28

compliments and the bringing of ashtrays and the striking of matches. Terry had never seen the apartment before; Mrs Gardenia and the Castevets had had a falling-out shortly after her arrival, and soon afterwards Mrs Gardenia had gone into the coma from which she had never emerged. 'It's a lovely apartment,' Terry said.

'It will be,' Rosemary said. 'We're not even halfway furnished yet.'

'I've *got* it!' Guy cried with a handclap. He pointed triumphantly at Terry. 'Anna Maria Alberghetti!'

4

A package came from Bonniers, from Hutch; a tall teakwood ice bucket with a bright orange lining. Rosemary called him at once and thanked him. He had seen the apartment after the painters left but not since she and Guy had moved in; she explained about the chairs that were a week late and the sofa that wasn't due for another month. 'For God's sake don't even think yet about entertaining,' Hutch said. 'Tell me how everything is.'

Rosemary told him, in happy detail. 'And the neighbours certainly don't *seem* abnormal,' she said. 'Except normal abnormal like homosexuals; there are two of them, and across the hall from us there's a nice old couple named Gould with a place in Pennsylvania where they breed Persian cats. We can have one any time we want.'

'They shed,' Hutch said.

'And there's another couple that we haven't actually met yet who took in this girl who was hooked on drugs, whom we *have* met, and they completely cured her and are putting her through secretarial school.'

'It sounds as if you've moved into Sunnybrook Farm,' Hutch said; 'I'm delighted.'

'The basement is kind of creepy,' Rosemary said. 'I curse you every time I go down there.'

'Why on earth me?'

'Your *stories*.'

'If you mean the ones I write, I curse me too; if you mean the ones

I told you, you might with equal justification curse the fire alarm for the fire and the weather bureau for the typhoon.'

Rosemary, cowed, said, 'It won't be so bad from now on. That girl I mentioned is going down there with me.'

Hutch said, 'It's obvious you've exerted the healthy influence I predicted and the house is no longer a chamber of horrors. Have fun with the ice bucket and say hello to Guy.'

The Kapps in apartment 7D appeared; a stout couple in their middle thirties with an inquisitive two-year-old daughter named Lisa. 'What's your name?' Lisa asked, sitting in her stroller. 'Did you eat your egg? Did you eat your Captain Crunch?'

'My name is Rosemary,' Rosemary said. 'I ate my egg but I've never even *heard* of Captain Crunch. Who is he?'

On Friday night, September 17th, Rosemary and Guy went with two other couples to a preview of a play called *Mrs Dally* and then to a party given by a photographer, Dee Bertillon, in his studio on West Forty-eighth Street. An argument developed between Guy and Bertillon over Actors Equity's policy of blocking the employment of foreign actors – Guy thought it was right, Bertillon thought it was wrong – and though the others present buried the disagreement under a quick tide of jokes and gossip, Guy took Rosemary away soon after, at a few minutes past twelve-thirty.

The night was mild and balmy and they walked; and as they approached the Bramford's blackened mass they saw on the sidewalk before it a group of twenty or so people gathered in a semicircle at the side of a parked car. Two police cars waited double-parked, their roof lights spinning red.

Rosemary and Guy walked faster, hand in hand, their senses sharpening. Cars on the avenue slowed questioningly; windows scraped open in the Bramford and heads looked out beside gargoyles' heads. The night doorman Toby came from the house with a tan blanket that a policeman turned to take from him.

The roof of the car, a Volkswagen, was crumpled to the side; the windshield was crazed with a million fractures. 'Dead,' someone said, and someone else said, 'I took up and I think it's some kind of a big bird zooming down, like an eagle or something.'

Rosemary and Guy stood on tiptoes, craned over people's shoulders. 'Get back now, will you?' a policeman at the centre said. The shoulders separated, a sport-shirted back moved away. On the sidewalk Terry lay, watching the sky with one eye, half of her face gone to red pulp. Tan blanket flipped over her. Settling, it reddened in one place and then another.

Rosemary wheeled, eyes shut, right hand making an automatic cross. She kept her mouth tightly closed, afraid she might vomit.

Guy winced and drew air in under his teeth. 'Oh, Jesus,' he said, and groaned. 'Oh my God.'

A policeman said, 'Get back, will you?'

'We know her,' Guy said.

Another policeman turned and said, 'What's her name?'

'Terry.'

'Terry what?' He was forty or so and sweating. His eyes were blue and beautiful, with thick black lashes.

Guy said, 'Ro? What was her name? Terry what?'

Rosemary opened her eyes and swallowed. 'I don't remember,' she said. 'Italian, with a G. A long name. She made a joke about spelling it. Not being able to.'

Guy said to the blue-eyed policeman. 'She was staying with people named Castevet, in apartment seven A.'

'We've got that already,' the policeman said.

Another policeman came up, holding a sheet of pale yellow notepaper. Mr Micklas was behind him, tight-mouthed, in a raincoat over striped pyjamas. 'Short and sweet,' the policeman said to the blue-eyed one, and handed him the yellow paper. 'She stuck it to the window sill with a band-aid so it wouldn't blow away.'

'Anybody there?'

The other shook his head.

The blue-eyed policeman read what was written on the sheet of paper, sucking thoughtfully at his front teeth. 'Theresa Gionoffrio,' he said. He pronounced it as an Italian would. Rosemary nodded.

Guy said, 'Wednesday night you wouldn't have guessed she had a sad thought in her mind.'

'Nothing but sad thoughts,' the policeman said, opening his pad holder. He laid the paper inside it and closed the holder with a width of yellow sticking out.

'Did you know her?' Mr Micklas asked Rosemary.

'Only slightly,' she said.

'Oh, of course,' Mr Micklas said; 'you're on seven too.'

Guy said to Rosemary, 'Come on, honey, let's go upstairs.'

The policeman said, 'Do you have any idea where we can find these people Castevet?'

31

'No, none at all,' Guy said. 'We've never even met them.'

'They're usually at home now,' Rosemary said. 'We hear them through the wall. Our bedroom is next to theirs.'

Guy put his hand on Rosemary's back. 'Come on, hon,' he said. They nodded to the policeman and Mr Micklas, and started towards the house.

'Here they come now,' Mr Micklas said. Rosemary and Guy stopped and turned. Coming from downtown, as they themselves had come, were a tall, broad, white-haired woman and a tall, thin, shuffling man. 'The Castevets?' Rosemary asked. Mr Micklas nodded.

Mrs Castevet was wrapped in light blue, with snow-white dabs of gloves, purse, shoes, and hat. Nurse-like she supported her husband's forearm. He was dazzling, in an every-colour seersucker jacket, red slacks, a pink bow tie, and a grey fedora with a pink band. He was seventy-five or older; she was sixty-eight or nine. They came closer with expressions of young alertness, with friendly quizzical smiles. The policeman stepped forward to meet them and their smiles faltered and fell away. Mrs Castevet said something worryingly; Mr Castevet frowned and shook his head. His wide, thin-lipped mouth was rosy-pink, as if lipsticked; his cheeks were chalky, his eyes small and bright in deep sockets. She was big-nosed, with a sullen fleshy underlip. She wore pink-rimmed eyeglasses on a neckchain that dipped down from behind plain pearl earrings.

The policeman said, 'Are you folks the Castevets on the seventh floor?'

'We are,' Mr Castevet said in a dry voice that had to be listened for.

'You have a young woman named Theresa Gionoffrio living with you?'

'We do,' Mr Castevet said. 'What's wrong? Has there been an accident?'

'You'd better brace yourselves for some bad news,' the policeman said. He waited, looking at each of them in turn and then he said, 'She's dead. She killed herself.' He raised a hand, the thumb pointing back over his shoulder. 'She jumped out of the window.'

They looked at him with no change of expression at all, as if he hadn't spoken yet; then Mrs Castevet leaned sideways, glanced beyond him at the red-stained blanket, and stood straight again and looked him in the eyes. 'That's not possible,' she said in her loud midwestern Roman-bring-me-some-root-beer voice. 'It's a mistake.

Somebody else is under there.'

The policeman, not turning from her, said, 'Artie, would you let these people take a look, please?'

Mrs Castevet marched past him, her jaw set.

Mr Castevet stayed where he was. 'I knew this would happen,' he said. 'She got deeply depressed every three weeks or so. I noticed it and told my wife, but she pooh-poohed me. She's an optimist who refuses to admit that everything doesn't always turn out the way she wants it to.'

Mrs Castevet came back. 'That doesn't mean that she killed herself,' she said. 'She was a very happy girl with no *reason* for self-destruction. It must have been an accident. She must have been cleaning the windows and lost her hold. She was always surprising us by cleaning things and doing things for us.'

'She wasn't cleaning windows at midnight,' Mr Castevet said.

'Why not?' Mrs Castevet said angrily. 'Maybe she was!'

The policeman held out the pale yellow paper, having taken it from his pad holder.

Mrs Castevet hesitated, then took it and turned it around and read it. Mr Castevet tipped his head in over her arm and read it too, his thin vivid lips moving.

'Is that her handwriting?' the policeman asked.

Mrs Castevet nodded. Mr Castevet said, 'Definitely. Absolutely.'

The policeman held out his hand and Mrs Castevet gave him the paper. He said, 'Thank you. I'll see you get it back when we're done with it.'

She took off her glasses, dropped them on their neckchain, and covered both her eyes with white-gloved fingertips. 'I don't believe it,' she said. 'I just don't believe it. She was so happy. All her troubles were in the past.' Mr Castevet put his hand on her shoulder and looked at the ground and shook his head.

'Do you know the name of her next-of-kin?' the policeman asked.

'She didn't have any,' Mrs Castevet said. 'She was all alone. She didn't have anyone, only us.'

'Didn't she have a brother?' Rosemary asked.

Mrs Castevet put on her glasses and looked at her. Mr Castevet looked up from the ground, his deep-socketed eyes glinting under his hat brim.

'Did she?' the policeman asked.

'She said she did,' Rosemary said. 'In the Navy.'

The policeman looked to the Castevets.

'It's news to me,' Mrs Castevet said, and Mr Castevet said, 'To both of us.'

The policeman asked Rosemary, 'Do you know his rank or where he's stationed?'

'No, I don't,' she said, and to the Castevets: 'She mentioned him to me the other day, in the laundry room. I'm Rosemary Woodhouse.'

Guy said, 'We're in seven E.'

'I feel just the way you do, Mrs Castevet,' Rosemary said. 'She seemed so happy and full of – of good feelings about the future. She said *wonderful* things about you and your husband; how grateful she was to both of you for all the help you were giving her.'

'Thank you,' Mrs Castevet said, and Mr Castevet said 'It's nice of you to tell us that. It makes it a little easier.'

The policeman said, 'You don't know anything else about this brother except that he's in the Navy?'

'That's all,' Rosemary said. 'I don't think she liked him very much.'

'It should be easy to find him,' Mr Castevet said, 'with an uncommon name like Gionoffrio.'

Guy put his hand on Rosemary's back again and they withdrew towards the house. 'I'm so stunned and so sorry,' Rosemary said to the Castevets; and Guy said, 'It's such a pity. It's—'

Mrs Castevet said, 'Thank you,' and Mr Castevet said something long and sibilant of which only the phrase 'her last days' was understandable.

They rode upstairs ('Oh, my!' the night elevator man Diego said; 'Oh, my! Oh, my!'), looked ruefully at the now-haunted door of 7A, and walked through the branching hallway to their own apartment. Mr Kellogg in 7G peered out from behind his chained door and asked what was going on downstairs. They told him.

They sat on the edge of their bed for a few minutes, speculating about Terry's reason for killing herself. Only if the Castevets told them some day what was in the note, they agreed, would they ever learn for certain what had driven her to the violent death they had nearly witnessed. And even knowing what was in the note, Guy pointed out, they might still not know the full answer, for part of it had probably been beyond Terry's own understanding. Something had led her to drugs and something had led her to death; what that something was, it was too late now for anyone to know.

Remember what Hutch said?' Rosemary asked. 'About there being more suicides here than in other buildings?'

'Ah, Ro,' Guy said, 'that's crap, honey, that ''danger zone'' business.'

'Hutch believes it.'

'Well, it's *still* crap.'

'I can imagine what he's going to say when he hears about this.'

'Don't tell him,' Guy said. 'He sure as hell won't read about it in the papers.' A strike against the New York newspapers had begun that morning, and there were rumours that it might continue a month or longer.

They undressed, showered, resumed a stopped game of Scrabble, stopped it, made love, and found milk and a dish of cold spaghetti in the refrigerator. Just before they put the lights out at two-thirty, Guy remembered to check the answering service and found that he had got a part in a radio commercial for Cresta Blanca wines.

Soon he was asleep, but Rosemary lay awake beside him, seeing Terry's pulped face and her one eye watching the sky. After a while, though, she was at Our Lady. Sister Agnes was shaking her fist at her, ousting her from leadership of the second-floor monitors. 'Sometimes I wonder how come you're the leader of *anything*!' she said. A bump on the other side of the wall woke Rosemary, and Mrs Castevet said, 'And please don't tell me what Laura-Louise said because I'm not interested!' Rosemary turned over and burrowed into her pillow.

Sister Agnes was furious. Her piggy-eyes were squeezed to slits and her nostrils were bubbling the way they always did at such moments. Thanks to Rosemary it had been necessary to brick up all the windows, and now Our Lady had been taken out of the beautiful-school competition being run by the *World-Herald*. 'If you'd listened to *me*, we wouldn't have *had* to do it!' Sister Agnes cried in a hoarse midwestern bray. 'We'd have been all set to go now instead of starting all over from scratch!' Uncle Mike tried to hush her. He was the principal of Our Lady, which was connected by passageways to his body shop in South Omaha. 'I *told* you not to tell her anything in advance,' Sister Agnes continued lower, piggy-eyes glinting hatefully at Rosemary. '*I told* you she wouldn't be open-minded. Time enough *later* to let her in on it.' (Rosemary had told Sister Veronica about the windows being bricked up and Sister Veronica had withdrawn the school from the competition; otherwise no one would have noticed and they would have won. It had been right to tell, though, Sister Agnes notwithstanding. A Catholic school shouldn't win by trickery.) 'Anybody! Anybody!' Sister Agnes said. 'All she has to be is young, healthy, and not a virgin. She doesn't have to be a no-good drug-addict whore out of the gutter. Didn't I say that in the beginning? Anybody. As long as she's young and healthy and not a virgin.' Which didn't make sense at all, not even to Uncle Mike; so Rosemary turned over and it was Saturday afternoon, and she and Brian and Eddie and Jean were at the candy counter in the Orpheum, going in to see Gary Cooper and Patricia Neal in *The Fountainhead*, only it was live, not a movie.

5

On the following Monday morning Rosemary was putting away the last of a double armload of groceries when the doorbell rang; and the peephole showed Mrs Castevet, white hair in curlers under a blue-and-white kerchief, looking solemnly straight ahead as if waiting for the click of a passport photographer's camera.

Rosemary opened the door and said, 'Hello. How are you?'

Mrs Castevet smiled bleakly. 'Fine,' she said. 'May I come in for a minute?'

'Yes, of course; please do.' Rosemary stood back against the wall and held the door wide open. A faint bitter smell brushed across her as Mrs Castevet came in, the smell of Terry's silver good luck charm filled with spongy greenish-brown. Mrs Castevet was wearing toreador pants and shouldn't have been; her hips and thighs were massive, slabbed with wide bands of fat. The pants were lime green under a blue blouse; the blade of a screwdriver poked from her hip pocket. Stopping between the doorways of the den and kitchen, she turned and put on her neckchained glasses and smiled at Rosemary. A dream Rosemary had had a night or two earlier sparked in her mind – something about Sister Agnes bawling her out for bricking up windows – and she shook it away and smiled attentively, ready to hear what Mrs Castevet was about to say.

'I just came over to thank you,' Mrs Castevet said, 'for saying those nice things to us the other night, poor Terry telling you she was grateful to us for what we done. You'll never know how comforting it was to hear something like that in such a shock moment, because in both of our minds was the thought that maybe we had failed her in some way and *drove* her to it, although her note made it crystal clear, of course, that she did it of her own free will; but anyway it was a blessing to hear the words spoken out loud like that by somebody Terry had confided in just before the end.'

'Please, there's no reason to thank me,' Rosemary said. 'All I did was tell you what she said to me.'

'A lot of people wouldn't have bothered,' Mrs Castevet said. 'They'd have just walked away without wanting to spend the air and the little bit of muscle power. When you're older you'll come to realize that acts of kindness are few and far between in this world of ours. So I *do* thank you, and Roman does too. Roman is my hubby.'

Rosemary ducked her head in concession, smiled, and said, 'You're welcome. I'm glad that I helped.'

'She was cremated yesterday morning with no ceremony,' Mrs Castevet said. 'That's the way she wanted it. Now we have to forget and go on. It certainly won't be easy; we took a lot of pleasure in having her around, not having children of our own. Do you have any?'

'No, we don't,' Rosemary said.

Mrs Castevet looked into the kitchen. 'Oh, that's nice,' she said, 'the pan's hanging on the wall that way. And look how you put the table, isn't that interesting.'

'It was in a magazine,' Rosemary said.

'You certainly got a nice paint job,' Mrs Castevet said, fingering the door jamb appraisingly. 'Did the house do it? You must have been mighty openhanded with the painters; they didn't do this kind of work for *us*.'

'All we gave them was five dollars each,' Rosemary said.

'Oh, is that all?' Mrs Castevet turned around and looked into the den. 'Oh, that's nice,' she said, 'a TV room.'

'It's only temporary,' Rosemary said. 'At least I hope it is. It's going to be a nursery.'

'Are you pregnant?' Mrs Castevet asked, looking at her.

'Not yet,' Rosemary said, 'but I hope to be, as soon as we're settled.'

'That's wonderful,' Mrs Castevet said. 'You're young and healthy; you ought to have lots of children.'

'We plan to have three,' Rosemary said. 'Would you like to see the rest of the apartment?'

'I'd love to,' Mrs Castevet said. 'I'm dying to see what you've done to it. I used to be in here almost every day. The woman who had it before you was a dear friend of mine.'

'I know,' Rosemary said, easing past Mrs Castevet to lead the way; 'Terry told me.'

'Oh, did she,' Mrs Castevet said, following along. 'It sounds like you two had some long talks together down there in the laundry room.'

'Only one,' Rosemary said.

The living-room startled Mrs Castevet. 'My goodness!' she said. 'I can't get over the change! It looks so much *brighter*! Oh and look at that chair. Isn't that handsome?'

'It just came Friday,' Rosemary said.

'What did you pay for a chair like that?'

Rosemary, disconcerted, said, 'I'm not sure. I think it was about two hundred dollars.'

'You don't mind my asking, do you?' Mrs Castevet said, and tapped her nose. 'That's how I got a big nose, by being nosy.'

Rosemary laughed and said, 'No, no, it's all right. I don't mind.'

Mrs Castevet inspected the living-room, the bedroom, and the bathroom, asking how much Mrs Gardenia's son had charged them for the rug and the vanity, where they had got the night-table lamps, exactly how old Rosemary was, and if an electric toothbrush was really any better than the old kind. Rosemary found herself enjoying this open forthright old woman with her loud voice and her blunt questions. She offered coffee and cake to her.

'What does your hubby do?' Mrs Castevet asked, sitting at the kitchen table idly checking prices on cans of soup and oysters. Rosemary, folding a Chemex paper, told her. 'I knew it!' Mrs Castevet said. 'I said to Roman yesterday, "He's so good-looking I'll bet he's a movie actor!" There's three-four of them in the building, you know. What movies was he in?'

'No movies,' Rosemary said. 'He was in two plays called *Luther* and *Nobody Loves An Albatross* and he does a lot of work in television and radio.'

They had the coffee and cake in the kitchen, Mrs Castevet refusing to let Rosemary disturb the living-room on her account. 'Listen, Rosemary,' she said, swallowing cake and coffee at once, 'I've got a two-inch-thick sirloin steak sitting defrosting right this minute, and half of it's going to go to waste with just Roman and me there to eat it. Why don't you and Guy come over and have supper with us tonight, what do you say?'

'Oh, no, we couldn't,' Rosemary said.

'Sure you could; why not?'

'No, really, I'm sure you don't want to—'

'It would be a big help to us if you would,' Mrs Castevet said. She looked into her lap, then looked up at Rosemary with a hard-to-carry smile. 'We had friends with us last night and Saturday,' she said, 'but this'll be the first night we'll be alone since –the other night.'

Rosemary leaned forward feelingly. 'If you're *sure* it won't be trouble for you,' she said.

'Honey, if it was trouble I wouldn't ask you,' Mrs Castevet said. 'Believe me, I'm as selfish as the day is long.'

Rosemary smiled. 'That isn't what Terry told me,' she said.

'Well,' Mrs Castevet said with a pleased smile, 'Terry didn't know what she was talking about.'

'I'll have to check with Guy,' Rosemary said, 'but you go ahead and count on us.'

Mrs Castevet said happily, 'Listen! You tell him I won't take no for an answer! I want to be able to tell folks I knew him when!'

They ate their cake and coffee, talking of the excitements and hazards of an acting career, the new season's television shows and how bad they were, and the continuing newspaper strike.

'Will six-thirty be too early for you?' Mrs Castevet asked at the door.

'It'll be perfect,' Rosemary said.

'Roman don't like to eat any later than that,' Mrs Castevet said. 'He has stomach trouble and if he eats too late he can't get to sleep. You know where we are, don't you? Seven A, at six-thirty. We'll be looking forward. Oh, here's your mail, dear; I'll get it. Ads. Well, it's better than getting nothing, isn't it?'

Guy came home at two-thirty in a bad mood; he had learned from his agent that, as he had feared, the grotesquely named Donald Baumgart had won the part he had come within a hair of getting. Rosemary kissed him and installed him in his new easy chair with a melted cheese sandwich and a glass of beer. She had read the script of the play and not liked it; it would probably close out of town, she told Guy, and Donald Baumgart would never be heard of again.

'Even if it folds,' Guy said, 'it's the kind of part that gets noticed.

You'll see; he'll get something else right after.' He opened the corner of his sandwich, looked in bitterly, closed it, and started eating.

'Mrs Castevet was here this morning,' Rosemary said. 'To thank me for telling them that Terry was grateful to them. I think she really just wanted to see the apartment. She's absolutely the nosiest person I've ever seen. She actually asked the prices of things.'

'No kidding,' Guy said.

'She comes right out and *admits* she's nosy, though, so it's kind of funny and forgivable instead of annoying. She even looked into the medicine chest.'

'Just like that?'

'Just like that. And guess what she was wearing.'

'A Pillsbury sack with three X's on it.'

'No, toreador pants.'

'*Toreador* pants?'

'Lime-green ones.'

'Ye gods.'

Kneeling on the floor between the bay windows, Rosemary drew a line on brown paper with crayon and a yardstick and then measured the depth of the window seats. 'She invited us to have dinner with them this evening,' she said, and looked at Guy. 'I told her I'd have to check with you, but that it would probably be okay.'

'Ah, Jesus, Ro,' Guy said, 'we don't want to do that, do we?'

'I think they're lonely,' Rosemary said. 'Because of Terry.'

'Honey,' Guy said, 'if we get friendly with an old couple like that we're *never* going to get them off our necks. They're right here on the same floor with us, they'll be looking in six times a day. Especially if she's nosy to begin with.'

'I told her she could count on us,' Rosemary said.

'I thought you told her you had to check first.'

'I did, but I told her she could count on us too.' Rosemary looked helplessly at Guy. 'She was so anxious for us to come.'

'Well, it's not my night for being kind to Ma and Pa Kettle,' Guy said. 'I'm sorry, honey, call her up and tell her we can't make it.'

'All right, I will,' Rosemary said, and drew another line with the crayon and the yardstick.

Guy finished his sandwich. 'You don't have to sulk about it,' he said.

'I'm not sulking,' Rosemary said. 'I see exactly what you mean about them being on the same floor. It's a valid point and you're absolutely right. I'm not sulking at all.'

'Oh hell,' Guy said, 'we'll go.'

'No, no, what for? We don't have to. I shopped for dinner before she came, so *that's* no problem.'

'We'll go,' Guy said.

'We don't have to if you don't want to. That sounds so phony but I really mean it, really I do.'

'We'll go. It'll be my good deed for the day.'

'All right, but only if you want to. And we'll make it very clear to them that it's only this one time and not the beginning of anything. Right?'

'Right.'

6

At a few minutes past six-thirty Rosemary and Guy left their apartment and walked through the branches of dark green hallway to the Castevets' door. As Guy rang the doorbell the elevator behind them clanged open and Mr Dubin or Mr DeVore (they didn't know which was which) came out carrying a suit swathed in cleaner's plastic. He smiled and, unlocking the door of 7B next to them, said, 'You're in the wrong place, aren't you?' Rosemary and Guy made friendly laughs and he let himself in, calling 'Me!' and allowing them a glimpse of a black sideboard and red-and-gold wallpaper.

The Castevets' door opened and Mrs Castevet was there, powdered and rouged and smiling broadly in light green silk and a frilled pink apron. 'Perfect timing!' she said. 'Come on in! Roman's making Vodka Blushes in the blender. My, I'm glad you could come, Guy! I'm fixing to tell people I knew you when! "Had dinner right off that plate, he did – Guy Woodhouse in person!" I'm not going to wash it when you're done; I'm going to leave it just as is!'

Guy and Rosemary laughed and exchanged glances; *Your friend*, his said, and hers said, *What can I do?*

There was a large foyer in which a rectangular table was set for four, with an embroidered white cloth, plates that didn't all match, and bright ranks of ornate silver. To the left the foyer opened on a living-room easily twice the size of Rosemary and Guy's but otherwise much like it. It had one large bay window instead of two smaller ones, and a huge pink marble mantel sculptured with lavish scrollwork. The room was oddly furnished; at the fireplace end there were a settee and a lamp table and a few chairs, and at the opposite end an officelike clutter of file cabinets, bridge tables piled with newspapers, overfilled bookshelves, and a typewriter on a metal stand. Between the two ends of the room was a twenty-foot field of brown wall-to-wall carpet, deep and new-looking, marked with the trail of a vacuum cleaner. In the centre of it, entirely alone, a small round table stood holding *Life* and *Look* and *Scientific American*.

Mrs Castevet showed them across the brown carpet and seated them on the settee; and as they sat Mr Castevet came in, holding in both hands a small tray on which four cocktail glasses ran over with clear pink liquid. Staring at the rims of the glasses he shuffled forward across the carpet, looking as if with every step he would trip and fall disastrously. 'I seem to have overfilled the glasses,' he said. 'No, no, don't get up. Please. Generally I pour these out as precisely as a bartender, don't I, Minnie?'

Mrs Castevet said, 'Just watch the carpet.'

'But this evening,' Mr Castevet continued, coming closer, 'I made a little too much, and rather than leave the surplus in the blender, I'm afraid I thought I . . . There we are. Please, sit down. Mrs Woodhouse?'

Rosemary took a glass, thanked him, and sat. Mrs Castevet quickly put a paper cocktail napkin in her lap.

'Mr Woodhouse? A Vodka Blush. Have you ever tasted one?'

'No,' Guy said, taking one and sitting.

'Minnie,' Mr Castevet said.

'It looks delicious,' Rosemary said, smiling vividly as she wiped the base of her glass.

'They're very popular in Australia,' Mr Castevet said. He took the final glass and raised it to Rosemary and Guy. 'To our guests,' he said. 'Welcome to our home.' He drank and cocked his head critically, one eye partway closed, the tray at his side dripping on the carpet.

Mrs Castevet coughed in mid-swallow. 'The carpet!' she choked, pointing.

Mr Castevet looked down. 'Oh dear,' he said, and held the tray up uncertainly.

Mrs Castevet thrust aside her drink, hurried to her knees, and laid a paper napkin carefully over the wetness. 'Brand-new carpet,' she said. 'Brand-new carpet. This man is so clumsy!'

The Vodka Blushes were tart and quite good.

'Do you come from Australia?' Rosemary asked, when the carpet had been blotted, the tray safely kitchened, and the Castevets seated in straight-backed chairs.

'Oh no,' Mr Castevet said, 'I'm from right here in New York City. I've been there though. I've been everywhere. Literally.' He sipped Vodka Blush, sitting with his legs crossed and a hand on his knee. He was wearing black loafers with tassels, grey slacks, a white blouse, and a blue-and-gold striped ascot. 'Every continent, every country,' he said. 'Every major city. You name a place and I've been there. Go ahead. Name a place.'

Guy said, 'Fairbanks, Alaska.'

'I've been there,' Mr Castevet said. 'I've been all over Alaska; Fairbanks, Juneau, Anchorage, Nome, Seward; I spent four months there in 1938 and I've made a lot of one-day stop-overs in Fairbanks and Anchorage on my way to places in the Far East. I've been in small towns in Alaska too; Dillingham and Akulurak.'

'Where are *you* folks from?' Mrs Castevet asked, fixing the folds at the bosom of her dress.

'I'm from Omaha,' Rosemary said, 'and Guy is from Baltimore.'

'Omaha is a good city,' Mr Castevet said. 'Baltimore is too.'

'Did you travel for business reasons?' Rosemary asked him.

'Business and pleasure both,' he said. 'I'm seventy-nine years old and I've been going one place or another since I was ten. You name it, I've been there.'

'What business were you in?' Guy asked.

'Just about every business,' Mr Castevet said. 'Wool, sugar, toys, machine parts, marine insurance, oil . . .'

A bell pinged in the kitchen. 'Steak's ready,' Mrs Castevet said, standing up with her glass in her hand. 'Don't rush your drinks now; take them along to the table. Roman, take your pill.'

'It will end on October third,' Mr Castevet said; 'the day before the Pope gets here. No Pope ever visits a city where the newspapers are on strike.'

'I heard on TV that he's going to postpone and wait till it's over,' Mrs Castevet said.

Guy smiled. 'Well,' he said, 'that's show biz.'

Mr and Mrs Castevet laughed, and Guy along with them. Rosemary smiled and cut her steak. It was overdone and juiceless, flanked by peas and mashed potatoes under flour-laden gravy.

Still laughing, Mr Castevet said, 'It *is*, you know! That's *just* what it is; show biz!'

'You can say *that* again,' Guy said.

'The costumes, the rituals,' Mr Castevet said; 'every religion, not only Catholicism. Pageants for the ignorant.'

Mrs Castevet said, 'I think we're offending Rosemary.'

'No, no, not at all,' Rosemary said.

'You aren't religious, my dear, are you?' Mr Castevet asked.

'I was brought up to be,' Rosemary said, 'but now I'm an agnostic. I wasn't offended. Really I wasn't.'

'And you, Guy?' Mr Castevet asked. 'Are you an agnostic too?'

'I guess so,' Guy said. 'I don't see how anyone can be anything else. I mean, there's no absolute proof one way or the other, is there?'

'No, there isn't,' Mr Castevet said.

Mrs Castevet, studying Rosemary, said, 'You looked uncomfortable before, when we were laughing at Guy's little joke about the Pope.'

'Well he *is* the Pope,' Rosemary said. 'I guess I've been conditioned to have respect for him and I still do, even if I don't think he's holy any more.'

'If you don't think he's holy,' Mr Castevet said, 'you should have no respect for him at *all*, because he's going around deceiving people and pretending he *is* holy.'

'Good point,' Guy said.

'When I *think* what they spend on robes and jewels,' Mrs Castevet said.

'A good picture of the hypocrisy behind organized religion,' Mr Castevet said, 'was given, in *Luther*. Did you ever get to play the leading part, Guy?'

'Me? No,' Guy said.

'Weren't you Albert Finney's understudy?' Mr Castevet asked.

'No,' Guy said, 'the fellow who played Weinand was. I just covered two of the smaller parts.'

'That's strange,' Mr Castevet said; 'I was quite certain that *you* were his understudy. I remember being struck by a gesture you made and checking in the programme to see who you were; and I could swear you were listed as Finney's understudy.'

'What gesture do you mean?' Guy asked.

'I'm not sure now; a movement of your—'

'I used to do a thing with my arms when Luther had the fit, a sort of involuntary reaching—'

'Exactly,' Mr Castevet said. 'That's just what I meant. It had a wonderful authenticity to it. In contrast, may I say, to everything Mr Finney was doing.'

'Oh, come on now,' Guy said.

'I thought his performance was considerably overrated,' Mr Castevet said. 'I'd be most curious to see what *you* would have done with the part.'

Laughing, Guy said, 'That makes two of us,' and cast a bright-eyed glance at Rosemary. She smiled back, pleased that Guy was pleased; there would be no reproofs from him now for an evening wasted talking with Ma and Pa Settle. No, Kettle.

'My father was a theatrical producer,' Mr Castevet said, 'and my early years were spent in the company of such people as Mrs Fiske and Forbes-Robertson, Otis Skinner and Modjeska. I tend, therefore, to look for something more than mere competence in actors. You have a most interesting inner quality, Guy. It appears in your television work, too, and it should carry you very far indeed; provided, of course, that you get those initial "breaks" upon which even the greatest actors are to some degree dependent. Are you preparing for a show now?'

'I'm up for a couple of parts,' Guy said.

'I can't believe that you won't get them,' Mr Castevet said.

'*I* can,' Guy said.

Mr Castevet stared at him. 'Are you serious?' he asked.

Dessert was a homemade Boston cream pie that, though better than the steak and vegetables, had for Rosemary a peculiar and unpleasant sweetness. Guy, however, praised it heartily and ate a second helping. Perhaps he was only acting, Rosemary thought; repaying compliments with compliments.

After dinner Rosemary offered to help with the cleaning up. Mrs Castevet accepted the offer instantly and the two women cleared the table while Guy and Mr Castevet went into the living-room.

The kitchen, opening off the foyer, was small, and made smaller still by the miniature greenhouse Terry had mentioned. Some three feet long, it stood on a large white table near the room's one window. Goosenecked lamps leaned close around it, their bright bulbs reflecting in the glass and making it blinding white rather than transparent. In the remaining space the sink, stove, and refrigerator stood close together with cabinets jutting out above them on all sides. Rosemary wiped dishes at Mrs Castevet's elbow, working diligently and conscientiously in the pleasing knowledge that her own kitchen was larger and more graciously equipped. 'Terry told me about that greenhouse,' she said.

'Oh yes,' Mrs Castevet said. 'It's a nice hobby. You ought to do it too.'

'I'd like to have a spice garden some day,' Rosemary said. 'Out of the city, of course. If Guy ever gets a movie offer we're going to grab it and go live in Los Angeles. I'm a country girl at heart.'

'Do you come from a big family?' Mrs Castevet asked.

'Yes,' Rosemary said. 'I have three brothers and two sisters. I'm the baby.'

'Are your sisters married?'

'Yes, they are.'

Mrs Castevet pushed a soapy sponge up and down inside a glass. 'Do they have children?' she asked.

'One has two and the other has four,' Rosemary said. 'At least that was the count the last I heard. It could be three and five by now.'

'Well, that's a good sign for *you*,' Mrs Castevet said, still soaping the glass. She was a slow and thorough washer. 'If your sisters have lots of children, chances are you will too. Things like that go in families.'

'Oh, we're fertile, all right,' Rosemary said, waiting towel in hand for the glass. 'My brother Eddie has *eight* already and he's only twenty-six.'

'My goodness!' Mrs Castevet said. She rinsed the glass and gave it to Rosemary.

'All told I've got twenty nieces and nephews,' Rosemary said. 'I haven't even *seen* half of them.'

'Don't you go home every once in a while?' Mrs Castevet asked.

'No, I don't,' Rosemary said. 'I'm not on the best of terms with my family, except one brother. They feel I'm the black sheep.'

'Oh? How is that?'

'Because Guy isn't Catholic, and we didn't have a church wedding.'

'Tsk,' Mrs Castevet said. 'Isn't it something the way people fuss about religion? Well, it's *their* loss, not yours; don't you let it bother you any.'

'That's more easily said than done,' Rosemary said, putting the glass on a shelf. 'Would you like me to wash and you wipe for a while?'

'No, this is fine, dear,' Mrs Castevet said.

Rosemary looked outside the door. She could see only the end of the living-room that was bridge tables and file cabinets; Guy and Mr Castevet were at the other end. A plane of blue cigarette smoke lay motionless in the air.

'Rosemary?'

She turned. Mrs Castevet, smiling, held out a wet plate in a green rubber-gloved hand.

It took almost an hour to do the dishes and pans and silver, although Rosemary felt she could have done them alone in less than half that time. When she and Mrs Castevet came out of the kitchen and into the living-room, Guy and Mr Castevet were sitting facing each other on the settee, Mr Castevet driving home point after point with repeated strikings of his forefinger against his palm.

'Now Roman, you stop bending Guy's ear with your Modjeska stories,' Mrs Castevet said. 'He's only listening 'cause he's polite.'

'No, it's interesting, Mrs Castevet,' Guy said.

'You see?' Mr Castevet said.

'*Minnie*,' Mrs Castevet told Guy. 'I'm Minnie and he's Roman; okay?' She looked mock-defiantly at Rosemary. 'Okay?'

Guy laughed. 'Okay, Minnie,' he said.

They talked about the Goulds and the Bruhns and Dubin-and-DeVore; about Terry's sailor brother who had turned out to be in a civilian hospital in Saigon; and, because Mr Castevet was reading a book critical of the Warren Report, about the Kennedy assassination. Rosemary, in one of the straight-backed chairs, felt oddly out of things, as if the Castevets were old friends of Guy's to whom she had just been introduced. 'Do *you* think it could have been a plot of some kind?' Mr Castevet asked her, and she answered awkwardly, aware that a considerate host was drawing a leftout guest into conversation. She excused herself and followed Mrs Castevet's directions to the bathroom, where there were flowered paper towels inscribed *For Our Guest* and a book called *Jokes for The John* that wasn't especially funny.

They left at ten-thirty, saying 'Goodbye, Roman' and 'Thank you, Minnie' and shaking hands with an enthusiasm and an implied promise of more such evenings together that, on Rosemary's part, was completely false. Rounding the first bend in the hallway and hearing the door close behind them, she blew out a relieved sigh and grinned happily at Guy when she saw him doing exactly the same.

'Naow Roman,' he said, working his eyebrows comically, 'yew stop bendin' Guy's ee-yurs with them thar Mojesky storees!'

Laughing, Rosemary cringed and hushed him, and they ran hand in hand on ultra-quiet tiptoes to their own door, which they unlocked, opened, slammed, locked, bolted, chained; and Guy nailed it over with imaginary beams, pushed up three imaginery boulders, hoisted an imaginary drawbridge, and mopped his brow and panted while Rosemary bent over double and laughed into both hands.

'About that steak,' Guy said.

'Oh my God!' Rosemary said. 'The pie! How did you eat two pieces of it? It was *weird*!'

'Dear girl,' Guy said, 'that was an act of superhuman courage and self-sacrifice. I said to myself, "Ye gods, I'll bet nobody's ever asked this old bat for seconds on *anything* in her entire life!" So I did it.' He waved a hand grandly. 'Now and again I get these noble urges.'

They went into the bedroom. 'She raises herbs and spices,' Rosemary said, 'and when they're full-grown she throws them out the window.'

'Shh, the walls have ears,' Guy said. 'Hey, how about that silverware?'

'Isn't that funny?' Rosemary said, working her feet against the floor to unshoe them; 'only three dinner plates that match, and they've got that beautiful, beautiful silver.'

'Let's be nice; maybe they'll will it to us.'

'Let's be nasty and buy our own. Did you go to the bathroom?'

'There? No.'

'Guess what they've got in it.'

'A bidet.'

'No, *Jokes for The John*.'

'No.'

Rosemary shucked off her dress. 'A book on a hook,' she said. 'Right next to the toilet.'

Guy smiled and shook his head. He began taking out his cufflinks, standing beside the armoire. 'Those stories of Roman's, though,' he said, 'were pretty damn interesting, actually. I'd never even heard of Forbes-Robertson before, but he was a very big star in his day.' He worked at the second link, having trouble with it. 'I'm going to go over there again tomorrow night and hear some more,' he said.

Rosemary looked at him, disconcerted. 'You are?' she asked.

'Yes,' he said, 'he asked me.' He held out his hand to her. 'Can you get this off for me?'

She went to him and worked at the link, feeling suddenly lost and uncertain. 'I thought we were going to do something with Jimmy and Tiger,' she said.

'Was that definite?' he asked. His eyes looked into hers. 'I thought we were just going to call and see.'

'It wasn't *definite*,' she said.

He shrugged. 'We'll see them Wednesday or Thursday.'

She got the link out and held it on her palm. He took it. 'Thanks,' he said. 'You don't have to come along if you don't want to; you can stay here.'

'I think I will,' she said. 'Stay here.' She went to the bed and sat down.

'He knew Henry Irving too,' Guy said. 'It's really terrifically interesting.'

Rosemary unhooked her stockings. 'Why did they take down the pictures,' she said.

'What do you mean?'

'Their pictures; they took them down. In the living-room and in the hallway leading back to the bathroom. There are hooks in the wall and clean places. And the one picture that *is* there, over the mantel, doesn't fit. There are two inches of clean at both sides of it.'

Guy looked at her. 'I didn't notice,' he said.

'And why do they have all those files and things in the living-room?' she asked.

'*That* he told me,' Guy said, taking off his shirt. 'He puts out a newsletter for stamp collectors. All over the world. That's why they get so much foreign mail.'

'Yes, but why in the living-room?' Rosemary said. 'They have three or four other rooms, all with the doors closed. Why doesn't he use one of those?'

Guy went to her, shirt in hand, and pressed her nose with a firm fingertip. 'You're getting nosier than Minnie,' he said, kissed air at her, and went out to the bathroom.

Ten or fifteen minutes later, while in the kitchen putting on water for coffee, Rosemary got the sharp pain in her middle that was the night-before signal of her period. She relaxed with one hand against the corner of the stove, letting the pain have its brief way, and then she got out a Chemex paper and the can of coffee, feeling disappointed and forlorn.

She was twenty-four and they wanted three children two years apart; but Guy 'wasn't ready yet' – nor would he ever be ready, she feared, until he was as big as Marlon Brando and Richard Burton put together. Didn't he know how handsome and talented he was, how sure to succeed? So her plan was to get pregnant by 'accident'; the pills gave her headaches, she said, and rubber gadgets were repulsive. Guy said that subconsciously she was still a good Catholic, and she protested enough to support the explanation. Indulgently he studied the calendar and avoided the 'dangerous days', and she said, 'No, it's safe today, darling; I'm sure it is.'

And again this month he had won and she had lost, in this undignified contest in which he didn't even know they were engaged. 'Damn!' she said, and banged the coffee can down on the stove. Guy, in the den, called, 'What happened?'

'I bumped my elbow!' she called back.

At least she knew now why she had become depressed during the evening.

Double damn! If they were living together and not married she would have been pregnant fifty times by now!

7

The following evening after dinner Guy went over to the Castevets'. Rosemary straightened up the kitchen and was debating whether to work on the window-seat cushions or get into bed with *Manchild in The Promised Land* when the doorbell rang. It was Mrs Castevet, and with her another woman, short, plump, and smiling, with a Buckley-for-Mayor button on the shoulder of a green dress.

'Hi, dear, we're not bothering you, are we?' Mrs Castevet said when Rosemary had opened the door. 'This is my dear friend Laura-Louise McBurney, who lives up on twelve. Laura-Louise, this is Guy's wife Rosemary.'

'Hello, Rosemary. Welcome to the Bram!'

'Laura-Louise just met Guy over at our place and she wanted to meet you too, so we came on over. Guy said you were staying in not doing anything. Can we come in?'

With resigned good grace Rosemary showed them into the living-room.

'Oh, you've got new chairs,' Mrs Castevet said. 'Aren't they beautiful!'

'They came this morning,' Rosemary said.

'Are you all right, dear? You look worn.'

'I'm fine,' Rosemary said and smiled. 'It's the first day of my period.'

'And you're up and around?' Laura-Louise asked, sitting. 'On *my* first days I experienced such pain that I couldn't move or eat or *anything*. Dan had to give me gin through a straw to kill the pain and we were one-hundred-per-cent Temperance at the time, with that one exception.'

'Girls today take things more in their stride than we did,' Mrs Castevet said, sitting too. 'They're healthier than we were, thanks to vitamins and better medical care.'

Both women had brought identical green sewing bags and, to Rosemary's surprise, were opening them now and taking out crocheting (Laura-Louise) and darning (Mrs Castevet); settling down for a long evening of needlework and conversation. 'What's that over there?' Mrs Castevet asked. 'Seat covers?'

'Cushions for the window seats,' Rosemary said, and thinking *Oh all right, I will*, went over and got the work and brought it back and joined them.

Laura-Louise said, 'You've certainly made a tremendous change in the apartment, Rosemary.'

'Oh, before I forget,' Mrs Castevet said, 'this is for you. From Roman and me.' She put a small packet of pink tissue paper into Rosemary's hand, with a hardness inside it.

'For me?' Rosemary asked. 'I don't understand.'

'It's just a little present is all,' Mrs Castevet said, dismissing Rosemary's puzzlement with quick hand-waves. 'For moving in.'

'But there's no reason for you to . . .' Rosemary unfolded the leaves of used-before tissue paper. Within the pink was Terry's silver filigree ball-charm and its clustered-together neck-chain. The smell of the ball's filling made Rosemary pull her head away.

'It's real old,' Mrs Castevet said. 'Over three hundred years.'

'It's lovely,' Rosemary said, examining the ball and wondering whether she should tell that Terry had shown it to her. The moment for doing so slipped by.

'The green inside is called tannis root,' Mrs Castevet said. 'It's good luck.'

Not for Terry, Rosemary thought, and said, 'It's lovely, but I can't accept such a—'

'You already have,' Mrs Castevet said, darning a brown sock and not looking at Rosemary. 'Put it on.'

Laura-Louise said, 'You'll get used to the smell before you know it.'

'Go on,' Mrs Castevet said.

'Well, thank you,' Rosemary said; and uncertainly she put the chain over her head and tucked the ball into the collar of her dress. It dropped down between her breasts, cold for a moment and obtrusive. *I'll take it off when they go*, she thought.

Laura-Louise said, 'A friend of ours made the chain entirely by hand. He's a retired dentist and his hobby is making jewellery out of silver and gold. You'll meet him at Minnie and Roman's on – on some night soon, I'm sure, because they entertain so much. You'll probably meet all their friends, all *our* friends.'

Rosemary looked up from her work and saw Laura-Louise pink with embarrassment that had hurried and confused her last words. Minnie was busy darning, unaware. Laura-Louise smiled and Rosemary smiled back.

'Do you make your own clothes?' Laura-Louise asked.

'No, I don't,' Rosemary said, letting the subject be changed. 'I try to every once in a while but nothing ever hangs right.'

It turned out to be a fairly pleasant evening. Minnie told some amusing stories about her girlhood in Oklahoma, and Laura-Louise showed Rosemary two useful sewing tricks and explained feelingly how Buckley, the Conservative mayoral candidate, could win the coming election despite the high odds against him.

Guy came back at eleven, quiet and oddly self-contained. He said hello to the women and, by Rosemary's chair, bent and kissed her cheek. Minnie said. '*Eleven*? My land! Come on, Laura-Louise.' Laura-Louise said, 'Come and visit me any time you want, Rosemary; I'm in twelve F.' The two women closed their sewing bags and went quickly away.

'Were his stories as interesting as last night?' Rosemary asked.

'Yes,' Guy said. 'Did you have a nice time?'

'All right. I got some work done.'

'So I see.'

'I got a present too.'

She showed him the charm. 'It was Terry's,' she said. 'They gave it to her; she showed it to me. The police must have – given it back.'

'She probably wasn't even wearing it,' Guy said.

'I'll bet she was. She was a proud of it as – as if it was the first gift anyone had ever given her.' Rosemary lifted the chain off over her head and held the chain and the charm on her palm, jiggling them and looking at them.

'Aren't you going to wear it?' Guy asked.

'It smells,' she said. 'There's stuff in it called tannis root.' She held out her hand. 'From the famous greenhouse.'

Guy smelled and shrugged. 'It's not bad,' he said.

Rosemary went into the bedroom and opened a drawer in the vanity where she had a tin Louis Sherry box full of odds and ends. 'Tannis, anybody?' she asked herself in the mirror, and put the charm in the box, closed it, and closed the drawer.

Guy, in the doorway, said, 'If you took it, you ought to wear it.'

That night Rosemary awoke and found Guy sitting beside her smoking in the dark. She asked him what was the matter. 'Nothing,' he said. 'A little insomnia, that's all.'

Roman's stories of old-time stars, Rosemary thought, might have depressed him by reminding him that his own career was lagging behind Henry Irving's and Forbes-Whos-it's. His going back for more of the stories might have been a form of masochism.

She touched his arm and told him not to worry.

'About what?'

'About anything.'

'All right,' he said, 'I won't.'

'You're the greatest,' she said. 'You know? You are. And it's all going to come out right. You're going to have to learn karate to get rid of the photographers.'

He smiled in the glow of his cigarette.

'Any day now,' she said. 'Something big. Something worthy of you.'

'I know,' he said. 'Go to sleep, honey.'

'Okay. Watch the cigarette.'

'I will.'

'Wake me if you can't sleep.'

'Sure.'

'I love you.'

'I love *you*, Ro.'

A day or two later Guy brought home a pair of tickets for the Saturday night performance of *The Fantasticks*, given to him, he explained, by Dominick, his vocal coach. Guy had seen the show years before when it first opened; Rosemary had always been meaning to see it. 'Go with Hutch,' Guy said; 'it'll give me a chance to work on the *Wait Until Dark* scene.'

Hutch had seen it too, though, so Rosemary went with Joan Jellico, who confided during dinner at the Bijou that she and Dick were separating, no longer having anything in common except their address. The news upset Rosemary. For days Guy had been distant and preoccupied, wrapped in something he would neither put aside nor share. Had Joan and Dick's estrangement begun in the same way? She grew angry at Joan, who was wearing too much make-up and applauding too loudly in the small theatre. No wonder she and Dick could find nothing in common; she was loud and vulgar, he was reserved, sensitive; they should never have married in the first place.

When Rosemary came home Guy was coming out of the shower, more vivacious and *there* than he had been all week. Rosemary's spirits leaped. The show had been even better than she expected, she told him, and bad news, Joan and Dick were separating. They really were birds of completely different feathers though, weren't they? How had the *Wait Until Dark* scene gone? Great. He had it down cold.

'Damn that tannis root,' Rosemary said. The whole bedroom smelled of it. The bitter prickly odour had even found its way into the bathroom. She got a piece of aluminium foil from the kitchen and wound the charm in a tight triple wrapping, twisting the ends to seal them.

'It'll probably lose its strength in a few days,' Guy said.

'It better,' Rosemary said, spraying the air with a deodorant bomb. 'If it doesn't, I'm going to throw it away and tell Minnie I lost it.'

They made love – Guy was wild and driving – and later, through the wall, Rosemary heard a party in progress at Minnie and Roman's; the same flat unmusical singing she had heard the last time, almost like religious chanting, and the same flute or clarinet weaving in and around and underneath it.

Guy kept his keyed-up vivacity all through Sunday, building shelves and shoe racks in the bedroom closets and inviting a bunch of *Luther* people over for Moo Goo Gai Woodhouse; and on Monday he painted the shelves and shoe racks and stained a bench Rosemary had found in a thrift shop, cancelling his session with Dominick and keeping his ear stretched for the phone, which he caught every time before the first ring was finished. At three in the afternoon it rang again, and Rosemary, trying out a different arrangement of the living-room chairs, heard him say, 'Oh God, no. Oh, the poor guy.'

She went to the bedroom door.

'Oh God,' Guy said.

He was sitting on the bed, the phone in one hand and a can of Red Devil paint remover in the other. He didn't look at her. 'And they don't have any idea what's causing it?' he said. 'My God, that's awful, just awful.' He listened, and straightened as he sat. 'Yes, I am,' he said. And then, 'Yes, I would. I'd hate to get it this way, but I—' He listened again. 'Well, you'd have to speak to Allan about that end of it,' he said,—Allan Stone, his agent—'but I'm sure there won't be any problem, Mr Weiss, not as far as we're concerned.'

He had it. The Something Big. Rosemary held her breath, waiting.

'Thank *you*, Mr Weiss,' Guy said. 'And will you let me know if there's any news? Thanks.'

He hung up and shut his eyes. He sat motionless, his hand staying on the phone. He was pale and dummylike, a Pop Art wax statue with real clothes and props, real phone, real can of paint remover.

'Guy?' Rosemary said.

He opened his eyes and looked at her.

'What is it?' she asked.

He blinked and came alive. 'Donald Baumgart,' he said.

'He's gone blind. He woke up yesterday and – he can't see.'

'Oh no,' Rosemary said.

'He tried to hang himself this morning. He's in Bellevue now, under sedation.'

They looked painfully at each other.

'I've got the part,' Guy said. 'It's a hell of a way to get it.' He looked at the paint remover in his hand and put it on the night table. 'Listen,' he said, 'I've got to get out and walk around.' He stood up. 'I'm sorry. I've got to get outside and absorb this.'

'I understand, go ahead,' Rosemary said, standing back from the doorway.

He went as he was, down the hall and out the door, letting it swing closed after him with its own soft slam.

She went into the living-room, thinking of poor Donald Baumgart and lucky Guy; lucky she-and-Guy, with the good part that would get attention even if the show folded, would lead to other parts, to movies maybe, to a house in Los Angeles, a spice garden, three children two years apart. Poor Donald Baumgart with his clumsy name that he didn't change. He must have been good, to have won out over Guy, and there he was in Bellevue, blind and wanting to kill himself, under sedation.

Kneeling on a window seat, Rosemary looked out the side of its bay and watched the house's entrance far below, waiting to see Guy come out. When would rehearsals begin? she wondered. She would go out of town with him, of course; what fun it would be! Boston? Philadelphia? Washington would be exciting. She had never been there. While Guy was rehearsing afternoons, she could sightsee; and evenings, after the performance, everyone would meet in a restaurant or club to gossip and exchange rumours . . .

She waited and watched but he didn't come out. He must have used the Fifty-fifth Street door.

Now, when he should have been happy, he was dour and troubled, sitting with nothing moving except his cigarette hand and his eyes. His eyes followed her around the apartment; tensely, as if she were dangerous. 'What's *wrong*?' she asked a dozen times.

'Nothing,' he said. 'Don't you have your sculpture class today?'

'I haven't gone in two months.'

'Why don't you go?'

She went; tore away old plasticine, reset the armature, and began anew, doing a new model among new students. 'Where've you been?' the instructor asked. He had eye-glasses and an Adam's apple and made miniatures of her torso without watching his hands.

'In Zanzibar,' she said.

'Zanzibar is no more,' he said, smiling nervously. 'It's Tanzania.'

One afternoon she went down to Macy's and Gimbels, and when she came home there were roses in the kitchen, roses in the living-room, and Guy coming out of the bedroom with one rose and a forgive-me smile, like a reading he had once done for her of Chance Wayne in *Sweet Bird*.

'I've been a living turd,' he said. 'It's from sitting around hoping that Baumgart won't regain his sight, which is what I've been doing, rat that I am.'

'That's natural,' she said. 'You're bound to feel two ways about—'

'Listen,' he said, pushing the rose to her nose, 'even if this thing falls through, even if I'm Charley Cresta Blanca for the rest of my days, I'm going to stop giving you the short end of the stick.'

'You haven't—'

'Yes I have. I've been so busy tearing my hair out over *my* career that I haven't given Thought One to yours. Let's have a baby, okay? Let's have three, one at a time.'

She looked at him.

'A baby,' he said. 'You know. Goo, goo? Diapers? Waa, waa?'

'Do you mean it?' she asked.

'Sure I mean it,' he said. 'I even figured out the right time to start. Next Monday and Tuesday. Red circles on the calendar, please.'

'You *really* mean it, Guy?' she asked, tears in her eyes.

'No, I'm kidding,' he said. '*Sure* I mean it. Look, Rosemary, for God's sake don't cry, all right? Please. It's going to upset me very much if you cry, so stop right now, all right?'

'All right,' she said. 'I won't cry.'

'I really went rose-nutty, didn't I?' he said, looking around brightly. 'There's a bunch in the bedroom too.'

8

She went to upper Broadway for swordfish steaks and across town to Lexington Avenue for cheeses; not because she couldn't get swordfish steaks and cheeses right there in the neighbourhood but simply because on that snappy bright-blue morning she wanted to be all over the city, walking briskly with her coat flying, drawing second glances for her prettiness, impressing tough clerks with the precision and know-how of her orders. It was Monday, October fourth, the day of Pope Paul's visit to the city, and the sharing of the event made people more open and communicative than they ordinarily were;

How nice it is, Rosemary thought, *that the whole city is happy on a day when I'm so happy.*

She followed the Pope's rounds on television during the afternoon, moving the set out from the wall of the den (soon nursery) and turning it so she could watch from the kitchen while readying the fish and vegetables and salad greens. His speech at the UN moved her, and she was sure it would help ease the Vietnam situation. 'War never again,' he said; wouldn't his words give pause to even the most hardheaded statesman?'

At four-thirty, while she was setting the table before the fireplace, the telephone rang.

'Rosemary? How are you?'

'Fine,' she said. 'How are you?' It was Margaret, the elder of her two sisters.

'Fine,' Margaret said.

'Where are you?'

'In Omaha.'

They had never got on well. Margaret had been a sullen, resentful girl, too often used by their mother as the caretaker of the younger children. To be called by her like this was strange; strange and frightening.

'Is everyone all right?' Rosemary asked. *Someone's dead,* she thought. *Who? Ma? Pa? Brian?*

'Yes, everyone's fine.'

'They are?'

'Yes. Are you?'

'Yes; I said I was.'

'I've had the funniest feeling all day long, Rosemary. That something happened to you. Like an accident or something. That you were hurt. Maybe in the hospital.'

'Well, I'm not,' Rosemary said, and laughed. 'I'm fine. Really I am.'

'It was such a strong feeling,' Margaret said. 'I was *sure* something had happened. Finally Gene said why don't I call you and find out.'

'How is he?'

'Fine.'

'And the children?'

'Oh, the usual scrapes and scratches, but they're fine too. I've got another one on the way, you know.'

'No, I didn't know. That's wonderful. When is it due?' *We'll have one on the way soon too.*

'The end of March. How's your husband, Rosemary?'

'He's fine. He's got an important part in a new play that's going into rehearsal soon.'

'Say, did you get a good look at the Pope?' Margaret asked. 'There must be terrific excitement there.'

'There is,' Rosemary said. 'I've been watching it on television. It's in Omaha too, isn't it?'

'Not live? You didn't go out and see him live?'

'No, I didn't.'

'Really?'

'Really.'

'Honest to goodness, Rosemary,' Margaret said. 'Do you know Ma and Pa were going to *fly there* to see him but they couldn't because there's going to be a strike vote and Pa's seconding the motion? Lots of people did fly, though: the Donovans, and Dot and Sandy Wallingford; and you're right there, *living* there, and didn't go out and see him?'

'Religion doesn't mean as much to me now as it did back home,' Rosemary said.

'Well,' Margaret said, 'I guess that's inevitable,' and Rosemary heard, unspoken, *when you're married to a Protestant*. She said, 'It was nice of you to call, Margaret. There's nothing for you to worry about. I've never been healthier or happier.'

'It was such a strong feeling,' Margaret said. 'From the minute I woke up. I'm so used to taking care of you little brats . . .'

'Give my love to everyone, will you? And tell Brian to answer my letter.'

'I will. Rosemary—?'

'Yes?'

'I still have the feeling. Stay home tonight, will you?'

'That's just what we're planning to do,' Rosemary said, looking over at the partially set table.

'Good,' Margaret said. 'Take care of yourself.'

'I will,' Rosemary said. 'You too, Margaret.'

'I will. Goodbye.'

'Goodbye.'

She went back to setting the table, feeling pleasantly sad and nostalgic for Margaret and Brian and the other kids, for Omaha and the irretrievable past.

With the table set, she bathed; then powdered and perfumed herself, did her eyes and lips and hair, and put on a pair of burgundy silk lounging pyjamas that Guy had given her the previous Christmas.

He came home late, after six. 'Mmmm,' he said, kissing her. 'you look good enough to eat. Shall we? Damn!'

'What?'

'I forgot the pie.'

He had told her not to make a dessert; he would bring home his absolute all-time favourite, a Horn and Hardart pumpkin pie.

'I could *kick* myself,' he said. 'I passed *two* of those damn retail stores; not one but two.'

'It's all right,' Rosemary said. 'We can have fruit and cheese. That's the best dessert anyway, really.'

'It is not; Horn and Hardart pumpkin pie is.'

He went in to wash up and she put a tray of stuffed mushrooms into the oven and mixed the salad dressing.

In a few minutes Guy came to the kitchen door, buttoning the collar of a blue velour shirt. He was bright-eyed and a bit on edge, the way he had been the first time they slept together, when he knew it was going to happen. It pleased Rosemary to see him that way.

'Your pal the Pope really loused up traffic today,' he said.

'Did you see any of the television?' she asked. 'They've had fantastic coverage.'

'I got a glimpse up at Allan's,' he said. 'Glasses in the freezer?'

'Yes. He made a wonderful speech at the UN. "War never again," he told them.'

'Rotsa ruck. Hey, *those* look good.'

They had Gibsons and the stuffed mushrooms in the living-room. Guy put crumpled newspaper and sticks of kindling on the fireplace grate, and two big chunks of cannel coal. 'Here goes nothing,' he said, and struck a match and lit the paper. It flamed high and caught the kindling. Dark smoke began spilling out over the front of the mantel and up towards the ceiling. 'Good grief,' Guy said, and groped inside the fireplace. 'The paint, the paint!' Rosemary cried.

He got the flue opened; and the air conditioner, set at exhaust, drew out the smoke.

'Nobody, but nobody, has a fire tonight,' Guy said.

Rosemary, kneeling with her drink and staring into the spitting flame-wrapped coals, said, 'Isn't it gorgeous? I hope we have the coldest winter in eighty years.'

Guy put on Ella Fitzgerald singing Cole Porter.

They were halfway through the swordfish when the doorbell rang. 'Shit,' Guy said. He got up, tossed down his napkin, and went to answer it. Rosemary cocked her head and listened.

The door opened and Minnie said, 'Hi, Guy!' and more that was unintelligible. *Oh, no*, Rosemary thought. *Don't let her in, Guy. Not now, not tonight.*

Guy spoke, and then Minnie again: '. . . extra. We don't need them.' Guy again and Minnie again. Rosemary eased out held-in breath; it didn't sound as if she was coming in, thank God.

The door closed and was chained (*Good!*) and bolted (*Good!*). Rosemary watched and waited, and Guy sidled into the archway, smiling smugly, with both hands behind his back. '*Who* says there's nothing to ESP?' he said, and coming towards the table brought forth his hands with two white custard cups sitting one on each palm. 'Madame and Monsieur shall have ze dessairt after all,' he said, setting one cup by Rosemary's wineglass and the other by his own. '*Mousse au chocolat*,' he said, 'or "chocolate mouse", as Minnie calls it. Of course with her it could *be* chocolate mouse, so eat with care.'

Rosemary laughed happily. 'That's wonderful,' she said. 'It's what *I* was going to make.'

'See?' Guy said, sitting. 'ESP.' He replaced his napkin and poured more wine.

'I was afraid she was going to come charging in and stay all evening,' Rosemary said, forking up carrots.

'No,' Guy said, 'she just wanted us to try her chocolate mouse, seein' as how it's one of her speci-*al*-ities.'

'It *looks* good.'

'It does, doesn't it.'

The cups were filled with peaked swirls of chocolate. Guy's was topped with a sprinkling of chopped nuts, and Rosemary's with a half walnut.

'It's sweet of her, really,' Rosemary said. 'We shouldn't make fun of her.'

'You're right,' Guy said, 'you're right.'

The mousse was excellent, but it had a chalky undertaste that reminded Rosemary of blackboards and grade school. Guy tried but could find no 'undertaste' at all, chalky or otherwise. Rosemary put her spoon down after two swallows. Guy said, 'Aren't you going to finish it? That's silly, honey; there's no "undertaste". '

Rosemary said there was.

'Come on,' Guy said, 'the old bat slaved all day over a hot stove; eat it.'

'But I don't like it,' Rosemary said.

'It's delicious.'

'You can have mine.'

Guy scowled. 'All right, don't eat it,' he said; 'you don't wear the charm she gave you, you might as well not eat her dessert too.'

Confused, Rosemary said, 'What does one thing have to do with the other?'

'They're both examples of – well, unkindness, that's all,' Guy said. 'Two minutes ago you said we should stop making fun of her. That's a form of making fun too, accepting something and then not using it.'

'Oh—' Rosemary picked up her spoon. 'If it's going to turn into a big scene—' She took a full spoonful of the mousse and thrust it into her mouth.

'It isn't going to turn into a big scene,' Guy said. 'Look, if you really can't stand it, don't eat it.'

'Delicious,' Rosemary said, full-mouthed and taking another spoonful, 'no undertaste at all. Turn the records over.'

Guy got up and went to the record player. Rosemary doubled her napkin in her lap and plopped two spoonfuls of the mousse into it, and another half-spoonful for good measure. She folded the napkin closed and then showily scraped clean the inside of the cup and swallowed down the scrapings as Guy came back to the table. 'There, Daddy,' she said, tilting the cup towards him. 'Do I get a gold star on my chart?'

'Two of them,' he said. 'I'm sorry if I was stuffy.'

'You were.'

'I'm sorry.' He smiled.

Rosemary melted. 'You're forgiven,' she said. 'It's nice that you're considerate of old ladies. It means you'll be considerate of me when *I'm* one.'

They had coffee and crème de menthe.

'Margaret called this afternoon,' Rosemary said.

'Margaret?'

'My sister.'

'Oh. Everything okay?'

'Yes. She was afraid something had happened to me. She had a feeling.'

'Oh?'

'We're to stay home tonight.'

'Drat. And I made a reservation at Nedick's. In the Orange Room.'

'You'll have to cancel it.'

'How come you turned out sane when the rest of your family is nutty?'

The first wave of dizziness caught Rosemary at the kitchen sink as she scraped the uneaten mousse from her napkin into the drain. She swayed for a moment, then blinked and frowned. Guy, in the den, said, 'He isn't there yet. Christ, what a mob.' The Pope at Yankee Stadium.

'I'll be in in a minute,' Rosemary said.

Shaking her head to clear it, she rolled the napkins up inside the tablecloth and put the bundle aside for the hamper. She put the stopper in the drain, turned on the hot water, squeezed in some Joy, and began loading in the dishes and pans. She would do them in the morning, let them soak overnight.

The second wave came as she was hanging up the dish towel. It lasted longer, and this time the room turned slowly around and her legs almost slued out from under her. She hung on to the edge of the sink.

When it was over she said 'Oh boy,' and added up two Gibsons, two glasses of wine (or had it been three?), and one crème de menthe. No wonder.

She made it to the doorway of the den and kept her footing through the next wave by holding on to the knob with one hand and the jamb with the other.

'What is it?' Guy asked, standing up anxiously.

'Dizzy,' she said, and smiled.

He snapped off the TV and came to her, took her arm and held her surely around the waist. 'No wonder,' he said. 'All that booze. You probably had an empty stomach, too.'

He helped her towards the bedroom and, when her legs buckled, caught her up and carried her. He put her down on the bed and sat beside her, taking her hand and stroking her forehead sympathetically. She closed her eyes. The bed was a raft that floated on gentle ripples, tilting and swaying pleasantly. 'Nice,' she said.

'Sleep is what you need,' Guy said, stroking her forehead. 'A good night's sleep.'

'We have to make a baby.'

'We will. Tomorrow. There's plenty of time.'

'Missing the mass.'

'Sleep. Get a good night's sleep. Go on . . .'

'Just a nap,' she said, and was sitting with a drink in her hand on President Kennedy's yacht. It was sunny and breezy, a perfect day for a cruise. The President, studying a large map, gave terse and knowing instructions to a Negro mate.

Guy had taken off the top of her pyjamas. 'Why are you taking them off?' she asked.

'To make you more comfortable,' he said.

'I'm comfortable.'

'Sleep, Ro.'

He undid the snaps at her side and slowly drew off the bottoms. Thought she was asleep and didn't know. Now she had nothing on at all except a red bikini, but the other women on the yacht – Jackie Kennedy, Pat Lawford, and Sarah Churchill – were wearing bikinis too, so it was all right, thank goodness. The President was in his Navy uniform. He had completely recovered from the assassination and looked better than ever. Hutch was standing on the dock with armloads of weather-forecasting equipment. 'Isn't Hutch coming with us?' Rosemary asked the President.

'Catholics only,' he said, smiling. 'I wish we weren't bound by these prejudices, but unfortunately we are.'

'But what about Sarah Churchill?' Rosemary asked. She turned to point, but Sarah Churchill was gone and the family was there in her place: Ma, Pa, and everybody, with the husbands, wives, and children. Margaret was pregnant, and so were Jean and Dodie and Ernestine.

Guy was taking off her wedding ring. She wondered why, but was too tired to ask. 'Sleep,' she said, and slept.

It was the first time the Sistine Chapel had been opened to the public and she was inspecting the ceiling on a new elevator that carried the visitor through the chapel horizontally, making it possible to see the frescoes exactly as Michelangelo, painting them, had seen them. How glorious they were! She saw God extending his finger to Adam, giving him the divine spark of life; and the underside of a shelf partly covered with gingham contact paper as she was carried backward through the linen closet. 'Easy,' Guy said, and another man said, 'You've got her too high.'

'Typhoon!' Hutch shouted from the dock amid all his weather-forecasting equipment. 'Typhoon! It killed fifty-five people in London and it's heading this way!' And Rosemary knew he was right. She must warn the President. The ship was heading for disaster.

But the President was gone. Everyone was gone. The deck was infinite and bare, except for, far away, the Negro mate holding the wheel unremittingly on its course.

Rosemary went to him and saw at once that he hated all white people, hated her. 'You'd better go down below, Miss,' he said, courteous but hating her, not even waiting to hear the warning she had brought.

Below was a huge ballroom where on one side a church burned fiercely and on the other a black-bearded man stood glaring at her. In the centre was a bed. She went to it and lay down, and was suddenly surrounded by naked men and women, ten or a dozen, with Guy among them. They were elderly, the women grotesque and slack-breasted. Minnie and her friend Laura-Louise were there, and Roman in a black mitre and a black silk robe. With a thin black wand he was drawing designs on her body, dipping the wand's point in a cup of red held for him by a sun-browned man with a white moustache. The point moved back and forth across her stomach and down ticklingly to the insides of her thighs. The naked people were chanting – flat, unmusical, foreign-tongued syllables – and a flute or clarinet accompanied them. 'She's awake, she sees!' Guy whispered to Minnie. He was large-eyed, tense. 'She *don't* see,' Minnie said. 'As long as she ate the mouse she can't see nor hear. She's like dead. Now sing.'

Jackie Kennedy came into the ballroom in an exquisite gown of ivory satin embroidered with pearls. 'I'm so sorry to hear you aren't feeling well,' she said, hurrying to Rosemary's side.

Rosemary explained about the mouse-bite, minimizing it so Jackie wouldn't worry.

'You'd better have your legs tied down,' Jackie said, 'in case of convulsions.'

'Yes, I suppose so,' Rosemary said. 'There's always a chance it was rabid.' She watched with interest as white-smocked interns tied her legs, and her arms too, to the four bedposts.

'If the music bothers you,' Jackie said, 'let me know and I'll have it stopped.'

'Oh, no,' Rosemary said. 'Please don't change the programme on my account. It doesn't bother me at all, really it doesn't.'

Jackie smiled warmly at her. 'Try to sleep,' she said. 'We'll be waiting up on deck.' She withdrew, her satin gown whispering.

Rosemary slept a while, and then Guy came in and began making love to her. He stroked her with both hands – a long, relishing stroke that began at her bound wrists, slid down over her arms, breasts, and loins, and became a voluptuous tickling between her legs. He repeated the exciting stroke again and again, his hands hot and sharp-nailed, and then, when she was ready-ready-more-than-ready, he slipped a hand in under her buttocks, raised them, lodged his hardness against her, and pushed it powerfully in. Bigger he was than always; painfully, wonderfully big. He lay forward upon her, his other arm sliding under her back to hold her, his broad chest crushing her breasts. (He was wearing, because it was to be a costume party, a suit of coarse leathery armour.) Brutally, rhythmically, he drove his new hugeness. She opened her eyes and looked into yellow furnace-eyes, smelled sulphur and tannis root, felt wet breath on her mouth, heard lust-grunts and the breathing of onlookers.

This is no dream, she thought. *This is real, this is happening*. Protest woke in her eyes and throat, but something covered her face, smothering her in a sweet stench.

The hugeness kept driving in her, the leathery body banging itself against her again and again and again.

The Pope came in with a suitcase in his hand and a coat over his arm. 'Jackie tells me you've been bitten by a mouse,' he said.

'Yes,' Rosemary said. 'That's why I didn't come to see you.' She spoke sadly, so he wouldn't suspect she had just had an orgasm.

'That's all right,' he said. 'We wouldn't want you to jeopardize your health.'

'Am I forgiven, Father?' she asked.

'Absolutely,' he said. He held out his hand for her to kiss the ring. Its stone was a silver filigree ball less than an inch in diameter; inside it, very tiny, Anna Maria Alberghetti sat waiting.

Rosemary kissed it and the Pope hurried out to catch his plane.

9

'Hey, it's after nine,' Guy said, shaking her shoulder.

She pushed his hand away and turned over on to her stomach. 'Five minutes,' she said, deep in the pillow.

'*No*,' he said, and yanked her hair. 'I've got to be at Dominick's at ten.'

'Eat out.'

'The hell I will.' He slapped her behind through the blanket.

Everything came back: the dreams, the drinks, Minnie's chocolate mousse, the Pope, that awful moment of not-dreaming. She turned back over and raised herself on her arms, looking at Guy. He was lighting a cigarette, sleep-rumpled, needing a shave. He had pyjamas on. She was nude.

'What time is it?' she asked.

'Ten after nine.'

'What time did I go to sleep?' She sat up.

'About eight-thirty,' he said. 'And you didn't go to sleep, honey; you passed out. From now on you get cocktails *or* wine, not cocktails *and* wine.'

'The dreams I had,' she said, rubbing her forehead and closing her eyes. 'President Kennedy, the Pope, Minnie and Roman . . .' She opened her eyes and saw scratches on her left breast; two parallel hairlines of red running down into the nipple. Her thighs stung; she pushed the blanket from them and saw more scratches, seven or eight going this way and that.

'Don't yell,' Guy said. 'I already filed them down.' He showed short smooth fingernails.

Rosemary looked at him uncomprehendingly.

'I didn't want to miss Baby Night,' he said.

'You mean you—'

'And a couple of my nails were ragged.'

'While I was – out?'

He nodded and grinned. 'It was kind of fun,' he said, 'in a necrophile sort of way.'

She looked away, her hands pulling the blanket back over her thighs. 'I dreamed someone was – raping me,' she said. 'I don't know who. Someone – unhuman.'

'Thanks a lot,' Guy said.

'You were there, and Minnie and Roman, other people . . . It was some kind of ceremony.'

'I tried to wake you,' he said, 'but you were out like a light.'

She turned further away and swung her legs out on the other side of the bed.

What's the matter?' Guy asked.

'Nothing,' she said, sitting there, not looking around at him. 'I guess I feel funny about your doing it that way, with me unconscious.'

'I didn't want to miss the night,' he said.

'We could have done it this morning or tonight. Last night wasn't the only split second in the whole month. And even if it *had* been . . .'

'I thought you would have wanted me to,' he said, and ran a finger up her back.

She squirmed away from it. 'It's supposed to be shared, not one awake and one asleep,' she said. Then: 'Oh, I guess I'm being silly.' She got up and went to the closet for her housecoat.

'I'm sorry I scratched you,' Guy said. 'I was a wee bit loaded myself.'

She made breakfast and, when Guy had gone, did the sinkful of dishes and put the kitchen to rights. She opened windows in the living-room and bedroom – the smell of last night's fire still lingered in the apartment – made the bed, and took a shower; a long one, first hot and then cold. She stood capless and immobile under the downpour, waiting for her head to clear and her thoughts to find an order and conclusion.

Had last night really been, as Guy had put it, Baby Night? Was she now, at this moment, actually pregnant? Oddly enough, she didn't care. She was unhappy – whether or not it was silly to be so. Guy had taken her without her knowledge, had made love to her as a mindless body ('kind of fun in a necrophile sort of way') rather than as the complete mind-and-body person she was; and had done so, moreover, with a savage gusto that had produced scratches, aching soreness, and a nightmare so real and intense that she could almost see on her stomach the designs Roman had drawn with his red-dipped wand. She scrubbed soap on herself vigorously, resentfully. True, he had done it for the best motive in the world, to make a baby, and true too he had drunk as much as she had; but she wished that no motive and no number of drinks could have enabled him to take her that way, taking only her body without her soul or self or she-ness – whatever it was he presumably loved. Now, looking back over the past weeks and months, she felt a disturbing presence of overlooked signals just beyond memory, signals of a shortcoming in his love for her, of a disparity between what he said and what he felt. He was an actor; could anyone know when an actor was true and not acting?

It would take more than a shower to wash away these thoughts. She turned the water off and, between both hands, pressed out her streaming hair.

On the way out to shop she rang the Castevets' doorbell and returned the cups from the mousse. 'Did you like it, dear?' Minnie asked. 'I think I put a little too much cream de cocoa in it.'

'It was delicious,' Rosemary said. 'You'll have to give me the recipe.'

'I'd love to. You going marketing? Would you do me a teeny favour? Six eggs and a small Instant Sanka; I'll pay you later. I hate going out for just one or two things, don't you?'

There was distance now between her and Guy, but he seemed not to be aware of it. His play was going into rehearsal November first – *Don't I Know You From Somewhere?* was the name of it – and he spent a great deal of time studying his part, practising the use of the crutches and leg-braces it called for, and visiting the Highbridge section of the Bronx, the play's locale. They had dinner with friends more evenings than not; when they didn't, they made natural-sounding conversation about furniture and the ending-any-day-now newspaper strike and the World Series. They went to a preview of a new musical and a screening of a new movie, to parties and the opening of a friend's exhibit of metal constructions. Guy seemed never to be looking at her, always at a script or TV or at someone else. He was in bed and asleep before she was. One evening he went to the Castevets' to hear more of Roman's theatre stories, and she stayed in the apartment and watched *Funny Face* on TV.

'Don't you think we ought to talk about it?' she said the next morning at breakfast.

'About what?'

She looked at him; he seemed genuinely unknowing. 'The conversations we've been making,' she said.

'What do you mean?'

'The way you haven't been looking at me.'

'What are you *talking* about? I've been looking at you.'

69

'No you haven't.'

'I have *so*. Honey, what is it? What's the matter?'

'Nothing. Never mind.'

'No, don't say that. What is it? What's bothering you?'

'Nothing.'

'Ah look, honey, I know I've been kind of preoccupied, with the part and the crutches and all; is that it? Well gee whiz, Ro, it's *important*, you know? But it doesn't mean I don't love you, just because I'm not riveting you with a passionate *gaze* all the time. I've got to think about *practical* matters too.' It was awkward and charming and sincere, like his playing of the cowboy in *Bus stop*.

'All right,' Rosemary said. 'I'm sorry I'm being pesty.'

'You? You couldn't be pesty if you tried.'

He leaned across the table and kissed her.

Hutch had a cabin near Brewster where he spent occasional weekends. Rosemary called him and asked if she might use it for three or four days, possibly a week. 'Guy's getting into his new part,' she explained, 'and I really think it'll be easier for him with me out of the way.'

'It's yours,' Hutch said, and Rosemary went down to his apartment on Lexington Avenue and Twenty-fourth Street to pick up the key.

She looked in first at a delicatessen where the clerks were friends from her own days in the neighbourhood, and then she went up to Hutch's apartment, which was small and dark and neat as a pin, with an inscribed photo of Winston Churchill and a sofa that had belonged to Madame de Pompadour. Hutch was sitting barefoot between two bridge tables, each with its typewriter and piles of paper. His practice was to write two books at once, turning to the second when he struck a snag on the first, and back to the first when he struck a snag on the second.

'I'm really looking forward to it,' Rosemary said, sitting on Madame de Pompadour's sofa. 'I suddenly realized the other day that I've never been alone in my whole life – not for more than a few hours, that is. The idea of three or four days is heaven.'

'A chance to sit quietly and find out who you are; where you've been and where you're going.'

'Exactly.'

'All right, you can stop forcing that smile,' Hutch said. 'Did he hit you with a lamp?'

'He didn't hit me with anything,' Rosemary said. 'It's a very difficult part, a crippled boy who *pretends* that he's adjusted to his crippled-ness. He's got to work with crutches and leg-braces, and naturally he's preoccupied and – and, well, preoccupied.'

'I see,' Hutch said. 'We'll change the subject. The *News* had a lovely rundown the other day of all the gore we missed during the strike. Why didn't you tell me you'd had another suicide up there at Happy House?'

'Oh, didn't I tell you?' Rosemary asked.

'No, you didn't,' Hutch said.

'It was someone we knew. The girl I told you about; the one who'd been a drug addict and was rehabilitated by the Castevets, these people who live on our floor. I'm *sure* I told you *that*.'

'The girl who was going to the basement with you.'

'That's right.'

'They didn't rehabilitate her very successfully, it would seem. Was she living with them?'

'Yes,' Rosemary said. 'We've gotten to know them fairly well since it happened. Guy goes over there once in a while to hear stories about the theatre. Mr Castevet's father was a producer around the turn of the century.'

'I shouldn't have thought Guy would be interested,' Hutch said. 'An elderly couple, I take it?'

'He's seventy-nine; she's seventy or so.'

'It's an odd name,' Hutch said. 'How is it spelled?'

Rosemary spelled it for him.

'I've never heard it before,' he said. 'French, I suppose.'

'The name may be but they aren't,' Rosemary said. 'He's from right here and she's from a place called – believe it or not – Bushy-head, Oklahoma.'

'My God,' Hutch said. 'I'm going to use that in a book. That one. I know just where to put it. Tell me, how are you planning to get to the cabin? You'll need a car, you know.'

'I'm going to rent one.'

'Take mine.'

'Oh no, Hutch, I couldn't.'

'Do, please,' Hutch said. 'All I do is move it from one side of the street to the other. Please. You'll save me a great deal of bother.'

Rosemary smiled. 'All right,' she said. 'I'll do you a favour and take your car.'

Hutch gave her the keys to the car and the cabin, a sketch-map of the route, and a typed list of instructions concerning the pump, the refrigerator, and a variety of possible emergencies. Then he put on shoes and a coat and walked her down to where the car, an old light-blue Oldsmobile, was parked. 'The registration papers are in the glove compartment,' he said. 'Please feel free to stay as long as you like. I have no immediate plans for either the car or the cabin.'

'I'm sure I won't stay more than a week,' Rosemary said. 'Guy might not even want me to stay that long.'

When she was settled in the car, Hutch leaned in at the window and said, 'I have all kinds of good advice to give you but I'm going to mind my own business if it kills me.'

Rosemary kissed him. 'Thank you,' she said. 'For that and for this and for everything.'

She left on the morning of Saturday, October 16th, and stayed five days at the cabin. The first two days she never once thought about Guy – a fitting revenge for the cheerfulness with which he had agreed to her going. Did she *look* as if she needed a good rest? Very well, she would *have* one, a long one, never once thinking about him. She took walks through dazzling yellow-and-orange woods, went to sleep early and slept late, read *Flight of The Falcon* by Daphne du Maurier, and made glutton's meals on the bottled-gas stove. Never once thinking about him.

On the third day she thought about him. He was vain, self-centred, shallow, and deceitful. He had married her to have an audience, not a mate. (Little Miss Just-out-of-Omaha, what a *goop* she had been! 'Oh, I'm *used* to actors; I've been here almost a year now.' And she had all but followed him around the studio carrying his newspaper in her mouth.) She would give him a year to shape up and become a good husband; if he didn't make it she would pull out, and with no religious qualms whatever. And meanwhile she would go back to work and get again that sense of independence and self-sufficiency she had been so eager to get rid of. She would be strong and proud and ready to go if he failed to meet her standards.

Those glutton's meals – man-size cans of beef stew and chili con carne – began to disagree with her, and on that third day she was mildly nauseated and could eat only soup and crackers.

On the fourth day she awoke missing him and cried. What was she doing there, alone in that cold crummy cabin? What had he done that was so terrible? He had gotten drunk and had grabbed her with-out saying may I. Well that was really an earth-shaking offence, now wasn't it? There he was, facing the biggest challenge of his career, and *she* – instead of being there to help him, to cue and encourage him – was off in the middle of nowhere, eating herself sick and feeling sorry for herself. Sure he was vain and self-centred; he was an actor, wasn't he? Laurence *Olivier* was probably vain and self-centred. And yes he might lie now and then; wasn't that exactly what had attracted her and still did? – that freedom and nonchalance so different from her own boxed-in propriety?

She drove into Brewster and called him. Service answered, the Friendly One: 'Oh hi, dear, are you back from the country? Oh. Guy is out, dear; can he call you? *You'll* call *him* at five. Right. You've certainly got lovely weather. Are you enjoying yourself? Good.'

At five he was still out, her message waiting for him. She ate in a diner and went to the one movie theatre. At nine he was still out and Service was someone new and automatic with a message for her: she should call him before eight the next morning or after six in the evening.

That next day she reached what seemed like a sensible and realistic view of things. They were both at fault; he for being thoughtless and self-absorbed, she for failing to express and explain her discontent. He could hardly be expected to change until she showed him that change was called for. She had only to talk – no, *they* had only to talk, for he might be harbouring a similar discontent of which she was similarly unaware – and matters couldn't help but improve. Like so many unhappinesses, this one had begun with silence in the place of honest open talk.

She went into Brewster at six and called and he was there. 'Hi, darling,' he said. 'How are you?'

'Fine. How are you?'

'All right. I miss you.'

She smiled at the phone. 'I miss *you*,' she said. 'I'm coming home tomorrow.'

'Good, that's great,' he said. 'All kinds of things have been going on here. Rehearsals have been postponed until January.'

'Oh?'

'They haven't been able to cast the little girl. It's a break for me though; I'm going to do a pilot next month. A half-hour comedy series.'

'You are?'

'It fell into my lap, Ro. And it really looks good. ABC loves the idea. It's called *Greenwich Village*; it's going to be filmed there, and

I'm a way-out writer. It's practically the lead.'

'That's marvellous, Guy!'

'Allan says I'm suddenly very hot.'

'That's wonderful!'

'Listen, I've got to shower and shave; he's taking me to a screening that Stanley Kubrick is going to be at. When are you going to get in?'

'Around noon, maybe earlier.'

'I'll be waiting. Love you.'

'Love you!'

She called Hutch, who was out, and left word with his service that she would return the car the following afternoon.

The next morning she cleaned the cabin, closed it up and locked it, and drove back to the city. Traffic on the Saw Mill River Parkway was bottlenecked by a three-car collision, and it was close to one o'clock when she parked the car half-in half-out-of the bus stop in front of the Bramford. With her small suitcase she hurried into the house.

The elevator man hadn't taken Guy down, but he had been off duty from eleven-fifteen to twelve.

He was there, though. The *No Strings* album was playing. She opened her mouth to call and he came out of the bedroom in a fresh shirt and tie, headed for the kitchen with a used coffee cup in his hand.

They kissed, lovingly and fully, he hugging her one-armed because of the cup.

'Have a good time?' he asked.

'Terrible. Awful. I missed you so.'

'How are you?'

'Fine. How was Stanley Kubrick?'

'Didn't show, the fink.'

They kissed again.

She brought her suitcase into the bedroom and opened it on the bed. He came in with two cups of coffee, gave her one, and sat on the vanity bench while she unpacked. She told him about the yellow-and-orange woods and the still nights; he told her about *Greenwich Village*, who else was in it and who the producers, writers, and director were.

'Are you *really* fine?' he asked when she was zipping closed the empty case.

She didn't understand.

74

'Your period,' he said. 'It was due on Tuesday.'

'It was?'

He nodded.

'Well, it's just two days,' she said – matter-of-factly, as if her heart weren't racing, leaping. 'It's probably the change of water, or the food I ate up there.'

'You've never been late before,' he said.

'It'll probably come tonight. Or tomorrow.'

'You want to bet?'

'Yes.'

'A quarter?'

'Okay.'

'You're going to lose, Ro.'

'Shut up. You're getting me all jumpy. It's only two days. It'll probably come tonight.'

10

It didn't come that night or the next day. Or the day after that or the day after that. Rosemary moved gently, walked lightly, so as not to dislodge what might possibly have taken hold inside her.

Talk with Guy? No, that could wait.

Everything could wait.

She cleaned, shopped, and cooked, breathing carefully. Laura-Louise came down one morning and asked her to vote for Buckley. She said she would, to get rid of her.

'Give me my quarter,' Guy said.

'Shut up,' she said, giving his arm a backhand punch.

She made an appointment with an obstetrician and, on Thursday, October 28th, went to see him. His name was Dr Hill. He had been recommended to her by a friend, Elise Dunstan, who had used him through two pregnancies and swore by him. His office was on West Seventy-second Street.

He was younger than Rosemary had expected – Guy's age or even less – and he looked a little bit like Dr Kildare on television. She liked him. He asked her questions slowly and with interest, examined her, and sent her to a lab on Sixtieth Street where a nurse drew blood from her right arm.

He called the next afternoon at three-thirty.

'Mrs Woodhouse?'

'Dr Hill?'

'Yes. Congratulations.'

'Really?'

'Really.'

She sat down on the side of the bed, smiling past the phone. *Really, really, really, really, really.*

'Are you there?'

'What happens now?' she asked.

'Very little. You come in and see me again next month. And you get those Natalin pills and start taking them. One a day. And you fill out some forms that I'm going to mail you – for the hospital; it's best to get the reservation in as soon as possible.'

'When will it be?' she asked.

'If your last period was September twenty-first,' he said, 'it works out to June twenty-eighth.'

'That sounds so far away.'

'It is. Oh, one more thing, Mrs Woodhouse. The lab would like another blood sample. Could you drop by there tomorrow or Monday and let them have it?'

'Yes, of course,' Rosemary said. 'What for?'

'The nurse didn't take as much as she should have.'

'But – I'm pregnant, aren't I?'

'Yes, they did *that* test,' Dr Hill said, 'but I generally have them run a few others besides – blood sugar and so forth – and the nurse didn't know and only took enough for the one. It's nothing to be concerned about. You're pregnant. I give you my word.'

'All right,' she said. 'I'll go back tomorrow morning.'

'Do you remember the address?'

'Yes, I still have the card.'

'I'll put those forms in the mail, and let's see you again – the last week in November.'

They made an appointment for November 29th at one o'clock and Rosemary hung up feeling that something was wrong. The nurse at the lab had seemed to know exactly what she was doing, and Dr Hill's offhandedness in speaking about her hadn't quite rung true. Were they afraid a mistake had been made? – vials of blood mixed up and wrongly labelled? – and was there still a possibility that she wasn't pregnant? But wouldn't Dr Hill have told her so frankly and not have been as definite as he had?

She tried to shake it away. Of course she was pregnant; she had to be, with her period so long overdue. She went into the kitchen, where a wall calendar hung, and in the next's day square wrote *Lab*; and in the square for November 29th, *Dr Hill – 1:00*.

When Guy came in she went to him without saying a word and put a quarter in his hand. 'What's this for?' he asked, and then caught on. 'Oh, that's great, honey!' he said. 'Just great!' – and taking her by the shoulders he kissed her twice and then a third time.

'Isn't it?' she said.

'Just great. I'm so happy.'

'Father.'

'Mother.'

'Guy, listen,' she said, and looked up at him, suddenly serious. 'Let's make this a new beginning, okay? A new openness and talking-to-each-other. Because we haven't been open. You've been so wrapped up in the show and the pilot and the way things have been breaking for you – I'm not saying you shouldn't be; it wouldn't be normal if you weren't. But that's why I went to the cabin, Guy. To settle in my mind what was going wrong between us. And that's what it was, and is: a lack of openness. On my part too. On my part as much as yours.'

'It's true,' he said, his hands holding her shoulders, his eyes meeting hers earnestly. 'It's true. I felt it too. Not as much as you did, I guess. I'm so God-damned self-centred, Ro. That's what the whole trouble is. I guess it's why I'm in this idiot nutty profession to begin with. You know I love you though, don't you? I *do*, Ro. I'll try to make it plainer from now on, I swear to God I will. I'll be as open as—'

'It's my fault as much as—'

'Bull. It's mine. Me and my self-centredness. Bear with me, will you, Ro? I'll try to do better.'

'Oh, Guy,' she said in a tide of remorse and love and forgiveness, and met his kisses with fervent kisses of her own.

'Fine way for parents to be carrying on,' he said.

She laughed, wet-eyed.

'Gee, honey,' he said, 'do you know what I'd love to do?'

'What?'

'Tell Minnie and Roman.' He raised a hand. 'I know, I know; we're supposed to keep it a deep dark secret. But I told them we were trying and they were so pleased, and, well, with people that old,' – he spread his hands ruefully – 'if we wait too long they might never get to know at all.'

'Tell them,' she said, loving him.

He kissed her nose. 'Back in two minutes,' he said, and turned and hurried to the door. Watching him go, she saw that Minnie and Roman had become deeply important to him. It wasn't surprising; his mother was a busy self-involved chatterer and none of his fathers had been truly fatherly. The Castevets were filling a need in him, a need of which he himself was probably unaware. She was grateful to them and would think more kindly of them in the future.

She went into the bathroom and splashed cold water on her eyes and fixed her hair and lips. 'You're pregnant,' she told herself in the mirror. (*But the lab wants another blood sample. What for*?)

As she came back out they came in at the front door: Minnie in a housedress, Roman holding in both hands a bottle of wine, and Guy behind them flushed and smiling. 'Now *that's* what I call good news!' Minnie said. 'Con*grat-u-la*-tions!' She bore down on Rosemary, took her by the shoulders, and kissed her cheek hard and loud.

'Our best wishes to you, Rosemary,' Roman said, putting his lips to her other cheek. 'We're more pleased than we can say. We have no champagne on hand, but this 1961 Saint Julien, I think, will do just as nicely for a toast.'

Rosemary thanked them.

'When are you due, dear?' Minnie asked.

'June twenty-eighth.'

'It's going to be so exciting,' Minnie said, 'between now and then.'

'We'll do all your shopping for you,' Roman said.

'Oh, no,' Rosemary said. 'Really.'

Guy brought glasses and a corkscrew, and Roman turned with him to the opening of the wine. Minnie took Rosemary's elbow and they walked together into the living-room. 'Listen, dear,' Minnie said, 'do you have a good doctor?'

'Yes, a very good one,' Rosemary said.

'One of the top obstetricians in New York,' Minnie said, 'is a dear friend of ours. Abe Sapirstein. A Jewish man. He delivers all the Society babies and he would deliver yours too if we asked him. And he'd do it *cheap*, so you'd be saving Guy some of his hard-earned money.'

'Abe Sapirstein?' Roman asked from across the room. 'He's one of the finest obstetricians in the country, Rosemary. You've heard of him, haven't you?'

'I think so,' Rosemary said, recalling the name from an article in a newspaper or magazine.

'*I* have,' Guy said. 'Wasn't he on *Open End* a couple of years ago?'

'That's right,' Roman said. 'He's one of the finest obstetricians in the country.'

'Ro?' Guy said.

'But what about Dr Hill?' she asked.

'Don't worry, I'll tell him something,' Guy said. 'You know me.'

Rosemary thought about Dr Hill, so young, so Kildare, with his lab that wanted more blood because the nurse had goofed or the technician had goofed or *someone* had goofed, causing her needless bother and concern.

Minnie said, 'I'm not going to *let* you go to no Dr Hill that nobody heard of! The *best* is what *you're* going to have, young lady, and the best is Abe Sapirstein!'

Gratefully Rosemary smiled her decision at them. 'If you're sure he can take me,' she said. 'He might be too busy.'

'He'll take you,' Minnie said. 'I'm going to call him right now. Where's the phone?'

'In the bedroom,' Guy said.

Minnie went into the bedroom. Roman poured glasses of wine. 'He's a brilliant man,' he said, 'with all the sensitivity of his much-tormented race.' He gave glasses to Rosemary and Guy. 'Let's wait for Minnie,' he said.

They stood motionless, each holding a full wineglass, Roman holding two. Guy said, 'Sit down, honey,' but Rosemary shook her head and stayed standing.

Minnie in the bedroom said, 'Abe? Minnie. Fine. Listen, a dear friend of ours just found out today that she's pregnant. Yes, isn't it? I'm in her apartment now. We told her you'd be glad to take care of her and that you wouldn't charge none of your fancy Society prices neither.' She was silent, then said 'Wait a minute,' and raised her voice. 'Rosemary? Can you go see him tomorrow morning at eleven?'

'Yes, that would be fine,' Rosemary called back.

Roman said, 'You see?'

'Eleven's fine, Abe,' Minnie said. 'Yes. You too. No, not at all. Let's hope so. Goodbye.'

She came back. 'There you are,' she said. 'I'll write down his address for you before we go. He's on Seventy-ninth Street and Park Avenue.'

'Thanks a million, Minnie,' Guy said, and Rosemary said, 'I don't know how to thank you. Both of you.'

Minnie took the glass of wine Roman held out to her. 'It's easy,' she said. 'Just do everything Abe tells you and have a fine healthy baby; that's all the thanks we'll ever ask for.'

Roman raised his glass. 'To a fine healthy baby,' he said.

'Hear, hear,' Guy said, and they all drank; Guy, Minnie, Rosemary, Roman.

'Mmm,' Guy said. 'Delicious.'

'Isn't it?' Roman said. 'And not at all expensive.'

'Oh my,' Minnie said, 'I can't wait to tell the news to Laura-Louise.'

Rosemary said, 'Oh, please. Don't tell anyone else. Not yet. It's so early.'

'She's right,' Roman said. 'There'll be plenty of time later on for spreading the good tidings.'

'Would anyone like some cheese and crackers?' Rosemary asked.

'Sit down, honey,' Guy said. 'I'll get it.'

That night Rosemary was too fired with joy and wonder to fall asleep quickly. Within her, under the hands that lay alertly on her stomach, a tiny egg had been fertilized by a tiny seed. Oh miracle, it would grow to be Andrew or Susan! ('Andrew' she was definite about; 'Susan' was open to discussion with Guy.) What was Andrew-or-Susan now, a pin-point speck? No, surely it was more than that; after all, wasn't she in her second month already? Indeed she was. It had probably reached the early tadpole stage. She would have to find a chart or book that told month by month exactly what was happening. Dr Sapirstein would know of one.

A fire engine screamed by. Guy shifted and mumbled, and behind the wall Minnie and Roman's bed creaked.

There were so many dangers to worry about in the months ahead; fires, falling objects, car out of control; dangers that had never been dangers before but were dangers now, now that Andrew-or-Susan was begun and living. (Yes, living!) She would give up her occasional cigarette, of course. And check with Dr Sapirstein about cocktails.

If only prayer were still possible! How nice it would be to hold a crucifix again and have God's ear: ask Him for safe passage through the eight more months ahead; no German measles, please, no great new drugs with Thalidomide side effects. Eight good months, please, free of accident and illness, full of iron and milk and sunshine.

Suddenly she remembered the good luck charm, the ball of tannis root; and foolish or not, wanted it – no, needed it – around her neck. She slipped out of bed, tiptoed to the vanity, and got it from the Louis Sherry box, freed it from its aluminium-foil wrapping. The smell of the tannis root had changed; it was still strong but no longer repellent. She put the chain over her head.

With the ball tickling between her breasts, she tiptoed back to bed and climbed in. She drew up the blanket and, closing her eyes, settled her head down into the pillow. She lay breathing deeply and was soon asleep, her hands on her stomach shielding the embryo inside her.

PART TWO
1

Now she was alive; was doing, was being, was at last herself and complete. She did what she had done before – cooked, cleaned, ironed, made the bed, shopped, took laundry to the basement, went to her sculpture class – but did everything against a new and serene background of knowing that Andrew-or-Susan (or Melinda) was every day a little bit bigger inside her than the day before, a little bit more clearly defined and closer to readiness.

Dr Sapirstein was wonderful; a tall sunburned man with white hair and a shaggy white moustache (she had seen him somewhere before but couldn't think where; maybe on *Open End*) who despite the Miës van der Rohe chairs and cool marble tables of his waiting-room was reassuringly old-fashioned and direct. 'Please don't read books,' he said. 'Every pregnancy is different, and a book that tells you what you're going to feel in the third week of the third month is only going to make you worry. No pregnancy was ever exactly like the ones described in the books. And don't listen to your friends either. They'll have had experiences very different from yours and they'll be absolutely certain that their pregnancies were the normal ones and that yours is abnormal.'

She asked him about the vitamin pills Dr Hill had prescribed.

'No, no pills,' he said. 'Minnie Castevet has a herbarium and a blender; I'm going to have her make a daily drink for you that will be fresher, safer, and more vitamin-rich than any pill on the market. And another thing: don't be afraid to satisfy your cravings. The theory today is that pregnant women invent cravings because they feel it's expected of them. I don't hold with that. I say if you want pickles in the middle of the night, make your poor husband go out and get some, just like in the old jokes. *Whatever* you want, be sure you get it. You'll be surprised at some of the strange things your body will ask for in these next few months. And any questions you have, call me night or day. Call *me*, not your mother or your Aunt Fanny. That's what I'm here for.'

She was to come in once a week, which was certainly closer attention than Dr Hill gave his patients, and he would make a reservation at Doctors Hospital without any bother of filling out forms.

Everything was right and bright and lovely. She got a Vidal Sassoon haircut, finished with the dentist, voted on Election Day (for Lindsay for mayor), and went down to Greenwich Village to watch some of the outdoor shooting of Guy's pilot. Between takes – Guy, running with a stolen hotdog wagon down Sullivan Street – she crouched on her heels to talk to small children and smiled *Me too* at pregnant women.

Salt, she found, even a few grains of it, made food inedible. 'That's perfectly normal,' Dr Sapirstein said on her second visit. 'When your system needs it, the aversion will disappear. Meanwhile, obviously, no salt. Trust your aversions the same as you do your cravings.'

She didn't have any cravings though. Her appetite, in fact, seemed smaller than usual. Coffee and toast was enough for breakfast, a vegetable and a small piece of rare meat for dinner. Each morning at eleven Minnie brought over what looked like a watery pistachio milkshake. It was cold and sour.

'What's in it?' Rosemary asked.

'Snips and snails and puppy-dogs' tails,' Minnie said, smiling.

Rosemary laughed. 'That's fine,' she said, 'but what if we want a girl?'

'Do you?'

'Well of course we'll take what we get, but it *would* be nice if the first one were a *boy*.'

'Well there you are,' Minnie said.

Finished drinking, Rosemary said, 'No, really, what's in it?'

'A raw egg, gelatin, herbs . . .'

'Tannis root?'

'Some of that, some of some other things.'

Minnie brought the drink every day in the same glass, a large one with blue and green stripes, and stood waiting while Rosemary drained it.

One day Rosemary got into a conversation by the elevator with

Phyllis Kapp, young Lisa's mother. The end of it was a brunch invitation for Guy and her on the following Sunday, but Guy vetoed the idea when Rosemary told him of it. In all likelihood he would be in Sunday's shooting, he explained, and if he weren't he would need the day for rest and study. They were having little social life just then. Guy had broken a dinner-and-theatre date they had made a few weeks earlier with Jimmy and Tiger Haenigsen, and he had asked Rosemary if she would mind putting off Hutch for dinner. It was because of the pilot, which was taking longer to shoot than had been intended.

It turned out to be just as well though, for Rosemary began to develop abdominal pains of an alarming sharpness. She called Dr Sapirstein and he asked her to come in. Examining her, he said that there was nothing to worry about; the pains came from an entirely normal expansion of her pelvis. They would disappear in a day or two, and meanwhile she could fight them with ordinary doses of aspirin.

Rosemary, relieved, said, 'I was afraid it might be an ectopic pregnancy.'

'Ectopic?' Dr Sapirstein asked, and looked sceptically at her. She coloured. He said, 'I thought you weren't going to read books, Rosemary.'

'It was staring me right in the face at the drug store,' she said.

'And all it did was worry you. Will you go home and throw it away, please?'

'I will. I promise.'

'The pains will be gone in two days,' he said. ' "Ectopic pregnancy".' He shook his head.

But the pains weren't gone in two days; they were worse, and grew worse still, as if something inside her were encircled by a wire being drawn tighter and tighter to cut it in two. There would be pain for hour after hour, and then a few minutes of relative painlessness that was only the pain gathering itself for a new assault. Aspirin did little good, and she was afraid of taking too many. Sleep, when it finally came, brought harried dreams in which she fought against huge spiders that had cornered her in the bathroom, or tugged desperately at a small black bush that had taken root on the middle of the living-room rug. She woke tired, to even sharper pain.

'This happens sometimes,' Dr Sapirstein said. 'It'll stop any day now. Are you sure you haven't been lying about your age? Usually it's the older women with less flexible joints who have this sort of difficulty.'

Minnie, bringing in the drink, said, 'You poor thing. Don't fret, dear; a niece of mine in Toledo had exactly the same kind of pains and so did two other women I know of. And their deliveries were real easy and they had beautiful healthy babies.'

'Thanks,' Rosemary said.

Minnie drew back righteously. 'What do you mean? That's the gospel truth! I swear to God it is, Rosemary!'

Her face grew pinched and wan and shadowed; she looked awful. But Guy insisted otherwise. 'What are you talking about?' he said. 'You look great. It's that *haircut* that looks awful, if you want the truth, honey. That's the biggest mistake you ever made in your whole life.'

The pain settled down to a constant presence, with no respite whatever. She endured it and lived with it, sleeping a few hours a night and taking one aspirin where Dr Sapirstein allowed two. There was no going out with Joan or Elise, no sculpture class or shopping. She ordered groceries by phone and stayed in the apartment, making nursery curtains and starting, finally, on *The Decline and Fall of The Roman Empire*. Sometimes Minnie or Roman came in of an afternoon, to talk a while and see if there was anything she wanted. Once Laura-Louise brought down a tray of gingerbread. She hadn't been told yet that Rosemary was pregnant. 'Oh my, I *do* like that haircut, Rosemary,' she said. 'You look so pretty and up-to-date.' She was surprised to hear she wasn't feeling well.

When the pilot was finally finished Guy stayed home most of the time. He had stopped studying with Dominick, his vocal coach, and no longer spent afternoons auditioning and being seen. He had two good commercials on deck – for Pall Mall and Texaco – and rehearsals of *Don't I know You From Somewhere*? were definitely scheduled to begin in mid-January. He gave Rosemary a hand with the cleaning, and they played time-limit Scrabble for a dollar a game. He answered the phone and, when it was for Rosemary, made plausible excuses.

She had planned to give a Thanksgiving dinner for some of their friends who, like themselves, had no family nearby; with the constant pain, though, and the constant worry over Andrew-or-Melinda's well-being, she decided not to, and they ended up going to Minnie and Roman's instead.

2

One afternoon in December, while Guy was doing the Pall Mall commercial, Hutch called. 'I'm around the corner at City Centre picking up tickets for Marcel Marceau,' he said. 'Would you and Guy like to come on Friday night?'

'I don't think so, Hutch,' Rosemary said. 'I haven't been feeling too well lately. And Guy's got two commercials this week.'

'What's the matter with you?'

'Nothing, really. I've just been a bit under the weather.'

'May I come up for a few minutes?'

'Oh do; I'd love to see you.'

She hurried into slacks and a jersey top, put on lipstick and brushed her hair. The pain sharpened – locking her for a moment with shut eyes and clenched teeth – and then it sank back to its usual level and she breathed out gratefully and went on brushing.

Hutch, when he saw her, stared and said, 'My God.'

'It's Vidal Sassoon and it's very in,' she said.

'What's *wrong* with you?' he said. 'I don't mean your hair.'

'Do I look that bad?' She took his coat and hat and hung them away, smiling a fixed bright smile.

'You look terrible,' Hutch said. 'You've lost God-knows-how-many pounds and you have circles around your eyes that a panda would envy. You aren't on one of those "Zen diets", are you?'

'No.'

'Then what is it? Have you seen a doctor?'

'I suppose I might as well tell you,' Rosemary said. 'I'm pregnant. I'm in my third month.'

Hutch looked at her, nonplussed. 'That's ridiculous,' he said. 'Pregnant women *gain* weight, they don't lose it. And they look *healthy*, not—'

'There's a slight complication,' Rosemary said, leading the way into the living-room. 'I have stiff joints or something, so I have pains that keep me awake most of the night. Well, *one* pain, really; it just sort of continues. It's not serious, though. It'll probably stop any day now.'

'I never heard of "stiff joints" being a problem,' Hutch said.

'Stiff pelvic joints. It's fairly common.'

Hutch sat in Guy's easy chair. 'Well, congratulations,' he said doubtfully. 'You must be very happy.'

'I am,' Rosemary said. 'We both are.'

'Who's your obstetrician?'

'His name is Abraham Sapirstein. He's—'

'I know him,' Hutch said. 'Or *of* him. He delivered two of Doris's babies.' Doris was Hutch's elder daughter.

'He's one of the best in the city,' Rosemary said.

'When did you see him last?'

'The day before yesterday. And he said just what I told you; it's fairly common and it'll probably stop any day now. Of course he's been saying *that* since it started . . .'

'How much weight have you lost?'

'Only three pounds. It looks—'

'Nonsense! You've lost *far* more than that!'

Rosemary smiled. 'You sound like our bathroom scale,' she said. 'Guy finally threw it out, it was scaring me so. No, I've lost only three pounds and one little space more. And it's perfectly normal to lose a little during the first few months. Later on I'll be gaining.'

'I certainly hope so,' Hutch said. 'You look as if you're being drained by a vampire. Are you sure there aren't any puncture marks?' Rosemary smiled. 'Well,' Hutch said, leaning back and smiling too, 'we'll assume that Dr Sapirstein knows whereof he speaks. God knows he should; he charges enough. Guy must be doing sensationally.'

'He is,' Rosemary said. 'But we're getting bargain rates. Our neighbours the Castevets are close friends of his; they sent me to him and he's charging us his special non-Society prices.'

'Does that mean Doris and Axel are Society?' Hutch said. 'They'll be delighted to hear about it.'

The doorbell rang. Hutch offered to answer it but Rosemary wouldn't let him. 'Hurts less when I move around,' she said, going out of the room; and went to the front door trying to recall if there was anything she had ordered that hadn't been delivered yet.

It was Roman, looking slightly winded. Rosemary smiled and said, 'I mentioned your name two seconds ago.'

'In a favourable context, I hope,' he said. 'Do you need anything from outside? Minnie is going down in a while and our house phone doesn't seem to be functioning.'

'No, nothing,' Rosemary said. 'Thanks so much for asking. I phoned out for things this morning.'

Roman glanced beyond her for an instant, and then, smiling, asked if Guy was home already.

'No, he won't be back until six at the earliest,' Rosemary said; and, because Roman's pallid face stayed waiting with its questioning smile, added, 'A friend of ours is here.' The questioning smile stayed. She said, 'Would you like to meet him?'

'Yes, I would,' Roman said. 'If I won't be intruding.'

'Of course you won't.' Rosemary showed him in. He was wearing a black-and-white checked jacket over a blue shirt and a wide paisley tie. He passed close to her and she noticed for the first time that his ears were pierced – that the left one was, at any rate.

She followed him to the living-room archway. 'This is Edward Hutchins,' she said, and to Hutch, who was rising and smiling, 'This is Roman Castevet, the neighbour I just mentioned.' She explained to Roman: 'I was telling Hutch that it was you and Minnie who sent me to Dr Sapirstein.'

The two men shook hands and greeted each other. Hutch said, 'One of my daughters used Dr Sapirstein too. On two occasions.'

'He's a brilliant man,' Roman said. 'We met him only last spring but he's become one of our closest friends.'

'Sit down, won't you?' Rosemary said. The men seated themselves and Rosemary sat by Hutch.

Roman said, 'So Rosemary has told you the good news, has she?'

'Yes, she has,' Hutch said.

'We must see that she gets plenty of rest,' Roman said, 'and complete freedom from worry and anxiety.'

Rosemary said, 'That would be heaven.'

'I was a bit alarmed by her appearance,' Hutch said, looking at Rosemary as he took out a pipe and a striped rep tobacco pouch.

'Were you?' Roman said.

'But now that I know she's in Dr Sapirstein's care I feel considerably relieved.'

'She's only lost two or three pounds,' Roman said. 'Isn't that so, Rosemary?'

'That's right,' Rosemary said.

'And that's quite normal in the early months of pregnancy,' Roman said. 'Later on she'll gain – probably far too much.'

'So I gather,' Hutch said, filling his pipe.

Rosemary said, 'Mrs Castevet makes a vitamin drink for me every day, with a raw egg and milk and fresh herbs that she grows.'

'All according to Dr Sapirstein's directions, of course,' Roman said. 'He's inclined to be suspicious of commercially prepared vitamin pills.'

'Is he really?' Hutch asked, pocketing his pouch. 'I can't think of anything I'd be less suspicious of; they're surely manufactured under every imaginable safeguard.' He struck two matches as one and sucked flame into his pipe, blowing out puffs of aromatic white smoke. Rosemary put an ashtray near him.

'That's true,' Roman said, 'but commercial pills can sit for months in a warehouse or on a druggist's shelf and lose a great deal of their original potency.'

'Yes, I hadn't thought of that,' Hutch said; 'I suppose they can.'

Rosemary said, 'I like the *idea* of having everything fresh and natural. I'll bet expectant mothers chewed bits of tannis root hundreds and hundreds of years ago when nobody'd even heard of vitamins.'

'Tannis root?' Hutch said.

'It's one of the herbs in the drink,' Rosemary said. 'Or *is* it a herb?' She looked to Roman. 'Can a root be a herb?' But Roman was watching Hutch and didn't hear.

' "Tannis"?' Hutch said. 'I've never heard of it. Are you sure you don't mean "anise" or "orris root"?'

Roman said, 'Tannis.'

'Here,' Rosemary said, drawing out her charm. 'It's good luck too, theoretically. Brace yourself; the smell takes a little getting-used-to.' She held the charm out, leaning forward to bring it closer to Hutch.

He sniffed at it and drew away, grimacing. 'I should say it does,' he said. He took the chained ball between two fingertips and squinted at it from a distance. 'It doesn't look like root matter at all,' he said; 'it looks like mould or fungus of some kind.' He looked at Roman. 'Is it ever called by another name?' he asked.

'Not to my knowledge,' Roman said.

'I shall look it up in the encyclopedia and find out all about it,' Hutch said. 'Tannis. What a pretty holder or charm or whatever-it-is. Where did you get it?'

With a quick smile at Roman, Rosemary said, 'The Castevets gave it to me.' She tucked the charm back inside her top.

Hutch said to Roman, 'You and your wife seem to be taking better care of Rosemary than her own parents would.'

Roman said, 'We're very fond of her, and of Guy too.' He pushed against the arms of his chair and raised himself to his feet. 'If you'll excuse me, I have to go now,' he said. 'My wife is waiting for me.'

'Of course,' Hutch said, rising. 'It's a pleasure to have met you.'

'We'll meet again, I'm sure,' Roman said. 'Don't bother, Rosemary.'

'It's no bother.' She walked along with him to the front door. His right ear was pierced too, she saw, and there were many small scars on his neck like a flight of distant birds. 'Thanks again for stopping by,' she said.

'Don't mention it,' Roman said. 'I like your friend Mr Hutchins; he seems extremely intelligent.'

Rosemary, opening the door, said, 'He is.'

'I'm glad I met him,' Roman said. With a smile and a handwave he started down the hall.

''Bye,' Rosemary said, waving back.

Hutch was standing by the bookshelves. 'This room is glorious,' he said. 'You're doing a beautiful job.'

'Thanks,' Rosemary said. 'I was until my pelvis intervened. Roman has pierced ears. I just noticed it for the first time.'

'Pierced ears and piercing eyes,' Hutch said. 'What was he before he became a Golden Ager?'

'Just about everything. And he's been everywhere in the world. Really everywhere.'

'Nonsense; nobody has. Why did he ring your bell? – if I'm not being too inquisitive.'

'To see if I needed anything from outside. The house phone isn't working. They're fantastic neighbours. They'd come in and do the cleaning if I let them.'

'What's *she* like?'

Rosemary told him. 'Guy's gotten very close to them,' she said. 'I think they've become sort of parent-figures for him.'

'And you?'

'I'm not sure. Sometimes I'm so grateful I could kiss them, and sometimes I get a sort of smothery feeling, as if they're being *too* friendly and helpful. Yet how can I complain? You remember the power failure?'

'Shall I ever forget it? I was in an elevator.'

'No.'

'Yes indeed. Five hours in total darkness with three women and a John Bircher who were all sure that the Bomb had fallen.'

'How awful.'

'You were saying?'

'We were here, Guy and I, and two minutes after the lights went out Minnie was at the door with a handful of candles.' She gestured towards the mantel. 'Now how can you find fault with neighbours like that?'

'You can't, obviously,' Hutch said, and stood looking at the mantel. 'Are those the ones?' he asked. Two pewter candlesticks stood between a bowl of polished stones and a brass microscope; in them were three-inch lengths of black candle ribbed with drippings.

'The last survivors,' Rosemary said. 'She brought a whole month's worth. What is it?'

'Were they all black?' he asked.

'Yes,' she said. 'Why?'

'Just curious.' He turned from the mantel, smiling at her. 'Offer me coffee, will you? And tell me more about Mrs Castevet. Where does she grow those herbs of hers? In window boxes?'

They were sitting over cups at the kitchen table some ten minutes later when the front door unlocked and Guy hurried in. 'Hey, what a surprise,' he said, coming over and grabbing Hutch's hand before he could rise. 'How are you, Hutch? Good to see you!' He clasped Rosemary's head in his other hand and bent and kissed her cheek and lips. 'How you doing, honey?' He still had his make-up on; his face was orange, his eyes black-lashed and large.

'You're the surprise,' Rosemary said. 'What happened?'

'Ah, they stopped in the middle for a rewrite, the dumb bastards. We start again in the morning. Stay where you are, nobody move; I'll just get rid of my coat.' He went out to the closet.

'Would you like some coffee?' Rosemary called.

'Love some!'

She got up and poured a cup, and refilled Hutch's cup and her own. Hutch sucked at his pipe, looking thoughtfully before him.

Guy came back in with his hands full of packs of Pall Mall. 'Loot,' he said, dumping them on the table. 'Hutch?'

'No, thanks.'

Guy tore a pack open, jammed cigarettes up, and pulled one out. He winked at Rosemary as she sat down again.

Hutch said, 'It seems congratulations are in order.'

Guy, lighting up, said, 'Rosemary told you? It's wonderful, isn't it? We're delighted. Of course I'm scared stiff that I'll be a lousy father, but Rosemary'll be such a great mother that it won't make much difference.'

'When is the baby due?' Hutch asked.

Rosemary told him, and told Guy that Dr Sapirstein had delivered two of Hutch's grandchildren.

Hutch said, 'I met your neighbour, Roman Castevet.'

'Oh, did you?' Guy said. 'Funny old duck, isn't he? He's got some interesting stories, though, about Otis Skinner and Modjeska. He's quite a theatre buff.'

Rosemary said, 'Did you ever notice that his ears are pierced?'

'You're kidding,' Guy said.

'No I'm not; I saw.'

They drank their coffee, talking of Guy's quickening career and of a trip Hutch planned to make in the spring to Greece and Turkey.

'It's a shame we haven't seen more of you lately,' Guy said, when Hutch had excused himself and risen. 'With me so busy and Ro being the way she is, we really haven't seen anyone.'

'Perhaps we can have dinner together soon,' Hutch said; and Guy, agreeing, went to get his coat.

Rosemary said, 'Don't forget to look up tannis root.'

'I won't,' Hutch said. 'And you tell Dr Sapirstein to check his scale; I still think you've lost more than three pounds.'

'Don't be silly,' Rosemary said. 'Doctors' scales aren't wrong.'

Guy, holding open a coat, said, 'It's not mine, it must be yours.'

'Right you are,' Hutch said. Turning, he put his arms back into it. 'Have you thought about names yet?' he asked Rosemary, 'or is it too soon?'

'Andrew or Douglas if it's a boy,' she said. 'Melinda or Sarah if it's a girl.'

' "Sarah"?' Guy said. 'What happened to "Susan"?' He gave Hutch his hat.

Rosemary offered her cheek for Hutch's kiss.

'I do hope the pain stops soon,' he said.

'It will,' she said, smiling. 'Don't worry.'

Guy said, 'It's a pretty common condition.'

Hutch felt his pockets. 'Is there another one of these around?' he asked, and showed them a brown fur-lined glove and felt his pockets again.

Rosemary looked around at the floor and Guy went to the closet and looked down on the floor and up on to the shelf. 'I don't see it, Hutch,' he said.

'Nuisance,' Hutch said. 'I probably left it at City Centre. I'll stop back there. Let's really have that dinner, shall we?'

'Definitely,' Guy said, and Rosemary said, 'Next week.'

They watched him around the first turn of the hallway and then stepped back inside and closed the door.

'That was a nice surprise,' Guy said. 'Was he here long?'

'Not very,' Rosemary said. 'Guess what he said.'

'What?'

'I look terrible.'

'Good old Hutch,' Guy said, 'spreading cheer wherever he goes.' Rosemary looked at him questioningly. 'Well he *is* a professional crepe-hanger, honey,' he said. 'Remember how he tried to sour us on moving in here?'

'He isn't a professional crepe-hanger,' Rosemary said, going into the kitchen to clear the table.

Guy leaned against the door jamb. 'Then he sure is one of the top-ranking amateurs,' he said.

A few minutes later he put his coat on and went out for a news-paper.

The telephone rang at ten-thirty that evening, when Rosemary was in bed reading and Guy was in the den watching television. He answered the call and a minute later brought the phone into the bed-room. 'Hutch wants to speak to you,' he said, putting the phone on the bed and crouching to plug it in. 'I told him you were resting but he said it couldn't wait.'

Rosemary picked up the receiver. 'Hutch?' she said.

'Hello, Rosemary,' Hutch said. 'Tell me, dear, do you go out at all or do you stay in your apartment all day?'

'Well I haven't *been* going out,' she said, looking at Guy; 'but I could. Why?' Guy looked back at her, frowning, listening.

'There's something I want to speak to you about,' Hutch said. 'Can you meet me tomorrow morning at eleven in front of the Seagram Building?'

'Yes, if you want me to,' she said. 'What is it? Can't you tell me now?'

'I'd rather not,' he said. 'It's nothing terribly important so don't brood about it. We can have a late brunch or early lunch if you'd like.'

'That would be nice.'

'Good. Eleven o'clock then, in front of the Seagram Building.'

'Right. Did you get your glove?'

'No, they didn't have it,' he said, 'but it's time I got some new ones anyway. Goodnight, Rosemary. Sleep well.'

'You too. Goodnight.'

She hung up.

'What was that?' Guy asked.

'He wants me to meet him tomorrow morning. He has something he wants to talk to me about.'

'And he didn't say what?'

'Not a word.'

Guy shook his head, smiling. 'I think those boys' adventure stories are going to his head,' he said. 'Where are you meeting him?'

'In front of the Seagram Building at eleven o'clock.'

Guy unplugged the phone and went out with it to the den; almost immediately, though, he was back. 'You're the pregnant one and I'm the one with yens,' he said, plugging the phone back in and putting it on the night table. 'I'm going to go out and get an ice cream cone. Do you want one?'

'Okay,' Rosemary said.

'Vanilla?'

'Fine.'

'I'll be as quick as I can.'

He went out, and Rosemary leaned back against her pillows, looking ahead at nothing with her book forgotten in her lap. What was it Hutch wanted to talk about? Nothing terribly important, he had said. But it must be something not *un*-important too, or else he wouldn't have summoned her as he had. Was it something about Joan? – or one of the other girls who had shared the apartment?

Far away she heard the Castevets' doorbell give one short ring. Probably it was Guy, asking them if they wanted ice cream or a morning paper. Nice of him.

The pain sharpened inside her.

3

The following morning Rosemary called Minnie on the house phone and asked her not to bring the drink over at eleven o'clock; she was on her way out and wouldn't be back until one or two.

'Why, that's fine, dear,' Minnie said. 'Don't you worry about a thing. You don't have to take it at no fixed time; just so you take it *sometime*, that's all. You go on out. It's a nice day and it'll do you good to get some fresh air. Buzz me when you get back and I'll bring the drink in then.'

It was indeed a nice day; sunny, cold, clear, and invigorating. Rosemary walked through it slowly, ready to smile, as if she weren't carrying her pain inside her. Salvation Army Santa Clauses were on every corner, shaking their bells in their fool-nobody costumes. Stores all had their Christmas windows; Park Avenue had its centre line of trees.

She reached the Seagram Building at a quarter of eleven and, because she was early and there was no sign yet of Hutch, sat for a while on the low wall at the side of the building's forecourt, taking the sun on her face and listening with pleasure to busy footsteps and snatches of conversation, to cars and trucks and a helicopter's racketing. The dress beneath her coat was – for the first satisfying time – snug over her stomach; maybe after lunch she would go to Bloomingdale's and look at maternity dresses. She was glad Hutch had called her out this way (but what did he want to talk about?); pain, even constant pain, was no excuse for staying indoors as much as she had. She would fight it from now on, fight it with air and sunlight and activity, not succumb to it in Bramford gloom under the well-meant pamperings of Minnie and Guy and Roman. *Pain, begone!* she thought; *I will have no more of thee!* The pain stayed, immune to Positive Thinking.

At five of eleven she went and stood by the building's glass doors, at the edge of their heavy flow of traffic. Hutch would probably be coming from inside, she thought, from an earlier appointment; or else why had he chosen here rather than someplace else for their meeting? She scouted the out-coming faces as best she could, saw him but was mistaken, then saw a man she had dated before she met Guy and was mistaken again. She kept looking, stretching now and then on tiptoes; not anxiously, for she knew that even if she failed to see him, Hutch would see her.

He hadn't come by five after eleven, nor by ten after. At a quarter after she went inside to look at the building's directory, thinking she might see a name there that he had mentioned at one time or another and to which she might make a call of inquiry. The directory proved to be far too large and many-named for careful reading, though; she skimmed over its crowded columns and, seeing nothing familiar, went outside again.

She went back to the low wall and sat where she had sat before, this time watching the front of the building and glancing over occasionally at the shallow steps leading up from the sidewalk. Men and women met other men and women, but there was no sign of Hutch, who was rarely if ever late for appointments.

At eleven-forty Rosemary went back into the building and was sent by a maintenance man down to the basement, where at the end of a white institutional corridor there was a pleasant lounge area with black modern chairs, an abstract mural, and a single stainless-steel phone booth. A Negro girl was in the booth, but she finished soon and came out with a friendly smile. Rosemary slipped in and dialled the number at the apartment. After five rings Service answered; there were no messages for Rosemary, and the one message for Guy was from a Rudy Horn, not a Mr Hutchins. She had another dime and used it to call Hutch's number, thinking that his service might know where he was or have a message from him. On the first ring a woman answered with a worried non-service 'Yes?'

'Is this Edward Hutchins' apartment?' Rosemary asked.

'Yes. Who is this, please?' She sounded like a woman neither young nor old – in her forties, perhaps.

Rosemary said, 'My name is Rosemary Woodhouse. I had an eleven o'clock appointment with Mr Hutchins and he hasn't shown up yet. Do you have any idea whether he's coming or not?'

There was silence, and more of it. 'Hello?' Rosemary said.

'Hutch has told me about you, Rosemary,' the woman said. 'My name is Grace Cardiff. I'm a friend of his. He was taken ill last night. Or early this morning, to be exact.'

Rosemary's heart dropped. 'Taken ill?' she said.

'Yes. He's in a deep coma. The doctors haven't been able to find out yet what's causing it. He's at St Vincent's Hospital.'

'Oh, that's *awful*,' Rosemary said. 'I spoke to him last night around ten-thirty and he sounded *fine*.'

'I spoke to him not much later than that,' Grace Cardiff said, 'and he sounded fine to me too. But his cleaning woman came in this morning and found him unconscious on the bedroom floor.'

'And they don't know what from?'

'Not yet. It's early though, and I'm sure they'll find out soon. And when they do, they'll be able to treat him. At the moment he's totally unresponsive.'

'How awful,' Rosemary said. 'And he's never had anything like this before?'

'Never,' Grace Cardiff said. 'I'm going back to the hospital now, and if you'll give me a number where I can reach you, I'll let you know when there's any change.'

'Oh, thank you,' Rosemary said. She gave the apartment number and then asked if there was anything she could do to help.

'Not really,' Grace Cardiff said. 'I just finished calling his daughters, and that seems to be the sum total of what has to be done, at least until he comes to. If there should be anything else I'll let you know.'

Rosemary came out of the Seagram Building and walked across the forecourt and down the steps and north to the corner of Fifty-third Street. She crossed Park Avenue and walked slowly towards Madison, wondering whether Hutch would live or die, and if he died, whether she (selfishness!) would ever again have anyone on whom she could so effortlessly and completely depend. She wondered too about Grace Cardiff, who sounded silver-grey and attractive; had she and Hutch been having a quiet middle-aged affair? She hoped so. Maybe this brush with death – that's what it would be, a *brush* with death, not death itself; it couldn't be – maybe this brush with death would nudge them both towards marriage, and turn out in the end to have been a disguised blessing. Maybe. Maybe.

She crossed Madison, and somewhere between Madison and Fifth found herself looking into a window in which a small crèche was spotlighted, with exquisite porcelain figures of Mary and the Infant and Joseph, the Magi and the shepherds and the animals of the stable. She smiled at the tender scene, laden with meaning and emotion that survived her agnosticism; and then saw in the window glass, like a veil hung before the Nativity, her own reflection smiling, with the skeletal cheeks and black-circled eyes that yesterday had alarmed Hutch and now alarmed her.

'Well *this* is what I call the long arm of coincidence!' Minnie exclaimed, and came smiling to her when Rosemary turned, in a white mock-leather coat and a red hat and her neckchained eyeglasses. 'I said to myself, "As long as *Rosemary's* out, *I* might as well go out, and do the last little bit of my Christmas shopping." And here *you* are and here *I* am! It looks like we're just two of a kind that go the same places and do the same things! Why, what's the matter, dear? You look so sad and downcast.'

'I just heard some bad news,' Rosemary said. 'A friend of mine is very sick. In the hospital.'

'Oh, no,' Minnie said. 'Who?'

'His name is Edward Hutchins,' Rosemary said.

'The one Roman met yesterday afternoon? Why, he was going on for an *hour* about what a nice intelligent man he was! Isn't that a pity! What's troubling him?'

Rosemary told her.

'My land,' Minnie said, 'I hope it doesn't turn out the way it did for poor Lily Gardenia! And the doctors don't even know? Well at least they admit it; usually they cover up what they don't know with a lot of high-flown Latin. If the money spent putting those astronauts up where they are was spent on medical research down here, we'd *all* be a lot better off, if you want *my* opinion. Do you feel all right, Rosemary?'

'The pain is a little worse,' Rosemary said.

'You poor thing. You know what I think? I think we ought to be going home now. What do you say?'

'No, no, you have to finish your Christmas shopping.'

'Oh, shoot,' Minnie said, 'there's two whole weeks yet. Hold on to your ears.' She put her wrist to her mouth and blew stabbing shrillness from a whistle on a gold-chain bracelet. A taxi veered towards them. 'How's *that* for service?' she said. 'A nice big Checker one too.'

Soon after, Rosemary was in the apartment again. She drank the cold sour drink from the blue-and-green-striped glass while Minnie looked on approvingly.

4

She had been eating her meat rare; now she ate it nearly raw – broiled only long enough to take away the refrigerator's chill and seal in the juices.

The weeks before the holidays and the holiday season itself were dismal. The pain grew worse, grew so grinding that something shut down in Rosemary – some centre of resistance and remembered well-being – and she stopped reacting, stopped mentioning pain to Dr Sapirstein, stopped referring to pain even in her thoughts. Until now it had been inside her; now *she* was inside it; pain was the weather around her, was time, was the entire world. Numbed and exhausted, she began to sleep more, and to eat more too – more nearly raw meat.

She did what had to be done: cooked and cleaned, sent Christmas cards to the family – she hadn't the heart for phone calls – and put new money into envelopes for the elevator men, doormen, porters, and Mr Micklas. She looked at newspapers and tried to be interested in students burning draft cards and the threat of a city-wide transit strike, but she couldn't: this was news from a world of fantasy; nothing was real but her world of pain. Guy bought Christmas presents for Minnie and Roman; for each other they agreed to buy nothing at all. Minnie and Roman gave them coasters.

They went to nearby movies a few times, but most evenings they stayed in or went around the hall to Minnie and Roman's where they met couples named Fountain and Gilmore and Wees, a woman named Mrs Sabatini who always brought her cat, and Dr Shand, the retired dentist who had made the chain for Rosemary's tannischarm. These were all elderly people who treated Rosemary with kindness and concern, seeing, apparently, that she was less than well. Laura-Louise was there too, and sometimes Dr Sapirstein joined the group. Roman was an energetic host, filling glasses and launching new topics of conversation. On New Year's Eve he proposed a toast – 'To 1966, The Year One,' – that puzzled Rosemary, although everyone else seemed to understand and approve of it. She felt as if she had missed a literary or political reference – not that she really cared. She and Guy usually left early, and Guy would see her into bed and go back. He was the favourite of the women, who gathered around him and laughed at his jokes.

Hutch stayed as he was, in his deep and baffling coma. Grace Cardiff called every week or so. 'No change, no change at all,' she would say. 'They still don't know. He could wake up tomorrow morning or he could sink deeper and never wake up at all.'

Twice Rosemary went to St Vincent's Hospital to stand beside Hutch's bed and look down powerlessly at the closed eyes, the scarcely discernible breathing. The second time, early in January, his daughter Doris was there, sitting by the window working a piece of needlepoint. Rosemary had met her a year earlier at Hutch's apartment; she was a short pleasant woman in her thirties, married to a Swedish-born psychoanalyst. She looked, unfortunately, like a younger wigged Hutch.

Doris didn't recognize Rosemary, and when Rosemary had re-introduced herself she made a distressed apology.

'Please don't,' Rosemary said, smiling. 'I know. I look awful.'

'No, you haven't changed at all,' Doris said. 'I'm terrible with faces. I forget my *children*, really I do.'

She put aside her needlepoint and Rosemary drew up another chair and sat with her. They talked about Hutch's condition and watched a nurse come in and replace the hanging bottle that fed into his taped arm.

'We have an obstetrician in common,' Rosemary said when the nurse had gone; and then they talked about Rosemary's pregnancy and Dr Sapirstein's skill and eminence. Doris was surprised to hear that he was seeing Rosemary every week. 'He only saw me once a month,' she said. 'Till near the end, of course. Then it was every two weeks, and *then* every week, but only in the last month. I thought that was fairly standard.'

Rosemary could find nothing to say, and Doris suddenly looked distressed again. 'But I suppose every pregnancy is a law unto itself,' she said, with a smile meant to rectify tactlessness.

'That's what *he* told me,' Rosemary said.

That evening she told Guy that Dr Sapirstein had only seen Doris once a month. 'Something is wrong with me,' she said. 'And he knew it right from the beginning.'

'Don't be silly,' Guy said. 'He would tell you. And even if he wouldn't, he would certainly tell *me*.'

'Has he? Has he said *anything* to you?'

'Absolutely not, Ro. I swear to God.'

'Then why do I have to go every week?'

'Maybe that's the way he does it now. Or maybe he's giving you better treatment, because you're Minnie and Roman's friend.'

'No.'

'Well *I* don't know; ask *him*,' Guy said. 'Maybe you're more fun to examine than she was.'

She asked Dr Sapirstein two days later. 'Rosemary, Rosemary,' he said to her; 'what did I tell you about talking to your friends? Didn't I say that every pregnancy is different?'

'Yes, but—'

'And the treatment has to be different too. Doris Allert had had two deliveries before she ever came to me, and there had been no complications whatever. She didn't require the close attention a first-timer does.'

'Do you always see first-timers every week?'

'I try to,' he said. 'Sometimes I can't. There's nothing wrong with you, Rosemary. The pain will stop very soon.'

'I've been eating raw meat,' she said. 'Just warmed a little.'

'Anything else out of the ordinary?'

'No,' she said, taken aback; wasn't that enough?

'Whatever you want, eat it,' he said. 'I told you you'd get some strange cravings. I've had women eat paper. And stop worrying. I don't keep things from my patients; it makes life too confusing. I'm telling you the truth. Okay?'

She nodded.

'Say hello to Minnie and Roman for me,' he said. 'And Guy too.'

She began the second volume of *The Decline and Fall*, and began knitting a red-and-orange striped muffler for Guy to wear to rehearsals. The threatened transit strike had come about but it affected them little since they were both at home most of the time. Late in the afternoon they watched from their bay windows the slow-moving crowds far below. 'Walk, you peasants!' Guy said. 'Walk! Home, home, and be quick about it!'

Not long after telling Dr Sapirstein about the nearly raw meat, Rosemary found herself chewing on a raw and dripping chicken heart – in the kitchen one morning at four-fifteen. She looked at herself in the side of the toaster, where her moving reflection had caught her eye, and then looked at her hand, at the part of the heart she hadn't yet eaten held in red-dripping fingers. After a moment she went over and put the heart in the garbage, and turned on the water and rinsed her hand. Then, with the water still running, she bent over the sink and began to vomit.

When she was finished she drank some water, washed her face and hands, and cleaned the inside of the sink with the spray attachment. She turned off the water and dried herself and stood for a while, thinking; and then she got a memo pad and a pencil from one of the drawers and went to the table and sat down and began to write.

Guy came in just before seven in his pyjamas. She had the *Life* Cookbook open on the table and was copying a recipe out of it. 'What the hell are you doing?' he asked.

She looked at him. 'Planning the menu,' she said. 'For a party. We're giving a party on January twenty-second. A week from next Saturday.' She looked among several slips of paper on the table and picked one up. 'We're inviting Elise Dunstan and her husband,' she said, 'Joan and a date, Jimmy and Tiger, Allan and a date, Lou and Claudia, the Chens, the Wendells, Dee Bertillon and a date unless you don't want him, Mike and Pedro, Bob and Thea Goodman, the Kapps' – she pointed in the Kapps' direction – 'and Doris and Axel Allert, if they'll come. That's Hutch's daughter.'

'I know,' Guy said.

She put down the paper. 'Minnie and Roman are not invited,' she said. 'Neither is Laura-Louise. Neither are the Fountains and the Gilmores and the Weeses. Neither is Dr Sapirstein. This is a very special party. You have to be under sixty to get in.'

'Whew,' Guy said. 'For a minute there I didn't think I was going to make it.'

'Oh, you make it,' Rosemary said. 'You're the bartender.'

'Swell,' Guy said. 'Do you really think this is such a great idea?'

'I think it's the best idea I've had in months.'

'Don't you think you ought to check with Sapirstein first?'

'Why? I'm just going to give a party; I'm not going to swim the English Channel or climb Annapurna.'

Guy went to the sink and turned on the water. He held a glass under it. 'I'll be in rehearsal then, you know,' he said. 'We start on the seventeenth.'

'You won't have to do a thing,' Rosemary said. 'Just come home and be charming.'

'And tend bar.' He turned off the water and raised his glass and drank.

'We'll *hire* a bartender,' Rosemary said. 'The one Joan and Dick used to have. And when you're ready to go to sleep I'll chase everyone out.'

Guy turned around and looked at her.

'I want to see them,' she said. 'Not Minnie and Roman. I'm tired of Minnie and Roman.'

He looked away from her, and then at the floor, and then at her eyes again. 'What about the pain?' he asked.

She smiled drily. 'Haven't you heard?' she said. 'It's going to be gone in a day or two. Dr Sapirstein told me so.'

Everyone could come except the Allerts, because of Hutch's condition, and the Chens, who were going to be in London taking pictures of Charlie Chaplin. The bartender wasn't available but knew another one who was. Rosemary took a loose brown velvet hostess gown to the cleaner, made an appointment to have her hair done, and ordered wine and liquor and ice cubes and the ingredients of a Chilean seafood casserole called *chupe*.

On the Thursday morning before the party, Minnie came with the drink while Rosemary was picking apart crabmeat and lobster tails. 'That looks interesting,' Minnie said, glancing into the kitchen. 'What is it?'

Rosemary told her, standing at the front door with the striped glass cold in her hand. 'I'm going to freeze it and then bake it Saturday evening,' she said. 'We're having some people over.'

'Oh, you feel up to entertaining?' Minnie asked.

'Yes, I do,' Rosemary said. 'These are old friends whom we haven't seen in a long time. They don't even know yet that I'm pregnant.'

'I'd be glad to give you a hand if you'd like,' Minnie said. 'I could help you dish things out.'

'Thank you, that's sweet of you,' Rosemary said, 'but I really can manage by myself. It's going to be buffet, and there'll be very little to do.'

'I could help you take the coats.'

'No, really, Minnie, you do enough for me as it is. Really.'

Minnie said, 'Well, let me know if you change your mind. Drink your drink now.'

Rosemary looked at the glass in her hand. 'I'd rather not,' she said, and looked up at Minnie. 'Not this minute. I'll drink it in a little while and bring the glass back to you.'

Minnie said, 'It doesn't do to let it stand.'

'I won't wait long,' Rosemary said. 'Go on. You go back and I'll bring the glass to you later on.'

'I'll wait and save you the walk.'

'You'll do no such thing,' Rosemary said. 'I get very nervous if anyone watches me while I'm cooking. I'm going out later so I'll be passing right by your door.'

'Going out?'

'Shopping. Scoot now, go on. You're too nice to me, really you are.'

Minnie backed away. 'Don't wait too long,' she said. 'It's going to lose its vitamins.'

Rosemary closed the door. She went into the kitchen and stood for a moment with the glass in her hand, and then went to the sink and tipped out the drink in a pale green spire drilling straight down into the drain.

She finished the *chupe*, humming and feeling pleased with herself. When it was covered and stowed away in the freezer compartment she made her own drink out of milk, cream, an egg, sugar, and sherry. Shaken in a covered jar, it poured out tawny and delicious-looking. 'Hang on, David-or-Amanda,' she said, and tasted it and found it great.

5

For a little while around half past nine it looked as if no one was going to come. Guy put another chunk of cannel coal on the fire, then racked the tongs and brushed his hands with his handkerchief; Rosemary came from the kitchen and stood motionless in her pain and her just-right hair and her brown velvet; and the bartender, by the bedroom door, found things to do with lemon peel and napkins and glasses and bottles. He was a prosperous-looking Italian named Renato who gave the impression that he tended bar only as a pastime and would leave if he got more bored than he already was.

Then the Wendells came – Ted and Carole – and a minute later Elise Dunstan and her husband Hugh, who limped. And then Allan Stone, Guy's agent, with a beautiful Negro model named Rain Morgan, and Jimmy and Tiger, and Lou and Claudia Comfort and Claudia's brother Scott.

Guy put the coats on the bed; Renato mixed drinks quickly, looking less bored. Rosemary pointed and gave names: 'Jimmy, Tiger, Rain, Allan, Elise, Hugh, Carole, Ted – Claudia and Lou and Scott.'

Bob and Thea Goodman brought another couple, Peggy and Stan Keeler. 'Of *course* it's all right,' Rosemary said; 'don't be silly, the more the merrier!' The Kapps came without coats. 'What a trip!' Mr Kapp ('It's Bernard') said. 'A bus, three trains, and a ferry! We left five hours ago!'

'Can I look around?' Claudia asked. 'If the rest of it's as nice as this I'm going to cut my throat.'

Mike and Pedro brought bouquets of bright red roses. Pedro, with his cheek against Rosemary's, murmured, 'Make him feed you baby; you look like a bottle of iodine.'

Rosemary said, 'Phyllis, Bernard, Peggy, Stan, Thea, Bob, Lou, Scott, Carole . . .'

She took the roses into the kitchen. Elise came in with a drink and a fake cigarette for breaking the habit. 'You're so lucky,' she said; 'it's the greatest apartment I've ever seen. Will you look at this kitchen? Are you all right, Rosie? You look a little tired.'

'Thanks for the understatement,' Rosemary said. 'I'm not all right but I will be. I'm pregnant.'

'You aren't! How *great*! When?'

'June twenty-eighth. I go into my fifth month on Friday.'

'That's *great*!' Elise said. 'How do you like C. C. Hill? Isn't he the dreamboy of the western world?'

'Yes, but I'm not using him,' Rosemary said.

'No!'

'I've got a doctor named Sapirstein, an older man.'

'What *for*? He can't be better than Hill!'

'He's fairly well known and he's a friend of some friends of ours,' Rosemary said.

Guy looked in.

Elise said, 'Well congratulations, Dad.'

'Thanks,' Guy said. 'Weren't nothin' to it. Do you want me to bring in the dip, Ro?'

'Oh, yes, would you? Look at these roses! Mike and Pedro brought them.'

Guy took a tray of crackers and a bowl of pale pink dip from the table. 'Would you get the other one?' he asked Elise.

'Sure,' she said, and took a second bowl and followed after him.

'I'll be out in a minute,' Rosemary called.

Dee Bertillon brought Portia Haynes, an actress, and Joan called to say that she and her date had got stuck at another party and would be there in half an hour.

Tiger said, 'You dirty stinking secret-keeper!' She grabbed Rosemary and kissed her.

'Who's pregnant?' someone asked, and someone else said, 'Rosemary is.'

She put one vase of roses on the mantel – 'Congratulations,' Rain

Morgan said, 'I understand you're pregnant' – and the other in the bedroom on the dressing table. When she came out Renato made a Scotch and water for her. 'I make the first ones strong,' he said, 'to get them happy. Then I go light and conserve.'

Mike wig-wagged over heads and mouthed *Congratulations*. She smiled and mouthed *Thanks*.

'The Trench sisters lived here,' someone said; and Bernard Kapp said, 'Adrian Marcato too, and Keith Kennedy.'

'And Pearl Ames,' Phyllis Kapp said.

'The Trent sisters?' Jimmy asked.

'Trench,' Phyllis said. 'They ate little children.'

'And she doesn't mean just ate them,' Pedro said; 'she means *ate them*!'

Rosemary shut her eyes and held her breath as the pain wound tighter. Maybe because of the drink; she put it aside.

'Are you all right?' Claudia asked her.

'Yes, fine,' she said, and smiled. 'I had a cramp for a moment.'

Guy was talking with Tiger and Portia Haynes and Dee. 'It's too soon to say,' he said; 'we've only been in rehearsal six days. It plays much better than it reads, though.'

'It couldn't play much worse,' Tiger said. 'Hey, what ever happened to the other guy? Is he still blind?'

'I don't know,' Guy said.

Portia said, 'Donald Baumgart? You know who *he* is, Tiger; he's the boy Zöe Piper lives with.'

'Oh, is *he* the one?' Tiger said. 'Gee, I didn't know he was someone I knew.'

'He's writing a great play,' Portia said. 'At least the first two scenes are great. Really burning anger, like Osborne before he made it.'

Rosemary said, 'Is he still blind?'

'Oh, yes,' Portia said. 'They've pretty much given up hope. He's going through hell trying to make the adjustment. But this great play is coming out of it. He dictates and Zöe writes.'

Joan came. Her date was over fifty. She took Rosemary's arm and pulled her aside, looking frightened. 'What's the *matter* with you?' she asked. 'What's *wrong*?'

'Nothing's wrong,' Rosemary said. 'I'm pregnant, that's all.'

She was in the kitchen with Tiger, tossing the salad, when Joan and Elise came in and closed the door behind them.

Elise said, 'What did you say your doctor's name was?'

'Sapirstein,' Rosemary said.

Joan said, 'And he's satisfied with your condition?'

Rosemary nodded.

'Claudia said you had a cramp a while ago.'

'I have a pain,' she said. 'But it's going to stop soon; it's not abnormal.'

Tiger said, 'What kind of a pain?'

'A – a *pain*. A sharp pain, that's all. It's because my pelvis is expanding and my joints are a little stiff.'

Elise said, 'Rosie, I've had that – two times – and all it ever meant was a few days of like a Charley horse, an ache through the whole area.'

'Well, everyone is different,' Rosemary said, lifting salad between two wooden spoons and letting it drop back into the bowl again. 'Every pregnancy is different.'

'Not *that* different,' Joan said. 'You look like Miss Concentration Camp of 1966. Are you sure this doctor knows what he's doing?'

Rosemary began to sob, quietly and defeatedly, holding the spoons in the salad. Tears ran from her cheeks.

'Oh, God,' Joan said, and looked for help to Tiger, who touched Rosemary's shoulder and said, 'Shh, ah, shh, don't cry, Rosemary. Shh.'

'It's good,' Elise said. 'It's the best thing. Let her. She's been wound up all night like – like I-don't-*know*-what.'

Rosemary wept, black streaks smearing down her cheeks. Elise put her into a chair; Tiger took the spoons from her hands and moved the salad bowls to the far side of the table.

The door started to open and Joan ran to it and stopped and blocked it. It was Guy. 'Hey, let me in,' he said.

'Sorry,' Joan said. 'Girls only.'

'Let me speak to Rosemary.'

'Can't; she's busy.'

'Look,' he said, 'I've got to wash glasses.'

'Use the bathroom.' She shouldered the door click-closed and leaned against it.

'Damn it, open the door,' he said outside.

Rosemary went on crying, her head bowed, her shoulders heaving, her hands limp in her lap. Elise, crouching, wiped at her cheeks every few moments with the end of a towel; Tiger smoothed her hair and tried to still her shoulders.

The tears slowed.

'It hurts so much,' she said. She raised her face to them. 'And I'm so afraid the baby is going to die.'

'Is he doing anything for you?' Elise asked. 'Giving you any medicine, any treatment?'

'Nothing, nothing.'

Tiger said, 'When did it start?'

She sobbed.

Elise asked, 'When did the pain start, Rosie?'

'Before Thanksgiving,' she said. 'November.'

Elise said, '*In November?*' and Joan at the door said, '*What?*' Tiger said, '*You've been in pain since November and he isn't doing anything for you?*'

'He says it'll stop.'

Joan said, 'Has he brought in another doctor to look at you?'

Rosemary shook her head. 'He's a very good doctor,' she said with Elise wiping at her cheeks. 'He's well known. He was on *Open End*.'

Tiger said, 'He sounds like a sadistic *nut*, Rosemary.'

Elise said, 'Pain like that is a warning that something's not right. I'm sorry to scare you, Rosie, but you go see Dr Hill. See *somebody* besides that—'

'That nut,' Tiger said.

Elise said, 'He *can't* be right, letting you just go on suffering.'

'I won't have an abortion,' Rosemary said.

Joan leaned forward from the door and whispered, 'Nobody's *telling* you to have an abortion! Just go see another doctor, that's all.'

Rosemary took the towel from Elise and pressed it to each eye in turn. 'He said this would happen,' she said, looking at mascara on the towel. 'That my friends would think their pregnancies were normal and mine wasn't.'

'What do you mean?' Tiger asked.

Rosemary looked at her. 'He told me not to listen to what my friends might say,' she said.

Tiger said, 'Well you *do* listen! What kind of sneaky advice is *that* for a doctor to give?'

Elise said, 'All we're telling you to do is check with another doctor. I don't think any reputable doctor would object to that, if it would help his patient's peace of mind.'

'You do it,' Joan said. 'First thing Monday morning.'

'I will,' Rosemary said.

'You promise?' Elise asked.

Rosemary nodded. 'I promise.' She smiled at Elise, and at Tiger and Joan. 'I feel a lot better,' she said. 'Thank you.'

'Well you look a lot worse,' Tiger said, opening her purse. 'Fix your eyes. Fix everything.' She put large and small compacts on the table before Rosemary, and two long tubes and a short one.

'Look at my dress,' Rosemary said.

'A damp cloth,' Elise said, taking the towel and going to the sink with it.

'The garlic bread!' Rosemary cried.

'In or out?' Joan asked.

'In.' Rosemary pointed with a mascara brush at two foil-wrapped loaves on top of the refrigerator.

Tiger began tossing the salad and Elise wiped at the lap of Rosemary's gown. 'Next time you're planning to cry,' she said, 'don't wear velvet.'

Guy came in and looked at them.

Tiger said, 'We're trading beauty secrets. You want some?'

'Are you all right?' he asked Rosemary.

'Yes, fine,' she said with a smile.

'A little spilled salad dressing,' Elise said.

Joan said, 'Could the kitchen staff get a round of drinks, do you think?'

The *chupe* was a success and so was the salad. (Tiger said under her breath to Rosemary, 'It's the tears that give it the extra zing.')

Renato approved of the wine, opened it with a flourish, and served it solemnly.

Claudia's brother Scott, in the den with a plate on his knee, said, 'His name is Altizer and he's down in – Atlanta, I think; and what he says is that the death of God is a specific historic event that happened right now, in our time. That God literally died.' The Kapps and Rain Morgan and Bob Goodman sat listening and eating.

Jimmy, at one of the living-room windows, said, 'Hey, it's beginning to snow!'

Stan Keeler told a string of wicked Polish-jokes and Rosemary laughed out loud at them. 'Careful of the booze,' Guy murmured at her shoulder. She turned and showed him her glass, and said, still laughing, 'It's only ginger ale!'

Joan's over-fifty date sat on the floor by her chair, talking up to her earnestly and fondling her feet and ankles. Elise talked to Pedro; he nodded, watching Mike and Allan across the room. Claudia began reading palms.

They were low on Scotch but everything else was holding up fine.

She served coffee, emptied ashtrays, and rinsed out glasses. Tiger and Carole Wendell helped her.

Later she sat in a bay with Hugh Dunstan, sipping coffee and watching fat wet snowflakes shear down, an endless army of them, with now and then an outrider striking one of the diamond panes and sliding and melting.

'Year after year I swear I'm going to leave the city,' Hugh Dunstan said; 'get away from the crime and the noise and all the rest of it. And every year it snows or the New Yorker has a Bogart Festival and I'm still here.'

Rosemary smiled and watched the snow. 'This is why I wanted this apartment,' she said; 'to sit here and watch the snow, with the fire going.'

Hugh looked at her and said, 'I'll bet you still read Dickens.'

'Of course I do,' she said. 'Nobody stops reading Dickens.'

Guy came looking for her. 'Bob and Thea are leaving,' he said.

By two o'clock everyone had gone and they were alone in the living-room, with dirty glasses and used napkins and spilling-over ashtrays all around. ('Don't forget,' Elise had whispered, leaving. Not very likely.)

'The thing to do now,' Guy said, 'is move.'

'Guy.'

'Yes?'

'I'm going to Dr Hill. Monday morning.'

He said nothing, looking at her.

'I want him to examine me,' she said. 'Dr Sapirstein is either lying or else he's – I don't know, out of his mind. Pain like this is a warning that something is wrong.'

'Rosemary,' Guy said.

'And I'm not drinking Minnie's drink any more,' she said. 'I want vitamins in pills, like everybody else. I haven't drunk it for three days now. I've made her leave it here and I've thrown it away.'

'You've—'

'I've made my own drink instead,' she said.

He drew together all his surprise and anger and, pointing back over his shoulder towards the kitchen, cried it at her. 'Is *that* what those bitches were giving you in there? Is *that* their hint for today? Change doctors?'

'They're my friends,' she said; 'don't call them bitches.'

'They're a bunch of not-very-bright *bitches* who ought to mind their own God-damned business.'

'All they said was get a second opinion.'

'You've got the best doctor in New York, Rosemary. Do you know what Dr Hill is? *Charley Nobody*, that's what he is.'

'I'm tired of hearing how great Dr Sapirstein is,' she said, starting to cry, 'when I've got this *pain* inside me since before Thanksgiving and all he does is tell me it's going to stop!'

'You're not changing doctors,' Guy said. 'We'll have to pay Sapirstein and pay Hill too. It's out of the question.'

'I'm not going to *change*,' Rosemary said; 'I'm just going to let Hill examine me and give his opinion.'

'I won't let you,' Guy said. 'It's – it's not fair to Sapirstein.'

'Not fair to—*What are you talking about*? What about what's fair to *me*?'

'You want another opinion? All right. *Tell* Sapirstein; let *him* be the one who decides who gives it. At least have *that* much courtesy to the top man in his field.'

'I want Dr *Hill*,' she said. 'If you won't pay I'll pay my—' She stopped short and stood motionless, paralysed, no part of her moving. A tear slid on a curved path towards the corner of her mouth.

'Ro?' Guy said.

The pain had stopped. It was gone. Like a stuck auto horn finally put right. Like anything that stops and is gone and is gone for good and won't ever be back again, thank merciful heaven. Gone and finished and oh, how good she might possibly feel as soon as she caught her breath!

'Ro?' Guy said, and took a step forward, worried.

'It stopped,' she said. 'The pain.'

'Stopped?' he said.

'Just now.' She managed to smile at him. 'It stopped. Just like that.' She closed her eyes and took a deep breath, and deeper still, deeper than she had been allowed to breathe for ages and ages. Since before Thanksgiving.

When she opened her eyes Guy was still looking at her, still looking worried.

'What was in the drink you made?' he asked.

Her heart dropped out of her. She had killed the baby. With the sherry. Or a bad egg. Or the combination. The baby had died, the pain had stopped. The pain was the baby and she had killed it with her arrogance.

'An egg,' she said. 'Milk. Cream. Sugar.' She blinked, wiped at her cheek, looked at him. 'Sherry,' she said, trying to make it sound non-toxic.

'How *much* sherry?' he asked.

Something moved in her.

'A lot?'

Again, where nothing had ever moved before. A rippling little pressure. She giggled.

'*Rosemary, for Christ's sake, how much?*'

'It's alive,' she said, and giggled again. 'It's moving. It's all right; it isn't dead. It's moving.' She looked down at her brown-velvet stomach and put her hands on it and pressed in lightly. Now two things were moving, two hands or feet; one here, one there.

She reached for Guy, not looking at him; snapped her fingers quickly for his hand. He came closer and gave it. She put it to the side of her stomach and held it there. Obligingly the movement came. 'You feel it?' she asked, looking at him. 'There, again; you feel it?'

He jerked his hand away, pale. 'Yes,' he said. 'Yes. I felt it.'

'It's nothing to be afraid of,' she said, laughing. 'It won't bite you.'

'It's wonderful,' he said.

'Isn't it?' She held her stomach again, looking down at it. 'It's alive. It's kicking. It's in there.'

'I'll clean up some of this mess,' Guy said, and picked up an ashtray and a glass and another glass.

'All right now, David-or-Amanda,' Rosemary said, 'you've made your presence known, so kindly settle down and let Mommy attend to the cleaning up.' She laughed. 'My God,' she said, 'it's so active! That means a boy, doesn't it?'

She said, 'All right, you, just take it easy. You've got five more months yet, so save your energy.'

And laughing, 'Talk to it, Guy; you're its father. Tell it not to be so impatient.'

And she laughed and laughed and was crying too, holding her stomach with both hands.

6

As bad as it had been before, that was how good it was now. With the stopping of the pain came sleep, great dreamless ten-hour spans of it; and with the sleep came hunger, for meat that was cooked, not raw, for eggs and vegetables and cheese and fruit and milk. Within days Rosemary's skull-face had lost its edges and sunk back behind filling-in flesh; within weeks she looked the way pregnant women are supposed to look: lustrous, healthy, proud, prettier than ever.

She drank Minnie's drink as soon as it was given to her, and drank it to the last chill drop, driving away as by a ritual the remembered guilt of *I-killed-the-baby*. With the drink now came a cake of white gritty sweet stuff like marzipan; this too she ate at once, as much from enjoyment of its candy-like taste as from a resolve to be the most conscientious expectant mother in all the world.

Dr Sapirstein might have been smug about the pain's stopping, but he wasn't, bless him. He simply said 'It's about time' and put his stethoscope to Rosemary's really-showing-now belly. Listening to the stirring baby, he betrayed an excitement that was unexpected in a man who had guided hundreds upon hundreds of pregnancies. It was this undimmed first-time excitement, Rosemary thought, that probably marked the difference between a great obstetrician and a merely good one.

She bought maternity clothes; a two-piece black dress, a beige suit, a red dress with white polka dots. Two weeks after their own party, she and Guy went to one given by Lou and Claudia Comfort. 'I can't get over the *change* in you!' Claudia said, holding on to both Rosemary's hands. 'You look a hundred per cent better, Rosemary! A *thousand* per cent!'

And Mrs Gould across the hall said, 'You know, we were quite concerned about you a few weeks ago; you looked so drawn and uncomfortable. But now you look like an entirely different person, really you do. Arthur remarked on the change just last evening.'

'I feel much better now,' Rosemary said. 'Some pregnancies start out bad and turn good, and some go the other way around. I'm glad I've had the bad first and have gotten it out of the way.'

She was aware now of minor pains that had been overshadowed by the major one – aches in her spinal muscles and her swollen breasts – but these discomforts had been mentioned as typical in the paperback book Dr Sapirstein had made her throw away; they *felt* typical too, and they increased rather than lessened her sense of well-being. Salt was still nauseating, but what, after all, was salt?

Guy's show, with its director changed twice and its title changed three times, opened in Philadelphia in mid-February. Dr Sapirstein didn't allow Rosemary to go along on the try-out tour, and so on the afternoon of the opening, she and Minnie and Roman drove to Philadelphia with Jimmy and Tiger, in Jimmy's antique Packard. The drive was a less than joyous one. Rosemary and Jimmy and Tiger had seen a bare-stage run-through of the play before the company left New York and they were doubtful of its chances. The best they hoped for was that Guy would be singled out for praise by one or more of the critics, a hope Roman encouraged by citing instances of great actors who had come to notice in plays of little or no distinction.

With sets and costumes and lighting the play was still tedious and verbose; the party afterwards was broken up into small separate enclaves of silent gloom. Guy's mother, having flown down from Montreal, insisted to their group that Guy was superb and the play was superb. Small, blonde, and vivacious, she chirped her confidence to Rosemary and Allan Stone and Jimmy and Tiger and Guy himself and Minnie and Roman. Minnie and Roman smiled serenely; the others sat and worried. Rosemary thought that Guy had been even better than superb, but she had thought so too on seeing him in *Luther* and *Nobody Loves An Albatross*, in neither of which he had attracted critical attention.

Two reviews came in after midnight; both panned the play and lavished Guy with enthusiastic praise, in one case two solid paragraphs of it. A third review, which appeared the next morning, was headed *Dazzling Performance Sparks New Comedy-Drama* and spoke of Guy as 'a virtually unknown young actor of slashing authority' who was 'sure to go on to bigger and better productions'.

The ride back to New York was far happier than the ride out.

Rosemary found much to keep her busy while Guy was away. There was the white-and-yellow nursery wallpaper finally to be ordered, and the crib and the bureau and the bathinette. There were long-postponed letters to be written, telling the family all the news; there were baby clothes and more maternity clothes to be shopped for; there were assorted decisions to be made, about birth announcements and breast-or-bottle and the name, the name, the name. Andrew or Douglas or David; Amanda or Jenny or Hope.

And there were exercises to be done, morning and evening, for she was having the baby by Natural Childbirth. She had strong feelings on the subject and Dr Sapirstein concurred with them whole-heartedly. He would give her an anaesthetic only if at the very last moment she asked for one. Lying on the floor, she raised her legs straight up in the air and held them there for a count of ten; she prac-tised shallow breathing and panting, imagining the sweaty trium-phant moment when she would see whatever-its-name-was coming inch by inch out of her effectively helping body.

She spent evenings at Minnie and Roman's, one at the Kapps', and another at Hugh and Elise Dunstan's. ('You don't have a nurse yet?' Elise asked. 'You should have arranged for one long ago; they'll all be booked by now.' But Dr Sapirstein, when she called him about it the next day, told her that he had lined up a fine nurse who would stay with her for as long as she wanted after the delivery. Hadn't he mentioned it before? Miss Fitzpatrick; one of the best.)

Guy called every second or third night after the show. He told Rosemary of the changes that were being made and of the rave he had got in *Variety*; she told him about Miss Fitzpatrick and the wall-paper and the shaped-all-wrong bootees that Laura-Louise was knitting.

The show folded after fifteen performances and Guy was home again, only to leave two days later for California and a Warner Brothers screen test. And then he was home for good, with two great next-season parts to choose from and thirteen half-hour *Greenwich Village*'s to do. Warner Brothers made an offer and Allan turned it down.

The baby kicked like a demon. Rosemary told it to stop or she would start kicking back.

Her sister Margaret's husband called to tell of the birth of an eight-pound boy, Kevin Michael, and later a too-cute announcement came – an impossibly rosy baby megaphoning his name, birth date, weight, and length. (Guy said, 'What, no blood type?') Rosemary decided on simple engraved announcements, with nothing but the baby's name, their name, and the date. And it would be Andrew John or Jennifer Susan. Definitely. Breast-fed, not bottle-fed.

They moved the television set into the living-room and gave the rest of the den furniture to friends who could use it. The wallpaper came, was perfect, and was hung; the crib and bureau and bathinette came and were placed first one way and then another. Into the bureau Rosemary put receiving blankets, waterproof pants, and shirts so tiny that, holding one up, she couldn't keep from laughing.

'Andrew John Woodhouse,' she said, '*stop* it! You've got two whole months yet!'

They celebrated their second anniversary and Guy's thirty-third birthday; they gave another party – a sit-down dinner for the Dunstans, the Chens, and Jimmy and Tiger; they saw *Morgan!* and a preview of *Mame*.

Bigger and bigger Rosemary grew, her breasts lifting higher atop her ballooning belly that was drum-solid with its navel flattened away, that rippled and jutted with the movements of the baby inside it. She did her exercises morning and evening, lifting her legs, sitting on her heels, shallow-breathing, panting.

At the end of May, when she went into her ninth month, she packed a small suitcase with the things she would need at the hospital – nightgowns, nursing brassieres, a new quilted housecoat and so on – and set it ready by the bedroom door.

On Friday, June 3rd, Hutch died in his bed at St Vincent's Hospital. Axel Allert, his son-in-law, called Rosemary on Saturday morning and told her the news. There would be a memorial service on Tuesday morning at eleven, he said, at the Ethical Culture Centre on West Sixty-fourth Street.

Rosemary wept, partly because Hutch was dead and partly because she had all but forgotten him in the past few months and felt now as if she had hastened his dying. Once or twice Grace Cardiff had called and once Rosemary had called Doris Allert; but she hadn't gone to see Hutch; there had seemed no point in it when he was still frozen in coma, and having been restored to health herself, she had been averse to being near someone sick, as if she and the baby might somehow have been endangered by the nearness.

Guy, when he heard the news, turned bloodless grey and was silent and self-enclosed for several hours. Rosemary was surprised by the depth of his reaction.

She went alone to the memorial service; Guy was filming and couldn't get free and Joan begged off with a virus. Some fifty people were there, in a handsome panelled auditorium. The service began soon after eleven and was quite short. Axel Allert spoke, and then another man who apparently had known Hutch for many years. Afterwards Rosemary followed the general movement towards the front of the auditorium and said a word of sympathy to the Allerts and to Hutch's other daughter, Edna, and her husband. A woman touched her arm and said, 'Excuse me, you're Rosemary, aren't you?' – a stylishly dressed woman in her early fifties, with grey hair and an exceptionally fine complexion. 'I'm Grace Cardiff.'

Rosemary took her hand and greeted her and thanked her for the phone calls she had made.

'I was going to mail this last evening,' Grace Cardiff said, holding a book-size brown-paper package, 'and then I realized that I'd probably be seeing you this morning.' She gave Rosemary the package; Rosemary saw her own name and address printed on it, and Grace Cardiff's return address.

'What is it?' she asked.

'It's a book Hutch wanted you to have; he was very emphatic about it.'

Rosemary didn't understand.

'He was conscious at the end for a few minutes,' Grace Cardiff said. 'I wasn't there, but he told a nurse to tell me to give you the book on his desk. Apparently he was reading it the night he was stricken. He was very insistent, told the nurse two or three times and made her promise not to forget. And I'm to tell you that "the name is an anagram". '

'The name of the book?'

'Apparently. He was delirious, so it's hard to be sure. He seemed to fight his way out of the coma and then die of the effort. First he thought it was the next morning, the morning after the coma began, and he spoke about having to meet you at eleven o'clock—'

'Yes, we had an appointment,' Rosemary said.

'And then he seemed to realize what had happened and he began telling the nurse that I was to give you the book. He repeated himself a few times and that was the end.' Grace Cardiff smiled as if she were making pleasant conversation. 'It's an English book about witchcraft,' she said.

Rosemary, looking doubtfully at the package, said, 'I can't imagine why he wanted me to have it.'

'He did though, so there you are. And the name is an anagram. Sweet Hutch. He made everything sound like a boy's adventure, didn't he?'

They walked together out of the auditorium and out of the building on to the sidewalk.

'I'm going uptown; can I drop you anywhere?' Grace Cardiff asked.

'No, thank you,' Rosemary said. 'I'm going down and across.'

They went to the corner. Other people who had been at the service

117

were hailing taxis; one pulled up, and the two men who had got it offered it to Rosemary. She tried to decline and, when the men insisted, offered it to Grace Cardiff, who wouldn't have it either. 'Certainly not,' she said. 'Take full advantage of your lovely condition. When is the baby due?'

'June twenty-eighth,' Rosemary said. Thanking the men, she got into the cab. It was a small one and getting into it wasn't easy.

'Good luck,' Grace Cardiff said, closing the door.

'Thank you,' Rosemary said, 'and thank you for the book.' To the driver she said, 'The Bramford, please.' She smiled through the open window at Grace Cardiff as the cab pulled away.

7

She thought of unwrapping the book there in the cab, but it was a cab that had been fitted out by its driver with extra ashtrays and mirrors and hand-lettered pleas for cleanliness and consideration, and the string and the paper would have been too much of a nuisance. So she went home first and got out of her shoes, dress, and girdle, and into slippers and a new gigantic peppermint-striped smock.

The doorbell rang and she went to answer it holding the still-unopened package; it was Minnie with the drink and the little white cake. 'I heard you come in,' she said. 'It certainly wasn't very long.'

'It was nice,' Rosemary said, taking the glass. 'His son-in-law and another man talked a little about what he was like and why he'll be missed, and that was it.' She drank some of the thin pale-green.

'That sounds like a sensible way of doing it,' Minnie said. 'You got mail already?'

'No, someone gave it to me,' Rosemary said, and drank again, deciding not to go into *who* and *why* and the whole story of Hutch's return to consciousness.

'Here, I'll hold it,' Minnie said, and took the package – 'Oh, thanks,' Rosemary said – so that Rosemary could take the white cake.

Rosemary ate and drank.

'A book?' Minnie asked, weighing the package.

'Mm-hmm. She was going to mail it and then she realized she'd be seeing me.'

Minnie read the return address. 'Oh, I know that house,' she said. 'The Gilmores used to live there before they moved over to where they are now.'

'Oh?'

'I've been there lots of times. "Grace." That's one of my favourite names. One of your girl friends?'

'Yes,' Rosemary said; it was easier than explaining and it made no difference really.

She finished the cake and the drink, and took the package from Minnie and gave her the glass. 'Thanks,' she said, smiling.

'Say listen,' Minnie said, 'Roman's going down to the cleaner in a while; do you have anything to go or pick up?'

'No, nothing, thanks. Will we see you later?'

'Sure. Take a nap, why don't you?'

'I'm going to. 'Bye.'

She closed the door and went into the kitchen. With a paring knife she cut the string of the package and undid its brown paper. The book within was *All Of Them Witches* by J. R. Hanslet. It was a black book, not new, its gold lettering all but worn away. On the flyleaf was Hutch's signature, with the inscription *Torquay, 1934* beneath it. At the bottom of the inside cover was a small blue sticker imprinted *J. Waghorn & Son, Booksellers*.

Rosemary took the book into the living-room, riffling its pages as she went. There were occasional photographs of respectable-looking Victorians, and, in the text, several of Hutch's underlinings and marginal checkmarks that she recognized from books he had lent her in the Higgins-Eliza period of their friendship. One underlined phrase was 'the fungus they call "Devil's Pepper". '

She sat in one of the window bays and looked at the table of contents. The name Adrian Marcato jumped to her eye; it was the title of the fourth chapter. Other chapters dealt with other people – all of them, it was to be presumed from the book's title, witches: Gilles de Rais, Jane Wenham, Aleister Crowley, Thomas Weir. The final chapters were *Witch Practices* and *Witchcraft and Satanism*.

Turning to the fourth chapter, Rosemary glanced over its twenty-odd pages; Marcato was born in Glasgow in 1846, he was brought soon after to New York (underlined), and he died on the island of Corfu in 1922. There were accounts of the 1896 tumult when he claimed to have called forth Satan and was attacked by a mob outside the Bramford (not in the lobby as Hutch had said), and of similar happenings in Stockholm in 1898 and Paris in 1899. He was a hypnotic-eyed black-bearded man who, in a standing portrait, looked fleetingly familiar to Rosemary. Overleaf there was a less formal photograph of him sitting at a Paris café table with his wife Hessia and his son Steven (underlined).

Was this why Hutch had wanted her to have the book; so that she could read in detail about Adrian Marcato? But why? Hadn't he issued his warnings long ago, and acknowledged later on that they were unjustified? She flipped through the rest of the book, pausing near the end to read other underlinings. 'The stubborn fact remains,' one read, 'that whether or not *we* believe, *they* most assuredly do.' And a few pages later: 'the universally held belief in the power of fresh blood'. And 'surrounded by candles, which needless to say are also black.'

The black candles Minnie had brought over on the night of the power failure. Hutch had been struck by them and had begun asking questions about Minnie and Roman. Was this the book's meaning; that they were *witches*? Minnie with her herbs and tannis-charms, Roman with his piercing eyes? But there *were* no witches, were there? Not *really*.

She remembered then the other part of Hutch's message, that the name of the book was an anagram. *All Of Them Witches*. She tried to juggle the letters in her head, to transpose them into something meaningful, revealing. She couldn't; there were too many of them to keep track of. She needed a pencil and paper. Or better yet, the Scrabble set.

She got it from the bedroom and, sitting in the bay again, put the unopened board on her knees and picked out from the box beside her the letters to spell *All Of Them Witches*. The baby, which had been still all morning, began moving inside her. *You're going to be a born Scrabble-player*, she thought, smiling. It kicked. 'Hey, easy,' she said.

With *All Of Them Witches* laid out on the board, she jumped the letters and mixed them around, then looked to see what else could be made of them. She found *comes with the fall* and, after a few minutes of rearranging the flat wood tiles, *how is hell fact met*. Neither of which seemed to mean anything. Nor was there revelation in *who shall meet it, we that chose ill*, and *if she shall come*, all of which weren't real anagrams anyway, since they used less than the full complement of letters. It was foolishness. How could the title of a book have a hidden anagram message for her and her alone? Hutch had been delirious; hadn't Grace Cardiff said so? Time-wasting. *Elf shot lame witch. Tell me which fatso.*

But maybe it was the name of the author, not the book, that was the anagram. Maybe J. R. Hanslet was a pen name; it didn't sound like a real one, when you stopped to think about it.

She took new letters.

The baby kicked.

J. R. Hanslet was *Jan Shrelt*. Or *J. H. Snartle*.

Now that *really* made sense.

Poor Hutch.

She took up the board and tilted it, spilling the letters back into the box.

The book, which lay open on the window seat beyond the box, had turned its pages to the picture of Adrian Marcato and his wife and son. Perhaps Hutch had pressed hard there, holding it open while he underlined 'Steven'.

The baby lay quiet in her, not moving.

She put the board on her knees again and took from the box the letters of *Steven Marcato*. When the name lay spelled before her, she looked at it for a moment and then began transposing the letters. With no false moves and no wasted motion she made them into *Roman Castevet*.

And then again into *Steven Marcato*.

And then again into *Roman Castevet*.

The baby stirred ever so slightly.

She read the chapter on Adrian Marcato and the one called *Witch Practices*, and then she went into the kitchen and ate some tuna salad and lettuce and tomatoes, thinking about what she had read.

She was just beginning the chapter called *Witchcraft and Satanism* when the front door unlocked and was pushed against the chain. The doorbell rang as she went to see who it was. It was Guy.

'What's with the chain?' he asked when she had let him in.

She said nothing, closing the door and rechaining it.

'What's the matter?' He had a bunch of daisies and a box from Bronzini.

'I'll tell you inside,' she said as he gave her the daisies and a kiss.

'Are you all right?' he asked.

'Yes,' she said. She went into the kitchen.

'How was the memorial?'

'Very nice. Very short.'

'I got the shirt that was in *The New Yorker*,' he said, going to the bedroom. 'Hey,' he called, '*On A Clear Day* and *Skyscraper* are both closing.'

She put the daisies in a blue pitcher and brought them into the living-room. Guy came in and showed her the shirt. She admired it. Then she said, 'Do you know who Roman really is?'

Guy looked at her, blinked, and frowned. 'What do you mean, honey?' he said. 'He's Roman.'

'He's Adrian Marcato's son,' she said. 'The man who said he conjured up Satan and was attacked downstairs by a mob. Roman is his son Steven. "Roman Castevet" is "Steven Marcato" rearranged – an anagram.'

Guy said, 'Who told you?'

'Hutch,' Rosemary said. She told Guy about *All Of Them Witches* and Hutch's message. She showed him the book, and he put aside his shirt and took it and looked at it, looked at the title page and the table of contents and then sprung the pages out slowly from under his thumb, looking at all of them.

'There he is when he was thirteen,' Rosemary said. 'See the eyes?'

'It might just *possibly* be a coincidence,' Guy said.

'And another coincidence that he's living here? In the same house Steven Marcato was brought up in?' Rosemary shook her head. 'The ages match too,' she said. 'Steven Marcato was born in August, 1886, which would make him seventy-nine now. Which is what Roman is. It's no coincidence.'

'No, I guess it's not,' Guy said, springing out more pages. 'I guess he's Steven Marcato, all right. The poor old geezer. No wonder he switched his name around, with a crazy father like that.'

Rosemary looked at Guy uncertainly and said, 'You don't think he's – the same as his father?'

'What do you mean?' Guy said, and smiled at her. 'A witch? A devil worshipper?'

She nodded.

'*Ro*,' he said. 'Are you *kidding*? Do you *really*—' He laughed and gave the book back to her. 'Ah, Ro, *honey*,' he said.

'It's a religion,' she said. 'It's an early religion that got – pushed into the corner.'

'All right,' he said, 'but *today*?'

'His father was a *martyr* to it,' she said. 'That's how it must look to him. Do you know where Adrian Marcato died? In a stable. On

Corfu. Wherever *that* is. Because they wouldn't let him into the hotel. Really. "No room at the inn." So he died in the stable. And *he* was with him. Roman. Do you think he's given it up after *that*?'

'Honey, it's 1966,' Guy said.

'This book was published in 1933,' Rosemary said; 'there were covens in Europe – that's what they're called, the groups, the congregations; covens – in Europe, in North and South America, in Australia; do you think they've all died out in just thirty-three years? They've got a coven *here*, Minnie and Roman, with Laura-Louise and the Fountains and the Gilmores and the Weeses; those parties with the flute and the chanting, those are *sabbaths* or *esbats* or whatever-they-are!'

'Honey,' Guy said, 'don't get excited. Let's—'

'Read what they do, Guy,' she said, holding the book open at him and jabbing a page with her forefinger. 'They use *blood* in their rituals, because blood has *power*, and the blood that has the *most* power is a *baby's* blood, a baby that hasn't been baptized; and they use *more* than the blood, they use the *flesh* too!'

'For God's sake, Rosemary!'

'Why have they been so friendly to us?' she demanded.

'Because they're friendly people! What do you think they are, maniacs?'

'Yes! Yes. Maniacs who think they have magic power, who think they're real storybook witches, *who perform all sorts of crazy rituals and practices* because they're – sick and crazy maniacs!'

'Honey—'

'Those black candles Minnie brought us were from the black mass! That's how Hutch caught on. And their living-room is clear in the middle so that they have *room*.'

'Honey,' Guy said, 'they're old people and they have a bunch of old friends, and Dr Shand happens to play the recorder. You can get black candles right down in the hardware store, and red ones and green ones and blue ones. And their living-room is clear because Minnie is a lousy decorator. Roman's father was a nut, okay; but that's no reason to think that Roman is too.'

'They're not setting foot in this apartment ever again,' Rosemary said. 'Either one of them. Or Laura-Louise or any of the others. And they're not coming within fifty feet of the baby.'

'The fact that Roman changed his name *proves* that he's not like his father,' Guy said. 'If he were he'd be proud of the name and would have kept it.'

'He did keep it,' Rosemary said. 'He switched it around, but he didn't really change it for something else. And this way he can get into hotels.' She went away from Guy, to the window where the Scrabble set lay. 'I won't let them in again,' she said. 'And as soon as the baby is old enough I want to sublet and move. I don't want them near us. Hutch was right; we never should have moved in here.' She looked out the window, holding the book clamped in both hands, trembling.

Guy watched her for a moment. 'What about Dr Sapirstein?' he said. 'Is he in the coven too?'

She turned and looked at him.

'After all,' he said, 'there've been maniac doctors, haven't there? His big ambition is probably to make house calls on a broomstick.'

She turned to the window again, her face sober. 'No, I don't think he's one of them,' she said. 'He's – too intelligent.'

'And besides, he's Jewish,' Guy said and laughed. 'Well, I'm glad you've exempted *somebody* from your McCarthy-type smear campaign. Talk about witch-hunting, wow! And guilt by association.'

'I'm not saying they're really witches,' Rosemary said. 'I know they haven't got *real* power. But there are people who *do* believe, even if we don't; just the way my family believes that God hears their prayers and that the wafer is the actual body of Jesus. Minnie and Roman believe *their* religion, believe it and practise it, I know they do; and I'm not going to take any chances with the baby's safety.'

'We're not going to sub-let and move,' Guy said.

'Yes we are,' Rosemary said, turning to him.

He picked up his new shirt. 'We'll talk about it later,' he said.

'He lied to you,' she said. 'His father wasn't a producer. He didn't have anything to do with the theatre at all.'

'All right, so he's a bullthrower,' Guy said; 'who the hell isn't?' He went into the bedroom.

Rosemary sat down next to the Scrabble set. She closed it and, after a moment, opened the book and began again to read the final chapter, *Witchcraft and Satanism*.

Guy came back in without the shirt. 'I don't think you ought to read any more of that,' he said.

Rosemary said, 'I just want to read this last chapter.'

'Not today, honey,' Guy said, coming to her; 'you've got yourself worked up enough as it is. It's not good for you *or* the baby.' He put his hand out and waited for her to give him the book.

'I'm not worked up,' she said.

'You're shaking,' he said. 'You've *been* shaking for five minutes now. Come on, give it to me. You'll read it tomorrow.'

'Guy—'

'No,' he said. 'I mean it. Come on, give it to me.'

She said 'Ohh' and gave it to him. He went over to the book-shelves, stretched up, and put it as high as he could reach, across the tops of the two Kinsey Reports.

'You'll read it tomorrow,' he said. 'You've had too much stirring-up today already, with the memorial and all.'

8

Dr Sapirstein was amazed. 'Fantastic,' he said. 'Absolutely fantastic. What did you say the name was, "Machado"?'

'Marcato,' Rosemary said.

'Fantastic,' Dr Sapirstein said. 'I had no idea whatsoever. I think he told me once that his father was a coffee importer. Yes, I remember him going on about different grades and different ways of grinding the beans.'

'He told Guy that he was a producer.'

Dr Sapirstein shook his head. 'It's no wonder he's ashamed of the truth,' he said. 'And it's no wonder that *you*'re upset at having dis-covered it. I'm as sure as I am of anything on earth that Roman doesn't hold any of his father's weird beliefs, but I can understand completely how disturbed you must be to have him for a close neigh-bour.'

'I don't want anything more to do with him or Minnie,' Rosemary said. 'Maybe I'm being unfair, but I don't want to take even the slightest chance where the baby's safety is concerned.'

'Absolutely,' Dr Sapirstein said. 'Any mother would feel the same way.'

Rosemary leaned forward. 'Is there any chance at all,' she said, 'that Minnie put something harmful in the drink or in those little cakes?'

Dr Sapirstein laughed. 'I'm sorry, dear,' he said; 'I don't mean to laugh, but really, she's such a kind old woman and so concerned for the baby's well-being . . . No, there's no chance at all that she gave you anything harmful. I would have seen evidence of it long ago, in you or in the baby.'

'I called her on the house phone and told her I wasn't feeling well. I won't take anything else from her.'

'You won't have to,' Dr Sapirstein said. 'I can give you some pills that will be more than adequate in these last few weeks. In a way this may be the answer to Minnie and Roman's problem too.'

'What do you mean?' Rosemary said.

'They want to go away,' Dr Sapirstein said, 'and rather soon. Roman isn't well, you know. In fact, and in the strictest of confidence, he hasn't got more than a month or two left in him. He wants to pay a last visit to a few of his favourite cities and they were afraid you might take offence at their leaving on the eve of the baby's birth, so to speak. They broached the subject to me the night before last, wanted to know how I thought you would take it. They don't want to upset you by telling you the real reason for the trip.'

'I'm sorry to hear that Roman isn't well,' Rosemary said.

'But glad at the prospect of his leaving?' Dr Sapirstein smiled. 'A perfectly reasonable reaction,' he said, 'all things considered. Suppose we do this, Rosemary: I'll tell them that I've sounded you out and you aren't at all offended by the idea of their going; and until they do go – they mentioned Sunday as a possibility – you continue as before, not letting Roman know that you've learned his true identity. I'm sure he would be embarrassed and unhappy if he knew, and it seems a shame to upset him when it's only a matter of three or four more days.'

Rosemary was silent for a moment, and then she said, 'Are you sure they'll be leaving on Sunday?'

'I know they'd like to,' Dr Sapirstein said.

Rosemary considered. 'All right,' she said; 'I'll go on as before, but only until Sunday.'

'If you'd like,' Dr Sapirstein said, 'I can have those pills sent over to you tomorrow morning; you can get Minnie to leave the drink and the cake with you and throw them away and take a pill instead.'

'That would be wonderful,' Rosemary said. 'I'd be much happier that way.'

'That's the main thing at this stage,' Dr Sapirstein said, 'keeping you happy.'

Rosemary smiled. 'If it's a boy,' she said, 'I may just name him Abraham Sapirstein Woodhouse.'

'God forbid,' Dr Sapirstein said.

Guy, when he heard the news, was as pleased as Rosemary. 'I'm sorry Roman is on his last lap,' he said, 'but I'm glad for your sake that they're going away. I'm sure you'll feel more relaxed now.'

'Oh, I will,' Rosemary said. 'I feel better already, just knowing about it.'

Apparently Dr Sapirstein didn't waste any time in telling Roman about Rosemary's supposed feelings, for that same evening Minnie and Roman stopped by and broke the news that they were going to Europe. 'Sunday morning at ten,' Roman said. 'We fly directly to Paris, where we'll stay for a week or so, and then we'll go on to Zürich, Venice, and the loveliest city in all the world, Dubrovnik, in Yugoslavia.'

'I'm green with envy,' Guy said.

Roman said to Rosemary, 'I gather this doesn't come as a complete bolt from the blue, does it, my dear?' A conspirator's gleam winked from his deep-socketed eyes.

'Dr Sapirstein mentioned you were thinking of going,' Rosemary said.

Minnie said, 'We'd have loved to stay till the baby came—'

'You'd be foolish to,' Rosemary said, 'now that the hot weather is here.'

'We'll send you all kinds of pictures,' Guy said.

'But when Roman gets the wanderlust,' Minnie said, 'there's just no holding him.'

'It's true, it's true,' Roman said. 'After a lifetime of travelling I find it all but impossible to stay in one city for more than a year; and it's been fourteen months now since we came back from Japan and the Philippines.'

He told them about Dubrovnik's special charms, and Madrid's, and the Isle of Skye's. Rosemary watched him, wondering which he really was, an amiable old talker or the mad son of a mad father.

The next day Minnie made no fuss at all about leaving the drink and the cake; she was on her way out with a long list of going-away jobs to do. Rosemary offered to pick up a dress at the cleaner's for her and buy toothpaste and dramamine. When she threw away the drink and the cake and took one of the large white capsules Dr Sapirstein had sent, she felt just the slightest bit ridiculous.

On Saturday morning Minnie said, 'You know, don't you, about who Roman's father was.'

Rosemary nodded, surprised.

'I could tell by the way you turned sort of cool to us,' Minnie said.

'Oh, don't apologize, dear; you're not the first and you won't be the last. I can't say that I really blame you. Oh, I could *kill* that crazy old man if he wasn't dead already! He's been the bane in poor Roman's existence! That's why he likes to travel so much; he always wants to leave a place before people can find out who he is. Don't let on to him that you know, will you? He's so fond of you and Guy, it would near about break his heart. I want him to have a real happy trip with no sorrows, because there aren't likely to be many more. Trips, I mean. Would you like the perishables in my icebox? Send Guy over later on and I'll load him up.'

Laura-Louise gave a bon voyage party Saturday night in her small dark tannis-smelling apartment on the twelfth floor. The Weeses and the Gilmores came, and Mrs Sabatini with her cat Flash, and Dr Shand. (How had Guy known that it was Dr Shand who played the recorder? Rosemary wondered. And that it was a recorder, not a flute or a clarinet? She would have to ask him.) Roman told of his and Minnie's planned itinerary, surprising Mrs Sabatini who couldn't believe they were bypassing Rome and Florence. Laura-Louise served home-made cookies and a mildly alcoholic fruit punch. Conversation turned to tornadoes and civil rights. Rosemary, watching and listening to these people who were much like her aunts and uncles in Omaha, found it hard to maintain her belief that they were in fact a coven of witches. Little Mr Wees, listening to Guy talking about Martin Luther King; could such a feeble old man, even in his dreams, imagine himself a caster of spells, a maker of charms? And dowdy old women like Laura-Louise and Minnie and Helen Wees; could they really bring themselves to cavort naked in mock-religious orgies? (Yet hadn't she seen them that way, seen all of them naked? No, no, that was a dream, a wild dream that she'd had a long, long time ago.)

The Fountains phoned a goodbye to Minnie and Roman, and so did Dr Sapirstein and two or three other people whose names Rosemary didn't know. Laura-Louise brought out a gift that everyone had chipped in for, a transistor radio in a pigskin carrying case, and Roman accepted it with an eloquent thank-you speech, his voice breaking. *He knows he's going to die*, Rosemary thought, and was genuinely sorry for him.

Guy insisted on lending a hand the next morning despite Roman's protests; he set the alarm clock for eight-thirty and, when it went off, hopped into chinos and a T shirt and went around to Minnie and Roman's door. Rosemary went with him in her peppermint-striped smock. There was little to carry; two suitcases and a hatbox. Minnie wore a camera and Roman his new radio. 'Anyone who needs more than one suitcase,' he said as he double-locked their door, 'is a tourist, not a traveller.'

On the sidewalk, while the doorman blew his whistle at oncoming cars, Roman checked through tickets, passport, traveller's cheques and French currency. Minnie took Rosemary by the shoulders. 'No matter where we are,' she said, 'our thoughts are going to be with you every minute, darling, till you're all happy and thin again with your sweet little boy or girl lying safe in your arms.'

'Thank you,' Rosemary said, and kissed Minnie's cheek. 'Thank you for everything.'

'You make Guy send us lots of pictures, you hear?' Minnie said, kissing Rosemary back.

'I will. I will,' Rosemary said.

Minnie turned to Guy. Roman took Rosemary's hand. 'I won't wish you luck,' he said, 'because you won't need it. You're going to have a happy, happy life.'

She kissed him. 'Have a wonderful trip,' she said, 'and come back safely.'

'Perhaps,' he said, smiling. 'But I may stay on in Dubrovnik, or Pescara or maybe Mallorca. We shall see, we shall see . . .'

'Come back,' Rosemary said, and found herself meaning it. She kissed him again.

A taxi came. Guy and the doorman stowed the suitcases beside the driver. Minnie shouldered and grunted her way in, sweating under the arms of her white dress. Roman folded himself in beside her. 'Kennedy Airport,' he said; 'the TWA Building.'

There were more goodbyes and kisses through open windows, and then Rosemary and Guy stood waving at the taxi that sped away with hands ungloved and white-gloved waving from either side of it.

Rosemary felt less happy than she had expected.

That afternoon she looked for *All of Them Witches*, to reread parts of it and perhaps find it foolish and laughable. The book was gone. It wasn't atop the Kinsey Reports or anywhere else that she could see. She asked Guy and he told her he had put it in the garbage Thursday morning.

'I'm sorry, honey,' he said, 'but I just didn't want you reading any more of that stuff and upsetting yourself.'

She was surprised and annoyed. 'Guy,' she said, 'Hutch *gave* me that book. He *left* it to me.'

'I didn't think about that part of it,' Guy said. 'I just didn't want you upsetting yourself. I'm sorry.'

'That's a *terrible* thing to do.'

'I'm sorry. I wasn't thinking about Hutch.'

'Even if he *hadn't* given it to me, you don't throw away another person's books. If I want to read something, I want to read it.'

'I'm sorry,' he said.

It bothered her all day long. And she had forgotten something that she meant to ask him; that bothered her too.

She remembered it in the evening, while they were walking back from La Scala, a restaurant not far from the house. 'How did you you know Dr Shand plays the recorder?' she said.

He didn't understand.

'The other day,' she said, 'when I read the book and we argued about it; you said that Dr Shand just happened to play the recorder. How did you know?'

'Oh,' Guy said. 'He told me. A long time ago. And I said we'd heard a flute or something through the wall once or twice, and he said that was him. How did you *think* I knew?'

'I didn't think,' Rosemary said. 'I just wondered, that's all.'

She couldn't sleep. She lay awake on her back and frowned at the ceiling. The baby inside her was sleeping fine, but she couldn't; she felt unsettled and worried, without knowing what she was worried about.

Well the *baby* of course, and whether everything would go the way it should. She had cheated on her exercises lately. No more of *that*; solemn promise.

It was really Monday already, the thirteenth. Fifteen more days. Two weeks. Probably all women felt edgy and unsettled two weeks before. And couldn't sleep from being sick and tired of sleeping on their backs! The first thing she was going to do after it was all over was sleep twenty-four solid hours on her stomach, hugging a pillow with her face snuggled deep down into it.

She heard a sound in Minnie and Roman's apartment, but it must have been from the floor above or the floor below. Sounds were masked and confused with the air conditioner going.

They were in Paris already. Lucky them. Some day she and Guy would go, with their three lovely children.

The baby woke up and began moving.

9

She bought cotton balls and cotton swabs and talcum powder and baby lotion; engaged a diaper service and rearranged the baby's clothing in the bureau drawers. She ordered the announcements – Guy would phone in the name and date later – and addressed and stamped a boxful of small ivory envelopes. She read a book called *Summerhill* that presented a seemingly irrefutable case for permissive child-rearing, and discussed it at Sardi's East with Elise and Joan, their treat.

She began to feel contractions; one one day, one the next, then none, then two.

A postcard came from Paris, with a picture of the Arc de Triomphe and a neatly written message: *Thinking of you both. Lovely weather, excellent food. The flight over was perfect. Love, Minnie.*

The baby dropped low inside her, ready to be born.

Early in the afternoon of Friday, June 24th, at the stationery counter at Tiffany's where she had gone for twenty-five more envelopes, Rosemary met Dominick Pozzo, who in the past had been Guy's vocal coach. A short, swarthy, hump-backed man with a voice that was rasping and unpleasant, he seized Rosemary's hand and congratulated her on her appearance and on Guy's recent good fortune, for which he disavowed all credit. Rosemary told him of the play Guy was signing for and of the latest offer Warner Brothers had made. Dominick was delighted; now, he said, was when Guy could truly benefit from intensive coaching. He explained why, made Rosemary promise to have Guy call him, and, with final good wishes, turned towards the elevators. Rosemary caught his arm. 'I never thanked you for the tickets to *The Fantasticks*,' she said. 'I just loved it. It's going to go on and on forever, like that Agatha Christie play in London.'

'*The Fantasticks*?' Dominick said.

'You gave Guy a pair of tickets. Oh, long ago. In the fall. I went with a friend. Guy had seen it already.'

'I never gave Guy tickets for *The Fantasticks*,' Dominick said.

'You did. Last fall.'

'No, my dear. I never gave *anybody* tickets to *The Fantasticks*; I never had any to give. You're mistaken.'

'I'm sure he said he got them from you,' Rosemary said.

'Then *he* was mistaken,' Dominick said. 'You'll tell him to call me, yes?'

'Yes. Yes, I will.'

It was strange, Rosemary thought when she was waiting to cross Fifth Avenue. Guy *had* said that Dominick had given him the tickets, she was certain of it. She remembered wondering whether or not to send Dominick a thank-you note and deciding finally that it wasn't necessary. She *couldn't* be mistaken.

Walk, the light said, and she crossed the avenue.

But *Guy* couldn't have been mistaken either. He didn't get free tickets every day of the week; he *must* have remembered who gave them to him. Had he deliberately lied to her? Perhaps he hadn't been given the tickets at all, but had found and kept them. No, there might have been a scene at the theatre; he wouldn't have exposed her to that.

She walked west on Fifty-seventh Street, walked very slowly with the bigness of the baby hanging before her and her back aching from withstanding its forward-pulling weight. The day was hot and humid; ninety-two already and still rising. She walked very slowly.

Had he wanted to get her out of the apartment that night for some reason? Had he gone down and bought the tickets himself? To be free to study the scene he was working on? But there wouldn't have been any need for trickery if that had been the case; more than once in the old one-room apartment he had asked her to go out for a couple of hours and she had gone gladly. Most of the time, though, he wanted her to stay, to be his line-feeder, his audience.

Was it a girl? One of his old flames for whom a couple of hours hadn't been enough, and whose perfume he had been washing off in the shower when she got home? No, it was tannis root not perfume that the apartment had smelled of that night; she had had to wrap the charm in foil because of it. And Guy had been far too energetic and amorous to have spent the earlier part of the night with someone else. He had made unusually violent love to her, she remembered; later, while he slept, she had heard the flute and the chanting at Minnie and Roman's.

No, not the flute. Dr Shand's recorder.

Was that how Guy knew about it? Had he been there that evening? At a sabbath . . .

She stopped and looked in Henri Bendel's windows, because she didn't want to think any more about witches and covens and baby's blood and Guy being over there. Why had she met that stupid Dominick? She should never have gone out today at all. It was too hot and sticky.

There was a great raspberry crepe dress that looked like a Rudi Gernreich. After Tuesday, after she was her own real shape again, maybe she would go in and price it. And a pair of lemon-yellow hip-huggers and a raspberry blouse . . .

Eventually, though, she had to go on. Go on walking, go on thinking, with the baby squirming inside her.

The book (*which Guy had thrown away*) had told of initiation ceremonies, of covens inducting novice members with vows and baptism, with anointing and the infliction of a 'witch mark'. Was it possible (the shower to wash away the smell of a tannis anointing) that Guy had joined the coven? That he (no, he couldn't be!) was one of them, with a secret mark of membership somewhere on his body?

There had been a flesh-coloured band-aid on his shoulder. It had been there in his dressing-room in Philadelphia ('That damn pimple,' he had said when she had asked him) and it had been there a few months before ('Not the same one!' she had said). Was it still there now?

She didn't know. He didn't sleep naked any more. He had in the past, especially in hot weather. But not any more, not for months and months. Now he wore pyjamas every night. When had she last seen him naked?

A car honked at her; she was crossing Sixth Avenue. 'For God's sake, lady,' a man behind her said.

But why, *why*? He was *Guy*, he wasn't a crazy old man with nothing better to do, with no other way to find purpose and self-esteem! He had a *career*, a busy, exciting, every-day-getting-better career! What did he need with wands and witch knives and censers and – and *junk*; with the Weeses and the Gilmores and Minnie and Roman? What could they give him that he couldn't get elsewhere?

She had known the answer before she asked herself the question. Formulating the question had been a way to put off facing the answer.

The blindness of Donald Baumgart.

If you believed.

But she didn't. She didn't.

Yet there Donald Baumgart was, blind, only a day or two after that Saturday. With Guy staying home to grab the phone every time it rang. Expecting the news.

The blindness of Donald Baumgart.

Out of which had come everything; the play, the reviews, the new play, the movie offer . . . Maybe Guy's part in *Greenwich Village*, too, would have been Donald Baumgart's if he hadn't gone inexplicably blind a day or two after Guy had joined (maybe) a coven (maybe) of witches (maybe).

There were spells to take an enemy's sight or hearing, the book had said. *All Of Them Witches*. (Not Guy!) The united mental force of the whole coven, a concentrated battery of malevolent wills, could blind, deafen, paralyse, and ultimately kill the chosen victim.

Paralyse and ultimately kill.

'Hutch?' she asked aloud, standing motionless in front of Carnegie Hall. A girl looked up at her, clinging to her mother's hand.

He had been reading the book that night and had asked her to meet him the next morning. To tell her that Roman was Steven Marcato. And Guy knew of the appointment, and knowing, went out for – what, ice cream? – and rang Minnie and Roman's bell. Was a hasty meeting called? The united mental force . . . But how had they known what Hutch would be telling her? She hadn't known herself; only he had known.

Suppose, though, that 'tannis root' wasn't 'tannis root' at all. Hutch hadn't heard of it, had he? Suppose it was – that other stuff he underlined in the book, Devil's Fungus or whatever it was. He had told Roman he was going to look into it; wouldn't that have been enough to make Roman wary of him? And right then and there Roman had taken one of Hutch's gloves, because the spells can't be cast without one of the victim's belongings! And then, when Guy told them about the appointment for the next morning, they took no chances and went to work.

But no, Roman couldn't have taken Hutch's glove; she had shown him in and shown him out, walking along with him both times.

Guy had taken the glove. He had rushed home with his make-up still on – which he *never* did – and had gone by himself to the closet. Roman must have called him, must have said, 'This man Hutch is getting suspicious about "tannis root"; go home and get one of his belongings, just in case!' And Guy had obeyed. To keep Donald Baumgart blind.

Waiting for the light at Fifty-fifth Street, she tucked her handbag and the envelopes under her arm, unhooked the chain at the back of her neck, drew the chain and the tannis-charm out of her dress and dropped them together down through the sewer grating.

So much for 'tannis root'. Devil's Fungus.

She was so frightened she wanted to cry.

Because she knew what Guy was giving them in exchange for his success.

The baby. To use in their rituals.

He had never *wanted* a baby until after Donald Baumgart was blind. He didn't like to feel it moving; he didn't like to talk about it; he kept himself as distant and busy as if it weren't his baby at all.

Because he knew what they were planning to do to it as soon as he gave it to them.

In the apartment, in the blessedly-cool shaded apartment, she tried to tell herself that she was mad. *You're going to have your baby in four days, Idiot Girl. Maybe even less. So you're all tense and nutty and you've built up a whole lunatic persecution thing out of a bunch of completely unrelated coincidences. There are no real witches. There are no real spells. Hutch died a natural death, even if the doctors* couldn't *give a name to it. Ditto for Donald Baumgart's blindness. And how, pray tell, did Guy get one of Donald Baumgart's belongings for the big spell-casting? See, Idiot Girl? It all falls apart when you pick at it.*

But why had he lied about the tickets?

She undressed and took a long cool shower, turned clumsily around and around and then pushed her face up into the spray, trying to think sensibly, rationally.

There *must* be another reason why he had lied. Maybe he'd spent the day hanging around Downey's, yes, and had gotten the tickets from one of the gang there; wouldn't he then have said Dominick had given them to him, so as not to let her know he'd been goofing off?

Of course he would have.

There, you see, Idiot Girl?

But why hadn't he shown himself naked in so many months and months?

She was glad, anyway, that she had thrown away that damned charm. She should have done it long ago. She never should have taken it from Minnie in the first place. What a pleasure it was to be rid of its revolting smell! She dried herself and splashed on cologne, lots and lots of it.

He hadn't shown himself naked because he had a little rash of some kind and was embarrassed about it. Actors are vain, aren't they? Elementary.

But why had he thrown out the book? And spent so much time at Minnie and Roman's? And waited for the news of Donald Baumgart's blindness? And rushed home wearing his make-up just before Hutch missed his glove?

She brushed her hair and tied it, and put on a brassiere and panties. She went into the kitchen and drank two glasses of cold milk.

She didn't know.

She went into the nursery, moved the bathinette away from the wall, and thumbtacked a sheet of plastic over the wallpaper to protect it when the baby splashed in its bath.

She didn't know.

She didn't know if she was going mad or going sane, if witches had only the longing for power or power that was real and strong, if Guy was her loving husband or the treacherous enemy of the baby and herself.

It was almost four. He would be home in an hour or so.

She called Actors Equity and got Donald Baumgart's telephone number.

The phone was answered on the first ring with a quick impatient 'Yeh?'

'Is this Donald Baumgart?'

'That's right.'

'This is Rosemary Woodhouse,' she said. 'Guy Woodhouse's wife.'

'Oh?'

'I wanted—'

'My God,' he said, 'you must be a happy little lady these days! I hear you're living in baronial splendour in the "Bram", sipping vintage wine from crystal goblets, with scores of uniformed lackeys in attendance.'

She said, 'I wanted to know how you are; if there's been any improvement.'

He laughed. 'Why bless your heart, Guy Woodhouse's wife,' he said, 'I'm fine! I'm splendid! There's been enormous improvement! I only broke six glasses today, only fell down three flights of stairs, and only went tap-a-tap-tapping in front of two speeding fire engines! Every day in every way I'm getting better and better and better and better.'

Rosemary said, 'Guy and I are both very unhappy that he got his break because of your misfortune.'

Donald Baumgart was silent for a moment, and then said, 'Oh, what the hell. That's the way it goes. Somebody's up, somebody's down. He would've made out all right anyway. To tell you the truth, after that second audition we did for *Two Hours of Solid Crap*, I was dead certain he was going to get the part. He was terrific.'

'He thought *you* were going to get it,' Rosemary said. 'And he was right.'

'Briefly.'

'I'm sorry I didn't come along that day he came to visit you,' Rosemary said. 'He asked me to, but I couldn't.'

'Visit me? You mean the day we met for drinks?'

'Yes,' she said. 'That's what I meant.'

'It's good you *didn't* come,' he said; 'they don't allow women, do they? No, after four they *do*, that's right; and it was after four. That was awfully good-natured of Guy. Most people wouldn't have had the – well, *class*, I guess. *I* wouldn't have had it, I can tell you that.'

'The loser buying the winner a drink,' Rosemary said.

'And little did we know that a week later – less than a week, in fact—'

'That's right,' Rosemary said. 'It was only a few days before you—'

'Went blind. Yes. It was a Wednesday or Thursday, because I'd been to a matinee – Wednesday, I think – and the following Sunday was when it happened. Hey,' – he laughed – 'Guy didn't put anything *in* that drink, did he?'

'No, he didn't,' Rosemary said. Her voice was shaking. 'By the way,' she said, 'he has something of yours, you know.'

'What do you mean?'

'Don't you know?'

'No,' he said.

'Didn't you miss anything that day?'

'No. Not that I remember.'

'You're sure?'

'You don't mean my tie, do you?'

'Yes,' she said.

'Well he's got mine and I've got his. Does he want his back? He can have it; it doesn't matter to *me* what tie I'm wearing, or if I'm wearing one at all.'

'No, he doesn't want it back,' Rosemary said. 'I didn't understand. I thought he had only borrowed it.'

'No, it was a trade. It sounded as if you thought he had *stolen* it.'

'I have to hang up now,' Rosemary said. 'I just wanted to know if there was any improvement.'

'No, there isn't. It was nice of you to call.'

She hung up.

It was nine minutes after four.

She put on her girdle and a dress and sandals. She took the emergency money Guy kept under his underwear – a not very thick fold of bills – and put it into her handbag, put in her address book too and the bottle of vitamin capsules. A contraction came and went, the second of the day. She took the suitcase that stood by the bedroom door and went down the hallway and out of the apartment.

Halfway to the elevator, she turned and doubled back.

She rode down in the service elevator with two delivery boys.

On Fifty-fifth Street she got a taxi.

Miss Lark, Dr Sapirstein's receptionist, glanced at the suitcase and said, smiling, 'You aren't in labour, are you?'

'No,' Rosemary said, 'but I have to see the doctor. It's very important.'

Miss Lark glanced at her watch. 'He has to leave at five,' she said, 'and there's Mrs Byron' – she looked over at a woman who sat reading and then smiled at Rosemary – 'but I'm sure he'll see you. Sit down. I'll let him know you're here as soon as he's free.'

'Thank you,' Rosemary said.

She put the suitcase by the nearest chair and sat down. The handbag's white patent was damp in her hands. She opened it, took out a tissue, and wiped her palms and then her upper lip and temples. Her heart was racing.

'How is it out there?' Miss Lark asked.

'Terrible,' Rosemary said. 'Ninety-four.'

Miss Lark made a pained sound.

A woman came out of Dr Sapirstein's office, a woman in her fifth or sixth month whom Rosemary had seen before. They nodded at each other. Miss Lark went in.

'You're due any day now, aren't you?' the woman said, waiting by the desk.

'Tuesday,' Rosemary said.

'Good luck,' the woman said. 'You're smart to get it over with before July and August.'

Miss Lark came out again. 'Mrs Byron,' she said, and to Rosemary, 'He'll see you right after.'

'Thank you,' Rosemary said.

Mrs Byron went into Dr Sapirstein's office and closed the door. The woman by the desk conferred with Miss Lark about another appointment and then went out, saying goodbye to Rosemary and wishing her luck again.

Miss Lark wrote. Rosemary took up a copy of *Time* that lay at her elbow. *Is God Dead?* it asked in red letters on a black background. She found the index and turned to Show Business. There was a piece on Barbra Streisand. She tried to read it.

'That smells nice,' Miss Lark said, sniffing in Rosemary's direction. 'What is it?'

'It's called "Detchema",' Rosemary said.

'It's a big improvement over your regular, if you don't mind my saying.'

'That wasn't a cologne,' Rosemary said. 'It was a good luck charm. I threw it away.'

'Good,' Miss Lark said. 'Maybe the doctor will follow your example.'

Rosemary, after a moment, said, 'Dr Sapirstein?'

Miss Lark said, 'Mm-hmm. He has the after-shave. But it isn't, is it? Then he has a good luck charm. Only he isn't superstitious. I don't *think* he is. *Anyway*, he has the same *smell* once in a while, *whatever* it is, and when he does, I can't come within five feet of him. Much stronger than yours was. Haven't you ever noticed?'

'No,' Rosemary said.

'I guess you haven't been here on the right days,' Miss Lark said. 'Or maybe you thought it was your own you were smelling. What is it, a chemical thing?'

Rosemary stood up and put down *Time* and picked up her suitcase. 'My husband is outside; I have to tell him something,' she said. 'I'll be back in a minute.'

'You can leave your suitcase,' Miss Lark said.

Rosemary took it with her though.

10

She walked up Park to Eighty-first Street, where she found a glass-walled phone booth. She called Dr Hill. It was very hot in the booth.

A service answered. Rosemary gave her name and the phone number. 'Please ask him to call me back right away,' she said. 'It's an emergency and I'm in a phone booth.'

'All right,' the woman said and clicked to silence.

Rosemary hung up and then lifted the receiver again, but kept a hidden finger on the hook. She held the receiver to her ear as if listening, so that no one should come along and ask her to give up the phone. The baby kicked and twisted in her. She was sweating. *Quickly, please, Dr Hill. Call me. Rescue me.*

All of them. All of them. They were all in it together. Guy, Dr Sapirstein, Minnie, and Roman. All of them witches. *All of Them Witches.* Using her to produce a baby for them, so that they could take it and – *Don't you worry, Andy-or-Jenny, I'll kill them before I let them touch you*!

The phone rang. She jumped her finger from the hook. 'Yes?'

'Is this Mrs Woodhouse?' It was the service again.

'Where's Dr *Hill*?' she said.

'Did I get the name right?' the woman asked. 'Is it "Rosemary Woodhouse"?'

'Yes!'

'And you're Dr Hill's patient?'

She explained about the one visit back in the fall. 'Please, please,' she said, 'he *has* to speak to me! It's important! It's – *please. Please tell him to call me.*'

'All right,' the woman said.

Holding the hook again, Rosemary wiped her forehead with the back of her hand. *Please, Dr Hill.* She cracked open the door for air and then pushed it closed again as a woman came near and waited. 'Oh, I didn't know that,' Rosemary said to the mouthpiece, her finger on the hook. 'Really? What else did he say?' Sweat trickled down her back and from under her arms. The baby turned and rolled.

It had been a mistake to use a phone so near Dr Sapirstein's office. She should have gone to Madison or Lexington. 'That's wonderful,' she said. 'Did he say anything else?' At this very moment he might be out of the door and looking for her, and wouldn't the nearest phone booth be the first place he'd look? She should have gotten right into a taxi, gotten far away. She put her back as much as she could in the direction he would come from if he came. The woman outside was walking away, thank God.

And now, too, Guy would be coming home. He would see the suitcase gone and call Dr Sapirstein, thinking she was in the hospital. Soon the two of them would be looking for her. And all the others too; the Weeses, the—

'Yes?' – stopping the ring in its middle.

'Mrs Woodhouse?'

It was Dr Hill, Dr Saviour-Rescuer-Kildare-Wonderful-Hill. 'Thank you,' she said. 'Thank you for calling me.'

'I thought you were in California,' he said.

'No,' she said. 'I went to another doctor, one some friends sent me to, and he isn't good, Dr Hill; he's been lying to me and giving me unusual kinds of – drinks and capsules. The baby is due on Tuesday – remember, you told me, June twenty-eighth? – and I want *you* to deliver it. I'll pay you whatever you want, the same as if I'd been coming to you all along.'

'Mrs Woodhouse—'

'Please, let me talk to you,' she said, hearing refusal. 'Let me come and explain what's been going on. I can't stay too long where I am right now. My husband and this doctor and the people who sent me to him, they've all been involved in – well, in a plot; I know that sounds crazy, Doctor, and you're probably thinking, "My God, this poor girl has completely flipped," but I *haven't* flipped, Doctor, I swear by all the saints I haven't. Now and then there *are* plots against people, aren't there?'

'Yes, I suppose there are,' he said.

'There's one against me and my baby,' she said, 'and if you'll let me come talk to you I'll tell you about it. And I'm not going to ask you to do anything unusual or wrong or anything; all I want you to do is get me into a hospital and deliver my baby for me.'

He said, 'Come to my office tomorrow after—'

'Now,' she said. 'Now. Right now. They're going to be looking for me.'

'Mrs Woodhouse,' he said, 'I'm not at my office now, I'm home. I've been up since yesterday morning and—'

'I beg you,' she said. 'I beg you.'

He was silent.

She said, 'I'll come there and explain to you. I can't stay here.'

'My office at eight o'clock,' he said. 'Will that be all right?'

'Yes,' she said. 'Yes. Thank you. Dr Hill?'

'Yes?'

'My husband may call you and ask if I called.'

'I'm not going to speak to *anyone*,' he said. 'I'm going to take a nap.'

'Would you tell your service? Not to say that I called? Doctor?'

'All right, I will,' he said.

'Thank you,' she said.

'Eight o'clock.'

'Yes. Thank you.'

A man with his back to the booth turned as she came out; he wasn't Dr Sapirstein though, he was somebody else.

She walked to Lexington Avenue and uptown to Eighty-sixth Street, where she went into the theatre there, used the ladies' room, and then sat numbly in the safe cool darkness facing a loud colour movie. After a while she got up and went with her suitcase to a phone booth, where she placed a person-to-person collect call to her brother Brian. There was no answer. She went back with her suitcase and sat in a different seat. The baby was quiet, sleeping. The movie changed to something with Keenan Wynn.

At twenty of eight she left the theatre and took a taxi to Dr Hill's office on West Seventy-second Street. It would be safe to go in, she thought; they would be watching Joan's place and Hugh and Elise's, but not Dr Hill's office at eight o'clock, not if his service had said she hadn't called. To be sure, though, she asked the driver to wait and watch until she was inside the door.

Nobody stopped her. Dr Hill opened the door himself, more pleasantly than she had expected after his reluctance on the telephone. He had grown a moustache, blond and hardly noticeable, but he still looked like Dr Kildare. He was wearing a blue-and-yellow plaid sport shirt.

They went into his consulting room, which was a quarter the size of Dr Sapirstein's, and there Rosemary told him her story. She sat with her hands on the chair arms and her ankles crossed and spoke quietly and calmly, knowing that any suggestion of hysteria would make him disbelieve her and think her mad. She told him about Adrian Marcato and Minnie and Roman; about the months of pain she had suffered and the herbal drinks and the little white cakes;

about Hutch and *All Of Them Witches* and the *Fantasticks* tickets and black candles and Donald Baumgart's necktie. She tried to keep everything coherent and in sequence but she couldn't. She got it all out without getting hysterical though; Dr Shand's recorder and Guy throwing away the book and Miss Lark's final unwitting revelation.

'Maybe the coma and the blindness were only coincidences,' she said, 'or maybe they *do* have some kind of ESP way of hurting people. But that's not important. The important thing is that they want the baby. I'm sure they do.'

'It certainly seems that way,' Dr Hill said, 'especially in light of the interest they've taken in it right from the beginning.'

Rosemary shut her eyes and could have cried. He believed her. He didn't think she was mad. She opened her eyes and looked at him, staying calm and composed. He was writing. Did all his patients love him? Her palms were wet; she slid them from the chair arms and pressed them against her dress.

'The doctor's name is Shand, you say,' Dr Hill said.

'No, Dr Shand is just one of the group,' Rosemary said. 'One of the coven. The doctor is Dr Sapirstein.'

'Abraham Sapirstein?'

'Yes,' Rosemary said uneasily. 'Do you know him?'

'I've met him once or twice,' Dr Hill said, writing more.

'Looking at him,' Rosemary said, 'or even talking to him, you would never think he—'

'Never in a million years,' Dr Hill said, putting down his pen, 'which is why we're told not to judge books by their covers. Would you like to go into Mount Sinai right now, this evening?'

Rosemary smiled. 'I would *love* to,' she said. 'Is it possible?'

'It'll take some wire-pulling and arguing,' Dr Hill said. He rose and went to the open door of his examining room. 'I want you to lie down and get some rest,' he said, reaching into the darkened room behind him. It blinked into ice-blue fluorescent light. 'I'll see what I can do and then I'll check you over.'

Rosemary hefted herself up and went with her handbag into the examining room. 'Anything they've got,' she said. 'Even a broom closet.'

'I'm sure we can do better than that,' Dr Hill said. He came in after her and turned on an air conditioner in the room's blue-curtained window. It was a noisy one.

'Shall I undress?' Rosemary asked.

'No, not yet,' Dr Hill said. 'This is going to take a good half-hour of high-powered telephoning. Just lie down and rest.' He went out and closed the door.

Rosemary went to the day bed at the far end of the room and sat down heavily on its blue-covered softness. She put her handbag on a chair.

God bless Dr Hill.

She would make a sampler to that effect some day.

She shook off her sandals and lay back gratefully. The air conditioner sent a small stream of coolness to her; the baby turned over slowly and lazily, as if feeling it.

Everything's okay now, Andy-or-Jenny. We're going to be in a nice clean bed at Mount Sinai Hospital, with no visitors and—

Money. She sat up, opened her handbag, and found Guy's money that she had taken. There was a hundred and eighty dollars. Plus sixteen-and-change of her own. It would be enough, certainly, for any advance payments that had to be made, and if more were needed Brian would wire it or Hugh and Elise would lend it to her. Or Joan. Or Grace Cardiff. She had plenty of people she could turn to.

She took the capsules out, put the money back in, and closed the handbag; and then she lay back again on the day bed, with the handbag and the bottle of capsules on the chair beside her. She would give the capsules to Dr Hill; he would analyse them and make sure there was nothing harmful in them. There *couldn't* be. They would want the baby to be healthy, wouldn't they, for their insane rituals?

She shivered.

The – monsters.

And Guy.

Unspeakable, unspeakable.

Her middle hardened in a straining contraction, the strongest one yet. She breathed shallowly until it ended.

Making three that day.

She would tell Dr Hill.

She was living with Brian and Dodie in a large contemporary house in Los Angeles, and Andy had just started talking (though only four months old) when Dr Hill looked in and she was in his examining room again, lying on the day bed in the coolness of the air conditioner. She shielded her eyes with her hand and smiled at him. 'I've been sleeping,' she said.

He pushed the door all the way open and withdrew. Dr Sapirstein and Guy came in.

Rosemary sat up, lowering her hand from her eyes.

They came and stood close to her. Guy's face was stony and blank. He looked at the walls, only at the walls, not at her. Dr Sapirstein said, 'Come with us quietly, Rosemary. Don't argue or make a scene, because if you say anything more about witches or witchcraft we're going to be forced to take you to a mental hospital. The facilities there for delivering the baby will be less than the best. You don't want that, do you? So put your shoes on.'

'We're just going to take you home,' Guy said, finally looking at her. 'No one's going to hurt you.'

'Or the baby,' Dr Sapirstein said. 'Put your shoes on.' He picked up the bottle of capsules, looked at it, and put it in his pocket.

She put her sandals on and he gave her her handbag.

They went out, Dr Sapirstein holding her arm, Guy touching her other elbow.

Dr Hill had her suitcase. He gave it to Guy.

'She's fine now,' Dr Sapirstein said. 'We're going to go home and rest.'

Dr Hill smiled at her. 'That's all it takes, nine times out of ten,' he said.

She looked at him and said nothing.

'Thank you for your trouble, Doctor,' Dr Sapirstein said, and Guy said, 'It's a shame you had to come in here and—'

'I'm glad I could be of help, sir,' Dr Hill said to Dr Sapirstein, opening the front door.

They had a car. Mr Gilmore was driving it. Rosemary sat between Guy and Dr Sapirstein in back.

Nobody spoke.

They drove to the Bramford.

The elevator man smiled at her as they crossed the lobby towards him. Diego. Smiled because he liked her, favoured her over some of the other tenants.

The smile, reminding her of her individuality, wakened something in her, revived something.

She snicked open her handbag at her side, worked a finger through her key ring, and, near the elevator door, turned the handbag all the way over, spilling out everything except the keys. Rolling lipstick, coins, Guy's tens and twenties fluttering, everything. She looked down stupidly.

They picked things up, Guy and Dr Sapirstein, while she stood mute, pregnant-helpless. Diego came out of the elevator, making tongue-teeth sounds of concern. He bent and helped. She backed in to get out of the way and, watching them, toed the big round floor button. The rolling door rolled. She pulled closed the inner gate.

Diego grabbed for the door but saved his fingers; smacked on the outside of it. 'Hey, Mrs Woodhouse!'

Sorry, Diego.

She pushed the handle and the car lurched upward.

She would call Brian. Or Joan or Elise or Grace Cardiff. Someone.

We're not through yet, Andy!

She stopped the car at nine, then at six, then halfway past seven, and then close enough to seven to open the gate and the door and step four inches down.

She walked through the turns of hallway as quickly as she could. A contraction came but she marched right through it, paying no heed.

The service elevator's indicator blinked from four to five and she knew it was Guy and Dr Sapirstein coming up to intercept her.

So of course the key wouldn't go into the lock.

But finally did, and she was inside, slamming the door as the elevator door opened, hooking in the chain as Guy's key went into the lock. She turned the bolt and the key turned it right back again. The door opened and pushed in against the chain.

'Open up, Ro,' Guy said.

'Go to hell,' she said.

'I'm not going to hurt you, honey.'

'You promised them the baby. Get away.'

'I didn't promise them anything,' he said. 'What are you talking about? Promised who?'

'Rosemary,' Dr Sapirstein said.

'You too. Get away.'

'You seem to have imagined some sort of conspiracy against you.'

'Get away,' she said, and pushed the door shut and bolted it.

It stayed bolted.

She backed away, watching it, and then went into the bedroom. It was nine-thirty.

She wasn't sure of Brian's number and her address book was in the

146

lobby or Guy's pocket, so the operator had to get Omaha Information. When the call was finally put through there was still no answer. 'Do you want me to try again in twenty minutes?' the operator asked.

'Yes, please,' Rosemary said; 'in *five* minutes.'

'I can't try again in five minutes,' the operator said, 'but I'll try in twenty minutes if you want me to.'

'Yes, please,' Rosemary said and hung up.

She called Joan, and Joan was out too.

Elise and Hugh's number was – she didn't know. Information took forever to answer but, having answered, supplied it quickly. She dialled it and got an answering service. They were away for the weekend. 'Are they anywhere where I can reach them? This is an emergency.'

'Is this Mr Dunstan's secretary?'

'No, I'm a close friend. It's very important that I speak to them.'

'They're on Fire Island,' the woman said. 'I can give you a number.'

'Please.'

She memorized it, hung up, and was about to dial it when she heard whispers outside the doorway and footsteps on the vinyl floor. She stood up.

Guy and Mr Fountain came into the room – 'Honey, we're *not* going to hurt you,' Guy said – and behind them Dr Sapirstein with a loaded hypodermic, the needle up and dripping, his thumb at the plunger. And Dr Shand and Mrs Fountain and Mrs Gilmore. 'We're your friends,' Mrs Gilmore said, and Mrs Fountain said, 'There's nothing to be afraid of, Rosemary; honest and truly there isn't.'

'This is nothing but a mild sedative,' Dr Sapirstein said. 'To calm you down so that you can get a good night's sleep.'

She was between the bed and the wall, and too gross to climb over the bed and evade them.

They came towards her – 'You know I wouldn't let anyone hurt you, Ro,' – and she picked up the phone and struck with the receiver at Guy's head. He caught her wrist and Mr Fountain caught her other arm and the phone fell as he pulled her around with startling strength. '*Help me, sombod*—' she screamed, and a handkerchief or something was jammed into her mouth and held there by a small strong hand.

They dragged her away from the bed so Dr Sapirstein could come in front of her with the hypodermic and a dab of cotton, and a contraction far more gruelling than any of the others clamped her middle and clenched shut her eyes. She held her breath, then sucked air in through her nostrils in quick little pulls. A hand felt her belly, deft all-over fingertipping, and Dr Sapirstein said, 'Wait a minute, wait a minute now; we happen to be in labour here.'

Silence; and someone outside the room whispered the news: 'She's in labour!'

She opened her eyes and stared at Dr Sapirstein, dragging air through her nostrils, her middle relaxing. He nodded to her, and suddenly took her arm that Mr Fountain was holding, touched it with cotton, and stabbed it with the needle.

She took the injection without trying to move, too afraid, too stunned.

He withdrew the needle and rubbed the spot with his thumb and then with the cotton.

The women, she saw, were turning down the bed.

Here?

Here?

It was supposed to be Doctors Hospital! Doctors Hospital with equipment and nurses and everything clean and sterile!

They held her while she struggled, Guy saying in her ear, 'You'll be all right, honey, I swear to God you will! I swear to God you're going to be perfectly all right! Don't go on fighting like this, Ro, please don't! I give you my absolute word of honour you're going to be perfectly all right!'

And then there was another contraction.

And then she was on the bed, with Dr Sapirstein giving her another injection.

And Mrs Gilmore wiped her forehead.

And the phone rang.

And Guy said, 'No, just cancel it, operator.'

And there was another contraction, faint and disconnected from her floating eggshell head.

All the exercises had been for nothing. All wasted energy. This wasn't Natural Childbirth at all; she wasn't helping, she wasn't seeing.

Oh, Andy, Andy-or-Jenny! I'm sorry, my little darling! Forgive me!

PART THREE
1

Light.

The ceiling.

And pain between her legs.

And Guy. Sitting beside the bed, watching her with an anxious, uncertain smile.

'Hi,' he said.

'Hi,' she said back.

The pain was terrible.

And then she remembered. It was over. It was over. The baby was born.

'Is it all right?' she asked.

'Yes, fine,' he said.

'What is it?'

'A boy.'

'Really? A boy?'

He nodded.

'And it's all right?'

'Yes.'

She let her eyes close, then managed to open them again.

'Did you call Tiffany's?' she asked.

'Yes,' he said.

She let her eyes close and slept.

Later she remembered more. Laura-Louise was sitting by the bed reading the *Reader's Digest* with a magnifying glass.

'Where is it?' she asked.

Laura-Louise jumped. 'My goodness, dear,' she said, the magnifying glass at her bosom showing red ropes interwoven, 'what a *start* you gave me, waking up so suddenly! My goodness!' She closed her eyes and breathed deeply.

'The baby; where is it?' she asked.

'You just wait here a minute,' Laura-Louise said, getting up with the *Digest* closed on a finger. 'I'll get Guy and Doctor Abe. They're right in the kitchen.'

'Where's the baby?' she asked, but Laura-Louise went out the door without answering.

She tried to get up but fell back, her arms boneless. And there was pain between her legs like a bundle of knife points. She lay and waited, remembering, remembering.

It was night. Five after nine, the clock said.

They came in, Guy and Dr Sapirstein, looking grave and resolute.

'Where's the baby?' she asked them.

Guy came around to the side of the bed and crouched down and took her hand. 'Honey,' he said.

'Where is it?'

'Honey . . .' He tried to say more and couldn't. He looked across the bed for help.

Dr Sapirstein stood looking down at her. A shred of coconut was caught in his moustache. 'There were complications, Rosemary,' he said, 'but nothing that will affect future births.'

'It's—'

She stared at him.

'Dead,' he said.

He nodded.

She turned to Guy.

He nodded too.

'It was in the wrong position,' Dr Sapirstein said. 'In the hospital I might have been able to do something, but there simply wasn't time to get you there. Trying anything here would have been – too dangerous for you.'

Guy said, 'We can have others, honey, and we will, just as soon as you're better. I promise you.'

Dr Sapirstein said, 'Absolutely. You can start on another in a very few months and the odds are thousands to one against anything similar happening. It was a tragic one-in-ten-thousand mishap; the baby itself was perfectly healthy and normal.'

Guy squeezed her hand and smiled encouragingly at her. 'As soon as you're better,' he said.

She looked at them, at Guy, at Dr Sapirstein with the shred of coconut in his moustache. 'You're lying,' she said. 'I don't believe you. You're both lying.'

'Honey,' Guy said.

'It didn't die,' she said. 'You took it. You're lying. You're witches. You're lying. You're lying! You're lying! *You're lying! You're lying! You're lying!*'

Guy held her shoulders to the bed and Dr Sapirstein gave her an injection.

She ate soup and triangles of buttered white bread. Guy sat on the side of the bed, nibbling at one of the triangles. 'You were crazy,' he said. 'You were really ka-pow out of your mind. It happens sometimes in the last couple of weeks. That's what Abe says. He has a name for it. Prepartum I-don't-know, some kind of hysteria. You had it, honey, and with a vengeance.'

She said nothing. She took a spoonful of soup.

'Listen,' he said, 'I know where you got the idea that Minnie and *Roman* were witches, but what made you think Abe and I had joined the party?'

She said nothing.

'That's stupid of me, though,' he said. 'I guess prepartum whatever-it-is doesn't *need* reasons.' He took another of the triangles and bit off first one point and then another.

She said, 'Why did you trade ties with Donald Baumgart?'

'Why did I – well what has *that* got to do with anything?'

'You needed one of his personal belongings,' she said, 'so they could cast the spell and make him blind.'

He stared at her. 'Honey,' he said, 'for God's sake what are you *talking* about?'

'You know.'

'Holy mackerel,' he said. 'I traded ties with him because I liked his and didn't like mine, and *he* liked mine and didn't like his. I didn't tell you about it because afterwards it seemed like a slightly faggy thing to have done and I was a little embarrassed about it.'

'Where did you get the tickets for *The Fantasticks*?' she asked him.

'*What*?'

'You said you got them from Dominick,' she said; 'you didn't.'

'Boy oh *boy*,' he said. 'And that makes me a witch? I got them from a girl named Norma-something that I met at an audition and had a couple of drinks with. What did Abe do? Tie his shoelaces the wrong way?'

'He uses tannis root,' she said. 'It's a witch thing. His receptionist told me she smelled it on him.'

'Maybe Minnie gave him a good luck charm, just the way she gave you one. You mean only witches use it? That doesn't sound very likely.'

Rosemary was silent.

'Let's face it, darling,' Guy said, 'you had the prepartum crazies. And now you're going to rest and get over them.' He leaned closer to her and took her hand. 'I know this has been the worst thing that ever happened to you,' he said, 'but from now on everything's going to be roses. Warners is within an inch of where we want them, and suddenly Universal is interested too. I'm going to get some more good reviews and then we're going to blow this town and be in the beautiful hills of Beverly, with the pool and the spice garden and the whole schmeer. And the kids too, Ro. Scout's honour. You heard what Abe said.' He kissed her hand. 'Got to run now and get famous.'

He got up and started for the door.

'Let me see your shoulder,' she said.

He stopped and turned.

'Let me see your shoulder,' she said.

'Are you kidding?'

'No,' she said. 'Let me see you. Your left shoulder.'

He looked at her and said, 'All right, whatever you say, honey.'

He undid the collar of his shirt, a short-sleeved blue knit, and peeled the bottom of it up and over his head. He had a white T shirt on underneath. 'I generally prefer doing this to music,' he said, and took off the T shirt too. He went close to the bed and, leaning, showed Rosemary his left shoulder. It was unmarked. There was only the faint scar of a boil or pimple. He showed her his other shoulder and his chest and his back.

'This is as far as I go without a blue light,' he said.

'All right,' she said.

He grinned. 'The question now,' he said, 'is do I put my shirt back on or do I go out and give Laura-Louise the thrill of a lifetime.'

Her breasts filled with milk and it was necessary to relieve them, so Dr Sapirstein showed her how to use a rubber-bulbed breast pump, like a glass auto horn; and several times a day Laura-Louise or Helen Wees or whoever was there brought it in to her with a Pyrex measuring cup. She drew from each breast an ounce or two of thin faintly-green fluid that smelled ever so slightly of tannis root – in a process that was a final irrefutable demonstration of the baby's absence. When the cup and the pump had been carried from the room she would lie against her pillows broken and lonely beyond tears.

Joan and Elise and Tiger came to see her, and she spoke with Brian for twenty minutes on the phone. Flowers came – roses and carnations and a yellow azalea plant – from Allan, and Mike and Pedro, and Lou and Claudia. Guy bought a new remote-control television set and put it at the foot of the bed. She watched and ate and took pills that were given to her.

A letter of sympathy came from Minnie and Roman, a page from each of them. They were in Dubrovnik.

The stitches gradually stopped hurting.

One morning, when two or three weeks had gone by, she thought she heard a baby crying. She rayed off the television and listened. There was a frail far away wailing. Or was there? She slipped out of bed and turned off the air conditioner.

Florence Gilmore came in with the pump and the cup.

'Do you hear a baby crying?' Rosemary asked her.

Both of them listened.

Yes, there it was. A baby crying.

'No, dear, I don't,' Florence said. 'Get back into bed now; you know you're not supposed to be walking around: Did you turn off the air conditioner? You mustn't do that; it's a *terrible* day. People are actually dying, it's so hot.'

She heard it again that afternoon, and mysteriously her breasts began to leak . . .

'Some new people moved in,' Guy said out of nowhere that evening. 'Up on eight.'

'And they have a baby,' she said.

'Yes. How did you know?'

She looked at him for a moment. 'I heard it crying,' she said.

She heard it the next day. And the next.

She stopped watching television and held a book in front of her, pretending to read but only listening, listening . . .

It wasn't up on eight; it was right there on seven.

And more often than not, the pump and the cup were brought to her a few minutes after the crying began; and the crying stopped a few minutes after her milk was taken away.

'What do you do with it?' she asked Laura-Louise one morning, giving her back the pump and the cup and six ounces of milk.

'Why throw it away, of course,' Laura-Louise said, and went out.

That afternoon, as she gave Laura-Louise the cup, she said, 'Wait a minute,' and started to put a used coffee spoon into it.

Laura-Louise jerked the cup away. 'Don't do that,' she said, and caught the spoon in a finger of the hand holding the pump.

'What difference does it make?' Rosemary asked.

'It's just messy, that's all,' Laura-Louise said.

2

It was alive.

It was in Minnie and Roman's apartment.

They were keeping it there, feeding it her milk and please God taking care of it, because, as well as she remembered from Hutch's book, August first was one of their special days, Lammas or Leamas, with special maniacal rituals. Or maybe they were keeping it until Minnie and Roman came back from Europe. For their share.

But it was still alive.

She stopped taking the pills they gave her. She tucked them down into the fold between her thumb and her palm and faked the swallowing, and later pushed the pills as far as she could between the mattress and the box spring beneath it.

She felt stronger and more wide-awake.

Hang on, Andy! I'm coming!

She had learned her lesson with Dr Hill. This time she would turn to no one, would expect no one to believe her and be her saviour. Not the police, not Joan or the Dunstans or Grace Cardiff, not even Brian. Guy was too good an actor, Dr Sapirstein too famous a doctor; between the two of them they'd have even him, even Brian, thinking she had some kind of post-losing-the-baby madness. This time she would do it alone, would go in there and get him herself, with her longest sharpest kitchen knife to fend away those maniacs.

And she was one up on them. Because she knew – and they didn't *know* she knew – that there was a secret way from the one apartment to the other. The door had been chained that night – she knew that as she knew the hand she was looking at was a hand, not a bird or a battleship – and still they had all come pouring in. So there had to be another way.

Which could only be the linen closet, barricaded by dead Mrs Gardenia, who surely had died of the same witchery that had frozen and killed poor Hutch. The closet had been put there to break the one big apartment into two smaller ones, and if Mrs Gardenia had belonged to the coven – she'd given Minnie her herbs; hadn't Terry said so? – then what was more logical than to open the back of the closet in some way and go to and fro with so many steps saved and the Bruhns and Dubin-and-DeVore never knowing of the traffic?

It *was* the linen closet.

In a dream long ago she had been carried through it. That had been no dream; it had been a sign from heaven, a divine message to be stored away and remembered now for assurance in a time of trial.

Oh Father in heaven, forgive me for doubting! Forgive me for turning from you, Merciful Father, and help me, help me in my hour of need! Oh Jesus, dear Jesus, help me save my innocent baby!

The pills, of course, were the answer. She squirmed her arm in under the mattress and caught them out one by one. Eight of them, all alike; small white tablets scored across the middle for breaking in half. Whatever they were, three a day had kept her limp and docile; eight at once, surely, would send Laura-Louise or Helen Wees into sound sleep. She brushed the pills clean, folded them up in a piece of magazine cover, and tucked them away at the bottom of her box of tissues.

She pretended still to be limp and docile; ate her meals and looked at magazines and pumped out her milk.

It was Leah Fountain who was there when everything was right. She came in after Helen Wees had gone out with the milk and said, 'Hi, Rosemary! I've been letting the other girls have the fun of visiting with you, but now *I'm* going to take a turn. You're in a regular movie theatre here! Is there anything good on tonight?'

Nobody else was in the apartment. Guy had gone to meet Allan and have some contracts explained to him.

They watched a Fred Astaire-Ginger Rogers picture, and during a break Leah went into the kitchen and brought back two cups of coffee. 'I'm a little hungry too,' Rosemary said when Leah had put the cups on the night table. 'Would you mind very much fixing me a cheese sandwich?'

'Of course I wouldn't mind, dear,' Leah said. 'How do you like it, with lettuce and mayonnaise?'

She went out again and Rosemary got the fold of magazine cover from her tissue box. There were eleven pills in it now. She slid them all into Leah's cup and stirred the coffee with her own spoon, which she then wiped off with a tissue. She picked up her own coffee, but it shook so much that she had to put it down again.

She was sitting and sipping calmly though when Leah came in with the sandwich. 'Thanks, Leah,' she said, 'that looks great. The coffee's a little bitter; I guess it was sitting too long.'

'Shall I make fresh?' Leah asked.

'No, it's not that bad,' Rosemary said.

Leah sat down beside the bed, took her cup, and stirred it and tasted. 'Mm,' she said and wrinkled her nose; she nodded, agreeing with Rosemary.

'It's drinkable though,' Rosemary said.

They watched the movie, and after two more breaks Leah's head drooped and snapped up sharply. She put down her cup and saucer, the cup two-thirds empty. Rosemary ate the last piece of her sandwich and watched Fred Astaire and two other people dancing on turntables in a glossy unreal fun house.

During the next section of the movie Leah fell asleep.

'Leah?' Rosemary said.

The elderly woman sat snoring, her chin to her chest, her hands palm-upward in her lap. Her lavender-tinted hair, a wig, had slipped forward; sparse white hairs stuck out at the back of her neck.

Rosemary got out of bed, slid her feet into slippers, and put on the blue-and-white quilted housecoat she had bought for the hospital. Going quietly out of the bedroom, she closed the door almost all the way and went to the front door of the apartment and quietly chained and bolted it.

She then went into the kitchen and, from her knife rack, took the longest sharpest knife – a nearly new carving knife with a curved and pointed steel blade and a heavy bone handle with a brass butt. Holding it point-down at her side, she left the kitchen and went down the hallway to the linen-closet door.

As soon as she opened it she knew she was right. The shelves looked neat and orderly enough, but the contents of two of them had been interchanged; the bath towels and hand towels were where the winter blankets ought to have been and vice versa.

She laid the knife on the bathroom threshold and took everything out of the closet except what was on the fixed top shelf. She put towels and linens on the floor, and large and small boxes, and then lifted out the four gingham-covered shelves she had decorated and placed there a thousand thousand years ago.

The back of the closet, below the top shelf, was a single large white-painted panel framed with narrow white moulding. Standing close and leaning aside for better light, Rosemary saw that where the panel and the moulding met, the paint was broken in a continuous line. She pressed at one side of the panel and then at the other; pressed harder, and it swung inward on scraping hinges. Within was darkness; another closet, with a wire hanger glinting on the floor and one bright spot of light, a keyhole. Pushing the panel all the way open, Rosemary stepped into the second closet and ducked down. Through the keyhole she saw, at a distance of about twenty feet, a small curio cabinet that stood at a jog in the hallway of Minnie and Roman's apartment.

She tried the door. It opened.

She closed it and backed out through her own closet and got the knife; then went in and through again, looked out again through the keyhole, and opened the door just the least bit.

Then opened it wide, holding the knife shoulder-high, point forward.

The hallway was empty, but there were distant voices from the living-room. The bathroom was on her right, its door open, dark. Minnie and Roman's bedroom was on the left, with a bedside lamp burning. There was no crib, no baby.

She went cautiously down the hallway. A door on the right was locked; another, on the left, was a linen closet.

Over the curio cabinet hung a small but vivid oil painting of a church in flames. Before, there had been only a clean space and a hook; now there was this shocking painting. St Patrick's, it looked like, with yellow and orange flames bursting from its windows and soaring through its gutted roof.

Where had she seen it? A church burning . . .

In the dream. The one where they had carried her through the linen closet. Guy and somebody else. 'You've got her too high.' To a ballroom where a church was burning. Where *that* church was burning.

But how could it be?

Had she *really* been carried through the closet, seen the painting as they carried her past it?

Find Andy. Find Andy. Find Andy.

Knife high, she followed the jog to the left and the right. Other doors were locked. There was another painting; nude men and women dancing in a circle. Ahead were the foyer and the front door, the archway on the right to the living-room. The voices were louder. 'Not if he's still waiting for a plane, he isn't!' Mr Fountain said, and there was laughter and then hushing.

In the dream ballroom Jackie Kennedy had spoken kindly to her and gone away, and then all of *them* had been there, the whole coven, naked and singing in a circle around her. Had it been a real thing that had really happened? Roman in a black robe had drawn designs on her. Dr Sapirstein had held a cup of red paint for him. Red paint? Blood?

'Oh hell now, Hayato,' Minnie said, 'you're just making fun of me! "Pulling my leg" is what we say over here.'

Minnie? Back from Europe? And Roman too? But only yesterday there had been a card from Dubrovnik saying they were staying on!

Had they ever really been away?

She was at the archway now, could see the bookshelves and file cabinets and bridge tables laden with newspapers and stacked envelopes. The coven was at the other end, laughing, talking softly. Ice cubes clinked.

She bettered her grip on the knife and moved a step forward. She stopped, staring.

Across the room, in the one large window bay, stood a black bassinet. Black and only black it was; skirted with black taffeta, hooded and flounced with black organza. A silver ornament turned on a black ribbon pinned to its black hood.

Dead? But no, even as she feared it, the stiff organza trembled, the silver ornament quivered.

He was in there. In that monstrous perverted witches' bassinet.

The silver ornament was a crucifix hanging upside down, with the black ribbon wound and knotted around Jesus' ankles.

The thought of her baby lying helpless amid sacrilege and horror brought tears to Rosemary's eyes, and suddenly a longing dragged at her to do nothing but collapse and weep, to surrender completely before such elaborate and unspeakable evil. She withstood it though; she shut her eyes tight to stop the tears, said a quick Hail Mary, and drew together all her resolve and all her hatred too; hatred of Minnie, Roman, Guy, Dr Sapirstein – of all of them who had conspired to steal Andy away from her and make their loathsome uses of him. She wiped her hands on her housecoat, threw back her hair, found a fresh grip on the knife's thick handle, and stepped out where they could every one of them see her and know she had come.

Insanely, they didn't. They went right on talking, listening, sipping, pleasantly partying, as if she were a ghost, or back in her bed dreaming; Minnie, Roman, Guy (contracts!), Mr Fountain, the Weeses, Laura-Louise, and a studious-looking young Japanese with eyeglasses – all gathered under an over-the-mantel portrait of Adrian Marcato. He alone saw her. He stood glaring at her, motionless, powerful; but powerless, a painting.

Then Roman saw her too; put down his drink and touched Minnie's arm. Silence sprang up, and those who sat with their backs towards her turned around questioningly. Guy started to rise but sat down again. Laura-Louise clapped her hands to her mouth and began squealing. Helen Wees said, 'Get back in bed, Rosemary; you know you aren't supposed to be up and around.' Either mad or trying psychology.

'Is the mother?' the Japanese asked, and when Roman nodded, said 'Ah, sssssss,' and looked at Rosemary with interest.

'She killed Leah,' Mr Fountain said, standing up. 'She killed my Leah. Did you? Where is she? Did you kill my Leah?'

Rosemary stared at them, at Guy. He looked down, red-faced.

She gripped the knife tighter. 'Yes,' she said, 'I killed her. I stabbed her to death. And I cleaned my knife and I'll stab to death whoever comes near me. Tell them how sharp it is, Guy!'

He said nothing. Mr Fountain sat down, a hand to his heart. Laura-Louise squealed.

Watching them, she started across the room towards the bassinet.

'Rosemary,' Roman said.

'Shut up,' she said.

'Before you look at—'

'Shut up,' she said. 'You're in Dubrovnik. I don't hear you.'

'Let her,' Minnie said.

She watched them until she was by the bassinet, which was angled in their direction. With her free hand she caught the black-covered handle at the foot of it and swung the bassinet slowly, gently, around to face her. Taffeta rustled; the back wheels squeaked.

Asleep and sweet, so small and rosy-faced, Andy lay wrapped in a snug black blanket with little black mitts ribbon-tied around his wrists. Orange-red hair he had, a surprising amount of it, silky-clean and brushed. *Andy! Oh, Andy!* She reached out to him, her knife turning away; his lips pouted and he opened his eyes and looked at

159

her. His eyes were golden-yellow, all golden-yellow, with neither whites nor irises; all golden-yellow, with vertical black-slit pupils.

She looked at him.

He looked at her, golden-yellowly, and then at the swaying upside-down crucifix.

She looked at them watching her and knife-in-hand screamed at them, '*What have you done to his eyes?*'

They stirred and looked to Roman.

'He has His Father's eyes,' he said.

She looked at him, looked at Guy – whose eyes were hidden behind a hand – looked at Roman again. 'What are you *talking* about?' she said. 'Guy's eyes are *brown*, they're *normal*! What have you *done* to him, you maniacs?' She moved from the bassinet, ready to kill them.

'Satan is His Father, not Guy,' Roman said. '*Satan* is His Father, who came up from Hell and begat a Son of mortal woman! To avenge the iniquities visited by the God worshippers upon His never-doubting followers!'

'Hail Satan,' Mr Wees said.

'*Satan* is His Father and His name is Adrian!' Roman cried, his voice growing louder and prouder, his bearing more strong and forceful. 'He shall overthrow the mighty and lay waste their temples! He shall redeem the despised and wreak vengeance in the name of the burned and the tortured!'

'Hail Adrian,' they said. 'Hail Adrian.' 'Hail Adrian.' And 'Hail Satan.' 'Hail Adrian.' 'Hail Satan.'

She shook her head. 'No,' she said.

Minnie said, 'He chose *you* out of all the world, Rosemary. Out of all the women in the whole world, He chose *you*. He brought you and Guy to your apartment there, He made that foolish what's-her-name, Terry, made her get all scared and silly so we had to change our plans. He arranged everything that *had* to be arranged, 'cause He wanted *you* to be the mother of His only living Son.'

'His power is stronger than stronger,' Roman said.

'Hail Satan,' Helen Wees said.

'His might will last longer than longer.'

'Hair Satan,' the Japanese said.

Laura-Louise uncovered her mouth. Guy looked out at Rosemary from under his hand.

'No,' she said, 'no,' the knife hanging at her side. 'No. It can't *be*. No.'

160

'Go look at His hands,' Minnie said. 'And His feet.'

'And His tail,' Laura-Louise said.

'And the buds of His horns,' Minnie said.

'Oh God,' Rosemary said.

'God's dead,' Roman said.

She turned to the bassinet, let fall the knife, turned back to the watching coven. 'Oh God!' she said and covered her face. 'Oh God!' And raised her fists and screamed to the ceiling: *'Oh God! Oh God! Oh God! Oh God! Oh God!'*

'God is DEAD!' Roman thundered. *'God is dead and Satan lives! The year is One, the first year of our Lord! The year is One, God is done! The year is One, Adrian's begun!'*

'Hail Satan!' they cried. 'Hail Adrian!' 'Hail Adrian!' 'Hail Satan!'

She backed away – 'No, no' – backed farther and farther away until she was between two bridge tables. A chair was behind her; she sat down on it and stared at them. 'No.'

Mr Fountain hurried out and down the hallway. Guy and Mr Wees hurried after him.

Minnie went over and, grunting as she stooped, picked up the knife. She took it out to the kitchen.

Laura-Louise went to the bassinet and rocked it possessively, making faces into it. The black taffeta rustled; the wheels squeaked.

She sat there and stared. 'No,' she said.

The dream. The dream. It had been true. The yellow eyes she had looked up into. 'Oh God,' she said.

Roman came over to her. 'Clare is just putting on,' he said, 'holding his heart that way over Leah. He's not that sorry. Nobody really liked her; she was stingy, emotionally as well as financially. Why don't you help us out, Rosemary, be a real mother to Adrian; and we'll fix it so you don't get punished for killing her. So that nobody ever even finds out about it. You don't have to *join* if you don't want to; just be a mother to your baby.' He bent over and whispered: 'Minnie and Laura-Louise are too old. It's not right.'

She looked at him.

He stood straight again. 'Think about it, Rosemary,' he said.

'I didn't kill her,' she said.

'Oh?'

'I just gave her pills,' she said. 'She's asleep.'

'Oh,' he said.

The doorbell rang.

'Excuse me,' he said, and went to answer it. 'Think about it anyway,' he said over his shoulder.

'Oh *God*,' she said.

'Shut up with your "Oh God's" or we'll kill you,' Laura-Louise said, rocking the bassinet. 'Milk or no milk.'

'*You* shut up,' Helen Wees said, coming to Rosemary and putting a dampened handkerchief in her hand. 'Rosemary is His mother, no matter how she behaves,' she said. 'You remember that, and show some respect.'

Laura-Louise said something under her breath.

Rosemary wiped her forehead and cheeks with the cool handkerchief. The Japanese, sitting across the room on a hassock, caught her eye and grinned and ducked his head. He held up an opened camera into which he was putting film, and moved it back and forth in the direction of the bassinet, grinning and nodding. She looked down and started to cry. She wiped at her eyes.

Roman came in holding the arm of a robust, handsome, dark-skinned man in a snow-white suit and white shoes. He carried a large box wrapped in light blue paper patterned with Teddy bears and candy canes. Musical sounds came from it. Everyone gathered to meet him and shake his hand. 'Worried,' they said, and 'pleasure', and 'airport', and 'Stavropoulos', and 'occasion'. Laura-Louise brought the box to the bassinet. She held it up for the baby to see, shook it for him to hear, and put it on the window seat with many other boxes similarly wrapped and a few that were wrapped in black with black ribbon.

'Just after midnight on June twenty-fifth,' Roman said. 'Exactly half the year 'round from you-know. Isn't it perfect?'

'But why are you surprised?' the newcomer asked with both his hands outstretched. 'Didn't Edmond Lautréamont predict June twenty-fifth three hundred years ago?'

'Indeed he did,' Roman said, smiling, 'but it's such a novelty for one of his predictions to prove accurate!' Everyone laughed. 'Come, my friend,' Roman said, drawing the newcomer forward, 'come see Him. Come see the Child.'

They went to the bassinet, where Laura-Louise waited with a shopkeeper's smile, and they closed around it and looked into it silently. After a few moments the newcomer lowered himself to his knees.

Guy and Mr Wees came in.

They waited in the archway until the newcomer had risen, and then Guy came over to Rosemary. 'She'll be all right,' he said; 'Abe is in there with her.' He stood looking down at her, his hands rubbing at his sides. 'They promised me you wouldn't be hurt,' he said. 'And you haven't been, really. I mean, suppose you'd had a baby and lost it; wouldn't it be the same? And we're getting so much in return, Ro.'

She put the handkerchief on the table and looked at him. As hard as she could she spat at him.

He flushed and turned away, wiping at the front of his jacket. Roman caught him and introduced him to the newcomer, Argyron Stavropoulos.

'How proud you must be,' Stavropoulos said, clasping Guy's hand in both his own. 'But surely that isn't the mother there? Why in the name of—' Roman drew him away and spoke in his ear.

'Here,' Minnie said, and offered Rosemary a mug of steaming tea. 'Drink this and you'll feel a little better.'

Rosemary looked at it, and looked up at Minnie. 'What's in it?' she said; 'tannis root?'

'*Nothing* is in it,' Minnie said. 'Except sugar and lemon. It's plain ordinary Lipton tea. You drink it.' She put it down by the handkerchief.

The thing to do was kill it. Obviously. Wait till they were all sitting at the other end, then run over, push away Laura-Louise, and grab it and throw it out the window. And jump out after it. *Mother Slays Baby and Self at Bramford.*

Save the world from God-knows-what. From Satan-knows-what.

A tail! The buds of his horns!

She wanted to scream, to die.

She would do it, throw it out and jump.

They were all milling around now. Pleasant cocktail party. The Japanese was taking pictures; of Guy, of Stavropoulos, of Laura-Louise holding the baby.

She turned away, not wanting to see.

Those eyes! Like an animal's, a tiger's, not like a human being's!

He *wasn't* a human being, of course. He was – some kind of a half-breed.

And how dear and sweet he had looked before he had opened those yellow eyes! The tiny chin, a bit like Brian's; the sweet mouth; all that lovely orange-red hair . . . It would be nice to look at him again, if only he wouldn't open those yellow animal-eyes.

She tasted the tea. It was tea.

No, she *couldn't* throw him out the window. He was her baby, no matter who the father was. What she had to do was go to someone who would understand. Like a priest. Yes, that was the answer; a priest. It was a problem for the Church to handle. For the Pope and all the cardinals to deal with, not stupid Rosemary Reilly from Omaha.

Killing was wrong, no matter what.

She drank more tea.

He began whimpering because Laura-Louise was rocking the bassinet too fast, so of course the idiot began rocking it faster.

She stood it as long as she could and then got up and went over.

'Get away from here,' Laura-Louise said. 'Don't you come near Him. Roman!'

'You're rocking him too fast,' she said.

'Sit down!' Laura-Louise said, and to Roman, 'Get her out of here. Put her back where she belongs.'

Rosemary said, 'She's rocking him too fast; that's why he's whimpering.'

'Mind your own business!' Laura-Louise said.

'Let Rosemary rock Him,' Roman said.

Laura-Louise stared at him.

'Go on,' he said, standing behind the bassinet's hood. 'Sit down with the others. Let Rosemary rock Him.'

'She's liable—'

'*Sit down with the others, Laura-Louise.*'

She huffed, and marched away.

'Rock Him,' Roman said to Rosemary, smiling. He moved the bassinet back and forth towards her, holding it by the hood.

She stood still and looked at him. 'You're trying to – get me to be his mother,' she said.

'*Aren't* you His mother?' Roman said. 'Go on. Just rock Him till He stops complaining.'

She let the black-covered handle come into her hand, and closed her fingers around it. For a few moments they rocked the bassinet between them, then Roman let go and she rocked it alone, nice and slowly. She glanced at the baby, saw his yellow eyes, and looked to the window. 'You should oil the wheels,' she said. 'That could bother him too.'

'I will,' Roman said. 'You see? He's stopped complaining. He knows who you are.'

'Don't be silly,' Rosemary said, and looked at the baby again. He was watching her. His eyes weren't that bad really, now that she was prepared for them. It was the surprise that had upset her. They were pretty in a way. 'What are his hands like?' she asked, rocking him.

'They're very nice,' Roman said. 'He has claws, but they're very tiny and pearly. The mitts are only so He doesn't scratch Himself, not because His hands aren't attractive.'

'He looks worried,' she said.

Dr Sapirstein came over. 'A night of surprises,' he said.

'Go away,' she said, 'or I'm going to spit in your face.'

'Go away, Abe,' Roman said, and Dr Sapirstein nodded and went away.

'Not you,' Rosemary said to the baby. 'It's not *your* fault. I'm angry at *them*, because they tricked me and lied to me. Don't look so worried; I'm not going to hurt you.'

'He knows that,' Roman said.

'Then what does he look so worried for?' Rosemary said. 'The poor little thing. Look at him.'

'In a minute,' Roman said. 'I have to attend to my guests. I'll be right back.' He backed away, leaving her alone.

'Word of honour I'm not going to hurt you,' she said to the baby. She bent over and untied the neck of his gown. 'Laura-Louise made this too tight, didn't she. I'll make it a little looser and then you'll be more comfortable. You have a very cute chin; are you aware of that fact? You have strange yellow eyes, but you have a very cute chin.'

She tied the gown more comfortably for him.

Poor little creature.

He couldn't be *all* bad, he just *couldn't*. Even if he was half Satan, wasn't he half *her* as well, half decent, ordinary, sensible, human being? If she worked *against* them, exerted a good influence to counteract their bad one . . .

'You have a room of your own, do you know that?' she said, undoing the blanket around him, which was also too tight. 'It has white-and-yellow wallpaper and a white crib with yellow bumpers, and there isn't one drop of witchy old black in the whole place. We'll show it to you when you're ready for your next feeding. In case you're curious, *I* happen to be the lady who's been supplying all that milk you've been drinking. I'll bet you thought it comes in bottles, didn't you. Well it doesn't'; it comes in *mothers*, and I'm yours. That's right, Mr Worry-face. You seem to greet the idea with no enthusiasm whatsoever.'

Silence made her look up. They were gathering around to watch her, stopping at a respectful distance.

She felt herself blushing and turned back to tucking the blanket around the baby. '*Let* them watch,' she said; 'we don't care, do we? We just want to be all cosy and comfortable, like so. There. Better?'

'Hail Rosemary,' Helen Wees said.

The others took it up. 'Hail Rosemary.' 'Hail Rosemary.' Minnie and Stavropoulos and Dr Sapirstein. 'Hail Rosemary.' Guy said it too. 'Hail Rosemary.' Laura-Louise moved her lips but made no sound. 'Hail Rosemary, mother of Adrian!' Roman said. She looked up from the bassinet. 'It's Andrew,' she said. 'Andrew John Woodhouse.' 'Adrian Steven,' Roman said.

Guy said, 'Roman, look,' and Stavropoulos, at Roman's other side, touched his arm and said, 'Is the name of so great an importance?'

'It is. Yes. It is,' Roman said. 'His name is Adrian Steven.'

Rosemary said, 'I understand why you'd like to call him that, but I'm sorry; you can't. His name is Andrew John. He's my child, not yours, and this is one point that I'm not even going to argue about. This and the clothes. He can't wear black all the time.'

Roman opened his mouth but Minnie said, 'Hail Andrew' in a loud voice, looking right at him.

Everyone else said 'Hail Andrew' and 'Hail Rosemary, mother of Andrew' and 'Hail Satan.'

Rosemary tickled the baby's tummy. 'You didn't like "Adrian", did you?' she asked him. 'I should think not. "Adrian Steven"! Will you *please* stop looking so worried?' She poked the tip of of his nose. 'Do you know how to smile yet, Andy? Do you? Come on, little funny-eyes Andy, can you smile? Can you smile for Mommy?' She tapped the silver ornament and set it swinging. 'Come on, Andy,' she said. 'One little smile. Come on, Andy-candy.'

The Japanese slipped forward with his camera, crouched, and took two three four pictures in quick succession.

The Stepford Wives

'Today the combat takes a different shape; instead of wishing to put man in a prison, woman endeavours to escape from one; she no longer seeks to drag him into the realms of immanence but to emerge, herself, into the light of transcendence. Now the attitude of the males creates a new conflict; it is with a bad grace that the man lets her go.'

Simone de Beauvoir
The Second Sex

Completed in February 1972 and dedicated to Ellie and Joe Busman

1

The Welcome Wagon lady, sixty if she was a day but working at youth and vivacity (ginger hair, red lips, a sunshine-yellow dress), twinkled her eyes and teeth at Joanna and said, 'You're really going to like it here! It's a nice town with nice people! You couldn't have made a better choice!' Her brown leather shoulder-bag was enormous, old and scuffed; from it she dealt Joanna packets of powdered breakfast drink and soup mix, a toy-size box of non-polluting detergent, a booklet of discount slips good at twenty-two local shops, two cakes of soap, a folder of deodorant pads—

'Enough, enough,' Joanna said, standing in the doorway with both hands full. 'Hold. Halt. Thank you.'

The Welcome Wagon lady put a vial of cologne on top of the other things, and then searched in her bag - 'No, really,' Joanna said - and brought out pink-framed eye-glasses and a small embroidered notebook. 'I do the "Notes on Newcomers", ' she said, smiling and putting on the glasses. 'For the *Chronicle*.' She dug at the bag's bottom and came up with a pen, clicking its top with a red-nailed thumb.

Joanna told her where she and Walter had moved from; what Walter did and with which firm; Pete's and Kim's names and ages; what she had done before they were born; and which colleges she and Walter had gone to. She shifted impatiently as she spoke, standing there at the front door with both hands full and Pete and Kim out of earshot.

'Do you have any hobbies or special interests?'

She was about to say a time-saving no, but hesitated: a full answer, printed in the local paper, might serve as a signpost to women like herself, potential friends. The women she had met in the past few days, the ones in the nearby houses, were pleasant and helpful enough, but they seemed completely absorbed in their household duties. Maybe when she got to know them better she would find they had further-reaching thoughts and concerns, yet it might be wise to put up that signpost. So, 'Yes, several,' she said. 'I play tennis whenever I get the chance, and I'm a semi-professional photographer—'

'Oh?' the Welcome Wagon lady said, writing.

Joanna smiled. 'That means an agency handles three of my pictures,' she said. 'And I'm interested in politics and in the Women's Liberation movement. Very much so in that. And so is my husband.'

'*He* is?' The Welcome Wagon lady looked at her.

'Yes,' Joanna said. 'Lots of men are.' She didn't go into the benefits-for-both-sexes explanation; instead she leaned her head back into the entrance hall and listened: a TV audience laughed in the family-room, and Pete and Kim argued but below intervention level. She smiled at the Welcome Wagon lady. 'He's interested in boating and football too,' she said, 'and he collects Early American legal documents.' Walter's half of the signpost.

The Welcome Wagon lady wrote, and closed her notebook, clicked her pen. 'That's just fine, Mrs Eberhart,' she said, smiling and taking her glasses off. 'I know you're going to love it here,' she said, 'and I want to wish you a sincere and hearty "Welcome to Stepford". If there's any information I can give you about local shops and services, please feel free to call me; the number's right there on the front of the discount book.'

'Thank you, I will,' Joanna said. 'And thanks for all this.'

'Try them, they're good products!' the Welcome Wagon lady said. She turned away. 'Goodbye now!'

Joanna said goodbye to her and watched her go down the curving walk towards her battered red Volkswagen. Dogs suddenly filled its windows, a black and brown excitement of spaniels, jumping and barking, paws pressing glass. Moving whiteness beyond the Volkswagen caught Joanna's eye: across the sapling-lined street, in one of the Claybrooks' upstairs windows, whiteness moved again, leaving one pane and filling the next; the window was being washed. Joanna smiled in case Donna Claybrook was looking at her. The whiteness moved to a lower pane, and then to the pane beside it.

With a surprising roar the Volkswagen lunged from the kerb, and Joanna backed into the entrance hall and hipped the door closed.

Pete and Kim were arguing louder. 'BM! Diarrhoea!' 'Ow! Stop it!'

'Cut it out!' Joanna called, dumping the double handful of

samples on to the kitchen table.

'She's kicking me!' Pete shouted, and Kim shouted, 'I'm not! You diarrhoea!'

'Now *stop* it,' Joanna said, going to the port and looking through. Pete lay on the floor too close to the TV set, and Kim stood beside him, red-faced, keeping from kicking him. Both were still in their pyjamas. 'She kicked me twice,' Pete said, and Kim shouted, 'You changed the channel! He changed the channel!' 'I did not!' '*I was watching Felix the Cat!*'

'Quiet!' Joanna commanded. 'Absolute silence! Utter – complete – total – silence.'

They looked at her, Kim with Walter's wide blue eyes, Pete with her own grave dark ones. 'Race 'em to a flying finish!' the TV set cried. 'No electricity!'

'A, you're too close to the set;' Joanna said. 'B, turn it off; and C, get dressed, both of you. That green stuff outside is grass, and the yellow stuff coming down on it is sunshine.' Pete scrambled to his feet and pawed the TV's control panel, blanking its screen to a dying dot of light. Kim began crying.

Joanna groaned and went around into the family-room.

Crouching, she hugged Kim to her shoulder and rubbed her pyjama'd back, kissed her silk-soft ringlets. 'Ah, come on now,' she said. 'Don't you want to play with that nice Allison again? Maybe you'll see another chipmunk.'

Pete came over and lifted a strand of her hair. She looked up at him and said, 'Don't change *channels* on her.'

'Oh, all right,' he said, winding a finger in the dark strand.

'And don't *kick*,' she told Kim. She rubbed her back and tried to get kisses in at her squirming-away cheek.

It was Walter's turn to do the dishes, and Pete and Kim were playing quietly in Pete's room, so she took a quick cool shower and put on shorts and a shirt and her sneakers and brushed her hair. She peeked in on Pete and Kim as she tied her hair: they were sitting on the floor playing with Pete's space station.

She moved quietly away and went down the new-carpeted stairs. It was a good evening. The unpacking was done with, finally, and she was cool and clean, with a few free minutes – ten or fifteen if she was lucky – maybe to sit outside with Walter and look at their trees and their two-point-two acres.

She went around and down the hallway. The kitchen was spick-

and-span, the washer pounding. Walter was at the sink, leaning to the window and looking out towards the Van Sant house. A Rorschach-blot of sweat stained his shirt: a rabbit with its ears bent outwards. He turned around, and started and smiled. 'How long have you been here?' he asked, dishtowel-wiping his hands.

'I just came in,' she said.

'You look reborn.'

'That's how I feel. They're playing like angels. You want to go outside?'

'Okay,' he said, folding the towel. 'Just for a few minutes, though. I'm going over to talk with Ted.' He slid the towel on to a rod of the rack. 'That's why I was looking,' he said. 'They just finished eating.'

'What are you going to talk with him about?'

They went out on to the patio.

'I was going to tell you,' he said as they walked. 'I've changed my mind; I'm joining that Men's Association.'

She stopped and looked at him.

'Too many important things are centred there to just opt out of it,' he said. 'Local politicking, the charity drives and so on . . .'

She said, 'How can you join an *outdated, old-fashioned*—'

'I spoke to some of the men on the train,' he said. 'Ted, and Vic Stavros, and a few others they introduced me to. They *agree* that the no-women-allowed business is archaic.' He took her arm and they walked on. 'But the only way to change it is from inside,' he said. 'So I'm going to help do it. I'm joining Saturday night. Ted's going to brief me on who's on what committees.' He offered her his cigarettes. 'Are you smoking or non- tonight?'

'Oh – *smoking*,' she said, reaching for one.

They stood at the patio's far edge, in cool blue dusk twanging with crickets, and Walter held his lighter flame to Joanna's cigarette and to his own.

'Look at that sky,' he said. 'Worth every penny it cost us.'

She looked – the sky was mauve and blue and dark blue; lovely – and then she looked at her cigarette. 'Organizations can be changed from the outside,' she said. 'You get up petitions, you picket—'

'But it's easier from the inside,' Walter said. 'You'll see: if these men I spoke to are typical, it'll be the *Everybody's* Association before you know it. Co-ed poker. Sex on the pool table.'

'If these men you spoke to were typical,' she said, 'it would be the

Everybody's Association already. Oh, all right, go ahead and join; I'll think up slogans for placards. I'll have plenty of time when school starts.'

He put his arm around her shoulders and said, 'Hold off a little while. If it's not open to women in six months, I'll quit and we'll march together. Shoulder to shoulder. "Sex, yes; sexism, no." '

' "Stepford is out of step", ' she said, reaching for the ashtray on the picnic table.

'Not bad.'

'Wait till I really get going.'

They finished their cigarettes and stood arm in arm, looking at their dark wide runway of lawn and the tall trees, black against mauve sky, that ended it. Lights shone among the trunks of the trees: windows of houses on the next street over, Harvest Lane.

'Robert Ardrey is right,' Joanna said. 'I feel very territorial.'

Walter looked around at the Van Sant house and then squinted at his watch. 'I'm going to go in and wash up,' he said, and kissed her cheek.

She turned and took his chin and kissed his lips. 'I'm going to stay out a few minutes,' she said. 'Yell if they're acting up.'

'Okay,' he said. He went into the house by the living-room door.

She held her arms and rubbed them; the evening was growing cooler. Closing her eyes, she threw her head back and breathed the smell of grass and trees and clean air: delicious. She opened her eyes, to a single speck of star in dark blue sky, a trillion miles above her. 'Star light, star bright,' she said. She didn't say the rest of it, but she thought it.

She wished – that they would be happy in Stepford. That Pete and Kim would do well in school, and that she and Walter would find good friends and fulfilment. That he wouldn't mind the commuting – though the whole idea of moving had been his in the first place. That the lives of all four of them would be enriched, rather than diminished, as she had feared, by leaving the city – the filthy, crowded, crime-ridden, but so-alive city.

Sound and movement turned her towards the Van Sant house.

Carol Van Sant, a dark silhouette against the radiance of her kitchen doorway, was pressing the lid down on to a dustbin. She bent to the ground, red hair glinting, and came up with something large and round, a stone; she put it on top of the lid.

'Hi!' Joanna called.

Carol straightened and stood facing her, tall and leggy and naked-

173

seeming – but edged by the purple of a lighted-from-behind dress. 'Who's there?' she called.

'Joanna Eberhart,' Joanna said. 'Did I scare you? I'm sorry if I did.' She went towards the fence that divided her and Walter's property from the Van Sants'.

'Hi, Joanna,' Carol said in her nasal New Englandy voice. 'No, you didn't scay-er me. It's a nice night, isn't it?'

'Yes,' Joanna said. 'And I'm done with my unpacking, which makes it even nicer.' She had to speak loud; Carol had stayed by her doorway, still too far away for comfortable conversation even though she herself was now at the flower bed edging the split-rail fence. 'Kim had a great time with Allison this afternoon,' she said. 'They get along beautifully together.'

'Kim's a sweet little girl,' Carol said. 'I'm glad Allison has such a nice new friend next door. Goodnight, Joanna.' She turned to go in.

'Hey, wait a minute!' Joanna called.

Carol turned back. 'Yes?' she said.

Joanna wished that the flower bed and fence weren't there, so she could move closer. Or, darn it, that Carol would come to *her* side of the fence. What was so top-priority-urgent in that fluorescent-lighted copper-pot-hanging kitchen? 'Walter's coming over to talk with Ted,' she said, speaking loud to Carol's naked-seeming silhouette. 'When you've got the kids down, why don't you come over and have a cup of coffee with me?'

'Thanks, I'd like to,' Carol said, 'but I have to wax the family-room floor.'

'*Tonight?*'

'Night is the only time to do it, until school starts.'

'Well, can't it wait? It's only three more days.'

Carol shook her head. 'No, I've put it off too long as it is,' she said. 'It's all over scuff-marks. And besides, Ted will be going to the Men's Association later on.'

'Does he go every night?'

'Just about.'

Dear God! 'And you stay home and do housework?'

'There's always something or other that has to be done,' Carol said. 'You know how it is. I have to finish the kitchen now. Goodnight.'

'Goodnight,' Joanna said, and watched Carol go – profile of too-big bosom – into her kitchen and close the door. She reappeared almost instantly at the over-the-sink window, adjusting the water lever, taking hold of something and scrubbing it. Her red hair was neat and gleaming; her thin-nosed face looked thoughtful (and, damn it all, *intelligent*); her big purpled breasts bobbed with her scrubbing.

Joanna went back to the patio. No, she *didn't* know how it was, thank God. Not to be like that, a compulsive hausfrau. Who could blame Ted for taking advantage of such an asking-to-be-exploited patsy?

She could blame him, that's who.

Walter came out of the house in a light jacket. 'I don't think I'll be more than an hour or so,' he said.

'That Carol Van Sant is not to be believed,' she said. 'She can't come over for a cup of coffee because she has to *wax the family-room floor*. Ted goes to the Men's Association every night and *she* stays home doing *housework*.'

'Jesus,' Walter said, shaking his head.

'Next to *her*,' she said, 'my mother is Kate Millett.'

He laughed. 'See you later,' he said, and kissed her cheek and went away across the patio.

She took another look at her star, brighter now – *Get to work, you*, she thought to it – and went into the house.

The four of them went out together Saturday morning, seatbelted into their spotless new station wagon; Joanna and Walter in sunglasses, talking of stores and shopping, and Pete and Kim power-switching their windows down and up till Walter told them to stop it. The day was vivid and gem-edged, a signal of autumn. They drove to Stepford Centre (white frame Colonial shopfronts, postcard pretty) for discount-slip hardware and pharmaceuticals; then south on Route Nine to a large new shopping mall – discount-slip shoes for Pete and Kim (what a wait!) and a no-discount climbing frame; then east on Eastbridge Road to a McDonald's (Big Macs, chocolate shakes); and a little further east for antiques (an octagonal end-table, no documents); and then north-south-east-west all over Stepford – Anvil Road, Cold Creek Road, Hunnicutt, Beavertail, Burgess Ridge – to show Pete and Kim (Joanna and Walter had seen it all house-hunting) their new school and the schools they would go to later on, the you'd-never-guess-what-it-is-from-the-outside non-polluting incinerator plant, and the picnic grounds where a community pool was under construction. Joanna sang 'Good Morning Starshine' at Pete's request, and they all did 'MacNamara's Band' with

175

each one imitating a different instrument in the final part, and Kim threw up, but with enough warning for Walter to pull over and stop and get her unbuckled and out of the station wagon in time, thank God.

That quietened things down. They drove back through Stepford Centre – slowly, because Pete said that *he* might throw up too. Walter pointed out the white frame Library, and the Historical Society's two-hundred-year-old white frame cottage.

Kim, looking upwards through her window, lifted a sucked-thin Life Saver from her tongue and said, 'What's that big one?'

'That's the Men's Association house,' Walter said.

Pete leaned to his seatbelt's limit and ducked and looked. 'Is that where you're going tonight?' he asked.

'That's right,' Walter said.

'How do you get to it?'

'There's a driveway further up the hill.'

They had come up behind a truck with a man in khakis standing in its open back, his arms stretched to its sides. He had brown hair and a long lean face and wore eyeglasses. 'That's Gary Claybrook, isn't it?' Joanna said.

Walter pressed a fleeting horn-beep and waved his arm out of the window. Their across-the-street neighbour bent to look at them, then smiled and waved and caught hold of the truck. Joanna smiled and waved. Kim yelled, 'Hello, Mr Claybrook!' and Pete yelled, 'Where's Jeremy?'

'He can't hear you,' Joanna said.

'I wish I could ride a truck that way!' Pete said, and Kim said, 'Me too!'

The truck was creeping and grinding, fighting against the steep left-curving upgrade. Gary Claybrook smiled self-consciously at them. The truck was half filled with small cartons.

'What's he doing, moonlighting?' Joanna asked.

'Not if he makes as much as Ted says he does,' Walter said.

'Oh?'

'What's moonlighting?' Pete asked.

The truck's brake lights flashed; it stopped, its left-turn signal winking.

Joanna explained what moonlighting was.

A car shot down the hill, and the truck began moving across the left lane. 'Is that the driveway?' Pete asked, and Walter nodded and said, 'Yep, that's it.' Kim switched her window further down, shouting, 'Hello, Mr Claybrook!' He waved as they drove past him.

Pete sprung his seatbelt buckle and jumped around on to his knees. 'Can I go there sometime?' he asked, looking out the back.

'Mm-mmm, sorry,' Walter said. 'No kids allowed.'

'Boy, they've got a great big fence!' Pete said. 'Like in *Hogan's Heroes*!'

'To keep women out,' Joanna said, looking ahead, a hand to the rim of her sunglasses.

Walter smiled.

'Really?' Pete asked. 'Is that what it's for?'

'Pete took his belt off,' Kim said.

'Pete—' Joanna said.

They drove up Norwood Road, then west into Winter Hill Drive.

As a matter of principle she wasn't going to do any housework. Not that there wasn't plenty to do, God knows, and some that she actually *wanted* to do, like getting the living-room bookshelves squared away – but not tonight, no sir. It could darn well wait. She wasn't Carol Van Sant and she wasn't Mary Ann Stavros – pushing a vacuum cleaner past a downstairs window when she went to lower Pete's shade.

No sir. Walter was at the Men's Association, fine; he *had* to go there to join, and he'd have to go there once or twice a week to get it changed. But she wasn't going to do housework while he was there (at least not this first time) any more than *he* was going to do it when *she* was out somewhere – which she was going to be on the next clear moonlit night: down in the Centre getting some time exposures of those Colonial shopfronts. (The hardware store's irregular panes would wobble the moon's reflection, maybe interestingly.)

So once Pete and Kim were sound asleep she went down to the cellar and did some measuring and planning in the storage room that was going to be her darkroom, and then she went back up, checked Pete and Kim, and made herself a vodka and tonic and took it into the den. She put the radio on to some schmaltzy but nice Richard-Rodgersy stuff, moved Walter's contracts and things carefully from the centre of the desk, and got out her magnifier and red pencil and the contact sheets of her quick-before-I-leave-the-city pictures. Most of them were a waste of film, as she'd suspected when taking them – she was never any good when she was rushing – but she found one that really excited her, a shot of a well-dressed young black man with an attache case, glaring venomously at an empty cab that had just passed him. If his expression enlarged well, and if she darkened the background to bring up the blurred cab, it could be an arresting picture – one she was sure the agency would be willing to handle. There were plenty of markets for pictures dramatizing racial tensions.

She red-pencilled an asterisk beside the print and went on looking for others that were good or at least part good but croppable. She remembered her vodka and tonic and sipped it.

At a quarter past eleven she was tired, so she put her things away in her side of the desk, put Walter's things back where they had been, turned the radio off, and brought her glass into the kitchen and rinsed it. She checked the doors, turned the lights off – except the one in the entrance hall – and went upstairs.

Kim's elephant was on the floor. She picked it up and tucked it under the blanket beside the pillow; then pulled the blanket up on to Kim's shoulders and fondled her ringlets very lightly.

Pete was on his back with his mouth open, exactly as he had been when she had checked before. She waited until she saw his chest move, then opened his door wider, switched the hall light off, and went into her and Walter's room.

She undressed, braided her hair, showered, rubbed in face cream, brushed her teeth, and got into bed.

Twenty to twelve. She turned the lamp off.

Lying on her back, she swung out her right leg and arm. She missed Walter beside her, but the expanse of cool-sheet smoothness was pleasant. How many times had she gone to bed alone since they were married? Not many: the nights he'd been out of town on Marburg-Donlevy business; the times she'd been in the hospital with Pete and Kim; the night of the power failure; when she'd gone home for Uncle Bert's funeral – maybe twenty or twenty-five times in all, in the ten years and a little more. It wasn't a bad feeling. By God, it made her feel like Joanna Ingalls again. Remember her?

She wondered if Walter was getting bombed. That was liquor on that truck that Gary Claybrook had been riding in (or had the cartons been too small for liquor?). But Walter had gone in Vic Stavros's car, so let him get bombed. Not that he really was likely to; he hardly ever did. What if Vic Stavros got bombed? The sharp curves on Norwood Road—

Oh nuts. Why worry?

The bed was shaking. She lay in the dark seeing the darker dark of the open bathroom door, and the glint of the dresser's handles, and the bed kept shaking her in a slow steady rhythm, each shake accompanied by a faint spring-squeak, again and again and again. It was Walter who was shaking! He had a fever! Or the dts? She spun around and leaned to him on one arm, staring, reaching to find his brow. His eye-whites looked at her and turned instantly away; all of him turned from her, and the tenting of the blanket at his groin was gone as she saw it, replaced by the shape of his hip. The bed became still.

He had been – masturbating?

She didn't know what to say.

She sat up.

'I thought you had the dts,' she said. 'Or a fever.'

He lay still. 'I didn't want to wake you,' he said. 'It's after two.'

She sat there and caught her breath.

He stayed on his side, not saying anything.

She looked at the room, its windows and furniture dim in the glow from the night light in Pete and Kim's bathroom. She fixed her braid down straight and rubbed her hand on her midriff.

'You could have,' she said, 'woken me. I wouldn't have minded.'

He didn't say anything.

'Gee whiz, you don't have to do *that*,' she said.

'I just didn't want to wake you,' he said. 'You were sound asleep.'

'Well, next time wake me.'

He came over on to his back. No tent.

'Did you?' she asked.

'*No*,' he said.

'Oh,' she said. 'Well' – and smiled at him – 'now I'm up.' She lay down beside him, turning to him, and held her arm out over him; and he turned to her and they embraced and kissed. He tasted of Scotch. 'I mean, consideration is fine,' she said in his ear, 'but Jesus.'

It turned out to be one of their best times ever – for her, at least.

'Wow,' she said, coming back from the bathroom, 'I'm still weak.'

He smiled at her, sitting in bed and smoking.

She got in with him and settled herself comfortably under his arm, drawing his hand down on to her breast. 'What did they do,' she said, 'show you dirty movies or something?'

He smiled. 'No such luck,' he said. He put his cigarette by her lips, and she took a puff of it. 'They took eight-fifty from me in poker,' he said, 'and they chewed my ear off about the Zoning Board's evil intentions re Eastbridge Road.'

'I was afraid you were getting bombed.'

'Me? Two Scotches. They're not heavy drinkers. What did *you* do?'

She told him, and about her hopes for the picture of the black man. He told her about some of the men he had met: the pediatrician the Van Sants and the Claybrooks had recommended, the magazine illustrator who was Stepford's major celebrity, two other lawyers, a psychiatrist, the Police Chief, the manager of the Centre Market.

'The psychiatrist should be in favour of letting women in,' she said.

'He is,' Walter said. 'And so is Dr Verry. I didn't sound out any of the others; I didn't want to come on as too much of an activist my first time there.'

'When are you going again?' she asked – and was suddenly afraid (why?) that he would say *tomorrow*.

'I don't know,' he said. 'Listen, I'm not going to make it a way of life the way Ted and Vic do. I'll go in a week or so, I guess; I don't know. It's kind of provincial really.'

She smiled and snuggled closer to him.

She was about a third of the way down the stairs, going by foot-feel, holding the damn laundry basket to her face because of the damn banister, when wouldn't you know it, the double-damn phone rang.

She couldn't put the basket down, it would fall, and there wasn't enough room to turn around with it and go back up; so she kept going slowly down, foot-feeling and thinking *Okay, okay* to the phone's answer-me-this-instant ringing.

She made it to the bottom, put the basket down, and stalked to the den desk.

'Hello,' she said – the way she felt, with no put-on graciousness.

'Hi, is this Joanna Eberhart?' The voice was loud, happy, raspy; Peggy Clavenger-ish. But Peggy Clavenger had been with *Paris-Match* the last she'd heard, and wouldn't even know she was married, let alone where she was living.

'Yes,' she said. 'Who's this?'

'We haven't been formally introduced,' the no-not-Peggy-Clavenger voice said, 'but I'm going to do it right now. Bobbie, I'd like you to meet Joanna Eberhart. Joanna, I'd like you to meet Bobbie Markowe – that's *KOWE*. Bobbie has been living here in Ajax Country for five weeks now, and she'd like very much to know an "avid shutterbug with a keen interest in politics and the Women's Lib movement". That's you, Joanna, according to what it says here

180

in the *Stepford Chronicle*. Or *Chronic Ill*, depending on your journalistic standards. Have they conveyed an accurate impression of you? Are you really not deeply concerned about whether pink soap pads are better than blue ones or vice versa? Does even the finest furniture polish fail to excite you? Hello? Are you still there, Joanna? Hello?'

'Hello,' Joanna said. 'Yes, I'm here. *And how* I'm here! Hello! Son of a gun, it pays to advertise!'

'What a pleasure to see a messy kitchen!' Bobbie said. 'It doesn't quite come up to mine – you don't have the little peanut-butter hand-prints on the cabinets – but it's good, it's very good. Congratulations.'

'I can show you some dull dingy bathrooms if you'd like,' Joanna said.

'Thanks. I'll just take the coffee.'

'Is instant okay?'

'You mean there's something else?'

She was short and heavy-bottomed, in a blue Snoopy sweatshirt and jeans and sandals. Her mouth was big, with unusually white teeth, and she had blue take-in-everything eyes and short dark tufty hair. And small hands and dirty toes. And a husband named Dave who was a stock analyst, and three sons, ten, eight, and six. And an Old English sheepdog and a corgi. She looked a bit younger than Joanna, thirty-two or -three. She drank two cups of coffee and ate a Ring Ding and told Joanna about the women of Fox Hollow Lane.

'I'm beginning to think there's a – nationwide contest I haven't heard about,' she said, tonguing her chocolated fingertips. 'A million dollars and – Paul Newman for the cleanest house by next Christmas. I *mean*, it's scrub, scrub, *scrub*; wax, wax, *wax*—'

'It's the same around here,' Joanna said. 'Even at night! And the men all—'

'The Men's Association!' Bobbie cried.

They talked about it – the antiquated sexist unfairness of it, the real *injustice*, in a town with no women's organization, not even a League of Women Voters. 'Believe me, I've combed this place,' Bobbie said. 'There's the Garden Club, and a few old-biddy church groups – for which I'm not eligible anyway; "Markowe" is upward-mobile for "Markowitz" – and there's the very non-sexist Historical Society. Drop in and say hello to them. Corpses in lifelike positions.'

Dave was in the Men's Association, and like Walter, thought it

181

could be changed from within. But Bobbie knew better: 'You'll see, we'll have to chain ourselves to the fence before we get any action. How *about* that fence? You'd think they were refining opium!'

They talked about the possibility of having a get-together with some of their neighbours, a rap session to wake them to the more active role they could play in the town's life; but they agreed that the women they had met seemed unlikely to welcome even so small a step towards liberation. They talked about the National Organization for Women, to which they both belonged, and about Joanna's photography.

'My God, these are *great*!' Bobbie said, looking at the four mounted enlargements Joanna had hung in the den. 'They're *terrific*!'

Joanna thanked her.

' "Avid shutterbug!" I thought that meant Polaroids of the kids! These are *marvellous*!'

'Now that Kim's in kindergarten I'm really going to get to work,' Joanna said.

She walked Bobbie to her car.

'Damn it, *no*,' Bobbie said. 'We ought to *try* at least. Let's talk to these hausfraus; there must be *some* of them who resent the situation a little. What do you say? Wouldn't it be great if we could get a group together – maybe even an NOW chapter eventually – and give that Men's Association a good shaking up? Dave and Walter are kidding themselves; it's not going to change unless it's *forced* to change; fat-cat organizations never do. What do you say, Joanna? Let's ask around.'

Joanna nodded. 'We should,' she said. 'They can't all be as content as they seem.'

She spoke to Carol Van Sant. 'Gee, no, Joanna,' Carol said. 'That doesn't sound like the sort of thing that would interest me. Thanks for ay-isking me though.' She was cleaning the plastic divider in Stacy and Allison's room, wiping a span of its accordion folds with firm downstrokes of a large yellow sponge.

'It would only be for a couple of hours,' Joanna said. 'In the evening, or if it's more convenient for everybody, sometime during school hours.'

Carol, crouching to wipe the lower part of the span, said, 'I'm sorry, but I just don't have much time for that sort of thing.'

Joanna watched for a moment. 'Doesn't it bother you,' she said, 'that the central organization here in Stepford, the *only* organization that does anything significant as far as community projects are concerned, is off limits to women? Doesn't that seem a little archaic to you?'

' "Ar-kay-ic?" ' Carol said, squeezing her sponge in a bucket of sudsy water.

Joanna looked at her. 'Out of date, old fashioned,' she said.

Carol squeezed the sponge out above the bucket. 'No, it doesn't seem archaic to me,' she said. She stood up straight and reached the sponge to the top of the next span of folds. 'Ted's better equipped for that sort of thing than I am,' she said, and began wiping the folds with firm downstrokes, each one neatly overlapping the one before. 'And men need a place where they can relax and have a drink or two,' she said.

'Don't women?'

'No, not as much,' Carol shook her neat red-haired shampoo-commercial head, not turning from her wiping. 'I'm sorry, Joanna,' she said, 'I just don't have time for a get-together.'

'Okay,' Joanna said. 'If you change your mind, let me know.'

'Would you mind if I don't walk you downstairs?'

'No, of course not.'

She spoke to Barbara Chamalian, on the other side of the Van Sants. 'Thanks, but I don't see how I could manage it,' Barbara said. She was a square-jawed brown-haired woman, in a snug pink dress moulding an exceptionally good figure. 'Lloyd stays in town a lot,' she said, 'and the evenings he doesn't, he likes to go to the Men's Association. I'd hate to pay a sitter for just—'

'It could be during school hours,' Joanna said.

'No,' Barbara said, 'I think you'd better count me out.' She smiled, widely and attractively. 'I'm glad we've met, though,' she said. 'Would you like to come in and sit for a while? I'm ironing.'

'No, thanks,' Joanna said. 'I want to speak to some of the other women.'

She spoke to Marge McCormick ('I honestly don't think I'd be interested in that') and Kit Sundersen ('I'm afraid I haven't the time; I'm really sorry, Mrs Eberhart') and Donna Claybrook ('That's a nice idea, but I'm so busy these days. Thanks for asking me, though').

She met Mary Ann Stavros in an aisle in the Centre Market. 'No, I don't think I'd have time for anything like that. There's so much to do around the house. You know.'

'But you go out *sometimes*, don't you?' Joanna said.

'Of course I do,' Mary Ann said. 'I'm out now, aren't I?'

'I mean *out*. For relaxation.'

Mary Ann smiled and shook her head, swaying her sheaves of straight blonde hair. 'No, not often,' she said. 'I don't feel much need for relaxation. See you.' And she went away, pushing her grocery cart; and stopped, took a can from a shelf, looked at it, and fitted it down into her cart and went on.

Joanna looked after her, and into the cart of another woman going slowly past her. *My God*, she thought, *they even fill their carts neatly!* She looked into her own: a jumble of boxes and cans and jars. A guilty impulse to put it in order prodded her; but *I'm damned if I will!* she thought, and grabbed a box from the shelf – Ivory Snow – and tossed it in. Didn't even need the damn stuff!

She spoke to the mother of one of Kim's classmates in Dr Verry's waiting-room; and to Yvonne Weisgalt, on the other side of the Stavroses; and to Jill Burke, in the next house over. All of them turned her down; they either had too little time or too little interest to meet with other women and talk about their shared experiences.

Bobbie had even worse luck, considering that she spoke to almost twice as many women. 'One taker,' she told Joanna. 'One eighty-five-year-old widow who dragged me through her door and kept me prisoner for a solid hour of close-up saliva spray. Any time we're ready to storm the Men's Association, Eda Mae Hamilton is ready and willing.'

'We'd better keep in touch with her,' Joanna said.

'Oh no, we're not done yet!'

They spent a morning calling on women together, on the theory (Bobbie's) that the two of them, speaking in planned ambiguities, might create the encouraging suggestion of a phalanx of women with room for one more. It didn't work.

'Jee-*zus*!' Bobbie said, ramming her car viciously up Short Ridge Hill. 'Something *fishy* is going on here! We're in the Town That Time Forgot!'

One afternoon Joanna left Pete and Kim in the care of sixteen-year-old Melinda Stavros and took the train into the city, where she met Walter and their friends Shep and Sylvia Tackover at an Italian restaurant in the theatre district. It was good to see Shep and Sylvia again; they were a bright, homely, energetic couple who had survived several bad blows, including the death by drowning of a four-year-old son. It was good to be in the city again too; Joanna relished the colour and bustle of the busy restaurant.

She and Walter spoke enthusiastically about Stepford's beauty and quiet, and the advantages of living in a house rather than an apartment. She didn't say anything about how home-centred the Stepford women were, or about the absence of outside-the-home activities. It was vanity, she supposed; an unwillingness to make herself the object of commiseration, even Shep and Sylvia's. She told them about Bobbie and how amusing she was, and about Stepford's fine uncrowded schools. Walter didn't bring up the Men's Association and neither did she. Sylvia, who was with the city's Housing and Development Administration, would have had a fit.

But on the way to the theatre Sylvia gave her a sharp appraising look and said, 'A tough adjustment?'

'In ways,' she said.

'You'll make it,' Sylvia said, and smiled at her. 'How's the photography? It must be great for you up there, coming to everything with a fresh eye.'

'I haven't done a damn thing,' she said. 'Bobbie and I have been running around trying to drum up some Women's Lib activity. It's a bit of a backwater, to tell the truth.'

'Running and drumming isn't your work,' Sylvia said. 'Photography is, or ought to be.'

'I know,' she said. 'I've got a plumber coming in any day now to put in the darkroom sink.'

'Walter looks chipper.'

'He is. It's a good life really.'

The play, a musical hit of the previous season, was disappointing. In the train going home, after they had hashed it over for a few minutes, Walter put on his glasses and got out some paper work, and Joanna skimmed *Time* and then sat looking out the window and smoking, watching the darkness and the occasional lights riding through it.

Sylvia was right; photography was her work. To hell with the Stepford women. Except Bobbie, of course.

Both cars were at the station, so they had to ride home separately. Joanna went first in the station wagon and Walter followed her in the Toyota. The Centre was empty and stage-setty under its three streetlights – yes, she would take pictures there, *before* the darkroom was finished – and there were headlights and lighted windows up at the Men's Association house, and a car waiting to pull out of its driveway.

Melinda Stavros was yawning but smiling, and Pete and Kim were in their beds sound asleep.

In the family-room there were empty milk glasses and plates on the lamp table, and crumpled balls of white paper on the sofa and the floor before it, and an empty ginger-ale bottle on the floor among the balls of paper.

At least they don't pass it on to their daughters, Joanna thought.

The third time Walter went to the Men's Association he called at about nine o'clock and told Joanna he was bringing home the New Projects Committee, to which he had been appointed the time before. Some construction work was being done at the house (she could hear the whine of machinery in the background) and they couldn't find a quiet place where they could sit and talk.

'Fine,' she said. 'I'm getting the rest of the junk out of the dark-room, so you can have the whole—'

'No, listen,' he said, 'stay upstairs with us and get into the conversation. A couple of them are die-hard men-only's; it won't do them any harm to hear a woman make intelligent comments. I'm assuming you will.'

'Thanks. Won't they object?'

'It's our house.'

'Are you sure you're not looking for a waitress?'

He laughed. 'Oh God, there's no fooling her,' he said. 'Okay, you got me. But an intelligent waitress, all right? Would you? It really might do some good.'

'Okay,' she said. 'Give me fifteen minutes and I'll even be an intelligent *beautiful* waitress; how's that for cooperation?'

'Fantastic. Unbelievable.'

There were five of them, and one, a cheery little red-faced man of about sixty, with toothpick-ends of waxed moustache, was Ike Mazzard, the magazine illustrator. Joanna, shaking his hand warmly, said, 'I'm not sure I like you; you blighted my adolescence with those dream girls of yours!' And he, chuckling, said, 'You must have matched up pretty well.'

'Would you like to bet on that?' she said.

The other four were all late-thirties or early-forties. The tall black-haired one, laxly arrogant, was Dale Coba, the president of the association. He smiled at her with green eyes that disparaged her, and said, 'Hello, Joanna, it's a pleasure.' *One of the die-hard men-only's*, she thought; *women are to lay*. His hand was smooth, without pressure.

The others were Anselm or Axhelm, Sundersen, Roddenberry. 'I met your wife,' she said to Sundersen, who was pale and paunchy, nervous-seeming. 'If you're the Sundersen across the way, that is.'

'You did? We are, yes. We're the only ones in Stepford.'

'I invited her to a get-together, but she couldn't make it.'

'She's not very social.' Sundersen's eyes looked elsewhere, not at her.

'I'm sorry, I missed your first name,' she said.

'Herb,' he said, looking elsewhere.

She saw them all into the living-room and went into the kitchen for ice and soda, and brought them to Walter at the bar cabinet. 'Intelligent? Beautiful?' she said, and he grinned at her. She went back into the kitchen and filled bowls with potato crisps and peanuts.

There were no objections from the circle of men when, holding her glass, she said 'May I?' and eased into the sofa-end Walter had saved for her. Ike Mazzard and Anselm-or-Axhelm rose, and the others made I'm-thinking-of-rising movements – except Dale Coba, who sat eating peanuts out of his fist, looking across the cocktail table at her with his disparaging green eyes.

They talked about the Christmas-Toys project and the Preserve-the-Landscape project. Roddenberry's name was Frank, and he had a pleasant pug-nosed blue-chinned face and a slight stutter; and Coba had a nickname – Diz, which hardly seemed to fit him. They talked about whether this year there shouldn't be Chanukah lights as well as a creche in the Centre, now that there were a fair number of Jews in town. They talked about ideas for new projects.

'May I say something?' she said.

'Sure,' Frank Roddenberry and Herb Sundersen said. Coba was lying back in his chair looking at the ceiling (disparagingly, no doubt), his hands behind his head, his legs extended.

'Do you think there might be a chance of setting up some evening lectures for adults?' she asked. 'Or parent-and-teenager forums? In one of the school auditoriums?'

'On what subject?' Frank Roddenberry asked.

'On any subject there's general interest in,' she said. 'The drug thing, which we're all concerned about but which the *Chronicle* seems to sweep under the rug; what rock music is all about – I don't know, *anything* that would get people out and listening and talking to each other.'

'That's *interesting*,' Claude Anselm-or-Axhelm said, leaning forward and crossing his legs, scratching at his temple. He was thin and blond; bright-eyed, restless.

'And maybe it would get the *women* out too,' she said. 'In case you don't know it, this town is a disaster area for baby-sitters.'

Everyone laughed, and she felt good and at ease. She offered other possible forum topics, and Walter added a few, and so did Herb Sundersen. Other new-project ideas were brought up; she took part in the talk about them, and the men (except Coba, damn him) paid close attention to her – Ike Mazzard, Frank, Walter, Claude, even Herb looked right at her – and they nodded and agreed with her, or thoughtfully questioned her, and she felt very good indeed, meeting their questions with wit and good sense. *Move over, Gloria Steinem!*

She saw, to her surprise and embarrassment, that Ike Mazzard was sketching her. Sitting in his chair (next to still-watching-the-ceiling Dale Coba), he was pecking with a blue pen at a notebook on his dapper-striped knee, looking at her and looking at his pecking.

Ike Mazzard! Sketching *her*!

The men had fallen silent. They looked into their drinks, swirled their ice cubes.

'Hey,' she said, shifting uncomfortably and smiling, 'I'm no Ike Mazzard girl.'

'Every girl's an Ike Mazzard girl,' Mazzard said, and smiled at her and smiled at his pecking.

She looked to Walter; he smiled embarrassedly and shrugged.

She looked at Mazzard again, and – not moving her head – at the other men. They looked at her and smiled, edgily. 'Well *this* is a conversation killer,' she said.

'Relax, you can move,' Mazzard said. He turned a page and pecked again.

Frank said, 'I don't think another b-baseball field is all that important.'

She heard Kim cry 'Mommy!' but Walter touched her arm, and putting his glass down, got up and excused himself past Claude.

The men talked about new projects again. She said a word or two, moving her head but aware all the time of Mazzard looking at her and pecking. Try being Gloria Steinem when Ike Mazzard is drawing you! It was a bit show-offy of him; she wasn't any once-in-a-lifetime-mustn't-be-missed, not even in the Pucci loungers. And what were the *men* so tense about? Their talking seemed forced and gap-ridden. Herb Sundersen was actually blushing.

She felt suddenly as if she were naked, as if Mazzard were drawing her in obscene poses.

She crossed her legs; wanted to cross her arms too but didn't. *Jesus, Joanna, he's a show-offy artist, that's all. You're dressed.*

Walter came back and leaned down to her. 'Just a bad dream,' he said; and straightening, to the men, 'Anyone want a refill? Diz? Frank?'

'I'll take a small one,' Mazzard said, looking at her, pecking.

'Bathroom down that way?' Herb asked, getting up.

The talking went on, more relaxed and casual now.

New projects.

Old projects.

Mazzard tucked his pen into his jacket, smiling.

She said 'Whew!' and fanned herself.

Coba raised his head, keeping his hands behind it, and chin-against-chest looked at the notebook on Mazzard's knee. Mazzard turned pages, looking at Coba, and Coba nodded and said, 'You never cease to amaze me.'

'Do I get to see?' she asked.

'Of course!' Mazzard said, and half rose, smiling, holding out the open notebook to her.

Walter looked too, and Frank leaned in to see.

Portraits of her; there were page after page of them, small and precise – and flattering, as Ike Mazzard's work had always been. Full faces, three-quarter views, profiles; smiling, not smiling, talking, frowning.

'These are *beautiful*,' Walter said, and Frank said, 'Great, Ike!' Claude and Herb came around behind the sofa.

She leafed back through the pages. 'They're – wonderful,' she said. 'I wish I could say they were absolutely accurate—'

'But they *are*!' Mazzard said.

'God bless you.' She gave the notebook to him, and he put it on his knee and turned its pages, getting out his pen. He wrote on a page, and tore it out and offered it to her.

It was one of the three-quarter views, a non-smiling one, with the familiar no-capitals *ike mazzard* signature. She showed it to Walter; he said, 'Thanks, Ike.'

'My pleasure.'

She smiled at Mazzard. 'Thank you,' she said. 'I forgive you for blighting my adolescence.' She smiled at all of them. 'Does anyone want coffee?'

They all did, except Claude, who wanted tea.

She went into the kitchen and put the drawing on the place mats on top of the refrigerator. An Ike Mazzard drawing of *her*! Who'da thought it, back home when she was eleven or twelve, reading Mom's *Journals* and *Companions*? It was foolish of her to have gotten so up-tight about it. Mazzard had been nice to do it.

Smiling, she ran water into the coffee-maker, plugged it in, and put in the basket and spooned in coffee. She put the top on, pressed the plastic lid down on to the coffee can, and turned around. Coba leaned in the doorway watching her, his arms folded, his shoulder to the jamb.

Very cool in his jade turtleneck (matching his eyes, of course) and slate-grey corduroy suit.

He smiled at her and said, 'I like to watch women doing little domestic chores.'

'You came to the right town,' she said. She tossed the spoon into the sink and took the coffee can to the refrigerator and put it in.

Coba stayed there, watching her.

She wished Walter would come. 'You don't seem particularly dizzy,' she said, getting out a saucepan for Claude's tea. 'Why do they call you Diz?'

'I used to work at Disneyland,' he said.

She laughed, going to the sink. 'No, really,' she said.

'That's really.'

She turned around and looked at him.

'Don't believe me?' he asked.

'No,' she said.

'Why not?'

She thought, and knew.

'Why not?' he said. 'Tell me.'

To hell with him; she would. 'You don't look like someone who enjoys making people happy.'

Torpedoing forever, no doubt, the admission of women to the hallowed and sacrosanct Men's Association.

Coba looked at her – disparagingly. 'How little you know,' he said.

And smiled and got off the jamb, and turned and walked away.

'I'm not so keen on El Presidente,' she said, undressing, and Walter said, 'Neither am I. He's cold as ice. But he won't be in office forever.'

'He'd better not be,' she said, 'or women'll never get in. When are elections?'

'Right after the first of the year.'

'What does he do?'

'He's with Burnham-Massey, on Route Nine. So is Claude.'

'Oh listen, what's his last name?'

'Claude's? Axhelm.'

Kim began crying, and was burning hot; and they were up till after three, taking her temperature (a hundred and three at first), reading Dr Spock, calling Dr Verry, and giving her cool baths and alcohol rubs.

Bobbie found a live one. 'At least she is compared to the rest of these clunks,' her voice rasped from the phone. 'Her name is Charmaine Wimperis, and if you squint a little she turns into Raquel Welch. They're up on Burgess Ridge in a two-hundred-thousand-dollar contemporary, and she's got a maid and a gardener and – now hear this – a tennis court.'

'*Really?*'

'I thought that would get you out of the cellar. You're invited to play, and for lunch too. I'll pick you up around eleven-thirty.'

'Today? I can't! Kim is still home.'

'*Still?*'

'Could we make it Wednesday? Or Thursday, just to be safe.'

'*Wednesday*,' Bobbie said. 'I'll check with her and call you back.'

Wham! Pow! Slam! Charmaine was good, *too* goddamn good; the ball came zinging straight and hard, first to one side of the court and then to the other; it kept her racing from side to side and then drove her all the way back – a just-inside-the-liner that she barely caught. She ran in after it, but Charmaine smashed it down into the left net corner – ungettable – and took the game and the set, six-three. After taking the first set six-two. 'Oh God, I've had it!' Joanna said. 'What a fiasco! *Oh boy!*'

'One more!' Charmaine called, backing to the serve line. 'Come on, one more!'

'I can't! I'm not going to be able to walk tomorrow as it is!' She picked up the ball. 'Come on, Bobbie, you play!'

Bobbie, sitting cross-legged on the grass outside the mesh fence, her face trayed on a sun reflector, said, 'I haven't played since *camp*, for Chrisake.'

'Just a game then!' Charmaine called. 'One more game, Joanna!'

'All right, one more game!'

Charmaine won it.

'You killed me but it was great!' Joanna said as they walked off the court together. 'Thank you!'

Charmaine, patting her high-boned cheeks carefully with an end of her towel, said, 'You just have to get back in practice, that's all. You have a first-rate serve.'

'Fat lot of good it did me.'

'Will you play often? All I've got now are a couple of teen-age boys, both with permanent erections.'

Bobbie said, 'Send them to my place' – getting up from the ground.

They walked up the flagstone path towards the house.

'It's a terrific court,' Joanna said, towelling her arm.

'Then *use* it,' Charmaine said. 'I used to play every day with Ginnie Fisher – do you know her? – but she flaked out on me. Don't *you*, will you? How about tomorrow?'

'Oh I couldn't!'

They sat on a terrace under a Cinzano umbrella, and the maid, a slight grey-haired woman named Nettie, brought them a pitcher of Bloody Marys and a bowl of cucumber dip and crackers. 'She's marvellous,' Charmaine said. 'A German Virgo; if I told her to lick my shoes she'd do it. What are you, Joanna?'

'An American Taurus.'

'If you tell her to lick your shoes she spits in your eye,' Bobbie said. 'You don't really believe that stuff, do you?'

'I certainly do,' Charmaine said, pouring Bloody Marys. 'You would too if you came to it with an open mind.' (Joanna squinted at her: no, not Raquel Welch, but darn close.) 'That's why Ginnie Fisher flaked out on me,' she said. 'She's a Gemini; they change all the time. Taureans are stable and dependable. Here's to tennis galore.'

Joanna said, 'This particular Taurean has a house and two kids and no German Virgo.'

Charmaine had one child, a nine-year-old son named Merrill. Her husband Ed was a television producer. They had moved to Stepford in July. Yes, Ed was in the Men's Association, and no, Charmaine wasn't bothered by the sexist injustice. 'Anything that gets him out of the house nights is fine with me,' she said. 'He's Aries and I'm Scorpio.'

'Oh *well*,' Bobbie said, and put a dip-loaded cracker into her mouth.

'It's a very bad combination,' Charmaine said. 'If I knew then what I know now.'

'Bad in what way?' Joanna asked.

Which was a mistake. Charmaine told them at length about her and Ed's manifold incompatibilities – social, emotional and, above all, sexual. Nettie served them lobster Newburg and julienne potatoes – 'Oi, my hips,' Bobbie said, spooning lobster on to her plate – and Charmaine went on in candid detail. Ed was a sex fiend and a real weirdo. 'He had this *rubber suit* made for me, at God knows what cost, in England. I ask you, *rubber*? "Put it on one of your secretaries," I said, "you're not going to get *me* into it." Zippers and padlocks all over. You can't lock up a Scorpio. Virgos, any time; their thing is to serve. But a Scorpio's thing is to go his own way.'

'If *Ed* knew then what you know now,' Joanna said.

'It wouldn't have made the least bit of difference,' Charmaine said. 'He's crazy about me. Typical Aries.'

Nettie brought raspberry tarts and coffee. Bobbie groaned. Charmaine told them about other weirdos she had known. She had been a model and had known several.

She walked them to Bobbie's car. 'Now look,' she said to Joanna, 'I know you're busy, but any time you have a free hour, *any* time, just come on over. You don't even have to call; I'm almost always here.'

'Thanks, I will,' Joanna said. 'And thanks for today. It was great.'

'*Any* time,' Charmaine said. She leaned to the window. 'And look, both of you,' she said, 'would you do me a favour? Would you read *Linda Goodman's Sun Signs*? Just read it and see how right she is. They've got it in the Centre Pharmacy, in paperback. Will you? Please?'

They gave in, smiling, and promised they would.

'*Ciao!*' she called, waving to them as they drove away.

'Well,' Bobbie said, rounding the curve of the driveway, 'she may not be ideal N O W material, but at least she's not in love with her vacuum cleaner.'

'My God, she's beautiful,' Joanna said.

'Isn't she? Even for these parts, where you've got to admit they *look* good even if they don't think good. Boy, what a marriage! How about that business with the suit? And I thought *Dave* had spooky ideas!'

'Dave?' Joanna said, looking at her.

Bobbie side-flashed a smile. 'You're not going to get any true confessions out of *me*,' she said. 'I'm a Leo, and our thing is changing the subject. You and Walter want to go to a movie Saturday night?'

They had bought the house from a couple named Pilgrim, who had lived in it for only two months and had moved to Canada. The Pilgrims had bought it from a Mrs McGrath, who had bought it from the builder eleven years before. So most of the junk in the storage room had been left by Mrs McGrath. Actually it wasn't fair to call it junk: there were two good Colonial side chairs that Walter was going to strip and refinish some day; there was a complete twenty-volume *Book of Knowledge*, now on the shelves in Pete's room; and there were boxes and small bundles of hardware and oddments that, though not finds, at least seemed likely to be of eventual use. Mrs McGrath had been a thoughtful saver.

Joanna had transferred most of the not-really-junk to a far corner of the cellar before the plumber had installed the sink, and now she was moving the last of it – cans of paint and bundles of asbestos roof shingles – while Walter hammered at a plywood counter and Pete handed him nails. Kim had gone with the Van Sant girls and Carol to the Library.

Joanna unrolled a packet of yellowed newspaper and found inside it an inch-wide paintbrush, its clean bristles slightly stiff but still pliable. She began rolling it back into the paper, a half page of the *Chronicle*, and the words *WOMEN'S CLUB* caught her eye. *HEARS AUTHOR*. She turned the paper to the side and looked at it.

'For God's sake,' she said.

Pete looked at her, and Walter, hammering, said, 'What is it?'

She got the brush out of the paper and put it down, and held the half page open with both hands, reading.

Walter stopped hammering and turned and looked at her. 'What is it?' he asked.

She read for another moment, and looked at him; and looked at the paper, and at him. 'There was – a *women's* club here,' she said.

'Betty Friedan spoke to them. And *Kit Sundersen* was the president. Dale Coba's wife and Frank Roddenberry's wife were officers.'

'Are you kidding?' he said.

She looked at the paper, and read: ' "Betty Friedan, the author of *The Feminine Mystique*, addressed members of the Stepford Women's Club Tuesday evening in the Fairview Lane home of Mrs Herbert Sundersen, the club's president. Over fifty women applauded Mrs Friedan as she cited the inequities and frustrations besetting the modern-day housewife . . ." ' She looked at him.

'Can I do some?' Pete asked.

Walter handed the hammer to him. 'When *was* that?' he asked her.

She looked at the paper. 'It doesn't say, it's the bottom half,' she said. 'There's a picture of the officers. "Mrs Steven Margolies, Mrs Dale Coba, author Betty Friedan, Mrs Herbert Sundersen, Mrs Frank Roddenberry, and Mrs Duane T. Anderson." ' She opened the half page towards him, and he came to her and took a side of it. 'If this doesn't beat everything,' he said, looking at the picture and the article.

'I *spoke* to Kit Sundersen,' she said. 'She didn't say a *word* about it. She didn't have time for a get-together. Like all the others.'

'This must have been six or seven years ago,' he said, fingering the edge of the yellowed paper.

'Or more,' she said. 'The *Mystique* came out while I was still working. Andreas gave me his review copy, remember?'

He nodded, and turned to Pete, who was hammering vigorously at the counter top. 'Hey, take it easy,' he said, 'you'll make half moons.' He turned back to the paper. 'Isn't this something?' he said. 'It must have just petered out.'

'With fifty members?' she said. '*Over* fifty? Applauding Friedan, not hissing her?'

'Well, it's not here now, is it?' he said, letting the paper go. 'Unless they've got the world's worst publicity chairman. I'll ask Herb what happened next time I see him.' He went back to Pete. 'Say, that's good work,' he said.

She looked at the paper and shook her head. 'I can't believe it,' she said. 'Who were the women? They can't all have moved away.'

'Come on now,' Walter said, 'you haven't spoken to every woman in town.'

'Bobbie has, darn near,' she said. She took the paper, and folded it, and put it on the carton of her equipment. The paintbrush was there; she picked it up. 'Need a paintbrush?' she said.

Walter turned and looked at her. 'You don't expect me to *paint* these things do you?' he asked.

'No, no,' she said. 'It was wrapped in the paper.'

'Oh,' he said, and turned to the counter.

She put the brush down, and crouched and gathered a few loose shingles. 'How could she not have mentioned it?' she said. 'She was the *president*.'

As soon as Bobbie and Dave got into the car, she told them.

'Are you sure it's not one of those newspapers they print in penny arcades?' Bobbie said. ' "Fred Smith Lays Elizabeth Taylor"?'

'It's the *Chronic Ill*,' Joanna said. 'The bottom half of the front page. Here, if you can see.'

She handed it back to them, and they unfolded it between them. Walter turned on the top light.

Dave said, 'You could have made a lot of money by betting me and *then* showing me.'

'Didn't think,' she said.

' "Over fifty women"!' Bobbie said. 'Who the hell were they? What happened?'

'That's what *I* want to know,' she said. 'And why Kit Sundersen didn't mention it to me. I'm going to speak to her tomorrow.'

They drove into Eastbridge and stood in line for the nine o'clock showing of an X-rated English movie. The couples in the line were cheerful and talkative, laughing in clusters of four and six, looking to the end of the line, waving at other couples. None of them looked familiar except an elderly couple Bobbie recognized from the Historical Society; and the seventeen-year-old McCormick boy and a date, holding hands solemnly, trying to look eighteen.

The movie, they agreed, was 'bloody good', and after it they drove back to Bobbie and Dave's house, which was chaotic, the boys still up and the sheepdog galumphing all over. When Bobbie and Dave had got rid of the sitter and the boys and the sheepdog, they had coffee and cheesecake in the tornado-struck living-room.

'I *knew* I wasn't uniquely irresistible,' Joanna said, looking at an Ike Mazzard drawing of Bobbie tucked in the frame of the over-the-mantel picture.

'Every girl's an Ike Mazzard girl, didn't you know?' Bobbie said, tucking the drawing more securely into the frame's corner, making the picture more crooked than it already was. 'Boy, I wish I looked *half* this good.'

'You're fine the way you are,' Dave said, standing behind them.

'Isn't he a doll?' Bobbie said to Joanna. She turned and kissed Dave's cheek. 'It's *still* your Sunday to get up early,' she said.

'Joanna Eberhart,' Kit Sundersen said, and smiled. 'How are you? Would you like to come in?'

'Yes, I would,' Joanna said, 'if you have a few minutes.'

'Of course I do, come on in,' Kit said. She was a pretty woman, black-haired and dimple-cheeked, and only slightly older looking than in the *Chronicle's* unflattering photo. About thirty-three, Joanna guessed, going into the entrance hall. Its ivory vinyl floor looked as if one of those plastic shields in the commercials had just floated down on to it. Sounds of a baseball game came from the living-room.

'Herb is inside with Gary Claybrook,' Kit said, closing the front door. 'Do you want to say hello to them?'

Joanna went to the living-room archway and looked in: Herb and Gary were sitting on a sofa watching a large colour TV across the room. Gary was holding half a sandwich and chewing. A plate of sandwiches and two cans of beer stood on a cobbler's bench before them. The room was beige and brown and green; Colonial, immaculate. Joanna waited till a retreating ballplayer caught the ball, and said, 'Hi.'

Herb and Gary turned and smiled. 'Hello, Joanna,' they said, and Gary said, 'How are you?' Herb said, 'Is Walter here too?'

'Fine. No, he isn't,' she said. 'I just came over to talk with Kit. Good game?'

Herb looked away from her and Gary said, 'Very.'

Kit, beside her and smelling of Walter's mother's perfume, whatever it was, said, 'Come, let's go into the kitchen.'

'Enjoy,' she said to Herb and Gary. Gary, biting into his sandwich, eye-smiled through his glasses, and Herb looked at her and said, 'Thanks, we will.'

She followed Kit over the plastic-shield vinyl.

'Would you like a cup of coffee?' Kit asked.

'No, thanks.' She followed Kit into the coffee-smelling kitchen. It was immaculate, of course – except for the open dryer, and the clothes and the laundry basket on the counter on top of it. The washer's round port was storming. The floor was more plastic shield.

'It's right on the stove,' Kit said, 'so it wouldn't be any trouble.'

'Well, in that case . . .'

She sat at a round green table while Kit got a cup and saucer from a neatly filled cabinet, cups all hook-hung, the plates filed in racks. 'It's nice and quiet now,' Kit said, closing the cabinet and going towards the stove. (Her figure, in a short sky-blue dress, was almost as terrific as Charmaine's.) 'The kids are over at Gary and Donna's,' she said. 'I'm doing Marge McCormick's wash. She's got a bug of some kind and can barely move today.'

'Oh, that's a shame,' Joanna said.

Kit finger-tipped the top of a percolator and poured coffee from it. 'I'm sure she'll be good as new in a day or two,' she said. 'How do you take this, Joanna?'

'Milk, no sugar, please.'

Kit carried the cup and saucer towards the refrigerator. 'If it's about that get-together again,' she said, 'I'm afraid I'm still awfully busy.'

'It isn't that,' Joanna said. She watched Kit open the refrigerator. 'I wanted to find out what happened to the Women's Club,' she said.

Kit stood at the lighted refrigerator, her back to Joanna. 'The Women's Club?' she said. 'Oh my, that was years ago. It disbanded.'

'Why?' Joanna asked.

Kit closed the refrigerator and opened a drawer beside it. 'Some of the women moved away,' she said – she closed the drawer and turned, putting a spoon on the saucer – 'and the rest of us just lost interest in it. At least I did.' She came towards the table, watching the cup. 'It wasn't accomplishing anything useful,' she said. 'The meetings got boring after a while.' She put the cup and saucer on the table and pushed them closer to Joanna. 'Is that enough milk?' she asked.

'Yes, that's fine,' Joanna said. 'Thanks. How come you didn't tell me about it when I was here the other time?'

Kit smiled, her dimples deepening. 'You didn't ask me,' she said. 'If you had I would have told you. It's no secret. Would you like a piece of cake, or some cookies?'

'No, thanks,' Joanna said.

'I'm going to fold these things,' Kit said, going from the table.

Joanna watched her close the dryer and take something white from the pile of clothes on it. She shook it out – a T shirt. Joanna said, 'What's wrong with *Bill* McCormick? Can't *he* run a washer? I thought he was one of our aerospace brains.'

'He's taking care of Marge,' Kit said, folding the T shirt. 'These things came out nice and white, didn't they?' She put the folded T shirt into the laundry basket, smiling.

Like an actress in a commercial.

That's what she was, Joanna felt suddenly. That's what they *all* were, all the Stepford wives: actresses in commercials, pleased with detergents and floor wax, with cleansers, shampoos, and deodorants. Pretty actresses, big in the bosom but small in the talent, playing suburban housewives unconvincingly, too nicey-nice to be real.

'Kit,' she said.

Kit looked at her.

'You must have been very young when you were president of the club,' Joanna said. 'Which means you're intelligent and have a certain amount of drive. Are you happy now? Tell me the truth. Do you feel you're living a full life?'

Kit looked at her, and nodded. 'Yes, I'm happy,' she said. 'I feel I'm living a very full life. Herb's work is important, and he couldn't do it nearly as well if not for me. We're a unit, and between us we're raising a family, and doing optical research, and running a clean comfortable household, and doing community work.'

'Through the Men's Association.'

'Yes.'

Joanna said, 'Were the Women's Club meetings more boring than housework?'

Kit frowned. 'No,' she said, 'but they weren't as useful as housework. You're not drinking your coffee. Is anything wrong with it?'

'No,' Joanna said, 'I was waiting for it to cool.' She picked up the cup.

'Oh,' Kit said, and smiled, and turned to the clothes and folded something.

Joanna watched her. Should she ask who the other women had been? No, they would be like Kit; and what difference would it make? She drank from the cup. The coffee was strong and rich-flavoured, the best she'd tasted in a long time.

'How are your children?' Kit asked.

'Fine,' she said.

She started to ask the brand of the coffee, but stopped herself and drank more of it.

Maybe the Hardware Store's panes would have wobbled the moon's reflection interestingly, but there was no way of telling, not with the panes where *they* were and the moon where *it* was. *C'est la vie.* She mooched around the Centre for a while, getting the feel of the night-empty curve of street, the row of white shopfronts on one side, the rise to the hill on the other; the Library, the Historical Society cottage. She wasted some film on streetlights and litter baskets – cliche time – but it was only black-and-white so what the hell. A cat trotted down the path from the Library, a silver-grey cat with a black moon-shadow stuck to its paws; it crossed the street towards the market parking lot. No thanks, we're not keen on cat pix.

She set up the tripod on the Library lawn and took shots of the shopfronts, using the fifty-millimetre lens and making ten-, twelve-, and fourteen-second exposures. An odd medicinal smell soured the air – coming on the breeze at her back. It almost reminded her of something in her childhood, but fell short. A syrup she'd been given? A toy she had had?

She reloaded by moonlight, gathered the tripod, and backed across the street, scouting the Library for a good angle. She found one and set up. The white clapboard siding was black-banded in the overhead moonlight; the windows showing book-shelved walls lighted faintly from within. She focused with extra-special care, and starting at eight seconds, took each-a-second – longer exposures up to eighteen. One of them, at least, would catch the inside book-shelved walls without over-exposing the siding.

She went to the car for her sweater, and looked around as she went back to the camera. The Historical Society cottage? No, it was too tree-shadowed, and dull anyway. But the Men's Association house, up on the hill, had a surprisingly comic look to it: a square old nineteenth-century house, solid and symmetrical, tipsily parasolled by a glistening TV antenna. The four tall upstairs windows were vividly alight, their sashes raised. Figures moved inside.

She took the fifty-millimetre lens out of the camera and was putting in the one-thirty-five when headlight beams swept on to the street and grew brighter. She turned and a spotlight blinded her. Closing her eyes, she tightened the lens; then shielded her eyes and squinted.

The car stopped, and the spotlight swung away and died to an orange spark. She blinked a few times, still seeing the blinding radiance.

A police car. It stayed where it was, about thirty feet away from her on the other side of the street. A man's voice spoke softly inside it; spoke and kept speaking.

She waited.

The car moved forward, coming opposite her, and stopped. The young policeman with the unpolicemanlike brown moustache smiled at her and said, 'Evening, ma'am.' She had seen him several times, once in the stationery store buying packs of coloured crepe paper, one each of every colour they had.

'Hello,' she said, smiling.

He was alone in the car; he must have been talking on his radio. About her? 'I'm sorry I hit you with the spot that way,' he said. 'Is that your car there by the post office?'

'Yes,' she said. 'I didn't park it here because I was—'

'That's all right, I'm just checking.' He squinted at the camera. 'That's a good-looking camera,' he said. 'What kind is it?'

'A Pentax,' she said.

'Pentax,' he said. He looked at the camera, and at her. 'And you can take pictures at night with it?'

'Time exposures,' she said.

'Oh, sure,' he said. 'How long does it take on a night like this?'

'Well, that depends,' she said.

He wanted to know on what, and what kind of film she was using. And whether she was a professional photographer, and how much a Pentax cost, just roughly. And how it stacked up against other cameras.

She tried not to grow impatient; she should be glad she lived in a town where a policeman could stop and talk for a few minutes.

Finally he smiled and said, 'Well, I guess I'd better let you go ahead with it. Goodnight.'

'Goodnight,' she said, smiling.

He drove off slowly. The silver-grey cat ran through his headlight beams.

She watched the car for a moment, and then turned to the camera and checked the lens. Crouching to the viewfinder, she levered into a good framing of the Men's Association house and locked the tripod head. She focused, sharpening the finder's image of the high square tipsy-antenna'd house. Two of its upstairs windows were dark now; and another was shade-pulled down to darkness, and then the last one.

She straightened and looked at the house itself, and turned to the police car's faraway tail lights.

He had radio'd a message about her, and then he had stalled her with his questions while the message was acted on, the shades pulled down.

Oh come on, girl, you're getting nutty! She looked at the house again. They wouldn't have a radio up there. And what would he have been afraid she'd photograph? An orgy in progress? Call-girls from the city? (Or better yet, from right there in Stepford.) *ENLARGER REVEALS SHOCKING SECRET. Seemingly diligent housewives, conveniently holding still for lengthy time exposures, were caught Sunday night disporting at the Men's Association house by photographer Joanna Drew Eberhart of Fairview Lane . . .*

Smiling, she crouched to the viewfinder, bettered her framing and focus, and took three shots of the dark-windowed house – ten seconds, twelve, and fourteen.

She took shots of the post office, and of its bare flag-pole silhouetted against moonlit clouds.

She was putting the tripod into the car when the police car came by and slowed. 'Hope they all come out!' the young policeman called.

'Thanks!' she called back to him. 'I enjoyed talking!' To make up for her city-bred suspiciousness.

A senior partner in Walter's firm died of uraemic poisoning, and the records of the trusts he had administered were found to be disquietingly inaccurate. Walter had to stay two nights and a weekend in the city, and on the nights following he seldom got home before eleven o'clock. Pete took a fall on the school bus and knocked out his two front teeth. Joanna's parents paid a short-notice three-day visit on their way to a Caribbean vacation. (They loved the house and Stepford, and Joanna's mother admired Carol Van Sant. 'So serene and efficient! Take a leaf from *her* book, Joanna.')

The dishwasher broke down, and the pump; and Pete's eighth birthday came, calling for presents, a party, favours, a cake. Kim got a sore throat and was home for three days. Joanna's period was late but came, thank God and the Pill.

She managed to get in a little tennis, her game improving but still not as good as Charmaine's. She got the darkroom three-quarters set up and made trial enlargements of the black-man-and-taxi picture, and developed and printed the ones she had taken in the Centre, two of which looked very good. She took shots of Pete and Kim and Scott Chamalian playing on the climbing frame.

She saw Bobbie almost every day; they shopped together, and sometimes Bobbie brought her two younger boys Adam and Kenny over after school. One day Joanna and Bobbie and Charmaine got dressed to the nines and had a two-cocktail lunch at a French restaurant in Eastbridge.

By the end of October, Walter was getting home for dinner again, the dead partner's peculations having been unravelled, made good, and patched over. Everything in the house was working, everyone was well. They carved a huge pumpkin for Hallowe'en, and Pete went trick-or-treating as a front-toothless Batman, and Kim as Heckel or Jeckel (she was both she insisted). Joanna gave out fifty bags of candy and had to fall back on fruit and cookies; next year she would know better.

On the first Saturday in November they gave a dinner party: Bobbie and Dave, Charmaine and her husband Ed; and from the city, Shep and Sylvia Tackover, and Don Ferrault - one of Walter's partners - and his wife Lucy. The local woman Joanna got to help serve and clean up was delighted to be working in Stepford for a change. 'There used to be *so* much entertaining here!' she said. 'I had a whole *round* of women that used to *fight* over me! And now I have to go to *Nor*wood, and *East*bridge, and New *Shar*on! And I. *hate* night driving!' She was a plump quick-moving white-haired woman named Mary Migliardi. 'It's that Men's Association,' she said, jabbing tooth-picks into shrimp on a platter. 'Entertaining's gone right out the window since *they* started up! The men go out and the women stay in! If my old man was alive he'd have to knock me on the head before I'd let him join!'

'But it's a very old organization, isn't it?' Joanna said, tossing salad at arms' length because of her dress.

'Are you kidding?' Mary said. 'It's new! Six or seven years, that's all. Before, there was the Civic Association and the Elks and the Legion' - she tooth-picked shrimp with machine-like rapidity - 'but they all merged in with it once it got going. Except the Legion; they're still separate. Six or seven years, that's all. This isn't all you got for hors d'oeuvres, is it?'

'There's a cheese roll in the refrigerator,' Joanna said.

Walter came in, looking very handsome in his plaid jacket, carrying the ice bucket. 'We're in luck,' he said, going to the refrigerator. 'There's a good Creature Feature; Pete doesn't even want to come down. I put the Sony in his room.' He opened the freezer section and took out a bag of ice cubes.

'Mary just told me the Men's Association is new,' Joanna said.

'It's not *new*,' Walter said, tearing at the top of the bag. A white dab of tissue clung to his jaw-bone, pinned by a dot of dried blood.

'Six or seven years,' Mary said.

'Where we come from that's old.'

Joanna said, 'I thought it went back to the Puritans.'

'What gave you that idea?' Walter asked, spilling ice cubes into the bucket.

She tossed the salad. 'I don't know,' she said. 'The way it's set up, and that old house . . .'

'That was the Terhune place,' Mary said, laying a stretch of plastic over the toothpicked platter. 'They got it dirt cheap. Auctioned for taxes and no one else bid.'

The party was a disaster. Lucy Ferrault was allergic to something and never stopped sneezing; Sylvia was preoccupied; Bobbie, whom Joanna had counted on as a conversational star, had laryngitis. Charmaine was Miss Vamp, provocative and come-hithery in floor-length white silk cut clear to her navel; Dave and Shep were provoked and went thither. Walter (*damn* him!) talked law in the corner with Don Ferrault. Ed Wimperis – big, fleshy, well-tailored, stewed – talked television, clamping Joanna's arm and explaining in slow careful words why cassettes were going to change everything. At the dinner table Sylvia got unpreoccupied and tore into suburban communities that enriched themselves with tax-yielding light industry while fortressing themselves with two- and four-acre zoning. Ed Wimperis knocked his wine over. Joanna tried to get light conversation going, and Bobbie pitched in valiantly, gasping an explanation of where the laryngitis had come from: she was doing tape-recordings for a friend of Dave's who 'thinks 'e's a bleedin' 'Enry 'Iggins, 'e does'. But Charmaine, who knew the man and had taped for him herself, cut her short with 'Never make fun of what a Capricorn's doing; they *produce*,' and went into an around-the-table sign analysis that demanded everyone's attention. The roast was overdone, and Walter had a bad time slicing it. The souffle rose, but not quite as much as it should have – as Mary remarked while serving it. Lucy Ferrault sneezed.

'Never again,' Joanna said as she switched the outside lights off; and Walter, yawning, said, 'Soon enough for me.'

'Listen, you,' she said. 'How could you stand there talking to Don while three women are sitting like stones on the sofa?'

Sylvia called to apologize – she had been passed up for a promotion she damn well knew she deserved – and Charmaine called to say they'd had a great time and to postpone a tentative Tuesday tennis date. 'Ed's got a bee in his bonnet,' she said. 'He's taking a few days off, we're putting Merrill with the DaCostas – you don't know them, lucky you – and he and I are going to "rediscover each other". That means he chases me around the bed. And my period's not till next week, God damn it.'

'Why not let him catch you?' Joanna said.

'Oh God,' Charmaine said. 'Look, I just don't enjoy having a big cock shoved into me, that's all. Never have and never will. And I'm not a lez either, because I tried it and *that's* no big deal. I'm just not interested in sex. I don't think any woman is, really, not even Pisces women. Are you?'

'Well, I'm not a nympho,' Joanna said, 'but I'm interested in it, sure I am.'

'*Really*, or do you just feel you're supposed to be?'

'Really.'

'Well, to each his own,' Charmaine said. 'Let's make it Thursday, all right? He's got a conference he can't get out of, thank God.'

'Okay. Thursday, unless something comes up.'

'Don't *let* anything.'

'It's getting cold.'

'We'll wear sweaters.'

She went to a PTA meeting. Pete's and Kim's teachers were there, Miss Turner and Miss Gair, pleasant middle-aged women eagerly responsive to her questions about teaching methods and how the busing programme was working out. The meeting was poorly attended; aside from the group of teachers at the back of the auditorium there were only nine women and about a dozen men. The president of the association was an attractive blonde woman named Mrs Hollingsworth who conducted business with smiling unhurried efficiency.

She bought winter clothes for Pete and Kim, and two pairs of wool slacks for herself. She made terrific enlargements of 'Off Duty' and 'The Stepford Library', and took Pete and Kim to Dr Coe, the dentist.

'Did we?' Charmaine asked, letting her into the house.

'Of course we did,' she did. 'I said it was okay if nothing came up.'

Charmaine closed the door and smiled at her. She was wearing an apron over slacks and a blouse. 'Gosh, I'm sorry, Joanna,' she said.

'I completely forgot.'

'That's all right, go change,' she said.

'We can't play,' Charmaine said. 'For one thing, I've got too much work to do—'

'Work?'

'Housework.'

Joanna looked at her.

'We've let Nettie go,' Charmaine said. 'It's absolutely unbelievable, the sloppy job she was getting away with. The place looks clean at first glance, but boy, look in the corners. I did the kitchen and the dining-room yesterday, but I've still got all the other rooms. Ed shouldn't have to live with dirt.'

Joanna, looking at her, said, 'Okay, funny joke.'

'I'm not joking,' Charmaine said. 'Ed's a pretty wonderful guy, and I've been lazy and selfish. I'm through playing tennis, and I'm through reading those astrology books. From now on I'm going to do right by Ed, and by Merrill too. I'm lucky to have such a wonderful husband and son.'

Joanna looked at the pressed and covered racket in her hand, and at Charmaine. 'That's great,' she said, and smiled. 'But I honestly can't believe you're giving up tennis.'

'Go look,' Charmaine said.

Joanna looked at her.

'Go look,' Charmaine said.

Joanna turned and went into the living-room and across it to the glass doors. She slid one open, hearing Charmaine behind her, and went out onto the terrace. She crossed the terrace and looked down the slope of flagstone-path'd lawn.

A truck piled with sections of mesh fencing stood on the tyre-marked grass beside the tennis court. Two sides of the court's fence were gone, and the other two lay flat on the grass, a long side and a short one. Two men kneeled on the long side, working at it with long-handled cutters. They brought the handles up and together, and clicks of sound followed. A mountain of dark soil sat on the centre of the court; the net and the posts were gone.

'Ed wants a putting green,' Charmaine said, coming to Joanna's side.

'It's a *clay court*!' Joanna said, turning to her.

'It's the only level place we've got,' Charmaine said.

'My God,' Joanna said, looking at the men working the cutter handles. 'That's crazy, Charmaine!'

'Ed plays golf, he doesn't play tennis,' Charmaine said.

Joanna looked at her. 'What did he *do* to you?' she said. '*Hypnotize* you?'

'Don't be silly,' Charmaine said, smiling. 'He's a wonderful guy and I'm a lucky woman who ought to be grateful to him. Do you want to stay awhile? I'll make you some coffee. I'm doing Merrill's room but we can talk while I'm working.'

'All right,' Joanna said, but shook her head and said, 'No, no, I—' She backed from Charmaine, looking at her. 'No, there are things *I* should be doing too.' She turned and went quickly across the terrace.

'I'm sorry I forgot to call you,' Charmaine said, following her into the living-room.

'It's all right,' Joanna said, going quickly, stopping, turning, holding her racket before her with both hands. 'I'll see you in a few days, okay?'

'Yes,' Charmaine said, smiling. 'Please call me. And please give my regards to Walter.'

Bobbie went to see for herself, and called about it. 'She was moving the bedroom furniture. And they just moved in in July; how dirty can the place be?'

'It won't last,' Joanna said. 'It can't. People don't change that way.'

'Don't they?' Bobbie said. 'Around here?'

'What do you mean?'

'Shut up, Kenny! Give him that! Joanna, listen, I want to talk with you. Can you have lunch tomorrow?'

'Yes—'

'I'll pick you up around noon. I said *give* it to him! Okay? Noon, nothing fancy.'

'Okay. Kim! You're getting water all over the—'

Walter wasn't particularly surprised to hear about the change in Charmaine. 'Ed must have laid the law down to her,' he said, turning a fork of spaghetti against his spoon. 'I don't think he makes enough money for that kind of a set-up. A maid must be at *least* a hundred a week these days.'

'But her whole *attitude's* changed,' Joanna said. 'You'd think she'd be complaining.'

'Do you know what Jeremy's allowance is?' Pete said.

'He's two years older than you are,' Walter said.

'This is going to sound crazy, but I want you to listen to me without laughing, because either I'm right or I'm going off my rocker and need sympathy.' Bobbie picked at the bun of her cheeseburger.

Joanna, watching her, swallowed cheeseburger and said, 'All right, go ahead.'

They were at the McDonald's on Eastbridge Road, eating in the car.

Bobbie took a small bite of her cheeseburger, and chewed and swallowed. 'There was a thing in *Time* a few weeks ago,' she said. 'I looked for it but I must have thrown the issue out.' She looked at Joanna. 'They have a very low crime rate in El Paso, Texas,' she said. 'I *think* it was El Paso. Anyway, *somewhere* in Texas they have a very low crime rate, much lower than anywhere *else* in Texas; and the reason is, there's a chemical in the ground that gets into the water, and it tranquillizes everybody and eases the tension. God's truth.'

'I think I remember,' Joanna said, nodding, holding her cheese-burger.

'Joanna,' Bobbie said, 'I think there's something *here*. In Stepford. It's possible, isn't it? All those fancy plants on Route Nine – electronics, computers, aerospace junk, with Stepford Creek running right behind them – who knows *what* kind of crap they're dumping into the environment.'

'What do you *mean*?' Joanna said.

'Just think for a minute,' Bobbie said. She fisted her free hand and stuck out her little finger. 'Charmaine's changed and become a hausfrau,' she said. She stuck out her ring finger. 'The woman you spoke to, the one who was president of the club; *she* changed, didn't she, from what she must have been before?'

Joanna nodded.

Bobbie's next finger flicked out. 'The woman Charmaine played tennis with, before you; she changed too, Charmaine said so.'

Joanna frowned. She took a French fry from the bag between them. 'You think it's – because of a *chemical*?' she said.

Bobbie nodded. 'Either leaking from one of those plants, or just *around*, like in El Paso or wherever.' She took her coffee from the dashboard. 'It *has* to be,' she said. 'It can't be a coincidence that Stepford women are all the way they are. And some of the ones we spoke to *must* have belonged to that club. A few years ago they were *applauding Betty Friedan*, and look at them now. *They've changed too.*'

Joanna ate the French fry and took a bite of her cheeseburger. Bobbie took a bite of her cheeseburger and sipped her coffee.

'There's *something*,' Bobbie said. 'In the ground, in the water, in the air – *I* don't know. It makes women interested in housekeeping and nothing else but. Who knows what chemicals can do? *Nobel-prize winners* don't even really know yet. Maybe it's some kind of hormone thing; that would explain the fantastic boobs. You've got to have noticed.'

'I sure have,' Joanna said. 'I feel pre-adolescent every time I set foot in the market.'

'*I* do, for God's sake,' Bobbie said. She put her coffee on the dashboard and took French fries from the bag. 'Well?' she said.

'I suppose it's – possible,' Joanna said. 'But it sounds so – fantastic.' She took her coffee from the dashboard; it had made a patch of fog on the windshield.

'No more fantastic than El Paso,' Bobbie said.

'More,' Joanna said. 'Because it affects only women. What does Dave think?'

'I haven't mentioned it to him yet. I thought I'd try it out on you first.'

Joanna sipped her coffee. 'Well, it's in the realm of *possibility*,' she said. 'I *don't* think you're off your rocker. The thing to do, I guess, is write a very level-headed-sounding letter to the State – what, Department of Health? Environmental Commission? Whatever agency would have the authority to look into it. We could find out at the Library.'

Bobbie shook her head. 'Mm-mmm,' she said. 'I *worked* for a Government agency; forget it. *I* think the thing to do is move out. *Then* futz around with letters.'

Joanna looked at her.

'I mean it,' Bobbie said. 'Anything that can make a hausfrau out of *Charmaine* isn't going to have any special trouble with *me. Or* with *you.*'

'Oh come *on*,' Joanna said.

'There's something here, Joanna! I'm not kidding! This is Zombieville! And Charmaine moved in in July, *I* moved in in August, and *you* moved in in September!'

'All right, quiet down, I can hear.'

Bobbie took a large-mouthed bite of her cheeseburger. Joanna sipped her coffee and frowned.

'Even if I'm wrong,' Bobbie said with her mouth full, 'even if there's no chemical doing anything' – she swallowed – 'is this where you really want to live? We've each got one friend now, you after two months, me after three. Is *that* your idea of the ideal community? I went into Norwood to get my hair done for your party; I saw a *dozen* women who were rushed and sloppy and irritated and alive; I wanted to hug every one of them!'

'Find friends in Norwood,' Joanna said, smiling. 'You've got the car.'

'You're so damn independent!' Bobbie took her coffee from the dashboard. 'I'm asking Dave to move,' she said. 'We'll sell here and buy in Norwood or Eastbridge; all it'll mean is some headaches and bother and the moving costs – for which, if he insists, I'll hock the rock.'

'Do you think he'll agree?'

'He damn well better had, or his life is going to get mighty miserable. I wanted to buy in Norwood all along; too many WASPs, he said. Well I'd rather get stung by WASPs than poisoned by whatever's working around here. So you're going to be down to no friends at all in a little while – unless *you* speak to *Walter*.'

'About *moving*?'

Bobbie nodded. Looking at Joanna, she sipped her coffee.

Joanna shook her head. 'I couldn't ask him to move again,' she said.

'Why not? He wants you to be happy, doesn't he?'

'I'm not sure that I'm not. And I just finished the darkroom.'

'Okay,' Bobbie said, 'stick around. Turn into your next-door neighbour.'

'Bobbie, it *can't* be a chemical. I mean it *could*, but I honestly don't believe it. Honestly.'

They talked about it while they finished eating, and then they drove up Eastbridge Road and turned on to Route Nine. They passed the shopping mall and the antiques stores, and came to the industrial plants.

'Poisoner's Row,' Bobbie said.

Joanna looked at the neat low modern buildings, set back from the road and separated each from the next by wide spans of green lawn: Ulitz Optics (where Herb Sundersen worked), and CompuTech (Vic Stavros, or was he with Instatron?), and Stevenson Biochemical, and Haig-Darling Computers, and Burnham-Massey-Microtech (Dale Coba – hiss! – and Claude Axhelm), and Instatron, and Reed & Saunders (Bill McCormick – how was

Marge?), and Vesey Electronics, and AmeriChem-Willis.

'Nerve-gas research, I'll bet you five bucks.'

'In a *populated area*?'

Why not? With that gang in Washington?'

'Oh come *on*, Bobbie!'

Walter saw something was bothering her and asked her about it. She said, 'You've got the Koblenz agreement to do,' but he said, 'I've got all weekend. Come on, what is it?'

So while she scraped the dishes and put them in the washer, she told him about Bobbie's wanting to move and her 'El Paso' theory.

'That sounds pretty far-fetched to me,' he said.

'To me too,' she said. 'But women *do* seem to change around here, and what they change into is pretty damn dull. If Bobbie moves, and if Charmaine doesn't come back to her old self, which at least was—'

'Do *you* want to move?' he asked.

She looked uncertainly at him. His blue eyes, waiting for her answer, gave no clue to his feelings. 'No,' she said, 'not when we're all settled in. It's a good house . . . And yes, I'm sure I'd be happier in Eastbridge or Norwood. I wish we'd looked in either one of them.'

'*There's* an unequivocal answer,' he said. ' "No and yes." '

'About sixty-forty,' she said.

He straightened from the counter he had been leaning against. 'All right,' he said, 'if it gets to be zero-a hundred, we'll do it.'

'You would?' she said.

'Sure,' he said, 'if you were really unhappy. I wouldn't want to do it during the school year—'

'No, no, of course not.'

'But we could do it next summer. I don't think we'd lose anything, except the time and the moving costs.'

'That's what Bobbie said.'

'So it's just a matter of making up your mind.' He looked at his watch and went out of the kitchen.

'Walter?' she called, touching her hands to a towel.

'Yes?'

She went to where she could see him, standing in the hallway. 'Thanks,' she said, smiling. 'I feel better.'

'You're the one who has to be here all day, not me,' he said, and smiled at her and went into the den.

She watched him go, then turned and glanced through the port of

the family-room. Pete and Kim sat on the floor watching TV –
President Kennedy and President Johnson, surprisingly; no, figures
of them. She watched for a moment, and went back to the sink and
scraped the last few dishes.

Dave, too, was willing to move at the end of the school year. 'He
gave in so easily I thought I'd keel over,' Bobbie said on the phone
the next morning. 'I just hope we *make* it till June.'

'Drink bottled water,' Joanna said.

'You think I'm not going to? I just sent Dave to get some.'

Joanna laughed.

'Go ahead, laugh,' Bobbie said. 'For a few cents a day I'd rather
be safe than sorry. And I'm writing to the Department of Health.
The problem is, how do I do it without coming across like a little old
lady without all her marbles? You want to help, and co-sign?'

'Sure,' Joanna said. 'Come on over later. Walter is drafting a trust
agreement; maybe he'll lend us a few whereases.'

She made autumn-leaf collages with Pete and Kim, and helped
Walter put up the storm windows, and met him in the city for a part-
ners-and-wives dinner – the usual falsely-friendly clothes-
appraising bore. A cheque came from the agency: two hundred
dollars for four uses of her best picture.

She met Marge McCormick in the market – yes, she'd had a bug
but now she was fine, thanks – and Frank Roddenberry in the hardware store – 'Hello, Joanna, how've you b-been?' – and the Welcome Wagon lady right outside. 'A black family is moving in on
Gwendolyn Lane. But I think it's *good*, don't you?'

'Yes, I do.'

'All ready for winter?'

'I am now.' Smiling, she showed the sack of birdseed she'd just
bought.

'It's beautiful here!' the Welcome Wagon lady said. 'You're the
shutterbug, aren't you? You should have a field day!'

She called Charmaine and invited her for lunch. 'I can't, Joanna,
I'm sorry,' Charmaine said. 'I've got so much to do around the
house here. You know how it is.'

Claude Axhelm came over one Saturday afternoon – to see her, not
Walter. He had a briefcase with him.

'I've got this project I've been working on in my spare time,' he said, walking around the kitchen while she fixed him a cup of tea. 'Maybe you've heard about it. I've been getting people to tape-record lists of words and syllables for me. The men do it up at the house, and the women do it in their homes.'

'Oh yes,' she said.

'They tell me where they were born,' he said, 'and every place they've lived and for how long.' He walked around, touching cabinet knobs. 'I'm going to feed everything into a computer eventually, each tape with its geographical data. With enough samples I'll be able to feed in a tape *without* data' – he ran a finger-tip along a counter edge, looking at her with his bright eyes – 'maybe even a very *short* tape, a few words or a sentence – and the computer'll be able to give a geographical rundown on the person, where he was born and where he's lived. Sort of an electronic Henry Higgins. Not just a stunt, though; I see it as being useful in police work.'

She said, 'My friend Bobbie Markowe—'

'Dave's wife, sure.'

' – got laryngitis from taping for you.'

'Because she rushed it,' Claude said. 'She did the whole thing in two evenings. You don't have to do it that fast. I leave the recorder; you can take as long as you like. Would you? It would be a big help to me.'

Walter came in from the patio; he had been burning leaves out the back with Pete and Kim. He and Claude said hello to each other and shook hands. 'I'm sorry,' he said to Joanna. 'I was supposed to tell you Claude was coming to speak to you. Do you think you'll be able to help him?'

She said, 'I have so little free time—'

'Do it in odd minutes,' Claude said. 'I don't care if it takes a few *weeks*.'

'Well, if you don't mind leaving the recorder that long . . .'

'And you get a present in exchange,' Claude said, unstrapping his briefcase on the table. 'I leave an extra cartridge, you tape any little lullabies or things you like to sing to the kids, and I transcribe them on to a record. If you're out for an evening the sitter can play it.'

'Oh, that'd be nice,' she said, and Walter said, 'You could do "The Goodnight Song" and "Good Morning Starshine".'

'Anything you want,' Claude said. 'The more the merrier.'

'I'd better get back outside,' Walter said. 'The fire's still burning. See you, Claude.'

'Right,' Claude said.

Joanna gave Claude his tea, and he showed her how to load and use the tape recorder, a handsome one in a black leather case. He gave her eight yellow-boxed cartridges and a black looseleaf binder.

'My gosh, there's a lot,' she said, leafing through curled and mended pages typed in triple columns.

'It goes quickly,' Claude said. 'You just say each word clearly in your regular voice and take a little stop before the next one. And see that the needle stays in the red. You want to practice?'

They had Thanksgiving dinner with Walter's brother Dan and his family. It was arranged by Walter's and Dan's mother and was meant to be a reconciliation – the brothers had been on the outs for a year because of a dispute about their father's estate – but the dispute flared again, growing in bitterness as the disputed property had grown in value. Walter and Dan shouted, their mother shouted louder, and Joanna made difficult explanations to Pete and Kim in the car going home.

She took pictures of Bobbie's oldest boy Jonathan working with his microscope, and men in a cherry picker trimming trees on Norwood Road. She was trying to get up a portfolio of at least a dozen firstrate photos – to dazzle the agency into a contract.

The first snow fell on a night when Walter was at the Men's Association. She watched it from the den window: a scant powder of glittery white, swirling in the light of the walk lamp-post. Nothing that would amount to anything. But more would come. Fun, good pictures – and the bother of boots and snowsuits.

Across the street, in the Claybrooks' living-room window, Donna Claybrook sat polishing what looked like an athletic trophy, buffing at it with steady mechanical movements. Joanna watched her and shook her head. *They never stop, these Stepford wives*, she thought.

It sounded like the first line of a poem.

They never stop, these Stepford wives, They something something *all their lives*. Work like robots. Yes, that would fit. *They work like robots all their lives*.

She smiled. Try sending *that* to the *Chronicle*.

She went to the desk and sat down and moved the pen she had left as a placemark on the typed page. She listened for a moment – to the silence from upstairs – and switched the recorder on. With a finger to the page, she leaned towards the microphone propped against the framed Ike Mazzard drawing of her. 'Taker. Takes. Taking,' she said. 'Talcum. Talent. Talented. Talk. Talkative. Talked. Talker. Talking. Talks.'

2

She would only want to move, she decided, if she found an absolutely perfect house; one that, besides having the right number of right-sized rooms, needed practically no redecoration and had an existing darkroom or something darn close to one. And it would have to cost no more than the fifty-two-five they had paid (and could still get, Walter was sure) for the Stepford house.

A tall order, and she wasn't going to waste too much time trying to fill it. But she went out looking with Bobbie one cold bright early-December morning.

Bobbie was looking *every* morning – in Norwood, Eastbridge, and New Sharon. As soon as she found something right – and she was far more flexible in her demands than Joanna – she was going to pressure Dave for an immediate move, despite the boys' having to change schools in the middle of the year. 'Better a little disruption in their lives than a zombie-ized mother,' she said. She really was drinking bottled water, and wasn't eating any locally grown produce. 'You can buy bottled oxygen, you know,' Joanna said.

'Screw you. I can see you now, comparing Ajax to your present cleanser.'

The looking inclined Joanna to look more; the women they met – Eastbridge homeowners and a real-estate broker named Miss Kirgassa – were alert, lively, and quirky, confirming by contrast the blandness of Stepford women. And Eastbridge offered a wide range of community activities, for women and for men *and* women. There was even an NOW chapter in formation. 'Why didn't you look here first?' Miss Kirgassa asked, rocketing her car down a zigzag road at terrifying speed.

'My husband had heard—' Joanna said, clutching the armrest, watching the road, tramping on wished-for brakes.

'It's *dead* there. We're much more with-it.'

'We'd like to get back there to pack, though,' Bobbie said from in back.

Miss Kirgassa brayed a laugh. 'I can drive these roads blindfolded,' she said. 'I want to show you two more places after this one.'

On the way back to Stepford Bobbie said, 'That's for me. I'm going to be a broker. I just decided. You get out, you meet people, and you get to look in everyone's closets. And you can set your own hours. I mean it, I'm going to find out what the requirements are.'

They got a letter from the Department of Health, two pages long. It assured them that their interest in environmental protection was shared by both their state and county Governments. Industrial installations throughout the state were subject to stringent antipollutionary regulations such as the following. These were enforced not only by frequent inspection of the installations themselves, but also by regular examination of soil, water, and air samples. There was no indication whatsoever of harmful pollution in the Stepford area, nor of any naturally occurring chemical presence that might produce a tranquillizing or depressant effect. They could rest assured that their concern was groundless, but their letter was appreciated nonetheless.

'Bullshit,' Bobbie said, and stayed with the bottled water. She brought a thermos of coffee with her whenever she came to Joanna's.

Walter was lying on his side, facing away from her, when she came out of the bathroom. She sat down on the bed, turned the lamp off, and got in under the blanket. She lay on her back and watched the ceiling take shape over her.

'Walter?' she said.

'Mm?'

'Was that any good?' she asked. 'For you?'

'Sure it was,' he said. 'Wasn't it for you?'

'Yes,' she said.

He didn't say anything.

'I've had the feeling that it hasn't been,' she said. 'Good for you. The last few times.'

'No,' he said. 'It's been fine. Just like always.'

She lay seeing the ceiling. She thought of Charmaine, who wouldn't let Ed catch her (or had she changed in *that* too?), and she remembered Bobbie's remark about Dave's odd ideas.

'Goodnight,' Walter said.

'Is there anything,' she asked, 'that I – don't do that you'd like me to? Or that I *do* do that you'd like me not to?'

He didn't say anything, and then he said, 'Whatever *you* want to do, that's all.' He turned over and looked at her, up on his elbow. 'Really,' he said, and smiled, 'it's fine. Maybe I've been a little tired lately because of the commuting.' He kissed her cheek. 'Go to sleep,' he said.

'Are you – having an affair with Esther?'

'Oh for God's sake,' he said. 'She's going with a *Black Panther*. I'm not having an affair with anybody.'

'A Black Panther?'

'That's what Don's secretary told *him*. We don't even *talk* about sex; all I do is correct her spelling. Come on, let's get to sleep.' He kissed her cheek and turned away from her.

She turned over on to her stomach and closed her eyes. She shifted and stirred, trying to settle herself comfortably.

They went to a movie in Norwood with Bobbie and Dave, and spent an evening with them in front of the fire, playing Monopoly kiddingly.

A heavy snow fell on a Saturday night, and Walter gave up his Sunday-afternoon football-watching, not very happily, to take Pete and Kim sledding on Winter Hill while she drove to New Sharon and shot a roll and a half of colour in a bird sanctuary.

Pete got the lead in his class Christmas play; and Walter, on the way home one night, either lost his wallet or had his pocket picked.

She brought sixteen photos in to the agency. Bob Silverberg, the man she dealt with there, admired them gratifyingly but told her that the agency wasn't signing contracts with *anybody* at that time. He kept the photos, saying he would let her know in a day or two whether he felt any of them were marketable. She had lunch, disappointedly, with an old friend, Doris Lombardo, and did some Christmas shopping for Walter and her parents.

Ten of the pictures came back, including 'Off Duty', which she decided at once she would enter in the next *Saturday Review* contest. Among the six the agency had kept and would handle was 'Student', the one of Jonny Markowe at his microscope. She called Bobbie and told her. 'I'll give him ten per cent of whatever it makes,' she said.

'Does that mean we can stop giving him his allowance?'

'You'd better not. My best one's made a little over a thousand so far, but the other two have only made about two hundred each.'

'Well, that's not bad for a kid who looks like Peter Lorre,' Bobbie said. 'Him I mean, not you. Listen, I was going to call you. Can you take Adam for the weekend? Would you?'

'Sure,' she said. 'Pete and Kim would love it. Why?'

'Dave's had a brainstorm; we're going to have a weekend alone. Second-honeymoon time.'

A sense of beforeness touched her; deja vu. She brushed it away. 'That's great,' she said.

'We've got Jonny and Kenny booked in the neighbourhood,' Bobbie said, 'but I thought Adam would have a better time at your place.'

'Sure,' Joanna said, 'it'll make it easier to keep Pete and Kim out of each other's hair. What are you doing, going into the city?'

'No, just staying here. And getting snowed in, we hope. I'll bring him over tomorrow after school, okay? And pick him up late Sunday.'

'Fine. How's the house-hunting?'

'Not so good. I saw a beauty in Norwood this morning, but they're not getting out till April first.'

'So stick around.'

'No, thanks. Want to get together?'

'I can't; I've *got* to do some cleaning. Really.'

'You see? You're changing. That Stepford magic is starting to work.'

A black woman in an orange scarf and a striped fake-fur coat stood waiting at the library desk, her fingertips resting on a stack of books. She glanced at Joanna and nodded with a near smile; Joanna nodded and near-smiled back; and the black woman looked away – at the empty chair behind the desk, and book-shelves behind the chair. She was tall and tan-skinned, with close-cropped black hair and large dark eyes – exotic-looking and attractive. About thirty.

Joanna, going to the desk, took her gloves off and got the post-card out of her pocket. She looked at Miss Austrian's namestand on the desk, and at the books under the long slim fingers of the black woman a few feet away. *A Severed Head* by Iris Murdoch, with *I Know Why the Caged Bird Sings* and *The Magus* underneath it. Joanna looked at the postcard; Skinner, *Beyond Freedom & Dignity* would be held for her until 12/11. She wanted to say something friendly and welcoming – the woman was surely the wife or daughter of the black family the Welcome Wagon lady had mentioned – but she didn't want to be white-liberal patronizing. Would she say something if the woman *weren't* black? Yes, in a situation like this she – 'We could walk off with the whole place if we wanted to,' the black woman said, and Joanna smiled at her and said, 'We ought to; teach her to stay on the job.' She nodded towards the desk.

The black woman smiled. 'Is it always this empty?' she asked.

'I've never seen it *this* way before,' Joanna said. 'But I've only been here in the afternoon and on Saturdays.'

'Are you new in Stepford?'

'Three months.'

'Three *days* for me,' the black woman said.

'I hope you like it.'

'I think I will.'

Joanna put her hand out. 'I'm Joanna Eberhart,' she said, smiling.

'Ruthanne Hendry,' the black woman said, smiling and shaking Joanna's hand.

Joanna tipped her head and squinted. 'I *know* that name,' she said. 'I've seen it someplace.'

The woman smiled. 'Do you have any small children?' she asked.

Joanna nodded, puzzled.

'I've done a children's book, *Penny Has a Plan*,' the woman said. 'They've got it here; I checked the catalogue first thing.'

'Of *course*,' Joanna said. 'Kim had it out about two weeks ago. And loved it! I did too; it's so good to find one where a girl actually *does* something besides make tea for her dolls.'

'Subtle propaganda,' Ruthanne Hendry said, smiling.

'You did the illustrations too,' Joanna said. 'They were terrific!'

'Thank you.'

'Are you doing another one?'

Ruthanne Hendry nodded. 'I've got one laid out,' she said. 'I'll be starting the real work as soon as we get settled.'

'I'm sorry,' Miss Austrian said, coming limping from the back of the room. 'It's so quiet here in the morning that I – ' she stopped and blinked, and came limping on ' – work in the office. Have to get one of those bells people can tap on. Hello, Mrs Eberhart.' She smiled at Joanna, and at Ruthanne Hendry.

'Hello,' Joanna said. 'This is one of your authors. *Penny Has a Plan*. Ruthanne Hendry.'

'Oh?' Miss Austrian sat down heavily in the chair and held its arms with plump pink hands. 'That's a very popular book,' she said. 'We have two copies in circulation and they're both replacements.'

'I *like* this library,' Ruthanne Hendry said. 'Can I join?'

'Do you live in Stepford?'

'Yes, I just moved here.'

'Then you're welcome to join,' Miss Austrian said. She opened a drawer, took out a white card, and put it down beside the stack of books.

At the Centre Luncheonette's counter, empty except for two telephone repairmen, Ruthanne stirred her coffee, and looking at Joanna, said, 'Tell me something, on the level: was there much reaction to our buying here?'

'None at all that I heard of,' Joanna said. 'It's not a town where reactions can develop – to anything. There's no place where people really intersect, except the Men's Association.'

'*They're* all right,' Ruthanne said. 'Royal is joining tomorrow night. But the *women* in the neighbourhood—'

'Oh listen,' Joanna said, 'that doesn't have anything to do with *colour*, believe me. They're like that with everybody. No time for a cup of coffee, right? Riveted to their housework?'

Ruthanne nodded. 'I don't mind for myself,' she said. 'I'm very self-sufficient, otherwise I wouldn't have gone along with the move. But I—'

Joanna told her about Stepford women, and how Bobbie was even planning to move away to avoid becoming like them.

Ruthanne smiled. 'There's *nothing* that's going to make a hausfrau out of *me*,' she said. 'If *they're* that way, fine. I was just concerned about it being about colour because of the girls.' She had two of them, four and six; and her husband Royal was chairman of the sociology department of one of the city universities. Joanna told her about Walter and Pete and Kim, and about her photography.

They exchanged phone numbers. 'I turned into a hermit when I was working on *Penny*,' Ruthanne said, 'but I'll call you sooner or later.'

'I'll call *you*,' Joanna said. 'If you're busy, just say so. I want you to meet Bobbie; I'm sure you'll like each other.'

On the way to their cars – they had left them in front of the Library – Joanna saw Dale Coba looking at her from a distance. He stood with a lamb in his arms, by a group of men setting up a crèche near the Historical Society cottage. She nodded at him, and he, holding the live-looking lamb, nodded and smiled.

She told Ruthanne who he was, and asked her if she knew that Ike Mazzard lived in Stepford.

'Who?'

'Ike Mazzard. The illustrator.'

Ruthanne had never heard of him, which made Joanna feel very old. Or very white.

Having Adam for the weekend was a mixed blessing. On Saturday he and Pete and Kim played beautifully together, inside the house and out; but on Sunday, a freezing-cold overcast day when Walter laid claim to the family-room for football-watching (fairly enough after last Sunday's sledding), Adam and Pete became, serially, soldiers in a blanket-over-the-dining-table fort, explorers in the cellar ('Stay out of that darkroom!'), and Star Trek people in Pete's room – all of them sharing, strangely enough, a single common enemy called Kim-She's-Dim. They were loudly and scornfully watchful, preparing defences; and poor Kim *was* dim, wanting only to join them, not to crayon or help file negatives, not even – Joanna was desperate – to bake cookies. Adam and Pete ignored threats, Kim ignored blandishments, Walter ignored everything.

Joanna was glad when Bobbie and Dave came to pick Adam up.

But she was glad she had taken him when she saw how great they looked. Bobbie had had her hair done and was absolutely beautiful – either due to make-up or love-making, probably both. And Dave looked jaunty and keyed up and happy. They brought bracing coldness into the entrance hall. 'Hi, Joanna, how'd it go?' Dave said, rubbing leather-gloved hands; and Bobbie, wrapped in her raccoon coat, said, 'I hope Adam wasn't any trouble.'

'Not a speck,' Joanna said. 'You look marvellous, both of you!'

'We *feel* marvellous,' Dave said, and Bobbie smiled and said, 'It was a lovely weekend. Thank you for helping us manage it.'

'Forget it,' Joanna said. 'I'm going to plunk Pete with *you* one of these weekends.'

'We'll be glad to take him,' Bobbie said, and Dave said, 'Whenever you want, just say the word. *Adam? Time to go!*'

'He's up in Pete's room.'

Dave cupped his gloved hands and shouted, '*Ad-am! We're here! Get your stuff!*'

'Take your coats off,' Joanna said.

'Got to pick up Jon and Kenny,' Dave said, and Bobbie said, 'I'm sure you'd like some peace and quiet. It must have been hectic.'

'Well, it hasn't been my most *restful* Sunday,' Joanna said. 'Yesterday was great though.'

'Hi there!' Walter said, coming in from the kitchen with a glass in his hand.

Bobbie said, 'Hello, Walter,' and Dave said, 'Hi, buddy!'

'How was the second honeymoon?' Walter asked.

'Better than the first,' Dave said. 'Just shorter, that's all.' He grinned at Walter.

Joanna looked at Bobbie, expecting her to say something funny. Bobbie smiled at her and looked towards the stairs. 'Hello, gumdrop,' she said. 'Did you have a nice weekend?'

'I don't want to go,' Adam said, standing tilted to keep his shopping bag clear of the stair. Pete and Kim stood behind him. Kim said, 'Can't he stay another night?'

'No, dear, there's school tomorrow,' Bobbie said, and Dave said, 'Come on, pal, we've got to collect the rest of the Mafia.'

Adam came sulkily down the stairs, and Joanna went to the closet for his coat and boots. 'Hey,' Dave said, 'I've got some information on that stock you asked me about.' Walter said, 'Oh, good,' and he and Dave went into the living-room.

Joanna gave Adam's coat to Bobbie, and Bobbie thanked her and held it open for Adam. He put his shopping bag down and winged back his arms to the coat sleeves.

Joanna, holding Adam's boots, said, 'Do you want a bag for these?'

'No, don't bother,' Bobbie said. She turned Adam around and helped him with his buttons.

'You smell nice,' he said.

'Thanks, gumdrop.'

He looked at the ceiling and at her. 'I don't like you to *call* me that,' he said. 'I *used* to, but now I don't.'

'I'm sorry,' she said. 'I won't do it again.' She smiled at him and kissed him on the forehead.

Walter and Dave came out of the living-room, and Adam picked up his shopping bag and said goodbye to Pete and Kim. Joanna gave Adam's boots to Bobbie and touched cheeks with her. Bobbie's was still cool from outside, and she *did* smell nice. 'Speak to you tomorrow,' Joanna said.

'Sure,' Bobbie said. They smiled at each other. Bobbie moved to

Walter at the door and offered her cheek. He hesitated – Joanna wondered why – and pecked it.

Dave kissed Joanna, clapped Walter on the arm – 'So long, buddy' – and steered Adam out after Bobbie.

'Can we go in the family-room now?' Pete asked.

'It's all yours,' Walter said.

Pete ran away and Kim after him.

Joanna and Walter stood at the cold glass of the storm door, looking out at Bobbie and Dave and Adam getting into their car.

'Fantastic,' Walter said.

'Don't they look great?' Joanna said. 'Bobbie didn't even look that good at the party. Why didn't you want to kiss her?'

Walter didn't say anything, and then he said, 'Oh, I don't know, *cheek*-kissing. It's so damn show-business.'

'I never noticed you objecting before.'

'Then I've changed, I guess,' he said.

She watched the car doors close, and the headlights flash on. 'How about *us* having a weekend alone?' she said. 'They'll take Pete, they said they would, and I'm sure the Van Sants would take Kim.'

'That'd be great,' he said. 'Right after the holidays.'

'Or maybe the Hendrys,' she said. '*They've* got a six-year-old girl, and I'd like Kim to get to know a black family.'

The car pulled away, red tail-lights shining, and Walter closed the door and locked it and thumbed down the switch of the outside lights. 'Want a drink?' he asked.

'And how,' Joanna said. 'I need one after today.'

Ugh, what a Monday: Pete's room to be reassembled and all the others straightened out, the beds to be changed, washing (and she'd let it pile up, of course), tomorrow's shopping list to make up, and three pairs of Pete's pants to be lengthened. That was what she was *doing*; never mind what *else* had to be done – the Christmas shopping, and the Christmas-card addressing, and making Pete's costume for the play (thanks for *that*, Miss Turner). Bobbie didn't call, thank goodness; this wasn't a day for kaffee-klatsching. *Is she right*? Joanna wondered. *Am I changing*? Hell, no; the housework *had* to be caught up with once in a while, otherwise the place would turn into – well, into *Bobbie's* place. Besides, a real Stepford wife would sail through it all very calmly and efficiently, not running the vacuum cleaner over its cord and then mashing her fingers getting the cord out from around the damn roller thing.

She gave Pete hell about not putting toys away when he was done playing with them, and he sulked for an hour and wouldn't talk to her. And Kim was coughing.

And Walter begged off his turn at KP and ran out to get into Herb Sundersen's full car. Busy time at the Men's Association; the Christmas-Toys project. (Who for? Were there needy children in Stepford? She'd seen no sign of any.)

She cut a sheet to start Pete's costume, a snowman, and played a game of Concentration with him and Kim (who only coughed once but keep the fingers crossed); and then she addressed Christmas cards down through the L's and went to bed at ten. She fell asleep with the Skinner book.

Tuesday was better. When she had cleaned up the breakfast mess and made the beds, she called Bobbie – no answer; she was house-hunting – and drove to the Centre and did the week's main shopping. She went to the Centre again after lunch, took pictures of the creche, and got home just ahead of the school bus.

Walter did the dishes and *then* went to the Men's Association. The toys were for kids in the city, ghetto kids and kids in hospitals. Complain about *that*, Ms Eberhart. Or would she still be Ms Ingalls? Ms Ingalls-Eberhart?

After she got Pete and Kim bathed and into bed she called Bobbie. It was odd that Bobbie hadn't called *her* in two full days. 'Hello?' Bobbie said.

'Long time no speak.'

'Who's this?'

'*Joanna.*'

'Oh, hello,' Bobbie said. 'How are you?'

'Fine. Are you? You sound sort of blah.'

'No, I'm fine,' Bobbie said.

'Any luck this morning?'

'What do you mean?'

'House-hunting.'

'I went shopping this morning,' Bobbie said.

'Why didn't you call me?'

'I went very early.'

'I went around ten; we must have just missed each other.'

Bobbie didn't say anything.

'Bobbie?'

'Yes?'

'Are you *sure* you're okay?'

'Positive. I'm in the middle of some ironing.'

'At this hour?'

'Dave needs a shirt for tomorrow.'

'Oh. Call me in the morning then; maybe we can have lunch. Unless you're going house-hunting.'

'I'm not,' Bobbie said.

'Call me then, okay?'

'Okay,' Bobbie said. ''Bye, Joanna.'

'Goodbye.'

She hung up and sat looking at the phone and her hand on it. The thought struck her – ridiculously – that Bobbie had changed the way Charmaine had. No, not Bobbie; impossible. She must have had a fight with Dave, a major one that she wasn't ready to talk about yet. Or could she herself have offended Bobbie in some way without being aware of it? Had she said something Sunday about Adam's stay-over that Bobbie might have misinterpreted? But no, they'd parted as friendly as ever, touching cheeks and saying they'd speak to each other. (Yet even then, now that she thought about it, Bobbie had seemed different; she – hadn't said the sort of things she usually did, and she'd moved more slowly too.) Maybe she and Dave had been smoking pot over the weekend. They'd tried it a couple of times without much effect, Bobbie had said. Maybe this time . . .

She addressed a few Christmas cards.

She called Ruthanne Hendry, who was friendly and glad to hear from her. They talked about *The Magus*, which Ruthanne was enjoying as much as Joanna had, and Ruthanne told her about her new book, another Penny story. They agreed to have lunch together the following week. Joanna would speak to Bobbie, and the three of them would go to the French place in Eastbridge. Ruthanne would call her Monday morning.

She addressed Christmas cards, and read the Skinner book in bed until Walter came home. 'I spoke to Bobbie tonight,' she said. 'She sounded – different, washed out.'

'She's probably tired from all that running around she's been doing,' Walter said, emptying his jacket pockets on to the bureau.

'She seemed different Sunday too,' Joanna said. 'She didn't say—'

'She had some make-up on, that's all,' Walter said. 'You're not going to start in with that chemical business, are you?'

She frowned, pressing the closed book to her blanketed knees.

'Did Dave say anything about their trying pot again?' she asked.

'No,' Walter said, 'but maybe that's the answer.'

They made love, but she was tense and couldn't really give herself, and it wasn't very good.

Bobbie didn't call. Around one o'clock Joanna drove over. The dogs barked at her as she got out of the station wagon. They were chained to an overhead line behind the house, the corgi up on his hind legs, pawing air and yipping, the sheepdog standing shaggy and stockstill, barking 'Ruff, ruff, ruff, ruff, ruff.' Bobbie's blue Chevy stood in the driveway.

Bobbie, in her immaculate living-room – cushions all fluffed, woodwork gleaming, magazines fanned on the polished table behind the sofa-smiled at Joanna and said, 'I'm sorry, I was so busy it slipped my mind. Have you had lunch? Come on into the kitchen. I'll fix you a sandwich. What would you like?'

She looked the way she had on Sunday – beautiful, her hair done, her face made-up. And she was wearing some kind of padded high-uplift bra under her green sweater, and a hip-whittling girdle under the brown pleated skirt.

In her immaculate kitchen she said, 'Yes, I've changed. I realized I was being awfully sloppy and self-indulgent. It's no disgrace to be a good homemaker. I've decided to do my job conscientiously, the way Dave does his, and to be more careful about my appearance. Are you sure you don't want a sandwich?'

Joanna shook her hand. '*Bobbie*,' she said, 'I – Don't you see what's happened? Whatever's around here – it's got *you*, the way it got Charmaine!'

Bobbie smiled at her. 'Nothing's got me,' she said. 'There's nothing around. That was a lot of nonsense. Stepford's a fine healthy place to live.'

'You – don't want to move any more?'

'Oh no,' Bobbie said. 'That was nonsense too. I'm perfectly happy here. Can't I at least make you a cup of coffee?'

She called Walter at his office. 'Oh good ahfter*noon*!' Esther said. 'So nice to speak to you! It must be a *super* day up there, or are you hyar in town?'

'No, I'm at home,' she said. 'May I speak to Walter please?'

'I'm afraid he's in conference at the moment.'

'It's important. Please tell him.'

'Hold on a sec then.'

She held on, sitting at the den desk, looking at the papers and envelopes she had taken from the centre drawer, and at the calendar – *Tuesday, Dec 14th*, yesterday – and the Ike Mazzard drawing.

'He'll be right with you, Mrs Eberhart,' Esther said. 'Nothing wrong with Peter or Kim, I hope.'

'No, they're fine.'

'Good. They must be having a—'

'Hello?' Walter said.

'Walter?'

'Hello. What is it?'

'Walter, I want you to listen to me and don't argue,' she said. 'Bobbie *has* changed. I was over there. The house looks like – It's *spotless*, Walter; it's *immaculate*! And she's got herself all – Listen, do you have the bankbooks? I've been looking for them and I can't find them. Walter?'

'Yes, I've got them,' he said. 'I've been buying some stock, on Dave's recommendations. What do you want them for?'

'To see what we've got,' she said. 'There was a house I saw in Eastbridge that—'

'Joanna.'

' – was a little more than this one but – '

'Joanna, listen to me.'

'I'm not going to stay here another – '

'Listen to me, damn it!'

She gripped the handset. 'Go ahead,' she said.

'I'll try to get home early,' he said. 'Don't do anything till I get there. You hear me? Don't make any commitments or anything. I think I can get away in about half an hour.'

'I'm not going to stay here another day,' she said.

'Just wait till I get there, will you?' he said. 'We can't talk about this on the phone.'

'Bring the bankbooks,' she said.

'Don't do anything till I get there.' The phone clicked dead.

She hung up.

She put the papers and envelopes back into the centre drawer and closed it. Then she got the phone book from the shelf and looked up Miss Kirgassa's number in Eastbridge.

The house she was thinking of, the St Martin house, was still on the market. 'In fact I think they've come down a bit since you saw it.'

'Would you do me a favour?' she said. 'We may be interested; I'll know definitely tomorrow. Would you find out the rock-bottom price they'll take for an immediate sale, and let me know as soon as you can?'

'I'll get right back to you,' Miss Kirgassa said. 'Do you know if Mrs Markowe has found something? We had an appointment this morning but she didn't show up.'

'She changed her mind, she's not moving,' she said. 'But I am.'

She called Buck Raymond, the broker they'd used in Stepford. 'Just hypothetically,' she said, 'if we were to put the house on the market tomorrow, do you think we could sell it quickly?'

'No doubt about it,' Buck said. 'There's a steady demand here. I'm sure you could get what you paid, maybe even a little more. Aren't you happy in it?'

'No,' she said.

'I'm sorry to hear that. Shall I start showing it? There's a couple here right now who are—'

'No, no, not yet,' she said. 'I'll let you know tomorrow.'

'Now just hold on a minute,' Walter said, making spread-handed calming gestures.

'No,' she said, shaking her head. 'No. Whatever it is takes four months to work, which means I've got one more month to go. Maybe less; we moved here September fourth.'

'For God's sake, Joanna—'

'Charmaine moved here in July,' she said. 'She changed in November. Bobbie moved here in August and now it's December.' She turned and walked away from him. The sink's faucet was leaking; she hit the handle back hard and the leaking stopped.

'You *had* the letter from the Department of Health,' Walter said.

'Bullshit, to quote Bobbie.' She turned and faced him. 'There's *something*, there's *got* to be,' she said. 'Go take a look. Would you do that, please? She's got her bust shoved out to here, and her behind girdled down to practically nothing! The house is like a commercial. Like Carol's, and Donna's, and Kit Sundersen's!'

'She had to clean it sooner or later; it was a pigsty.'

'She's *changed*, Walter! She doesn't *talk* the same, she doesn't *think* the same – and I'm not going to wait around for it to happen to me!'

'We're not going to—'

Kim came in from the patio, her face red in its fur-edged hood.

228

'Stay out, Kim,' Walter said.

'We want some supplies,' Kim said. 'We're going on a hike.'

Joanna went to the cookie jar and opened it and got out cookies. 'Here,' she said, putting them into Kim's mittened hands. 'Stay near the house, it's getting dark.'

'Can we have chocolate fingers?'

'We don't *have* chocolate fingers. Go on.'

Kim went out. Walter closed the door.

Joanna brushed crumbs from her hand. 'It's a nicer house than this one,' she said, 'and we can have it for fifty-three-five. And we can get that for this one; Buck Raymond said so.'

'We're not moving,' Walter said.

'You *said* we would!'

'Next summer, not—'

'I won't be *me* next summer!'

'Joanna—'

'Don't you understand? It's going to happen to *me*, in *January*!'

'*Nothing's* going to happen to you!'

'That's what I told Bobbie! I kidded her about the bottled water!'

He came close to her. 'There's nothing in the water, there's nothing in the air,' he said. 'They changed for exactly the reasons they told you: because they realized they'd been lazy and negligent. If Bobbie's taking an interest in her appearance, it's about time. It wouldn't hurt *you* to look in a mirror once in a while.'

She looked at him, and he looked away, flushing, and looked back at her. 'I mean it,' he said. 'You're a very pretty woman and you don't do a damn thing with yourself any more unless there's a party or something.'

He turned away from her and went and stood at the stove. He twisted a knob one way and the other.

She looked at him.

He said, 'I'll tell you what we'll do—'

'Do you *want* me to change?' she asked.

'Of course not, don't be silly.' He turned around.

'Is *that* what you want?' she asked. 'A cute little gussied-up hausfrau?'

'All I said was—'

'Is *that* why Stepford was the only place to move? Did somebody pass the message to you? "Take her to Stepford, Wally old pal; there's something in the air there; she'll change in four months". '

'There's nothing in the air,' Walter said. 'The message I got was

229

good schools and low taxes. Now look, I'm trying to see this from your viewpoint and make some kind of fair judgement. You want to move because you're afraid you're going to "change"; and I think you're being irrational and – a little hysterical, and that moving at this point would impose an undue hardship on all of us, especially Pete and Kim.' He stopped and drew a breath. 'All right, let's do this,' he said. 'You have a talk with Alan Hollingsworth, and if he says you're—'

'With who?'

'Alan Hollingsworth,' he said. His eyes went from hers. 'The psychiatrist. You know.' His eyes came back. 'If he says you're not going through some—'

'I don't need a psychiatrist,' she said. 'And if I did, I wouldn't want Alan Hollingsworth. I saw his wife at the PTA; she's one of *them*. You *bet* he'd think I'm irrational.'

'Then pick someone else,' he said. 'Anyone you want. If you're not going through some kind of – delusion or something, then we'll move, as soon as we possibly can. I'll look at that house tomorrow morning, and even put a deposit on it.'

'I don't need a psychiatrist,' she said. 'I need to get out of Stepford.'

'Now come on, Joanna,' he said. 'I think I'm being damn fair. You're asking us to undergo a major upheaval, and I think you owe it to all of us, including yourself – *especially* yourself – to make sure you're seeing things as clearly as you think you are.'

She looked at him.

'Well?' he said.

She didn't say anything. She looked at him.

'Well?' he said. 'Doesn't that sound reasonable?'

She said, 'Bobbie changed when she was alone with Dave, and Charmaine changed when she was alone with Ed.'

He looked away, shaking his head.

'Is that when it's going to happen to *me*?' she asked. 'On *our* weekend alone?'

'It was *your idea*,' he said.

'Would *you* have suggested it if *I* hadn't?'

'Now you *see*?' he said. 'Do you hear how you're talking? I want you to think about what I said. You can't disrupt all our lives on the spur of the moment this way. It's unreasonable to expect to.' He turned around and went out of the kitchen.

She stood there, and put her hand to her forehead and closed her eyes. She stayed that way, and then lowered her hand, opened her eyes, and shook her head. She went to the refrigerator and opened it, and took out a covered bowl and a market-pack of meat. He sat at the desk, writing on a yellow pad. A cigarette in the ashtray ribboned smoke up into the lamplight. He looked at her and took his glasses off.

'All right,' she said. 'I'll – speak to someone. But a woman.'

'Good,' he said. 'That's a good idea.'

'And you'll put a deposit on the house tomorrow?'

'Yes,' he said. 'Unless there's something radically wrong with it.'

'There isn't,' she said. 'It's a good house and it's only six years old. With a good mortgage.'

'Fine,' he said.

She stood looking at him. '*Do* you want me to change?' she asked him.

'No,' he said. 'I'd just like you to put on a little lipstick once in a while. That's no big change. I'd like *me* to change a little too, like lose a few pounds for instance.'

She pushed her hair back straight. 'I'm going to work down in the darkroom for a while,' she said. 'Pete's still awake. Will you keep an ear open?'

'Sure,' he said, and smiled at her.

She looked at him, and turned and went away.

She called the good old Department of Health, and they referred her to the county medical society, and *they* gave her the names and phone numbers of five women psychiatrists. The two nearest ones, in Eastbridge, were booked solid through mid-January; but the third, in Sheffield, north of Norwood, could see her on Saturday afternoon at two. Dr Margaret Fancher; she sounded nice over the phone.

She finished the Christmas cards, and Pete's costume; bought toys and books for Pete and Kim, and a bottle of champagne for Bobbie and Dave. She had got a gold belt buckle for Walter in the city, and had planned to canvass the Route Nine antique stores for legal documents; instead she bought him a tan cardigan.

The first Christmas cards came in – from her parents and Walter's junior partners, from the McCormicks, the Chamalians, and the Van Sants. She lined them up on a living-room bookshelf.

A cheque came from the agency: a hundred and twenty-five dollars.

On Friday afternoon, despite two inches of snow and more falling, she put Pete and Kim into the station wagon and drove over to Bobbie's.

Bobbie welcomed them pleasantly; Adam and Kenny and the dogs welcomed them noisily. Bobbie made hot chocolate, and Joanna carried the tray into the family-room. 'Watch your step,' Bobbie said, 'I waxed the floor this morning.'

'I noticed,' Joanna said.

She sat in the kitchen watching Bobbie – beautiful, shapely Bobbie – cleaning the oven with paper towels and a spray can of cleaner. 'What have you *done* to yourself, for God's sake?' she asked.

'I'm not eating the way I used to,' Bobbie said. 'And I'm getting more exercise.'

'You must have lost ten pounds!'

'No, just two or three. I'm wearing a girdle.'

'Bobbie, will you *please* tell me what *happened* last weekened?'

'Nothing happened. We stayed in.'

'Did you smoke anything, take anything? Drugs, I mean.'

'No. Don't be silly.'

'Bobbie, you're not *you* any more! Can't you see that? You've become like the others!'

'Honestly, Joanna, that's nonsense,' Bobbie said. 'Of course I'm me. I simply realized that I was awfully sloppy and self-indulgent, and now I'm doing my job conscientiously, the way Dave does his.'

'I know, I know,' she said. 'How does *he* feel about it?'

'He's very happy.'

'I'll bet he is.'

'This stuff really works. Do you use it?'

I'm not crazy, she thought. *I'm not crazy.*

Jonny and two other boys were making a snowman in front of the house next door. She left Pete and Kim in the station wagon and went over and said hello to him. 'Oh, hi!' he said. 'Do you have any money for me?'

'Not yet,' she said, shielding her face against the downfall of thick flakes. 'Jonny, I – I can't get over the way your mother's changed.'

'Hasn't she?' he said, nodding, panting.

'I can't understand it,' she said.

'Neither can I,' he said. 'She doesn't shout any more, she makes hot breakfasts . . .' He looked over at the house and frowned. Snowflakes clung to his face. 'I hope it lasts,' he said, 'but I bet it doesn't.'

Dr Fancher was a small elfin-faced woman in her early fifties, with short swirls of greying brown hair, a sharp marionette nose, and smiling blue-grey eyes. She wore a dark-blue dress, a gold pin engraved with the Chinese Yang-and-Yin symbol, and a wedding ring. Her office was cheerful, with Chippendale furniture and Paul Klee prints, and striped curtains translucent against the brightness of sun and snow outside. There was a brown leather couch with a paper-covered headrest, but Joanna sat in the chair facing the mahogany desk, on which dozens of small white papers flag-edged the sides of a green blotter.

She said, 'I'm here at my husband's suggestion. We moved to Stepford early in September, and I want to move away as soon as possible. We've put a deposit on a house in Eastbridge, but only because I insisted on it. He feels I'm – being irrational.'

She told Dr Fancher why she wanted to move: about Stepford women, and how Charmaine and then Bobbie had changed and become like them. 'Have you been to Stepford?' she asked.

'Only once,' Dr Fancher said. 'I heard that it was worth looking at, which it is. I've also heard that it's an insular, unsocial community.'

'Which it is, believe me.'

Dr Fancher knew of the city in Texas with the low crime rate. 'Lithium is what's doing it, apparently,' she said. 'There was a paper about it in one of the journals.'

'Bobbie and I wrote to the Department of Health,' Joanna said. 'They said there was nothing in Stepford that could be affecting anyone. I suppose they thought we were crackpots. At the time, actually, I thought *Bobbie* – was being a little over-anxious. I only helped with the letter because she asked me to . . .' She looked at her clasped hands and worked them against each other.

Dr Fancher stayed silent.

'I've begun to suspect—' Joanna said. 'Oh Jesus, "suspect"; that sounds so—' She worked her hands together, looking at them.

Dr Fancher said, 'Begun to suspect what?'

She drew her hands apart and wiped them on her skirt. 'I've begun to suspect that the men are behind it,' she said. She looked at Dr Fancher.

Dr Fancher didn't smile or seem surprised. 'Which men?' she asked.

Joanna looked at her hands. 'My husband,' she said. 'Bobbie's

233

husband, Charmaine's.' She looked at Dr Fancher. 'All of them,' she said.

She told her about the Men's Association.

'I was taking pictures in the Centre one night a couple of months ago,' she said. 'That's where those Colonial shops are; the house overlooks them. The windows were open and there was – a smell in the air. Of medicine, or chemicals. And then the shades were pulled down, maybe because they knew I was out there; this policeman had seen me, he stopped and talked to me.' She leaned forward. 'There are a lot of sophisticated industrial plants on Route Nine,' she said, 'and a lot of the men who have high-level jobs in them live in Stepford and belong to the Men's Association. *Something* goes on there every night, and I don't think it's just fixing toys for needy children, and pool and poker. There's AmeriChem-Willis, and Stevenson Biochemical. They could be – concocting something that the Department of Health wouldn't know about, up there at the Men's Association . . .' She sat back in the chair, wiping her hands against her skirted thighs, not looking at Dr Fancher.

Dr Fancher asked her questions about her family background and her interest in photography; about the jobs she had held, and about Walter and Pete and Kim.

'Any move is traumatic to a degree,' Dr Fancher said, 'and particularly the city-to-the-suburbs move for a woman who doesn't find her housewife's role totally fulfilling. It can feel pretty much like being sent to Siberia.' She smiled at Joanna. 'And the holiday season doesn't help matters any,' she said. 'It tends to magnify anxieties, for everyone. I've often thought that one year we should have a *real* holiday and skip the whole business.'

Joanna made a smile.

Dr Fancher leaned forward, and joining her hands, rested her elbows on the desk. 'I can understand your not being happy in a town of highly home-orientated women,' she said to Joanna. '*I* wouldn't be either; no woman with outside interests would. But I do wonder-and I imagine your husband does too – whether you would be happy in Eastbridge, or anywhere else at this particular time.'

'I think I would be,' Joanna said.

Dr Fancher looked at her hands, pressing and flexing the wedding-ring'd one with the other. She looked at Joanna. 'Towns develop their character gradually,' she said, 'as people pick and choose among them. A few artists and writers came here to Sheffield a long

234

time ago; others followed, and people who found them too Bohemian moved away. Now we're an artists-and-writers town; not exclusively, of course, but enough to make us different from Norwood and Kimball. I'm sure Stepford developed its character in the same way. That seems to me far more likely than the idea that the men there have banded together to brainwash chemically the women. And could they really do it? They could tranquillize them; yes; but these women don't sound tranquillized to me; they're hardworking and industrious within their own small range of interests. That would be quite a job for even the most advanced chemists.'

Joanna said, 'I know it sounds—' She rubbed her temple.

'It sounds,' Dr Fancher said, 'like the idea of a woman who, like many women today, and with good reason, feels a deep resentment and suspicion of men. One who's pulled two ways by conflicting demands, perhaps more strongly than she's aware; the old conventions on the one hand, and the *new* conventions of the liberated woman on the other.'

Joanna, shaking her head, said, 'If only you could see what Stepford women are *like*. They're actresses in TV commercials, all of them. No, not even *that*. They're – they're like—' She sat forward. 'There was a programme four or five weeks ago,' she said. 'My children were watching it. These figures of all the Presidents, moving around, making different facial expressions. Abraham Lincoln stood up and delivered the Gettysburg Address; he was so lifelike you'd have—' She sat still.

Dr Fancher waited, had nodded. 'Rather than force an immediate move on your family,' she said, 'I think you should con—'

'Disneyland,' Joanna said. 'The programme was from *Disneyland* . . .'

Dr Fancher smiled. 'I know,' she said. 'My grandchildren were there last summer. They told me they "met" Lincoln.'

Joanna turned from her, staring.

'I think you should consider trying therapy,' Dr Fancher said. 'To identify and clarify your feelings. Then you can make the *right* move – maybe to Eastbridge, maybe back to the city; maybe you'll even find Stepford less oppressive.'

Joanna turned to her.

'Will you think about it for a day or two and call me?' Dr Fancher said. 'I'm sure I can help you. It's certainly worth a few hours' exploration, isn't it?'

Joanna sat still, and nodded.

Dr Fancher took a pen from its holder and wrote on a prescription pad.

Joanna looked at her. She stood up and took her handbag from the desk.

'These will help you in the meantime,' Dr Fancher said, writing. 'They're a mild tranquillizer. You can take three a day.' She tore off a slip and offered it to Joanna, smiling. 'They *won't* make you fascinated with housework,' she said.

Joanna took the slip.

Dr Fancher stood up. 'I'll be away Christmas week,' she said, 'but we could start the week of the third. Will you call me Monday or Tuesday and let me know what you've decided?'

Joanna nodded.

Dr Fancher smiled. 'It's *not* catastrophic,' she said. 'Really. I'm sure I can help you.' She held out her hand.

Joanna shook it and went out.

The library was busy. Miss Austrian said they were down in the cellar. The door on the left, the bottom shelf. Put them back in their proper order. No smoking. Put out the lights.

She went down the steep narrow stairs, touching the wall with one hand. There was no banister.

The door on the left. She found the light switch inside. An eye-sting of fluorescence; the smell of old paper; the whine of a motor, climbing in pitch.

The room was small and low-ceilinged. Walls of shelved magazines surrounded a library table and four kitchen chairs, chrome and red plastic.

Big brown-bound volumes jutted from the bottom shelf all around the room, lying flat, piled six high.

She put her handbag on the table, and took her coat off and laid it over one of the chairs.

She started five years back, leafing backward through the half-a-year volume.

CIVIC AND MEN'S ASSOCIATION TO MERGE. The proposed union of the Stepford Civic Association and the Stepford Men's Association has been endorsed by the members of both organizations and will take place within weeks. Thomas C. Miller III and Dale Coba, the respective presidents . . .

She leafed back, through Little League ball games and heavy

snowfalls, through thefts, collisions, school-bond disputes.

WOMEN'S CLUB SUSPENDS MEETINGS. The Stepford Women's Club is suspending its bi-weekly meetings because of declining membership, according to Mrs Richard Ockrey, who assumed the club's presidency only two months ago on the resignation of former president Mrs Alan Hollingsworth. 'It's only a temporary suspension,' Mrs Ockrey said in her home on Fox Hollow Lane. 'We're planning a full-scale membership drive and a resumption of meetings in the early spring . . .'

Do tell, Mrs Ockrey.

She leafed back through ads for old movies and low-priced food, through fire at the Methodist Church and the opening of the incinerator plant.

MEN'S ASSOCIATION BUYS TERHUNE HOUSE. Dale Coba, president of the Stepford . . .

A zoning-law change, a burglary at Compu-Tech.

She dropped the next-earlier volume down on to the other one. Sitting, she opened the volume at its back.

LEAGUE OF WOMEN VOTERS MAY CLOSE.

So what's so surprising about that?

Unless the recent fall-off in membership is reversed, the Stepford League of Women Voters may be forced to close its doors. So warns the league's new president, Mrs Theodore Van Sant of Fairview Lane . . .

Carol?

Back, back.

A drought was relieved, a drought grew worse.

MEN'S ASSOCIATION RE-ELECTS COBA. Dale Coba of Anvil Road was elected by acclamation to a second two-year term as president of the steadily expanding . . .

Back two years then.

She jumped three volumes.

A theft, a fire, a bazaar, a snowfall.

She flipped up the pages with one hand, turned them with the other; quickly, quickly.

MEN'S ASSOCIATION FORMED. A dozen Stepford men who repaired the disused barn on Switzer Lane and have been meeting in it for over a year, have formed the Stepford Men's Association and will welcome new members. Dale Coba of Anvil Road has been elected president of the association, Duane T. Anderson of Switzer Lane is vice-president, and Robert Sumner Jr of Gwendolyn Lane is secretary-treasurer. The purpose of the association, Mr Coba says, is 'strictly social – poker, man-talk, and the pooling of information on crafts and hobbies'. The Coba family seems especially apt at getting things started; Mrs Coba was among the founders of the Stepford Women's Club, although she recently withdrew from it, as did Mrs Anderson and Mrs Sumner. Other men in the Stepford Men's Association are Claude Axhelm, Peter J. Duwicki, Frank Ferretti, Steven Margolies, Ike Mazzard, Frank Roddenberry, James J. Scofield, Herbert Sundersen, and Martin I. Weiner. Men interested in further information should . . .

She jumped two more volumes, and now she turned pages in whole-issues clusters, finding each 'Notes on Newcomers' in its page-two box.

. . . *Mr Ferretti is an engineer in the systems development laboratory of the CompuTech Corporation.*

. . . *Mr Sumner, who holds many patents in dyes and plastics, recently joined the AmeriChem-Willis Corporation, where he is doing research in vinyl polymers.*

'Notes on Newcomers', 'Notes on Newcomers'; stopping only when she saw one of the names, skipping to the end of the article, telling herself she was right, she was right.

. . . *Mr Duwicki, known to his friends as Wick, is in the Instatron Corporation's microcircuitry department.*

. . . *Mr Weiner is with the Sono-Trak division of the Instatron Corporation.*

. . . *Mr Margolies is with Reed & Saunders, the makers of stabilizing devices whose new plant on Route Nine begins operation next week.*

She put volumes back, took other volumes out, dropping them heavily on the table.

. . . *Mr Roddenberry is associate chief of the CompuTech Corporation's systems development laboratory.*

. . . *Mr Sundersen designs optical sensors for Ulitz Optics, Inc.*

And finally she found it.

She read the whole article.

New neighbours on Anvil Road are Mr and Mrs Dale Coba and their sons Dale Jr, four, and Darren, two. The Cobas have come here from Anaheim, California, where they lived for six years. 'So far we like this part of the country,' Mrs Coba says. 'I don't know how we'll feel when winter comes. We're not used to cold weather.'

Mr and Mrs Coba attended UCLA, and Mr Coba did post-

graduate work at the California Institute of Technology. For the past six years he worked in 'audio-animatronics' at Disneyland, helping to create the moving and talking presidential figures featured in the August number of National Geographic. *His hobbies are hunting and piano-playing. Mrs Coba, who majored in languages, is using her spare time to write a translation of the classic Norwegian novel* The Commander's Daughters.

Mr Coba's work here will probably be less attention-getting than his work at Disneyland; he has joined the research and development department of Burnham-Massey-Microtech.

She giggled.

Research and development! And 'probably be less attention-getting'!

She giggled and giggled.

Couldn't stop.

Didn't *want* to!

She laughed, standing up and looking at that 'Notes on Newcomers' in its neat box of lines. '*Probably be less attention-getting!*' Dear God in heaven!

She closed the big brown volume, laughing, and picked it up with a volume beneath it and swung them down to their place on the shelf.

'Mrs Eberhart?' Miss Austrian upstairs. 'It's five of six; we're closing.'

Stop laughing, for God's sake. 'I'm done!' she called. 'I'm just putting them away!'

'Be sure you put them back in the right order.'

'I will!' she called.

'And put the lights out.'

'*Jawohl!*'

She put all the volumes away, in their right order more or less. 'Oh God in heaven!' she said, giggling. ' "*Probably*"! '

She took her coat and handbag, and switched the lights off, and went giggling up the stairs towards Miss Austrian peering at her. No wonder!

'Did you find what you were looking for?' Miss Austrian asked.

'Oh yes,' she said, swallowing the giggles. 'Thank you very much. You're a fount of knowledge, you and your library. Thank you. Goodnight.'

'Goodnight,' Miss Austrian said.

She went across to the Pharmacy, because God knows she *needed* a tranquillizer. The pharmacy was closing too; half dark, and nobody there but the Cornells. She gave the prescription to Mr Cornell, and he read it and said, 'Yes, you can have this now.' He went into the back.

She looked at combs on a rack, smiling. Glass clinked behind her and she turned around.

Mrs Cornell stood at the wall behind the side counter, outside the lighted part of the pharmacy. She wiped something with a cloth, wiped at the wall shelf, and put the something on it, clinking glass. She was tall and blonde, long-legged, full-bosomed; as pretty as – oh, say an Ike Mazzard girl. She took something from the shelf and wiped it, and wiped at the shelf, and put the something on it, clinking glass; and took something from the shelf and—

'Hi there,' Joanna said.

Mrs Cornell turned her head. 'Mrs Eberhart,' she said, and smiled. 'Hello. How are you?'

'Just fine,' Joanna said. 'Jim-dandy. How are *you*?'

'Very well, thank you,' Mrs Cornell said. She wiped what she was holding, and wiped at the shelf and put the something on it, clinking glass; and took something from the shelf and wiped it—

'You do that well,' Joanna said.

'It's just dusting,' Mrs Cornell said, wiping at the shelf.

A typewriter peck-peck-pecked from in back. Joanna said, 'Do you know the Gettysburg Address?'

'I'm afraid not,' Mrs Cornell said, wiping something.

'Oh come on,' Joanna said. 'Everybody does. "Fourscore and seven years—" '

'I know that but I don't know the rest of it,' Mrs Cornell said. She put the something on the shelf, clinking glass, and took something from the shelf and wiped it.

'Oh, I see, not necessary,' Joanna said. 'Do you know "This Little Piggy Went to Market"?'

'Of course,' Mrs Cornell said, wiping at the shelf.

'Charge?' Mr Cornell asked. Joanna turned. He held out a small white-capped bottle.

'Yes,' she said, taking it. 'Do you have some water? I'd like to take one now.'

He nodded and went in back.

Standing there with the bottle in her hand, she began to tremble. Glass clinked behind her. She pulled the cap from the bottle and pinched out the fluff of cotton. White tablets were inside; she tipped one into her palm, trembling, and pushed the cotton into the bottle and pressed the cap on. Glass clinked behind her.

Mr Cornell came with a paper cup of water.

'Thank you,' she said, taking it. She put the tablet on her tongue and drank and swallowed.

Mr Cornell was writing on a pad. The top of his head was white scalp, like an under-a-rock *thing*, a slug, with a few strands of brown hair pasted across it. She drank the rest of the water, put the cup down, and put the bottle into her handbag. Glass clinked behind her.

Mr Cornell turned the pad towards her and offered his pen, smiling. He was ugly; small-eyed, chinless.

She took the pen. 'You have a lovely wife,' she said, signing the pad. 'Pretty, helpful, submissive to her lord and master; you're a lucky man.' She held the pen out to him.

He took it, pink-faced. 'I know,' he said, looking downward.

'This town is full of lucky men,' she said. 'Goodnight.'

'Goodnight,' he said.

'Goodnight,' Mrs Cornell said. 'Come again.'

She went out into the Christmas-lighted street. A few cars passed by, their tyres squishing.

The Men's Association windows were alight; and windows of houses further up the hill. Red, green, and orange twinkled in some of them.

She breathed the night air deeply, and stomped boot-footed through a snowbank and across the street.

She walked down to the floodlit creche and stood looking at it; at Mary and Joseph and the Infant, and the lambs and calves around them. Very lifelike it all was, though a mite Disneyish.

'Do *you* talk too?' she asked Mary and Joseph.

No answer; they just kept smiling.

She stood there – she wasn't trembling any more – and then she walked back towards the Library.

She got into the car, started it, and turned on the lights; and cut across the street, backed, and drove past the creche and up the hill.

The door opened as she came up the walk, and Walter said, 'Where have you been?'

She kicked her boots against the doorstep. 'The Library,' she said.

'Why didn't you *call*? I thought you had an accident, with the snow . . .'

'The roads are clear,' she said, scuffing her boots on the mat.

'You should have called, for God's sake. It's after six.'

She went in. He closed the door.

She put her handbag on the chair and began taking her gloves off.

'What's she like?' he asked.

'She's very nice,' she said. 'Sympathetic.'

'What did she say?'

She put the gloves into her pockets and began unbuttoning her coat. 'She thinks I need a little therapy,' she said. 'To sort out my feelings before we move. I'm "pulled two ways by conflicting demands". ' She took the coat off.

'Well that sounds like sensible advice,' he said. 'To me, anyway. How does it sound to you?'

She looked at the coat, holding it by the lining at its collar, and let it drop over the handbag and the chair. Her hands were cold; she rubbed them palm against palm, looking at them.

She looked at Walter. He was watching her attentively, his head cocked. Stubble sanded his cheeks and darkened his chin-cleft. His face was fuller than she had thought – he was gaining weight – and below his wonderfully blue eyes pouches of flesh had begun to form. How old was he now? Forty on his next birthday, March third.

'To me,' she said, 'it sounds like a mistake, a very big mistake.' She lowered her hands and palmed her skirted sides. 'I'm taking Pete and Kim into the city,' she said. 'To Shep and—'

'What for?'

'—Sylvia's or to a hotel. I'll call you in a day or two. Or have someone call you. Another lawyer.'

He stared at her, and said, 'What are you *talking* about?'

'I *know*,' she said. 'I've been reading old *Chronicles*. I know what Dale Coba *used* to do, and I know what he's doing *now*, he and those other – CompuTech Instatron geniuses.'

He stared at her, and blinked. 'I don't know what you're talking about,' he said.

'Oh cut it out.' She turned away and went down the hallway and into the kitchen, switching on the lights. The port to the family-room showed darkness. She turned; Walter stood in the doorway. 'I haven't the foggiest idea what you're talking about,' he said.

She strode past him. 'Stop lying,' she said. 'You've been lying to me ever since I took my first picture.' She swung around and started up the stairs. 'Pete!' she called. 'Kim!'

'They're not here.'

She looked at him over the banisters as he came from the hallway.

'When you didn't show up,' he said, 'I thought it would be a good idea to get them out for the night. In case anything was wrong.'

She turned, looking down at him. 'Where are they?' she asked.

'With friends,' he said. 'They're fine.'

'*Which* friends?'

He came around to the foot of the stairs. 'They're fine,' he said.

She turned to face him, found the banister, held it. 'Our weekend alone?' she said.

'I think you ought to lie down awhile,' he said. He put a hand to the wall, his other hand on the banister. 'You're not making sense, Joanna,' he said. 'Diz, of all people; where does *he* come into things? And what you just said about my lying to you.'

'What did you do?' she said. 'Put a rush on the order? Is that why everyone was so busy this week? Christmas toys; *that's* a hoot. What were *you* doing, trying it for size?'

'I honestly don't know what you're—'

'The dummy!' she said. She leaned towards him, holding the banister. 'The robot! Oh very good; attorney surprised by a new allegation. You're wasting yourself in trusts and estates; you belong in a courtroom. What does it cost? Would you tell me? I'm dying to know. What's the going price for a stay-in-the-kitchen wife with big boobs and no demands? A fortune, I'll bet. Or do they do it dirt cheap, out of that good old Men's Association spirit? And what happens to the real ones? The incinerator? Stepford Pond?'

He looked at her, standing with his hands to the wall and the banister. 'Go upstairs and lie down,' he said.

'I'm going out,' she said.

He shook his head. 'No,' he said. 'Not when you're talking like this. Go upstairs and rest.'

She came down a step. 'I'm not going to stay here to be—'

'*You're not going out*,' he said. 'Now go up and rest. When you've calmed down we'll – try to talk sensibly.'

She looked at him standing there with his hands to the wall and the banister, looked at her coat on the chair – and turned and went quickly up the stairs. She went into the bedroom and closed the door; turned the key, switched on the lights.

She went to the dresser, pulled a drawer open, and got out a bulky white sweater; shook it unfolded and thrust her arms in and sleeved them. She pulled the turtleneck down over her head and gathered her hair and drew it free. The door was tried, tapped on.

'Joanna?'

'Scram,' she said, pulling the sweater down around her. 'I'm resting. You told me to rest.'

'Let me in for a minute.'

She stood watching the door, said nothing.

'Joanna, unlock the door.'

'Later,' she said. 'I want to be alone for a while.'

She stood without moving, watching the door.

'All right. Later.'

She stood and listened – to silence – and turned to the dresser and eased the top drawer open. She searched in it and found a pair of white gloves. She wriggled a hand into one and the other, and pulled out a long striped scarf and looped it around her neck.

She went to the door and listened, and switched the lights off.

She went to the window and raised the shade. The walk light shone. The Claybrooks' living-room was lighted but empty; their upstairs windows were dark.

She raised the window sash quietly. The storm window stood behind it.

She'd forgotten about the damn storm window.

She pushed at its bottom. It was tight, wouldn't budge. She hit at it with the side of her gloved fist, and pushed again with both hands. It gave, swinging outward a few inches – and would swing no farther. Small metal arms at its sides reached open to their fullest. She would have to unclamp them from the window frame.

Light fanned out on the snow below.

He was in the den.

She stood straight and listened; a tiny-toothed chittering came from behind her, from the phone on the night table; came again and again, long, short, long.

He was dialling the den phone.

Calling Dale Coba to tell him she was there. Proceed with plans. All systems go.

She tiptoed slowly to the door, listened, and turned the key back and eased the door open, a hand held against it. Pete's Star Trek gun lay by the threshold of his room. Walter's voice burred faintly.

She tiptoed to the stairs and started slowly, quietly down, pressing close to the wall, looking down through the banister supports at the corner of the den doorway.

'. . . not sure I can handle her myself . . .'

You're goddamn right you can't, counsellor.

But the chair by the front door was empty, her coat and handbag (car keys, wallet) gone.

Still, this was better than going through the window.

She made it down to the hall. He talked, and was quiet. Look for the handbag?

He moved in the den and she ducked into the living-room, stood at the wall, her back pressing tight.

His footsteps came into the hall, came near the doorway, stopped.

She held her breath.

A string of short hisses – his usual let's-see-now sound before tackling major projects; putting up storm windows, assembling a tricycle. (Killing a wife? Or did Coba the hunter perform that service?) She closed her eyes and tried not to think, afraid her thoughts would somehow beckon him.

His footsteps went up the stairs, slowly.

She opened her eyes and freed her breath bit by bit, waiting as he went higher.

She hurried quietly across the living-room, around chairs, the lamp table; unlocked the door to the patio and opened it, unlocked the storm door and pushed it against a base of drifted snow.

She squeezed herself out and ran over snow, ran and ran with her heart pounding; ran towards dark tree trunks over snow that was sled-tracked, Pete-and-Kim-boot-marked; ran, ran, and clutched a trunk and swung around it and rushed-stumbled-groped through tree trunks, tree trunks. She rushed, stumbled, groped, keeping to the centre of the long belt of trees that separated the houses on Fairview from the houses on Harvest.

She had to get to Ruthanne's. Ruthanne would lend her money and a coat, let her call an Eastbridge taxi or someone in the city – Shep, Doris, Andreas – someone with a car who would come pick her up.

Pete and Kim would be all right; she *had* to believe that. They'd be all right till she got to the city and spoke to people, spoke to a lawyer, got them back from Walter. They were probably being cared for beautifully by Bobbie or Carol or Mary Ann Stavros – by the things that were called by those names, that is.

And Ruthanne had to be *warned*. Maybe they could go together – though Ruthanne had time yet.

She came to the end of the belt of trees, made sure no cars were coming, and ran across Winter Hill Drive. Snow-pillowed spruce trees lined the far side of it; she hurried along behind them, her arms folded across her chest, her hands in their thin gloves burrowed in her armpits.

Gwendolyn Lane, where Ruthanne lived, was somewhere near Short Ridge Hill, out past Bobbie's; getting there would take almost an hour. More, probably, with the snow on the ground and the darkness. And she didn't dare hitch-hike because any car could be Walter, and she wouldn't know till too late.

Not only Walter, she realized suddenly. They would *all* be out looking for her, cruising the roads with flashlights, spotlights. How could they let her get away and tell? *Every* man was a threat, every car a danger. She would have to make sure Ruthanne's husband wasn't there before she rang the bell; look through the windows.

Oh God, *could* she get away? None of the others had.

But maybe none of the others had tried. Bobbie hadn't, Charmaine hadn't. Maybe she was the first one to find out in time. If it *was* in time . . .

She left Winter Hill and hurried down Talcott Lane. Headlights flashed, and a car swung from a driveway ahead on the other side. She crouched beside a parked car and froze, and light swam under her and the car drove past. She stood and looked: the car was going slowly, and sure enough, a spotlight beam lanced from it and slid a wobble of light over housefronts and lawns of snow.

She hurried down Talcott, past silent houses with Christmas-lighted windows and Christmas-light-trimmed doors. Her feet and legs were cold, but she was all right. At the end of Talcott was Old Norwood Road, and from there she would take either Chimney Road or Hunnicutt.

A dog barked nearby, barked ragingly; but the barking dropped behind her as she hurried on.

A black arm of tree branch lay on the trodden snow. She set her boot across it and broke off half of it, and hurried on, holding the cold wet strength of branch in her thin-gloved hand.

A flashlight gleamed in Pine Tree Lane. She ran between two houses, ran over snow towards a snowdome of bush; huddled behind it panting, holding the branch tightly in her aching-cold hand.

She looked out at the backs of houses, their windows alight. From the rooftop of one a stream of red sparks lofted and danced, dying among the stars.

The flashlight came swaying from between two houses, and she drew back behind the bush. She rubbed a stockinged knee, warmed the other in the crook of her elbow.

Wan light swept towards her over snow, and spots of light slid away over her skirt and gloved hand.

She waited, waited longer, and looked out. A dark man-shape went towards the houses, following a patch of lighted snow.

She waited till the man had gone, and rose and hurried towards the next street over. Hickory Lane? Switzer? She wasn't sure which it was, but both of them led towards Short Ridge Road.

Her feet were numb, despite the boots' fleece lining.

A light shone blindingly and she turned and ran. A light ahead swung towards her and she ran to the side, up a cleared driveway, past the side of a garage, and down a long slope of snow. She slipped and fell, clambered to her feet still holding the branch – the lights were bobbing towards her – and ran over level snow. A light swung towards her. She turned, towards snow with no hiding place, and turned, and stood where she was, panting. 'Get away!' she cried at the lights bobbing towards her, two on one side, one on the other. She raised the branch. 'Get away!'

Flashlights bobbed towards her, and slowed and stopped, their radiance blinding. 'Get away!' she cried, and shielded her eyes.

The light lessened. 'Put them out. We're not going to hurt you, Mrs Eberhart.' 'Don't be afraid. We're Walter's friends.' The light went; she lowered her hand. '*Your* friends too. I'm Frank Rodden-berry. You know me.' 'Take it easy, no one's going to hurt you.'

Shapes darker than the darkness stood before her. 'Stay away,' she said, raising the branch higher.

'You don't need that.'

'We're not going to hurt you.'

'Then get away,' she said.

'Everyone's out looking for you,' Frank Roddenberry's voice said. 'Walter's worried.'

'I'll bet he is,' she said.

They stood before her, four or five yards away; three men. 'You shouldn't be running around like this, no coat on,' one of them said.

'Get away,' she said.

'P-put it down,' Frank said. 'No one's going to hurt you.'

'Mrs Eberhart, I was on the phone with Walter not five minutes ago.' The man in the middle was speaking. 'We know about this idea you've got. It's *wrong*, Mrs Eberhart. Believe me, it's just not so.'

'Nobody's making robots,' Frank said.

'You must think we're a hell of a lot smarter than we really are,' the man in the middle said. 'Robots that can drive cars? And cook meals? And trim kids' hair?'

'And so real-looking that the kids wouldn't notice?' the third man said. He was short and wide.

'You must think we're a townful of geniuses,' the man in the middle said. 'Believe me, we're not.'

'You're the men who put us on the moon,' she said.

'*Who* is?' he said. 'Not me. Frank, did you put anybody on the moon? Bernie?'

'Not me,' Frank said.

The short man laughed. 'Not me, Wynn,' he said. 'Not that I know of.'

'I think you've got us mixed up with a couple of other fellows,' the man in the middle said. 'Leonardo da Vinci and Albert Einstein, maybe.'

'My gosh,' the short man said, 'we don't want *robots* for wives. We want real women.'

'Get away and let me go on,' she said.

They stood there, darker than the darkness. 'Joanna,' Frank said, 'if you were right and we could make robots that were so fantastic and lifelike, don't you think we'd cash in on it somehow?'

'That's right,' the man in the middle said. 'We could all be rich with that kind of knowhow.'

'Maybe you're going to,' she said. 'Maybe this is just the beginning.'

'Oh my Lord,' the man said, 'you've got an answer for everything. *You* should have been the lawyer, not Walter.'

Frank and the short man laughed.

'Come on, Joanna,' Frank said, 'p-put down that b-bat or whatever it is and—'

'Get away and let me go on!' she said.

'We can't do that,' the man in the middle said. 'You'll catch pneumonia. Or get hit by a car.'

'I'm going to a friend's house,' she said. 'I'll be inside in a few minutes. I'd be inside *now* if you hadn't – oh Jesus . . .' She lowered the branch and rubbed her arm; and rubbed her eyes and her forehead, shivering.

'Will you let us *prove* to you that you're wrong?' the man in the middle said. 'Then we'll take you *home*, and you can get some help if you need it.'

She looked at his dark shape. '*Prove* to me?' she said.

'We'll take you to the house, the Men's Association house—'

'Oh no.'

'Now just a second; just hear me out please. We'll take you to the house and you can check it over from stem to stern. I'm sure nobody'll object, under the circumstances. And you'll see there's—'

'I'm not setting foot in—'

'You'll see there's no robot factory there,' he said. 'There's a bar and a card-room and a few other rooms, and that's it. There's a projector and some very X-rated movies; that's our big secret.'

'And the slot machines,' the short man said.

'Yes. We've got some slot machines.'

'I wouldn't set foot in there without an armed guard,' she said. 'Of women soldiers.'

'We'll clear everyone out,' Frank said. 'You'll have the p-place all to yourself.'

'I won't go,' she said.

'Mrs Eberhart,' the man in the middle said, 'we're trying to be as gentle about this as we know how, but there's a limit to how long we're going to stand here parleying.'

'Wait a minute,' the short man said, 'I've got an idea. Suppose one of these women you think is a robot - suppose she was to cut herself on the finger, and bleed. Would *that* convince you she was a real person? Or would you say we made robots with blood under the skin?'

'For God's sake, Bernie,' the man in the middle said, and Frank said, 'You can't - ask someone to cut herself just to—'

'Will you let her answer the question, please? Well, Mrs Eberhart? Would that convince you? If she cut her finger and bled?'

'*Ber*nie . . .'

'Just let her answer, damn it!'

Joanna stood staring, and nodded. 'If she bled,' she said, 'I would - think she was - real . . .'

'We're not going to ask someone to cut herself. We're going to go to—'

'Bobbie would do it,' she said. 'If she's really Bobbie. She's my friend. Bobbie Markowe.'

'On Fox Hollow Lane?' the short man asked.

'Yes,' she said.

'You see?' he said. 'It's two minutes from here. Just think for a second will you? We won't have to go all the way in to the Centre; we won't even have to make Mrs Eberhart go somewhere she doesn't want to . . .'

Nobody said anything.

'I guess it's – not a b-bad idea,' Frank said. 'We could speak to Mrs Markowe . . .'

'She won't bleed,' Joanna said.

'She will,' the man in the middle said. 'And when she does, you'll know you're wrong and you'll let us take you home to Walter, without any arguments.'

'*If* she does,' she said. 'Yes.'

'All right,' he said. 'Frank, you run on ahead and see if she's there and explain to her. I'm going to leave my flashlight on the ground here, Mrs Eberhart. Bernie and I'll go a little ahead, and you pick it up and follow us, as far behind as makes you comfortable. But keep the light on us so we know you're still there. I'm leaving my coat too; put it on. I can hear your teeth chattering.'

She was wrong, she knew it. She was wrong and frozen and wet and tired and hungry, and pulled eighteen ways by conflicting demands. Including to pee.

If they were killers, they'd have killed her then. The branch wouldn't have stopped them, three men facing one woman.

She lifted the branch and looked at it, walking slowly, her feet aching. She let the branch fall. Her glove was wet and dirty, her fingers frozen. She flexed them, and tucked her hand into her other armpit. She held the long heavy flashlight as steady as she could.

The men walked with small steps ahead of her. The short man wore a brown coat and a red leather cap; the taller man, a green shirt and tan pants tucked into brown boots. He had reddish-blonde hair.

His sheepskin coat lay warm on her shoulders. Its smell was strong and good – of animals, of life.

Bobbie would bleed. It was coincidence that Dale Coba had worked on robots at Disneyland, that Claude Axhelm thought he was Henry Higgins, that Ike Mazzard drew his flattering sketches. Coincidence, that she had spun into – into madness. Yes, madness. ('It's *not* catastrophic,' Dr Fancher said, smiling. 'I'm sure I can help you.')

Bobbie would bleed, and she would go home and get warm.

Home to Walter?

When had it begun, her distrust of him, the feeling of nothingness between them? Whose fault was it?

His face had grown fuller; why hadn't she noticed it before today? Had she been too busy taking pictures, working in the darkroom?

She would call Dr Fancher on Monday, would go and lie on the brown leather couch; would cry a little maybe, and try to become happy.

The men waited at the corner of Fox Hollow Lane.

She made herself walk faster.

Frank stood waiting in Bobbie's bright doorway. The men talked with him, and turned to her as she came slowly up the walk.

Frank smiled. 'She says sure,' he said. 'If it'll make you feel b-better she'll be glad to do it.'

She gave the flashlight to the green-shirted man. His face was broad and leathery, strong looking. 'We'll wait out here,' he said, lifting the coat from her shoulders.

She said, 'She doesn't have to . . .'

'No, go on,' he said. 'You'll only start wondering again later.'

Frank came out on to the doorstep. 'She's in the kitchen,' he said.

She went into the house. Its warmth surrounded her. Rock music blared and thumped from upstairs.

She went down the hallway, flexing her aching hands.

Bobbie stood waiting in the kitchen, in red slacks and an apron with a big daisy on it. 'Hi, Joanna,' she said, and smiled. Beautiful bosomy Bobbie. But not a robot.

'Hi,' she said. She held the doorjamb, and leaned to it and rested the side of her head against it.

'I'm sorry to hear you're in such a state,' Bobbie said.

'Sorry to be in it,' she said.

'I don't mind cutting my finger a little,' Bobbie said, 'if it'll ease your mind for you.' She walked to a counter. Walked smoothly, steadily, gracefully. Opened a drawer.

'Bobbie . . .' Joanna said. She closed her eyes, and opened them. 'Are you really Bobbie?' she asked.

'Of course I am,' Bobbie said, a knife in her hand. She went to the sink. 'Come here,' she said. 'You can't see from there.'

The rock music blared louder. 'What's going on upstairs?' Joanna asked.

'I don't know,' Bobbie said. 'Dave has the boys up there. Come

251

here. You can't see.'

The knife was large, its blade pointed. 'You'll amputate your whole hand with that thing,' Joanna said.

'I'll be careful,' Bobbie said, smiling. 'Come on.' She beckoned, holding the large knife.

Joanna raised her head from the jamb, and took her hand from it. She went into the kitchen – so shining and immaculate, so un-Bobbie-like.

She stopped. *The music is in case I scream*, she thought. *She isn't going to cut her finger; she's going to—*

'Come on,' Bobbie said, standing by the sink, beckoning, holding the point-bladed knife.

Not catastrophic, Dr Fancher? Thinking they're robots not women? Thinking Bobbie would kill me? Are you sure you can help me?

'You don't have to do it,' she said to Bobbie.

'It'll ease your mind,' Bobbie said.

'I'm seeing a shrink after New Year,' she said. '*That*'ll ease my mind. At least I hope it will.'

'Come on,' Bobbie said. 'The men are waiting.'

Joanna went forward, towards Bobbie standing by the sink with the knife in her hand, so real-looking – skin, eyes, hair, hands, rising-falling aproned bosom – that she *couldn't* be a robot, she simply *couldn't* be, and that was all there was to it.

The men stood on the doorstep, blowing out steamy breath, their hands deep in their pockets. Frank hipped from side to side with the beat of the loud rock music.

Bernie said, 'What's taking so long?'

Wynn and Frank shrugged.

The rock music blared.

Wynn said, 'I'm going to call Walter and tell him we found her.' He went into the house.

'Get Dave's car keys!' Frank called after him.

252

3

The market parking lot was pretty well filled, but she found a good place up near the front; and that, plus the sun's warmth and the moist sweet smell of the air when she got out of the car, made her feel less bothered about having to be shopping. A *little* less bothered, anyway.

Miss Austrian came limping and caning towards her from the market's entrance, with a small paper bag in her hand and – she didn't believe it – a friendly smile on her Queen-of-Hearts white face. For her? 'Good morning, Mrs Hendry,' Miss Austrian said.

What do you know, black is bearable. 'Good morning,' she said.

'March is certainly going out like a lamb, isn't it?'

'Yes,' she said. 'It seemed like it was going to be a two-headed lion.'

Miss Austrian stopped and stood looking at her. 'You haven't been in the library in months,' she said. 'I hope we haven't lost you to television.'

'Oh no, not me,' she said, smiling. 'I've been working.'

'On another book?'

'Yes.'

'Good. Let me know when it's going to be published; we'll order a copy.'

'I will,' she said. 'And I'll be in soon. I'm almost done with it.'

'Have a good day,' Miss Austrian said, smiling and caning away.

'Thanks. You too.'

Well, there was *one* sale.

Maybe she'd been hypersensitive. Maybe Miss Austrian was cold to whites too until they'd been there a few months.

She went through the market's opening-by-themselves doors and found an empty cart. The aisles were the usual Saturday-morning parade.

She went quickly, taking what she needed, manoeuvring the cart in and out and around. 'Excuse me. Excuse me, please.' It still bugged her the way they shopped so languidly, gliding along as if they never sweated. How white could you get? Even filling their *carts* just so! She could shop the whole market in the time they did one aisle.

Joanna Eberhart came towards her, looking terrific in a tightly belted pale-blue coat. She had a fine figure and was prettier than Ruthanne remembered, her dark hair gleaming in graceful drawn-back wings. She came along slowly, looking at the shelves.

'Hello, Joanna,' Ruthanne said.

Joanna stopped and looked at her with thick-lashed brown eyes. 'Ruthanne,' she said, and smiled. 'Hello. How are you?' Her bow lips were red, her complexion pale-rose and perfect.

'I'm fine,' Ruthanne said, smiling. 'I don't have to ask how *you* are; you look marvellous.'

'Thanks,' Joanna said. 'I've been taking better care of myself lately.'

'It certainly shows,' Ruthanne said.

'I'm sorry I haven't called you,' Joanna said.

'Oh that's all right.' Ruthanne hitched her cart over in front of Joanna's so people could get by them.

'I meant to,' Joanna said, 'but there's been so much to do around the house. You know how it is.'

'That's all right,' Ruthanne said. 'I've been busy too. I'm almost done with my book. Just one more main drawing and a few small ones.'

'Congratulations,' Joanna said.

'Thanks,' Ruthanne said. 'What have *you* been up to? Have you taken any interesting pictures?'

'Oh no,' Joanna said. 'I don't do much photography any more.'

'You don't?' Ruthanne said.

'No,' Joanna said. 'I wasn't especially talented, and I was wasting a lot of time that I really have better uses for.'

Ruthanne looked at her.

'I'll call you one of these days when I get caught up with things,' Joanna said, smiling.

'What are you doing then, besides your housework?' Ruthanne asked her.

'Nothing, really,' Joanna said. 'Housework's enough for me. I used to feel I had to have other interests, but I'm more at ease with myself now. I'm much happier too, and so is my family. That's what really counts, isn't it?'

'Yes, I guess so,' Ruthanne said. She looked down at their carts, her own jumble-filled one against Joanna's neatly filled one. She hitched hers out of Joanna's way. 'Maybe we can have that lunch,' she said, looking at Joanna. 'Now that I'm finishing the book.'

'Maybe we can,' Joanna said. 'It was nice seeing you, Ruthanne.'

'Same here,' Ruthanne said.

Joanna, smiling, walked away – and stopped, took a box from a shelf, looked at it, and fitted it down into her cart. She went away down the market aisle.

Ruthanne stood watching her, and turned and went on in the other direction.

She couldn't get to work. She paced and turned in the close-walled room; looked out the window at Chickie and Sara playing with the Cohane girls; leafed through the stack of finished drawings and found them not as amusing and skilful as she'd thought they were.

When she finally got going on Penny at the wheel of the *Bertha P. Moran*, it was practically five o'clock.

She went down to the den.

Royal sat reading *Men in Groups*, his feet in blue socks on the hassock. He looked up at her. 'Done?' he asked. He had fixed the frame of his glasses with adhesive tape.

'Hell, no,' she said. 'I just got started.'

'How come?'

'*I* don't know,' she said. '*Something's* been bugging me. Listen, would you do me a favour? Now that it's moving I want to stay with it.'

'Supper?' he said.

She nodded. 'Would you take them to the pizza place? Or to McDonald's?'

He took his pipe from the table. 'All right,' he said.

'I want to get it done with,' she said. 'Otherwise I won't enjoy next weekend.'

He laid the open book down across his lap and took his pipe-cleaning gadget from the table.

She turned to go, and looked back at him. 'You sure you don't mind?' she asked.

He twisted the gadget back and forth in the pipe bowl. 'Sure,' he said. 'Stay with it.' He looked up at her and smiled. 'I don't mind,' he said.

A Kiss Before Dying

For
My Parents

The persons and incidents described in this book are fictional; any similarity to specific individuals and events is unintended by the author. The places, too – with the exception of certain points of interest in New York City – are imaginary and not intended to represent specific places.

Acknowledgement is due to Leeds Music Ltd., holders of the copyright, for permission to reprint part of the lyric of *On Top of Old Smoky*.

PART ONE
DOROTHY
1

His plans had been running so beautifully, so goddamned beautifully, and now *she* was going to smash them all. Hate erupted and flooded through him, gripping his face with jaw-aching pressure. That was all right though; the lights were out.

And she, she kept on sobbing weakly in the dark, her cheek pressed against his bare chest, her tears and her breath burning hot. He wanted to push her away.

Finally his face relaxed. He put his arm around her and stroked her back. It was warm, or rather his hand was cold; all of him was cold, he discovered; his armpits were creeping with sweat and his legs were quivering the way they always did when things took a crazy turn and caught him helpless and unprepared. He lay still for a moment, waiting for the trembling to subside. With his free hand he drew the blanket up around her shoulders. 'Crying isn't going to do any good,' he told her gently.

Obediently, she tried to stop, catching her breath in long choking gasps. She rubbed her eyes with the worn binding of the blanket. 'It's just – the holding it in for so long. I've known for days – weeks. I didn't want to say anything until I was sure—'

His hand on her back was warmer. 'No mistake possible?' He spoke in a whisper, even though the house was empty.

'No.'

'How far?'

'Two months almost.' She lifted her cheek from his chest, and in the dark he could sense her eyes on him. 'What are we going to do?' she asked.

'You didn't give the doctor your right name, did you?'

'No. He knew I was lying though. It was awful—'

'If your father ever finds out—'

259

She lowered her head again and repeated the question, speaking against his chest. 'What are we going to do?' She waited for his answer.

He shifted his position a bit, partially to give emphasis to what he was about to say, and partially in the hope that it would encourage her to move, for her weight on his chest had become uncomfortable.

'Listen, Dorrie,' he said. 'I know you want me to say we'll get married right away – tomorrow. And I want to marry you. More than anything else in the world. I swear to God I do.' He paused, planning his words with care. Her body, curled against his, was motionless, listening. 'But if we marry this way, me not even meeting your father first, and then a baby comes seven months later, you know what he'd do.'

'He couldn't *do* anything,' she protested. 'I'm over eighteen. Eighteen's all you have to be out here. What could he do?'

'I'm not talking about an annulment or anything like that.'

'Then what? What do you mean?' she appealed.

'The money,' he said. 'Dorrie, what kind of man is he? What did you tell me about him – him and his holy morals? Your mother makes a single slip; he finds out about it eight years later and divorces her, divorces her not caring about you and your sisters, not caring about her bad health. Well what do you think he would do to you? He'd forget you ever existed. You wouldn't see a penny.'

'I don't *care*,' she said earnestly. 'Do you think I care?'

'But I do, Dorrie.' His hand began moving gently on her back again. 'Not for me. I swear to God not for me. But for you. What will happen to us? We'll both have to quit school; you for the baby, me to work. And what will I do? – another guy with two years' college and no degree. What will I be? A clerk? Or an oiler in some textile mill or something?'

'It doesn't matter—'

'It does! You don't know how much it does. You're only nineteen and you've had money all your life. You don't know what it means not to have it. I do. We'd be at each other's throats in a year.'

'No, no, we wouldn't!'

'All right, we love each other so much we never argue. So where are we? In a furnished room with – with paper drapes? Eating spaghetti seven nights a week? If I saw you living that way and I knew it was my fault' – he paused for an instant, then finished very softly – 'I'd take out insurance and jump in front of a car.'

She began sobbing again.

He closed his eyes and spoke dreamly, intoning the words in a sedative chant. 'I had it planned so beautifully. I would have come to New York this summer and you would have introduced me to him. I could have gotten him to like me. You would have told me what he's interested in, what he likes, what he dislikes—' He stopped short, then continued. 'And after graduation we would have been married. Or even this summer. We could have come back here in September for our last two years. A little apartment of our own, right near the campus—'

She lifted her head from his chest. 'What are you trying to do?' she begged. 'Why are you saying these things?'

'I want you to see how beautiful, how wonderful, it could have been.'

'I see. Do you think I don't see?' The sobs twisted her voice. 'But I'm pregnant. I'm two months pregnant.' There was silence, as though unnoticed motors had suddenly stopped. 'Are – are you trying to get out of it? To get away? Is that what you're trying to do?'

'No! God no, Dorrie!' He grabbed her by the shoulders and pulled her up until her face was next to his. 'No!'

'Then what are you doing to me? We *have* to get married now! We don't have any choice!'

'We *do* have a choice, Dorrie,' he said.

He felt her body stiffen against his.

She gave a small terrified whisper, 'No!' and began shaking her head violently from side to side.

'Listen, Dorrie!' he pleaded, hands gripping her shoulders, 'No operation. Nothing like that.' He caught her jaw in one hand, fingers pressing into her cheeks, holding her head rigid. 'Listen!' He waited until the wildness of her breathing subsided. 'There's a guy on campus, Hermy Godsen. His uncle owns the drugstore on University and Thirty-fourth. Hermy sells things. He could get some pills.'

He let go of her jaw. She was silent.

'Don't you see, baby? We've got to try! It means so much!'

'Pills—' she said gropingly, as though it were a new word.

'We've got to try. It could be so wonderful.'

She shook her head in desperate confusion. 'Oh God, I don't know—'

He put his arms around her. 'Baby, I *love* you. I wouldn't let you take anything that might hurt you.'

261

She collapsed against him, the side of her head striking his shoulder. 'I don't know – I don't know—'

He said, 'It would be so wonderful,' his hand caressing, 'A little apartment of our own; no waiting for a damn landlady to go to the movies—'

Finally she said, 'How – how do you know they would work? What if they didn't work?'

He took a deep breath. 'If they don't work,' he kissed her forehead, and her cheek, and the corner of her mouth. 'If they don't work we'll get married right away and to hell with your father and Kingship Copper Incorporated. I swear we will, baby.'

He had discovered that she liked to be called 'baby'. When he called her 'baby' and held her in his arms he could get her to do practically anything. He had thought about it, and decided it had something to do with the coldness she felt towards her father.

He kept kissing her gently, talking to her with warm low words, and in a while she was calm and easy.

They shared a cigarette. Dorothy holding it first to his lips and then to hers, when the pink glow of each puff would momentarily touch the feathery blonde hair and the wide brown eyes.

She turned the burning end of the cigarette towards them and moved it around and around, back and forth, painting circles and lines of vivid orange in the darkness. 'I bet you could hypnotize someone this way,' she said. Then she swung the cigarette slowly before his eyes. In its wan light her slim-finger hand moved sinuously. 'You are my slave,' she whispered, lips close to his ear. 'You are my slave and completely in my power! You must obey my every bidding!' She was so cute he couldn't help smiling.

When they finished the cigarette he looked at the luminous dial of his watch. Waving his hand before her, he intoned, 'You must get dressed. You must get dressed because it is twenty past ten and you must be back at the dorm by eleven.'

2

He was born in Menasset, on the outskirts of Fall River, Massachusetts; the only child of a father who was an oiler in one of the Fall River textile mills and a mother who sometimes had to take in sewing when the money ran low. They were of English extraction with some French intermixed along the way, and they lived in a neighbourhood populated largely by Portuguese. His father found no reason to be bothered by this, but his mother did. She was a bitter and unhappy woman who had married young, expecting her husband to make more of himself than a mere oiler.

At an early age he became conscious of his good looks. On Sundays guests would come and exclaim over him – the blondness of his hair, the clear blue of his eyes – but his father was always there, shaking his head admonishingly at the guests. His parents argued a great deal, usually over the time and money his mother devoted to dressing him.

Because his mother had never encouraged him to play with the children of the neighbourhood, his first few days at school were an agony of insecurity. He was suddenly an anonymous member of a large group of boys, some of whom made fun of the perfection of his clothes and the obvious care he took to avoid the puddles in the school yard. One day, when he could bear it no longer, he went up to the ringleader of the hazers and spat on his shoes. The ensuing fight was brief but wild, and at the end of it he had the ringleader flat on his back and was kneeling on his chest, banging his head against the ground again and again. A teacher came running and broke up the fight. After that, everything was all right. Eventually he accepted the ringleaders as one of his friends.

His marks in school were good, which made his mother glow and even won reluctant praise from his father. His marks became still better when he started sitting next to an unattractive but brilliant girl who was so beholden to him for some awkward cloakroom kisses that she neglected to cover her paper during examinations.

His school days were the happiest of his life; the girls liked him for his looks and his charm; the teachers liked him because he was polite and attentive, nodding when they stated important facts, smiling when they attempted feeble jokes; and to the boys he showed his dislike of both girls and teachers just enough so that they liked him too. At home, he was a god. His father finally gave in and joined his mother in deferent admiration.

When he started dating, it was with the girls from the better part of the town. His parents argued again, over his allowance and the amount of money spent on his clothes. The arguments were short though, his father only sparring half-heartedly. His mother began to talk about his marrying a rich man's daughter. She only said it jokingly, of course, but she said it more than once.

He was president of his senior class in high school and was graduated with the third highest average and honours in mathematics and science. In the school year-book he was named the best dancer, the most popular, and the most likely to succeed. His parents gave a party for him which was attended by many young people from the better part of town.

Two weeks later he was drafted.

For the first few days of Basic Training, he coasted along on the glory he had left behind. But then reality rubbed off the insulation, and he found the impersonal authority of the army to be a thousand times more degrading than his early schooldays had been. And here, if he went up to the sergeant and spat on his shoes, he'd probably spend the rest of his life in the glasshouse. He cursed the blind system which had dropped him into the infantry, where he was surrounded by coarse, comic-book-reading idiots. After a while he read comic-books too, but only because it was impossible to concentrate on the copy of *Anna Karenina* he had brought with him. He made friends with some of the men, buying them beers in the canteen, and inventing obscene and fantastically funny biographies of all the officers. He was contemptuous of everything that had to be learned and everything that had to be done.

When he was shipped out of San Francisco, he vomited all the way across the Pacific, and he knew it was only partly from the lift and drop of the ship. He was sure he was going to be killed.

On an island still partially occupied by the Japanese, he became separated from the other members of his company and stood terrified in the midst of a silent jungle, desperately shifting this way and that, not knowing in which direction safety lay. A rifle slapped, sent a bullet keening past his ear. Jagged bird screams split the air. He dropped to his stomach and rolled under a bush, sick with the certainty that this was the moment of his death.

The bird sounds fluttered down into silence. He saw a gleam in a tree up ahead, and knew that that was where the sniper waited. He found himself inching forward under the bushes, dragging his rifle with one hand. His body was clammy cold and alive with sweat; his legs were trembling so badly that he was sure the Jap would hear the leaves rustling under them. The rifle weighed a ton.

Finally he was only twenty feet from the tree, and looking up, he could discern the figure crouched in it. He lifted his rifle; he aimed, and fired. The bird chorus shrieked. The tree remained motionless. Then suddenly a rifle dropped from it, and he saw the sniper slide clumsily down a vine and drop to the ground with his hands high in the air; a little yellow man grotesquely festooned with leaves and branches, his lips emitting a terrified sing-song chatter.

Keeping the rifle trained on the Jap, he stood up. The Jap was as scared as he was; the yellow face twitched wildly and the knees shivered; more scared, in fact, for the front of the Jap's pants was dark with a spreading stain.

He watched the wretched figure with contempt. His own legs steadied. His sweating stopped. The rifle was weightless, like an extension of his arms, immobile, aimed at the trembling caricature of a man that confronted him. The Jap's chatter had slowed to a tone of entreaty. The yellow-brown fingers made little begging motions in the air.

Quite slowly, he squeezed the trigger. He did not move with the recoil. Insensate to the kick of the butt in his shoulder, he watched attentively as a black-red hole blossomed and swelled in the chest of the Jap. The little man slid clawing to the jungle floor. Bird screams were like a handful of coloured cards thrown into the air.

After looking at the slain enemy for a minute or so, he turned and walked away. His step was as easy and certain as when he had crossed the stage of the auditorium after accepting his diploma.

He received an honourable discharge in January of 1947, and left the army with the Bronze Star and the Purple Heart, and the record of a shell fragment traced in a vein of thin scar tissue over his dextral ribs. Returning home, he found that his father had been killed in an automobile accident while he was overseas.

He was offered several jobs in Menasset, but rejected them as being of too little promise. His father's insurance money was sufficient to support his mother and she was taking in sewing again besides, so after two months of drawing admiration from the townspeople and twenty dollars a week from the federal government, he decided to go to New York. His mother argued, but he was over twenty-one, if only by a few months, so he had his way. Some of the neighbours expressed surprise that he did not intend to go to college, especially when the government would pay for it. He felt, however, that college would only be an unnecessary stopover on the road to the success he was certain awaited him.

His first job in New York was in a publishing house, where the personnel manager assured him there was a fine future for the right man. Two weeks, however, was all he could take of the shipping-room.

His next job was with a department store, where he was a sales clerk in the men's wear department. The only reason he remained there an entire month was that he was able to buy his clothes on a twenty per cent discount.

By the end of August, when he had been in New York five months and had had six jobs, he was again prey to the awful insecurity of being one among many rather than one alone; unadmired and with no tangible sign of success. He sat in his furnished room and devoted some time to serious self-analysis. If he had not found what he wanted in these six jobs, he decided, it was unlikely that he would find it in the next six. He took out his fountain pen and made what he considered to be a completely objective list of his qualities, abilities, and talents.

In September, he enrolled in a dramatic school under the G.I. Bill. The instructors expressed great hopes for him at first; he was handsome, intelligent, and had a fine speaking voice, although the New England accent would have to be eliminated. He had great hopes too, at first. Then he discovered how much work and study were involved in becoming an actor. The exercises the instructors gave – 'Look at this photograph and act out the emotions it brings to mind' – struck him as ridiculous, although the other students seemed to take them seriously. The only study to which he applied himself was diction; he had been dismayed to hear the world 'accent' used in relation to himself, having always thought of it as something someone else had.

In December, on his twenty-second birthday, he met a fairly attractive widow. She was in her forties and she had a good deal of money. They met on the corner of Fifth Avenue and Fifty-fifth Street – quite romantically, they later agreed. Stepping back on to the kerb to avoid a bus, she tripped and fell into his arms. She was embarrassed and terribly shaken. He made some humorous comments on the ability and thoughtfulness of Fifth Avenue bus drivers, and then they went down the street to a dignified bar where they had two Martinis each, for which he paid the check. In the weeks that followed they attended small East Side art movies and dined in restaurants where there were three or four people to be tipped at the end of the meal. He paid many more checks, although not again with his own money.

Their attachment lasted for several months, during which time he weaned himself away from the dramatic school – no painful process – and devoted his afternoons to squiring her on shopping tours, some of which were for him. At first he was somewhat embarrassed at being seen with her because of the obvious discrepancy in their ages, but he soon found himself getting over that. He was, however, dissatisfied with the relationship on two accounts: firstly, while her face was fairly attractive, her body unfortunately, was not; secondly, and of greater importance, he learned from the elevator operator in her apartment house that he was only one of a series of young men, each of whom had been replaced with equinoctial regularity at the end of six months. It seemed, he reflected humorlessly, that this was another position with no future. At the end of five months, when she began to exhibit less curiosity about how he spent the nights he was not with her, he anticipated her move and told her that he had to return home because his mother was deathly ill.

He did return home, after reluctantly excising the custom tailor's labels from his suits and pawning a Patek Philippe wristwatch. He spent the early part of June lounging around the house, silently lamenting the fact that the widow had not been younger, prettier, and open to a more permanent sort of alliance.

That was when he began to make his plans. He decided he would go to college after all. He took a summer job in a local dry goods store because, while the G.I. Bill would cover his tuition, his living expenses would be quite high; he was going to attend a good school.

He finally chose Stoddard University in Blue River, Iowa, which was supposed to be something of a country club for the children of the mid-western wealthy. There was no difficulty in his gaining admission. He had such a fine high school record.

In his first year he met a lovely girl, a senior, the daughter of the vice-president of an internationally organized farm equipment concern. They took walks together, cut classes together, and slept together. In

May, she told him that she was engaged to a boy back home and she hoped he hadn't taken it too seriously.

In his sophomore year, he met Dorothy Kingship.

3

He got the pills, two greyish-white capsules, from Hermy Godsen. They cost him five dollars.

At eight o'clock he met Dorothy at their regular meeting-place, a tree-shrouded bench in the centre of the wide stretch of lawn between the Fine Arts and Pharmacy buildings. When he left the white concrete path and cut across the darkness of the lawn he saw that Dorothy was already there, sitting stiffly with her fingers locked in her lap, a dark coat cloaking her shoulders against the April coolness. A street lamp off to the side cast leaf shadows on her face.

He sat down beside her and kissed her cheek. She greeted him softly. From the rectangle of lighted windows in the Fine Arts Building drifted the conflicting themes of a dozen pianos. After a moment he said, 'I got them.'

A couple crossed the lawn towards them and, seeing the bench occupied, turned back to the white path. The girl's voice said, 'My God, they're all taken.'

He took the envelope from his pocket and put it into Dorothy's hand. Her fingers felt the capsules through the paper. 'You're to take both of them together,' he said. 'You're liable to get a little fever, and you'll probably feel nauseous.'

She put the envelope in her coat pocket. 'What's in them?' she asked.

'Quinine, some other things. I'm not sure.' He paused. 'They can't hurt you.'

He looked at her face and saw that she was staring off at something beyond the Fine Arts Building. He turned and followed her gaze to a winking red light miles away. It marked the local radio station's transmitting tower, which stood atop Blue River's tallest structure, the Municipal Building – where the Marriage Licence Bureau was. He wondered if she were staring at the light because of that, or only because it was a winking red light in a sky of darkness. He touched her hands and found them cold. 'Don't worry, Dorrie. Everything will be all right.'

They sat in silence for a few minutes, and then she said, 'I'd like to go to a movie tonight. There's a Joan Fontaine picture at the Uptown.'

'I'm sorry,' he said, 'but I've got a ton of Spanish homework.'

'Let's go over to the Student Union. I'll help you with it.'

'What are you trying to do, corrupt me?'

He walked her back across the campus. Opposite the low modern shape of the Girls' Dormitory, they kissed good night. 'See you in class tomorrow,' he said. She nodded, and kissed him again. She was trembling. 'Look baby, there's nothing to worry about. If they don't work we get married. Haven't you heard? – love conquers all.' She was waiting for him to say more. 'And I love you very much,' he said, and kissed her. When their lips parted, hers were pressed into an unsteady smile.

'Good night, baby,' he said.

He returned to his room, but he couldn't do his Spanish. He sat with his elbows planted on the bridge table, his head in his hands, thinking about the pills. Oh God, they must work! They *will* work!

But Hermy Godsen had said: 'I can't give you no written guarantee. If this girl-friend of yours is two months gone already—'

He tried not to think about it. He got up and went to the bureau and opened the bottom drawer. From under the neatly folded pyjamas he took two pamphlets whose supple covers gleamed with a copper finish.

On first meeting Dorothy and discovering, through one of the student-secretaries in the Registrar's office, that she was not merely one of the 'Kingship Copper' Kingships but actually a daughter of the corporation's president, he had written a business-like letter to the organization's New York office. In it he represented himself as contemplating an investment in Kingship Copper (which was not entirely an untruth), and requested descriptive brochures of its holdings.

Two weeks later, when he was reading *Rebecca* and pretending to love it because it was Dorothy's favourite book, and when she was doggedly knitting him bulky argyle socks because a previous boy-friend had liked them and so the knitting of them had become the badge of her devotion, the pamphlets arrived. He opened their envelope with ceremonial care. They proved wonderful – *Technical Information on Kingship Copper and Copper Alloys and Kingship Copper, Pioneer in Peace and War* they were called, and they were crammed with photographs: mines and furnaces, concentrators and converters, reversing mills, rolling mills, rod mills, and tube mills. He read them a hundred times and knew every caption by heart. He returned to them at odd moments, a musing smile on his lips, like a woman with a love letter.

Tonight they were no good. 'Open-cut mine in Landers, Michigan. From this single mine, a year output . . . '

What angered him most was that in a sense the responsibility for the entire situation rested with Dorothy. He had wanted to take her to his room only once – a down-payment guaranteeing the fulfilment of a contract. It was Dorothy, with her gently closed eyes and her passive, orphan hunger, who had wished for further visits. He struck the table. It really was her fault! Damn her!

He dragged his mind back to the pamphlets, but it was no use; after a minute he pushed them away and rested his head in his hands again. If the pills didn't work – leave school? Ditch her? It would be futile; she knew his Menasset address. Even if she should be reluctant to seek him out, her father would hasten to do so. Of course there could be no legal action (or could there?), but Kingship could still cause him plenty of trouble. He imagined the wealthy as a closely knit, mutually protective clan, and he could hear Leo Kingship: 'Watch out for this young man. He's no good. I feel it my duty as a parent to warn you—' And what would be left for him then? Some shipping-room?

Or if he married her. Then she would have the baby and they'd never get a cent out of Kingship. Again the shipping-room, only this time saddled with a wife and child. Oh God!

The pills *had* to work. That was all there was to it. If they failed, he didn't know what he'd do.

The book of matches was white, with *Dorothy Kingship* stamped on it in copper leaf. Every Christmas Kingship Copper gave personalized matches to its executives, customers, and friends. It took her four strokes to light the match, and when she held it to her cigarette the flame trembled as though in a breeze. She sat back, trying to relax, but she couldn't tear her eyes from the open bathroom door, the white envelope waiting on the edge of the sink, the glass of water . . .

She closed her eyes. If only she could speak to Ellen about it. A letter had come that morning – 'The weather has been beautiful . . . president of the refreshment committee for the Junior Prom . . . have you read Marquand's new novel?' – another of the mean-ingless mechanical notes that had been drifting between them since Christmas and the argument. If only she could get Ellen's advice, talk to her the way they used to talk . . .

Dorothy had been five and Ellen six when Leo Kingship divorced his wife. A third sister, Marion, was ten. When the three girls lost their mother, first through the divorce and then through her death a year later, Marion felt the loss most deeply of all. Recalling clearly the accusations and denunciations which had preceded the divorce, she recounted them in bitter detail to her sisters as they grew up. She exaggerated Kingship's cruelty to some degree. As the years passed she grew apart, solitary, and withdrawn.

Dorothy and Ellen, however, turned to each other for the affec-tion which they received neither from their father, who met their coldness with coldness, nor from the series of odourless and precise governesses to whom he transferred the custody the courts had granted him. The two sisters went to the same schools and camps, joined the same clubs and attended the same dances (taking care to return home at the hour designated by their father). Where Ellen led, Dorothy followed.

But when Ellen entered Caldwell College, in Caldwell, Wisconsin, and Dorothy made plans to follow her there the next year, Ellen said no; Dorothy should grow up and become self-reliant. Their father agreed, self-reliance being a trait he valued in himself and in others. A measure of compromise was allowed, and Dorothy was sent to Stoddard, slightly more than a hundred miles from Caldwell, with the understanding that the sisters would visit one another on week-ends. A few visits were made, the length of time between them increasing progressively, until Dorothy austerely announced that her first year of college had made her completely self-reliant, and the visits stopped altogether. Finally, this past Christmas, there had been an argument. It had started on nothing – 'If you want to borrow my blouse you might at least have asked me!' – and had swollen because Dorothy had been in a depressed mood all during her vacation. When the girls returned to school, the letters between them faded to brief, infrequent notes . . .

There was still the telephone. Dorothy found herself staring at it. She could get Ellen on the line in an instant . . . But no; why should she be the one to give in first and chance a rebuff? She squashed her cigarette in an ashtray. Besides, now that she had calmed down, what was there to hesitate about? She would take the pills; if they worked, all well and good. If not; marriage. She thought about how wonderful that would be, even if her father did have a fit. She didn't want any of *his* money, anyway.

She went to the hall door and locked it, feeling a slight thrill in the unaccustomed and somewhat melodramatic act.

In the bathroom, she took the envelope from the edge of the sink and tilted the capsules into her palm. They were grey-white, their gelatin coating lustrous, like elongated pearls. Then, as she dropped the envelope into the waste-basket, the thought flashed into her mind – 'What if I don't take them?'

They would be married tomorrow! Instead of waiting until the summer, or more likely until graduation – over two years – they'd be married by tomorrow night!

But it wouldn't be fair. She had promised she would try. Still, tomorrow . . .

She lifted the glass, clapped the pills into her mouth, and drained the water in a single draught.

4

The classroom, in one of Stoddard's new buildings, was a clean rectangle with one wall of aluminium-framed glass. Eight rows of seats faced the lecturer's platform. There were ten grey metal seats to a row, each with a right arm that curved in and fanned to form a writing surface.

He sat at the back of the room, in the second seat from the window. The seat on his left, the window seat, the empty seat, was hers. It was the first class of the morning, a daily Social Science lecture, and their only class together this semester. The speaker's voice droned in the sun-filled air.

Today of all days she could have made an effort to be on time. Didn't she know he'd be frozen in an agony of suspense? Heaven or hell. Complete happiness, or the awful mess he didn't even want to think about. He looked at his watch; 9.08. Damn her.

He shifted in his seat, fingering his key-chain nervously. He stared at the back of the girl in front of him and started to count the polka dots on her blouse.

The door at the side of the room opened quietly. His head jerked around.

She looked awful. Her face was pasty white so that the rouge was like paint. There were grey arcs under her eyes. She was looking at him the instant the door opened, and with a barely perceptible motion, she shook her head.

Oh God! He turned back to the key-chain in his fingers and stared at it, numb. He heard her coming around behind him, slipping into the seat on his left. He heard her books being put on the floor in the aisle between them, and then the scratching of a pen on paper, and finally the sound of a page being torn from a spiral-bound pad.

He turned. Her hand was extended towards him, holding a folded piece of blue-lined paper. She was watching him, her wide eyes anxious.

He took the paper and opened it in his lap:

I had a terrible fever and I threw up. But nothing happened.

He closed his eyes for a moment, then opened them again and turned to her, his face expressionless. Her lips made a tight nervous smile. He tried to make himself return the smile, but he couldn't. His eyes went back to the note in his hand. He folded the paper in half, then folded it again and again, until it was a tight wad, which he placed in his pocket. Then he sat with his fingers locked firmly together, watching the lecturer.

After a few minutes, he was able to turn to Dorothy, give her a reassuring smile, and form the words 'Don't worry' with silent lips.

When the bell sounded at 9.55, they left the room with the other students who were laughing and pushing and complaining about coming exams and overdue papers and dates. Outside, they moved from the crowded path and stood in the shadow of the concrete-walled building.

The colour was beginning to return to Dorothy's cheeks. She

273

spoke quickly. 'It'll be all right. I know it will. You won't have to quit school. You'll get more money from the government, won't you? With a wife?'

'A hundred and five a month.' He couldn't keep the sourness out of his voice.

'Others get along on it – the ones in the trailer camp. We'll manage.'

He put his books down on the grass. The important thing was to get time, time to think. He was afraid his knees were going to start shaking. He took her by the shoulders, smiling. 'That's the spirit. You just don't worry about anything.' He took a breath. 'Friday afternoon we'll go down to the Municipal—'

'Friday?'

'Baby, it's Tuesday. Three days won't make any difference now.'

'I thought we'd go today.'

He fingered the collar of her coat. 'Dorrie, we can't. Be practical. There are so many things to be taken care of. I think I have to take a blood test first. I'll have to check on that. And then, if we get married Friday we can have the week-end for a honeymoon. I'm going to get us a reservation at the New Washington House—'

She frowned indecisively.

'What difference will three days make?'

'I guess you're right,' she sighed.

'That's my baby.'

She touched his hand. 'I – I know it isn't the way we wanted it, but – you're happy, aren't you?'

'Well, what do you think? Listen, the money isn't that important. I just thought that for your sake—'

Her eyes were warm, reaching.

He looked at his watch. 'You have a ten o'clock, don't you?'

'*Solamente el Espanol.* I can cut it.'

'Don't. We'll have better reasons to cut our morning classes.' She squeezed his hand. 'I'll see you at eight,' he said. 'At the bench.' Reluctantly, she turned to go. 'Oh, Dorrie—'

'Yes?'

'You haven't said anything to your sister, have you?'

'Ellen? No.'

'Well you better not. Not until after we're married.'

'I thought I'd tell her before. We've been so close. I'd hate to do it without telling her.'

'If she's been so rotten to you the past two years—'

274

'Not rotten.'

'That was the word you used. Anyhow, she's liable to tell your father. He might do something to stop us.'

'What could he do?'

'I don't know. He would try anyway, wouldn't he?'

'All right. Whatever you say.'

'Afterwards you'll call her up right away. We'll tell everybody.'

'All right.' A final smile, and then she was walking to the sunbright path, her hair glinting gold. He watched her until she disappeared behind the corner of a building. Then he picked up his books and walked away in the opposite direction. A braking car screeched somewhere, making him start. It sounded like a bird in a jungle.

Without forming a conscious decision he was cutting the rest of the day's classes. He walked all the way through the town and down to the river, which was not blue but a dull muddy brown. Leaning on the rail of the black-girded Morton Street Bridge, he looked into the water and smoked a cigarette.

Here it was. The dilemma had finally caught up with him and engulfed him like the filthy water that pounded the abutments of the bridge. Marry her or leave her. A wife and a child and no money, or be hounded and blackballed by her father. 'You don't know me, sir. My name is Leo Kingship. I'd like to speak to you about the young man you have just employed – the young man your daughter is going with – I think you should know—' Then what? There would be no place to go to but home. He thought of his mother. Years of complacent pride, patronizing sneers for the neighbours' children, and then she sees him clerking in a dry goods store, not just for the summer, but permanently. Or even some lousy mill! His father had failed to live up to her expectations, and he'd seen what love she'd had for the old man burn itself into bitterness and contempt. Was that in store for him too? People talking behind his back. Oh Jesus! Why hadn't the goddamned pills killed the girl?

If only he could get her to undergo an operation. But no, she was determined to get married, and even if he pleaded she'd still want to consult Ellen before taking such a drastic measure. And anyway, where would they get the money? And suppose something happened, suppose she died. He would be involved because he would have been the one who arranged for the operation. He'd be right where he started – with her father out to get him. Her death

275

wouldn't do him a bit of good.

Not if she died that way.

There was a heart scratched into the black paint of the railing, with initials on either side of the arrow that pierced it. He concentrated on the design, picking at it with his fingernail, trying to blank his mind of what had finally welled to the surface. The scratches had exposed cross-sections of paint layers: black, orange, black, orange, black, orange. It reminded him of the pictures of rock strata in a geology text. Records of dead ages.

Dead.

After a while he picked up his books and slowly walked from the bridge. Cars flew towards him and passed with a rushing sound.

He went into a dingy riverside restaurant and ordered a ham sandwich and coffee. He ate the sandwich at a little corner table. While sipping the coffee, he took out his memorandum book and fountain pen.

The first thing that had entered his mind was the Colt .45 he had taken on leaving the army. Bullets could be obtained with little difficulty. But assuming he wanted to do it, a gun would be no good. It would have to look like an accident, or suicide. The gun would complicate matters too much.

He thought of poison. But where would he get it? Hermy Godsen? No. Maybe the Pharmacy Building. The supply room there shouldn't be too hard to get into. He would have to do some research at the library, to see which poison . . .

It would have to look like an accident or suicide, because if it looked like anything else, he would be the first one the police would suspect.

There were so many details – assuming he wanted to do it. Today was Tuesday; the marriage could be postponed no later than Friday or she might get worried and call Ellen. Friday would be the deadline. It would require a great deal of fast, careful planning.

He looked at the notes he had written:

1. *Gun* (n.g.)
2. *Poison*
   (a) *Selection*
   (b) *Obtaining*
   (c) *Administering*
   (d) *Appearance of* (1) *accident*
           or (2) *suicide*

Assuming, of course, that he wanted to do it. At present it was all purely speculative: he would explore the details a little. A mental exercise.

But his stride, when he left the restaurant and headed back through town, was relaxed and sure and steady.

5

He reached the campus at three o'clock and went directly to the library. In the card catalogue he found listed six books likely to contain the information he wanted; four of them were general works on toxicology; the other two, manuals of criminal investigation whose file cards indexed chapters on poisons. Rather than have a librarian get the books for him, he registered at the desk and went into the stacks himself.

He had never been in the stacks before. There were three floors filled with bookshelves, a metal staircase spiralling up through them. One of the books on his list was out. He found the other five without difficulty on the shelves on the third floor. Seating himself at one of the small study tables that flanked a wall of the room, he turned on the lamp, arranged his pen and memorandum book in readiness, and began to read.

At the end of an hour, he had a list of five toxic chemicals likely to be found in the Pharmacy supply room, any one of which, by virtue of its reaction time and the symptoms it produced prior to death, would be suitable for the plan whose rudimentary outline he had already formulated during the walk from the river.

He left the library and the campus, and walked in the direction of the house where he roomed. When he had gone two blocks he came upon a dress shop whose windows were plastered with big-lettered sale signs. One of the signs had a sketch of an hour-glass with the legend *Last Days of Sale*.

He looked at the hour-glass for a moment. Then he turned around and walked back towards the campus.

He went to the University Bookstore. After consulting the mimeo-graphed booklist tacked to the bulletin board, he asked the clerk for a copy of *Pharmaceutical Techniques*, the laboratory manual used by the advanced pharmacy students. 'Pretty late in the semester,' the clerk commented, returning from the rear of the store with the manual in his hand. It was a large thin book with a distinctive green-paper cover. 'Lose yours?'

'No. It was stolen.'

'Oh. Anything else?'

'Yes. I'd like some envelopes, please.'

'What size?'

'Regular envelopes. For letters.'

The clerk put a pack of white envelopes on the book. 'That's a dollar-fifty and twenty-five. Plus tax – a dollar seventy-nine.'

The College of Pharmacy was housed in one of Stoddard's old build-ings, three storeys of ivy-masked brick. Its front had broad stone steps that led up to the main entrance. At either side of the building were steps leading down to a long corridor which cut straight through the basement, where the supply-room was located. There was a Yale lock on the supply-room door. Keys to this lock were in the possession of the usual university functionaries, the entire faculty of the College of Pharmacy, and those advanced students who had received permission to work without supervision. This was the regular arrangement followed in all departments of the univer-sity which used enough equipment to necessitate the maintenance of a supply-room. It was an arrangement familiar to almost everyone on campus.

He came in at the main entrance and crossed the hall to the lounge. Two bridge games were in session and some other students sat around, reading and talking. A few of them glanced up when he entered. He went directly to the long clothes rack in the corner and put his books on the shelf above it. Removing his corduroy jacket, he hung it on one of the hooks. He took the pack of envelopes from among his books, removed three of them and folded them into his hip pocket. He but the rest of the envelopes back with the books, took the lab. manual, and left the room.

He went downstairs to the basement corridor. There was a men's room to the right of the stairwell. He entered it and after looking under the doors to make sure the booths were empty, dropped the manual on the floor. He stepped on it a few times and then kicked it all the way across the tiled floor. When he picked it up it had lost its blatant newness. He put it on the ledge of a sink. Watching himself in the mirror, he unbuttoned the cuffs of his shirt and rolled the sleeves half-way up his arms. He unfastened his collar and lowered the knot of his tie. Tucking the manual under his arm, he stepped out into the corridor.

The door to the supply room was midway between the central stairwell and one end of the corridor. On the wall a few feet beyond it was a bulletin board. He walked down to the board and stood before it, looking at the notices tacked there. He stood with his back turned slightly towards the end of the corridor, so that from the corner of his eye he could see the stairwell. He held the manual under his left arm. His right arm was at his side, fingers by his key-chain.

A girl came out of the supply-room, closing the door behind her. She carried one of the green manuals and a beaker half full of a milky fluid. He watched her as she went down the corridor and turned to climb the stairs.

Some people entered from the door behind him. They walked past, talking. Three men. They went straight down the corridor and out the door at the other end. He kept looking at the bulletin board.

At five o'clock bells rang, and for a few minutes there was a great deal of activity in the hallway. It subsided quickly though, and he was alone again. One of the notices on the board was an illustrated folder about summer sessions at the University of Zurich. He began to read it.

A bald-headed man emerged from the stairwell. He had no manual, but it was apparent from the angle at which he approached and the movement of his hand towards his key-chain that he was coming to the supply-room. There was, however, the look of an instructor . . . Putting his back towards the approaching man, he turned a page of the Zurich pamphlet. He heard the sound of a key in the door, and then the door opening and closing. A minute later, it opened and closed again, and the sound of the man's footsteps diminished and then changed to a stair-climbing rhythm.

He resumed his former position and lit a cigarette. After one puff he dropped it and ground it under his foot; a girl had appeared, coming towards him. There was a lab. manual in her hand. She had lanky brown hair and horn-rimmed glasses. She was taking a brass key from the pocket of her smock.

He lessened the pressure of the manual under his arm, letting it drop down into his left hand, conspicuous with its green cover. With a last casual finger-flick at the Zurich folder, he moved to the supply-room door, not looking at the approaching girl. He fumbled with his key-chain as though the keys had caught in the pocket's lining. When he finally brought out the bunch of keys the girl was already at the door. His attention was on the keys, shuffling through them, apparently looking for a certain one. It seemed as though he didn't become conscious of the girl's presence until she had inserted her key in the lock, turned it and pushed the door partially open, smiling up at him 'Oh, thanks,' he said, reaching over her to push the door wide, his other hand tucking the keys back in his pocket. He followed the girl in and closed the door behind them.

It was a small room with counters and shelves filled with labelled bottles and boxes and odd-looking apparatus. The girl touched a wall switch, making fluorescent tubes wink to life, incongruous among the room's old-fashioned fittings. She went to the side of the room and opened her manual on the counter there. 'Are you in Aberson's class?' she asked.

He went to the opposite side. He stood with his back to the girl, facing a wall of bottles. 'Yes,' he said.

Faint clinkings of glass and metal sounded in the room. 'How's his arm?'

'About the same, I guess,' he said. He touched the bottles, pushing them against each other, so the girl's curiosity should not be aroused.

'Isn't that the craziest thing?' she said. 'I hear he's practically blind without his glasses.' She lapsed into silence.

Each bottle had a white label with black lettering. A few bore an additional label that glared POISON in red. He scanned the rows of bottles quickly, his mind registering only the red-labelled ones. The list was in his pocket, but the names he had written on it shimmered in the air before him as though printed on a gauze screen.

He found one. The bottle was a bit above eye level not two feet from where he stood. *White Arsenic* – As_4O_6 – POISON. It was half filled with white powder. His hand moved towards it, stopped.

He turned slowly until he could see the girl from the corner of his eye. She was pouring some yellow powder from the tray of a balance into a glass cup. He turned back to the wall and opened his manual on the counter. He looked at meaningless pages of diagrams and instructions.

At last the girl's movements took on sounds of finality; the balance being put away, a drawer closing. He leaned more closely over the manual, following the lines of print with a careful finger. Her footsteps moved to the door. 'So long,' she said.

'So long.'

The door opened and closed. He looked around. He was alone.

He took his handkerchief and the envelopes from his pocket. With the handkerchief draped over his right hand, he lifted the arsenic bottle from the shelf, put it on the counter, and removed the stopper. The powder was like flour. He poured about a tablespoonful into the envelope; it fell in whispering puffs. He folded the envelope into a tight pack, folded that into a second envelope and pocketed it. After he had stoppered and replaced the bottle he moved slowly around the room, reading the labels on drawers and boxes, the third envelope held open in his hand.

He found what he wanted within several minutes: a box filled with empty gelatine capsules, glittering like oval bubbles. He took six of them, to be on the safe side. He put them in the third envelope and slipped it gently into his pocket, so as not to crush the capsules. Then, when everything appeared as he had found it, he took the manual from the counter, turned out the lights, and left the room.

After retrieving his books and his jacket, he left the campus again. He felt wonderfully secure; he had devised a course of action and had executed its initial steps with speed and precision. Of course it was still only a tentative plan and he was in no way committed to carry it through to its goal. He would see how the next steps worked out. The police would never believe that Dorrie had taken a lethal dose of arsenic by accident. It would have to look like suicide, like obvious, indisputable suicide. There would have to be a note or something equally convincing. Because if they ever suspected that it wasn't suicide and started an investigation, the girl who had let him into the supply-room would always be able to identify him.

He walked slowly, conscious of the fragile capsules in the lefthand pocket of his trousers.

He met Dorothy at eight o'clock. They went to the Uptown, where the Joan Fontaine picture was still playing.

The night before, Dorothy had been anxious to go; her world had been as grey as the pills he had given her. But tonight – tonight everything was radiant. The promise of immediate marriage had swirled away her problems the way a fresh wind swirls away dead leaves; not only the looming problem of her pregnancy, but all the problems she had ever had; the loneliness, the insecurity. The only hint of grey remaining was the inevitable day when her father, having already been appalled by a hasty unquestioning marriage, would learn the truth about its cause. But even that seemed of trifling importance tonight. She had always hated his unyielding morality and had defied it only in secrecy and guilt. Now she would be able to display her defiance openly, from the security of a husband's arms. Her father would make an ugly scene of it, but in her heart she looked forward to it a little.

She envisioned a warm and happy life in the trailer camp, still warmer and happier when the baby came. She was impatient with the motion picture, which distracted her from a reality more beautiful than any movie could ever be.

He, on the other hand, had not wanted to see the picture on the previous night. He was not fond of movies, and he especially disliked pictures that were founded on exaggerated emotions. Tonight, however, in comfort and darkness, with his arm about Dorothy and his hand resting lightly on the upper slope of her breast, he relished the first moments of relaxation he had known since Sunday night, when she had told him she was pregnant.

He surrendered all his attention to the picture, as though answers to eternal mysteries were hidden in the windings of its plot. He enjoyed it immensely.

Afterwards he went home and made up the capsules.

He funnelled the white powder from a folded sheet of paper into the tiny gelatine cups, and then fitting the slightly larger cups that were the other halves of the capsules over them. It took him almost an hour, since he ruined two capsules, one squashed and the other softened by the moisture of his fingers, before he was able to complete two good ones.

When he was finished, he took the damaged capsules and the remaining capsules and powder into the bathroom and flushed them down the toilet. He did the same with the paper from which he had poured the arsenic and the envelopes in which he had carried it, first tearing them into small pieces. Then he put the two arsenic capsules into a fresh envelope and hid them in the bottom drawer of his bureau, under the pyjamas and the Kingship Copper pamphlets, the sight of which brought a wry smile to his face.

One of the books he had read that afternoon had listed the lethal dose of arsenic as varying from one-tenth to one-half of a gram. By rough computation, he estimated that the two capsules contained a total of five grams.

6

He followed his regular routine on Wednesday, attending all his classes, but he was no more a part of the life and activity that surrounded him than is the diver in his diving bell a part of the alien world in which he is submerged. All of his energies were turned inward, focused on the problem of beguiling Dorothy into writing a suicide note or, if that could not be contrived, finding some other way to make her death seem self-induced. While in this state of laboured concentration he unconsciously dropped the pretence of being undecided as to whether or not he would actually go through with his plans; he was going to kill her; he had the poison and he already knew how he was going to administer it; there was only this one problem left, and he was determined to solve it. At times during the day, when a loud voice or the chalk's screech made him momentarily aware of his surroundings, he looked at his classmates with mild surprise. Seeing their brows contracted over a stanza in Browning or a sentence in Kant, he felt as though he had suddenly come upon a group of adults playing hopscotch.

A Spanish class was his last of the day, and the latter half of it was devoted to a short unannounced examination. Because it was his poorest subject, he forced himself to lower the focus of his concentration to the translating of a page of the florid Spanish novel which the class was studying.

Whether the stimulus was the actual work he was doing or the comparative relaxation which the work offered after a day of more rigorous thinking, he could not say. But in the midst of his writing the idea came to him. It rose up fully formed, a perfect plan, unlikely to fail and unlikely to arouse Dorothy's suspicion. The contemplation of it so occupied his mind that when the period ended he had completed only half the assigned page. The inevitable failing mark in the quiz troubled him very little. By ten o'clock the following morning Dorothy would have written her suicide note.

That evening, his landlady having gone to an Eastern Star meeting, he brought Dorothy back to his room. During the two hours they spent there, he was as warm and tender as she had ever wished him to be. In many ways he liked her a great deal, and he was conscious of the fact that this was to be her last such experience.

Dorothy, noticing his new gentleness and devotion, attributed it to the nearness of their wedding. She was not a religious girl, but she deeply believed that the state of wedlock carried with it something of holiness.

Afterwards they went to a small restaurant near the campus. It was a quiet place and not popular with the students; the elderly proprietor, despite the pains he took to decorate his windows with blue and white crêpe paper and Stoddard pennants, was irascible with the noisy and somewhat destructive university crowd.

Seated in one of the blue-painted wall booths, they had cheese-burgers and chocolate malteds, while Dorothy chattered on about a new type of bookcase that opened out into a full-size dining-table. He nodded unenthusiastically, waiting for a pause in the monologue.

'Oh, by the way,' he said, 'do you still have that picture I gave you? The one of me.'

'Of course I do.'

'Well let me have it back for a couple of days. I want to have a copy made to send to my mother. It's cheaper than getting another print from the studio.'

She took a green wallet from the pocket of the coat folded on the seat beside her. 'Have you told your mother about us?'

'No, I haven't.'

'Why not?'

He thought for a moment. 'Well, as long as you can't tell your family until after, I thought I wouldn't tell my mother. Keep it our secret.' He smiled. 'You haven't told anyone, have you?'

'No,' she said. She was holding a few snapshots she had taken from the wallet. He looked at the top one from across the table. It was of Dorothy and two other girls – her sisters, he supposed. Seeing his glance, she passed the picture to him. 'The middle one is Ellen, and Marion's on the end.'

The three girls were standing in front of a car, a Cadillac, he noticed. The sun was behind them, their faces shadowed, but he could still discern a resemblance among them. All had the same wide eyes and prominent cheekbones. Ellen's hair seemed to be of a shade midway between Dorothy's light and Marion's dark. 'Who's the prettiest?' he asked. 'After you, I mean.'

'Ellen,' Dorothy said. 'And before me. Marion could be very pretty too, only she wears her hair like this.' She pulled her hair back severely and frowned. 'She's the intellectual. Remember?'

'Oh. The Proust fiend.'

She handed him the next snapshot, which was of her father. 'Grrrr,' he growled, and they both laughed. Then she said, 'And this is my fiancé,' and passed him his own picture.

He looked at it speculatively, seeing the symmetry of the clear planes. 'I don't know,' he drawled, rubbing his chin. 'Looks kind of dissolute to me.'

'But so handsome,' she said. 'So very handsome.' He smiled and pocketed the picture with a satisfied air. 'Don't lose it,' she warned seriously.

'I won't.' He looked around, his eyes bright. On the wall next to them was a selector for the jukebox at the rear of the restaurant. 'Music,' he announced, producing a nickel and dropping it into the slot. He traced a finger up and down the twin rows of red buttons as he read the names of the songs. He paused at the button opposite *Some Enchanted Evening*, which was one of Dorothy's favourites, but then his eyes caught *On Top of Old Smoky* further down the row, and he thought a moment and chose that instead. He pushed the button. The jukebox bloomed into life, casting a pink radiance on Dorothy's face.

She leaned at her wrist-watch, then leaned back, eyes closed rapturously. 'Oh gee, just think,' she murmured, smiling. 'Next week no rushing back to the dorm!' Introductory guitar chords sounded from the jukebox. 'Shouldn't we put in an application for one of the trailers?'

'I was down there this afternoon,' he said. 'It may take a couple of weeks. We can stay at my place. I'll speak to my landlady.' He took a paper napkin and began tearing careful bits from its folded edges.

A girl's voice sang:

> *On top of old Smoky,*
> *All covered with snow,*
> *I lost my true loved one,*
> *For courtin' too slow . . .*

'Folk songs,' Dorothy said, lighting a cigarette. The flame glinted

285

on the copper-stamped match-book.

'The trouble with you,' he said, 'is you're a victim of your aristocratic upbringing.'

> *Now courtin's a pleasure,*
> *But partin's a grief,*
> *And a false-hearted lover*
> *Is worse than a thief . . .*

'Did you take the blood test?'

'Yes. I did that this afternoon too.'

'Don't I have to take one?'

'No.'

'I looked in the Almanac. It said "blood test required" for Iowa. Wouldn't that mean for both?'

'I asked. You don't have to.' His fingers picked precisely at the napkin.

> *A thief he will rob you*
> *And take what you have,*
> *But a false-hearted lover*
> *Will lead you to the grave . . .*

'It's getting late—'

'Just let's stay to the end of the record, okay? I like it.'

He picked symmetrically and the paper became a web of intricate lace. He spread his handiwork on the table admiringly.

> *The grave will decay you,*
> *And turn you to dust.*
> *Not one man in a hundred*
> *A poor girl can trust . . .*

'See what we women have to put up with?'

'A pity. A real pity. My heart bleeds.'

Back in his room, he held the photograph over an ashtray and touched a lighted match to its lowest corner. It was a print of the year-book photo and a good picture of him; he hated to burn it, but he had written 'To Dorrie, with all my love' across the bottom of it.

7

As usual she was late for the nine o'clock class. Sitting at the back of the room, he watched the rows of seats fill up with students. It was raining outside and ribbons of water sluiced down the wall of windows. The seat on his left was still empty when the lecturer mounted the platform and began talking about the city manager form of government.

He had everything in readiness. His pen poised over the notebook opened before him and the Spanish novel, *La Casa de las Flores Negras*, was balanced on his knee. A sudden heart-stopping thought hit him; what if she picked today to cut? Tomorrow was Friday, the deadline. This was the only chance he would have to get the note, and he had to have it by tonight. What would he do if she cut?

At ten past nine, though, she appeared; out of breath, her books in one arm, her raincoat over the other, a smile for him lighting her face the moment she eased through the door. Tiptoeing across the room behind him, she draped the raincoat over the back of her chair and sat down. The smile was still there as she sorted her books, keeping a notebook and a small assignment pad before her and putting the remaining books in the aisle between their seats.

Then she saw the book that he held open on his knee, and her eyebrows lifted questioningly. He closed the book, keeping his finger between the pages, and tilted it towards her so that she could see the title. Then he opened it again and with his pen ruefully indicated the two exposed pages and his notebook, meaning that that was how much translation he had to do. Dorothy shook her head condolingly. He pointed to the lecturer and to her notebook – she should take notes and he would copy them later. She nodded.

After he had worked for a quarter of an hour, carefully following the words of the novel, slowly writing in his notebook, he glanced cautiously at Dorothy and saw that she was intent on her own work. He tore a piece of paper about two inches square from the corner of one of the notebook's pages. One side of it he covered with doodling; words written and crossed out, spirals and zigzagging lines. He turned that side downward. With a finger stabbing the print of the novel, he began shaking his head and tapping his foot in impatient perplexity.

Dorothy noticed. Inquiringly, she turned to him. He looked at her and expelled a troubled sigh. Then he lifted his finger in a gesture that asked her to wait a moment before returning her attention to the lecturer. He began to write, squeezing words on to the small piece of paper, words that he was apparently copying from the novel. When he was through, he passed the paper to her.

Traducción, por favour, he had headed it. Translation, please:
Querido,
Espero que me perdonares por la infelicidad que causaré. No hay ninguna otra cosa que puedo hacer.

She gave him a mildly puzzled glance, because the sentences were quite simple. His face was expressionless, waiting. She picked up her pen and turned the paper over, but the back of it was covered with doodling. So she tore a page from her assignment pad and wrote on that.

She handed him the translation. He read it and nodded. '*Muchas gracias*,' he whispered. He hunched forward and wrote in his notebook. Dorothy crumpled the paper on which he had written the Spanish and dropped it to the floor. From the corner of his eye he saw it land. There was another bit of paper near it, and some cigarette butts..At the end of the day they would all be swept together and burned.

He looked at the paper again, at Dorothy's small slanted handwriting:

Darling,
I hope you will forgive me for the unhappiness that I will cause. There is nothing else that I can do.

He tucked the paper carefully into the pocket on the inner cover of the notebook, and closed it. He closed the novel and placed it on top of the notebook. Dorothy turned, looked at the books and then at him. Her questioning glance asked if he were finished.

He nodded and smiled.

They were not to see each other that evening. Dorothy wanted to wash and set her hair and pack a small valise for their week-end honeymoon at the New Washington House. But at 8.30 the phone on her desk rang.

'Listen, Dorrie. Something's come up. Something important.'

'What do you mean?'

'I've got to see you right away.'

'But I can't. I can't come out. I just washed my hair.'

'Dorrie, this is important.'

'Can't you tell me now?'

'No. I have to see you. Meet me at the bench in half an hour.'

'It's *drizzling* out. Can't you come to the lounge downstairs?'

'No. Listen, you know that place where we had the cheeseburgers last night? Gideon's? Well, meet me there. At nine.'

'I don't see why you can't come to the lounge—'

'Baby, please—'

'Is - is it anything to do with tomorrow?'

'I'll explain everything at Gideon's.'

'Is it?'

'Well, yes and no. Look, everything's going to be all right. I'll explain everything. You just be there at nine.'

'All right.'

At ten minutes to nine he opened the bottom drawer of his bureau and took two envelopes from under the pyjamas. One envelope was stamped, sealed, and addressed:

> Miss Ellen Kingship
> North Dormitory
> Caldwell College
> Caldwell, Wisconsin.

He had typed the address that afternoon in the Student Union lounge, on one of the typewriters available for general student use. In the envelope was the note that Dorothy had written in class that morning. The other envelope contained the two capsules.

He put one envelope in each of the inner pockets of his jacket, taking care to remember which envelope was on which side. Then he put on his trenchcoat, belted it securely, and with a final glance in the mirror, left the room.

When he opened the front door of the house he was careful to step out with his right foot forward, smiling indulgently at himself as he did so.

8

Gideon's was practically empty when he arrived. Only two booths were occupied; in one, a pair of elderly men sat frozen over a chessboard; in the other, across the room, Dorothy sat with her hands clasped around a cup of coffee, gazing down at it as though it were a crystal ball. She had a white kerchief tied about her head. The hair that showed in front was a series of flattened damp-darkened rings, each transfixed by a bobby pin.

She became aware of him only when he was standing at the head of the booth taking off his coat. Then she looked up, her brown eyes worried. She had no make-up on. Her pallor and the closeness of her hair made her seem younger. He put his coat on a hook beside her raincoat and eased into the seat opposite her. 'What is it?' she asked anxiously.

Gideon, a sunken-cheeked old man, came to their table. 'What's yours?'

'Coffee.'

'Jest coffee?'

'Yes.'

Gideon moved away, his slippered feet dragging audibly. Dorothy leaned forward. 'What is it?'

He kept his voice low, matter-of-fact. 'When I got back to my place this afternoon there was a message for me. Hermy Godsen called.'

Her hands squeezed tighter around the coffee cup. 'Hermy Godsen—'

'I called him back.' He paused for a moment, scratching the table-top. 'He made a mistake with those pills the other day. His uncle—' He cut off as Gideon approached with a cup of coffee rattling in his hand. They sat motionless, eyes locked, until the old man was gone. 'His uncle switched things around in the drugstore or something. Those pills weren't what they were supposed to be.'

'What were they?' She sounded frightened.

'Some kind of emetic. You said you threw up.' Lifting his cup, he put a paper napkin in the saucer to absorb the coffee that Gideon's shaking hand had spilled. He pressed the bottom of the cup into the napkin to wipe it.

She breathed relief. 'Well that's all *over* with. They didn't hurt me. The way you spoke on the phone, you got me so worried—'

'That's not the point, baby.' He put the soggy napkin to one side. 'I saw Hermy just before I called you. He gave me the right pills, the ones we should have had last time.'

Her face sagged. 'No—'

'Well there's nothing tragic. We're right where we were Monday, that's all. It's a second chance. If they work, everything's rosy. If not, we can still get married tomorrow.' He stirred his coffee slowly, watching it swirl. 'I've got them with me. You can take them tonight.'

'But—'

'But what?'

'I don't *want* a second chance. I don't *want* any more *pills*—' She leaned forward, hands knotted white on the table. 'All I've been thinking about is tomorrow, how wonderful, how happy—' She closed her eyes, the lids pressing out tears.

Her voice had risen. He glanced across the room to where the chess players sat with Gideon watching. Fishing a nickel from his pocket, he pushed it into the jukebox selector and jabbed one of the buttons. Then he clasped her clenched hands, forced them open, held them. 'Baby, baby,' he soothed, 'do we have to go through it all again? It's you I'm thinking of. You, not me.'

'No.' She opened her eyes, staring at him. 'If you were thinking of me you'd want what I want.' Music blared up, loud brassy jazz.

'What *do* you want, baby? To starve? This is no movie; this is real.'

'We *wouldn't* starve. You're making it worse that it would be. You'd get a good job even if you didn't finish school. You're smart, you're—'

'You don't know,' he said flatly. 'You just don't know. You're a kid who's been rich all her life.'

Her hands tried to clench within his. 'Why must everyone always throw that at me? Why must *you*? Why do you think that's so important?'

'It is important, Dorrie, whether you like it or not. Look at you – a pair of shoes to match every outfit, handbag to match every pair of shoes. You were brought up that way. You can't—'

'Do you think that matters? Do you think I care?' She paused. Her hands relaxed, and when she spoke again the anger in her voice had softened to a straining earnestness. 'I know you smile at me sometimes, at the movies I like, at my being romantic. Maybe it's because you're five years older than I am, or because you were in the army, or

291

because you're a man – I don't know. But I believe, I truly believe, that if two people really love each other – the way I love you, the way you say you love me – then nothing else matters very much – money, things like that, they just don't matter. I believe that, I really do—' Her hands pulled away from his and flew to her face.

He drew a handkerchief from his breast pocket and touched it to the back of her hand. She took it and held it against her eyes. 'Baby, I believe that too. You know I do,' he said gently. 'Do you know what I did today?' He paused. 'Two things. I bought a wedding ring for you, and I put a classified ad. in the Sunday *Clarion*. An ad. for a job. Night work.' She patted her eyes with the handkerchief. 'Maybe I did paint things too black. Sure, we'll manage to get along, and we'll be happy. But let's be just a *little* realistic, Dorrie. We'll be even happier if we can get married this summer with your father's approval. You can't deny that. And all you have to do for us to have a chance at that extra happiness is just take these pills.' He reached into his inner pocket and brought out the envelope, pressing it to make sure it was the right one. 'There isn't one logical reason why you should refuse.'

She folded the handkerchief and turned it in her hands, looking at it. 'Since Tuesday morning I've been dreaming about tomorrow. It changed everything – the whole world.' She pushed the handkerchief over to him. 'All my life I've been arranging things to suit my father.'

'I know you're disappointed, Dorrie. But you've got to think of the future.' He extended the envelope to her. Her hands, folded on the table, made no move to accept it. He put it on the table between them, a white rectangle slightly swollen by the capsules inside. 'I'm prepared to take a night job now, to quit school at the end of this term. All I'm asking you to do is to swallow a couple of pills.'

Her hands remained folded, her eyes on the sterile whiteness of the envelope.

He spoke with cool authority: 'If you refuse to take them, Dorothy, you're being stubborn, unrealistic, and unfair. Unfair more to yourself than to me.'

The jazz record ended, the coloured lights died, and there was silence.

They sat with the envelope between them.

Across the room there was the whisper of a chessman being placed and an old man's voice said, 'Check.'

Her hands parted slightly and he saw the glisten of sweat in her palms. His own hands were sweating too, he realized. Her eyes lifted from the envelope to meet his.

'Please, baby—'

She looked down again, her face rigid.

She took the envelope. She pushed it into the handbag on the bench beside her and then sat gazing at her hands on the table.

He reached across the table and touched her hand, caressed the back of it, clasped it. With his other hand he pushed his untouched coffee over to her. He watched her lift the cup and drink. He found another nickel in his pocket and, still holding her hand, dropped the coin into the selector and pressed the button opposite *Some Enchanted Evening*.

They walked the wet concrete paths in silence, divorced by the privacy of their thoughts, holding hands through habit. The rain had stopped, but face-tingling moisture filled the air, defining the scope of each street-lamp in shifting grey.

Across the street from the dorm, they kissed. Her lips under his were cool and compressed. When he tried to part them she shook her head. He held her for a few minutes, whispering persuasively, and then they exchanged good nights. He watched as she crossed the street and passed into the yellow-lighted hall of the building.

He went to a nearby bar, where he drank two glasses of beer and tore a paper napkin into a delicate filigreed square of admirable detail. When half an hour had passed, he stepped into the telephone booth and dialled the number of the dorm. He asked the girl at the switchboard for Dorothy's room.

She answered after two rings. 'Hello?'

'Hello, Dorrie?' Silence at her end. 'Dorrie, did you do it?'

A pause. 'Yes.'

'When?'

'A few minutes ago.'

He drew a deep breath. 'Baby, does that girl on the switchboard ever listen in?'

'No. They fired the last girl for—'

'Well listen, I didn't want to tell you before, but – they might hurt a little.' She said nothing. He continued, 'Hermy said you'll probably throw up, like before. And you might get a sort of burning sensation in your throat and some pains in your stomach. Whatever

happens, don't get frightened. It'll just mean that the pills are working. Don't call anyone.' He paused, waiting for her to say something, but she was silent. 'I'm sorry I didn't tell you before but, well,
it won't hurt too much. And it'll be over before you know it.' A
pause. 'You're not angry with me, are you, Dorrie?'

'No.'

'You'll see, it'll all be for the best.'

'I know. I'm sorry I was stubborn.'

'That's all right, baby. Don't apologize.'

'I'll see you tomorrow.'

'Yes.'

There was silence for a moment and then she said, 'Well, good
night.'

'Good-bye, Dorothy,' he said.

9

Striding into the classroom Friday morning he felt weightless and tall
and wonderful. It was a beautiful day; sunlight poured into the room
and bounced off the metal chairs to spangle the walls and ceiling.
Taking his seat in the back of the room, he stretched his legs all the
way out and folded his hands across his chest, watching the other
students crowd in. The morning's radiance had inflamed them all,
and tomorrow was the first Varsity baseball game, with the Spring
Dance in the evening; there was chattering, shouting, grinning and
laughter.

Three girls stood off to the side and whispered excitedly. He
wondered if they were dorm girls, if they could possibly be talking
about Dorothy. She couldn't have been found yet. Why would anyone enter her room? They would think she wanted to sleep late. He
was counting on her not being found for several hours; he held his
breath until the girls' whispering erupted into laughter.

No, it was unlikely that she would be found before one o'clock or
so. 'Dorothy Kingship wasn't at breakfast and she wasn't at lunch
either' – then they would knock on her door and get no answer.
They'd most likely have to get the house mother or someone with a

key. Or it might not even happen then. Many of the dorm girls slept through breakfast, and some of them ate lunch out occasionally. Dorrie hadn't had any close friends who would miss her right away. No, if his luck held, they might not find her until Ellen's phone call came.

The night before, after saying good-bye to Dorothy on the telephone, he had returned to the dorm. In the mailbox on the corner he had posted the envelope addressed to Ellen Kingship, the envelope containing Dorothy's suicide note. The first mail collection of the morning was at six; Caldwell was only a hundred miles away and so the letter would be delivered this afternoon. If Dorothy were found in the morning, Ellen, notified by her father, might leave Caldwell for Blue River before the letter arrived, which would mean that an investigation of some sort would almost certainly be launched, because the suicide note would not be found until Ellen returned to Caldwell. It was the only risk, but it was a small one and unavoidable; it had been impossible for him to sneak into the Girls' Dormitory to plant the note in Dorothy's room, and impractical to secrete it in the pocket of her coat or in one of her books prior to giving her the pills, in which case there would have been the far greater risk of Dorothy finding the note and throwing it away or, still worse, putting two and two together.

He had decided upon noon as the safety mark. If Dorothy were found after twelve, Ellen would have received the note by the time the school authorities contacted Leo Kingship and Kingship in turn contacted her. If his luck *really* held, Dorothy would not be discovered until late afternoon, a frantic phone call from Ellen leading to the discovery. Then everything would be neat and in its proper order.

There would be an autopsy, of course. It would reveal the presence of a great deal of arsenic and a two-month embryo – the way and the why of her suicide. That and the note would more than satisfy the police. Oh, they would make a perfunctory check of the local drugstores, but it would net them only a fat zero. They might even consider the Pharmacy supply-room. They would ask the students, 'Did you see this girl in the supply-room or anywhere in the Pharmacy Building? – displaying photograph of the deceased. Which would produce another zero. It would be a mystery, but hardly an important one; even if they couldn't be sure of the source of the arsenic, her death would still be an indisputable suicide.

Would they look for the man in the case, the lover? He considered that unlikely. For all they knew she was as promiscuous as a bunny. That was hardly their concern. But what about Kingship? Would outraged morality inaugurate a private inquiry? 'Find the man who ruined my daughter!' Although, from the description of her father that Dorothy had painted, Kingship would be more likely to think 'Aha, she was ruined all along. Like mother, like daughter.' Still, there might be an inquiry . . .

He would certainly be dragged into that. They had been seen together, though not as frequently as might be expected. In the beginning, when success with Dorothy had been in question, he had not taken her to popular places; there had been that other rich girl last year, and if Dorothy didn't work out as he planned there would be others in the future; he didn't want the reputation of a money-chaser. Then, when Dorothy did work out, they had gone to movies, to his room, and to quiet places like Gideon's. Meeting at the bench rather than in the dorm lounge had become a custom.

He would be involved in any inquiry all right, but Dorothy hadn't told anyone they were going steady, so other men would be involved too. There was the red-headed one she'd been chatting with outside the classroom the day he first saw her and noticed the copper-stamped *Kingship* on her matches, and the one she'd started knitting argyle socks for, and every man she'd dated once or twice – they would *all* be brought into it, and then it would be anybody's guess as to who had 'ruined' her because all would deny it. And as thorough as the investigation might be, Kingship could never be certain that he hadn't completely overlooked the 'guilty' party. There would be suspicion directed at all the men, proof against none.

No, everything would be perfect. There would be no quitting school, no shipping clerk's job, no oppressing wife and child, no vengeful Kingship. Only one tiny shadow . . . Suppose he were pointed out around campus as one of the men who'd gone with Dorothy. Suppose that the girl who had let him into the supply-room should see him again, hear who he was, learn that he wasn't a Pharmacy student at all . . . But even that was unlikely, out of twelve thousand students . . . But suppose the very worst happened. Suppose she saw him, remembered, and went to the police. Even then, it would be no evidence. So he was in the supply-room. He could make up some kind of excuse and they would have to believe him, because there would still be the note, the note in Dorothy's handwriting. How could they explain—

The door at the side of the room opened, creating a draft that lifted the pages of his notebook. He turned to see who it was. It was Dorothy.

Shock burst over him, hot as a wave of lava. He half-rose, blood rushing to his face, his chest a block of ice. Sweat dotted his body and crawled like a million insects. He knew it was written on his face in swollen eyes and burning cheeks, written for her to see, but he couldn't stop it. She was looking at him wonderingly, the door closing behind her. Like any other day; books under her arm, green sweater, plaid skirt. Dorothy. Coming to him, made anxious by his face.

His notebook slapped to the floor. He bent down, seizing the momentary escape. He stayed with his face near the side of the seat, trying to breathe. What happened? Oh God! She didn't take the pills! She couldn't have! She lied! The bitch. The lying goddamned bitch! The note on its way to Ellen – Oh Jesus, Jesus!

He heard her sliding into her seat. Her frightened whisper – '*What's wrong? What's the matter*?' He picked up the notebook and sat erect, feeling the blood drain from his face, from his entire body, leaving him dead cold with sweat drops moving. '*What's wrong*?' He looked at her. Like any other day. There was a green ribbon in her hair. He tried to speak but it was as if he were empty inside with nothing to make a sound. '*What is it*?' Students were turning to look. Finally he scraped out, 'Nothing – I'm all right—'

'You're sick! Your face is as grey as—'

'I'm all right. It's – it's this,' touching his side where she knew he had the army scar. 'It gives me a twinge once in a while—'

'God, I thought you were having a heart attack or something,' she whispered.

'No. I'm all right.' He kept looking at her, trying for one good breath, his hands clutching his knees in rigid restraint. Oh God, what could he do? The bitch! She had planned also, planned to get married!

He saw the anxiety for him melt from her face, a flushed tension replacing it. She ripped a page from her assignment pad, scribbled on it, and passed it to him:

The pills didn't work.

The liar! The goddamned liar! He crumpled the paper and

squeezed it in his hand, fingernails biting into his palm. Think! Think! His danger was so enormous he couldn't grasp it all at once. Ellen would receive the note – when? Three o'clock? Four? – and call Dorothy – 'What does this mean? Why did you write this?' – 'Write what?' – then Ellen would read the note and Dorothy would recognize it . . . Would she come to him? What explanation could he invent? Or would she see the truth – blurt out the whole story to Ellen – call her father. If she had kept the pills – if she hadn't thrown them away, there would be proof! Attempted murder. Would she take them to a drugstore, have them analysed? There was no figuring her now. She was an unknown quantity. He'd thought he could predict every little twitch of her goddamned brain, and now . . .

He could feel her looking at him, waiting for some kind of reaction to the words she'd written. He tore paper from his notebook and pulled open his pen. He shielded his hand so she couldn't see how it was shaking. He couldn't write. He had to print, digging the point of the pen so hard that it shredded the surface of the paper. Make it sound natural!

Okay. We tried, that's all. Now we get married as per schedule.

He handed it to her. She read it and turned to him, and her face was warm and radiant as the sunlight. He pressed a smile back at her, praying she wouldn't notice the stiffness of it.

It still wasn't too late. People wrote suicide notes and then stalled around before actually doing it. He looked at his watch: 9.20. The earliest Ellen could get the note would be – three o'clock. Five hours and forty minutes. No step by step planning now. It would have to be quick, positive. No trickery that counted on her doing a certain thing at a certain time. No poison. How else do people kill themselves? In five hours and forty minutes she must be dead.

10

At ten o'clock they left the building arm in arm, going out into the crystalline air that rang with the shouts of between-class students. Three girls in cheerleaders' uniforms pushed by, one beating a tin pie pan with a wood spoon, the other two carrying a big sign advertising a baseball pep rally.

'Does your side still hurt you?' Dorothy asked, concerned for his grim expression.

'A little,' he said.

'Do you get those twinges often?'

'No. Don't worry.' He looked at his watch. 'You're not marrying an invalid.'

They stepped off the path on to the lawn. 'When will we go?' She pressed his hand.

'This afternoon. Around four.'

'Shouldn't we go earlier?'

'Why?'

'Well, it'll take time, and they probably close around five or so.'

'It won't take long. We just fill out the application for the licence and then there's someone right on the same floor who can marry us.

'I'd better bring proof that I'm over eighteen.'

'Yes.'

She turned to him, suddenly serious, remorse flushing her cheeks. Not even a good liar, he thought. 'Are you terribly sorry the pills didn't work?' she asked anxiously.

'No, not terribly.'

'You *were* exaggerating, weren't you? About how things will be?'

'Yes. We'll make out okay. I just wanted you to try the pills. For your sake.'

She flushed more deeply. He turned away, embarrassed by her transparency. When he looked at her again, the joy of the moment had crowded out her compunctions and she was hugging her arms and smiling. 'I *can't* go to my classes! I'm cutting.'

'Good. I am too. Stay with me.'

'What do you mean?'

'Until we go down to the Municipal Building. We'll spend the day together.'

'I can't, darling. Not the whole day. I have to get back to the dorm, finish packing, dress – Don't you have to pack?'

'I left a suitcase down at the hotel when I made the reservation.'

'Oh. Well you have to dress, don't you. I expect to see you in your blue suit.'

He smiled. 'Yes, ma'am. You can give me *some* of your time, anyway. Until lunch.'

'What'll we do?' They sauntered across the lawn.

'I don't know,' he said. 'Maybe go for a walk. Down to the river.'

'In these shoes?' She lifted a foot, displaying a soft leather loafer. 'I'd get fallen arches. There's no support in these things.'

'Okay,' he said, 'no river.'

'I've got an idea.' She pointed to the Fine Arts Building ahead of them. 'Let's go to the record-room in Fine Arts and listen to some records.'

'I don't know, it's such a beautiful day I'd like to stay—' He paused as her smile faded.

She was looking beyond the Fine Arts Building to where the needle of station KBRI's transmission tower speared the sky. 'The last time I was in the Municipal Building it was to see that doctor,' she said soberly.

'It'll be different this time,' he said. And then he stopped walking.

'What is it?'

'Dorrie, you're right. Why should we wait until four o'clock? Let's go now!'

'Get married *now*?'

'Well, after you pack and dress and everything. Look, you go back to the dorm now and get ready. What do you say?'

'Oh, yes! Yes! Oh, I want to go now!'

'I'll call you up in a little while and tell you when I'll pick you up.'

'Yes. Yes.' She stretched up and kissed his cheek excitedly. 'I love you so much,' she whispered.

He grinned at her.

She hurried away, flashing a smile back over her shoulder, walking as fast as she could.

He watched her go. Then he turned and looked again at the KBRI tower, which marked the Blue River Municipal Building; the tallest building in the city; fourteen storeys above the hard slabs of the sidewalk.

11

He went into the Fine Arts Building where a telephone booth was jammed under the slope of the main stairway. Calling Information, he obtained the number of the Marriage Licence Bureau.

'Marriage Licence Bureau.'

'Hello. I'm calling to find out what hours the Bureau is open today.'

'Till noon and from one to five-thirty.'

'Closed between twelve and one?'

'That's right.'

'Thank you.' He hung up, dropped another coin into the phone and dialled the dorm. When they buzzed Dorothy's room there was no answer. He replaced the receiver, wondering what could have detained her. At the rate she had been walking she should have been in her room already.

He had no more change, so he went out and crossed the campus to a luncheonette, where he broke a dollar bill and glared at the girl who occupied the phone booth. When she finally abdicated he stepped into the perfume-smelling booth and closed the door. This time Dorothy answered.

'Hello?'

'Hi. What took you so long? I called a couple of minutes ago.'

'I stopped on the way. I had to buy a pair of gloves.' She sounded breathless and happy.

'Oh. Listen, it's – twenty-five after ten now. Can you be ready at twelve?'

'Well, I don't know. I want to take a shower—'

'Twelve-fifteen?'

'Okay.'

'Listen, you're not going to sign out for the week-end, are you?'

'I have to. You know the rules.'

'If you sign out, you'll have to put down where you're going to be, won't you?'

'Yes.'

'Well?'

'I'll put down "New Washington House". If the house mother asks, I'll explain to her.'

'Look, you can sign out later this afternoon. We have to come back here, anyway. About the trailer. We have to come back about that.'

'We do?'

'Yes. They said I couldn't make the formal application until were actually married.'

'Oh. Well if we're coming back later, I won't take my valise now.'

'No. Take it now. As soon as we're through with the ceremony we'll check in at the hotel and have lunch. It's only a block or so from the Municipal Building.'

'Then I might as well sign out now too. I don't see what difference it'll make.'

'Look, Dorrie, I don't think the school is exactly crazy about having out-of-town girls running off to get married. Your house mother is sure to slow us up somehow. She'll want to know if your father knows. She'll give you a lecture, try to talk you into waiting until the end of the term. That's what house mothers are there for.'

'All right. I'll sign out later.'

'That's the girl. I'll be waiting for you outside the dorm at a quarter after twelve. On University Avenue.'

'On University?'

'Well you're going to use the side door, aren't you? – leaving with a valise and not signing out.'

'That's right. I didn't think of that. Gee, we're practically eloping.'

'Just like a movie.'

She laughed warmly. 'A quarter after twelve.'

'Right. We'll be downtown by twelve-thirty.'

'Good-bye, groom.'

'So long, bride.'

He dressed meticulously in his navy blue suit, with black shoes and socks, a white-on-white shirt, and a pale blue tie of heavy Italian silk patterned with black and silver fleurs-de-lis. On surveying himself in the mirror, however, he decided that the beauty of the tie was a trifle too conspicuous, and so he changed it for a simple pearl grey knit. Viewing himself again as he refastened his jacket, he wished he could as easily exchange his face, temporarily, for one of less distinctive design. There were times, he realized, when being so handsome was a definite handicap. As a step, at least, in the direction of appearing commonplace, he reluctantly donned his one hat, a dove grey fedora, settling the unfamiliar weight cautiously, so as not to disturb his hair.

At five minutes past twelve he was on University Avenue, across the street from the side of the dorm. The sun was almost directly overhead, hot and bright. In the sultry air the occasional sounds of birds and footfalls and grinding tramcars had a rarefied quality, as though coming from behind a glass wall. He stood with his back to the dorm, staring into the window of a hardware store.

At twelve-fifteen, reflected in the window, he saw the door across the street open and Dorothy's green-clad figure appear. For once in her life she was punctual. He turned. She was looking from right to left, her pivoting glance, overlooking him completely. In one white-gloved hand she held a purse, in the other, a small valise covered in tan airplane cloth with wide red stripes. He lifted his arm and in a moment she noticed him. With an eager smile she stepped from the kerb, waited for a break in the passing traffic, and came towards him.

She was beautiful. Her suit was dark green, with a cluster of white silk sparkling at the throat. Her shoes and purse were brown alligator, and there was a froth of dark green veil floating in her feathery golden hair. When she reached him, he grinned and took the valise from her hand. 'All brides are beautiful,' he said, 'but you especially.'

'*Gracias, señor.*' She looked as though she wanted to kiss him.

A taxicab cruised by and slowed in passing. Dorothy looked at him inquiringly, but he shook his head. 'If we're going to economize, we'd better get in practice.' He peered down the avenue. In the glittering air a tramcar approached.

Dorothy drank in the world as if she had been indoors for months. The sky was a shell of perfect blue. The campus, unfolding at the front of the dorm and stretching seven blocks down University Avenue, was quiet, shaded by freshly-green trees. A few students walked the paths; others sprawled on the lawns. 'Just think,' she marvelled, 'When we come back this afternoon, we'll be married.'

The tramcar clattered up and groaned to a halt. They got on.

They sat towards the back of the car, saying little, each enfolded in thoughts. The casual observer would have been uncertain as to whether or not they travelled together.

The lower eight floors of the Blue River Municipal Building were given over to the offices of the city and of Rockwell County, of which Blue River was the county seat. The remaining six floors were rented to private tenants, most of whom were lawyers, doctors, and dentists. The building itself was a mixture of modern and classical architecture, a compromise between the functional trend of the thirties and resolute Iowa conservatism. Professors teaching the introductory architecture courses at Stoddard's College of Fine Arts referred to it as an architectural abortion, causing freshmen to laugh self-consciously.

Viewed from above, the building was a hollow square, an airshaft plunging down through the core of it. From the side, setbacks at the eighth and twelfth storeys gave it the appearance of three blocks of decreasing size piled one atop the other. Its lines were graceless and stark, its window lintels were traced with factitious Grecian designs, and its three bronze and glass revolving doors were squeezed between giant pillars whose capitals were carved into stylized ears of corn. It was a monstrosity, but on alighting from the tramcar Dorothy turned, paused, and gazed up at it as though it were the cathedral at Chartres.

It was twelve-thirty when they crossed the street, mounted the steps, and pushed through the central revolving door. The marble-floored lobby was filled with people going to and from lunch, people hurrying to appointments, people standing and waiting. The sound of voices and the surf of shoes on marble hung susurrant under the vaulted ceiling.

He dropped a pace behind Dorothy, letting her lead the way to the directory board at the side of the lobby. 'Would it be under R for Rockwell County or M for Marriage?' she asked, her eyes intent on the board as he came up beside her. He looked at the board as though oblivious of her presence. 'There it is,' she said triumphantly. 'Marriage Licence Bureau – six-oh-four.' He turned towards the elevators, which were opposite the revolving doors. Dorothy hurried along beside him. She reached for his hand but the valise was in it. He apparently did not notice her gesture, for he made no move to change hands.

One of the four elevators stood open, half-filled with waiting passengers. As they approached it, he stepped back a bit, allowing Dorothy to enter first. Then an elderly woman came up and he waited until she too had gone in before entering. The woman smiled at him, pleased by his air of gallantry, doubly unexpected from a young man in a busy office building. She seemed a bit disappointed when he failed to remove his hat. Dorothy smiled at him also, over the head of the woman, who had somehow got between them. He returned the smile with an almost invisible curving of his lips.

They left the car at the sixth floor, along with two men with brief-cases who turned to the right and walked briskly down the corridor. 'Hey, wait for me!' Dorothy protested in an amused whisper as the elevator door clanged shut behind her. She had been the last to leave the car, and he the first. He had turned to the left and walked some fifteen feet, for all the world as though he were alone. He turned, appearing flustered, as she caught up with him and gaily took his arm. Over her head he watched the men with the briefcases reach the other end of the corridor, turn to the right, and vanish down the side of the square. 'Where you running?' Dorothy teased.

'Sorry,' he smiled. 'Nervous bridegroom.' They walked along arm in arm, following the left turn the corridor made. Dorothy recited the numbers painted on the doors as they passed them 'Six-twenty, six-eighteen, six-sixteen . . .' They had to take another left turn before they reached 604, which was at the back of the square, across from the elevators. He tried the door. It was locked. They read the hours listed on the frosted glass panel and Dorothy moaned dejectedly.

'Damn,' he said. 'I should have called to make sure.' He put down the valise and looked at his watch. 'Twenty-five to one.'

'Twenty-five minutes,' Dorothy said. 'I guess we might as well go downstairs.'

'Those crowds—' he muttered, then paused. 'Hey, I've got an idea.'

'What?'

'The roof. Let's go up on the roof. It's such a beautiful day. I bet we'll be able to see for miles!'

'Are we allowed?'

'If nobody stops us, we're allowed.' He picked up the valise. 'Come on, get your last look at the world as an unmarried woman.'

She smiled and they began walking, retracing their path around the square to the bank of elevators where, in a few moments, there glowed above one of the doors a white arrow pointing upwards.

When they left the car at the fourteenth floor, it happened again that they were separated by the other alighting passengers. In the corridor they waited until these had hurried around the turns or into offices, and then Dorothy said, 'Let's go,' in a conspiratorial whisper. She was making an adventure of it.

Again they had to make a half-circuit of the building, until, next to room 1402, they found a door marked *Stairway*. He pushed it open and they entered. The door sighed closed behind them. They were on a landing, with black metals stairs leading up and down. Dim light sifted through a dirt-fogged skylight. They walked upwards; eight steps, a turn, and eight more steps. A door confronted them, heavy reddish-brown metal. He tried the knob.

'Is it locked?'

'I don't think so.'

He put his shoulder to the door and pushed.

'You're going to get your suit filthy.'

The door rested on a ledge, a sort of giant threshold that raised its bottom a foot above the level of the landing. The ledge jutted out, making it difficult for him to apply his weight squarely. He put down the valise, braced his shoulder against the door, and tried again.

'We can go downstairs and wait,' Dorothy said. 'That door probably hasn't been opened in—'

He clenched his teeth. With the side of his left foot jammed against the base of the ledge, he swung back and then smashed his shoulder against the door with all his strength. It gave, groaning open. The chain of a counterweight clattered. A slice of electric blue sky hit their eyes, blinding after the obscurity of the stairway. There was the quick flutter of pigeons' wings.

He picked up the valise, stepped over the ledge, and put the valise down again where it would be clear of the door's swing. Pushing the door further open, he stood with his back to it. He extended one hand to Dorothy. With the other he gestured towards the expanse of roof as a head waiter gestures towards his finest table. He gave her a mock bow and his best smile. 'Enter, mam'selle,' he said.

Taking his hand, she stepped gracefully over the ledge and on to the black tar of the roof.

12

He wasn't nervous at all. There had been a moment of near-panic when he couldn't get the door open, but it had dissolved the instant the door had yielded to the force of his shoulder, and now he was calm and secure. Everything was going to be perfect. No mistakes, no intruders. He just *knew* it. He hadn't felt so good since – Jesus, since high school!

He swung the door partly closed, leaving a half inch between it and the jamb, so that it wouldn't give him any trouble when he left. He would be in a hurry then. Bending over, he moved the valise so that he would be able to pick it up with one hand while opening the door with the other. As he straightened up he felt his hat shift slightly with the motion. He took it off, looked at it, and placed it on the valise. Christ, he was thinking of everything! A little thing like that hat would probably louse up somebody else. They would push her over and then a breeze or the force of the movement might send their hat sailing down to land beside her body. Bam! They might as well throw themselves over after it. Not he, though; he had anticipated, prepared. An act of God, the crazy kind of little thing that was always screwing up perfect plans – and he had anticipated it. Jesus! He ran a hand over his hair, wishing there were a mirror.

'Come look at this.'

He turned. Dorothy was standing a few feet away, her back towards him, the alligator purse tucked under one arm. Her hands rested on the waist-high parapet that edged the roof. He came up behind her. 'Isn't it something?' she said. They were at the back of the building, facing south. The city sprawled before them, clear and sharp in the brilliant sunlight. 'Look' – Dorothy pointed to a green spot far away – 'I think that's the campus.' He put his hands on her shoulders. A white-gloved hand reached up to touch his.

He had planned to do it quickly, as soon as he got her up there, but now he was going to take it slow and easy, drawing it out as long as he safely could. He was entitled to that, after a week of nerve-twisting tension. Not just a week – years. Ever since high school it had been nothing but strain and worry and self-doubt. There was no need to rush this. He looked down at the top of her head against his chest, the dark green veiling buoyant in the yellow hair. He blew, making the fine net tremble. She tilted her head back and smiled up at him.

When her eyes returned to the panorama, he moved to her side, keeping one arm about her shoulders. He leaned over the parapet. Two storeys below, the red-tiled floor of a wide balcony extended like a shelf across the width of the building. The top of the twelfth storey setback. It would be on all four sides. That was bad; a two-storey drop wasn't what he wanted. He turned and surveyed the roof.

It was perhaps a hundred and fifty square, edged by the brick parapet whose coping was flat white stone, a foot wide. A identical wall rimmed the airshaft, a square hole some thirty feet across, in the centre of the roof. On the left side of the roof was a vast stilt-supported water storage tank. On the right, the KBRI tower reared up like a smaller Eiffel, its girdered pattern black against the sky. The staircase entrance, a slant-roofed shed, was in front of him and a bit to his left. Beyond the airshaft, at the north side of the building, was a large rectangular structure, the housing of the elevator machinery. The entire roof was dotted with chimneys and ventilator pipes that stuck up like piers from a tarry sea.

Leaving Dorothy, he walked across to the parapet of the airshaft. He leaned over. The four walls funnelled down to a tiny area fourteen storeys below, its corners banked with trash cans and wooden crates. He looked for a moment, then stopped and pried a rain-faded match-book from the gummy surface of the roof. He held the folder out beyond the parapet – and dropped it, watching as it drifted down, down, down, and finally became invisible. He glanced at the walls of the shaft. Three were striped with windows. The fourth, which faced him and evidently backed on the elevator shafts, was blank, windowless. This was the spot. The south side of the airshaft. Right near the stairway, too. He slapped the top of the parapet, his lips pursed thoughtfully. Its height was greater than he had anticipated.

Dorothy came up behind him and took his arm. 'It's so quiet,' she said. He listened. At first there seemed to be absolute silence, but then the sounds of the roof asserted themselves: the throbbing of the elevator motors, a gentle wind strumming the cables that guyed the radio tower, the squeak of a slow-turning ventilator cap . . .

They began walking slowly. He led her around the airshaft and past the elevator housing. As they strolled she brushed his shoulder clean of the dust from the door. When they reached the northern rim of the roof they were able to see the river, and with the sky reflected in it, it was really blue, as blue as the rivers painted on maps. 'Do you have a cigarette?' she asked.

He reached into his pocket and touched a pack of Chesterfields. Then his hand came out empty. 'No, I don't. Do you have any?'

'They're buried in here some-place.' She dug into her purse, pushing aside a gold compact and a turquoise handkerchief, and finally produced a crushed pack of Herbert Tareytons. They took one. He lit them and she returned the pack to her purse.

'Dorrie, there's something I want to tell you' – she was blowing a stream of smoke against the sky, hardly listening – 'about the pills.'

Her face jerked around, going white. She swallowed.

'What?'

'I'm glad they didn't work,' he said, smiling. 'I really am.'

She looked at him uncomprehendingly. 'You're glad?'

'Yes. When I called you last night, I was going to tell you not to take them, but you already had.' Come on, he thought, confess. Get it off your chest. It must be killing you.

Her voice was shaky. 'Why? You were so . . . what made you change your mind?'

'I don't know. I thought it over. I suppose I'm as anxious to get married as you are.' He examined his cigarette. 'Besides, I guess it's really a sin to do something like that.' When he looked up again her cheeks were flushed and her eyes glistened.

'Do you mean that?' she asked breathlessly. 'Are you really glad?'

'Of course I am. I wouldn't say it if I weren't.'

'Oh, thank God!'

'What's the matter, Dorrie?'

'Please, don't be angry. I – I didn't take them.' He tried to look surprised. The words poured from her lips: 'You said you were going to get a night job and I knew we could manage, everything would work out, and I was counting on it so much, *so* much. I knew I was right.' She paused. 'You aren't angry, are you?' she beseeched. 'You understand?'

'Sure, baby, I'm not angry. I told you I was glad they didn't work.'

Her lips made a quivering smile of relief. 'I felt like a criminal, lying to you. I thought I would never be able to tell you. I – I can't believe it!'

He took the neatly-folded handkerchief from his breast pocket and touched it to her eyes. 'Dorrie, what did you do with the pills?'

'Threw them away.' She smiled shamefacedly.

'Where?' he asked casually, replacing the handkerchief.

'The john.'

That was what he wanted to hear. There would be no questions about why she had taken such a messy way out when she had already gone to the trouble of obtaining poison. He dropped his cigarette and stepped on it.

Dorothy, taking a final puff, did the same with hers. 'Oh, gee,' she marvelled, 'everything's perfect now. Perfect.'

He put his hands on her shoulders and kissed her gently on the lips. 'Perfect,' he said.

He looked down at the two stubs, hers edged with lipstick, his clean. He picked his up. Splitting it down the middle with his thumbnail, he let the tobacco blow away and rolled the paper into a tiny ball. He flicked it out over the parapet. 'That's the way we used to do it in the army,' he said.

She consulted her watch. 'It's ten to one.'

'You're fast,' he said, glancing at his. 'We've got fifteen minutes yet.' He took her arm. They turned and walked leisurely away from the edge of the roof.

'Did you speak to your landlady?'

'Wha—? Oh, yes. It's all set.' They passed the elevator housing. 'Monday we'll move your stuff from the dorm.'

Dorothy grinned. 'Will they be surprised, the girls in the dorm.' They strolled around the parapet of the airshaft. 'Do you think your landlady'll be able to give us some more closet space?'

'I think so.'

'I can leave some of my stuff, the winter things, in the attic at the dorm. There won't be too much.'

They reached the south side of the airshaft. He stood with his back against the parapet, braced his hands on the top of it, and hitched himself up. He sat with his heels kicking against the side of the wall.

'Don't sit there,' Dorothy said apprehensively.

'Why not?' he asked, glancing at the white stone coping. 'It's a foot wide. You sit on a bench a foot wide and you don't fall off.' He patted the stone on his left. 'Come on.'

'No,' she said.

'Chicken.'

She touched her rear. 'My suit—'

He took out his handkerchief, whipped it open, and spread it on the stone beside him. 'Sir Walter Raleigh,' he said.

She hesitated a moment, then gave him her purse. Turning her back to the parapet, she gripped the top on either side of the handkerchief and lifted herself up. He helped her. 'There,' he said, putting his arm around her waist. She turned her head slowly, peeking over her shoulder. 'Don't look down,' he warned. 'You'll get dizzy.'

He put the purse on the stone to his right and they sat in silence for a moment, her hands still fastened upon the front of the coping. Two pigeons came out from behind the staircase shed and walked around, watching them cautiously, their claws ticking against the tar.

'Are you going to call or write when you tell your mother?' Dorothy asked.

'I don't know.'

'I think I'll write Ellen and father. It's an awfully hard thing to just say over the phone.'

A ventilator cap creaked. After a minute, he took his arm from her waist and put his hand over hers, which gripped the stone between them. He braced his other hand on the coping and eased himself down from the parapet. Before she could do likewise he swung around and was facing her, his waist against her knees, his hands covering both of hers. He smiled at her and she smiled back. His gaze dropped to her stomach. 'Little mother,' he said. She chuckled.

His hands moved to her knees, cupped them, his fingertips caressing under the hem of her skirt.

'We'd better be going, hadn't we, darling?'

'In a minute, baby. We still have time.'

His eyes caught hers, held them, as his hands descended and moved behind to rest curving on the slope of her calves. At the periphery of his field of vision he could make out her white-gloved hands; they still clasped the front of the coping firmly.

'That's a beautiful blouse,' he said, looking at the fluffy silk bow at her throat. 'Is it new?'

'New? It's as old as the hills.'

His gaze became critical. 'The bow is a little off centre.'

One hand left the stone and rose to finger the bow. 'No,' he aid, 'now you've got it worse.' Her other detached itself from the top of the parapet.

His hands moved down over the silken swell of her calves, as low as he could reach without bending. His right foot dropped back, poised on the toe in readiness. He held his breath.

She adjusted the bow with both hands. 'Is that any bett—'

With cobra speed he ducked – hands streaking down to catch her heels – stepped back, and straightened up, lifting her legs high. For one frozen instant, as his hands shifted from cupping her heels to a flat grip on the soles of her shoes, their eyes met, stupefied terror bursting in hers, a cry rising in her throat. Then, with all his strength, he pushed against her fear-rigid legs.

Her shriek of petrified anguish trailed down into the shaft like a burning wire. He closed his eyes. The scream died. Silence, then a god-awful deafening crash. Wincing, he remembered the cans and crates piled far below.

He opened his eyes to see his handkerchief billowing as the breeze pulled it free of the stone's rough surface. He snatched it up. Wheeling, he raced to the stairway door, grabbed hat and valise with one hand and pulled the door open, wiping the knob with the handkerchief as he did so. He stepped quickly over the threshold ledge, pulled the door closed, and wiped its inner knob. He turned and ran.

He clattered down flight after flight of black metal steps, the valise banging against his legs, his right hand burning over the banisters. His heart galloped and the image of whirling walls dizzied him. When he finally stopped he was on the seventh floor landing.

He clung to the newel post, gasping. The phrase 'physical release of tension' danced in his mind. That was why he had run that way – physical release of tension – not panic, not panic. He caught his breath. Putting down the valise, he reshaped his hat, which had been crushed in his grasp. He put it on, his hands trembling slightly. He looked at them. The palms were dirty grey from the soles of . . . he wiped them clean and jammed the handkerchief into his pocket. After a few straightening tugs at his jacket, he picked up the valise, opened the door, and stepped out into the corridor.

Every door was open. People rushed across the corridor from offices on the outer circumference to those on the inner, where windows faced the airshaft. Men in business suits, stenographers with paper cuffs clipped to their blouses, shirt-sleeved men with green eyeshades; all with jaws clenched, eyes wide, faces bloodless. He walked towards the elevators at a moderate pace, paused when someone darted before him, then continuing on his way. Passing the doorway of each inner office, he glanced in and saw the backs of people crammed around the open windows, their voices a murmur of excitement and tense speculation.

Shortly after he reached the bank of elevators, a down car came. He squeezed in and faced the front of the car. Behind him the other passengers avidly exchanged fragments of information, the customary elevator coldness shattered by the violence at their backs.

The easy bustle of normality filled the lobby. Most of the people

there, having just entered from outside, were unaware of any distur-
bance. Swinging the valise lightly, he made his way across the
marbled expanse and out into the bright noisy afternoon. As he
jogged down the steps that fronted the building, two policemen
passed him, going up. He turned and watched the blue uniforms
vanish into a revolving door. At the foot of the steps he paused and
examined his hands once again. They were steady as rocks. Not a
tremor. He smiled. Turning, he looked at the revolving doors, wondering how dangerous it would be for him to go back, mingle with
the crowd, see her . . .

He decided against it.

A University tramcar rumbled past. He walked double-time to the
corner, where the car was detained by a red light. Swinging himself
on, he dropped a dime in the box and walked to the rear of the car.
He stood looking out of the window. When the car had gone about
four blocks, a white ambulance clanged by, the pitch of its bell
dropping as it passed. He watched it grow smaller and smaller and
finally cut through traffic to pull up in front of the Municipal
Building. Then the tramcar turned on to University Avenue, and he
could see no more.

13

The baseball pep rally began at nine that night, taking place on an
empty lot next to the stadium, but the news of a student's suicide (for
how could she have fallen when the *Clarion* clearly stated there was a
three and a half foot wall?) put a damper on the entire affair. In the
orange glow of the bonfire, the students, the girls especially, spread
their blankets and sat huddled in conversation. The business manager of the baseball team and the members of the cheerleading squad
tried vainly to make the rally what it should be. They spurred the
boys to the gathering of more and more fuel, throwing on crates and
cartons until the flaming pillar was so high it threatened to topple,
but it was to no avail.

The half-hearted cheers wavered and died before half the school's
name was spelled out.

He had not attended many of the pep rallies before, but he attended this one. He walked the dark streets from his rooming house at a slow liturgic pace, bearing a carton in his arms.

In the afternoon he had emptied Dorothy's valise, hiding her clothes under the mattress of his bed. Then, although it was a warm day, he had donned his trenchcoat, and after filling its pockets with the bottles and small containers of cosmetics that had been lodged among the clothes, he left the house with the valise, from which he had stripped the tags bearing Dorothy's New York and Blue River addresses. He had gone downtown and checked the valise in a locker at the bus terminal. From there he had walked to the Morton Street Bridge, where he dropped the locker key and then the bottles, one by one, into the umber water, opening them first so that trapped air would not keep them afloat. Ghosts of pink lotion rode the water and thinned and faded. On his way home from the bridge he stopped at a grocery store, where he secured a tan corrugated carton that had once contained cans of pineapple juice.

He carried the carton to the rally and picked his way through the mass of squatting and reclining figures orange-sketched in the darkness. Stepping gingerly between blanket corners and blue-jeaned legs, he advanced to the flaming centre of the field.

The heat and the glare were intense in the clearing that surrounded the roaring twelve-foot fire. He stood for a moment, staring at the flames. Suddenly the baseball manager and a cheerleader came dashing around from the other side of the clearing. 'That's it! That's the boy!' they cried, and seized the carton from his hands.

'Hey,' the manager said, hefting the box. 'This isn't empty.'

'Books – old notebooks.'

'Ah! Magnifico!' The manager turned to the encircling crowd. 'Attention! Attention! The burning of the books!' A few people looked up from their conversations. The manager and the cheerleader took the carton between them, swinging it back and forth towards the rippling flames. 'All the way to the top!' the manager shouted.

'Hey—'

'Don't worry, friend. We never miss! Book-burning a specialty!' They swung the carton; one, two, *three*! It sailed up parallel to the cone-shaped pyre, arced over, and landed with a gush of sparks at the very top. It teetered a moment, then held. There was a spattering of applause from the onlookers. 'Hey, here comes Al with a packing-case!' cried the cheerleader. He dashed around to the other side of the fire, the manager running after him.

He stood watching as the carton turned black, sheets of flame sliding up past its sides. Suddenly the foundation of the fire shifted, pushing out showers of sparks. A flaming brand hit his foot. He jumped back. Sparks glowed all over the front of his trousers. Nervously he slapped them out, his hands coppery in the fire's glare.

When the last sparks were extinguished, he looked up to make certain that the carton was still secure. It was. Flames ripped up through its top. Its contents, he thought, were probably completely burned by now.

These had included the Pharmacy lab. manual, the Kingship Copper pamphlets, the tags from the valise, and the few articles of clothing that Dorothy had prepared for their brief honeymoon; a cocktail dress of grey taffeta, a pair of black suede pumps, stockings, a half-slip, bra and panties, two handkerchiefs, a pair of pink satin mules, a pink negligee, and a nightgown; silk and lace, delicate, scented, white . . .

14

From the Blue River *Clarion-Ledger*; Friday, April 28, 1950:

STODDARD CO-ED DIES IN PLUNGE

MUNICIPAL BUILDING TRAGEDY FATAL TO DAUGHTER OF COPPER MAGNATE

Dorothy Kingship, nineteen-year-old Stoddard University sophomore, was killed today when she fell or jumped from the roof of the fourteenth-storey Blue River Municipal Building. The attractive blonde girl, whose home was in New York City, was a daughter of Leo Kingship, president of Kingship Copper Inc.

At 12.58 p.m., workers in the building were startled by a loud scream and a crashing sound from the wide airshaft which runs through the structure. Rushing to their windows, they saw the contorted figure of a young woman. Dr Harvey C. Hess, of 57 Wood-

315

bridge Circle, who was in the lobby at the time, reached the scene seconds later to pronounce the girl dead.

The police, arriving shortly thereafter, found a purse resting on the three and a half foot wall that encircles the airshaft. In the purse were a birth certificate and a Stoddard University registration card which served to identify the girl. Police also found a fresh cigarette stub on the roof, stained with lipstick of the shade Miss Kingship wore, leading them to conclude that she had been on the roof for several minutes prior to the plunge which ended her life . . .

Rex Cargill, an elevator operator, told police that he took Miss Kingship to the sixth or seventh floor half an hour before the tragedy. Another operator, Andrew Vecci, believes he took a woman dressed similarly to Miss Kingship to the fourteenth floor shortly after 12.30, but is uncertain of the floor at which she entered his car.

According to Stoddard's Dean of Students, Clark D. Welch, Miss Kingship was doing satisfactory work in all her studies. Shocked residents of the dormitory where she lived could offer no reason why she might have taken her own life. They described her as quiet and withdrawn. 'Nobody knew her too well,' said one girl.

From the Blue River *Clarion-Ledger*; Saturday, April 29, 1950:

CO-ED'S DEATH WAS SUICIDE
SISTER RECEIVES NOTE IN MAIL

The death of Dorothy Kingship, Stoddard co-ed who plunged from the roof of the Municipal Building yesterday afternoon, was a suicide, Chief of Police Eldon Chesser told reporters last night. An unsigned note in a handwriting definitely established to be that of the dead girl was received through the mail late yesterday afternoon by her sister, Ellen Kingship, a student of Caldwell, Wisconsin. Although the exact wording of the note has not been made public, Chief Chester characterized it as 'a clear expression of suicidal intent'. The note was mailed from this city, postmarked yesterday at 6.30 a.m.

On receiving the note, Ellen Kingship attempted to reach her sister by telephone. The call was transferred to Stoddard's Dean of Students, Clark D. Welsh, who informed Miss Kingship of the nineteen-year-old girl's death. Miss Kingship left immediately for Blue River, arriving here yesterday evening. Her father, Leo

Kingship, president of Kingship Copper, Inc., is expected to arrive some time today, his plane having been grounded in Chicago because of bad weather.

LAST PERSON TO SPEAK TO SUICIDE DESCRIBES HER AS TENSE, NERVOUS
by La Verne Breen

'She laughed a lot and was smiling the whole time she was in my room. And she kept moving around. I thought at the time that she was very happy about something, but now I realize that those were all symptoms of the terrible nervous strain she was under. Her laughs were tense laughs, not happy ones. I should have recognized that right away, being a psychology major.' Thus Annabelle Koch, Stoddard sophomore, describes the behaviour of Dorothy Kingship two hours before the latter's suicide.

Miss Koch, a native of Boston, is a petite and charming young lady. Yesterday she was confined to her dormitory-room because of a severe head cold. 'Dorothy knocked on the door around a quarter past eleven,' says Miss Koch. 'I was in bed. She came in and I was a little surprised, because we hardly knew each other. As I said, she was smiling and moving around a great deal. She was wearing a bathrobe. She asked if I would loan her the belt to my green suit. I should mention that we both have the same green suit. I got mine in Boston and she got hers in New York, but they're exactly the same. We both wore them to dinner last Saturday night, and it was really embarrassing. Anyway, she asked if I would loan her my belt because the buckle of hers was broken. I hesitated at first, because it's my new spring suit, but she seemed to want it so badly that I finally told her which drawer it was in and she got it. She thanked me very much and left.'

Here Miss Koch paused and removed her glasses. 'Now here's the strange part. Later, when the police came and searched her room for a note, *they found my belt on her desk*! I recognized it by the way the gold finish was rubbed off the tooth of the buckle. I had been very disappointed about that, because it was an expensive suit. The police kept the belt.

'I was very puzzled by Dorothy's actions. She had pretended to want my belt, but she hadn't used it at all. She was wearing her green suit when – when it happened. The police checked and her belt buckle wasn't the least bit broken. It all seemed very mysterious.

'Then I realized that the belt must have been just a pretext to talk to me. Laying out the suit probably reminded her of me, and everyone knew I was incapacitated with a cold, so she came in and pretended she needed the belt. She must have been desperate for someone to talk with. If only I'd recognized the signs at the time. I can't help feeling that if I had gotten her to talk out her troubles, whatever they might have been, maybe all this wouldn't have happened.'

. . . As we left Annabelle Koch's room, she added a final word. 'Even when the police return the belt to me,' she said, 'I know I won't be able to wear my green suit again.'

15

He found the last six weeks of the school year disappointingly flat. He had expected the excitement created by Dorothy's death to linger in the air like the glow of a rocket; instead it had faded almost immediately. He had anticipated more campus conversations and newspaper articles, allowing him the luxuriant superiority of the omniscient; instead – nothing. Three days after Dorothy died campus gossip veered away to pounce on a dozen marijuana cigarettes that had been discovered in one of the smaller dormitories. As for the newspapers, a short paragraph announcing Leo Kingship's arrival in Blue River marked the last time the Kingship name appeared in the *Clarion-Ledger*. No word of an autopsy nor of her pregnancy, although surely when an unmarried girl committed suicide without stating a reason, that must be the first thing they looked for. Keeping it out of the papers must have cost Kingship plenty.

He told himself he should be rejoicing. If there had been any kind of inquiry he certainly would have been sought for questioning. But there had been no questions, no suspicion – hence no investigation. Everything had fallen into place perfectly. Except that business of the belt. That puzzled him. Why on earth had Dorothy taken that Koch girl's belt when she hadn't wanted to wear it? Maybe she really did want to talk to someone – about the wedding – and then had thought better of it. Thank God for that. Or maybe the buckle of her belt had really been broken, but she had managed to fix it after she had already taken Koch's. Either way, though, it was an unimportant incident. Koch's interpretation of it only strengthened the picture of a suicide, added to the flawless success of his plans. He should be walking on air, smiling at strangers, toasting himself with secret champagne. Instead there was this dull, leaden, letdown feeling. He couldn't understand it.

His depression became worse when he returned to Menasset early in June. Here he was, right where he'd been last summer after the daughter of the farm equipment concern had told him about the boy back home, and the summer before, after he had left the widow. Dorothy's death had been a defensive measure; all his planning hadn't advanced him in the slightest.

He became impatient with his mother. His correspondence from school had been limited to a weekly postcard, and now she badgered him for details; did he have pictures of the girls he'd gone out with? – expecting them to be the most beautiful, the most sought after – Did he belong to this club, to that club? – expecting him to be the president of each – What was his standing in philosophy, in English, in Spanish? – expecting him to be the leader in all. One day he lost his temper. 'It's about time you realized I'm not the king of the world!' he shouted, storming from the room.

He took a job for the summer; partly because he needed money, partly because being in the house with his mother all day made him uneasy. The job didn't do any good towards taking his mind off things though; it was in a haberdashery shop whose fixtures were of angular modern design; the glass display counters were bound with inch wide strips of burnished copper.

Towards the middle of July, however, he began to slough off his dejection. He still had the newspaper clippings about Dorothy's death, locked in a small grey strongbox he kept in his bedroom closet. He began taking them out once in a while, skimming through them, smiling at the officious certainty of Chief of Police Eldon Chesser and the half-baked theorizing of Annabelle Koch.

He dug up his old library card, had it renewed, and began withdrawing books regularly: Pearson's *Studies in Murder*, Bolitho's *Murder for Profit*, volumes in the *Regional Murder Series*. He read about Landru, Smith, Pritchard, Crippen; men who had failed where he had succeeded. Of course it was only the failures whose stories got written – God knows how many successful ones there were. Still, it was flattering to consider how many had failed.

Until now he had always thought of what happened at the Municipal Building as 'Dorrie's death'. Now he began to think of it as 'Dorrie's murder'.

Sometimes, when he had lain in bed and read several accounts in one of the books, the enormous daring of what he had done would overwhelm him. He would get up and look at himself in the mirror over the dresser. I got away with murder, he would think. Once he whispered it aloud: 'I got away with murder!'

So what if he wasn't rich yet! Hell, he was only twenty-four.

PART TWO
ELLEN
1

LETTER FROM ANNABELLE KOCH TO LEO KINGSHIP:
Girls' Dormitory
Stoddard University
Blue River, Iowa
March 5, 1951

Dear Mr Kingship,

I suppose you are wondering who I am, unless you remember my name from the newspapers. I am the young woman who loaned a belt to your daughter Dorothy last April. I was the last person to speak to her. I would not bring up this subject as I am sure it must be a very painful subject to you, except that I have a good reason.

As you may recall Dorothy and I had the same green suit. She came to my room and asked to borrow my belt. I loaned it to her and later the police found it (or what I thought was it) in her room. They kept it for over a month until they got around to returning it to me by that time it was quite late in the season so I did not wear the green suit again last year.

Now spring is approaching again and last night I tried on my spring clothes. I tried on my green suit and it fitted perfectly. But when I put on the belt I found to my surprise that it was Dorothy's belt all along. You see, the notch that is marked from the buckle is two notches too big for my waist. Dorothy was quite slender but I am even more so. In fact to be frank I am quite thin. I *know* that I certainly did not lose any weight because the suit still fits me perfectly, as I said above, so the belt must be Dorothy's. When the police first showed it to me I thought it was mine because the gold finish on the tooth of the buckle was rubbed off. I should have realized that since both suits were made by the same manufacturer the finish would have come off *both* buckles.

321

So now it seems that Dorothy could not wear her own belt for some reason, even though it was not broken at all, and took mine instead. I cannot understand it. At the time I thought she only pretended to need my belt because she wanted to speak to me.

Now that I know the belt is Dorothy's I would feel funny wearing it. I am not superstitious, but after all it does not belong to me and it did belong to poor Dorothy. I thought of throwing it away but I would feel funny doing that also, so I am sending it to you in a separate package and you can keep it or dispose of it as you see fit.

I can still wear the suit because all the girls here are wearing wide leather belts this year anyway.

> Yours truly,
> Annabelle Koch

LETTER FROM LEO KINGSHIP TO ELLEN KINGSHIP:
March 8, 1951

My dear Ellen,

I received your last letter and am sorry not to have replied sooner, but the demands of business have been especially pressing of late.

Yesterday being Wednesday, Marion came here to dinner. She is not looking too well. I showed her a letter which I received yesterday and she suggested that I send it on to you. You will find it enclosed. Read it now, and then continue with my letter.

Now that you have read Miss Koch's letter, I will explain why I forwarded it.

Marion tells me that ever since Dorothy's death you have been rebuking yourself for your imagined callousness to her. Miss Koch's unfortunate story of Dorothy's 'desperate need for someone to talk with' made you feel, according to Marion, that that someone should have been you and would have been you, had you not pushed Dorothy out on her own too soon. You believe, although this is something which Marion has only deduced from your letters, that had there been a difference in your attitude towards Dorothy, she might not have chosen the path she did.

I credit what Marion says since it explains your wishful thinking, for I can only call it that, of last April, when you stubbornly refused to believe that Dorothy's death had been a suicide, despite the incontestable evidence of the note which you yourself received. You felt that if Dorothy had committed suicide you were in some way responsible, and so it was several weeks before you were able to accept her death for what it was, and accept also the burden of an imagined responsibility.

This letter from Miss Koch makes it clear that Dorothy went to the girl because, for some peculiar reason of her own, she did want her belt; she was *not* in desperate need of someone to whom she could talk. She had made up her mind to do what she was going to do, and there is absolutely no reason for you to believe that she would have come to you first if you two had not had that argument the previous Christmas. (And don't forget it was *she* who was in a sullen mood and started the argument.) As for the initial coldness on Dorothy's part, remember that I agreed with you that she should go to Stoddard rather than Caldwell, where she would only have become more dependent on you. True, if she had followed you to Caldwell the tragedy would not have happened, but 'if' is the biggest word in the world. Dorothy's punishment may have been excessively severe, but she was the one who chose it. I am not responsible, you are not responsible; no one is but Dorothy herself.

The knowledge that Miss Koch's original interpretation of Dorothy's behaviour was erroneous will I hope, rid you of any feelings of self-recrimination that may remain.

Your loving,
Father

P.S. Please excuse my indecipherable handwriting. I thought this letter too personal to dictate to Miss Richardson.

LETTER FROM ELLEN KINGSHIP TO BUD CORLISS:
March 12, 1951
8.35 a.m.

Dear Bud,

Here I sit in the club car with a Coke (at this hour – ugh!) and a pen and paper, trying to keep my writing hand steady against the motion of the train and trying to give a 'lucid if not brilliant' explanation – as Prof. Mulholland would say – of why I am making this trip to Blue River.

I'm sorry about tonight's basketball game, but I'm sure Connie or Jane will be glad to go in my place, and you can think of me between the halves.

Now first of all, this trip is *not* impulsive! I thought about it all last night. You'd think I was running off to Cairo, Egypt! Second of all, I *will not* be missing work, because *you* are going to take complete notes in each class, and anyway I doubt if I'll be gone more than a week. And besides, since when do they flunk seniors for overcuts? Third of all, I won't be wasting my time, because I'll never know until I've tried, and until I try I'll never have a moment's peace.

Now that the objections are out of the way, let me explain why I am going. I'll fill in a little background first.

From the letter I received from my father Saturday morning, you know that Dorothy originally wanted to come to Caldwell and I opposed her for her own good, or so I convinced myself at the time. Since her death I've wondered whether it wasn't pure selfishness on my part. My life at home had been restrained both by my father's strictness and Dorothy's dependence on me, although I didn't realize it at the time. So when I got to Caldwell I really let go. During my first three years I was the rah-rah girl; beer parties, hanging around with the Big Wheels, etc. You wouldn't recognize me. So as I say, I'm not sure whether I prevented Dorothy from coming in order to encourage her independence or to avoid losing mine, Caldwell being the everybody-knows-what-everybody-else-is-doing-type place that it is.

My father's analysis (probably second-hand via Marion) of my reaction to Dorothy's death is absolutely right. I didn't want to admit it was suicide because that meant that I was partly responsible. I thought I had other reasons for doubt besides emotional ones however. The note she sent me, for instance. It was her handwriting – I can't deny that – but it didn't sound like her. It sounded kind of stilted, and she addressed me as 'Darling', when before it had always been 'Dear Ellen' or 'Dearest Ellen'. I mentioned that to the police, but they said that naturally she was under a strain when she wrote the note and couldn't be expected to sound her usual self, which I had to admit seemed logical. The fact that she carried her birth certificate with her also bothered me, but they explained that away too. A suicide will often take pains to make sure he is immediately identified, they said. The fact that other things which she always carried in her wallet (Stoddard registration card, etc.) would have been sufficient identification didn't seem to make any impression on them. And when I told them that she just wasn't the suicidal type, they didn't even bother to answer me. They swept away every point I raised.

So there I was. Of course I finally had to accept the fact that Dorothy committed suicide – and that I was partly to blame. Annabelle Koch's story was only the clincher. The motive for

Dorothy's suicide made me even more responsible, for rational girls today do not kill themselves if they become pregnant – not, I thought, unless they have been brought up to depend on someone else and then that someone else suddenly isn't there.

But Dorothy's pregnancy meant that another person had deserted her too – the man. If I knew anything about Dorothy it was that she did not treat sex lightly. She wasn't the kind for quick flings. The fact that she was pregnant meant that there was one man whom she had loved and had intended to marry some day.

Now early in the December before her death, Dorothy had written me about a man she had met in her English class. She had been going out with him for quite some time, and this was the Real Thing. She said she would give me all the details over Christmas vacation. But we had an argument during Christmas, and after that she wouldn't even give me the right time. And when we returned to school our letters were almost like business letters. So I never even learned his name. All I knew about him was what she had mentioned in that letter; that he had been in her English class in the fall, and that he was handsome and somewhat like Len Vernon – he is the husband of a cousin of ours – which meant that Dorothy's man was tall, blond, and blue-eyed.

I told my father about this man, urging him to find out who he was and punish him somehow. He refused, saying that it would be impossible to prove he was the one who had gotten Dorothy into trouble, and futile even if we could prove it. She had punished herself for her sins; it was a closed case as far as he was concerned.

That's how things stood until Saturday, when I received my father's letter with the one from Annabelle Koch enclosed. Which brings us to my big scene.

The letters did not have the effect my father had hoped for – not at first – because as I said, Annabelle Koch's story was far from the sole cause of my melancholy. But then I began to wonder; if Dorothy's belt was in perfect condition, why had she lied about it and taken Annabelle's instead? Why couldn't Dorothy wear her own belt? My father was content to let it pass, saying she had 'some peculiar reason of her own', but I wanted to know what that reason was, because there were three other seemingly inconsequential things which Dorothy did on the day of her death that puzzled me then and that still puzzled me. Here they are:

1. At 10.15 that morning she bought an inexpensive pair of white cloth gloves in a shop across the street from her dormitory. (The

owner reported it to the police after seeing her picture in the papers.)
First she asked for a pair of stockings, but because of a rush of business for the Spring Dance scheduled for the following night, they
were out of her size. She then asked for gloves, and bought a pair for
$1.50. She was wearing them when she died, yet in the bureau in her
room was a beautiful pair of hand-made white cloth gloves, perfectly
spotless, that Marion had given her the previous Christmas. Why
didn't she wear those?

2. Dorothy was a careful dresser. She was wearing her green suit
when she died. With it she wore an inexpensive white silk blouse
whose floppy out-of-style bow was all wrong for the lines of the suit.
Yet in her closet was a white silk blouse, also perfectly spotless,
which had been *specially made* to go with the suit. Why didn't she
wear that blouse?

3. Dorothy was wearing dark green, with brown and white
accessories. Yet the handkerchief in her purse was bright blue, as
wrong as could be for the outfit she wore. In her room were at least a
dozen handkerchiefs that would have matched her outfit perfectly.
Why didn't she take one of those?

At the time of her death I mentioned these points to the police.
They dismissed them as quickly as they had dismissed the others I
brought up. She was distracted. It was ridiculous to expect her to
dress with her ordinary care. I pointed out that the glove incident was
the reverse of carelessness; she had gone out of her way to get them.
If there was conscious preparation behind one incident, it wasn't
unreasonable to assume that all three had some kind of purpose.
Their comeback was, 'You can't figure a suicide'.

Annabelle Koch's letter added a fourth incident which followed
the pattern of the other three. Her own belt was perfectly all right,
but Dorothy wore Annabelle's instead. In each case she rejected an
appropriate item for one that was less appropriate. Why?

I batted that problem around in my head all day Saturday, and
Saturday night too. Don't ask me what I expected to prove. I felt that
there had to be some kind of meaning to it all, and I wanted to find
out as much as I could about Dorothy's state of mind at the time.
Like poking a bad tooth with your tongue, I guess.

I'd have to write reams to tell you all the mental steps I went
through, searching for some relationship among the four rejected
items. Price, where they came from, and a thousand other thoughts,
but nothing made sense. The same thing happened when I tried to get
common characteristics in the wrong things she had actually worn. I

even took sheets of paper and headed them Glove, Handkerchief, Blouse, and Belt, and put down everything I knew about each, looking for a meaning. Apparently, there just wasn't a meaning. Size, age, ownership, cost, colour, quality, place of purchase – none of the significant characteristics appeared on all four lists. I tore up the papers and went to bed. You can't figure a suicide.

It came to me about an hour later, so startlingly that I shot up straight in bed, suddenly cold. The out-of-style blouse, the gloves she'd bought that morning. Annabelle Koch's belt, the turquoise handkerchief – Something old, something new, something borrowed, and something blue.

It might – I keep telling myself – be a coincidence. But in my heart I don't believe that.

Dorothy went to the Municipal Building, not because it is the tallest building in Blue River, but because a Municipal Building is where you go when you want to get married. She wore something old, something new, something borrowed, and something blue – poor romantic Dorothy – and she carried her birth certificate with her to prove she was over eighteen. And you don't make a trip like that alone. Dorothy can only have gone with one person – the man who made her pregnant, the man she'd been going with for a long time, the man she loved – the handsome blue-eyed blond of her fall English class. He got her up to the roof somehow. I'm almost certain that's the way it was.

The note? All it said was 'I hope you will forgive me for the unhappiness I will cause. There is nothing else that I can do.' Where is there mention of suicide? She was referring to the marriage! She knew Father would disapprove of a hasty step like that, but there was nothing else she could do because she was pregnant. The police were right when they said the stilted tone was the result of strain, only it was the strain of an eloping bride, not of a person contemplating suicide.

'Something old, something new' was enough to set me going, but it would never be enough to make the police reclassify a suicide with note as an unsolved murder, especially when they would be prejudiced against me – the crank who pestered them last year. You know that's true. So I'm going to find this man and do some *very cautious* Sherlocking. As soon as I turn up anything that supports my suspicions, anything strong enough to interest the police, I promise to go straight to them. I've seen too many movies where the heroine accuses the murderer in his sound-proof penthouse and he says 'Yes, I did it, but you'll never live to tell the tale.' So don't worry about me, and don't get impatient and don't write my father as he would probably explode. Maybe it is 'crazy and impulsive' to rush into it this way, but how can I sit and wait when I know what has to be done and there is no one else to do it?

Perfect timing. We're just entering Blue River now. I can see the Municipal Building from the window.

I'll wind this letter up later in the day, when I'll be able to tell you where I'm staying and what progress, if any, I've made. Even though Stoddard is ten times as big as Caldwell, I have a pretty good idea of how to begin. Wish me luck . . .

2

Dean Welch was plump, with round grey eyes like buttons pressed into the shiny pink clay of his face. He favoured suits of clergy-black flannel, single-breasted so as to expose his Phi Beta Kappa key. His office was dim and chapel-like, with dark wood and draperies and, in its centre, a broad field of meticulously accoutred desk-top.

After releasing the button on the inter-office speaker, the Dean rose and faced the door, his customary moist-lipped smile replaced by an expression of solemnity suitable for greeting a girl whose sister had taken her own life while nominally under his care. The ponderous notes of the noon-day carillon floated into the chamber, muffled by distance and draperies. The door opened and Ellen Kingship entered.

By the time she had closed the door and approached his desk, the Dean of Students had measured and evaluated her with the complacent certainty of one who has dealt with younger people for many years. She was neat; he liked that. And quite pretty. Red-brown hair in thick bangs, brown eyes, a smile whose restraint acknowledged the unfortunate past. Determined looking. Probably not brilliant, but a plodder – second quarter of her class. Her coat and dress were shades of dark blue, a pleasant contrast to the usual student polychrome. She seemed a bit nervous, but then, weren't they all?

'Miss Kingship,' he murmured with a nod, indicating the visitor's chair. They sat. The Dean folded his pink hands. 'Your father is well, I hope.'

'Very well, thank you.' Her voice was low-pitched and breathy.

The Dean said, 'I had the pleasure of meeting him – last year.' There was a moment of silence. 'If there's anything I can do for you—'

She shifted in the stiff-backed chair. 'We – my father and I – are trying to locate a certain man, a student here.' The Dean's eyebrows lifted in polite curiosity. 'He lent my sister a fairly large sum of money a few weeks before her death. She wrote me about it. I happened to come across her cheque-book last week and it reminded me of the incident. There's nothing in the cheque-book to indicate that she ever repaid the debt, and we thought he might have felt awkward about claiming it.'

The Dean nodded.

'The only trouble,' Ellen said, 'is that I don't recall his name. But I do remember Dorothy mentioning that he was in her English class during the fall semester, and that he was blond. We thought perhaps you could help us locate him. It was a fairly large sum of money—' She took a deep breath.

'I see,' said the Dean. He pressed his hands together as though comparing their size. His lips smiled at Ellen. 'Can do,' he snapped with military briskness. He held the pose for an instant, then jabbed one of the buttons on the inter-office speaker. 'Miss Platt,' he snapped, and released the button.

He brought his chair into more perfect alignment with the desk, as if he were preparing for a long campaign.

The door opened and a pale efficient-looking woman stepped into the room. The Dean nodded at her and then leaned back in his chair and stared at the wall beyond Ellen's head, mapping his strategy. Several moments passed before he spoke. 'Get the programme card of Kingship, Dorothy, fall semester, nineteen forty-nine. See which English section she was in and get the enrolment list for that section. Bring me the folders of all the male students whose names appear on the list.' He looked at the secretary. 'Got that?'

'Yes, sir.'

He made her repeat the instructions.

'Fine,' he said. She went out. 'On the double,' he said to the closed door. He turned back to Ellen and smiled complacently. She returned the smile.

By degrees the air of military efficiency faded, giving way to one of avuncular solicitude. The Dean leaned forward, his fingers softly clustered on the desk. 'Surely you haven't come to Blue River solely for this purpose,' he said.

'I'm visiting friends.'

'Ahh.'

Ellen opened her handbag. 'May I smoke?'

'By all means.' He pushed a crystal ashtray to her side of the desk. 'I smoke myself,' he admitted graciously. Ellen offered him a cigarette, but he demurred. She lit hers with a match drawn from a white folder on which *Ellen Kingship* was printed in copper letters.

The Dean regarded the match-book thoughtfully. 'Your conscientiousness in financial matters is admirable,' he said, smiling. 'If only everyone we dealt with were similarly conscientious.' He examined a bronze letter opener. 'We are at present beginning the construction of a new gymnasium and fieldhouse. Several people who pledged contributions have failed to live up to their words.'

Ellen shook her head sympathetically.

'Perhaps your father would be interested in making a contribution,' the Dean speculated. 'A memorial to your sister—'

'I'll be glad to mention it to him.'

'Would you? I would certainly appreciate that.' He replaced the letter-opener. 'Such contributions are tax-deductible,' he added.

A few minutes later the secretary entered with a stack of manilla folders in her arm. She set them before the Dean. 'English fifty-one,' she said, 'section six. Seventeen male students.'

'Fine,' said the Dean. As the secretary left he straightened his chair and rubbed his hands, the military man once more. He opened the top folder and leafed through its contents until he came to an application form. There was a photograph pasted in the corner of it. 'Dark hair,' he said, and put the folder on his left.

When he had gone though all of them, there were two uneven piles. 'Twelve with dark hair and five with light,' the Dean said.

Ellen leaned forward. 'Dorothy once told me he was handsome—'

The Dean drew the pile of five folders to the centre of his desk blotter and opened the first one. 'George Speiser,' he said thoughtfully. 'I doubt if you'd call Mr Speiser handsome.' He lifted out the application form and turned it towards Ellen. The face in the photograph was a chinless, gimlet-eyed teenager. She shook her head.

The second man was an emaciated young man with thick eyeglasses.

The third was fifty-three years old and his hair was white, not blond.

Ellen's hands were damp on her purse.

The Dean opened the fourth folder. 'Gordon Gant,' he said. 'Does that sound like the name?' He turned the application form towards her.

He was blond and unarguably handsome; light eyes under full brows, a long firm jaw, and a cavalier grin. 'I think so,' she said. 'Yes, I think he—'

'Or could it be Dwight Powell?' the Dean asked, displaying the fifth application form in his other hand.

The fifth photograph showed a square-jawed, serious-looking young man, with a cleft chin and pale-toned eyes.

'Which name sounds familiar?' the Dean asked.

Ellen looked impotently from one picture to the other.

They were both blond; they were both blue-eyed; they were both handsome.

She came out of the Administration Building and stood at the head of the stone steps surveying the campus, dull grey under a clouded sky. Her purse was in one hand, a slip of paper from the Dean's memo pad in the other.

Two . . . It would slow her up a little, that's all. It should be simple to find out which was the one – and then she would watch him, even meet him perhaps – though not as Ellen Kingship. Watch for the darting eye, the guarded answer. Murder must leave marks. (It *was* murder. It *must* have been murder.)

She was getting ahead of herself. She looked at the paper in her hand:

> *Gordon C. Gant*
> *1312 West Twenty-sixth Street*
> *Dwight Powell*
> *1520 West Thirty-fifth Street.*

3

Her lunch, eaten in a small restaurant across the street from the campus, was a hasty mechanical affair, her mind racing with swift thoughts. How to begin? Ask a few discreet questions of their friends? But where do you start? Follow each man, learn the identity of his friends, meet them, find the ones who had known him last year? Time, time, time . . . If she remained in Blue River too long, Bud might call her father. Her fingers tapped impatiently. Who would be *sure* to know about Gordon Gant and Dwight Powell? Their families. Or if they were from out of town, a landlady or a room-mate. It would be impetuous to go straight to the centre of things, to the people nearest them, but still, no time could be wasted . . . She bit her lower lip, her fingers still tapping.

After a minute she put down her half-finished cup of coffee, rose from the table and threaded her way to the phone booth. Hesitantly she ruffled the pages of the thin Blue River book. There was no Gant at all, no Powell on Thirty-fifth Street. That meant they either had no phones, which seemed unlikely, or they were living with families other than their own.

She called Information and obtained the number of the telephone at 1312 West Twenty-sixth Street; 2-2014:

'Hello?' The voice was a woman's; dry, middle-aged.

'Hello.' Ellen swallowed. 'Is Gordon Gant there?'

A pause. 'Who's calling?'

'A friend of his. Is he there?'

'No.' Snapped out sharply.

'Who is this?'

'His landlady.'

'When do you expect him back?'

'Won't be back till late tonight.' The woman's voice was quick with annoyance. There was a click as she hung up.

Ellen looked at the dead receiver and placed it on the hook. When she got back to her table the coffee was cold.

He would be gone all day. Go there? A single conversation with the landlady might establish that Gant was the one who had gone with Dorothy. Or, by elimination, it might prove that Powell was the one. Speak to the landlady – but under what pretext?

Why, any pretext! Provided the woman believed it, what harm could the wildest story do? – even if its falseness were completely obvious to Gant when the landlady reported it. Either he wasn't the man, in which case let him puzzle over a mysterious questioner pretending to be a friend or a relative, or he *was* the man, in which case: (*a*) he had not killed Dorothy – again let him puzzle over a mysterious questioner; or (*b*) he *had* killed Dorothy – and the story of a girl seeking information about him would make him uneasy. Yet his uneasiness would not interfere with her plans, for should she later make his acquaintance, he would have no reason to associate her with the girl who had questioned his landlady. Uneasiness on his part might even be a help to her, making him tense, more likely to betray himself. Why, he might even decide to take no chances and leave town – and that would be all she'd need to convince the police that there was a sound basis to her suspicions. They would investigate, find the proof . . .

Go straight to the centre of things. Impetuous? When you thought about it, it was really the most logical thing to do.

She looked at her watch. Five past one. Her visit shouldn't be made too soon after the telephone call or the landlady might connect the two and become suspicious. Forcing herself to sit back in the chair. Ellen caught the waitress's eye and ordered another cup of coffee.

At a quarter to two she entered the 1300 block of West Twenty-sixth Street. It was a quiet, tired-looking street, with pallid two-storey frame houses sitting behind pocked brown lawns still hard from winter. A few old Fords and Chevvies stood immobile along the kerb, some ageing naturally, some trying to stay young with unprofessional paint jobs, bright coloured but lustreless. Ellen walked with the enforced slowness of attempted nonchalance, the sound of her heels the only sound in the still air.

The house where Gordon Gant lived, 1312, was the third one from the corner: mustard coloured, its brown trim the shade of stale chocolate. After looking at it for a moment, Ellen walked up the cracked concrete path that bisected the dead lawn and led to the porch. There she read the nameplate on the mailbox affixed to one of the posts: *Mrs Minna Arquette*. She stepped to the door. Its bell was of the old-fashioned kind; a fan-shaped metal tab protruded from the centre of the door. Drawing a deep initiatory breath, she gave the tab a quick twist. The bell within rang gratingly. Ellen waited.

Presently footsteps sounded inside, and then the door opened. The woman who stood in the doorway was tall and lank, with frizzy grey hair clustered above a long equine face. Her eyes were pink and rheumy. A busily printed housedress hung from her sharp shoulders. She looked Ellen up and down. 'Yes?' – the dry midwestern voice of the telephone.

'You must be Mrs Arquette,' Ellen declared.

'That's right.' The woman twitched a sudden smile, displaying teeth of an unnatural perfection.

Ellen smiled back at her. 'I'm Gordon's cousin.'

Mrs Arquette arched thin eyebrows. 'His cousin?'

'Didn't he mention that I'd be here today?'

'Why, no. He didn't say anything about a cousin. Not a word.'

'That's funny. I wrote him I'd be passing through. I'm on my way to Chicago and I purposely came this way so I could stop off and see him. He must have forgotten to—'

'When did you write him?'

Ellen hesitated. 'The day before yesterday. Saturday.'

'Oh.' The smile flashed again. 'Gordon leaves the house early in the morning and the first mail don't come till ten. Your letter is probably sitting in his room this minute.'

'Ohh—'

'He isn't here right—'

'Couldn't I come in for a few minutes?' Ellen cut in quickly. 'I took the wrong tramcar from the station and I had to walk about ten blocks.'

Mrs Arquette took a step back into the house. 'Of course. Come on in.'

'Thank you very much.' Ellen crossed the threshold, entering a hallway that was stale-smelling and – once the front door was closed – dimly lighted. A flight of stairs rose along the right wall. On the left an archway opened on to a parlour which had the stiff look of seldom used rooms.

'Miz Arquette?' a voice called from the back of the house.

'Coming!' she answered. She turned to Ellen. 'You mind sitting in the kitchen?'

'Not at all,' Ellen said. The Arquette teeth shone again, and then Ellen was following the tall figure down the hallway, wondering why the woman, so pleasant now, had been so irritable over the telephone.

The kitchen was painted the same mustard colour as the exterior of the house. There was a white porcelain-topped table in the middle of the room, with a set of anagrams laid out on it. An elderly bald-headed man with thick glasses sat at the table, pouring the last of a bottle of Dr Pepper into a flower jar that had once held cheese. 'This is Mr Fishback from next door,' said Mrs Arquette. 'We play anagrams.'

'Nickel a word,' added the old man, raising his glasses to look at Ellen.

'This is Miss—' Mrs Arquette waited.

'Gant,' said Ellen.

'Miss Gant, Gordon's cousin.'

'How do you do,' said Mr Fishback. 'Gordon's a nice boy.' He dropped his glasses back into place, his eyes swelling up behind them. 'It's your go,' he said to Mrs Arquette.

She took the seat opposite to Mr Fishback. 'Sit down,' she said to Ellen, indicating one of the empty chairs. 'You want some pop?'

'No, thank you,' Ellen said, sitting. She slipped her arms from the sleeves of her coat and dropped it back over the chair.

Mrs Arquette stared at the dozen turned up letters in the ring of black-backed wooden squares. 'Where you on your way from?' she inquired.

'California.'

'I didn't know Gordon had family in the west.'

'No, I was just visiting there. I'm from the east.'

'Oh.' Mrs Arquette looked at Mr Fishback. 'Go ahead, I give up. Can't do anything with no vowels.'

'It's my turn?' he asked. She nodded. With a grin Mr Fishback snatched at the turned-up letters. 'You missed it, you missed it!' he crowed. 'C-R-Y-P-T. Crypt. What they bury folks in.' He pushed the letters together and added the word to the other ranged before him.

'That's not fair,' Mrs Arquette protested. 'You had all that time to think while I was at the door.'

'Fair is fair,' Mr Fishback declared. He turned up two more letters and placed them in the centre of the ring.

'Oh, shoot,' Mrs Arquette muttered, sitting back in her chair.

'How is Gordon these days?' Ellen asked.

'Oh, fine,' said Mrs Arquette. 'Busy as a bee, what with school and the programme.'

'The programme?'

'You mean you don't know about Gordon's programme?'

'Well, I haven't heard from him in quite a while—'

'Why, he's had it for almost three months now!' Mrs Arquette

335

drew herself up grandly. 'He plays records and talks. A disc jockey. "The Discus Thrower" he's called. Every night except Sunday, from eight to ten over KBRI.'

'That's wonderful!' Ellen exclaimed.

'Why, he's a real celebrity,' the landlady continued, turning up a letter as Mr Fishback nodded to her. 'They had an interview on him in the paper a couple of Sundays back. Reporter come here and everything. And girls he don't even know calling him up at all hours. Stoddard girls. They get his number out of the Student Directory and call up just to hear his voice over the telephone. He don't want anything to do with them, so I'm the one's got to answer. It's enough to drive a person crazy,' Mrs Arquette frowned at the anagrams. 'Go ahead, Mr Fishback,' she said.

Ellen fingered the edge of the table. 'Is Gordon still going out with that girl he wrote me about last year?' she asked.

'Which one's that?'

'A blonde girl, short, pretty. Gordon mentioned her in a few of his letters last year – October, November, all the way up through April. I thought he was really interested in her. But he stopped writing about her in April.'

'Well I'll tell you,' Mrs Arquette said, 'I don't ever get to see the girls Gordon goes out with. Before he got the programme he used to go out three – four times a week but he never brought any of the girls here. Not that I'd expect him to. I'm only his landlady. He never talks about them neither. Other boys I had here before him used to tell me all about their girls, but college boys were younger then. Nowadays they're mostly veterans and I guess they get a little older, they don't chatter so much. Least Gordon don't. Not that I'd want to pry, but I'm interested in people.' She turned over a letter. 'What was the girl's name? You tell me her name I can probably tell you if he's still going out with her, because sometimes when he's using the phone over by the stairs there, I'm in the parlour and can't help hearing part of the conversation.'

'I don't remember her name,' Ellen said, 'but he was going with her last year, so maybe if *you* remember the names of some of the girls he spoke to then, I'll be able to recognize it.'

'Let's see,' Mrs Arquette pondered, mechanically arranging anagrams in search of a word. 'There was a Louella. I remember that one because I had a sister-in-law by that name. And then there was a—' her watery eyes closed in concentration – 'a Barbara. No, that was the year before, his first year. Let's see, Louella.' She shook her head. 'There was others, but I'm hanged if I can remember them.'

The game of anagrams went on in silence for a minute. Finally Ellen said, 'I think this girl's name was Dorothy.'

Mrs Arquette waved a go-ahead at Mr Fishback. 'Dorothy.' Her eyes narrowed. 'No – if the name's Dorothy, I don't think he's going out with her. I haven't heard him talking to any Dorothy lately. I'm sure of that. Of course he goes down to the corner some-times to make a real personal call or a long distance.'

'But he *was* going with a Dorothy last year?'

Mrs Arquette looked up at the ceiling. 'I don't know. I don't *remember* a Dorothy, but I don't *not remember* one either, if you know what I mean.'

'Dottie?' Ellen tried.

Mrs Arquette considered for a moment and then gave a noncom-mittal shrug.

'Your go,' Mr Fishback said petulantly.

The wooden squares clicked softly as Mrs Arquette manoeuvred them about. 'I think,' said Ellen, 'that he must have broken up with this Dorothy in April when he stopped writing about her. He must have been in a bad mood around the end of April. Worried, ner-vous—' She looked at Mrs Arquette questioningly.

'Not Gordon,' she said. 'He had a real spring fever last year. Going around humming. I joshed him about it.' Mr Fishback fidgeted impatiently. 'Oh, go ahead,' Mrs Arquette said.

Choking over his Dr Pepper, Mr Fishback pounced on the ana-grams. 'You missed one again!' he cried, clawing up letters. 'F-A-N-E. Fane!'

'What're you talking about, fane? No such word!' Mrs Arquette turned to Ellen. 'You ever hear of a word "Fane"?'

'You should know better'n to argue with me!' Mr Fishback shrilled. 'I don't know what it means, but I know it's a word. I seen it!' He turned to Ellen. 'I read three books a week, regular as clockwork.'

'Fane,' snorted Mrs Arquette.

'Well look it up in the dictionary!'

'That little pocket one with nothing in it? Every time I look up one of your words and it ain't there you blame it on the dictionary!'

Ellen looked at the two glaring figures. 'Gordon must have a dic-tionary,' she said. She stood up. 'I'll be glad to get it if you'll tell me which room is his.'

'That's right,' Mrs Arquette said decisively. 'He *does* have one.'

She rose. 'You sit down, dear. I know just where it is.'

'May I come along then? I'd like to see Gordon's room. He's told me what a nice place—'

'Come on,' said Mrs Arquette, stalking out of the kitchen. Ellen hurried after her.

'You'll see,' Mr Fishback's voice chased them, 'I know more words than you'll *ever* know, even if you live to be a hundred!'

They sped up the darkwood stairs, Mrs Arquette in the fore muttering indignantly. Ellen followed her through a door adjacent to the head of the stairway.

The room was bright with flowered wallpaper. There was a green-covered bed, a dresser, easy chair, table . . . Mrs Arquette, having snatched a book from the top of the dresser, stood by the window ruffling the pages. Ellen moved to the dresser and scanned the titles of the books ranked across its top. A diary maybe. Any kind of notebook. *Prize Stories of 1950, An Outline of History, Radio Announcer's Handbook of Pronunciation, The Brave Bulls, A History of American Jazz, Swann's Way, Elements of Psychology, Three Famous Murder Novels*, and *A Sub-Treasury of American Humour*.

'Oh, shoot,' said Mrs Arquette. She stood with her forefinger pressed to the open dictionary. 'Fane,' she read, 'a temple; hence a church.' She slammed the book shut. 'Where does he get words like that?'

Ellen eased over to the table, where three envelopes were fanned out. Mrs Arquette, putting the dictionary on the dresser, glanced at her. 'The one without a return address is yours, I guess.'

'Yes, it is,' Ellen said. The two letters with return addresses were from *Newsweek* and the National Broadcasting Company.

Mrs Arquette was at the door. 'Coming?'

'Yes,' Ellen said.

They trudged down the stairs and walked slowly into the kitchen, where Mr Fishback was waiting. As soon as he observed Mrs Arquette's dejection he burst into gleeful cackling. She gave him a dirty look. 'It means a church,' she said, slumping into her chair. He laughed some more. 'Oh, shut up and get on with the game,' Mrs Arquette grumbled. Mr Fishback turned over two letters.

Ellen took her purse from the coat-draped chair in which she had sat. 'I guess I'll be going now,' she said dispiritedly.

'Going?' Mrs Arquette looked up, the thin eyebrows arching.

Ellen nodded.

'Well for goodness' sake, aren't you going to wait for Gordon?' Ellen went cold. Mrs Arquette looked at the clock on the refrigerator next to the door. 'It's ten after two,' she said. 'His last class ended at two o'clock. He should be here any minute.'

She couldn't speak. The image of Mrs Arquette's upturned face swayed sickeningly. 'You – you told me he would be gone all day—' she strained out finally.

Mrs Arquette looked injured. 'Why, I never told you no such thing! Why on earth you been sitting here if not waiting for him?'

'The telephone—'

The landlady's jaw dropped. 'Was that you? Around one o'clock?'

Ellen nodded helplessly.

'Well why didn't you tell me it was you? I thought it was one of those fool girls. Whenever someone calls and won't give a name I tell them he's gone for the day. Even if he's here. He told me to. He—' The expression of earnestness drained from Mrs Arquette's face. The dull eye, the thin-lipped mouth became grim, suspicious. 'If you thought he was out for the day,' she demanded slowly, 'then why did you come here at all?'

'I – I wanted to meet you. Gordon wrote so much—'

'Why were you asking all those questions?' Mrs Arquette stood up.

Ellen reached for her coat. Suddenly Mrs Arquette was holding Ellen's arms, the long bony fingers clutching painfully. 'Let go of me. Please—'

'Why were you snooping in his room?' The horse-like face pressed close to Ellen's, the eyes swelling with anger, the rough skin red. 'What did you want in there? You take something while my back was turned?'

Behind Ellen, Mr Fishback's chair scraped and his voice piped frightenedly. 'Why'd she want to steal anything from her own cousin?'

'Who says she's his cousin?' Mrs Arquette snapped.

Ellen worked futilely in her grasp, 'Please, you're hurting me—'

The pale eyes narrowed. 'And I don't think she's one of those damn girls looking for a souvenir or something either. Why was she asking all those questions?'

'I'm his cousin! I am!' Ellen tried to steady her voice. 'I want to go now. You can't keep me here. I'll see him later.'

'You'll see him now,' Mrs Arquette said. 'You're staying here until Gordon comes.' She glanced over Ellen's shoulder. 'Mr Fishback, get over by the back door.' She waited, her eyes following Mr Fishback's slow passage, and then she released Ellen. Moving quickly to the front doorway, she blocked it, her arms folded across her chest. 'We'll find out what this is all about,' she said.

Ellen rubbed her arms where Mrs Arquette's fingers had clamped them. She looked at the man and woman blocking the doors at either end of the kitchen; Mr Fishback with his glass-magnified eyes blinking nervously; Mrs Arquette standing grim, monolithic. 'You can't do this.' She retrieved her purse from the floor. She took her coat from the chair and put it over her arm. 'Let me out of here,' she said firmly.

Neither of them moved.

They heard the front door slam and footsteps on the stairs. 'Gordon!' Mrs Arquette shouted, 'Gordon!' The footsteps stopped. 'What is it, Mrs Arquette?' The landlady turned and ran down the hallway.

Ellen faced Mr Fishback, 'Please,' she implored. 'Let me out of here. I didn't mean any harm.'

He shook his head slowly.

She stood motionless, hearing the excited rasping of Mrs Arquette's voice far behind her. Footsteps approached and the voice grew louder. 'She kept asking all kinds of questions about what girls you were going out with last year, and she even tricked me into taking her to your room. She was looking at your books and the letters on your table.' Mrs Arquette's voice suddenly flooded the kitchen. 'There she is!'

Ellen turned. Mrs Arquette stood to the left of the table, one arm lifted, pointing accusation. Gant was in the doorway leaning against the jamb, tall and spare in a pale-blue topcoat, books in one hand. He looked at her for a moment, then his lips curved a smile over his long jaw and one eyebrow lifted slightly.

He detached himself from the jamb and stepped into the room, putting his books on the refrigerator without taking his eyes from her. 'Why, Cousin Hester,' he marvelled softly, his eye flicking down then up again in considered appraisal. 'You've passed through adolescence magnificently.' He ambled around the table, placed his hands on Ellen's shoulders, and kissed her fondly on the cheek.

4

'You – mean she really *is* your cousin?' Mrs Arquette gasped.

'Arquette, my love,' said Gant, moving to Ellen's left, 'ours was a communal teething ring.' He patted Ellen's shoulder. 'Wasn't it, Hester?'

She eyed him crazily, her face flushed, her mouth slack. Her gaze moved to Mrs Arquette at the left of the table, to the hallway beyond it, to the coat and purse in her hands . . . She darted to the right, sped around the table and through the door and down the hallway hearing Arquette's 'Running away!' and Gant's pursuing shout; 'She's from the psychotic side of the family!' Wrenching open the heavy front door, she fled from the house, her toes biting the concrete path. At the sidewalk she turned to the right and reined to swift bitter strides, wrestling into her tangled coat. Oh God, everything messed up! She clenched her teeth, feeling the hot pressure of tears behind her eyes. Gant caught up with her and matched her strides with long easy legs. She flung a fiery glance at the grinning face and then glared straight ahead, her whole being compressed with unreasoned fury at herself and him.

'Isn't there a secret word?' he asked. 'Aren't you supposed to press a message into my hand and whisper "Southern Comfort" or something? Or is this the one where the heavy in the dark suit has been following you all day and you sought refuge in the nearest door-way? I like them equally well, so whichever it is—' She strode along in acid silence. 'You ever read the Saint stories? I used to. Old Simon Templar was *always* running into beautiful women with strange behaviour patterns. Once one of them swam on to his yacht in the middle of the night. Said she was a channel swimmer gone astray, I believe. Turned out to be an insurance investigator.' He caught her arm. 'Cousin Hester, I have the most insatiable curiosity—'

She pulled her arm free. They had reached an intersecting avenue along the other side of which a taxi cruised. She waved and the cab began a U-turn. 'It was a joke,' she said tightly. 'I'm sorry. I did it on a bet.'

'That's what the girl on the yacht told the Saint.' His face went serious. 'Fun is fun, but why all the questions about my sordid past?'

The cab pulled up. She tried to open the door but he braced his hand against it. 'Look here, cousin, don't be fooled by my disc jockey dialogue. I'm not kidding . . .'

'Please,' she moaned exhaustedly, tugging at the doorhandle. The cabbie appeared at the front window, looking up at them and appraising the situation. 'Hey mister,' he said. His voice was a menacing rumble.

With a sigh, Gant released the door. Ellen opened it, ducked in, and slammed it closed. She sank into soft worn leather. Outside Gant was leaning over, his hands on the door, staring in at her through the glass as though trying to memorize the details of her face. She looked away.

She waited until the cab had left the kerb before telling the driver her destination.

It took ten minutes to reach the New Washington House, where Ellen had registered before calling on the Dean – ten minutes of lip-biting and quick-handed smoking and bitter self-denunciation, the release of the tension which had been built up before Gant's arrival and which had been left hanging, unspent, by his anti-climatic asinine banter. Cousin Hester! Oh, she had really messed things up! She had bet half her chips and got nothing in return. Still in the dark as to whether or not he was *the* man, she had made further questioning of him or his landlady completely impossible. If investigation of Powell should show he wasn't the man, proving that Gant was, she might as well give up and go back to Caldwell because if – always the second, the big 'if' – if Gant had killed Dorothy, he would be on guard, knowing Ellen's face and knowing what she was after by the questions she had asked Mrs Arquette. A killer on guard, ready perhaps to kill again. She wouldn't risk tangling with that – not when he had seen her face. Better to live in doubt than to die in certainty. Her only other course would be to go to the police, and she would still have nothing more to offer them than 'something old, something new', so they would nod solemnly and usher her politely from the station.

Oh, she had made a fine start!

The hotel room had beige walls and clumsy brown furniture and the same clean, impersonal, transient air as the miniature paper-wrapped cake of soap in the adjoining bathroom. The only mark of its occupancy was the suitcase with the Caldwell stickers on the rack at the foot of the double bed.

After hanging her coat in the closet, Ellen seated herself at the writing-table by the window. She took her fountain pen and the letter to Bud from her purse. Staring down at the addressed but still unsealed envelope, she debated whether or not to mention, in addition to an outline of the interview with Dean Welch, the story of the Gant fiasco. No – if Dwight Powell turned out to be the one then the Gant business meant nothing. It *must* be Powell. Not Gant, she told herself – not with that lighthearted chatter. But what had he said? – Look here, cousin, don't be fooled by my disc jockey dialogue. I'm not kidding . . .

There was a knock at the door. She jumped to her feet. 'Who is it?'

'Towels,' a high feminine voice answered.

Ellen crossed the room and grasped the door-knob. 'I – I'm not dressed. Could you leave them outside please?'

'All right,' the voice said.

She stood there for two minutes, hearing occasional passing footsteps and the muffled sound of the elevator down the hall, while the knob grew damp in her hand. Finally she smiled at her nervousness, visualizing herself peering under the bed old-maid fashion before going to sleep. She opened the door.

Gant lounged with one elbow against the jamb, the hand propping up his blond head. 'Hi, Cousin Hester,' he said. 'I believe I mentioned my insatiable curiosity.' She tried to close the door, but his foot was in the way, immovable. He smiled. 'Much fun. Follow that cab!' His right hand described a zigzag course. 'Shades of the Warner Brothers. The driver got such a kick out of it he almost refused the tip. I told him you were running away from my bed and board.'

'Get away!' she whispered fiercely. 'I'll call the manager!'

'Look, Hester,' the smile dropped, 'I think I could have you arrested for illegal entry or impersonating a cousin or something like that, so why don't you invite me in for a small confab? If you're worried about what the bell-hops will think, you can leave the door open.' He pushed gently on the door, forcing Ellen to retreat a step. 'That's a good girl,' he said as he eased through the opening. He eyed her dress with exaggerated disappointment. ' "I'm not dressed," she says. I should have known you were a habitual liar.' He strolled to the bed and sat down on the edge of it. 'Well for pity's sake, coz, stop shaking! I'm not going to eat you.'

'What – what do you want?'

'An explanation.'

She swung the door all the way open and remained standing in the doorway, as though it were his room and she the visitor. 'It's – very simple. I listen to your programme all the time—'

He glanced at the suitcase. 'In Wisconsin?'

'It's only a hundred miles away. We get KBRI. We really do.'

'Go ahead.'

'I listen to you all the time, and I like your programme very much. I'm in Blue River, so I thought I'd try to meet you.'

'And when you meet me you run away.'

'Well what would you have done? I didn't plan it *that* way. I pretended to be your cousin because I – I wanted to get information about you – what kind of girls you like—'

Rubbing his jaw doubtfully, he stood up. 'How did you get my phone number?'

'From the Student Directory.'

He moved to the foot of the bed and touched the suitcase. 'If you go to Caldwell, how did you get a Stoddard directory?'

'From one of the girls here.'

'Who?'

'Annabelle Koch. She's a friend of mine.'

'Annabelle—' He had recognized the name. He squinted at Ellen incredulously. 'Hey, is this really on the level?'

'Yes.' She looked down at her hands. 'I know it was a crazy thing to do, but I like your programme so much.' When she looked up again he was by the window.

He said, 'Of all the stupid, idiotic—' and suddenly he was staring at the hallway beyond her, his eyes baffled. She turned. There was nothing out of the ordinary to be seen. She looked back at Gant and he was facing the window, his back to her. 'Well, Hester,' he said, 'that was a flattering explanation' – he turned, taking his hand from inside his jacket – 'and one I shall long remember.' He glanced at the partially open bathroom door. 'Do you mind if I utilize your facilities?' he asked, and before she could say anything he had ducked into the bathroom and closed the door. The lock clicked.

Ellen gazed blankly at the door, wondering whether or not Gant had believed her. Her knees quivered. Drawing a deep steady breath, she crossed the room to the writing-table and took a cigarette from her purse. She broke two matches before she got it lighted, and then she stood looking out the window, nervously rolling her fountain pen back and forth over the surface of the table which was bare except for her purse. Bare – the letter. The letter to Bud! Gant had been standing near the table and he had tricked her into turning towards the hallway and then he had been facing the window and he turned, taking his hand from inside his jacket!

Frantically she hammered on the bathroom door. 'Give me that letter! Give it to me!'

Several seconds passed before Gant's deep-toned voice said, 'My curiosity is especially insatiable when it comes to phoney cousins with flimsy stories.'

She stood in the doorway with one hand on the jamb and her coat in the other, looking from the still-closed bathroom door to the hallway and smiling inanely at the occasional passers-by. A bellhop asked if there were anything he could do for her. She shook her head.

Gant finally came out. He was folding the letter carefully into its envelope. He put it on the writing-table. 'Well,' he said. He viewed her ready-to-flee figure. 'Well.' He smiled somewhat uncomfortably. 'As my grandmother said when the man on the phone asked for Lana Turner, "Boy, have you got the wrong number!" '

Ellen did not move.

'Look,' he said. 'I didn't even know her. I said hello to her once or twice. There were other blond guys in that class. I didn't even know her name until her picture was in the papers. The teacher had taken attendance by seat numbers, never called the roll. I didn't even know her name.'

Ellen didn't move.

'Well, for God's sake, if you want to break a speed record that coat's only going to be in the way.'

She didn't move.

In two swift strides he was at the bedside table, snatching up the Gideon Bible. He raised his right hand. 'I swear on this Bible that I never went out with your sister, or said more than two words to her - or anything—' He put the Bible down. 'Well?'

'If Dorothy was killed,' Ellen said, 'the man who did it would swear on a dozen Bibles. And if she thought he loved her, then he was a good actor too.'

Gant rolled his eyes heavenward and extended his wrists for the handcuffs. 'All right,' he said, 'I'll go quietly.'

'I'm glad you think this is something to joke about.'

He lowered his hands. 'I'm sorry,' he said sincerely. 'But how the hell am I supposed to convince you that—'

'You can't,' Ellen said. 'You might as well go.'

'There were other blond guys in the class,' he insisted. He snapped his fingers. 'There was one she used to come in with all the time!

Cary Grant chin, tall—'

'Dwight Powell?'

'That's right!' He stopped short. 'Is he on your list?'

She hesitated a moment, and then nodded.

'He's the one!'

Ellen looked at him suspiciously.

He threw up his hands. 'Okay. I give up. You'll see, it was Powell.' He moved towards the door; Ellen backed into the hallway. 'I would just like to leave, as you suggested,' Gant said loftily.

He came into the hallway. 'Unless you want me to go on calling you Hester, you ought to tell me what your name really is.'

'Ellen.'

Gant seemed reluctant to go. 'What are you going to do now?'

After a moment she said, 'I don't know.'

'If you barge into Powell's place, don't pull a fluff like you did this afternoon. He may be no one to fool around with.'

Ellen nodded.

Gant looked her up and down. 'A girl on a mission,' he mused. 'Never thought I'd live to see the day.' He started to go and then turned back. 'You wouldn't be in the market for a Watson, would you?'

'No, thanks,' she said in the doorway. 'I'm sorry but—'

He shrugged and smiled. 'I figured my credentials wouldn't be in order. Well, good luck.' He turned and walked down the hallway.

Ellen backed into her room and slowly closed the door.

. . . It's 7.30 now, Bud, and I'm comfortably settled in a very nice room at the New Washington House – just had dinner and am ready to take a bath and turn in after a full day.

I spent most of the afternoon in the waiting-room of the Dean of Students. When I finally got to see him I told a fabulous story about an unpaid debt which Dorothy owed to a handsome blond in her fall English class. After much digging through records and examining a rogues gallery of application blank photos, we came up with the man – Mr Dwight Powell of 1520 West Thirty-fifth Street, on whom the hunting season opens tomorrow morning.

How's that for an efficient start? Never underestimate the power of a woman!

Love,
Ellen.

At eight o'clock she paused in her undressing and dropped a quarter into the coin-operated bedside radio. She pushed the button marked KBRI. There was a low humming and then, smooth and sonorous, Gant's voice swelled into the room. ' . . . another session with the Discus Thrower, or as our engineer puts it, "Puff and Pant with Gordon Gant", which shows the limitations of a purely scientific education. On to the agenda. The first disc of the evening is an oldie, and it's dedicated to Miss Hester Holmes of Wisconsin—'

A jumpy orchestral introduction, nostalgically dated, burst from the radio and faded under the singing of a sugary, little-girl voice.

Smiling, Ellen went into the bathroom. The tiled walls rang with the sound of water pounding into the tub. She kicked off her slippers and hung her robe on a hook beside the door. She reached over and turned off the water. In the sudden silence, the wispy voice sifted in from the next room.

5

'Hello?' The voice was a woman's.

'Hello,' Ellen said. 'Is Dwight Powell there?'

'No, he isn't.'

'When do you expect him back?'

'I couldn't say for sure. I know he works over at Folger's between his classes and afterwards, but I don't know to what time he works.'

'Aren't you his landlady?'

'No. I'm her daughter-in-law come over to clean. Mrs Honig is in Iowa City with her foot. She cut it last week and it got infected. My husband had to take her to Iowa City.'

'Oh, I'm sorry—'

'If you have a message for Dwight, I can leave him a note.'

'No, thanks. I have a class with him in a couple of hours, so I'll see him then. It wasn't anything important.'

'Okay. Good-bye.'

'Good-bye.'

Ellen hung up. She certainly wasn't going to wait to speak to the landlady. She was already more or less convinced that Powell was the man who had been going with Dorothy; checking with the land-lady would only have been a sort of formality; verification could be obtained just as easily from Powell's friends. Or from Powell him-self.

She wondered what kind of place it was where he worked. Folger's. It would have to be near the campus if he went there in free hours between classes. If it were a store of some sort, where he waited on customers . . .

She picked up the telephone book, turned to the F's and skimmed through the listings.

Folger Drugs, 1448 Univ. Av. . . . . . . 2 – 3800.

It was between Twenty-eighth and Twenty-ninth Streets across the avenue from the campus; a squat brick structure with a long green sign stretched across its brow; *Folger Drugs* and in smaller letters *Prescriptions* and in still smaller letters *Fountain Service*. Ellen paused outside the glass door and smoothed her bangs. Drawing her-self up as though making an entrance on to a stage, she pushed open the door and went in.

The fountain was on the left; mirrors, chrome, grey marble; fronted by a line of round-topped red leatherette stools. It was not yet noon so only a few people were seated at the forward end.

Dwight Powell was behind the counter, wearing a snug white mess jacket and a white cap which rode the waves of his fine blond hair like an overturned ship. His square-jawed face was lean and he had a moustache; a thin carefully-trimmed line of almost colourless hairs, visible only when the light gleamed on it; a feature which evidently had been added some time after the taking of the photograph which the Dean had shown. Powell was squirting whipped cream from a metal canister on to a gummy-looking sundae. There was a sullen set to his lips that made it clear he disliked his job.

Ellen walked towards the far end of the counter. As she passed Powell, who was placing the sundae before a customer, she sensed him glance up. She went on, eyes straight ahead, to the empty sec-tion. Taking off her coat, she folded it and put it with her purse on one of the row of empty stools. She seated herself on the next stool. With her hands flat on the cold marble, she examined her reflection in the mirrored wall opposite. Her hands left the marble, dropped to the bottom of her powder-blue sweater and pulled it down tight.

Powell approached along the gangway behind the counter. He put a glass of water and a paper napkin before her. His eyes were deep blue, the skin immediately below them grey-shadowed. 'Yes, miss?'

he said in a low-pitched voice. His eyes met hers and then strayed downwards momentarily.

She looked at the mirrored wall, at the pictures of sandwiches fixed to it. The grill was directly opposite her. 'A cheeseburger,' she said, looking back at him. His eyes were on hers again. 'And a cup of coffee.'

'Cheeseburger and coffee,' he said, and smiled. It was a stiff smile that vanished quickly, as though his facial muscles were unaccustomed to the exercise. He turned and opened a locker under the grill, taking out a patty of meat on a piece of waxed paper. Kicking the locker door shut, he slapped the meat on to the grill and peeled the waxed paper off its back. The meat sizzled. He took a hamburger roll from a bin next to the grill and began slicing it down the centre with a long knife. She watched his face in the mirror. He glanced up and smiled again. She returned the smile faintly; I am not interested, but I am not completely *un*interested. He put the two halves of the roll face down beside the hamburger and turned to Ellen. 'Coffee now or later?'

'Now, please.'

He produced a tan cup and saucer and a spoon from under the counter. He arranged them before her and then moved a few paces down the gangway, to return with a glass pot of coffee. He poured the steaming liquid slowly into her cup. 'You go to Stoddard?' he asked.

'No, I don't.'

He rested the coffee pot on the marble and with his free hand brought a jigger of cream up from under the counter.

'You?' Ellen asked.

He nodded.

Down the counter a spoon chinked against glass. Powell answered the call with the sullen compression returning to his lips.

He was back a minute later, picking up a spatula and turning the hamburger. He opened the locker again and took out a slice of American cheese which he put on top of the meat. They looked at each other in the mirror as he arranged the roll and a couple of slices of pickle on a plate. 'You haven't been in here before, have you,' he said.

'No. I've only been in Blue River a couple of days.'

'Oh. Staying or passing through?' He spoke slowly, like a circling hunter.

'Staying. If I can find a job.'

'As what?'

'A secretary.'

He turned around, the spatula in one hand, the plate in the other. 'That should be easy to find.'

'Ha,' she said.

There was a pause. 'Where you from?' he asked.

'Des Moines.'

'It should be easier to find a job there than it is here.'

She shook her head. 'All the girls looking for jobs go to Des Moines.'

Turning back to the grill, he lifted the cheeseburger with the spatula and slid it on to the roll. He set the plate before her and produced a bottle of ketchup from below the counter. 'You have relatives here?'

She shook her head. 'Don't know a soul in town. Except the woman at the employment agency.'

A spoon tapped glass again down the counter. 'Damn,' he muttered. 'Maybe you want *my* job?' He stalked away.

In a few minutes he returned. He began scraping the top of the grill with the edge of the spatula. 'How's the cheeseburger?'

'Fine.'

'You want something else? Some more coffee?'

'No, thanks.'

The grill was perfectly clean but he continued scraping it, watching Ellen in the mirror. She dabbed at her lips with the napkin. 'Check, please,' she said.

He turned, taking a pencil and a green pad from a clip on his belt. 'Listen,' he said, not looking up from his writing, 'there's a very good revival at the Paramount tonight. *Lost Horizon*. You want to see it?'

'I—'

'You said you didn't know anybody in town.'

She seemed to debate for a moment. 'All right,' she said finally.

He looked up and smiled, this time effortlessly. 'Swell. Where can I meet you?'

'The New Washington House. In the lobby.'

'Eight o'clock okay?' He tore the check from the pad. 'My name is Dwight,' he said. 'As in Eisenhower. Dwight Powell, ' He looked at her, waiting.

'Mine is Evelyn Kittredge.'

'Hi,' he said, smiling. She flashed a broad smile in return. Something flickered over Powell's face; surprise? – memory?

'What's wrong?' Ellen asked. 'Why do you look at me that way?'

'Your smile,' he said uneasily. 'Exactly like a girl I used to know.'

There was a pause, then Ellen said decisively, 'Joan Bacon or Bascomb or something. I've been in this town only two days and two people have told me I look like this Joan—'

'No,' Powell said, 'this girl's name was Dorothy.' He folded the check. 'Lunch is on me.' He waved his arm, trying to attract the attention of the cashier up front. Craning his neck, he pointed to the check, to Ellen and to himself, and then tucked the check into his pocket. 'All taken care of,' he said.

Ellen was standing, putting on her coat. 'Eight o'clock in the New Washington lobby,' Powell reiterated. 'Is that where you're staying?'

'Yes.' She made herself smile. She could see his mind following the path; easy pick-up, stranger in town, staying at a hotel. 'Thanks for lunch.'

'Don't mention it.'

She picked up her purse.

'See you tonight, Evelyn.'

'Eight o'clock,' she said. She turned and walked towards the front of the store, keeping her pace slow, feeling his eyes on her back. At the door she turned. He lifted a hand and smiled. She returned the gesture.

Outside, she found that her knees were shaking.

6

Ellen was in the lobby at 7.30, so that Powell would not have the occasion to ask the desk clerk to ring Miss Kittredge's room. He arrived at five to eight, the thin line of his moustache glinting over an edgy smile. (Easy pick-up, stranger in town . . .) He had ascertained that *Lost Horizon* went on at 8.06, so they took a cab to the theatre although it was only five blocks away. Midway through the picture Powell put his arm around Ellen, resting his hand on her shoulder. She kept seeing it from the corner of her eye, the hand that had caressed Dorothy's body, had pushed powerfully . . . maybe . . .

The Municipal Building was three blocks from the theatre and less than two from the New Washington House. They passed it on their way back to the hotel. A few windows were lighted in the upper floors of the looming façade across the street. 'Is that the tallest building in the city?' Ellen asked, looking at Powell.

'Yes' he said. His eyes were focused some twenty feet ahead on the sidewalk.

'How high is it?'

'Fourteen storeys.' The direction of his gaze had not altered. Ellen thought: When you ask a person the height of something that's in his presence, he instinctively turns to look at it, even if he already knows the answer. Unless he has some reason for not wanting to look at it.

They sat in a booth in the hotel's black-walled, soft-pianoed cocktail lounge and drank whisky sours. Their conversation was intermittent, Ellen pushing it against the up hill slope of Powell's slow deliberate speech. The taut buoyancy with which he had begun the evening had faded in passing the Municipal Building, had risen again on entering the hotel, and now was waning steadily the longer they sat in the red-upholstered booth.

They spoke about jobs. Powell disliked his. He had held it for two months and planned to quit as soon as he could find something better. He was saving his money for a summer study tour of Europe.

What was he studying? His major was English. What did he plan to do with it? He wasn't sure. Advertising, maybe, or get into publishing. His plans for the future seemed sketchy.

They spoke about girls. 'I'm sick of these college girls,' he said. 'Immature – they take everything too seriously.' Ellen thought this was the beginning of a line, the one that leads straight to 'You place too much importance on sex. As long as we like each other, what's the harm in going to bed?' It wasn't though. It seemed to be something that was troubling him. He weighed his words carefully, twisting the stem of the third cocktail glass between long restless fingers. 'You get one of them on your neck,' he said, the blue eyes clouded, 'and you can't get her off.' He watched his hand. 'Not without making a mess.'

Ellen closed her eyes, her hands damp on the slick black table top.

'You can't help feeling sorry for people like that,' he went on, 'but you've got to think of yourself first.'

'People like what?' she said, not opening her eyes.

'People who throw themselves on other people.' There was the loud snap of his hand hitting the table top. Ellen opened her eyes. He was taking cigarettes from a pack on the table, smiling. 'The trouble with me is too many whisky sours,' he said. His hand, holding a match to her cigarette, was unsteady. 'Let's talk about you.'

She made up a story about a secretarial school in Des Moines run by an elderly Frenchman who pitched spitballs at the girls when they weren't looking. When it was finished Powell said, 'Look, let's get out of here.'

'You mean go to another place?' Ellen asked.

'If you want to,' he said unenthusiastically.

Ellen reached for the coat beside her. 'If you don't mind, I'd just as soon we didn't. I was up very early this morning.'

'Okay,' Powell said. 'I'll escort you to your door.' The edgy smile which had begun the evening made its return.

She stood with her back to the door of her room, the brass-tagged key in her hand. 'Thank you very much,' she said. 'It really was a nice evening.'

His arm with both their coats over it went around her back. His lips came towards her and she turned away, catching the kiss on her cheek. 'Don't be coy,' he said flatly. He caught her jaw in his hand and kissed her mouth hard.

'Let's go in – have a last cigarette,' he said.

She shook her head.

'Evvie—' His hand was on her shoulder.

She shook her head again. 'Honestly, I'm dead tired.' It was a refusal, but the modest curling of her voice implied that things might be different some other night.

He kissed her a second time. She pushed his hand back up to her shoulder. 'Please – someone might—' Still holding her, he drew back a bit and smiled at her. She smiled back, trying to make it the same broad smile she had given him in the drugstore.

It worked. It was like touching a charged wire to an exposed nerve. The shadow flickered across his face.

He drew her close, both arms around her, his chin over her shoulder as if to avoid seeing her smile. 'Do I still remind you of that girl?' she asked. And then, 'I'll bet she was another girl you went out with just once.'

'No,' he said, 'I went out with her for a long time.' He pulled back. 'Who says I'm going out with you just once? You doing anything tomorrow night?'

'No.'

'Same time, same place?'

'If you'd like.'

He kissed her cheek and held her close again. 'What happened?' she asked.

'What do you mean?' His words vibrated against her temple.

'That girl. Why did you stop going with her?' She tried to make it light, casual. 'Maybe I can profit by her mistakes.'

'Oh.' There was a pause. Ellen stared at the cloth of his lapel, seeing the precise weaving of the slate-blue threads. 'It was like I said downstairs – we got too involved. Had to break it off.' She heard him take a deep breath. 'She was very immature,' he added.

After a moment, Ellen made a withdrawing movement. 'I think I'd better—' '

He kissed her again, a long one. She closed her eyes sickly.

Easing from his arms, she turned and put the key in the door without looking at him. 'Tomorrow night at eight,' he said. She had to turn around to take her coat, and there was no avoiding his eyes. 'Good night, Evvie.'

She opened the door behind her and steped back, forcing a smile to her lips. 'Good night.' She shut the door.

She was sitting motionless on the bed, the coat still in her hands, when the telephone rang five minutes later. It was Gant.

'Keeping late hours, I see.'

She sighed. 'Is it a relief to talk to you!'

'Well!' he said, stretching the word. 'Well, well, *well*! I gather that my innocence has been clearly and conclusively established.'

'Yes. Powell's the one who was going with her. And I'm right about it not being suicide. I know I am. He keeps talking about girls who throw themselves on other people and take things too seriously and get involved and things like that.' The words tumbled quickly, freed of the strain of guarded conversation.

'Good Lord, your efficiency astounds me. Where did you get your information?'

'From him.'

'What?'

'I picked him up in the drugstore where he works. I'm Evelyn Kittredge, unemployed secretary, of Des Moines, Iowa. I just tightroped through the evening with him.'

There was a long silence from Gant's end of the line. 'Tell all,' he said finally, wearily. 'When do you plan to beat the written confession out of him?'

She told him of Powell's sudden dejection when passing the Municipal Building, repeating as accurately as she could the remarks he had made under the influence of the doldrums and the whisky sours.

When Gant spoke again he was serious. 'Listen, Ellen, this doesn't sound like anything to play around with.'

'Why? As long as he thinks I'm Evelyn Kittredge—'

'How do you know he does? What if Dorothy showed him a picture of you?'

'She had only one, and that was a very fuzzy group snap-shot with our faces in the shade. If he did see it, it was almost a year ago. He couldn't possibly recognize me. Besides, if he suspected who I am he wouldn't have said the things he did.'

'No, I guess he wouldn't have,' Gant admitted reluctantly. 'What do you plan to do now?'

'This afternoon I went down to the library and read all the newspaper reports of Dorothy's death. There were a few details that were never mentioned, little things like the colour of her hat, and the fact that she was wearing gloves. I have another date with him tomorrow night. If I can get him talking about her "suicide" maybe he'll let drop one of those things that he couldn't know unless he was with her.'

'It wouldn't be conclusive evidence,' Gant said. 'He could claim he was in the building at the time and he saw her after she—'

'I'm not *looking* for conclusive evidence. All I want is something that will prevent the police from thinking that I'm just a crank with an overactive imagination. If I can prove he was anywhere near her at the time, it should be enough to start them digging.'

'Well will you please tell me how the hell you expect to get him to talk in such detail without making him suspicious? He's not an idiot, is he?'

'I have to try,' she argued. 'What else is there to do?'

Gant thought for a moment. 'I am the owner of an old ballpeen hammer,' he said. 'We could beat him over the head, drag him to the scene of the crime, and sweat it out of him.'

'You see,' Ellen said seriously, 'There's no other way to—' Her voice faded.

'Hello?'

'I'm still here,' she said.

'What happened? I thought we were cut off.'

'I was just thinking.'

'Oh. Look, seriously – be careful, will you? And if it's at all possible, call me tomorrow evening, just to let me know where you are and how things are going.'

'Why?'

'Just to be on the safe side.'

'He thinks I'm Evelyn Kittredge.'

'Well call me anyway. It can't hurt. Besides, my hair greys easily.'

'All right.'

'Good night, Ellen.'

'Good night, Gordon.'

She replaced the receiver and remained sitting on the bed, biting her lower lip and drumming her fingers the way she always did when she was toying with an idea.

7

Snapping shut her purse, Ellen looked up and smiled across the lobby at Powell's approaching figure. He was wearing a grey topcoat and a navy blue suit, and the same smile he had worn the previous evening. 'Hi,' he said, dropping down beside her on the leather divan. 'You certainly don't keep your dates waiting.'

'Some of them I do.'

His smile broadened. 'How's the job-hunting?'

'Pretty good,' she said. 'I think I've got something. With a lawyer.'

'Swell. You'll be staying in Blue River then, right?'

'It looks that way.'

'Swell,' he drew the word out caressingly. Then his eyes flicked to his wrist-watch. 'We'd better get on our horses. I passed the Glo-Ray Ballroom on my way over here and there was a line all the way—'

'Ohh,' she lamented.

'What's the matter?'

Her face was apologetic. 'I've got an errand to do first. This lawyer. I have to bring him a letter – a reference.' She tapped her purse.

'I didn't know secretaries needed references. I thought they just tested your shorthand or something.'

'Yes, but I mentioned that I had this letter from my last employer and he said he'd like to see it. He's going to be at his office till eight-thirty.' She signed. 'I'm awfully sorry.'

'That's all right.'

Ellen touched his hand. 'I'd just as soon not go dancing,' she confided. 'We can go some place, have a few drinks—'

'Okay,' he said more cheerfully. They stood up. 'Where is this lawyer?' Powell asked, standing behind her, helping her on with her coat.

'Not far from here,' Ellen said. 'The Municipal Building.'

At the head of the steps that fronted the Municipal Building, Powell stopped. Ellen, in the quadrant of a revolving door, relaxed her about-to-push hand and looked at him. He was pale, but that might have been the greyish light filtering out from the lobby. 'I'll wait for you down here, Evvie.' His jaw was rigid, the words coming out stiffly.

'I wanted you to come up with me,' she said. 'I could have brought this letter over here before eight o'clock, but I thought it was kind of odd, his telling me to bring it in the evening. He's a greasy-looking character.' She smiled. 'You're my protection.'

'Oh,' Powell said.

Ellen pushed around through the door, and after a moment Powell followed her. She had turned and was watching him when he came out of the door. He was breathing through partially-opened lips, his face barren of expression.

The vast marbled lobby was silent and empty. Three of the four elevators were black behind latticed metal gates. The fourth was a yellow-lighted cell with wooden walls the colour of honey. They walked towards it side by side, their footsteps drawing whispering echoes from the domed ceiling.

In the cell a tan-uniformed Negro operator stood reading a copy of *Look*. He tucked the magazine under his arm, toed the floor button that released the big sliding metal door, and threw the latticed gate across after it. 'Floor please,' he said.

'Fourteen,' Ellen said.

They stood in silence, watching the steadily advancing position of the lighted numeral in the row of unlighted numerals over the door: 7-8-9 . . . Powell rubbed his moustache with the side of his forefinger.

When the light jumped from 13 to 14, the car came to a smooth automatic top-floor stop. The operator drew in the gate and pulled down on the jointed bar that opened the outer door.

Ellen stepped out into the deserted corridor, Powell following her. Behind them the door slid shut with a hollow clangour. They heard the gate closing and then the decrescent hum of the car. 'It's this way,' Ellen said, moving towards the right. 'Room fourteen-oh-five.' They walked to the bend of the corridor and made the right turn. There was light behind only two of the frosted door panels in the stretch of straight-lined corridor before them. There was no sound except their feet on the polished rubber tiles. Ellen groped for something to say, 'It won't take long. I just have to give him the letter.'

'Do you think you'll get the job?'

'I think so. It's a good letter.'

They reached the end of the corridor and turned right again. One door was lighted, up ahead in the left wall, and Powell angled towards it. 'No, that not the one,' Ellen said. She went to an unlighted door on the right. Its frosted panel was inscribed *Frederic H. Clausen, Attorney-at-Law*. Powell came up behind her as she futilely tried the knob and looked at her watch. 'How do you like that?' she said bitterly. 'Not even a quarter after and he said he'd be here till eight-thirty.' (The secretary on the telephone had said, 'The office closes at five.')

'What now?' Powell asked.

'I guess I'll leave it under the door,' she said, opening her purse. She took out a large white envelope and her fountain pen. Uncapping the pen, she held the envelope flat against the purse and began to write. 'It's a shame about the dancing,' she said.

'That's okay,' said Powell. 'I wasn't too keen on it myself.' He was breathing more easily, like a novice aerialist passing the middle of the taut wire and becoming less uncertain of his footing.

'On second thought,' Ellen said, glancing up at him, 'if I leave the letter now I'll only have to come back for it tomorrow, anyway. I might as well bring it over in the morning.' She recapped the pen and put it back in her purse. She held the envelope at an angle to the light, saw that the ink was still wet, and began to wave the envelope with quick fan-like motions. Her gaze drifted to a door across the corridor, the door marked *Stairway*. Her eyes lighted. 'You know what I'd like to do?' she asked.

'What?'

'. . . Before we go back and have those drinks.'

'What?' He smiled.

She smiled back at him, waving the envelope. 'Go up to the roof.'

The aerialist looked down and saw the net being drawn out from under him. 'What do you want to do that for?' he asked slowly.

'Didn't you see the moon? And the stars? It's a perfect night. The view must be tre*men*dous.'

'I think we might still be able to get into the Glo-Ray,' he said.

'Oh, neither of us are crazy about going.' She slipped the envelope into her purse and snapped it shut. 'Come on,' she said gaily, turning from him and crossing the corridor. 'What happened to all that romance you displayed in the hall last night?' His hand reached out for her arm and caught empty air.

She pushed the door open and looked back, waiting for him to follow.

'Evvie, I – heights make me dizzy,' He forced a thin smile.

'You don't have to look down,' she said lightly. 'You don't even have to go near the edge.'

'The door's probably locked.'

'I don't think they can lock a door to a roof. Fire laws.' She frowned in mock disgust. 'Oh, come on! You'd think I was asking you to go over Niagara Falls in a barrel or something!' She backed through the doorway on to the landing, holding the door, smiling, waiting for him.

He came with a slow trance-like helplessness, as though there were part of him that perversely wanted to follow her. When he was on the landing she released the door. It swung closed with a soft pneumatic hissing, cutting off the light from the corridor and leaving a ten-watt bulb to fight a losing battle against the shadows of the stairwell.

They climbed eight steps, turned, and climbed eight more. There was a dark metal door with a warning painted on it in large white letters: *Entrance Strictly Forbidden Except in Emergency*. Powell read it aloud, stressing the words 'strictly forbidden'.

'Signs,' Ellen said disdainfully. She tried the knob.

'It must be locked,' Powell said.

'If it were locked they wouldn't have *that*.' Ellen indicated the sign. 'You try.'

He took the knob, pushed. 'It's stuck, then.'

'Oh, come on. Give a real try.'

'Okay,' he said, 'okay, okay,' with to-hell-with-it abandon. He drew back and slammed his shoulder against the door full-force. It flew open almost dragging him with it. He stumbled across the high threshold on to the tarred deck. 'Okay, Evvie,' he said sullenly, straightening himself, holding the door wide, 'come look at your gorgeous moon.'

'Sourpuss,' Ellen said, the light tone of her voice stripping his bitterness of significance. She stepped over the ledge and breezed a few steps past Powell, advancing from the shadow of the staircase housing out on to the expanse of roof like a cold-legged skater pretending not to worry about thin ice. She heard the door closing behind her, and then Powell came up on her left.

'Sorry,' he said, 'it's just that I almost broke my shoulder on the damn door, that's all.' He managed a starchy smile.

They were facing the KBRI tower; skeletal, black against the blue-black star-spattered sky; at the very top of it a slowly flashing red light whose steady pulsing flushed the roof with intermittent rose. Between the red throbs there was the soft light of the quarter moon overhead.

Ellen glanced at Powell's upturned tense-jawed profile; first dim white, then bathed with red, then white again. Beyond him she saw the wall that rimmed the airshaft, its white stone top distinct in the night. She remembered a diagram that had appeared in one of the newspapers; the X at the south side of the square – the side nearest them. Suddenly she was caught by a crazy desire to go there, look over, see where Dorothy . . . A sick wave swept over her. The focus of her vision realigned on Powell's white-edged profile and involuntarily she drew away.

It's all right, she told herself, I'm safe – safer than pushing conversation in some cocktail lounge. I'm all right, I'm Evelyn Kittredge.

He became conscious of her gaze. 'I thought you want to look at the sky,' he said, not lowering his own skyward face. She looked up and the sudden lifting of her head heightened the dizziness. The stars wheeled . . .

She broke away, went to the right, to the outer edge of the roof. Abrading her hands against the roughness of the coping, she gasped lungfuls of the cold night air. This is where he killed her. He's bound to betray himself – enough to go to the police. I'm safe . . . Finally her head cleared. She looked at the panorama below, the myriad lights glittering off into blackness. 'Dwight, come look.'

He turned and walked towards the parapet, but he stopped a few feet away.

'Isn't it beautiful?' She spoke without looking back.

'Yes,' he said.

He looked for a moment, while a breeze plucked softly at the tower cables, and then he turned slowly around until he was facing the airshaft. He stared at the parapet. Then his right foot extended itself and his legs began to walk. They carried him forward with silent relentless efficiency, like the legs of a reformed alcoholic carrying him to the bar for just one little drink. They carried him straight up to the airshaft parapet and his hands rose and set themselves flat on the cool stone. He leaned over and looked down.

Ellen felt his absence. She turned round and probed the quarter-moon obscurity. Then the tower light flashed on, its crimson glow showing him at the wall of the airshaft, and her heart jumped chokingly. The red glow vanished, but knowing where he was she could still distinguish him in the wan moonlight. She began moving forward, her steps noiseless on the resilient tar.

He looked down. A few yellow beams from lighted windows criss-crossed the square funnel of the shaft. One light was far below, at the very bottom, illuminating the small grey concrete square that was the focus of the converging walls.

'I thought heights made you dizzy.'

He whirled.

There were sweat beads on his brow and above his moustache. A nervous smile shot to his lips. 'They do,' he said, 'but I can't help looking. Self-torture.' The smile faded. 'That's my specialty.' He took a deep breath. 'You ready to go now?' he asked.

'We just got here,' Ellen protested lightly. She turned and walked towards the eastern rim of the roof, threading her way between the gaunt shapes of ventilator pipes. Powell followed reluctantly. Reaching the edge, Ellen stood with her back to the parapet and gazed up at the rearing red-limned tower beside them. 'It's nice up here,' she said. Powell, looking out over the city, his hands folded on the parapet, said nothing. 'Have you ever been here at night?' Ellen asked.

'No,' he said. 'I've never been here before at all.'

She turned to the parapet and leaned over, looking down at the shelf of the setback two storeys below. She frowned thoughtfully. 'Last year,' she said slowly, 'I think I read about some girl falling from here.'

A ventilator cap cracked. 'Yes,' Powell said. His voice was dry. 'A suicide. She didn't fall.'

'Oh.' Ellen kept looking at the setback. 'I don't see how she could have gotten killed,' she said. 'It's only two storeys.'

He lifted a hand, the thumb pointing back over his shoulder. 'Over there – the shaft.'

'Oh, that's right.' She straightened up. 'I remember now. The Des Moines newspapers gave it a very big write-up.' She put her purse on the ledge and held it squarely with both hands, as though testing the rigidity of its frame. 'She was a Stoddard girl, wasn't she?'

'Yes,' he said. He pointed far out towards the horizon. 'You see that roundish building there, with the lights on it? That's the Stoddard Observatory. Had to go out there for a Physical Science project once. They have a—'

'Did you know her?'

The red light stained his face. 'Why do you ask?' he said.

'I just thought you might have known her. That's a natural thing to think, both going to Stoddard.'

'Yes,' he said sharply, 'I knew her and she was a very nice girl. Now let's talk about something else.'

'The only reason the story stuck in my mind,' she said, 'was because of the hat.'

Powell gave an exasperated sigh. Wearily he said, 'What hat?'

'She was wearing a red hat with a bow on it and I had just bought a red hat with a bow on it the day that it happened.'

'Who said she was wearing a red hat?' Powell asked.

'Wasn't she? The Des Moines papers said—' Tell me they were wrong, she prayed, tell me it was green.

There was silence for a moment. 'The *Clarion* never mentioned a red hat,' Powell said. 'I read the articles carefully, knowing her.'

'Just because the Blue River paper never mentioned it doesn't mean that it wasn't so,' Ellen said.

He didn't say anything. She looked and saw him squinting at his wrist-watch. 'Look,' he said brusquely, 'it's twenty-five to nine. I've had enough of this magnificent view.' He turned away abruptly, heading for the staircase housing.

Ellen hurried after him. 'We can't go yet,' she wheedled, catching his arm just outside the slant-roofed shed.

'Why not?'

Behind a smile her mind raced. 'I – I want a cigarette.'

'Oh, for—' His hand jerked towards a pocket, then stopped short. 'I don't have any. Come on, we'll get some downstairs.'

'I have some,' she said quickly, flashing her purse. She backed away, the position of the airshaft behind her as clear in her mind as if she were looking at the newspaper diagram. X marks the spot. Turning slightly, she sidled back towards it, opening the purse, smiling at Powell, saying inanely, 'It'll be nice to smoke a cigarette up here.' The parapet reared against her hip. X. She fumbled in her purse. 'You want one?'

He came towards her with resignation and compressed-lip anger. She shook the crumpled pack of cigarettes until one white cylinder protruded, thinking – it has to be tonight, because he won't ask Evelyn Kittredge for another date. 'Here,' she offered. He snatched the cigarette grimly.

Her fingertips dug for another one, and as they did her eyes roved and apparently became aware of the airshaft for the first time. She turned towards it slightly. 'Is this where—?' She turned back to him.

His eyes were narrowed, his jaw tightened by the last threads of a fast-ravelling patience. 'Listen, Evvie,' he said, 'I asked you not to talk about it. Now will you just do me that one favour? Will you please?' He jabbed the cigarette between his lips.

She didn't take her eyes from his face. Drawing a cigarette from the pack, she put it calmly to her lips and dropped the pack back into her purse. 'I'm sorry,' she said coolly, tucking the purse under her left arm. 'I don't know what you're so touchy about.'

'Can't you understand? I *knew* the girl.'

She struck a match and held it to his cigarette, the orange glow lighting his face, showing the blue eyes simmering with about-to-break strain, the jaw muscles tight as piano wires. One more jab, one more jab. She withdrew the match from his lighted cigarette, held it before his face. 'They never did say why she did it, did they?' His eyes closed painfully. 'I'll bet she was pregnant,' she said.

His face flared from flame orange to raw red as the match died and the tower light flashed on. The wire-tight muscles burst and the blue eyes shot open like dams exploding. Now! Ellen thought triumphantly. Now! Let it be something good, something damning!

'All right!' he blazed, 'all right! You know why I won't talk about it? You know why I didn't want to come up here at all? Why I didn't even want to come into this goddamn building?' He flung away his cigarette. 'Because the girl who committed suicide here was the girl I told you about last night! The one you smile like!' His eyes dropped from her face. 'The girl who I—'

The words cut off guillotine-sharp. She saw his downcast eyes dilate with shock and then the tower light faded and she could see him only as a dim form confronting her. Suddenly his hand caught her left wrist, gripping it with paralysing pressure. A scream pushed the cigarette from her lips. He was wrenching at the fingers of her captive hand, clawing at them. The purse slid out from under her arm and thudded to her feet. Futilely her right hand flailed his head. He was thumbing the muscles of her hand, forcing the fingers open . . . Releasing her, he stepped back and became a dimly outlined form again.

'What did you do?' she cried. 'What did you take?' Dazedly she stooped and retrieved her purse. She flexed her left hand, her jarred senses vainly trying to recall the imprint of the object she had been holding.

Then the red light flashed on again and she saw it resting in the palm of his hand as though he had been examining it even in the dark. The match-book. With the coppered letters glinting sharp and clear: *Ellen Kingship*.

Coldness engulfed her. She closed her eyes, sickly, nauseous fear ballooning in her stomach. She swayed; her back felt the hard edge of the airshaft parapet.

8

'Her sister,' he faltered, 'her sister.'

She opened her eyes. He was staring at the match-book with glazed incomprehension. He looked up at her. 'What is this?' he asked dully. Suddenly he hurled the match-book at her feet and his voice flared loud again. 'What do you want from me?'

'Nothing, nothing,' she said quickly, 'nothing.' Her eyes darted desperately. He was standing between her and the stairway shed. If only she could circle around him. She began inching to her left, her back pulling against the parapet.

He rubbed his forehead. 'You – you pick me up, you ask me questions about her, you get me up here.' Now his voice was entreating: 'What do you *want* from me?'

'Nothing – nothing.' warily sidestepping.

'Then why did you *do* this?' His body flexed to move forward.

'Stop!' she cried.

The ball-poised feet dropped flat, frozen.

'If anything happens to me,' she said, forcing herself to speak slowly, evenly, 'there's somebody else who knows all about you. He knows I'm with you tonight, and he knows all about you, so if anything happens, anything at all—'

'If anything—?' His brow furrowed. 'What are you talking about?'

'You know what I mean. If I fall—'

'Why should you?' He stared unbelievingly. 'You think I'd—?' One hand gestured limply towards the parapet. 'Jesus!' he whispered. 'What are you, crazy?'

She was a good fifteen feet from him. She began edging away from the parapet, cutting across to get on a straight line with the stairway door that was behind him and on his right. He pivoted slowly, following her cautious transverse path. 'What's this "knows all about me?" ' he demanded. 'Knows what?'

'Everything,' she said. 'Everything. And he's waiting downstairs. If I'm not down in five minutes he's calling the police.'

He slapped his forehead exhaustedly. 'I give up,' he moaned. 'You want to go downstairs? You want to go? Well go ahead!' He turned and backed to the airshaft parapet, to the spot where Ellen had been standing originally, leaving her a clear path to the door. He stood with his elbows resting on the stone behind him. 'Go ahead! Go on!'

She moved towards the door slowly, suspiciously, knowing that he could still beat her there, cut her off. He didn't move.

'If I'm supposed to be arrested,' he said. 'I'd just like to know what for. Or is that too much to ask?'

She made no answer until she had the door open in her hand. Then she said, 'I expected you to be a convincing actor. You had to be, to make Dorothy believe you were going to marry her.'

'What?' This time his surprise seemed deeper, painful. 'Now listen, I never said *anything* to make her believe I was going to marry her. That was all on *her* side, all *her* idea.'

'You liar,' she clenched hatefully. 'You filthy liar.' She ducked behind the shield of the open door and stepped over the high threshold.

'Wait!' As though sensing that any forward moment would send her running, he dropped back along the parapet and then cut out from it, following the same path Ellen had taken before. He stopped when he was opposite the doorway, some twenty feet from it. Within the shed Ellen turned to face him, one hand on the door-knob, ready to pull it closed.

'For God's sake,' he said earnestly, 'will you just tell me what this is all about? Please?'

'You think I'm bluffing. You think we really don't know.'

'Jesus—' he whispered furiously.

'All right,' she glared. 'I'll itemize it for you. One; she was pregnant. Two: you didn't want—'

'*Pregnant*?' It hit him like a rock in the stomach. He leaned forward. 'Dorothy was *pregnant*? Is *that* why she did it? Is *that* why she killed herself?'

'She didn't kill herself!' Ellen cried. 'You killed her!' She pulled the door shut, turned and ran.

She ran clatteringly down the metal steps, her heels ringing, clutching at the banister and swinging round the turn at each landing and before she had gone two and a half flights she heard him thundering down after her shouting, '*Evvie! Ellen! Wait!*' and then it was too late to take the elevator because by the time she ran all the way around the corridor and it came and took her down he would be waiting there already so there was nothing to do but keep on running with her heart beating and legs aching down the fourteen flights from roof to lobby which were really twenty-eight half flights spiralling down through the gloomy stairwell with twenty-seven landings to swing out arm-pullingly banging against the wall with him thundering closer behind all the way down to the main floor half-slipping with the damn heels and coming out into a marble-corridor and running around clattering echoing into the slippery-floored cathedral of a lobby where the startled Negro head popped out of the elevator then pushing exhaustedly out through the heavy revolving door and down more steps to treacherous marble and almost bumping into a woman on the sidewalk and running down to the left down towards Washington Avenue down the small-town night-deserted street and finally slowing with her heart hard-pumping to snatch one backward look before rounding the corner and there he was running down the marble steps waving and shouting, '*Wait! Wait!*' She wheeled around the corner running again ignoring the couple that turned to stare and the boys in the car shouting '*Want a ride?*' and seeing the hotel down the block with its glass doors glowing like an ad. for hotels getting nearer – he's getting nearer too but don't look back just keep on running – until at last she reached the beautiful glass doors and a man smiling amusedly held one of them open. 'Thank you, thank you,' and finally she was in the lobby, the lobby, the safe warm lobby, with bell-hops, and loungers and men behind newspapers. She was dying to drop into one of the chairs but she went straight to the corner phone booths because if Gant went to the police with her, Gant who was a local celebrity, then they'd be more inclined to listen to her, believe her, investigate. Panting, she seized the phone book and flipped to the K's – it was five to nine so he'd be at the studio. She slapped away pages, gaspingly catching her breath. There is was: KBRI – 5 – 1000. She opened her purse, and hunted for coins. Five-one-thousand, five-one-thousand, as she turned from the phone book rack and looked up.

Powell confronted her. He was flushed and panting, his blond hair wild. She wasn't afraid; there were bright lights and people. Hate levelled her rough breathing like a glacier: 'You should have run the other way. It won't do you any good, but I would start running if I were you.'

And he looked at her with a sick-dog, pleading, near-tears expression that was so pathetically sad-looking it had to be true, and he said softly, hurtfully, 'Ellen, I loved her.'

'I have a phone call to make,' she said, 'if you'll get out of the way.'

'Please, I've got to talk to you,' he pleaded. 'Was she? Was she really pregnant?'

'I have a phone call to make.'

'Was she?' he demanded.

'You know she was!'

'The papers said nothing! Nothing . . .?' Suddenly his brow furrowed and his voice dropped low, intense. 'What month was she in?'

'Will you please get out of my—'

'What month was she in?' His voice was demanding again.

'Oh God! The second.'

He let out a tremendous weight-dropping sigh of relief.

'Now will you *please* get out of my way?'

'Not until you explain what's going on. This Evelyn Kittredge act—'

Her glare was acid.

He whispered confusedly, 'You mean you really think I killed her?' and saw no change in the narrow stabbing of her eyes. 'I was in New York!' he protested. 'I can prove it! I was in New York all last spring!'

It shook her, but only for a moment. Then she said, 'I suppose you could figure out a way to prove you were in Cairo, Egypt, if you wanted to.'

'Jesus,' he hissed, exasperated. 'Will you just let me speak to you for five minutes? Five minutes?' He glanced around and caught a glimpse of a man's head vanishing behind a quickly lifted newspaper. 'People are listening,' he said. 'Just come into the cocktail lounge for five minutes. What harm can it do? I couldn't "do anything" to you there, if that's what you're worried about.'

'What *good* can it do?' she argued. 'If you were in New York and you didn't kill her, then why did you avoid looking at the Municipal Building when we passed it last night? And why didn't you want to go up on the roof tonight? And why did you stare down into the airshaft the way you did?'

He looked at her awkwardly, painfully. 'I can explain it,' he said haltingly, 'only I don't know whether you'll be able to understand it. You see, I felt' – he groped for a word – 'I felt *responsible* for her suicide.'

Most of the booths in the black-walled lounge were empty. Glasses clinked and the soft piano dallied with some Gershwin themes. They took the seats they had occupied the night before, Ellen sitting back stiffly against the upholstered partition as though to repudiate any suggestion of intimacy. When the waiter appeared they ordered whisky sours, and it wasn't until the drinks were on the table between them and Powell had taken the first sip of his that, realizing Ellen's intention to maintain a non-committal silence, he began to speak. The words came slowly at first, and with embarrassment.

'I met her a couple of weeks after classes began last year,' he said. 'Last school year, I mean. Late September. I'd seen her before – she was in two of my classes and she'd been in one of my classes in freshman year – but I never spoke to her until this particular day because I usually wind up with a seat in the first or second row and she always sat at the back, in the corner. Well, on the night before this day when I spoke to her, I'd been talking with some guys and one of them had said how the quiet girls were the ones who—' He paused, fingering his glass and looking down at it. 'You're more likely to have good time with a quiet girl. So when I saw her the next day, sitting at the back in the corner where she always sat. I remembered what this guy had said.

'I started a conversation with her, going out of the room at the end of the period. I told her I'd forgotten to take down the assignment and would she give it to me, and she did, I think she knew it was just an excuse to talk, but still she responded so – so eagerly it surprised me. I mean, usually a pretty girl will take a thing like that lightly, give you smart answers, you know. But she was so – unsophisticated, she made me feel a little guilty.

'Well anyway, we went out that Saturday night, went to a movie and to Frank's Florentine Room, and we really had a nice time. I don't mean fooling around or anything. Just a nice time. We went out again the next Saturday night and two times the week after that, and then three times until finally, just before we broke up, we were seeing each other almost every night. Once we got to know each other, she was a lot of fun. Not at all like she'd been in class. Happy, I like her.

'Early November it turned out that that guy was right, what he said about quiet girls. About Dorothy, anyway.' He glanced up, his eyes meeting Ellen's squarely. 'You know what I mean?'

'Yes,' she said coolly, impassive as a judge.

'This is a hell of a thing to tell a girl's sister.'

'Go on.'

'She was a *nice* girl,' he said, still looking at her. 'It was just that she was – love-starved. Not sex. Love.' His glance fell. 'She told me about things at home, about her mother – your mother, about how she'd wanted to go to school with you.'

A tremor ran through her; she told herself it was only the vibration caused by someone sitting down in the booth behind her.

'Things went on that way for a while,' Powell continued, talking more swiftly now, his shame melting into a confessionary satisfaction. 'She was really in love, hanging on to my arm and smiling up at me all the time. I mentioned once I liked argyle socks; she knitted me three pairs of them.' He scratched the table-top carefully. 'I loved her too, only it wasn't the same. It was – sympathy-love. I felt sorry for her. Very nice of me.

'The middle of December she started to talk about marriage. Very indirectly. It was just before Christmas vacation and I was going to stay here in Blue River. I've got no family and all I've got in Chicago are a couple of cousins and some high school and navy friends. So she wanted me to go to New York with her. Meet the family. I told her no, but she kept bringing it up again and finally there was a showdown.

'I told her I wasn't ready to get tied down yet, and she said that plenty of men were engaged and even married by twenty-two and if it was the future I was worrying about, her father would find a place for me. I didn't want that though. I had ambitions. I'll have to tell you about my ambitions some day. I was going to revolutionize American advertising. Well anyway, she said we could both get jobs when we finished school, and I said she could never live that way having been rich all her life. She said I didn't love her as much as she loved me, and I said I guessed she was right. That was it, of course, more than any of the other reasons.

'There was a scene and it was terrible. She cried and said I'd be sorry and all the things a girl says. Then after a while she changed her tack and said she was wrong; we would wait and go on the way we had been. But I'd been feeling sort of guilty all along, so I figured that since we'd had this half-way break, we might as well make it complete, and right before a vacation was the best to do it. I told her it was all over, and there was more crying and more "You'll be sorry" and that's the way it ended. Couple of days later she left for New York.'

Ellen said, 'All during that vacation she was in such a bad mood. Sulking, picking arguments—'

Powell printed wet rings on the table with the bottom of his glass. 'After vacation,' he said, 'it was bad. We still had those two classes together. I would sit in the front of the room not daring to look back. We kept bumping into each other all over campus. So I decided I'd had enough of Stoddard and applied for a transfer to NYU.' He saw the downcast expression on Ellen's face. 'What's the matter?' he said. 'Don't you believe me? I can prove all this. I've got a transcript from NYU and I think I've still got a note that Dorothy sent me when she returned a bracelet I'd given her.'

'No,' Ellen said dully. 'I believe you. That's just the trouble.'

He gave her a baffled look, and then continued. 'Just before I left, towards the end of January, she was starting to go with another guy. I saw—'

'Another man?' Ellen leaned forward.

'I saw them together a couple of times. It hadn't been such a big blow to her after all, I thought. I left with a nice clean conscience. Even felt a bit noble.'

'Who was he?' Ellen asked.

'Who?'

'The other man.'

'I don't know. A man. I think he was in one of my classes. Let me finish.

'I read about her suicide the first of May, just a paragraph in the New York papers. I raced up to Times Square and got a *Clarion-Ledger* at the Out-of-Town Newspaper stand. I bought a *Clarion* every day of that week, waiting for them to say what was in the note she sent you. They never did. They never said why she did it.

'Can you imagine how I felt? I didn't think she had done it just on account of me, but I did think that it was sort of a – general despondency. Which I was a major cause of.

'My work fell off after that. I was bucking too hard. I guess I felt I had to get terrific marks to justify what I'd done to her. I broke into a cold sweat before every exam, and my marks turned out pretty poor. I told myself it was because of the transfer; at NYU I had to make up a lot of required courses that weren't required at Stoddard, and I'd lost about sixteen credits besides. So I decided to come back to Stoddard in September, to get myself straightened out.' He smiled wryly. 'Also maybe to try to convince myself that I didn't feel guilty.

'Anyway, it was a mistake. Every time I saw one of the places we used to go to, or the Municipal Building—' He frowned. 'I kept telling myself it was her fault, that any other girl would have been mature enough to shrug it off – but it didn't do much good. It got to the point where I found myself going out of my way to walk past the building, needling myself, like looking into the airshaft tonight, visualizing her—'

'I know,' Ellen said, hurrying him, 'I wanted to look too. I guess it's a natural reaction.'

'No,' Powell said, 'you don't know what it means to feel *responsible*—' He paused, seeing Ellen's humourless smile. 'What are you smiling at?'

'Nothing.'

'Well – that's it. Now you tell me she did it because she was pregnant – two months. It's a rotten thing of course, but it makes me feel a whole lot better. I guess she still wouldn't be dead if I hadn't ditched her, but I couldn't be expected to know how things would turn out, could I? I mean, there's a limit to responsibility. If you keep going back you could blame it on anyone.' He drained the rest of his drink. 'I'm glad to see you've stopped running for the police,' he said. 'I don't know where you got the idea that I killed her.'

'Someone did kill her,' Ellen said. He looked at her wordlessly. The piano paused between selections, and in the sudden stillness she could hear the faint cloth rustlings of the person in the booth behind her.

Leaning forward, she began talking, telling Powell of the ambiguously worded note, of the birth certificate, of something old, something new, something borrowed, and something blue.

He was silent until she had finished. Then he said, 'My God. It *can't* be a coincidence,' as eager as she to disprove suicide.

'This man you saw her with,' Ellen said. 'You're sure you don't know who he was?'

'I think he was in one of my classes that semester, but the two times I saw them together were fairly late in January, when exams had started and there were no more classes, so I couldn't make sure or find out his name. And right afterwards I left for New York.'

'Haven't you seen him again?'

'I don't know,' Powell said. 'I'm not sure. Stoddard's a big campus.'

'And you're absolutely certain you don't know his name?'

'I don't know it now,' Powell said, 'but I can find it out in about an hour.' He smiled. 'You see, I've got his address.'

9

'I told you I saw them together a couple of times,' he said. 'Well the second time was one afternoon in a luncheonette across from the campus. I never expected to see Dorothy there; it wasn't a very popular place. That's why I was there. I didn't notice them until I'd sat down at the counter and then I didn't want to get up and leave because she'd already seen me in the mirror. I was sitting at the end of the counter, then two girls, then Dorothy and this guy. They were drinking malteds.

'The minute she saw me she started talking to him and touching his arm a lot; you know, trying to show me she had someone new. It made me feel awful, her doing that. Embarrassed for her. Then, when they were ready to leave, she gave a nod to those two girls sitting between us, turned to him, and said in a louder-than-necessary voice, "Come on, we can drop our books at your place." To show me how chummy they were, I figured.

'As soon as they were gone one of the girls commented to the other about how good-looking he was. The other one agreed, and then she said something like, "He was going with so-and-so last year. It looks as if he's only interested in the ones who have money."

'Well, I figured that if Dorothy was a sitting duck because she was on the rebound from me, then I ought to make sure that she wasn't being taken in by some gold-digger. So I left the luncheonette and followed them.

'They went to a house a few blocks north of the campus. He rang the bell a couple of times and then he took some keys out of his pocket and unlocked the door and they went in. I walked by on the other side of the street and copied down the address on one of my notebooks. I thought I would call up later, when someone else was there, and find out his name. I had a vague idea about speaking to some of the girls around school about him.

'I never did it though. On the way back to the campus, the – presumption of the whole thing hit me. I mean, where did I come off asking questions about this guy just on the basis of some remark made by a girl who probably had a bad case of sour grapes? It was a cinch he couldn't treat Dorothy any worse than I had. And that "on the rebound" stuff; how did I know they weren't fine for each other?'

'But you still have the address?' Ellen asked anxiously.

'I'm pretty sure I do. I've got all my old notes in a suitcase in my room. We can go over there and get it right now if you want.'

'Yes,' she agreed quickly. 'Then all we'll have to do is call up and find out who he is.'

'He isn't necessarily the right one,' Powell said, taking out his wallet.

'He must be. It can't be anyone she started going with much later than that.' Ellen stood up. 'There's still a phone call I'd like to make before we go.'

'To your assistant? The one who was waiting downstairs ready to call the police if you didn't show up in five minutes?'

'That's right,' she admitted, smiling. 'He wasn't waiting downstairs, but there really is someone.'

She went to the back of the dimly-lit room, where a telephone booth painted black to match the walls stood like an up-ended coffin. She dialled 5–1000.

'KBRI, good evening,' a woman's voice chirruped.

'Good evening. May I speak to Gordon Gant please?'

'I'm sorry, but Mr Gant's programme is on the air now. If you call again at ten o'clock you might be able to catch him before he leaves the building.'

'Couldn't I speak to him while a record is on?'

'I'm sorry, but no telephone calls may be directed to a studio from which a programme is being broadcast.'

'Well would you take a message for him?'

The woman sing-songed that she would be glad to take a message, and Ellen told her that Miss Kingship – spelled out – said that Powell – spelled out – was all right but had an idea as to who wasn't, and Miss Kingship was going to Powell's home and would be there at ten o'clock, when Mr Gant could call her.

'Any telephone number?'

'Darn,' Ellen said, opening the purse in her lap. 'I don't have the number, but the address' – managing to unfold the slip of paper without dropping the purse – 'is Fifteen-twenty West Thirty-fifth Street.'

The woman read the message back. 'That's right,' Ellen said. 'You'll be sure he gets it?'

'Of course I will,' the woman declared frostily.

'Thank you very much.'

Powell was feeding coins on to a small silver tray in the hand of a rapt waiter when Ellen returned to their booth. A smile appeared momentarily on the waiter's face and he vanished, trailing a mumbled thank you. 'All set,' Ellen said. She reached for her coat which was folded on the banquette where she had been sitting. 'By the way, what does he look like, our man? Aside from being so handsome that girls comment on it.'

'Blond, tall . . .' Powell said, pocketing his wallet.

'Another blond,' sighed Ellen.

'Dorothy went for us Nordic types.'

Ellen smiled, pulling on her coat. 'Our father is blond – or was until he lost his hair. All three of us—' Ellen's empty coat-sleeve slapped over the top of the booth partition as her hand groped for it. 'Excuse me,' she said, glancing back over her shoulder, and then she saw that the next booth had been vacated. There were a cocktail glass and a dollar bill on the table, and a paper napkin which had been carefully torn into a delicate lacework web.

Powell helped her with the obstinate sleeve. 'Ready?' he asked, putting on his own coat.

'Ready,' she said.

It was 9.50 when the cab pulled up in front of Powell's house. West Thirty-fifth Street was silent, feebly lighted by street lamps whose beams had to strain their way through meshing tree branches. Yellow windowed houses faced each other on either side, like timid armies showing flags across no-man's land.

As the roar of the departing cab faded away, Ellen and Powell mounted the steps of a dark, creaking-floored porch. After a few unsuccessful stabs for the keyhole, Powell unlocked the door and pushed it open. He stepped aside and followed Ellen in, throwing the door closed with one hand and flicking a light switch with the other.

They were in a pleasant-looking living-room full of fat chintz-and-maple furniture. 'You'd better stay down here,' Powell said, going towards a staircase at the left side of the room. 'Everything's in a mess upstairs. My landlady is in the hospital and I wasn't expecting company.' He paused on the first step. 'It'll probably take me a few minutes to find that book. There's some instant coffee in the kitchen back there. You want to fix some?'

'All right,' Ellen said, slipping out of her coat.

Powell jogged up the stairs and swung around the newel post. The door to his room was opposite the side of the stairwell. He went in, flipping on the light, and shucked off his coat. The unmade bed, on the right against the windows, was littered with pyjamas and discarded clothes. He tossed his coat on top of the whole business and squatted down, about to pull a suitcase from under the bed; but with a sharp finger-snap he straightened up, turned, and stepped over to the bureau, which stood squeezed between a closet door and an armchair. He opened the top drawer and rummaged through papers and small boxes and scarves and broken cigarette lighters. He found the paper he wanted at the bottom of the drawer. Pulling it free with a flourish, he went into the hall and leaned over the stairwell banister. 'Ellen!' he called.

In the kitchen, Ellen adjusted the sighing gas flame under a pan of water. 'Coming!' she answered. She hurried through the dining-room and into the living-room. 'Got it already?' she asked, going to the stairs and looking up.

Powell's head and shoulders jutted into the stairwell. 'Not yet,' he said. 'But I thought you'd like to see this.' He let go of a stiff sheet of paper that came side-slipping down. 'Just in case you have any lingering doubts.'

It landed on the stairs before her. Picking it up, she saw that it was a photostat of his NYU record, the words *Student Copy* stamped on it. 'If I had any lingering doubts,' she said, 'I wouldn't be here, would I?'

'True,' Powell said, 'true' – and vanished from the stairwell.

Ellen took another look at the transcript and noted that his marks had indeed been pretty poor. Putting the paper on a table she returned through the dining-room to the kitchen. It was a depressing room with old-fashioned appliances and cream-coloured walls that were brown in the corners and behind the stove. There was, however, a pleasant breeze blowing through from the back.

She found cups and saucers and a can of Nescafé in the various cupboards, and while she was spooning the powder into the cups, she noticed a radio with a cracked plastic case on the counter next to the stove. She turned it on, and once it had warmed up, slowly twisted the selector knob until she found KBRI. She almost passed over it because the small celluloid-vibrating set made Gant's voice sound unfamiliarly thin. '. . . and a little too much about things political,' he was saying, 'so let's get back to music. We've just got time for one more record, and it's the late Buddy Clark singing *If This Isn't Love*.'

Powell, having dropped the transcript down to Ellen, turned around and went back into his room. Squatting before the bed, he shot his hand underneath it – to bang his fingertips painfully against the suitcase, which had been pulled forward from its usual position flush against the wall. He jerked his hand out, waggling the fingers and blowing on them, and cursing his landlady's daughter-in-law who apparently had not been satisfied with only secreting his shoes beneath the bureau.

He reached under the bed again, more cautiously this time, and dragged the heavy-as-lead suitcase all the way out into the open. He took a bunch of keys from his pocket, found the right one and twisted it in the two locks springing them. Replacing the keys, he lifted the lid. The suitcase was filled with text-books, a tenis racket, a bottle of Canadian Club, golf shoes. . . . He took out the larger items and put them on the floor so that it would be easier to get at the notebooks underneath.

There were nine of them: pale-green spiral-bound notebooks. He gathered them into a bundle, stood up with the bundle in his arm and began inspecting them one at a time; examining both covers, dropping the books one by one back into the suitcase.

It was on the seventh one, on the back cover. The pencilled address was rubbed and smudged, but it was still legible. He dropped the other two notebooks into the suitcase and turned around, his mouth opening to form Ellen's name in a triumphant shout.

The shout didn't come through. The exultant expression clung to his face for a moment, like a stopped movie, and then it cracked and slid slowly away, like thick snow cracking and sliding from a canted roof.

The closet door was open and a man in a trenchcoat stood framed there. He was tall and blond, and a gun bulked large in his gloved right hand.

10

He was sweating. Not cold sweat though; hot healthy sweat from standing in the sweat-box of an airless closet in the sweat-suit of an imporous trenchcoat. His hands too; the gloves were brown leather with a fuzzy lining and elastic cuffs that held in the heat even more; his hands were sweating so much that the fuzzy lining was sodden and caked.

But the automatic (weightless now like part of him after dragging heavily in his pocket all evening) was motionless; the inevitable trajectory of the bullet as palpable in the air as a dotted line in a diagram. Point A: the rock-steady muzzle; Point B: the heart under the lapel of the cheesy-looking probably-bought-in-Iowa suit. He looked down at the Colt .45 as though to verify its blue steel existence, so light it was, and then he took a step forward from the mouth of the closet, reducing by a foot the length of dotted line AB.

Well say something, he thought, enjoying the slow stupid melting of Mister Dwight Powell's face. Start talking. Start pleading. Probably can't. Probably he's all talked out after the – what's that word? – logorrhoea of a cocktail lounge. Good word.

'I bet you don't know what logorrhoea means,' he said, standing there powerfully with the gun in his hand.

Powell stared at the gun. 'You're the one – with Dorothy,' he said.

'It means what *you've* got. Diarrhoea of the mouth. Words keep running. I thought my ear would fall off in that cocktail lounge.' He smiled at Powell's widening eyes. 'I was responsible for poor Dorothy's death,' he mimicked. 'A pity. A real pity.' He stepped closer. 'The notebook, *por favor*,' he said, extending his left hand. 'And don't try anything.'

From downstairs, singing of a dance tune came softly.

He took the notebook that Powell held out, dropped back a step and pressed it against his side, bending it in half length wise cracking the cover, never taking his eyes or the gun off Powell. 'I'm awfully sorry you found this. I was standing in there hoping you wouldn't.' He stuck the folded notebook into his coat pocket.

'You really killed her,' Powell said.

'Let's keep the voice low.' He moved the gun admonishingly. 'We don't want to disturb the girl detective, do we?' It annoyed him the way Mister Dwight Powell was standing there so blankly. Maybe he was too stupid to realize . . . 'Maybe you don't realize it, but this is a real gun, and it's loaded.'

Powell didn't say anything. He just went on looking at this gun, not even staring now – just looking at it with mildly distasteful interest, as though it were the first ladybug of the year.

'Look, I'm going to kill you.'

Powell didn't say anything.

'You're such a great one for analysing yourself – tell me, how do you feel now? I bet your knees are shaking, aren't they? Cold sweat all over you?'

Powell said, 'She thought she was going there to get married.'

'Forget about her! You've got yourself to worry about.' Why wasn't he trembling? Didn't he have brains enough . . .?

'Why did you kill her?' Powell's eyes finally lifted from the gun. 'If you didn't want to marry her, you could have left her. That would have been better than killing her.'

'Shut up about her! What's the matter with you? You think I'm bluffing? Is that it? You think—'

Powell leaped forward.

Before he had gone six inches a loud explosion roared; dotted line AB was solidified and fulfilled by tearing lead.

Ellen had been standing in the kitchen looking out through the closed window and listening to the fading theme of Gordon Gant's programme, when she suddenly realized that with the window closed, where was that pleasant breeze coming from?

There was a shadowed alcove in a rear corner of the room. She went to it and saw the back door, with the pane of glass nearest the knob smashed in and lying in fragments on the floor. She wondered if Dwight knew about it. You'd think he would have swept up the—

That was when she heard the shot. It smacked loudly through the house, and as the sound died the ceiling light shivered as if something upstairs had fallen. Then there was silence.

The radio said, 'At the sound of the chime, ten p.m., Central Standard Time,' and a chime toned.

'Dwight?' Ellen said.

There was no answer.

She went into the dining-room. She called the name louder: 'Dwight?'

In the living-room she moved hesitantly to the staircase. There was no sound from overhead. This time she spoke the name with dry-throated apprehension: 'Dwight?'

The silence held for another moment. Then a voice said, 'It's all right, Ellen. Come on up.'

She hurried up the stairs with her heart drumming. 'In here,' the voice said from the right. She pivoted around the newel post and swept to the lighted doorway.

The first thing she saw was Powell lying on his back in the middle of the room, limbs sprawled loosely. His jacket had fallen away from his chest. On his white shirt blood was flowering from a black core over his heart.

She steadied herself against the jamb. Then she raised her eyes to the man who stood beyond Powell, the man with the gun in his hand.

Her eyes dilated, her face went rigid with questions that couldn't work their way to her lips.

He shifted the gun from the firing position to a flat appraising weight on his gloved palm. 'I was in the closet,' he said, looking her straight in the eye, answering the unasked questions. 'He opened the suitcase and took out this gun. He was going to kill you. I jumped him. The gun went off.'

'No – oh God—' She rubbed her forehead dizzily. 'But how – how did you—?'

He put the gun in the pocket of his coat. 'I was in the cocktail lounge,' he said. 'Right behind you. I heard him talking you into coming up here. I left while you were in the phone booth.'

'He told me he—'

'I heard what he told you. He was a good liar.'

'Oh God, I believed him – I believed him—'

'That's just your trouble,' he said with an indulgent smile. 'You believe everybody.'

'Oh God—' she shivered.

He came to her, stepping between Powell's spraddled legs.

She said, 'But I still don't understand – How were you there, in the lounge?'

'I was waiting for you in the lobby. I missed you when you went out with him. Got there too late. I kicked myself for that. But I waited around. What else could I do?'

'But how – how—?'

He stood before her with his arms wide, like a soldier returning home. 'Look, a heroine isn't supposed to question her nick-of-time rescuer. Just be glad you gave me his address. I may have thought you were being a fool, but I wasn't going to take any chances on having you get your head blown off.'

She threw herself in his arms, sobbing with relief and retrospective fear. The leather-tight hands patted her back comfortingly. 'It's all right, Ellen,' he said softly. 'Everything's all right now.'

She buried her cheek against his shoulder. 'Oh Bud,' she sobbed, 'thank God for you! Thank God for you, Bud!'

11

The telephone rang downstairs.

'Don't answer it,' he said as she started to draw away.

There was a lifeless glaze to her voice: 'I know who it is.'

'No, don't answer it. Listen' – his hands were solid and convincing on her shoulders – 'someone is sure to have heard that shot. The police will probably be here in a few minutes. Reporters, too.' He let that sink in. 'You don't want the papers to make a big story out of this, do you? Dragging up everything about Dorothy, pictures of you—'

'There's no way to stop them.'

'There is. I have a car downstairs. I'll take you back to the hotel and then come right back here.' He turned off the light. 'If the police haven't shown up yet, I'll call them. Then you won't be here for the reporters to jump on, and I'll refuse to talk until I'm alone with the police. They'll question you later, but the papers won't know you're involved.' He led her out into the hallway. 'By that time you'll have called your father; he's got enough influence to keep the police from letting out anything about you or Dorothy. They can say Powell was drunk and started a fight with me, or something like that.'

The telephone stopped ringing.

'I wouldn't feel right about leaving—' she said as they started down the stairs.

'Why not? I'm the one who did it, not you. It's not as if I'm going to lie about your being here; I'll need you to back up my story. All I want to do is prevent the papers from having a field day with this.' He turned to her as they descended into the living-room. 'Trust me, Ellen,' he said, touching her hand.

· She sighed deeply, gratefully letting tension and responsibility drop from her shoulders. 'All right,' she said. 'But you don't have to drive me. I can get a cab.'

'Not at this hour, not without phoning. And I think the tramcars stop running at ten.' He picked up her coat and held it for her.

'Where did you get a car?' she asked dully.

'I borrowed it.' He gave her her purse. 'From a friend.' Turning off the lights, he opened the door to the porch. 'Come on,' he said, 'we haven't got too much time.'

He had parked the car across the street and some fifty feet down the block. It was a black Buick sedan, two or three years old. He opened the door for Ellen, then went around to the other side and slipped in behind the wheel. He fumbled with the ignition key. Ellen sat silently, hands folded in her lap. 'You feel all right?' he asked.

'Yes,' she said, her voice thin and tired. 'It's just that – he was going to kill me.' She sighed. 'At least I was right about Dorothy. I *knew* she didn't commit suicide.' She managed a reproachful smile. 'And you tried to talk me out of making this trip—'

He got the motor started. 'Yes,' he said. 'You were right.'

She was silent for a moment. 'Anyway, there's a sort of silver lining to all this,' she said.

'What's that?' He shifted gears and the car glided forward.

'Well, you saved my life,' she said. 'You really saved my life. That should cut short whatever objections my father might have, when you meet him and we speak to him about us.'

After they had been driving down Washington Avenue for a few minutes, she moved closer to him and hesitantly took his arm, hoping it wouldn't interfere with his driving. She felt something hard pressing against her hip and realized that it was the gun in his pocket, but she didn't want to move away.

'Listen, Ellen,' he said. 'This is going to be a lousy business you know.'

'What do you mean?'

'Well, I'll be held for manslaughter.'

'But you didn't mean to kill him! You were trying to get the gun away from him.'

'I know, but they'll still have to hold me – all kinds of red tape—' He stole a quick glance at the downcast figure beside him and then returned his gaze to the traffic ahead. 'Ellen – when we get to the hotel, you could just pick up your things and check out. We could be back in Caldwell in a couple of hours—'

'Bud!' Her voice was sharp with surprised reproach. 'We couldn't do a thing like that!'

'Why not? He killed your sister, didn't he? He got what was coming to him. Why should we have to get mixed up—'

'We can't do it,' she protested. 'Aside from its being such a – a *wrong* thing to do, suppose they found out anyway that you – killed him. Then they'd never believe the truth, not if you ran away.'

'I don't see how they could find out it was me,' he said. 'I'm wearing gloves, so there can't be any fingerprints. And nobody saw me there, except you and him.'

'But suppose they *did* find out! Or suppose they blamed someone else for it! How would you feel then?' He was silent. 'As soon as I get to the hotel, I'll call my father. Once he's heard the story, I know he'll take care of lawyers and everything. I guess it *will* be a terrible business. But to run away—'

'It was a foolish suggestion,' he said. 'I didn't really expect you to agree.'

'No, Bud, you wouldn't want to do a thing like that, would you?'

'I only tried it as a last resort,' he said. Suddenly he swung the car in a wide left turn from the brightly lighted orbit of Washington Avenue to the darkness of a northbound road.

'Shouldn't you stay on Washington?' Ellen asked.

'Quicker this way. Avoid traffic.'

'What I can't understand,' she said, tapping her cigarette on the edge of the dashboard tray, 'is why he didn't do anything to me there, on the roof.' She was settled comfortably, turned towards Bud with her left leg drawn up under her, the cigarette suffusing her with sedative warmth.

'You must have been pretty conspicuous, going there at night,' he said. 'He was probably afraid that an elevator man or someone would remember his face.'

'Yes, I suppose so. But wouldn't it have been less risky than taking me back to his house and – doing it there?'

'Maybe he didn't intend to do it there. Maybe he was going to force you into a car and drive you out into the country some place.'

'He didn't have a car.'

'He could have stolen one. It's not such a hard thing to steal a car.' A street-light flashing brushed his face with white, then dropped it back into the darkness where the cleanly-hewn features were touched only by the dashboard's nebulous green.

'The lies he told me! "I loved her. I was in New York. I felt responsible." ' She mashed the cigarette into the ashtray, shaking her head bitterly. 'Oh, my God!' she gasped.

He flicked a glance at her. 'What is it?'

Her voice had taken on the sick glaze again. 'He showed me his transcript – from NYU. He *was* in New York—'

'That was probably a fake. He must have known someone in the registrar's office there. They could fake something like that.'

'But suppose it wasn't. Suppose he was telling the truth!'

'He was coming after you with a gun. Isn't that proof enough he was lying?'

'Are you sure, Bud? Are you sure he didn't – maybe take the gun out to get at something else? The notebook he mentioned?'

'He was going to the door with the gun.'

'Oh God, if he really didn't kill Dorothy—' She was silent for a moment. 'The police will investigate,' she said positively. 'They'll prove he was right here in Blue River! They'll prove he killed Dorothy!'

'That's right,' he said.

'But even if he didn't. Bud, even if it was a – a terrible mistake – they wouldn't blame you for anything. You couldn't know; you saw him with the gun. They could never blame you for anything.'

'That's right,' he said.

Shifting uncomfortably, she drew her folded leg out from under her. She squinted at her watch in the dashboard's glow. 'It's twenty-five after ten. Shouldn't we be there already!'

He didn't answer her.

She looked out of the window. There were no more street-lights, no more buildings. There was only the pitch blackness of fields, under the star-heightened blackness of the sky. 'Bud, this isn't the way into town.'

He didn't answer her.

Ahead of the car a white onrush of highway narrowed to implied infinity always beyond the headlights' reach.

'Bud, you're going the wrong way!'

12

'What you want from *me*?' Chief of Police Eldon Chesser asked blandly. He lay supine, his long legs supported beneath the ankles by an arm of the chintz-covered sofa, his hands laced loosely across the front of his red flannel shirt, his large brown eyes vaguely contemplating the ceiling.

'Get after the car. That's what I want,' Gordon Gant said, glaring at him from the middle of the living-room.

'Ha,' said Chesser. 'Ha ha. A dark car is all the man next door knows; after he called about the shot he saw a man and a woman go down the block and get into a dark car. A dark car with a man and a woman. You know how many dark cars there are driving around town with a man and woman in them? We didn't even have a description of the girl until you come shooting in. By that time they could've been half-way to Cedar Rapids. Or parked in some garage two blocks from here, for all we know.'

Gant paced malevolently. 'So what are we supposed to do?'

'Wait, is all. I notified the highway boys, didn't I? Maybe this is bank night. Why don't you sit down?'

'Sure, sit down,' Gant snapped. 'She's liable to be murdered!' Chesser was silent. 'Last year her sister - now her.'

'Here we go again,' Chesser said. 'The brown eyes closed in weariness. 'Her sister committed suicide,' he articulated slowly. 'I saw the note with my own two eyes. A handwriting expert—' Gant made a noise. 'And who killed her?' Chesser demanded. 'You said Powell was supposed to be the one, only now it couldn't've been him 'cause the girl left a message for you that he was all right, and you found this paper here from New York U. that makes it look like he wasn't even in these parts last spring. So if the only suspect didn't do it, who did? Answer: nobody.'

His voice tight with the exasperation of repetition, Gant said, 'Her message said that Powell had an idea who it was. The murderer must have known that Powell—'

'There *was* no murderer, until tonight,' Chesser said flatly. 'The sister committed suicide,' His eyes blinked open and regarded the ceiling.

Gant glared at him and resumed his bitter pacing.

After a few minutes Chesser said, 'Well, I guess I got it all reconstructed now.'

'Yeah?' Gant said.

'Yeah. You didn't think I was laying here just to be lazy, did you? This is the way to think, with your feet higher'n your head. Blood goes to the brain.' He cleared his throat. 'The guy breaks in about a quarter to ten - man next door heard the glass break but didn't think anything of it. No sign of any of the other rooms having been gone through, so Powell's must have been the first one he hit. A couple of minutes later Powell and the girl come in. The guy is stuck upstairs.

He hides in Powell's closet – the clothes are all pushed to the side. Powell and the girl go into the kitchen. She starts making coffee, turns on the radio. Powell goes upstairs to hang up his coat, or maybe he heard a noise. The guy comes out. He's already tried to open the suitcase – we found glove smudges on it. He makes Powell unlock it and goes through it. Stuff all over the floor. Maybe he finds something, some money. Anyway, Powell jumps him. The guy shoots Powell. Probably panics, probably didn't intend to shoot him – they never do; they only carry the guns to scare people. Always wind up shooting 'em. Forty-five shell. Most likely an army Colt. Million of 'em floating around.

'Next thing the girl comes running upstairs – same prints on the door frame up there as on the cups and stuff in the kitchen. The guy is panicky, no time to think – he forces her to leave with him.'

'Why? Why wouldn't he have left her here – the way he left Powell?'

'Don't ask me. Maybe he didn't have the nerve. Or maybe he got ideas. Sometimes they get ideas when they're holding a gun and there's a pretty girl on the other end of it.'

'Thanks,' Gant said. 'That makes me feel a whole lot better. Thanks a lot.'

Chesser sighed. 'You might as well sit down,' he said. 'There ain't a damn thing we can do but wait.'

Gant sat down. He began rubbing his forehead with the heel of his hand.

Chesser finally turned his face from the ceiling. He watched Gant sitting across the room. 'What is she? Your girl friend?' he asked.

'No,' Gant said. He remembered the letter he had read in Ellen's room. 'No, there's some guy in Wisconsin.'

13

Behind the racing island of the headlights' reach, the car arrowed over the tight line of highway, tarred seams in concrete creating a regular rhythm under the tyres. The speedometer's luminous green needle split the figure fifty. The foot on the accelerator was steady as the foot of a statue.

He drove with his left hand, occasionally giving the steering wheel an inappreciable right or left movement to relieve the hypnotic monotony of the highway. Ellen was huddled all the way over against the door, her body knotted tight, her eyes staring brokenly at the handkerchief-twisting hands in her lap. On the seat between them, snake-like, lay his gloved right hand with the gun in it, the muzzle riveted against her hip.

She had cried; long throat-dragging animal moans; more sound and shaking than actual tears.

He had told her everything, in a bitter voice, glancing frequently at her green-touched face in the darkness. There were moments of awkward hesitancy in his narration, as an on-leave soldier telling how he won his medals hesitates before describing to the gentle townsfolk how his bayonet ripped open an enemy's stomach, then goes on and describes it because they asked how he won his medals, didn't they? – describes it with irritation and mild contempt for the gentle townsfolk who never had had to rip open anyone's stomach. So he told Ellen about the pills and the roof and why it had been necessary to kill Dorothy, and why it had then been the most logical course to transfer to Caldwell and go after *her*, Ellen, knowing her likes and dislikes from conversations with Dorothy, knowing how to make himself the man she was waiting for – not only the most logical and inevitable course, going after the girl with whom he had such an advantage, but also the course most ironically satisfying, the course most compensatory for past bad luck (the course most law-defying, back-slapping, ego-preening) he told her these things with irritation and contempt; this girl with her hands over her mouth in horror had had everything given her on a silver platter; she didn't know what it was to live on a swaying catwalk over the chasm of failure, stealing perilously inch by inch towards the solid ground of success so many miles away.

She listened with the muzzle of his gun jabbing painfully into her hip; painfully only at first, then numbingly, as though that part of her were already dead, as though death came from the gun not in a swift bullet but in slow radiation from the point of contact. She listened and then she cried, because she was so sickened and beaten and shocked that there was nothing else she could do to express it all. Her cries were long throat-dragging animal moans; more sound and shaking than actual tears.

And then she sat staring brokenly at the handkerchief-twisting hands in her lap.

'I *told* you not to come,' he said querulously. 'I *begged* you to stay in Caldwell, didn't I?' He glanced at her as though expecting an affirmation. 'But *no*. No, you had to be the girl detective! Well this is what happens to girl detectives.' His eyes returned to the highway. 'If you only *knew* what I've gone through since Monday,' he clenched, remembering how the world had dropped out from under him Monday morning when Ellen had phoned – 'Dorothy didn't commit suicide! I'm leaving for Blue River!' – running down to the station, barely catching her, futilely desperately trying to keep her from leaving but she stepped on to the train – 'I'll write you this minute! I'll explain the whole thing!' – leaving him standing there, watching her glide away, sweating, terrified. It made him sick just thinking about it.

Ellen said something faintly.

'What?'

'They'll catch you—'

After a moment's silence he said, 'You know how many don't get caught? More than fifty per cent, that's how many. Maybe a *lot* more.' After another moment he said, 'How are they going to catch me? Fingerprints? – none. Witnesses? – none. Motive? – none that they know about. They won't even think of me. The gun? I have to go over the Mississippi to get back to Caldwell; good-bye gun. This car? – two or three in the morning I leave it a couple of blocks from where I took it; they think it was some crazy high school kids. Juvenile delinquents.' He smiled. 'I did it last night too. I was sitting two rows behind you and Powell in the threatre and I was right around a bend in the hall when he kissed you good night.' He glanced at her to see her reaction; none was visible. His gaze returned to the road and his face clouded again, 'That letter of yours – how I sweated till it came! When I first started to read it I thought I was safe; you were looking for someone she'd met in her English class in the fall; I didn't meet her till January, and it was in Philosophy. But then I realized who that guy youwere looking for actually was – Old Argyle-Socks, my predecessor. We'd had Math, together, and he'd seen me with Dorrie. I thought he might know my name. I knew that if he ever convinced you he didn't have anything to do with Dorrie's murder – if he ever mentioned my name to you—'

Suddenly he jammed down on the brake pedal and the car screeched to a halt. Reaching left-handed around the steering column, he shifted gears. When he stepped on the gas again, the car rolled slowly backwards. On their right, the dark form of a house slid into view, low-crouching behind a broad expanse of empty parking lot. The headlights of the retreating car caught a large upright sign at the highway's edge: *Lillie and Doane's - The Steak Supreme.* A smaller sign hung swaying from the gallows of the larger one: *Reopening April 15th.*

He shifted back into first, spun the wheel to the right, and stepped on the gas. He drove across the parking lot and pulled up at the side of the low building, leaving the motor running. He pressed the horn ring; a loud blast banged through the night. He waited a minute, then sounded the horn again. Nothing happened. No window was raised, no light went on. 'Looks like nobody's home,' he said, turning off the headlights.

'Please,' she said, 'please—'

In the darkness the car rolled forward, turned to the left, moved behind the house where the asphalt into the dirt of a field that swept off to meet the blackness of the sky. It swung all the way around until it was facing the direction from which it had come.

He set the emergency brake and left the motor running.

'Please—' she said.

He looked at her. 'You think I want to do this? You think I like the idea? We were almost engaged?' He opened the door on his left. 'You had to be smart—' He stepped out on to the asphalt, keeping the gun aimed at her huddled figure. 'Come here,' he said. 'Come out on this side.'

'Please—'

'Well what am I supposed to do, Ellen? I can't let you go, can I? I asked you to go back to Caldwell without saying anything, didn't I?' The gun made an irritated gesture. 'Come out.'

She pulled herself across the seat, clutching her purse. She stepped out on to the asphalt.

The gun directed her in a semicircular path until she stood with the field at her back, the gun between her and the car.

'Please,' she said, holding up the purse in a futile shielding gesture, 'please—'

14

From the Blue River *Clarion-Ledger*; Thursday, March 15, 1951:

DOUBLE SLAYING HERE
POLICE SEEK MYSTERY GUNMAN

Within a period of two hours last night, an unknown gunman committed two brutal murders. His victims were Ellen Kingship, twenty-one, of New York City, and Dwight Powell, twenty-three, of Chicago, a junior at Stoddard University . . .

Powell's slaying occurred at 10 p.m., in the home of Mrs Elizabeth Honig, 1520 West Thirty-fifth Street, where Powell was a roomer. As police reconstruct the events, Powell, entering the house at 9.50 in the company of Miss Kingship, went to his second-floor room where he encountered an armed burglar who had earlier broken into the house through the back door . . .

. . . the medical examiner established the time of Miss Kingship's death as somewhere near midnight. Her body, however, was not discovered until 7.20 this morning, when Willard Herne, eleven, of nearby Randalia, crossed through a field adjacent to the restaurant . . . Police learned from Gordon Gant, KBRI announcer and a friend of Miss Kingship, that she was the sister of Dorothy Kingship who last April committed suicide by jumping from the roof of the Blue River Municipal Building . . .

Leo Kingship, president of Kingship Copper Inc., and father of the slain girl, is expected to arrive in Blue River this afternoon, accompanied by his daughter, Marion Kingship.

An Editorial from the *Clarion-Ledger*; Thursday, April 19, 1951:
DISMISSAL OF GORDON GANT
In dismissing Gordon Gant from their employ (story on page five) the management of KBRI points out that 'despite frequent warnings, he has persisted in using (KBRI'S) microphones to harass and malign the Police Department in a manner bordering on the slanderous.' The matter involved was the month-old Kingship-Powell slayings, in which Mr Gant has taken a personal and somewhat acrimonious interest. His public criticism of the police was, to say the least, indiscreet, but considering that no progress has been made towards reaching a solution of the case, we find ourselves forced to agree with the appropriateness of his remarks, if not with their propriety.

15

At the end of the school year he returned to Menasset and sat around the house in sombre depression. His mother tried to combat his sullenness and then began to reflect it. They argued, like hot coals boosting each other into flame. To get out of the house and out of himself, he reclaimed his old job at the haberdashery shop. From nine to five-thirty he stood behind a glass display counter not looking at the binding-strips of gleaming burnished copper.

One day in July he took the small grey strongbox from his closet. Unlocking it on his desk, he took out the newspaper clippings about Dorothy's murder. He tore them into small pieces and dropped them into the waste-basket. He did the same with the clippings on Ellen and Powell. Then he took out the Kingship Copper pamphlets; he had written away for them a second time when he started to go with Ellen. As his hands gripped them, ready to tear, he smiled ruefully. Dorothy, Ellen . . .

It was like thinking 'Faith, Hope . . . ' 'Charity' pops into the mind to fulfil the sequence.

Dorothy, Ellen – Marion.

He smiled at himself and gripped the pamphlets again.

But he found that he couldn't tear them. Slowly he put them down on the desk, mechanically smoothing the creases.

He pushed the strongbox and the pamphlets to the back of the desk and sat down. He headed a sheet of paper *Marion* and divided it into two columns with a vertical line. He headed one column *Pro*; the other *Con*.

There were so many things to list under *Pro*: months of conversations with Dorothy, months of conversations with Ellen; all studded with passing references to Marion; her likes, her dislikes, her opinions, her past. He knew her like a book without even having met her; lonely, bitter, living alone . . . A perfect set-up.

Emotion was on the *Pro* side too. Another chance. Hit a home run and the two strikes that preceded it are washed away. And three was the lucky number – third time lucky – all the childhood fairy tales with the third try and the third wish and the third suitor . . .

He couldn't think of a thing to list under *Con*.

That night he tore up the *Pro* and *Con* list and began another one, of Marion Kingship's characteristics, opinions, likes, and dislikes. He made several notations and, in the weeks that followed, added regularly to the list. In every spare moment he pushed his mind back to conversations with Dorothy and Ellen; conversations in luncheonettes, between classes, while walking, while dancing; dredging words, phrases, and sentences up from the pool of his memory. Sometimes he spent entire evenings flat on his back, remembering, a small part of his mind probing the larger, less conscious part like a Geiger counter that clicked on *Marion*.

As the list grew, his spirits swelled. Sometimes he would take the paper from the strongbox even when he had nothing to add – just to admire it; the keenness, the planning, the potence displayed. It was almost as good as having the clippings on Dorothy and Ellen.

'You're crazy,' he told himself aloud one day, looking at the list. 'You're a crazy nut,' he said affectionately. He didn't really think that; he thought he was daring, audacious, brilliant, intrepid, and bold.

'I'm not going back to school,' he told his mother one day in August.

'What?' She stood small and thin in the doorway of his room, one hand frozen in mid-passage over her straggly grey hair.

'I'm going to New York in a few weeks.'

'You got to finish *school*,' she said plaintively. He was silent. 'What is it, you got a job in New York?'

'I don't but I'm going to get one. I've got an idea I want to work on. A – a project, sort of.'

'But you got to finish school, Bud,' she said hesitantly.

'I don't "got to" do anything!' he snapped. There was silence. 'If this idea flops, which I don't think it will, I can always finish school next year.'

Her hands wiped the front of her housedress nervously. 'Bud, you're past twenty-five. You got to – have to finish school and get yourself started some place. You can't keep—'

'Look, will you just let me live my own life?'

She stared at him. 'That's what your father used to give me,' she said quietly, and went away.

He stood by his desk for a few moments, hearing the angry clanking of cutlery in the kitchen sink. He picked up a magazine and looked at it, pretending he didn't care.

A few minutes later he went into the kitchen. His mother was at the sink, her back towards him. 'Mom,' he said pleadingly, 'you know I'm as anxious as you are to see myself get some place.' She didn't turn around. 'You know I wouldn't quit school if this idea wasn't something important.' He went over and sat down at the table, facing her back. 'If it doesn't work, I'll finish school next year. I *promise* I will, Mom.'

Reluctantly, she turned. 'What kind of idea is it?' she asked slowly, 'An invention?'

'No. I can't tell you,' he said regretfully. 'It's only in the – the planning stage. I'm sorry—'

She sighed and wiped her hands on a towel. 'Can't it wait till next year? When you'd be through with school?'

'Next year might be too late, Mom.'

She put down the towel. 'Well I wish you could tell me what it is.'

'I'm sorry, Mom. I wish I could too. But it's one of those things that you just can't explain.'

She went around behind him and laid her hands on his shoulders. She stood there for a moment, looking down at his anxiously upturned face. 'Well,' she said, pressing his shoulders, 'I guess it must be a *good* idea.'

He smiled up at her happily.

PART THREE
MARION
1

When Marion Kingship was graduated from college (Columbia University, an institution demanding long hours of earnest study; unlike that Midwestern Twentieth-Century-Fox playground that Ellen was entering) her father offhandedly mentioned the fact to the head of the advertising agency which handled the Kingship Copper account, and Marion was offered a job as a copy writer. Although she wanted very much to write advertising copy, she refused the offer. Eventually she managed to find a position with a small agency where Kingship was a name stamped on the washroom plumbing and where Marion was assured that in the not-too-distant future she would be permitted to submit copy for some of the smaller accounts, provided that the writing of the copy did not interfere with her secretarial duties.

A year later, when Dorothy inevitably followed Ellen's lead and went off to football cheers and campus kisses, Marion found herself alone in an eight-room apartment with her father, the two of them like charged metal pellets that drift and pass but never touch. She decided, against her father's obvious though unvoiced disapproval, to find a place of her own.

She rented a two-room apartment on the top-floor of a converted brownstone house in the East Fifties. She furnished it with a great deal of care. Because the two rooms were smaller than those she had occupied in her father's home, she could not take all her possessions with her. Those that she did take, therefore, were the fruit of a thoughtful selection. She told herself she was choosing the things she liked best, the things that meant the most to her, which was true; but as she hung each picture and placed each book upon the shelf, she saw it not only through her own eyes but also through the eyes of a visitor who would some day come to her apartment, a visitor as yet unidentified except as to his sex. Every article was invested with significance, an index to her self; the furniture and the lamps and the ashtrays (modern but not modernistic), the reproduction of her favourite painting (Charles Demuth's *My Egypt*; not quite realistic; its planes accentuated and enriched by the eye of the artist), the records (some of the jazz and some of the Stravinsky and Bartók, but mostly the melodic listen-in-the-dark themes of Grieg and Brahms and Rachmaninoff), and the books – especially the books, for what better index of the personality is there? (The novels and plays, the non-fiction and verse, all chosen in proportion and representation of her tastes.) It was like the concentrated abbreviation of a Help Wanted ad. The egocentricity which motivated it was not that of the spoiled, but of the too little spoiled; the lonely. Had she been an artist she would have painted a self-portrait; instead she decorated two rooms, changing them with objects which some visitor, some day, would recognize and understand. And through that understanding he would divine all the capacities and longings she had found in herself and was unable to communicate.

The map of her week was centred about two landmarks; on Wednesday evenings she had dinner with her father, and on Saturdays she thorough-cleaned her two rooms. The first was a labour of duty; the second, of love. She waxed wood and polished glass, and dusted and replaced objects with sacramental care.

There were visitors. Dorothy and Ellen came when they were home on vacation, unconvincingly envying Marion as a woman of the world. Her father came, puffing from the three flights of stairs, looking dubiously at the small living-bedroom and smaller kitchen and shaking his head. Some girls from the office came, playing Canasta as though life and honour were at stake. And a man came once; the bright young junior account executive; very nice, very intelligent. His interest in the apartment manifested itself in sidelong glances at the studio couch.

When Dorothy committed suicide, Marion returned to her father's apartment for two weeks, and when Ellen died, she stayed with him for a month. They could no more get close to each other than could charged metal pellets, no matter how they tried. At the end of the month, he suggested with a diffidence unusual in him that she move back permanently. She couldn't; the thought of relinquishing her own apartment was unimaginable, as though she had locked too much of herself into it. After that though, she had dinner at her father's three evenings a week instead of only one.

On Saturdays she cleaned the rooms, and once each month she opened all the books to prevent their bindings from growing stiff.

One Saturday morning in September, the telephone rang. Marion, on her knees in the act of polishing the underside of a plate-glass coffee table, froze at the sound of the bell. She gazed down through the blue-toned glass at the flattened dust-cloth, hoping that it was a mistake, that someone had dialled the wrong number, had realized it at the last moment and hung up. The phone rang again. Reluctantly she rose to her feet and went over to the table beside the studio couch, still holding the dustcloth in her hand.

'Hello,' she said flatly.

'Hello.' It was a man's voice, unfamiliar. 'Is this Marion Kingship?'

'Yes.'

'You don't know me. I was – a friend of Ellen's.' Marion felt suddenly awkward; a friend of Ellen's; someone handsome and clever and fast-talking . . . Someone dull underneath, someone *she* wouldn't care for anyway. The awkwardness retreated. 'My name,' the man continued, 'is Burton Corliss – Bud Corliss.'

'Oh, yes. Ellen told me about you.' ('I love him so much,' Ellen had said during the visit that had proved to be her last, 'and he loves me too' – and Marion, though happy for her, had for some reason been sombre the rest of the evening.)

'I wonder if I could see you,' he said. 'I have something that belonged to Ellen. One of her books. She lent it to me just before – before she went to Blue River, and I thought you might like to have it.'

Probably some book-of-the-month novel, Marion thought, and then, hating herself for her smallness, said, 'Yes, I'd like very much to have it. Yes, I would.'

For a moment there was silence from the other end of the wire. 'I could bring it over now,' he said. 'I'm in the neighbourhood.'

'No,' she said quickly, 'I'm going out.'

'Well then, some time tomorrow—'

'I – I won't be in tomorrow either.' She drifted uncomfortably, ashamed of her lying, ashamed that she didn't want him in her apartment. He was probably likeable enough, and he'd loved Ellen and Ellen was dead, and he was going out of his way to give her Ellen's book . . . 'We could meet some place this afternoon,' she offered.

'Fine,' he said. 'That would be fine.'

'I'm going to be – around Fifth Avenue.'

'Then suppose we meet, say, in front of the statue at Rockefeller Centre, the one of Atlas holding up the world.'

'All right.'

'At three o'clock?'

'Yes. Three o'clock. Thank you very much for calling. It's very nice of you.'

'Don't mention it,' he said. 'Good-bye, Marion.' There was a pause. 'I'd feel funny calling you Miss Kingship. Ellen spoke about you so much.'

'That's all right.' She felt awkward again, and self-conscious. 'Good-bye,' she said, unable to decide whether to call him Bud or Mr Corliss.

'Good-bye,' he repeated.

She replaced the receiver and stood looking at the telephone for a moment. Then turned and went to the coffee table. Kneeling, she resumed her work, sweeping the dustcloth in unaccustomedly hurried arcs, because now the whole afternoon was broken up.

2

In the shadow of the towering bronze statue, he stood with his back to the pedestal, immaculate in grey flannel, a paper-wrapped package under his arm. Before him passed intermeshing streams of oppositely-bound people slow-moving against a backdrop of roaring buses and impatient taxis. He watched their faces carefully. The Fifth Avenue set; men with unpadded shoulders and narrowly knotted ties; women self-consciously smart in tailored suits, kerchiefs crisp at their throats, their beautiful heads lifted high, as though photographers might be waiting farther down the street. And, like transient sparrows tolerated in an aviary, the pink rural faces gawking at the statue and the sun-sharpened spires of Saint Patrick's across the street. He watched them all carefully, trying to recall the snapshot Dorothy had shown him so long ago. 'Marion could be very pretty, only she wears her hair like this.' He smiled, remembered Dorrie's fierce frown as she pulled her hair back primly. His fingers toyed with a fold in the wrapping of the package.

She came from the north, and he recognized her when she was still a hundred feet away. She was tall and thin, a bit too thin, and dressed much like the women around her; a brown suit, a gold kerchief, a small Vogue-looking felt hat, a shoulder-strap handbag. She seemed stiff and uncomfortable in the outfit, though, as if it had been made to someone else's measure. Her pulled-back hair was brown. She had Dorothy's large brown eyes, but in her drawn face they were too large, and the high cheekbones that had been so beautiful in her sisters were, in Marion, too sharply defined. As she came nearer, she saw him. With an uncertain, questioning smile, she approached, appearing ill at ease in the spotlight of his gaze. Her lipstick, he noticed, was the pale rose he associated with timorously experimenting adolescents.

'Marion?'

'Yes.' She offered her hand hesitantly. 'How do you do,' she said, directing a too-quick smile at a point somewhere below his eyes.

Her hand in his was long-fingered and cold. 'Hello,' he said. 'I've been looking forward to meeting you.'

They went to a determinedly Early American cocktail lounge around the corner. Marion, after some indecision, ordered a Daquiri.

'I – I can't stay long, I'm afraid,' she said, sitting erect on the edge of her chair, her fingers stiff around the cocktail glass.

'Where are they always running, these beautiful women?' he inquired smilingly – and immediately saw that it was the wrong approach; she smiled tensely and seemed to grow more uncomfortable. He looked at her curiously, allowing the echo of his words to fade. After a moment he began again. 'You're with an advertising agency, aren't you?'

'Camden and Galbraith,' she said. 'Are you still at Caldwell?'

'No.'

'I thought Ellen said you were a junior.'

'I was, but I had to quit school.' He sipped his Martini. 'My father is dead. I didn't want my mother to work any more.'

'Oh, I'm sorry—'

'Maybe I'll be able to finish up next year. Or I may go to night school. Where did you go to school?'

'Columbia. Are you from New York?'

'Massachusetts.'

Every time he tried to steer the conversation around to her, she turned it back towards him. Or to the weather. Or to a waiter who bore a startling resemblance to Claude Rains.

Eventually she asked, 'Is that the book?'

'Yes. *Dinner at Antoine's*. Ellen wanted me to read it. There are some personal notes she scribbled on the flyleaf, so I thought you might like to have it.' He passed the package to her.

'Personally,' he said, 'I go for books that have a little more meaning.'

Marion stood up. 'I'll have to be leaving now,' she said apologetically.

'But you haven't finished your drink yet.'

'I'm sorry,' she said quickly, looking down at the package in her hands. 'I have an appointment. A business appointment. I couldn't possibly be late.'

He rose. 'But—'

'I'm sorry.' She looked at him uncomfortably.

He put money on the table.

They walked back to Fifth Avenue. At the corner she offered her hand again. It was still cold. 'It's been very nice meeting you, Mr Corliss,' she said. 'Thank you for the drink. And the book. I appreciate it – very thoughtful—' She turned and melted into the stream of people.

Emptily, he stood on the corner for a moment. Then his lips clenched and he started walking.

He followed her. The brown felt hat had a gold ornament that glittered brightly. He stayed some thirty feet behind it.

She walked up to Fifty-fourth Street, where she crossed the avenue, heading east towards Madison. He knew where she was going; he remembered the address from the telephone book. She crossed Madison and Park. He stopped on the corner and watched her climb the steps of the brown-stone house.

'Business appointment,' he muttered. He waited around for a few minutes, not knowing exactly why he waited, and then he turned and walked slowly back towards Fifth Avenue.

3

Sunday afternoon Marion went to the Museum of Modern Art. The main floor was still occupied by an automobile exhibit which she had seen before and found uninteresting, and the second floor was unusually crowded, so she continued up the turning stairway to the third floor, there to wander among the pleasantly familiar paintings and sculptures; the arched white smoothness of the *Girl Washing Her Hair*, the perfect spear of *Bird in Space*.

Two men were in the room that held the Lehmbruck sculptures, but they went out soon after Marion entered, leaving her alone in the cool grey cube with the two statues, the male and female, he standing and she kneeling in opposite quarters of the room, their bodies elongated and gauntly beautiful. The attention of the statues gave them an unearthly air, almost like religious art, so that Marion had always been able to look at them with none of the slight embarrassment she usually felt on viewing nude sculptures. She moved slowly around the figure of the young man.

'Hello.' The voice was behind her, pleasantly surprised.

It must be for me, she thought, there's no one else here. She turned around.

Bud Corliss smiled in the doorway.

'Hello,' Marion said confusedly.

'It really *is* a small world,' he said, coming to her. 'I came in right behind you downstairs, only I wasn't sure it was you. How are you?'

'Fine, thank you.' There was an uncomfortable pause. 'How are you?' she added.

'Fine, thanks.'

They turned to the statue. Why did she feel so clumsy? Because he was handsome? Because he had been part of Ellen's circle? – had shared football cheers and campus kisses and love . . .

'Do you come here often?' he asked.

'Yes.'

'So do I.'

The statue embarrassed her now, because Bud Corliss was standing beside her. She turned away and moved towards the figure of the kneeling woman. He followed at her side. 'Did you make the appointment on time?'

'Yes,' she said. What brought him here? You'd think he'd be

strolling in Central Park with some poised flawless Ellen, her hand on his arm . . .

They looked at the statue. After a moment, he said, 'I really didn't think it was you downstairs.'

'Why not?'

'Well, Ellen wasn't the museum type—'

'Sisters aren't exactly alike,' she said.

'No, I guess not.' He began to circle around the kneeling figure. 'The Fine Arts department at Caldwell had a small museum,' he said. 'Mostly reproductions and copies. I dragged Ellen there once or twice. Thought I'd indoctrinate her.' He shook his head. 'No luck.'

'She wasn't interested in art.'

'No,' he said. 'It's funny the way we try to push our tastes on people we like.'

Marion looked at him, facing her on the other side of the statue. 'I once took Ellen and Dorothy – Dorothy was our youngest sister—'

'I know—'

'I took them here once when they were just going into their teens. They were bored, though. I guess it was too young.'

'I don't know,' he said, retracing his semicircular path towards her. 'If there'd been a museum in my home town when I was that age – Did *you* come here when you were twelve or thirteen?'

'Yes.'

'See?' he said. His smile made them fellow members of a group to which Ellen and Dorothy had never belonged.

A man and woman with two children in tow came bursting into the room.

'Let's move on,' he suggested, at her side again.

'I—'

'It's Sunday,' he said. 'No business appointments to run to.' He smiled at her; a very nice smile, soft and lenitive. 'I'm alone; you're alone.' He took her elbow gently. 'Come on,' he said, with the persuasive smile.

They went through the third floor and half of the second, commenting on the works they saw, and then they went down to the main floor, past the gleaming automobiles incongruous within a building, and out through the glass doors to the garden behind the museum. They strolled from statue to statue, pausing before each. They came to the Maillol woman, full-bodied, strident.

'The last of the red-hot mammas,' Bud said.

Marion smiled. 'I'll tell you something,' she said. 'I always get a little embarrassed looking at - statues like this.'

'This one embarrasses *me* a little,' he said, smiling. 'It's not a nude; it's a naked.' They both laughed.

When they had looked at all the statues, they sat down on one of the benches at the back of the garden and lit cigarettes.

'You and Ellen were going steady, weren't you.'

'Not exactly.'

'I thought—'

'Not officially, I mean. Anyway, going steady in college doesn't always mean as much as going steady outside of college.'

Marion smoked in silence.

'We had a great many things in common, but they were mainly surface things; having the same classes, knowing the same people - things having to do with Caldwell. Once we were through with college though, I don't think we would've gotten married.' He stared at his cigarette. 'I was fond of Ellen. I liked her better than any girl I've ever known. I was miserable when she died. But - I don't know - she wasn't a very *deep* person.' He paused. 'I hope I'm not offending you.'

Marion shook her head, watching him.

'Everything was like that museum business. I thought I could at least get her interested in some of the uncomplicated artists, like Hopper or Wood. But it didn't work. She wasn't interested at all. And it was the same thing with books or politics - anything serious. She always wanted to be *doing* something.'

'She'd led a restricted life at home. I guess she was making up for it.'

'Yes,' he said. 'And then, she was four years younger than I.' He put out his cigarette. 'But she was the sweetest girl I've ever known.'

There was a pause.

'Didn't they ever find out *anything* about who did it?' he asked incredulously.

'Nothing. Isn't it awful—'

They sat in silence for a moment. Then they began to talk again; about how many interesting things there were to do in New York, what a pleasant place the museum was, about the Matisse exhibit that was coming soon.

'Do you know who I like?' he asked.

'Who?'

'I don't know if you're familiar with his work,' he said. 'Charles Demuth.'

4

Leo Kingship sat with his elbows propped on the table, his fingers interlocked around a cold-frosted glass of milk which he studied as though it were a beautifully coloured wine. 'You've been seeing him frequently, haven't you,' he said, trying to sound casual.

With elaborate care, Marion placed her coffee cup in the indentation of the blue and gold Aynsley saucer, and then looked across the crystal and silver and damask at her father. His full red face was bland. Reflected light blanked the lenses of his glasses, masking his eyes. 'Bud?' she said, knowing it was Bud he meant.

Kingship nodded.

'Yes,' Marion said squarely, 'I've been seeing him frequently.' She paused. 'He's calling for me tonight, in about fifteen minutes.' She watched her father's expressionless face with waiting eyes, hoping that there would not be an argument because it would tarnish the entire evening, and hoping that there *would* be one because it would try the strength of what she felt for Bud.

'This job of his,' Kingship said, setting down the milk. 'What are its prospects?'

After a cold moment Marion said, 'He's on the executive training squad. He should be a section manager in a few months. Why all the questions?' She smiled with her lips only.

Kingship removed his glasses. His blue eyes wrestled uncomfortably with Marion's cool stare. 'You brought him here to dinner, Marion,' he said. 'You never brought anyone to dinner before. Doesn't that entitle me to ask a few questions?'

'He lives in a rooming house,' Marion said. 'When he doesn't eat with me, he eats alone. So I brought him to dinner one night.'

'The nights you don't dine here, you dine with him?'

'Yes, most of them. Why should we both eat alone? We work only five blocks from each other.' She wondered why she was being evasive; she hadn't been caught doing something wrong. 'We eat together because we enjoy each other's company,' she said firmly. 'We like each other very much.'

'Then I do have a right to ask some questions, don't I,' Kingship pointed out quietly.

'He's someone I like. Not someone applying for a job with Kingship Copper.'

'Marion—'

She plucked a cigarette from a silver cup and lit it with a silver table-lighter. 'You don't like him, do you?'

'I didn't say that.'

'Because he's poor,' she said.

'That's not true, Marion, and you know it.'

There was silence for a moment.

'Oh, yes,' Kingship said, 'he's poor all right. He took pains to mention it exactly three times the other night. And that anecdote he dragged in, about the woman his mother did sewing for.'

'What's wrong with his mother taking in sewing?'

'Nothing, Marion, nothing. It's the way he alluded to it so casually, so very casually. Do you know who he reminded me of? There's a man at the club who has a bad leg, limps a little. Every time we play golf he says, "You boys go on ahead. Old Peg-leg'll catch up with you." So everyone walks extra slowly and you feel like a heel if you beat him.'

'I'm afraid the similarity escapes me,' Marion said. She rose from the table and went out towards the living-room, leaving Kingship to rub a hand despairingly over the few yellow-white hairs that thinly crossed his scalp.

In the living-room there was a large window that looked out over the East River. Marion stood before it, one hand on the thick cloth of the draperies. She heard her father come into the room behind her.

'Marion, believe me, I only want to see you happy.' He spoke awkwardly. 'I know I haven't always been so – concerned, but haven't I – done better since Dorothy and Ellen—'

'I know,' she admitted reluctantly. She fingered the drapes. 'But I'm practically twenty-five – a grown woman. You don't have to treat me as if—'

'I just don't want you rushing into anything, Marion.'

'I'm not,' she said softly.

'That's all I want.'

Marion stared out the window. 'Why do you dislike him?' she asked.

'I don't dislike him. He – I don't know, I—'

'Is it that you're afraid I'll go away from you?' She spoke the question slowly, as though the idea surprised her.

'You're already away from me, aren't you? In that apartment.'

She turned from the window and faced Kingship at the side of the room. 'You know, you really should be grateful to Bud,' she said. 'I'll tell you something. I didn't want him to have dinner here. As soon as I suggested, I was sorry. But he insisted. "He's your father," he said. "Think of his feelings." You see, Bud is strong on family ties, even if I'm not. So you should be grateful to him, not antagonistic. Because if he does anything, it will be to bring us closer together.' She faced the window again.

'All right,' Kingship said. 'He's probably a wonderful boy. I just want to make sure you don't make any mistakes.'

'What do you mean?' She turned from the window again, this time more slowly, her body stiffening.

'I just don't want you to make any mistakes, that's all,' Kingship said uncertainly.

'Are you asking other questions about him?' Marion demanded. 'Asking other people? Do you have someone checking on him?'

'No!'

'Like you did with Ellen?'

'Ellen was seventeen at the time! And I was right, wasn't I? Was that boy any good?'

'Well I'm twenty-five and I know my own mind! If you have anyone checking on Bud—'

'The idea never entered my mind!'

Marion's eyes stung him. 'I like Bud,' she said slowly, her voice tight. 'I like him very much. Do you know what that means, to finally find someone you like?'

'Marion, I—'

'So if you do *anything*, anything at all, to make him feel unwelcome or unwanted, to make him feel that he's not good enough for me – I'll never forgive you. I swear to God I'll never speak to you again as long as I live.'

She turned back to the window.

'The idea never entered my mind. Marion, I swear—' He looked futilely at her rigid back and then sank into a chair with a weary sigh.

A few minutes later the chimes of the front door sounded. Marion left the window and crossed the room towards the double door that led to the foyer.

'Marion.' Kingship stood up.

She paused and looked back at him. From the foyer came the sound of the front door opening and the murmur of voices in conversation.

'Ask him to stay a few minutes – have a drink.'

A moment passed. 'All right,' she said. At the doorway she hesitated for a second. 'I'm sorry I spoke the way I did.' She went out.

Kingship watched her go. Then he turned and faced the fireplace. He took a step back and regarded himself in the mirror tilted over the mantel. He looked at the well-fed man in the three hundred and forty dollar suit in the seven hundred dollar a month living-room.

Then he straightened up, put a smile on his face, turned, and walked towards the doorway, extending his right hand. 'Good evening, Bud,' he said.

5

Marion's birthday fell on a Saturday early in November. In the morning she cleaned her apartment hastily. At one o'clock she went to a small building in a quiet tributary of Park Avenue, where a discreet silver plaque beside a white door confided that the premises were occupied, not by a psychiatrist nor an interior decorator, but by a restaurant. Leo Kingship was waiting within the white door, sitting gingerly on a Louis Quinze sofa and scanning a management-owned copy of *Gourmet*. He put down the magazine, rose, kissed Marion on the cheek, and wished her a happy birthday. A *maître d'hôtel* with fluttering fingers and neon teeth ushered them to their table, swooped away a Reserved placard and seated them with Gallic effusion. There was a centre-piece of roses on the table, and, at Marion's place, a small box wrapped in white paper and clouds of gold ribbon. Kingship pretended not to be aware of it. While he was occupied with the wine card and 'If I may suggest, Monsieur', Marion freed the box of its gold entanglement, excitement colouring her cheeks and shining her eyes. Nested between layers of cotton was a golden disc, its surface constellated with tiny pearls. Marion exclaimed over the brooch, and when the *maître d'hôtel* had gone, thanked her father happily, squeezing his hand, which lay as if by chance near hers on the table.

The brooch was not one which she would have chosen herself; its design was too elaborate for her taste. Her happiness, however, was genuine, inspired by the giving if not by the gift. In the past, Leo Kingship's standard birthday present to his daughters had been a one hundred dollar gift certificate redeemable at a Fifth Avenue department store, a matter automatically attended to by his secretary.

After leaving her father, Marion spent some time at a beauty salon and then returned to her apartment. Late in the afternoon the buzzer sounded. She pressed the button that released the door downstairs. A few minutes later a messenger appeared at her door, panting dramatically, as though he had been carrying something much heavier than a florist's box. The receipt of a quarter soothed his respiration.

In the box, under green waxed paper, was a white orchid arranged in a corsage. The card with it said simply, 'Bud.' Standing before a mirror, Marion held the bloom experimentally to her hair, her wrist, and her shoulder. Then she went into the kitchen and placed the flower in its box and in the waist-high refrigerator, first sprinkling a few drops of water on its thick-veined tropical petals.

He arrived promptly at six. He gave the button next to Marion's nameplate two quick jabs and stood waiting in the stuffy hallway, removing a grey suede glove to pick a speck of lint from the lapel of his navy blue coat. Soon footsteps sounded on the stairs. The dingily curtained door opened and Marion appeared, radiant, the orchid bursting whitely on her black coat. They clasped each other's hands. Wishing her the happiest of birthdays, he kissed her on the cheek so as not to smudge her lipstick, which he noticed was of a deeper shade than she had worn when first he met her.

They went to a steak house on Fifty-second Street. The prices on the menu, although considerably lower than those on the one from which she had selected her lunch, seemed exorbitant to Marion, because she was seeing them through Bud's eyes. She suggested that he order for both of them. They had black onion soup and sirloin steaks, preceded by champagne cocktails – 'To you, Marion.' At the end of the meal, placing eighteen dollars on the waiter's salver, Bud caught Marion's faint frown. 'Well, it's your birthday, isn't it?' he said, smiling.

From the restaurant they took a taxi to the theatre where *Saint Joan* was playing. They sat in the orchestra, sixth row centre. During the intermission Marion was unusually voluble, her doelike eyes glittering brightly as she talked of Shaw and the acting and a celebrity who was seated in the row in front of them. During the play their hands were warm in each other's.

Afterwards – because, she told herself, Bud had already spent so much money that evening – Marion suggested that they go to her apartment.

'I feel like a pilgrim who's finally being permitted to enter the shrine,' he said as he slipped the key into the slit of the lock. He turned the key and door-knob simultaneously.

'It's nothing fancy,' Marion said, her voice quick. 'Really. They call it two rooms but it's more like one, the kitchen is so tiny.'

He pushed the door open, withdrawing the key which he handed to Marion. She stepped into the apartment and reached for a wall switch beside the door. Lamps filled the room with diffused light. He entered, closing the door behind him. Marion turned to watch his face. His eyes were ranging over the deep grey walls, the blue and white striped drapes, the limed oak furniture. He gave an appreciative murmur.

'It's very small,' Marion said.

'But nice,' he said. '*Very* nice.'

'Thank you.' She turned away from him, unpinning the orchid from her coat, suddenly as ill at ease as when they first met. She put the corsage on a sideboard and started to remove her coat. His hands helped her. 'Beautiful furniture,' he said over her shoulder.

She hung their coats in the closet mechanically, and then turned to the mirror over the sideboard. With fumbling fingers, she pinned the orchid to the shoulder of her russet dress, her eyes focused beyond her own reflection, on Bud's image. He had walked down to the centre of the room. Standing before the coffee table, he picked up a square copper plate. His face, in profile, was expressionless, giving no indication whether he liked or disliked the piece. Marion found herself motionless. 'Mmmm,' he said at last, liking it. 'A present from your father, I bet.'

'No.' Marion said into the mirror, 'Ellen gave it to me.'

'Oh.' He looked at it for a moment and then put it down.

Fingering the collar of her dress, Marion turned from the mirror and watched as he crossed the room with three easy strides. He stood before the low bookcase and looked at the picture on the wall above it. Marion watched him. 'Our old friend Demuth,' he said. He glanced at her, smiling. She smiled back. He looked at the picture again.

After a moment, Marion moved forward and went to his side.

'I never could figure out why he called a picture of a grain elevator "My Egypt",' Bud said.

'Is that what it is? I was never sure.'

'It's a beautiful picture, though.' He turned to Marion. 'What's the matter? Have I got some dirt on my nose or something?'

'What?'

'You were looking—'

'Oh. No. Would you like something to drink?'

'Mmm-hmm.'

'There's nothing but wine.'

'Perfect.'

Marion turned towards the kitchen.

'Before you go.' He took a small tissue-wrapped box from his pocket. 'Happy Birthday.'

'Oh, Bud, you shouldn't have!' 'I shouldn't have,' he mimicked simultaneously. 'But aren't you glad I did?'

There were silver earrings in the box, simple polished triangles. 'Oh, thank you! They're lovely!' Marion exclaimed, and kissed him.

She hurried to the sideboard to try them on. He came up behind her, looking at her in the mirror. When she had fastened both earrings, he turned her around. 'Lovely is right,' he said.

When the kiss ended he said, 'Now where's that wine we were talking about?'

Marion came out of the kitchen with a raffia-covered bottle of Bardolino and two glasses on a tray. Bud, his jacket off, was sitting crosslegged on the floor in front of the bookcase, a book opened on his lap. 'I didn't know you liked Proust,' he said.

'Oh, I do!' She set the tray on the coffee table.

'Here,' he said, pointing to the bookcase. Marion transferred the tray to the bookcase. She filled the two glasses and handed one to

Bud. Holding the other, she worked her feet out of her shoes and lowered herself to the floor beside him. He leafed through the pages of the book. 'I'll show you the part I'm crazy about,' he said.

He pressed the switch. The tone arm swung slowly and dipped down to touch with its serpent's head the rim of the spinning record. Closing the cover of the phonograph, he crossed the room and sat beside Marion on the blue-covered studio couch. The first deep piano notes of the Rachmaninoff Second Concerto sounded. 'Just the right record,' Marion said.

Leaning back against the thick bolster that ran along the wall, Bud scanned the room, now softly lighted by a single lamp. 'Everything's so perfect here,' he said. 'Why haven't you asked me up before?'

She picked at a filament of raffia that had got caught on one of the buttons on the front of her dress. 'I don't know,' she said. 'I – I thought maybe you wouldn't like it.'

'How could I not like it?' he asked.

His fingers worked dexterously down the row of buttons. Her hands, warm, closed over his, restraining them between her breasts.

'Bud, I've never – done anything before.'

'I know that, darling. You don't have to tell me that.'

'I've never loved anyone before.'

'Neither have I. I've never loved anyone. Not until you.'

'Do you mean that? Do you?'

'Only you.'

'Not even Ellen?'

'Only you. I swear it.'

He kissed her again.

Her hands freed his and rose to find his cheeks.

6

From the *New York Times*; Monday, December 24, 1951:

MARION J. KINGSHIP TO BE WED SATURDAY

Miss Marion Joyce Kingship, daughter of Mr Leo Kingship of Manhattan and the late Phyllis Hatcher, will be married to Mr Burton Corliss, son of Mrs Joseph Corliss of Menasset, Mass., and the late Mr Corliss, on the afternoon of Saturday, December 29, in the home of her father.

Miss Kingship was graduated from the Spence School in New York and is an alumna of Columbia University. Until last week she was with the advertising agency of Camden and Galbraith.

The prospective bridegroom, who served with the army during the Second World War and attended Caldwell College in Caldwell, Wis., has recently joined the domestic sales division of the Kingship Copper Corporation.

7

Seated at her desk, Miss Richardson stretched out her right hand in a gesture she considered quite graceful and squinted at the gold bracelet that constricted the plumpness of her wrist. It was definitely too young-looking for her mother, she decided. She would get something else for mother and keep the bracelet for herself.

Beyond her hand the background suddenly turned blue. With white pin-stripes. She looked up, starting to smile, but stopped when she saw that it was the pest again.

'Hello,' he said cheerfully.

Miss Richardson opened a drawer and busily ruffled the edges of some blank typing paper. 'Mr Kingship is still at lunch,' she said frigidly.

'Dear lady, he was at lunch at twelve o'clock. It is now three o'clock. What is he, a rhinoceros?'

411

'If you wish to make an appointment for later in the week—'

'I would like an audience with His Eminence this afternoon.'

Miss Richardson closed the drawer grimly. 'Tomorrow is Christmas,' she said. 'Mr Kingship is interrupting a four-day weekend by coming in today. He wouldn't do that unless he were very busy. He gave me strict orders not to disturb him on any account. On no account whatsoever.'

'Then he isn't at lunch.'

'He gave me strict orders—'

The man sighed. Slinging his folded coat over one shoulder, he drew a slip of paper from the rack next to Miss Richardson's telephone. 'May I?' he asked, already having taken the paper. Placing it on a large blue book which he held in the crook of his arm, he removed Miss Richardson's pen from its onyx holder and began to write.

'Well I never!' said Miss Richardson. 'Honestly!' she said.

Finished writing, the man replaced the pen and blew on the paper. He folded it carefully into quarters and handed it to Miss Richardson. 'Give him this,' he said. 'Slip it under the door, if need be.'

Miss Richardson glared at him. Then she calmly unfolded the paper and read it.

Uncomfortably, she looked up. 'Dorothy and Ellen—?'

His face was expressionless.

She hoisted herself from the chair. 'He told me not to distrub him on any account,' she repeated softly, as though seeking guidance in the incantation. 'What's your name?'

'Just give him that, please, like the angel you are.'

'Now look—'

He was doing just that; looking at her quite seriously, despite the lightness of his voice. Miss Richardson frowned, glanced again at the paper, and refolded it. She moved to a heavily pannelled door. 'All right,' she said darkly, 'but you'll see. He gave me strict orders.' Gingerly she tapped on the door. Opening it, she slipped in with the paper held appeasingly before her.

She reappeared a minute later with a betrayed expression on her face. 'Go ahead,' she said sharply, holding the door open.

The man breezed past her, his coat over his shoulder, the book under his arm. 'Keep smiling,' he whispered.

At the faint sound of the door closing, Leo Kingship looked up from the slip of paper in his hand. He was standing behind his desk in his

412

shirt-sleeves, his jacket draped on the back of the chair behind him. His glasses were pushed up on his pink forehead. Sunlight, sliced by a Venetian blind, striped his stocky figure. He squinted anxiously at the man approaching him across the panelled and carpeted room.

'Oh,' he said, when the man came close enough to block the sunlight, enabling Kingship to recognize his face. 'You.' He looked down at the slip of paper and crumpled it, his expression of anxiety turning to relief and then to annoyance.

'Hello, Mr Kingship,' the man said, offering his hand.

Kingship took it half-heartedly. 'No wonder you wouldn't give your name to Miss Richardson.'

Smiling, the man dropped into the visitor's chair. He settled his coat and the book in his lap.

'But I'm afraid I've forgotten it,' Kingship said. 'Grant?' he ventured.

'Gant.' The long legs crossed comfortably. 'Gordon Gant.'

Kingship remained standing. 'I'm extremely busy, Mr Gant,' he said firmly, indicating the paper-strewn desk. 'So if this "information about Dorothy and Ellen",' – he held up the crumpled slip of paper – 'consists of the same "theories" you were expounding back in Blue River—'

'Partially,' Gant said.

'Well, I'm sorry. I don't want to listen.'

'I gathered that I wasn't number one on your Hit Parade.'

'You mean I didn't like you? That isn't so. Not at all. I realized your motives were of the best; you had taken a liking to Ellen; you showed a – a youthful enthusiasm. But it was misdirected, misdirected in a way that was extremely painful to me. Barging into my hotel room so soon after Ellen's death – bringing up the past at such a moment.' He looked at Gant appealingly. 'Do you think I wouldn't have liked to believe that Dorothy didn't take her own life?'

'She didn't.'

'The note,' he said wearily, 'the note—'

'A couple of ambiguously worded sentences that could have referred to a dozen things beside suicide. Or that she could have been tricked into writing.' Gant leaned forward. 'Dorothy went to the Municipal Building to get married. Ellen's theory was right; the fact that she was killed proves it.'

'It does no such thing,' Kingship snapped. 'There was no connection. You heard the police—'

'A housebreaker!'

'Why not? Why not a housebreaker?'

'Because I *don't* believe in coincidences. Not that kind.'

'A sign of immaturity, Mr Gant.'

After a moment Gant said flatly, 'It was the same person both times.'

Kingship braced his hands tiredly on the desk, looking down at the papers there. 'Why do you have to revive all this?' he sighed. 'Intruding in other people's business. How do you think I feel—?' He pushed his glasses down into place and fingered the papers of a ledger. 'Would you please go now.'

Gant made no move to rise. 'I'm home on vacation,' he said. 'Home is White Plains. I didn't spend an hour on the New York Central just to rehash what was already said last March.'

'What then?' Kingship looked warily at the long-jawed face.

'There was an article in this morning's *Times* – the society page.'

'My daughter?'

Gant nodded. He took a pack of cigarettes from his breast pocket. 'What do you know about Bud Corliss?' he asked.

Kingship eyed him in silence. 'Know about him?' he said slowly. 'He's going to be my son-in-law. What do you mean, know about him?'

'Do you know that he and Ellen were going together?'

'Of course,' Kingship straightened up. 'What are you driving at?'

'It's a long story,' Gant said. The blue eyes were sharp and steady under the thick blond brows. He gestured towards Kingship's chair. 'And my delivery is bound to suffer if you stand towering over me.'

Kingship sat down. He kept his hands on the edge of the desk before him, as though ready to rise again in an instant.

Gant lit his cigarette. He sat silently for a moment, regarding it thoughtfully and working his lower lip with his teeth, as though awaiting a time signal. Then he began to speak in the easy, fluid, announcer's voice.

'When she left Caldwell,' he said, 'Ellen wrote a letter to Bud Corliss. I happened to read that letter soon after Ellen arrived in Blue River. It made quite an impression on me, since it described a murder suspect whom I resembled much too closely for comfort.' He smiled. 'I read the letter twice, and carefully, as you can imagine.

'On the night Ellen was killed, Eldon Chesser, that lover of prima facie evidence, asked me if Ellen were my girlfriend. It was probably the only constructive thing he ever did during his entire detectival career, because it set me thinking of friend Corliss. Partly to take my mind off Ellen, who was God-knows-where with an armed killer, and partly because I liked her and wondered what kind of a man she liked. I thought about that letter which was still fresh in my mind and which was my only source of information about my "rival", Bud Corliss.'

Gant paused for a second, and then continued. 'At first it seemed to contain nothing; a name – Dear Bud – and an address on the envelope – Burton Corliss, something-or-other Roosevelt Street, Caldwell, Wisconsin. No other clues. But on further reflection I found several bits of information in Ellen's letter, and I was able to fit them together into an even bigger piece of information about Bud Corliss; it seemed insignificant at the time; a purely external fact about him rather than an indication of his personality, which was what I was really looking for. But that fact stayed with me, and today it seems significant indeed.'

'Go ahead,' Kingship said as Gant drew on his cigarette.

Gant leaned back comfortably. 'First of all: Ellen wrote Bud that she wouldn't fall behind in her work while away from Caldwell because she would be able to get all the notes from him. Now, Ellen was a senior, which meant that she was taking advanced courses. In every college senior courses are closed to freshmen and often to sophomores. If Bud shared *all* Ellen's classes – they probably made out their programmes together – it meant that he was conceivably a sophomore, but in all probability a junior or a senior.

'Secondly: at one point in the letter Ellen described her behaviour during her first three years at Caldwell, which apparently differed from her behaviour after Dorothy's death. She described how she had been "the rah-rah girl", and then she said, and I think I remember the exact words, "You wouldn't recognize me." Which meant, as clearly as could possibly be, that Bud had not seen her during those first three years. This would be highly conceivable at a good-sized university like Stoddard, but we come to thirdly.'

'Thirdly: Caldwell is a very small college; one-tenth the size of Stoddard, Ellen wrote, and she was giving it the benefit of the doubt. I checked in the almanac this morning; Stoddard has over twelve thousand students; Caldwell, barely eight hundred. Furthermore, Ellen mentioned in the letter that she hadn't wanted Dorothy to come to Caldwell precisely because it was the kind of place where everybody knew everybody else and knew what they were doing.

'So, we add one, two and three: Bud Corliss, who is at least in his third year of college, was a stranger to Ellen at the beginning of her fourth year, despite the fact that they both attended a very small school where, I understand, the social side of life plays hob with the scholastic. All of which can be explained in only one way and can be condensed to a simple statement of fact; the fact which seemed insignificant last March, but today seems like the most important fact in Ellen's letter: *Bud Corliss was a transfer student, and he transferred to Caldwell in September of 1950, at the beginning of Ellen's fourth year and after Dorothy's death.*'

Kingship frowned. 'I don't see what—'

'We come now to today, December 24, 1951,' Gant said, crushing his cigarette in an ashtray, 'when my mother, bless her, brings the prodigal son breakfast in bed, along with the *New York Times*. And there, on the society page, is the name of Kingship. Miss Marion Kingship to wed Mr Burton Corliss. Imagine my surprise. Now, my mind, in addition to being insatiably curious and highly analytical, is also very dirty. It looks to me, says I, as though the new member of the domestic sales division was determined not to be disqualified from the Kingship Copper sweepstakes.'

'Now look here, Mr Gant—'

'I considered,' Gant went on, 'how when one sister was killed he proceeded directly to the next one. Beloved of two of the Kingship daughters. Two out of three. Not a bad score.

'And then the analytical side and the dirty side of my brain blended, and I thought: three out of three would have been an even better score for Mr Burton Corliss who transferred to Caldwell College in September of 1950.'

Kingship stood up, staring at Gant.

'A random thought,' Gant said. 'Wildly improbable. But easily removed from the realm of doubt. A simple matter of sliding out from under the breakfast tray, going to the book-case, and taking therefrom *The Stoddard Flame*, yearbook for 1950.' He displayed the large blue leatherette book with its white-lettered cover. 'In the sophomore section,' he said, 'there are several interesting photographs. One of Dorothy Kingship and one of Dwight Powell, both of whom are now dead. None of Gordon Gant; didn't have five spare bucks to have my face recorded for posterity. But many sophomores did, among them—' He opened the book to a page marked by a strip of newsprint, turned the volume around and put it down on the desk, his finger stabbing one of the checkerboard photographs. He recited the inscription beside it from memory: 'Corliss, Burton quote Bud unquote, Menasset, Mass., Liberal Arts.'

Kingship sat down again. He looked at the photograph, hardly larger than a postage stamp. Then he looked at Gant. Gant reached forward, turned a few pages, and pointed to another picture. It was Dorothy. Kingship looked at that, too. Then looked up again.

Gant said, 'It struck me as awfully odd. I thought you should know.'

'Why?' Kingship asked stolidly. 'What is this supposed to be leading up to?'

'May I ask you one question, Mr Kingship, before I answer that?'

'Go ahead.'

'He never told you he went to Stoddard, did he?'

'No. But we've never discussed things like that,' he explained quickly. 'He must have told Marion. Marion must know.'

'I don't think she does.'

'Why not?' Kingship demanded.

'The *Times*. Marion gave them the information for that article, didn't she? The bride-to-be usually does.'

'Well?'

'Well there's no mention of Stoddard. And in the other wedding and engagement articles, it's mentioned when someone's attended more than one school.'

'Maybe she just didn't bother to tell them.'

'Maybe. Or maybe she doesn't know. Maybe Ellen didn't know either.'

'All right, now what are you saying, mister?'

'Don't be sore at *me*, Mr Kingship. The facts speak for themselves; I didn't invent them.' Gant closed the yearbook and put it in his lap. 'There are two possibilities,' he said, 'Either Corliss told Marion that he attended Stoddard, in which case it might conceivably be a coincidence; he went to Stoddard and he transferred to Caldwell; he might not have known Dorothy any more than he knew me.' He paused. 'Or else, he *didn't* tell Marion he went there.'

'Which means?' Kingship challenged.

'Which means that he must have been involved with Dorothy in some way. Why else would he conceal it?' Gant looked down at the book in his lap. 'There was a man who wanted Dorothy out of the way because he had gotten her pregnant—'

Kingship stared at him. 'You're back to the same thing! Someone killed Dorothy, then killed Ellen. You've got this – this cockeyed moving picture theory and you don't want to admit—' Gant was silent. 'Bud?' Kingship asked incredulously. He sat back. He shook his head, smiling pityingly. 'Come on, now,' he said. 'That's crazy. Just crazy.' He kept shaking his head. 'What do you think that boy is, a maniac?' and smiling, 'You've got this crazy idea—'

'All right,' Gant said, 'it's crazy. For the time being. But if he didn't tell Marion he went to Stoddard, then in some way he must have been involved with Dorothy. And if he was involved with Dorothy, and then Ellen, and now with Marion – then he was goddamned good and determined to marry one of your daughters! Any one!'

The smile left Kingship's face slowly, draining it of expression. His hands were motionless on the edge of the desk.

'That *isn't* so crazy, I take it.'

Kingship removed his glasses. He blinked a couple of times and then straightened up. 'I have to speak to Marion,' he said.

Gant looked at the telephone.

'No,' Kingship said emptily. 'She's had her phone disconnected. She's giving up her apartment, staying with me until the wedding.' His voice faltered. 'After the honeymoon they're moving into an apartment I'm furnishing for them – Sutton Terrace. Marion didn't want to accept it at first, but he convinced her. He's been so good with her – made the two of us get along so much better.' They looked at each other for a moment; Gant's eyes steady and challenging, Kingship's apprehensive.

Kingship stood up.

'Do you know where she is?' Gant asked.

'At her place – packing things.' He put on his jacket. 'He *must* have told her about Stoddard.'

When they came out of the office Miss Richardson looked up from a magazine.

'That's all for today, Miss Richardson. If you'll just clear my desk.'

She frowned with frustrated curiosity. 'Yes, Mr Kingship. Merry Christmas.'

'Merry Christmas, Miss Richardson.'

They walked down a long corridor, on the walls of which were black and white photographs, matted and mounted between plates of glass held together by copper brackets at top and bottom. There were photographs of underground and open-pit mines, smelters, refineries, furnaces, rolling mills, and artistic close-ups of tubing and copper wire.

Waiting for the elevator Kingship said, 'I'm sure he told her.'

8

'Gordon Gant?' Marion said, exploring the name, when they had shaken hands. 'Don't I know that name?' She backed into the room, smiling, one hand finding Kingship's and drawing him with her, the other rising to the collar of her blouse and fingering the golden pearl-starred brooch.

'Blue River,' Kingship's voice was wooden as when he had performed the introduction, and his eyes were not quite on Marion's. 'I think I told you about him.'

'Oh, yes. You knew Ellen, wasn't that it?'

'That's right,' Gant said. He shifted his hand farther down the spine of the book at his side, to a spot where the leatherette wasn't damp, wishing he hadn't been so damned eager when Kingship had asked him to come up; the *Times* photo of Marion had offered no hint in its dotted greys of the lucency of her eyes, the radiance of her cheeks, the halo of I'm-getting-married-Saturday that glowed all over her.

She gestured at the room despairingly. 'I'm afraid there isn't even a place to sit down,' She moved towards a chair on which some shoe boxes were piled.

'Don't bother,' Kingship said. 'We just stopped by. Only for a minute. A lot of work waiting for me at the office.'

'You haven't forgotten tonight, have you?' Marion asked. 'You can expect us at seven or so. She's arriving at five, and I guess she'll want to stop at her hotel first.' She turned to Gant. 'My prospective mother-in-law,' she said significantly.

Oh Lord, Gant thought, I'm supposed to say, 'You're getting married?' 'Yes, Saturday.' 'Congratulations, good luck, best wishes!' He smiled wanly and didn't say anything. Nobody said anything.

'To what do I owe the pleasure of this visit?' Marion inquired, a curtsey in her voice.

Gant looked at Kingship, waiting for him to speak.

Marion looked at both of them. 'Anything special?'

After a moment, Gant said, 'I knew Dorothy, too. Very slightly.'

'Oh,' Marion said. She looked down at her hands.

'She was in one of my classes. I go to Stoddard.' He paused. 'I don't think Bud was ever in any of my classes though.'

She looked up. 'Bud?'

'Bud Corliss. Your—'

She shook her head, smiling. 'Bud was never at Stoddard,' she corrected him.

'He was, Miss Kingship.'

'No,' she insisted amusedly, 'he went to Caldwell.'

'He went to Stoddard, *then* to Caldwell.'

Marion smiled quizzically at Kingship, as though expecting him to offer some explanation for the obstinacy of the caller he had brought.

'He was at Stoddard, Marion,' Kingship said heavily. 'Show her the book.'

Gant opened the yearbook and handed it to Marion, pointing to the picture.

'Well for goodness' sake,' she said. 'I have to apologize. I never knew . . .' She glanced at the cover of the book. 'Nineteen-fifty.'

'He's in the forty-nine yearbook too,' Gant said. 'He went to Stoddard for two years and then transferred to Caldwell.'

'For goodness' sake,' she said. 'Isn't that funny? Maybe he knew Dorothy.' She sounded pleased, as though this were yet another bond between her and her fianc9. Her eyes slipped back to his picture.

'He never mentioned it to you at all?' Gant asked, despite Kingship's prohibitive headshakings.

'Why, no, he never said a—'

Slowly she looked up from the book, becoming aware for the first time of the strain and discomfort of the two men. 'What's the matter?' she asked curiously.

'Nothing,' Kingship said. He glanced at Gant, seeking corroboration.

'Then why are the two of you standing there as if—' She looked at the book again, and then at her father. There was a tightening

A KISS BEFORE DYING

moment in her throat. 'Is this why you came up here, to tell me this?' she asked.

'We – we only wondered if you knew, that's all.'

'Why?' she asked.

'We just wondered, that's all.'

Her eyes cut to Gant. 'Why?'

'Why should Bud conceal it,' Gant asked, 'unless—'

Kingship said, 'Gant!'

'*Conceal* it?' Marion said. 'What kind of a word is that? He didn't *conceal* it; we never talk about school much, because of Ellen; it just didn't come up.'

'Why should the girl he's marrying not know he spent two years at Stoddard,' Gant rephrased implacably, 'unless he was involved with Dorothy?'

'*Involved*? With *Dorothy*?' Her eyes, wide with incredulity, probed into Gant's, and then swung slowly, narrowing, to Kingship. 'What is this?'

Kingship's face flickered with small uneasy movements, as though dust were blowing at it.

'How much are you paying him?' Marion asked coldly.

'Paying him?'

'For snooping!' she flared. 'For digging up dirt! For *inventing* dirt!'

'He came to me of his own accord, Marion!'

'Oh, yes, he just *happened* to pop up!'

Gant said, 'I saw the article in the *Times*.'

Marion glared at her father. 'You swore you wouldn't do this,' she said bitterly. 'Swore! It would *never* enter your mind to ask *questions*, to investigate, treat him like a *criminal*. Oh, no, not much!'

'I *haven't* been asking questions,' Kingship protested.

Marion turned her back. 'I thought you changed,' she said. 'I really did. I thought you liked Bud. I thought you liked *me*. But you can't—'

'Marion—'

'No, not if you're doing this. The apartment, the job – and all along *this* has been going on.'

'*Nothing* is going on, Marion. I swear—'

'Nothing? I'll tell you *exactly* what's going on.' She faced him again. 'You think I don't know you? He was "involved" with

Dorothy – is he supposed to be the one who got her in trouble? And he was "involved" with Ellen, and now he's "involved" with me – all for the money, all for your precious money. That's what's going on – *in your mind*!' She thrust the yearbook into his hands.

'You've got it wrong, Miss Kingship,' Gant said. 'That's what's going on in *my* mind, not your father's.'

'See?' Kingship said. 'He came to me of his own accord.'

Marion stared at Gant. 'Just who are you? What makes this your business?'

'I knew Ellen.'

'So I understand,' she snapped. 'Do you know Bud?'

'I've never had the pleasure.'

'Then will you please explain to me what you're doing here, making accusations against him behind his back!'

'It's quite a story—'

'You've said enough, Gant,' Kingship interrupted.

Marion said, 'Are you jealous of Bud? Is that it? Because Ellen preferred him to you?'

'That's right,' Gant said drily. 'I'm consumed with jealousy.'

'And have you heard of the slander laws?' she demanded.

Kingship edged towards the door, signalling Gant with his eyes. 'Yes,' Marion said, 'you'd better go.'

'Wait a minute,' she said as Gant opened the door. 'Is this going to stop?'

Kingship said, 'There's nothing *to* stop, Marion.'

'Whoever's behind it' – she looked at Gant – 'it's got to stop. We never talked about school. Why should we, with Ellen? It just never came up.'

'All right, Marion,' Kingship said, 'all right.' He followed Gant into the hall and turned to pull the door closed.

'It's got to stop,' she said.

'All right,' He hesitated, and his voice dropped. 'You're still coming tonight aren't you, Marion?'

Her lips clenched. She thought for a moment. 'Because I don't want to hurt Bud's mother's feelings,' she said finally.

Kingship closed the door.

They went to a drugstore on Lexington Avenue, where Gant ordered coffee and cherry pie and Kingship, a glass of milk.

'So far, so good,' Gant said.

Kingship was gazing at a paper napkin he held. 'What do you mean?'

'At least we know where we stand. He didn't tell her about Stoddard. That makes it practically certain that—'

'You heard Marion,' Kingship said. 'They don't talk about school because of Ellen.'

Gant regarded him with slightly lifted eyebrows. 'Come on,' he said slowly, 'that may satisfy *her*; she's in love with him. But for a man not to tell his fiancée where he went to college—'

'It isn't as if he lied to her,' Kingship protested.

Sardonically Gant said, 'They just didn't talk about school.'

'Considering the circumstances, I think that's understandable.'

'Sure. The circumstances being that he was mixed up with Dorothy.'

'That's an assumption you have no right to make.'

Gant stirred his coffee slowly and sipped it. He added more cream and stirred it again. 'You're afraid of her, aren't you?' he said.

'Of Marion? Don't be ridiculous.' Kingship set his glass of milk down firmly. 'A man is innocent until he's proved guilty.'

'Then we've got to find proof, don't we?'

'You see? You're assuming he's a fortune hunter before you've started.'

'I'm assuming a hell of a lot more than that,' Gant said, lifting a forkful of pie to his mouth. When he had swallowed it he said, 'What are you going to do?'

Kingship was looking at the napkin again. 'Nothing.'

'You're going to let them get married?'

'I couldn't stop them even if I wanted to. They're both over twenty-one, aren't they?'

'You could hire detectives. There are four days yet. They might find something.'

'Might,' Kingship said. 'If there's anything to find. Or Bud might get wind of it and tell Marion.'

Gant smiled. 'I thought I was being ridiculous about you and Marion.'

Kingship sighed. 'Let me tell you something,' he said, not looking at Gant. 'I had a wife and three daughters. Two daughters were taken from me. My wife I pushed away myself. Maybe I pushed one of the daughters too. So now I have only one daughter. I'm fifty-seven years old and I have one daughter and some men I play golf and talk business with. That's all.'

After a moment Kingship turned to Gant, his face set rigidly. 'What about you?' he demanded. 'What *is* your real interest in this affair? Maybe you just enjoy chattering about your analytical brain and showing people what a clever fellow you are. You didn't have to go through that whole rigmarole, you know. In my office, about Ellen's letter. You could have just put the book on my desk and said, "Bud Corliss went to Stoddard." Maybe you just like to show off.'

'Maybe,' Gant said lightly. 'Also maybe I think he might have killed your daughters and I've got this quixotic notion that murderers should be punished.'

Kingship finished his milk. 'I think you'd better just go back to Yonkers and enjoy your vacation.'

'White Plains.' Gant scraped together the syrupy remains of the pie with the side of his fork. 'Do you have ulcers?' he asked, glancing at the empty milk glass.

Kingship nodded.

Gant leaned back on his stool and surveyed the man beside him. 'And about thirty pounds overweight, I'd say.' He put the red-clotted fork in his mouth and drew it out clean. 'I should estimate that Bud has you figured for ten more years, tops. Or maybe he'll get impatient in three or four years and try to hurry you on.'

Kingship got off his stool. He pulled a dollar from a money-clipped roll and put it on the counter. 'Good-bye, Mr Gant,' he said, and strode away.

The counterman came over and took the dollar. 'Anything else?' he asked.

Gant shook his head.

He caught the 5.19 for White Plains.

9

In writing to his mother, Bud had made only the most vague allusions to Kingship's money. Once or twice he had mentioned *Kingship Copper*, but never with any clarifying phrases, and he was certain that she, whose poverty-formed conception of wealth was as hazy and inexact as a pubert's visions of orgies, had not the slightest real comprehension of the luxuriance of living into which the presidency of such a corporation could be translated. He had looked forward eagerly, therefore, to the moment when he could introduce her to Marion and her father, and to the surrounding magnificence of Kingship's duplex apartment, knowing that in light of the coming marriage her awe-widened eyes would regard each inlaid table and glittering chandelier as evidence, not of Kingship's capabilities, but of his own.

The evening, however was a disappointment.

Not that his mother's reaction was anything less than he had anticipated; with mouth partially opened and teeth lightly touching her lower lip, she drew in her breath with soft sibilance, as though seeing not one but a series of miracles; the formally attired servant – a butler! – the velvety depth of the carpets, the wallpaper that wasn't paper at all but intricately textured cloth, the leather-bound books, the golden clock, the silver tray from which the butler served champagne – champagne! – in crystal goblets. Vocally, she restrained her admiration to a gently-smiling. 'Lovely, lovely,' accompanied by a slight nodding of the stiff newly-waved grey hair, giving the impression that such surroundings were by no means completely alien to her – but when her eyes met Bud's as the toast was drunk, the bursting pride she felt leaped out to him like a thrown kiss, while one work-roughened hand surreptitiously marvelled at the cloth of the couch on which she sat.

No, his mother's reaction was warming and wonderful. What made the evening a disappointment was the fact that Marion and Leo had apparently had an argument; Marion spoke to her father only when appearances made it inescapable. And furthermore, the argument must have been about him, since Leo addressed him with hesitant unfocused eyes, while Marion was determinedly, defiantly effusive, clinging to him and calling him 'dear' and 'darling', which she had never done before when others were present. The first faint worry began to sting him like a pebble in his shoe.

Dinner, then, was dismal. With Leo and Marion at the ends of the table and his mother and he at the sides, conversation passed only around the edges; father and daughter would not talk; mother and son could not talk, for anything they had to say would be personal and exclusive-sounding before these people who were still in a sense outsiders. So Marion called him 'darling' and told his mother about the Sutton Terrace apartment, and his mother spoke to Leo about 'the children', and Leo asked him to pass the bread please, not quite looking at him.

And he was silent, lifting each fork and spoon slowly as he selected it, so that his mother could see and do likewise; an affectionate conspiracy fallen into without words or signal, dramatizing the bond between them and forming the one enjoyable aspect of the meal – that and the smiles that passed across the table when Marion and Leo were looking down at their food, smiles prideful and loving and all the more pleasing to him because of the unsuspecting heads whose path they slipped across.

At the end of the meal, although there was a silver lighter on the table, he lit Marion's and his own cigarette with his matches, afterwards tapping the folder absentmindedly on the cloth until his mother had noticed the white cover on which *Bud Corliss* was stamped in copper leaf.

But all along there was the pebble in his shoe.

Later, it being Christmas Eve, they went to Church and after Church Bud expected to take his mother back to her hotel while Marion returned home with Leo. But Marion, to his annoyance, assumed an unfamiliar coquetry and insisted on accompanying them to the hotel, so Leo went off by himself as Bud squired the two women into a taxi. He sat between them, reciting to his mother the names of what landmarks they passed. The cab, at his direction, departed from its course so that Mrs Corliss, who had never been to New York before, might see Times Square at night.

He left her in the lobby of her hotel, outside the elevator. 'Are you very tired?' he asked, and when she said she was, he seemed disappointed. 'Don't go to sleep right away,' he said. 'I'll call you later.' They kissed good night and, still holding Bud's hand, Mrs Corliss kissed Marion happily on the cheek.

During the taxi ride back to Leo's, Marion was silent.

'What's the matter, darling?'

'Nothing,' she said, smiling unconvincingly. 'Why?'

He shrugged.

He had intended to leave her at the door of the apartment, but the pebble of worry was assuming the proportions of a sharp stone; he went in with her. Kingship had already retired. They went into the living-room where Bud lit cigarettes while Marion turned on the radio. They sat on the couch.

She told him that she liked his mother very much. He said he was glad, and he could tell that his mother liked her too. They began to speak of the future, and he sensed from the stiff casualness of her voice that she was working up to something. He leaned back with his eyes half closed, one arm around her shoulders, listening as he had never listened before, weighing every pause and inflection, fearful all the while of what it was leading up to. It couldn't be anything important! It couldn't be! He had slighted her somehow, forgotten something he'd promised to do, that was all. What could it be? He paused before each reply, examining his words before he spoke them, trying to determine what response they would bring, like a chess player touching pieces before making his move.

She worked the conversation around to children. 'Two,' she said.

His left hand, on his knee, pinched the crease of his trousers. He smiled. 'Or three,' he said. 'Or four.'

'Two,' she said. 'Then one can go to Columbia and one to Caldwell.'

Caldwell. Something about Caldwell. Ellen? 'They'll probably both wind up at Michigan or some place,' he said.

'Or if we only have one,' Marion went on, 'he can go to Columbia and then transfer to Caldwell. Or vice versa.' She leaned forward, smiling, and pressed her cigarette into an ashtray. Much more carefully than she usually put out her cigarettes, he observed. Transfer to Caldwell. Transfer to Caldwell . . . He waited in silence. 'No,' she said, 'I really wouldn't want him to do that' – followed up her statement with a tenacity she never would have applied to mere idle chatter – 'because he would lose credits. Transferring must be very involved.'

They sat side by side, silently for a moment.

'No, it isn't,' he said.

'Isn't it?' she asked.

'No,' he said. 'I didn't lose any credits.'

'You didn't transfer, did you?' She sounded surprised.

'Of course,' he said. 'I told you.'

'No you didn't. You never said—'

'I did, honey. I'm sure I told you. I went to Stoddard University, and then to Caldwell.'

'Why, that's where my sister Dorothy went, Stoddard!'

'I know. Ellen told me.'

'Don't tell me you *knew* her.'

'No. Ellen showed me her picture though, and I think I remember seeing her around. I'm sure I told you, that first day, in the museum.'

'No, you didn't. I'm positive.'

'Well sure, I was at Stoddard two years. And you mean to say you

427

didn't—' Marion's lips stopped the rest of the sentence, kissing him fervidly, atoning for doubt.

A few minutes later he looked at his watch. 'I'd better be leaving,' he said. 'I want to get as much sleep as I can this week, because I have an idea I won't be getting much sleep at all next week.'

It only meant that Leo had somehow learned he'd been at Stoddard. There was no real danger. There wasn't! Trouble maybe; the wedding plans might be blown up – oh Jesus! – but there was no *danger*, no police danger. There's no law against going after a rich girl is there?

But why so late? If Leo wanted to check on him, why hadn't he done it sooner? Why today? The announcement in the *Times* – of course! Someone had seen it, someone who'd been at Stoddard. The son of one of Leo's friends or someone like that. 'My son and your future son-in-law were at Stoddard together.' So Leo puts two and two together, Dorothy, Ellen, Marion – gold-digger. He tells Marion, and that was their argument.

God damn, if only it had been possible to mention Stoddard at the beginning! That would have been crazy though; Leo would have suspected right off, and Marion would have listened to him then. But why did it have to come up now!

Still, what could Leo do, with only suspicions? They must be only suspicions; the old man couldn't know for sure that he'd known Dorothy, or else Marion wouldn't have been so happy when he himself told her he hadn't known her. Or could Leo have withheld part of his information from Marion? No, he would have tried to convince her, given her all the evidence he had. So Leo wasn't certain. Could he *make* certain? How? The kids at Stoddard, mostly seniors now, would they remember who Dorothy had gone with? They might. But it's Christmas! Vacation. They're scattered all over the country. Only four days to the wedding. Leo could never talk Marion into postponing.

All he had to do was sit tight and keep his fingers crossed. Tuesday, Wednesday, Thursday, Friday – *Saturday*. If worst came to worst, so he was after the money; that was all Leo could ever prove. He couldn't prove that Dorothy didn't commit suicide. He couldn't drag the Mississippi for a gun that was probably buried under twenty feet of mud.

And if best came to best, the wedding would go off as per schedule. Then what could Leo do even if the kids at Stoddard did remember? Divorce? Annulment? Not nearly enough grounds for either, even if Marion could be persuaded to seek one, which she probably couldn't. When then? Maybe Leo would try to buy him off . . .

Now *there* was a thought. How much would Leo be willing to pay to free his daughter from the big bad gold-digger? Quite a lot, probably.

But not nearly as much as Marion would have some day.

Bread now or cake later?

When he got back to his rooming house, he telephoned his mother.

'I hope I didn't wake you. I walked back from Marion's.'

'That's all right, darling. Oh Bud, she's a lovely girl! Lovely! So sweet – I'm so happy for you!'

'Thanks, Mom.'

'And Mr Kingship, such a fine man! Did you notice his hands?'

'What about them?'

'So clean!' He laughed. 'Bud,' her voice lowered, 'they must be rich, very rich—'

'I guess they are, Mom.'

'That apartment – like a movie! My goodness—!'

He told her about the Sutton Terrace apartment – 'Wait till you see it, Mom!' – and about the visit to the smelter – 'He's taking me there Thursday. He wants me to be familiar with the whole set-up!' – and towards the end of the conversation, she said:

'Bud, whatever happened to that idea of yours?'

'What idea?'

'The one why you didn't go back to school.'

'Oh, that,' he said. 'It didn't pan out.'

'Oh—' She was disappointed.

'You know that shaving cream?' he said. 'Where you press the button and it comes out of the can like whipped cream?'

'Yes?'

'Well that was it. Only they beat me to it.'

She breathed a drawn-out 'Oh' of commiseration. 'If that isn't a shame . . . You didn't talk to anyone about it, did you?'

'No. They just beat me to it.'

'Well,' she said with a sigh, 'things like that happen. It certainly is a shame though. An idea like that—'

When he had finished talking to her, he went into his room and stretched out on the bed, feeling good all over. Leo and his suspicions, nuts to him! Everything was going to be perfect.

Jesus, that was one thing he was going to do – see that she got some of the money.

10

The train, having passed through Stamford, Bridgeport, New Haven and New London, continued grinding eastward along the southern border of Connecticut, passing between flat snow on the left and flat water on the right; a segmented serpent from whose body trapped people vapidly gazed. Inside, aisles and vestibules were clogged with the Christmas Day overflow.

In one of the vestibules, facing a dirt-stained window, Gordon Gant occupied himself by counting codfish-cake billboards. It was, he reflected, a hell of a way to spend Christmas Day.

Shortly after six o'clock the train reached Providence.

In the station, Gant addressed several questions to the bored oracle of the information booth. Then, regarding his watch, he left the building. It was already dark outside. Crossing a wide and slushy thoroughfare, he entered an establishment which called itself a 'spa', where he made quick work of a steak sandwich, mincemeat pie, and coffee. Christmas dinner. He left the spa and went to a drugstore two doors away, where he purchased an inch-wide roll of Scotch Tape. He returned to the station. He sat on an uncomfortable bench and read a Boston tabloid. At ten minutes to seven he left the station again, proceeding to a nearby place where three buses stood waitng. He boarded a blue and yellow one marked *Menasset – Somerset – Fall River.*

At twenty minutes past seven the bus paused midway down Menasset's four block Main Street, discharging several passengers, Gant among them. After a brief acclimatizing glance, he entered a 1910-looking pharmacy where he consulted a thin directory, from which he copied an address and a telephone number. He tried the number in the phone booth and, when the phone on the other end of the line had rung ten times without answer, hung up.

The house was a shabby grey box, one storey, the sills of its darkened windows furred with snow. Gant looked at it closely as he passed. It was set back only a few yards from the sidewalk; the snow between door and sidewalk was undisturbed.

He walked to the end of the deserted block, turned and came back, passing the grey house again, this time paying more attention to the houses on either side of it. In one, framed in the window's home-made Christmas wreath, a Spanish-looking family was dining in an atmosphere of magazine cover warmth. In the house on the other side of the grey one, a solitary man was holding a globe of the world in his lap, spinning it in its frame and then stopping it with his finger and looking to see which country his finger had chosen. Gant passed, walked to the other end of the block, turned, and came back. This time, as he passed the grey house, he turned sharply, cutting between it and the Spanish-family house. He went around to the back.

There was a small porch. Facing it, across a little yard laced with stiff clothes-lines, was a high board fence. Gant went up on the porch. There were a door and a window, a garbage can and a basket of clothes-pins. He tried the door; it was locked. The window was locked also. Propped on the sill within was an ice company sign, a square placard with 5, 10, 25, and X printed around the four sides. The X side was uppermost. Gant took the roll of Scotch tape from his pocket. Tearing off a ten-inch length, he pressed it across one of the window's dozen panes, the one below the central latch. He fitted the ends of the tape over the pane's moulding and tore off another ten-inch strip.

In a few minutes he had cross-hatched the rectangular pane with cellophane strips. He struck it with his gloved fist. There was a cracking sound; the broken glass sagged, held in place by the tape. Gant began to pull the tape ends from the moulding. When that was done he drew the rectangle of cellophane and broken glass from the window and lowered it noiselessly to the bottom of the garbage can. Reaching through the window, he unfastened the latch and raised the lower section. The ice placard fell back into the darkness.

He took a pencil flashlight from his pocket and leaned through the open window. There was a chair piled with folded newspapers before it. He pushed the chair aside and climbed in, closing the window after him.

The flashlight's disc of pallid light glided swiftly over a cramped and shabby kitchen. Gant moved forward, threading softly on worn-through linoleum.

He came to a living-room. The chairs were fat and velvet, rubbed bald at the arms. Cream-coloured shades were drawn down over the windows, flanked by foral-patterned paper drapes. There were pictures of Bud all over; Bud as a child in short pants, Bud at high school graduation, Bud in a private's uniform. Bud in a dark suit, smiling. Snapshots were tucked in the frames of the portraits, surrounding the large smiling faces with smaller faces also smiling.

Gant went through the living-room to a hallway. The first room off the hallway was a bedroom; a bottle of lotion on the dresser, an empty dress box and tissue paper on the bed, a wedding picture, and a picture of Bud on the night table. The second room was the bathroom; the flashlight caught decals of swans on moisture-faded walls.

The third room was Bud's. It might have been a room in a second-class hotel; apart from the high-school diploma over the bed, it was barren of anything suggesting the occupant's individuality. Gant went in.

He inspected the titles of some books on a shelf; they were mainly college texts and a few classic novels. No diaries, no engagement books. He sat behind the desk and went through the drawers one at a time. There were stationery and blank scratch pads, back issues of *Life* and the *New Yorker*, term papers from college, road maps of New England. No letters, no calendars with appointments written in, no address books with names crossed out. He rose from the desk and went to the dresser. Half the drawers were empty. The other contained summer shirts and swimming trunks, a couple of pairs of argyle socks, underwear, tarnished cuff-links, celluloid collar stays, bow ties with broken clips. No papers lost in corners, no forgotten pictures.

Perfunctorily he opened the closet. On the floor in the corner there was a small grey strongbox.

He took it out and put it on the desk. It was locked. He lifted and shook it. Its contents shifted, sounding like packets of paper. He put the box down again and picked at its lock with the blade of a small knife he carried on his key-chain. Then he took it into the kitchen. He found a screwdriver in one of the drawers and tried that. Finally he wrapped the box in newspaper, hoping that it didn't contain Mrs Corliss's life's savings.

He opened the window, took the ice placard from the floor, and climbed out on to the porch. When he had closed and locked the window, he tore the placard to size and fitted it in the open pane, blank side out. With the strongbox under his arm, he moved quietly between the houses to the sidewalk.

11

Leo Kingship returned to his apartment at ten o'clock on Wednesday night, having worked late in order to compensate for some of the last hours Christmas had entailed. 'Is Marion in?' he asked the butler, giving him his coat.

'Out with Mr Corliss. She said she'd be in early though. There's a Mr Dettweiler waiting in the living-room.'

'Dettweiler?'

'He said Miss Richardson sent him about the securities. He has a little strongbox with him.'

'Dettweiler?' Kingship frowned.

He went into the living-room.

Gordon Gant rose from a comfortable chair adjacent to the fireplace. 'Hello,' he said pleasantly.

Kingship looked at him for a moment. 'Didn't Miss Richardson make it clear this afternoon that I don't want—' His hands fisted at his sides. 'Get out of here,' he said. 'If Marion comes in—'

'Exhibit A,' Gant pronounced, raising a pamphlet in each hand, 'in the case against Bud Corliss.'

'I don't want to—' The sentence hung unfinished. Apprehensively, Kingship came forward. He took the pamphlets from Gant's hands. 'Our publications—'

'In the possession of Bud Corliss,' Gant said. 'Kept in a strongbox which until last night resided in a closet in Menasset, Massachusetts.' He gave a light kick to the strongbox on the floor beside him. The open lid was bent out of shape. There were four oblong Manilla envelopes inside. 'I stole it,' Gant said.

'*Stole* it?'

He smiled. 'Fight fire with fire. I don't know where he's staying in New York, so I decided to sally forth to Menasset.'

'You crazy—' Kingship sat heavily on a couch that faced the fireplace. He stared at the pamphlets. 'Oh God,' he said.

Gant resumed his seat next to the couch. 'Observe the condition of Exhibit A, if you will. Frayed around the edges, soiled by many fingermarks, centre pages worked loose from the staples. I would say he had them for quite some time. I would say he drooled over them considerably.'

'That – that son of a bitch—' Kingship spoke the phrase distinctly, as though not accustomed to using it.

Gant prodded the strongbox with his toe. 'The History of Bud Corliss, a drama in four envelopes,' he said. 'Envelope one: newspaper clippings of the high school hero; class president, chairman of the prom. committee, most likely to succeed and so on and so forth. Envelope two: honourable discharge from the army, Bronze Star, Purple Heart, several interesting though obscene photographs and a pawn ticket which I have discovered may be exchanged for a wrist-watch if you have a couple of hundred dollars you don't need. Envelope three: college days; transcripts from Stoddard and Caldwell. Envelope four: two well-read brochures describing the magnitude of Kingship Copper Incorporated, and this' – he drew a folded sheet of blue-lined yellow paper from his pocket and passed it to Kingship – 'which I can't make head or tail of.'

Kinship unfolded the paper. He read half-way down it. 'What is it?'

'I'm asking you.'

He shook his head.

'It must have some bearing on this,' Gant said. 'It was in with the pamphlets.'

Kingship shook his head and handed the paper back to Gant, who returned it to his pocket. Kingship's gaze dropped to the pamphlets. The grip of his hands crackled the thick paper. 'How am I going to tell Marion?' he said. 'She *loves* him.' He looked at Gant dismally. Then slowly his face smoothed out. He glanced at the pamphlets and back at Gant, his eyes narrowing. 'How do I know these were in the strongbox? How do I know that you didn't put them there yourself?'

Gant's jaw dropped. 'Oh, for—'

Kingship went around the end of the couch and across the room. There was a telephone on a carved table. He dialled a number.

'Come on now,' Gant chided.

In the silence of the room the buzzing and the clicks of the phone were audible. 'Hello? Miss Richardson? This is Mr Kingship. I'd like to ask a favour of you. A big favour, I'm afraid. And absolutely confidential.' An unintelligible twittering emanated from the phone. 'Would you please go down to the office – yes, now. I wouldn't ask you, only it's terribly important, and I—' There was more twittering. 'Go to the public relations department,' Kingship said. 'Go through the files and see whether we've ever sent any promotional publications to – Bud Corliss.'

'Burton Corliss,' Gant said.

'Or Burton Corliss. Yes, that's right – Mr Corliss. I'm at my home, Miss Richardson. Call me as soon as you find out. Thank you. Thank you very much, Miss Richardson. I appreciate this—' He hung up.

Gant shook his head wryly. 'We're really grasping at straws, aren't we.'

'I have to be sure,' Kingship said. 'You have to be sure of your evidence in a thing like this.' He came back across the room and stood behind the couch.

'You're sure already, and you know damn well you are,' Gant said.

Kingship braced his hands on the couch, looking down at the pamphlets in the hollow of the cushion where he had been sitting.

'You know damn well you are,' Gant repeated.

After a moment Kingship's breath sighed out tiredly. He came around the couch, picked up the pamphlets, and sat down. 'How am I supposed to tell Marion?' he asked. He rubbed his knee. 'That son of a bitch – that God-damned son of a bitch—'

Gant leaned towards him, his elbows on his knees. 'Mr Kingship, I was right about this much. Will you admit I might be right all the way?'

'What "all the way"?'

'About Dorothy and Ellen.' Kingship drew an irritated breath. Gant spoke quickly: 'He didn't tell Marion he went to Stoddard. He *must* have been mixed up with Dorothy. He *must* be the one who got her pregnant. He killed her, and Powell and Ellen somehow found out it was him and he had to kill them too.'

'The note—'

'He could have tricked her into writing it! It's been done before – there was a case in the papers just last month about a guy who did it, and for the same reason; the girl was pregnant.'

Kingship shook his head. 'I'd believe it of him,' he said. 'After what he's done to Marion, I'd believe anything of him. But there's a flaw in your theory, a big flaw.'

'What?' Gant demanded.

'He's after the money, isn't he?' Gant nodded. 'And you "know" Dorothy was murdered because she was wearing something old, something new, something borrowed, something blue?' Gant nodded again. 'Well,' Kingship said, 'if he were the one who'd gotten her into trouble, and if she were ready to marry him that day, then why would he have killed her? He would have gone ahead and married her, wouldn't he? He would have married her and gotten in on the money.'

Gant looked at him wordlessly.

'You were right about this,' Kingship said, lifting the pamphlets, 'but you're wrong about Dorothy. All wrong.'

After a moment Gant rose. He turned and paced up to the window. He looked through it dully, gnawing his lower lip. 'I may jump,' he announced.

When the door chimes toned, Gant turned from the window. Kingship had risen and was standing before the fireplace, gazing at the birch logs neatly pyramided there. He turned reluctantly, holding the rolled pamphlets at his side, his face averted from Gant's watching eyes.

They heard the front door open, and then voices: '. . . come in for a while?'

'I don't think so, Marion. We'll have to get up early tomorrow.' There was a long silence. 'I'll be in front of my place at seven-thirty.'

'You'd better wear a dark suit. A smelter must be a filthy place.' Another silence. 'Good night, Bud.'

'Good night.'

The door closed.

Kingship wound the pamphlets into a tighter cylinder. 'Marion,' he called, but it came out too low. 'Marion,' he called again, louder.

'Coming,' her voice answered cheerfully.

The two men waited, suddenly conscious of a clock's ticking.

She appeared in the wide doorway, perking up the collar of her crisp white full-sleeved blouse. Her cheeks were luminous from the cold outside. 'Hi,' she said. 'We had a—'

She saw Gant. Her hand froze, dropped.

'Marion, we—'

She whirled and was gone.

'Marion!' Kingship hurried to the doorway and into the foyer. 'Marion!' She was half-way up the curving white staircase, her legs driving furiously. 'Marion!' he shouted grimly, commanding.

She stopped, facing rigidly up the stairs, one hand on the banister. 'Well?'

'Come down here,' he said. 'I have to speak to you. This is extremely important.' A moment passed. 'Come down here,' he said.

'All right.' She turned and descended the stairs with regal coldness. 'You can speak to me. Before I go upstairs and pack and get out of here.'

Kingship returned to the living-room. Gant was standing uncomfortably in the middle of the room, his hand on back of the couch. Kingship, shaking his head dolefully, went to his side.

She came into the room. Their eyes followed her as, without looking at them, she came up to the chair across from the one in which Gant had sat, at the end of the couch nearer the door. She sat down. She crossed her legs carefully, smoothing the red wool of her skirt. She put her hands on the arms of the chair. She looked up at them, standing behind the couch to her left. 'Well?' she said.

Kingship shifted uneasily, withering under her gaze. 'Mr Gant went to – Yesterday he—'

'Yes?'

Kingship turned to Gant helplessly.

Gant said: 'Yesterday afternoon, absolutely without your father's knowledge, I went to Menasset. I broke into your fiancçe's home—'

'No!'

'—and I took from it a strongbox I found in the closet in his room—'

She pressed back into the chair, her knuckles gripping white, her mouth clamped to a lipless line, her eyes shut.

'I brought it home and jimmied the cover—'

Her eyes shot open, flashing. 'What did you find? The plans of the atom bomb?'

They were silent.

'What did you find?' she repeated, her voice lowering, growing wary.

Kingship moved down to the end of the couch and handed her the pamphlets, awkwardly unrolling them.

She took them slowly and looked at them.

'They're old,' Gant said. 'He's had them for some time.'

Kingship said, 'He hasn't been back to Menasset since you started going with him. He had them before he met you.'

She smoothed the pamphlets carefully in her lap. Some of the corners were folded over. She bent them straight. 'Ellen must have given them to him.'

'Ellen never had any of our publications, Marion. You know that. She was as little interested as you are.'

She turned the pamphlets over and examined their backs. 'Were you there when he broke open the box? Do you know for certain they were in the box?'

'I'm checking on that,' Kingship said. 'But what reason would Mr Gant have for—'

She began turning the pages of one of the pamphlets; casually, as though it were a magazine in a waiting-room. 'All right,' she said stiffly, after a moment, 'maybe it *was* the money that attracted him at first.' Her lips formed a strained smile. 'For once in my life I'm grateful for your money.' She turned a page. 'What is it they say? It's as easy to fall in love with a rich girl as with a poor.' And another page. 'You really can't blame him too much, coming from such a poor family. Environmental influence—' She stood up and tossed the pamphlets on the couch. 'Is there anything else you wanted?' Her hands were trembling slightly.

'Anything else?' Kingship stared. 'Isn't that enough?'

'Enough?' she inquired. 'Enough for what? Enough for me to call off the wedding? No' – she shook her head – 'no, it isn't enough.'

'You *still* want to—'

'He *loves* me,' she said. 'Maybe it was the money that attracted him at first, but – well, suppose I were a very pretty girl; I wouldn't call off the wedding if I found out it was my looks that attracted him, would I?'

'At first?' Kingship said. 'The money is still what attracts him.'

'You have no right to say that!'

'Marion, you *can't* marry him now.'

'No? Come down to City Hall Saturday morning!'

'He's a no-good scheming—'

'Oh, yes! You always know just who's good and who's bad, don't you! You knew Mom was bad and you got rid of her, and you knew Dorothy was bad and that's why she killed herself because you brought us up with your good and bad, your right and wrong! Haven't you done enough with your good and bad?'

'You're *not* going to marry a man who's only after you for your money!'

'He *loves* me! Don't you understand English? He loves me! I love him! I don't care *what* brought us together! We think alike! Feel alike! We like the same books, the same plays, the same music, the same—'

'The same food?' Gant cut in. 'Would you both be fond of Italian and Armenian food?' She turned to him, her mouth ajar. He was unfolding a sheet of blue-lined yellow paper he had taken from his pocket. 'And those books,' he said, looking at the paper, 'would they include the works of Proust, Thomas Wolfe, Carson McCullers?'

Her eyes widened. 'How did you—? What is that?'

He came around the end of the couch. She turned to face him. 'Sit down,' he said.

'What are you . . .?' She moved back. The edge of the couch pressed against the back of her knees.

'Sit down, please,' he said.

She sat down. 'What is that?'

'This was in the strongbox with the pamphlets,' he said. 'In the same envelope. The printing is his, I presume.' He handed her the yellow paper. 'I'm sorry,' he said.

She looked at him confusedly, and then looked down at the paper.

Proust, T. Wolfe, C. McCullers, 'Madame Bovary,' 'Alice in
    Wonderland,' Eliz. B. Browning – Read!
ART (mostly modern) – Hopley or Hopper, DeMeuth (sp.?),
READ general books on mod. art.
Pink phase in high school.
Jealous of E.?
Renoir, Van Gogh
Italian and Armenian food – LOOK UP restaurants in NYC.
Theatre: Shaw, T. Williams – serious stuff . . .

She read barely a quarter of the closely-printed page, her cheeks draining of colour. Then she folded the paper with trembling care. 'Well,' she said, folding it again, not looking up, 'haven't I been the – trusting soul.' She smiled crazily at her father coming gently around the end of the couch to stand helplessly beside her. 'I should have known, shouldn't I?' The blood rushed back to her cheeks, burning red. Her eyes were swimming and her fingers were suddenly mashing and twisting the paper with steel strength. 'Too good to be true,' she smiled, tears starting down her cheeks, her fingers plucking at the paper. 'I really should have known . . .' Her hands released the yellow fragments and flew to her face. She began to cry.

Kingship sat beside her, his arm about her bended shoulders. 'Marion – Marion – be glad you didn't find out too late.'

Her back was shaking under his arm. 'You don't understand,' she sobbed through her hands, 'you can't understand . . .'

When the tears had stopped she sat numbly, her fingers knotted around the handkerchief Kingship had given her, her eyes on the pieces of yellow paper on the carpet.

'Do you want me to take you upstairs?' Kingship asked.

'No. Please – just – just let me sit here.'

He rose and joined Gant at the window. They were silent for a while, looking at the lights beyond the river. Finally Kingship said, 'I'll do *something* to him. I swear to God, I'll do *something*.'

A minute passed. Gant said, 'She referred to your "good and bad". Were you very strict with your daughters?'

Kingship thought for a moment. 'Not very,' he said.

'I thought you were, the way she spoke.'

'She was angry,' Kingship said.

Gant stared across the river at a Pepsi-Cola sign. 'In the drugstore the other day, after we left Marion's apartment, you said something about maybe having pushed one of your daughters away. What did you mean?'

'Dorothy,' Kingship said. 'Maybe if I hadn't been—'

'So strict?' Gant suggested.

'No. I *wasn't* very strict. I taught them right from wrong. Maybe I – over-emphasized a little, because of their mother.' He sighed. 'Dorothy shouldn't have felt that suicide was the only way out,' he said.

Gant took out a pack of cigarettes and removed one. He turned it between his fingers. 'Mr Kingship, what would you have done if Dorothy had married without first consulting you, and then had had a baby – too soon?'

After a moment Kingship said, 'I don't know.'

'He would have thrown her out,' Marion said quietly. The two men turned. She was sitting motionlessly on the couch, as she had been before. They could see her face in the canted mirror over the mantel. She was still looking at the papers on the floor.

'Well?' Gant said to Kingship.

'I don't think I would have thrown her out,' he protested.

'You would have,' Marion said tonelessly.

Kingship turned back to the window. 'Well,' he said finally, 'under those circumstances, shouldn't a couple be expected to assume the responsibilities of marriage, as well as the—' He left the sentence unfinished.

Gant lit his cigarette. 'There you are,' he said. 'That's why he killed her. She must have told him about you. He knew he wouldn't get near the money even if he did marry her, and if he didn't marry her he would get into trouble, so . . . Then he decides to have a second try, with Ellen, but she starts to investigate Dorothy's death and gets too close to the truth. So close that he has to kill her and Powell. And then he tries a third time.'

'Bud?' Marion said. She spoke the name blankly, her face in the mirror showing the barest flicker of surprise, as though her fiancé had been accused of having imperfect table manners.

Kingship stared narrow-eyed out the window. 'I'd believe it,' he said intently. 'I'd believe it.' But as he turned to Gant the resolution faded from his eyes. 'You're basing it all on his not telling Marion he went to Stoddard. We're not even sure he *knew* Dorothy, let alone he was the one she was – seeing. We have to be *sure*.'

'The girls at the dorm,' Gant said. 'Some of them must have known who she was going with.'

Kingship nodded. 'I could hire someone to go out there, speak to them—'

Gant pondered and shook his head. 'It's no good. It's vacation; by the time you managed to find one of the girls who knew, it would be too late.'

'Too late?'

'Once he knows the wedding is off' – he glanced at Marion; she was silent – 'he's not going to wait around to find out why, is he?'

'We'd find him,' Kingship said.

'Maybe. And maybe not. People disappear.' Gant smoked thoughtfully. 'Didn't Dorothy keep a diary or anything?'

The telephone rang.

Kingship went to the carved table and lifted the receiver. 'Hello?' There was a long pause. Gant looked at Marion; she was leaning forward, picking up the pieces of paper from the floor. 'When?' Kingship asked. She put the pieces of paper in her left hand and squeezed them together. She looked at them, not knowing what to do with them. She put them on the couch beside her, on top of the two pamphlets. 'Thank you,' Kingship said. 'Thank you very much.' There was the sound of the receiver being replaced, and then silence. Gant turned to look at Kingship.

He was standing beside the table, his pink face rigid. 'Miss Richardson,' he said. 'Promotional literature was sent to Burton Corliss in Caldwell, Wisconsin, on October 16, 1950.'

'Just when he must have started his campaign with Ellen,' Gant said.

Kingship nodded. 'But that was the second time,' he said slowly. 'Promotional literature was also sent to Burton Corliss on February 6, 1950, in Blue River, Iowa.'

Gant said, 'Dorothy—'

Marion moaned.

Gant remained after Marion had gone upstairs. 'We're still in the same boat Ellen was in,' he said. 'The police have Dorothy's "suicide note" and all we have are suspicions and a flock of circumstantial evidence.'

Kingship held one of the pamphlets. 'I'll make sure,' he said.

'Didn't they find *anything* at Powell's place? A fingerprint, a thread of cloth?'

'Nothing,' Kingship said. 'Nothing at Powell's place, nothing at that restaurant where Ellen—'

Gant sighed. 'Even if you could get the police to arrest him, a first-year law student could get him released in five minutes.'

'I'll get him somehow,' Kingship said. 'I'll make sure, and I'll get him.'

Gant said, 'We've either got to find out how he got her to write that note, or else find the gun he used on Powell and Ellen. And before Saturday.'

Kingship looked at the photograph on the pamphlet's cover. 'The smelter—' Sorrowfully he said, 'We're supposed to fly out there tomorrow. I wanted to show him around. Marion too. She was never interested before.'

'You'd better see that she doesn't let him know the wedding is off until the last possible moment.'

Kingship smoothed the pamphlet on his knee. He looked up. 'What?'

'I said you should see that she doesn't let him know the wedding is off until the last possible moment.'

'Oh,' Kingship said. His eyes returned to the pamphlet. A moment passed. 'He picked the wrong man,' he said softly, still looking at the photograph of the smelter. 'He should have picked on somebody else's daughters.'

12

Was there ever such a perfect day? That was all he wanted to know – was there? He grinned at the plane; it looked as impatient as he; it craned forward at the runway, its compact body gleaming, the coppered KINGSHIP and the crown trademark on its side emblazoned by the early morning sun. He grinned at the busy scene farther down the field, where *commercial* planes stood, their waiting passengers herded behind wire fences like dumb animals. Well, we all can't have private planes at our disposal! He grinned at the ceramic blue of the sky, then stretched and pounded his chest happily, watching his breath plume upwards. No, he decided judicially, there really never was such a perfect day. What, never? No, never! What, *never*? Well – hardly ever! He turned and strode back to the hangar, humming Gilbert and Sullivan.

Marion and Leo were standing in the shade, having one of their tight-lipped arguments. 'I'm going!' Marion insisted.

'What's the dif*few*culty?' he smiled, coming up to them.

Leo turned and walked away.

'What's the matter?' he asked Marion.

'Nothing's the matter. I don't feel well, so he doesn't want me to go.' Her eyes were on the plane beyond him.

'Bridal nerves?'

'No. I just don't feel well, that's all.'

'Oh,' he said knowingly.

They stood in silence for a minute, watching a pair of mechanics fuss with the plane's fuel tank, and then he moved towards Leo. Leave it to Marion to be off on a day like this. Well, it was probably all for the good; maybe she'd keep quiet for a change. 'All set to go?'

'A few minutes,' Leo said. 'We're waiting for Mr Dettweiler.'

'Who?'

'Mr Dettweiler. His father is on the board of directors.'

A few minutes later a blond man in a grey overcoat approached from the direction of the commercial hangars. He had a long jaw and heavy eyebrows. He nodded at Marion and came up to Leo. 'Good morning, Mr Kingship.'

'Good morning, Mr Dettweiler.' They shook hands. 'I'd like you to meet my prospective son-in-law, Bud Corliss. Bud, this is Gordon Dettweiler.'

'How do you do.'

443

'Well,' Dettweiler said, he had a handshake like a mangle, 'I've certainly been looking forward to meeting you. Yes, sir, I certainly have.' A character, Bud thought, or maybe he was trying to get in good with Leo.

'Ready, sir?' a man asked from within the plane.

'Ready,' Leo said. Marion came forward. 'Marion, I honestly wish you wouldn't—' but she marched right past Leo, up the three-step platform and into the plane. Leo shrugged and shook his head. Dettweiler followed Marion in. Leo said, 'After you, Bud.'

He jogged up the three steps and entered the plane. It was a six-seater, its interior done in pale blue. He took the last seat on the right, behind the wing. Marion was across the aisle. Leo took the front seat, across from Dettweiler.

When the engine coughed and roared to life, Bud fastened his seat-belt. Son of a gun, if it didn't have a copper buckle! He shook his head, smiling. He looked out of the window at the people waiting behind fences, and wondered if they could see him. . .

The plane began to roll forward. On the way. . .Would Leo be taking him to the smelter if he were still suspicious? Never! What, never? No, never! He leaned over, tapped Marion's elbow and grinned at her. She smiled back, looking ill all right, and returned to her window. Leo and Dettweiler were talking softly to each other over the aisle. 'How long will it take, Leo?' he asked cheerfully. Leo turned, 'Three hours. Less if the wind's good,' and turned back to Dettweiler.

Well, he hadn't wanted to talk to anyone anyway. He returned to his window and watched the ground slide past.

At the edge of the field the plane turned slowly around. The engine whined higher, building up power. . .

He stared out of the window, fingering the copper buckle. On the way to the smelter. . .The smelter? The grail! The fountainhead of wealth!

Why the hell did his mother have to be afraid of flying? Christ, it would have been *terrific* having her along!

The plane roared forward.

He was the first to spot it; far ahead and below, a small black geometric cluster on the bedsheet of snow; a small black cluster like a twig on the end of a curving stem of railroad tracks. 'There it is,' he heard Leo saying, and he was faintly conscious of Marion crossing the aisle and taking the seat in front of him. His breath fogged the window; he wiped it clean.

The twig vanished under the wind. He waited. He swallowed and his ears popped as the plane soared lower.

The smelter reappeared directly below him, sliding out from under the wing. There were half a dozen rectilinear brown roofs with thick tails of smoke dragging from their centres. They crowded together, huge and shadowless in the overhead sun, beside the glittering chain-mail patch of a filled parking lot. Railroad tracks looped and encircled them, merging below into a multi-veined stem, down which a freight train crawled, its smudge of smoke dwarfed by the giant black plumes behind it, its chain of cars scintillating with salmon-coloured glints.

His head turned slowly, his eyes locked to the smelter that slid towards the tail of the plane. Fields of snow followed it. Scattered houses appeared. The smelter was gone. There were more houses, then roads separating them into blocks. Still more houses, closer now, and stores and signs and creeping cars and dot-like people, a park, the cubist pattern of a housing development . . .

The plane banked, circling. The ground tilted away, then levelled, swept closer, and finally came slicing up under the wing of the plane. A jolt; the seat-belt's buckle bit his stomach. Then the plane rolled smoothly. He drew the pale blue webbing from the copper clamp.

There was a limousine waiting when they descended from the plane; a custom-built Packard, black and polished. He sat on a jump-seat next to Dettweiler. He leaned forward, looking over the driver's shoulder. He peered down the long perspective of the town's main street to a white hill far away on the horizon. At its summit, from the far side, columns of smoke arose. They were curving and black against the sky, like the cloud-fingers of a genie's hand.

The main street became a two-lane highway that speared between fields of snow, and the highway became an asphalt road that embraced the curve of the hill's base, and the asphalt road became a gravel one that jounced over the serried ribs of railroad tracks and turned to the left, rising up the hillside parallel to the tracks. First one slowly climbing train was overtaken, and then another. Sparks of hidden metal winked from ore-heaped gondola cars.

Ahead, the smelter rose up. Brown structures merged into a crude pyramid, their belching smoke-stacks ranked around the largest one. Nearer, the buildings swelled and clarified; their clifflike walls were streaky brown metal, laced in spots with girdered fretwork and irregularly patched with soot-stained glass; the shapes of the buildings were hard, geometric; they were bound together by chutes and catwalks. Still nearer, the building merged again, the sky space between them lost behind projecting angles. They became a single massive form, large hulks buttressing larger ones into an immense smoke-spired industrial cathedral. It loomed up mountainously, and then suddenly swept off to the side as the limousine veered away.

The car pulled up before a low brick building, at the door of which waited a lean, white-haired, unctuously smiling man in a dark grey suit.

He forgot what he was eating, that's how interested he was in lunch. He pulled his eyes from the window across the room, the window through which could be seen the buildings wherein heaps of grey-brown dirt were purified to gleaming copper, and looked down at his plate. Creamed chicken. He started eating more quickly, hoping the others would follow suit.

The carefully-dressed white-haired man had turned out to be a Mr Otto, the manager of the smelter. Leo having introduced him, Mr Otto had led them into a conference room and begun apologizing for things. He apologized smilingly for the tablecloth that left bare one end of the long table – 'We're not in the New York office, you know' – and he apologized suavely for cool food and warm wine – 'I'm afraid we lack the facilities of our big city brethren.' Mr Otto longed transparently for the New York office. Over the soup he spoke of the copper shortage and disparaged the suggestions of the National Production Authority for its mitigation. Occasionally he referred to copper as 'the red metal'.

'Mr Corliss.' He looked up. Dettweiler was smiling at him across the table. 'You'd better be careful,' Dettweiler said. 'I found a bone in mine.'

Bud glanced at his nearly empty plate and smiled back at Dettweiler. 'I'm anxious to see the smelter,' he said.

'Aren't we all,' Dettweiler remarked, still smiling.

'You found a bone in yours?' Mr Otto inquired. 'That woman! I told her to take care. These people can't even cut up a chicken properly.'

Now that they had at long last left the brick building and were crossing the asphalt yard to the buildings of the smelter itself, he walked slowly. The others, coatless, hurried ahead, but he drifted behind, savouring the climatic sweetness of the moment. He watched an ore-laden train disappear behind a steel wall at the left of the buildings. At the right, a train was being loaded; cranes swung copper into the cars; great square slabs like solidified flame that must have weighed five or six hundred pounds each. A heart! he thought, gazing up at the monstrous brown form that filled more and more of the sky – a giant heart of American industry, drawing in bad blood, pumping out good! Standing so close to it, about to enter it, it was impossible not to share the surging of its power!

The others had vanished into a doorway at the base of the towering steel mass. Now Mr Otto smiled within the doorway, beckoning.

He moved forward less slowly, like a lover going to a long awaited tryst. Success rewarded! Promise fulfilled! There should be a fanfare! he thought. There should be a fanfare!

A whistle screamed.

Thank you. *Muchas gracias.*

He went into the darkness of the doorway. The door closed after him.

The whistle screamed again, piercingly, like a bird in a jungle.

13

He stood on a chain-railed catwalk staring fascinatedly at an army of huge cylindrical furnaces ranked before him in diminishing perspective like an ordered forest of giant redwood trucks. At their bases men moved methodically, regulating incomprehensible controls. The air was hot and sulphurous.

'There are six hearths, one above the other, in each furnace,' Mr Otto lectured. 'The ore is introduced at the top. It's moved steadily downward from hearth to hearth by rotating arms attached to a central shaft. The roasting removes excess sulphur from the ore.'

He listened intently, nodding. He turned to the others to express his awe, but only Marion stood on his right, wooden-faced as she had been all day. Leo and that Dettweiler were gone. 'Where'd your father and Dettweiler go?' he asked her.

'I don't know. Dad said he wanted to show him something.'

'Oh.' He turned back to the furnaces. What would Leo want to show Dettweiler? Well . . . 'How many are there?'

'Furnaces?' Mr Otto dabbed perspiration from his upper lip with a folded handkerchief. 'Fifty-four.'

Fifty-four! Jesus! 'How much ore goes through them in a day?' he asked.

It was wonderful! He'd never been so interested in anything in his whole life! He asked a thousand questions and Mr Otto, visibly reacting to his fascination, answered them in detail, speaking only to him, while Marion trailed unseeingly behind.

In another building there were more furnaces; brick-walled, flat, and over a hundred feet long. 'The reverberatory furnaces,' Mr Otto said. 'The ore that comes from the roasting furnaces is about ten per cent copper. Here it's melted down. The lighter minerals flow off as slag. What's left is iron and copper – we call it "matte" – forty per cent copper.'

'What do you use for fuel?'

'Pulverized coal. The waste heat is used to generate steam for making power.'

He shook his head, whistling between his teeth.

Mr Otto smiled. 'Impressed?'

'It's wonderful,' Bud said. 'Wonderful.' He gazed down the endless stretch of furnaces. 'It makes you realize what a great country this is.'

'This,' Mr Otto said, pushing his voice over a roaring tide of sound, 'is probably the most spectacular part of the entire smelting process.'

'Jesus!'

'The converters,' Mr Otto said loudly.

The building was a vast steel shell, percussant with the sustained thunder of machines and men. A greenish haze obscured its far reaches, swimming around shafts of yellow-green sunlight that pillared down through crane tracks and catwalks from windows in the peaked roof dim and high above.

At the near end of the building, on either side, lay six massive dark cylindroid vessels, end to end, like giant steel barrels on their sides, dwarfing the workmen on railed platforms between them. Each vessel had an opening in its uppermost surface. Flames burst forth from these mouths: yellow, orange, red, blue; roaring up into funnel-like hoods overhead that swallowed and bore them away.

One of the converters was turned forward on the cogged rollers that supported it, so that its round mouth, scabrous with coagulated metal, was at the side; liquid fire rushed from the radiant throat, pouring down into an immense crucible on the floor. The molten flow, heavy and smoking, filled the steel container. The converter rolled back groaningly, its mouth dripping. The yoke of the crucible lifted, caught by a great blunt hook from whose block a dozen cables rose in unwavering ascension, rose higher than the converters, higher than the central spine of catwalk, up to the underbelly of a grimy cab that hung from a single-railed track below the dimness of the roof. The cables contracted; the crucible lifted in slow, weightless levitation. It rose until it was higher than the converters, some twenty-five feet above the ground, and then cab, cables, and crucible began to draw away, retreating towards the cupreous haze at the northern end of the building.

The centre of it all! The heart of the heart! With rapt eyes Bud followed the heat-shimmering column of air over the departing crucible.

'Slag,' Mr Otto said. They stood on an island of railed platform against the south wall, a few feet above the floor and midway between the two banks of converters. Mr Otto touched his handkerchief to his forehead. 'The molten matte from the reverberatory furnaces is poured into these converters. Silica is added, and then compressed air is blown in through pipes at the back. The impurities are oxidized; slag forms and is poured off, as you just saw. More matte is added, more slag forms, and so on. The copper keeps getting richer and richer until, after about five hours, it's ninety-nine per cent pure. Then it's poured out in the same way as the slag.'

'Will they be pouring copper soon?'

Mr Otto nodded. 'The converters are operated on a stagger system, so that there's a continuous output.'

'I'd like to see them pour the copper,' Bud said. He watched one of the converters on the right pouring off slag. 'Why are the flames different colours?' he asked.

'The colour changes as the process advances. That's how the operators tell what's going on inside.'

Behind them a door closed. Bud turned. Leo was standing beside Marion. Dettweiler leaned against a ladder that climbed the wall beside the door. 'Are you enjoying the tour?' Leo asked over the thunder.

'It's wonderful, Leo! Overpowering!'

'They're going to pour copper over there,' Mr Otto said loudly.

Before one of the converters on the left, a crane had lowered a steel vat, larger than the crucible into which the slag had been poured. Its steep sides were a three-inch thickness of dull grey metal, as high as a man. Its rim was seven feet across.

The mammoth cylinder of the converter began to turn, rumbling, rolling forward in its place. A wraith of blue flame flickered over its clotted mouth. It turned further; a volcanic radiance blasted from its interior, veils of white smoke arose, and then a flood of racing incandescence came bursting out. It spilled forward and fell gleamingly into the giant bowl. The steady molten flow seemed motionless, a solid, shining shaft between the converter and the depths of the vat. The converter turned further; new ribs twisted fluidly down the shaft, and again it was motionless. Within the vat the surface of the liquid appeared, slowly rising, clouded by whorls of smoke. The bitter smell of copper singed the air. The steaming shaft thinned, twisting, as the converter began rolling back. The thin stream petered out, its last few drops rolling over the swell of the cylinder and sparkling to the cement floor.

The smoke above the vat dissolved in vaporous wisps. The surface of the molten copper, a few inches below the vessel's rim, was an oblique disc of glistening oceanic green.

'It's green,' Bud said, surprised.

'When it cools it regains its usual colour,' Mr Otto said.

Bud stared at the restless pool. Blisters formed, swelled, and popped glutinously on its surface. 'What's the matter, Marion?' he heard Leo ask. The heated air above the vat trembled as though sheets of cellophane were being shaken.

'Matter?' Marion said.

Leo said, 'You look pale.'

Bud turned around. Marion seemed no paler than usual. 'I'm all right,' she was saying.

'But you're pale,' Leo insisted, and Dettweiler nodded agreement.

'It must be the heat or something,' Marion said.

'The fumes,' Leo said. 'Some people can't stand the fumes. Mr Otto, why don't you take my daughter back to the administration building. We'll be along in a few minutes.'

'Honestly, Dad,' she said tiredly, 'I feel—'

'No nonsense,' Leo smiled stiffly. 'We'll be with you in a few minutes.'

'But—' She hesitated a moment, looking annoyed, and then

shrugged and turned to the door. Dettweiler opened it for her.

Mr Otto followed after Marion. He paused in the doorway and turned back to Leo. 'I hope you're going to show Mr Corliss how we mould the anodes.' He turned to Bud. 'Very impressive,' he said, and went out. Dettweiler closed the door.

'Anodes?' Bud said.

'The slabs they were loading on the train outside,' Leo said. Bud noticed an odd mechanical quality in his voice, as though he were thinking of something else. 'They're shipped to the refinery in New Jersey. Electrolytic refining.'

'My God,' Bud said, 'it's some involved process.' He turned back to the converters on the left. The vat of copper, its angular handle hooked by the crane overhead, was about to be raised. The dozen cables tensed, vibrating, and then rigidified sharply. The vat listed from the floor.

Behind him Leo said, 'Did Mr Otto take you up on the catwalk?'

'No,' Bud said.

'You get a much better view,' Leo said. 'Would you like to go up?'

Bud turned. 'Do we have the time?'

'Yes.' Leo said.

Dettweiler, his back against the ladder, stepped aside. 'After you,' he smiled.

Bud went to the ladder. He grasped one of the metal rungs and looked upwards. The rungs, like oversize staples, ran narrowingly up the brown wall. They focused at a trap in the floor of the catwalk, which projected perpendicularly from the wall some fifty feet above.

'Bottle-neck,' Dettweiler murmured beside him.

He began to climb. The rungs were warm, their upper surfaces polished smooth. He climbed in a steady rhythm, keeping his eyes on the descending wall before him. He heard Dettweiler and Leo following after him. He tried to visualize the sight the catwalk would offer. To look down on the scene of industrial power . . .

He climbed the ladder up through the trap and stepped off on to the ridged metal floor of the catwalk. The thunder of the machines was diminished up here, but the air was hotter and the smell of copper stronger. The narrow runway, railed by heavy chain between iron stanchions, extended in a straight line down the spine of the building. It ended half-way down the building's length, where it was cut off by a broad strip of steel partition wall that hung from the roof to floor, some twelve feet wider than the catwalk. Overhead, on either side, crane tracks paralleled the runway. They passed clear of the partition that ended the catwalk and continued into the northern half of the building.

He peered over the left side of the catwalk, his hands folded over the top of one of the waist-high stanchions. He looked down upon the six converters, the men scurrying between them. . .

His eyes shifted. To his right, twenty feet below and ten feet out from the catwalk, hung the vat of copper, a steel rimmed pool of green on its slow procession towards the far end of the building. Ghosts of smoke rose from the liquid sheen of its surface.

He followed it, walking slowly, his left hand tracing over the dipping curves of the chain railing. He stayed far enough behind the vat so that he could just feel the fringe of its radiant heat. He heard Leo and Dettweiler following. His eyes climbed the vat's cables, six and six on either side of the block, up to the cab a dozen feet above him. He could see the shoulder of the operator inside. His eyes dropped back to the copper.

How much is in there? How many tons? What was it worth? One thousand? Two thousand? Three? Four? Five? . . .

He was nearing the steel partition, and now he saw that the catwalk didn't end there after all; instead it branched six feet to right and left, following the partition to its edges like the head of a long-stemmed T. The vat of copper vanished beyond the partition. He turned on to the left wing of the T. A three-foot chain swung across the catwalk's end. He put his left hand on the corner stanchion and his right on the edge of the partition, which was quite warm. He leaned forward a bit and peered around the partition at the receding vat. 'Where does it go now' he called out.

Behind him Leo said, 'Refining furnaces. Then it's poured into moulds.'

He turned around. Leo and Dettweiler faced him shoulder to shoulder, blocking the stem of the T. Their faces were oddly inflexible. He patted the partition on his left. 'What's behind here?' he asked.

'The refining furnaces,' Leo said. 'Any more questions?'

He shook his head, puzzled by the grimness of the two men.

'Then I've got one for you,' Leo said. His eyes were like blue marbles behind his glasses. 'How did you get Dorothy to write that suicide note?'

14

Everything fell away; the catwalk, the smelter, the whole world; everything melted away like sand castles sucked into the sea, leaving him suspended in emptiness with two blue marbles staring at him and the sound of Leo's question swelling and reverberating like being inside an iron bell.

Then Leo and Dettweiler confronted him again; the smelter's rumble welled up; the plates of the partition materialized slippery against his left hand, the knob of the stanchion damp under his right, the floor of the catwalk – but the floor didn't come back completely; it swayed anchorless and undulant beneath his feet, because his knees – Oh God! – were jelly, trembling and shaking. 'What're you—' he started to say, but nothing came out. He swallowed air. 'What're you – talking about—'

'Dorothy,' Dettweiler told him. Slowly he said, 'You wanted to marry her. For the money. But then she was pregnant. You knew you wouldn't get the money. You killed her.'

He shook his head in confused protest. 'No,' he said. 'No! She committed suicide! She sent a note to Ellen! You know that, Leo!'

'You tricked her into writing it,' Leo said.

'How – Leo, how could I do that? How the hell could I do *that*?'

'That's what you're going to tell us,' Dettweiler said.

'I hardly knew her!'

'You didn't know her at all,' Leo said. 'That's what you told Marion.'

'That's right! I didn't know her at all!'

'You just said you *hardly* knew her.'

'I didn't know her *at all*!'

Leo's fists clenched. 'You sent for our publications in February nineteen hundred and fifty!'

Bud stared, his hand bracing tightly against the partition. 'What publications?' It was a whisper; he had to say it again: 'What publications?'

Dettweiler said, 'The pamphlets I found in the strongbox in your room in Menasset.'

The catwalk dipped crazily. The strongbox! Oh, Jesus Christ! The pamphlets and what else? The clippings? He'd thrown them out, thank God! The pamphlets – *and the list on Marion*! Oh, Jesus! 'Who are you?' he exploded. 'Where the hell do you come off

453

breaking into a person's—'

'Stay back!' Dettweiler warned.

Withdrawing the single step he had advanced, Bud gripped the stanchion again. 'Who are you?' he shouted.

'Gordon Gant,' Dettweiler said.

Gant! The one on the radio, the one who'd kept needling the police! How the hell did he—

'I knew Ellen,' Gant said. 'I met her a few days before you killed her.'

'I—' He felt the sweat running. 'Crazy!' he shouted. 'You're crazy! Who else did I kill?' To Leo, 'You listen to him? Then you're crazy too! I never killed anybody!'

Gant said, 'You killed Dorothy and Ellen and Dwight Powell!'

'And almost killed Marion,' Leo said. 'When she saw that list—'

She saw the list! Oh God almighty! 'I never killed anybody! Dorrie committed suicide and Ellen and Powell were killed by a burglar!'

'Dorrie?' Gant snapped.

'I - everybody called her Dorrie! I - I never killed anybody! Only a Jap, and that was in the army!'

'Then why are your legs shaking?' Gant asked. 'Why is the sweat dripping down your cheek?'

He swiped at his cheek. Control! Self-control! He dragged a deep breath into his chest . . . Slow up, slow up . . . They can't prove a thing, not a goddamn thing! They know about the list, about Marion, about the pamphlets - okay - but they can't prove a thing about . . . He drew another breath . . .

'You can't prove a thing,' he said. 'Because there isn't anything to prove. You're crazy, both of you.' His hands wiped against his thighs. 'Okay,' he said, 'I knew Dorrie. So did a dozen other guys. And I've had my eyes on the money all along the way. Where's the law against that? So there's no wedding Saturday. Okay.' He straightened his jacket with stiff fingers. 'I'm probably better off poor than having a bastard like you for a father-in-law. Now get out of the way and let me pass. I don't feel like standing around talking to a couple of crazy lunatics.'

They didn't move. They stood shoulder to shoulder six feet away.

'Move,' he said.

'Touch the chain behind you,' Leo said.

'Get out of the way and let me pass!'

'Touch the chain behind you!'

454

He looked at Leo's stone-like face for a moment and then turned slowly.

He didn't have to touch the chain; he just had to look at it; the metal eye of the stanchion had been bent open into a loose C that barely engaged the first of the heavy links.

'We were up here when Otto was showing you around,' Leo said. 'Touch it.'

His hand came forward, brushed the chain. It collapsed. The free end clanked to the floor; it slid rattlingly off and swung down, striking noisily against the partition.

Fifty feet below cement floor yawned, seemed to sway . . . 'Not as much as Dorothy got,' Gant was saying, 'but enough.'

He turned to face them, clutching the stanchion and the edge of the partition, trying not to think of the void behind his heels. 'You wouldn't – dare—' he heard himself saying.

'Don't I have reason enough?' Leo asked. 'You killed my daughters!'

'I didn't, Leo! I swear to God I didn't!'

'Is that why you were sweating and shaking the minute I mentioned Dorothy's name? Is that why you didn't think it was a bad joke, and react the way an innocent person would have reacted?'

'Leo, I swear on the soul of my dead father—'

Leo stared at him coldly.

He shifted his grip on the stanchion. It was slick with sweat. 'You wouldn't do it,' he said. 'You'd never get away with it.'

'Wouldn't I?' Leo said. 'Do you think you're the only one who can plan something like this?' He pointed to the stanchion. 'The jaws of the wrench were wrapped in cloth; there are no marks on that ring. An accident, a terrible accident; a piece of iron, old, continually subjected to intense heat, weakens and bends when a six-foot man stumbles against the chain attached to it. A terrible accident. And how can you prevent it? Yell? No one will hear you over the noise. Wave your arms? The men down there have jobs to attend to, and even if they should look up, there's the haze and the distance. Attack us? One push and you're finished.' He paused. 'So tell me, why won't I get away with it? Why?

'Of course,' he continued after a moment, 'I would rather not do it. I would rather hand you over to the police.' He looked at his watch. 'So I'll give you three minutes. From now. I want something that will convince a jury, a jury that won't be able to take you by surprise and see the guilt written all over you.'

'Tell us where the gun is,' Gant said.

The two of them stood side by side; Leo with his left wrist lifted and his right hand holding back the cuff to expose his watch; Gant with his hands at his sides.

'How did you get Dorothy to write the note?' Gant asked.

His own hands were so tight against the partition and the stanchion that they throbbed with a leaden numbness. 'You're bluffing,' he said. They leaned forward to hear him. 'You're trying to scare me into admitting – to something I never did.'

Leo shook his head slowly. He looked at the watch. A moment passed. 'Two minutes and thirty seconds,' he said.

Bud whirled to the right, catching the stanchion with his left hand and shouting to the men over at the converters. 'Help!' he cried, 'Help! Help!' – bellowing as loud as he could, waving his right arm furiously, clutching the stanchion. 'Help!'

The men far off below might as well have been painted figures; their attention was centred on a converter pouring copper.

He turned back to Leo and Gant.

'You see?' Leo said.

'You'll be killing an innocent man, that's what you'll be doing!'

'Where's the gun?' Gant asked.

'There is no gun! I never had a gun!'

Leo said, 'Two minutes.'

They were bluffing! They must be! He looked around desperately; the main shaft of the catwalk, the roof, the crane tracks, the few windows, the . . . The crane tracks!

Slowly, trying not to make it too obvious, he glanced to the right again. The converter had rolled back. The vat before it was full and smoking, cables trailing slackly up to the cab above. The vat would be lifted; the cab, now over two hundred feet away, would bear the vat forward, approaching along the track that passed behind and above him; and the man in the cab – a dozen feet up? four feet out? – would be able to hear! To see!

If only they could be stalled! If only they could be stalled until the cab was near enough!

The vat lifted . . .

'One minute, thirty seconds,' Leo said.

Bud's eyes flicked back to the two men. He met their stares for a few seconds, and then risked another glance to the right, cautiously, so that they should not guess his plan. (Yes, a plan! Even now, at this moment, a plan!) The distant vat hung between floor and catwalk, its skein of cables seeming to shudder in the heat-vibrant air. The box-like cab was motionless under the track – and then it began to come forward, bearing the vat, growing imperceptibly larger. So slowly! Oh God, make it come faster!

He turned back to them.

'We aren't bluffing, Bud,' Leo said. And after a moment: 'One minute.'

He looked again; the cab was nearer – a hundred and fifty feet? One thirty? He could distinguish a pale shape behind the black square of its window.

'Thirty seconds.'

How could time race by so fast? 'Listen,' he said frantically, 'listen, I want to tell you something – something about Dorrie. She—' He groped for something to say – and then stopped wide-eyed; there had been a flicker of movement in the dimness at the far end of the catwalk. Someone else was up here! Salvation!

'Help!' he cried, his arm semaphoring. 'You! Come here! Help!'

The flicker of movement became a figure hurrying along the cat-walk, speeding towards them.

Leo and Gant looked over their shoulders in confusion.

Oh, dear God, thank you!

Then he saw that it was a woman.

Marion.

Leo cried out, 'What are you – Get out of here! For God's sake, Marion, go back down!'

She seemed not to hear him. She came up behind them, her face flushed and large-eyed above their compacted shoulders.

Bud felt her gaze rake his face and then descend to his legs. Legs that were trembling again . . . If he only had a gun . . . 'Marion,' he pleaded, 'stop them! They're crazy! They're trying to kill me! Stop them! They'll listen to you! I can explain about that list, I can explain everything! I swear I wasn't lying—'

She kept looking at him. Finally she said, 'The way you explained why you didn't tell me about Stoddard?'

'I love you! I swear to God I do! I started out thinking about the money, I admit that, but I love you! You know I wasn't lying about that!'

'*How* do I know?' she asked.

'I swear it!'

457

'You swore so many things—' Her fingers appeared curving over the men's shoulders; long, white, pink-nailed fingers; they seemed to be pushing.

'Marion! You wouldn't! Not when we – after we—'

Her fingers pressed forward into the cloth of the shoulders, pushing . . .

'Marion,' he begged futilely.

Suddenly he became aware of a swelling in the smelter's thunder, an added rumble. A wave of heat was spreading up his right side. The cab! He wheeled catching the stanchion with both hands. There it was! – not twenty feet away, grinding closer on the overhead track with the cables shooting down from its belly. Through the opening in its front end he could see a bent head in a visored grey cap. 'You!' he bellowed, his jaw muscles cording. 'You in the cab! Help! You!' Heat from the oncoming vat pressed heavily against his chest. 'Help! You! In the cab!' The grey cap, coming closer, never lifted. *Deaf*? Was the stupid bastard *deaf*? 'Help!' he roared chokingly again and again, but it was no use.

He turned from the swelling heat, wanting to cry in despair.

Leo said, 'The noisiest place in the smelter, up there in those cabs.' As he said it, he took a step forward. Gant moved up beside him. Marion followed behind.

'Look,' Bud said placatingly, clutching the partition in his left hand again. 'Please—' He stared at their faces, mask-like except for burning eyes.

They came another step closer.

The catwalk dipped and bucked like a shaken blanket. The baking heat on his right began extending itself across his back. They meant it! They weren't bluffing! They were going to kill him! Moisture trickled all over him.

'All right!' he cried. 'All right! She thought she was doing a Spanish translation! I wrote out the note in Spanish! I asked her to translate—' His voice faded and stopped.

What was the matter with them? Their faces – the mask-like blankness was gone, warped into – into embarrassment and sick contempt, and they were looking down at . . .

He looked down. The front of his pants was dark with a spreading stain that ran in a series of island blotches down his right trouser leg. Oh God! The Jap – the Jap he had killed – that wretched, trembling, chattering, pants-wetting caricature of a man – was that *him*? Was that *himself*?

The answer was in their faces.

'No!' he cried. He clapped his hands over his eyes, but their faces were still there. 'No! I'm not like him!' He wheeled away from them. His feet slipped on wetness and kicked out from under him. His hands flew from his face and flailed the air. Heat blasted up at him. Falling, he saw a giant disc of glistening green sliding into place below; gaseous, restless, shimmering—

Hardness in his hands! The cables! The weight of his body swung down and around, pulling at his armpits and tearing his hands on protruding steel threads. He hung with his legs swinging against the taut cables and his eyes staring at one of them, seeing the frayed fibres that were stabbing like needles into his hands above. A chaos of sound; a whistle shrieking, a woman screaming, voices above, voices below . . . He squinted up at his hands – blood was starting to trickle down the insides of his wrists – the oven-like heat was smothering, dizzying, engulfing him with the noxious stench of copper – voices shouted to him – he saw his hands starting to open – he was letting go because he wanted to, it wasn't the burning suffocation or the needles in his hands, he was letting go because he wanted to, just as he had jumped from the catwalk but instinct had made him grab the cables and now he was overcoming instinct – his left hand opened and fell – he hung by his right, turning slightly in the furnace heat – there was oil on the back of his hand from the stanchion or the chain or something – and they wouldn't have pushed him either – you think *anyone* can kill? – he had jumped and now he was letting go because he wanted to, that's all, and everything was all right and his knees weren't shaking any more, not that they had been shaking so much anyway, his knees weren't shaking any more because he was in command again – he hadn't noticed his right hand open but it must have opened because he was dropping into the heat, cables were shooting up, someone was screaming like Dorrie going into the shaft and Ellen when the first bullet wasn't enough – this person was screaming this godawful scream and suddenly it was himself and he couldn't stop! Why was he screaming? Why? Why on earth should he be—

The scream, which had knifed through the sudden stillness of the smelter, ended in a viscous splash. From the other side of the vat a sheet of green leaped up. Arcing, it sheared down to the floor where it splattered into a million pools and droplets. They hissed softly on the cement and slowly dawned from green to copper.

15

Kingship remained at the smelter. Gant accompanied Marion back to New York. In the plane they sat silent and immobile with the aisle between them.

After a while Marion took out a handkerchief and pressed it to her eyes. Gant turned to her, his face pale. 'We only wanted him to confess,' he said defensively. 'We weren't going to *do* it. And he *did* confess. What did he have to turn away like that for?'

The words took a long time to reach her. Almost inaudibly she said, 'Don't—'

He looked at her downcast face. 'You're crying,' he told her gently.

She gazed at the handkerchief in her hands, saw the damp places in it. She folded it and turned to the window at her side. Quietly she said, 'Not for him.'

They went to the Kingship apartment. When the butler took Marion's coat – Gant kept his – he said, 'Mrs Corliss is in the living-room.'

'Oh God,' Marion said.

They went into the living-room. In the late afternoon sunlight, Mrs Corliss was standing by a curio cabinet looking at the underside of a porcelain figurine. She put it down and turned to them. 'So soon?' she smiled. 'Did you enjoy—' She squinted through the light at Gant. 'Oh, I thought you were—' She came across the room, peering beyond them into the empty hallway.

Her eyes returned to Marion. Her eyebrows lifted and she smiled. 'Where's Bud?' she asked.